Catherine Alliott lived in London for some years, working as a copywriter in advertising. She now lives in Hertfordshire with her husband, a barrister, and their three children.

Catherine's first novel, THE OLD-GIRL NETWORK, was chosen by WHSmith for their Fresh Talent Promotion in 1994 and became an instant bestseller across the country, as did her subsequent novels, GOING TOO FAR, THE REAL THING, ROSIE MEADOWS REGRETS . . ., OLIVIA'S LUCK, A MARRIED MAN and THE WEDDING DAY.

The Old-Girl Network
and
Going Too Far

Catherine Alliott

THE OLD-GIRL NETWORK first published in Great Britain in 1994
by HEADLINE BOOK PUBLISHING

GOING TOO FAR first published in Great Britain in 1994
by HEADLINE BOOK PUBLISHING

First published in this omnibus edition in 2005
by HEADLINE BOOK PUBLISHING

A HEADLINE paperback

10 9 8 7 6 5 4 3 2 1

ISBN 0 7553 2652 0

Typeset in Times by Avon DataSet Ltd,
Bidford-on-Avon, Warwickshire

Printed and bound in Great Britain by
Mackays of Chatham plc, Chatham, Kent

Headline's policy is to use papers that are natural, renewable and
recyclable products and made from wood grown in sustainable
forests. The logging and manufacturing processes are expected to
conform to the environmental regulations of the country of origin.

HEADLINE BOOK PUBLISHING
A division of Hodder Headline
338 Euston Road
London NW1 3BH

www.headline.co.uk
www.hodderheadline.com

The Old-Girl Network

For George

Chapter One

I sat down and ran a practised eye over the ten people sitting opposite me. I saw at once that it wasn't a good day. In fact, it was a particularly bad day. Six women and only four men, and as if that wasn't bad enough, all four of the men looked as if they'd narrowly survived major car crashes. A singularly unpromising selection and I had to go to bed with one of them. Damn.

I sat back in my seat narrowing my rather myopic eyes and studied the four contenders: Too Fat, Too Young, Too Chinese and Too Ginger. Typical. Where was Too Handsome when I needed him most? Still, it was no good belly-aching about lack of talent; rules were rules, and one of these lucky guys was about to get even luckier. I gritted my teeth and appraised them individually, searching for hidden depths. I was going to have to dig pretty deep.

Number one was a fat slob masquerading as a businessman. The buttons of his blue nylon shirt were doing sterling work as they strained under the pressure of his ample bosom, and the waistband of his trousers was nowhere to be seen as his gut spilled out over the top of it. Lovely. Not only that, but he was bald too. Long flowing locks had been grown from somewhere beneath his left ear and swept carefully over the top à la Bobby Charlton, but that didn't fool anyone. Sensing early depression I dismissed him out of hand and moved smartly on to number two.

I suppressed a shudder. This callow youth was still grappling with something I'd got to grips with long ago and I didn't fancy going through it again. Puberty. As I cast a cold eye over his acne-festooned, hormone-infested face, his upper lip suddenly curled into a leer, a lazy eye winked at me, and a lolling hand scratched at the fly of his jeans. Good grief, the very idea! I tossed my head in disgust. Bloody nerve.

I swiftly turned my attention to number three. Ah. Now this was a tricky one. You see, I've nothing against Chinese men per se, in fact the one in my local takeaway couldn't be nicer, it's just that — well, on balance I prefer my men to be, er, you know — English. I'm quite sure the Chinese make wonderful lovers but, as I said, my personal preference is for something a little closer to home, like — well, like Harry, of course.

For one blissful moment I allowed a fleeting glimpse of the divine Harry Lloyd-Roberts to seep into my consciousness. Ah yes, there he was, with his mop of blond hair, his tanned, smiling face, his bright blue eyes, his long lean legs, his broad shoulders, his — I gave myself a little shake. Concentrate, Polly, Harry is not on the menu this morning, but this Oriental gentleman is and you'll have to do a little better than simply admitting to a preference for Englishmen.

I grudgingly appraised him again and realised, with joy, that he had a mighty peculiar set of teeth. I seized gratefully on his unusual dental arrangement. Oh no, I'm sorry, I simply have to have straight teeth; they must be regular and they must be white, I make a point of insisting on it. No, I wasn't being racist at all, I was just — yes, I was just being a little toothist, that was it!

As I rejected him I realised with a sinking heart that I was now left with only one contender and — oh, horrors, I was about to be gingerist too. I studied the red-headed gentleman before me and sighed. But not deeply. Because, hold on a minute, Polly McLaren, not so fast. On closer inspection this one wasn't so bad. Ginger, certainly, but not flaming carrots or nasty nasturtium red, more of a — well, more of an autumnal russet really. And was I seeing things, or weren't those features remarkably regular? And wasn't that face rather attractively tanned? And didn't we have here a particularly piercing pair of blue eyes? We did! Complete with crinkle-cut laughter lines at each corner! That very nearly did it, I'm a sucker for crinkle cuts, but I had the good sense to run an eye over the rest of the goods before I clinched the deal. Shoulders broad, legs long, no sign of a paunch, good.

He was wearing a pale blue Brooks Brothers shirt topped with an expensive navy jacket, a good quality leather belt and heavy cotton trousers — not too baggy, not too tight — and, more to the point (and how foolish of me not to have spotted it before), he was sporting a signet-ring on the little finger of his left hand. I leaned back in my seat, heady with relief. I had myself a winner.

There was no true competition, but I gave the opposition another cursory glance just to ensure fair play. Too Chinese and Too Young had never got off their starting blocks, Too Fat was definitely Too Bald and, let's face it, a girl has to have something to run her fingers through, even if it is red, so Ginger — I charitably omitted the 'Too' — it was. He'd run an easy race and won by an absence of baldness, hormones and buck teeth. What a lucky guy!

I stood up, flushed with success and pleased with my prize. So pleased, in fact, that I did something unforgivable. I smiled at the victor. It slipped out before I had a chance to retract it or even to turn it into something like a nasty little twitch. There it was, all turned up at the corners, wide and welcoming, teeth flashing away like beacons. Ginger looked up in surprise and returned the smile, blue eyes crinkling as predicted.

Horrified with myself, I wrapped my scarf around my

flushing neck and made for the sliding doors, just as — thank God — the tube pulled into South Kensington station. There was a nasty moment when the doors stuck for a second, but a minute later I was off and running — well, walking fast — in the direction of the escalator.

How ghastly! He must have thought I was sizing him up for real, propositioning him even! I glanced nervously over my shoulder as I joined the moronic trudge for the exit, but thankfully there was no sign of his russet locks hovering hopefully behind me.

But that was a lucky escape, Polly, I told myself sternly; don't do it again, for God's sake — who knows what sort of trouble it could get you into? It's bad enough that you stare at them every morning, without giving them the come-on too.

I grinned sheepishly as I thought of the way I amused myself on the way to work. Blind date without the blindfold, and without, of course, the actual date. Harmless fun, but these days increasingly depressing. Take yesterday, for example. I shuddered as I recalled. Yesterday, due to an unprecedented number of women commuters, I'd been forced to climb between the imaginary sheets with a slack-jawed octogenarian with bubbles on his lower lip. There'd been a moment back there when I could have become a lesbian, but no, I played the game. After all, it was my game, and I couldn't cheat on myself, could I?

As I jostled for position in the line up to the escalator, I spotted the leering Too Young ahead of me in the queue. Oh dear, he really didn't know the ropes did he? There he was, pushing his way through, and committing the unpardonable sin of standing firmly on the left which, as every urbane traveller knows, is for climbers only. I had the satisfaction of seeing him being bundled over to the right by a hoard of embattled commuters amidst a sea of shaking heads and tutting tongues. 'You stand on the right,' someone muttered by way of explanation — only muttered you understand, no one who did this on a regular basis would be so gauche as to talk. I joined in the 'glare past' on the way up to complete the ritual humiliation. To my surprise, he had the balls to leer back at me.

Oh well, I thought, as I trudged on up the moving staircase, its always nice to be ogled, even if it is by a spotty fourteen-year old: I must be looking quite good today.

We reached the top and I geared myself up to catch a glimpse of my reflection in the photo-booth mirror that everyone looks in and pretends not to. Christ, I thought as I caught my millisecond's worth, he must be desperate. Bad hair, bad make-up (too hurried) and a very bad jacket covered in dog hairs. Lottie's fault for buying a bloody Yorkshire Terrier. I brushed myself down, cursing my impulsive flatmate. At least it was all superficial. The hair could be washed, the jacket changed, and the make-up carefully reapplied in time for tonight's little excursion with the divine Harry. Please God, let there be an excursion! Please God, let him ring!

I allowed myself a moment's luxury as I considered the joys of going out with the utterly mouth-wateringly delicious Mr Harry Lloyd-Roberts. My heart pranced around in its usual foolish manner, but after an initial burst of skippy enthusiasm, sank a little too. I sighed. If only he wasn't so elusive. If only every date wasn't such a trumpet-blowing-red-carpeted-big-deal because they were so few and far between. If only — oh well. Don't bang on, Polly.

And that was another thing, I thought bitterly as I barged and elbowed my way towards the ticket barrier, it was all so time-consuming. I really didn't want to be the sort of girl who only thought about boys, but until I'd well and truly ensnared this one, I honestly didn't think I could get my mind around anything else. Of course it went without saying that once he was as besotted with me as I was with him I'd spend a lot more time thinking about — oh well, you know — Shakespeare, art, starving orphans, charity work, that kind of thing; but until that glorious, glorious day came, I'm afraid I just didn't have the time.

As I approached the barrier, I dug into my pocket for some change. The diminutive ticket collector already had his hand out, palm upward. It was a tacit agreement we had. He knew I was a lazy slut who couldn't be bothered to buy a ticket at the right station, and I knew he was a thieving bastard who pocketed my sixty pence. We smiled sweetly at one another, both happy with the arrangement, and London Transport was none the wiser.

As I walked up the few remaining steps to the main road, I felt as if I was walking into a Persil advert. South Kensington was awash with bright, primary colours bathed in sunshine. Tall white houses soared up into a bright blue sky, and the little patches of green grass at their feet played host to the very first signs of spring as snowdrops, crocuses and a few lonely daffodils bobbed around in the sunshine. It was a beautiful day, and my spirits rose.

They rose even higher as I turned the corner into Cresswell Gardens, for this was where I'd met Harry and it never failed to please. Number twenty-four, to be precise — yes, this was the one. I paused outside, allowing myself a moment of sentimental nostalgia.

If I say so myself, I'd looked pretty damn sexy that night; seductively clad in a black Alaia dress which clung to every curve — of which I have a few; some would say too many — and with a liberal sprinkling of Butler and Wilson's finest baubles at my ears and around my neck, my long, wavy blond hair freshly highlighted, and the remains of a tan still glowing . . . I hadn't looked bad.

The occasion had been a birthday drinks party, but to this day I can't remember being invited, although I do remember the hostess's look of surprise as I kissed her warmly on both cheeks. I'd obviously crashed it, probably with Lottie, who knows everyone. It had been a small, select gathering, and the venue had been the drawing room of this majestic townhouse. It was chock-a-block with original oil paintings, tasteful antiques, and other expensive and eminently breakable family heirlooms, and in fact the atmosphere had been so rarefied that people were talking in whispers. They didn't stray from their own little groups of two or three, and it seemed to me that everyone was in danger of turning to stone and joining the rest of the precious treasures dotted around the room.

Thankfully, as the evening limped along, the hostess was suddenly alive to this possibility, and hastily poured a two-litre bottle of brandy into the insipid punch. A rather horsy girl standing next to me said she thought it was the stupidest thing she'd ever seen. I thought it was inspired. Within twenty minutes the party was revving up like nobody's business, and I delved deep to summon up all the Dutch courage I possessed to chat up the most attractive man in the room.

He was standing by the window wearing a pair of ageing beige cords, a blue shirt and a bright red skiing jumper. An unruly mop of floppy blond hair was constantly falling into the bluest eyes I'd ever seen. He was such a cliché it was untrue. He was calmly eating pistachio nuts and staring out of the window to the street below, pretending he didn't know how divine he looked and what a commotion he was causing.

No less than three knock-out looking girls were prowling and circling around him, tossing back metres of silky hair and adjusting their hemlines up or down, according to whether they had good or bad legs. I decided to skip these formalities and move in for the kill. Buoyed up by too much bevvy and my revealing little black dress, I took a deep breath and dived in.

Somehow, and to this day I know not how, I managed to

monopolise him totally for the rest of the evening, engaging him with my witty repartee whilst at the same time staving off the competition. The circling harpies evidently decided I'd scored and limped away to nurse their egos and, within the hour, I'd secured myself a seat opposite him in a restaurant of my choice somewhere on the Fulham Road. Before you could say your place or mine, it was back to his for Rémy and rumpy-pumpy – and the rest, as they say, is history. Unfortunately I was under the distinct impression that, unless I could recapture some of that original wit and vitality, I was in danger of becoming history too. I bit my lip miserably. Why was love such bloody hard work? Perhaps I should have a few sun-beds.

I turned the corner into Egerton Street where the houses are even taller, even whiter and even lovelier. My second pause on the walk to work was just coming up, right . . . here. I stopped in front of one of the tallest and whitest and gazed up at it, for this was where Harry and I were going to live when we were married. I'd picked it out ages ago as being the perfect house. I could almost hear my Manolo Blahnik heels tip-tapping around the highly polished wooden floors as I checked on my beautiful blond children asleep in their bedrooms and adjusted my Chanel suit in the enormous hall mirror before skipping off to join my husband for dinner or the theatre – or both.

Before I went I would dispense a few last-minute instructions to the Swedish nanny – did I say Swedish? Lord, no, I meant Rumanian or, um . . . yes, Mongolian. Or did Mongolians have those rather attractive high cheekbones? I was rattled. Well then, we wouldn't have one at all, why bother? Baby-sitters were just as good, and cheaper. But younger. I sighed. Even I could see the poverty of my situation, when even in my fantasies Harry was incapable of keeping his hands to himself.

With these weighty problems still preying on my mind, I

climbed the steps to my workplace, Penhalligan and Waters, number thirty-three. I pressed the buzzer urgently, as if I'd been waiting there for some time and wasn't late at all.

'S'me!' I yelled into the metal squawk box, and another buzzer obligingly let me in.

The only delay I was now likely to encounter was Bob. I looked nervously around the marble hallway. Bob was a large black labrador who belonged to Maurice, the aged and grumpy commissionaire who fielded visitors and clients up to the various offices in the building. They say a dog resembles his owner, but these two really couldn't have been more different.

Maurice was a Yorkshireman; dour, miserable, grizzled and past it. Bob, on the other hand, was well-bred, bouncy, friendly, in peak condition and well up to it. He greeted most people simply with enthusiasm and affection, which was fine as long as his paws were clean and you weren't wearing white, but I was a different matter. Bob adored me. Let's face it, Bob had the hots for me. The mere smell of me would make his nose twitch with delight, and the sight of me would have him yelping with joy. Within seconds, his front paws would be up on my shoulders, his tongue frantically licking every scrap of make-up off my face. If I pushed him away, he'd think it was all part of the foreplay. He'd goose me in the crutch, whimpering with delight, and it wasn't funny because Bob was a big dog. There I'd be, pinned to the Regency staircase or the Georgian hall-table, with Bob on top of me, pleading with him, or Maurice, or both, to give me a break.

'Wants to play, by the look of things,' Maurice would observe at length from the safety of his chair.

'Yes – yes, he does, doesn't he?' I'd pant as Bob's big black head would give me another excruciating buck in the groin. 'Ooof! Geddof, Bob! But the thing is, Maurice, I'm just a teensy bit late, could you possibly — you know, call him off? Aarrhh!'

'Humph,' Maurice would grunt in an offended fashion. 'He's only being friendly like, better than being all aggressive like one of them Rottweilers, i'n't it?'

'Oh yes, yes, absolutely, much better,' I'd gasp, nodding furiously. 'It's just that — well, you know, I do have to get to work and I am rather late . . .'

'C'mon then, Bob,' Maurice would growl grudgingly, jerking his head. 'She don't want your attentions. Save them for them that do.'

Luckily Bob was remarkably obedient to Maurice's commands — probably terrified of him like the rest of us — and he'd respond immediately, slinking back to his basket. Muttering my thanks to Maurice, I'd then back gratefully up the stairs, flapping my skirt in a vain attempt to get the air to it and dry the nasty wet patch where he'd slobbered before I got upstairs.

This morning, thank goodness, there was no sign of the amorous Bob. Maurice appeared to be asleep behind his desk, so I tiptoed past, hoping Bob was also kipping deadly in his basket beside him or, even better, at home with a bad case of doggy flu.

I looked at my watch and leaped up the stairs two at a time — Christ! I hadn't realised I was that late. I flew down one of the many corridors in the grand old house, which at one time would have been full of oil paintings and family portraits. Now that the second floor housed an advertising agency, the walls were lined with stills from cat-food commercials and Tampax ads. I barged through reception shouting, 'Morning!' to Josie the receptionist, then, out of breath and panting heavily, shouldered open the nearest door and fell into the pit I share with Pippa.

Even by my standards it was a mess. It was a small office, dominated by two enormous desks which were almost totally obscured by magazines, newspapers, TV scripts, show reels, voice-over tapes, commercials, and the odd word processor or two. The walls were plastered with polaroid photos which appeared to chart the progress of a particularly debauched office party – a veritable collage of tongues, silly hats, bare bottoms, gin bottles and suspender belts. The windowsill, the filing cabinet, and any other spare surface area, spewed over with rampant Busy Lizzie plants and their offspring; cuttings of cuttings of cuttings had taken over in triffid-like proportions. The floor was covered with yet more magazines; in piles, in bundles, in general disarray. In the midst of this chaos, a young girl in a blue coat was slumped in a heap at her desk.

Pippa had obviously died at her typewriter. She was sitting with her head cradled in her arms, her face pressed nose-down on to her blotter. She was one of those girls who had an amazing capacity to look ravishingly attractive one day and hideously atrocious the next. Today it was obviously the latter. Her insatiable appetite for night clubs, late nights, gin and tonics and men – not necessarily in that order – was also instrumental in determining how she looked in the morning. My best friend, soul-mate and partner in grime at Penhalligan and Waters raised a pale green face from the blotter and peered at me through severely bloodshot eyes. 'Don't talk to me,' she whispered.

'Chocolate milk and bacon sandwich?' I ventured sympathetically.

'Please, if you're going.'

It was all she could manage. Her head dropped back on to her desk like a stone. I dumped my bag and moved a few papers around on my own desk to make it look as if I'd been in for hours.

'If Nick gets back from his meeting, say I've been in for ages and I've just popped out to the bank,' I commanded.

Pippa moaned in agreement and I galloped downstairs,

this time escaping through the back entrance, thereby avoiding Maurice and Bob.

I exchanged the usual pleasantries with the friendly Italians in the sandwich bar, in pidgin Italian on my part and in pidgin English on theirs, and with '*Arrivederci, Bella*!' still ringing in my ears, sped back to the patient, hangover cure in hand.

As I deposited it on her desk, I decided she'd improved, but only marginally. She was still wrapped up in her navy blue winter coat, even though it was a warm spring day, but her head was off the desk and she was at least indulging in some sort of activity. She was smoking her one, two, three — fourth cigarette of the morning, judging by the ashtray. If Pippa were having a frontal lobotomy, she'd find time to light a fag.

'Was he worth it?' I asked smugly, from my frightfully healthy position at the opposite desk.

'Oh, very definitely,' whispered Pippa, fumbling to open the chocolate milk and quietly ramming home the fact that I might be the picture of health, but I'd earned it by spending a mind-bendingly boring evening in front of the television, working my way through two chocolate oranges and a box of Maltesers. I'd suffered the added indignity of dog-sitting for Lottie whilst she too pursued life in the fast lane. Between them, Pippa and Lottie went to more clubs and parties than I'd had hot dates. What was the point of having a boyfriend if I never went out with him? I didn't voice this last complaint to Pippa, as I already knew her jaundiced views on the subject of Harry.

'And you?' It was a supreme effort on Pippa's part, but she managed to form the two short syllables. After all, the morning ritual of, 'What did you do last night?' had to be gone through, come hell, high water or hangover.

'Oh, you know, just a quiet evening in. Quite nice for a change,' I lied. I hoped she wasn't going to ask, 'With Harry?' but she was opening her mouth ominously, so I cut in quickly, 'No, not with Harry. Something came up.'

Pippa sighed. 'Probably his dinner.'

'What do you mean?' I pounced quickly, realising she had classified information.

'He was in the same restaurant as me last night, absolutely plastered.' It was still an effort to speak, but our code of honour meant this horrendous piece of news had to be transmitted as soon as possible. I felt cold as I waited for the inevitable bombshell.

'No, don't worry, he wasn't with anybody, just a whole crowd of hoorays having a bun fight.'

I breathed a sigh of relief and my heart slipped out of my mouth, down my throat, and back to a more normal position. So it hadn't been a candlelit tête-à-tête but, even so, why hadn't I been there? I like restaurants, I don't mind hoorays, and I'm game-on for a bun fight. I quizzed Pippa mercilessly, ignoring her frail condition, but she either didn't know much or was being very kind. Her answers were suspiciously diplomatic.

' . . . About ten of them, mostly men.'

' . . . No, he didn't see me.'

' . . . Um, a blondish girl on one side and a man on the other.'

' . . . No, not very pretty, more mousy than blonde actually.'

' . . . Oh, a blue dress, very Top Shop.'

' . . . Um, about twelve-thirty, I think, in a taxi.'

' . . . No, not with Top Shop, on his own — Polly, please don't bully me any more, you know he's a dead loss, what more can I tell you?'

Her body slumped forward again and her head dropped back into position. The interview was over. I sighed and lit what was for me a very premature cigarette. She was right, of course, he was a dead loss. Always out, but never with me. I decided for the millionth time to end what passed as our relationship the next time I saw him. For sure. Yes, definitely. The very next time. He simply wasn't worth it. Having made that little porky-pie of a resolution I felt better, and even had the appetite to tuck into my own daily fix of egg mayonnaise on brown and the *Daily Mail*.

Nick, my boss, and in fact *the* boss, was still in a client meeting, and when Nick was away the rest of the agency played. We lounged around on desks, sofas and – after a heavy lunch – floors. We draped ourselves decoratively around the reception area watching the television, exchanged dirty jokes, made calls to Australia, drank the 'strictly client meetings only' drinks cupboard dry, threw up in loos (new boys only), and generally behaved like any other normal advertising agency. When Nick was around we did exactly the same but made sure he didn't notice.

Which brings me to another sore point. Another bitter blow to add to my long and doleful list of disappointments. Nick Penhalligan.

When I switched from the overworked and underpaid world of publishing to the sexy and glamorous world of advertising six months ago, I had very definite ideas about what life at Penhalligan and Waters was going to be like. OK, it was a small agency, only fifteen people, but small agencies were by all accounts great fun. I was also going to be working for the chairman, which of course guaranteed me an enormous slice of the action.

I daydreamed about being an indispensable girl Friday to a wild and wacky ad-man full of crazy impulsive ideas like, 'Let's get out of the agency today and go and bounce a few ideas around in the wine bar.' I imagined a snappy sartorial dresser with a fine line in enormous red-framed spectacles and swivelling bow-ties who lived in a creative dreamworld and needed a sensible, reliable girl by his side to guide him through his hectic day.

I foresaw long boozy lunches in dimly lit Soho restaurants, where he'd confide in me and tell me all his marital problems, after which we'd pile into a taxi together and charge off to a shoot. As we swept into the studio, the crew would mutter, 'That's Nick Penhalligan: he's brilliant, but of course he can't *move* without Polly, she's his right arm; in fact I don't know where he'd be without her.' To illustrate this point, Nick would then discover he'd lost the script for the commercial and would rummage frantically through his briefcase as everyone waited.

'It's not here!' he'd cry, 'but I'm sure I put it in!'

There'd be an awkward silence, then I'd smile indulgently and produce a wad of paper from my handbag. 'Don't worry, Nick,' I'd say soothingly, 'I've got a copy.'

Everyone would heave great sighs of relief and say things like, 'Gosh, thank goodness for Polly,' and I'd spend the rest of the afternoon being chatted up by the director, the producer and Nigel Havers who happened to be starring in the commercial, before being whisked away to the Zanzibar for several large gin and tonics by my grateful boss. As you can see, I have quite a stranglehold on reality.

The real Nick Penhalligan turned out to be about as wacky as a filing cabinet, and the nearest I got to a shoot was nearly being fired on my first day.

I had arrived on day one of my employment dressed in what I imagined people in the ad-racket probably wore. Short leather mini-skirt, white Katherine Hamnett T-shirt complete with anti-establishment slogan, black biker's jacket, Doc Marten-type shoes and an extraordinary pair of dangly white earrings which Pippa later told me she'd thought were tampons. Dead trendy, or so I believed.

Pippa's eyes were out on stalks when she collected me in reception in her navy blue Puffa, Liberty print skirt and velvet hairband. She eyed what passed for my skirt in disbelief and mumbled something incoherent like 'shit', before leading me into Nick's office.

Nick didn't recognise me. Hardly surprising really, since the girl he'd interviewed for the job had been buttoned up to the eyeballs in Laura Ashley and bore no resemblance whatsoever to the apparition sitting in front of him now. He gaped at me for a long time, opening and closing his mouth a lot, and then very slowly the penny started to drop.

'Ah, yes, you're um . . . you must be Polly, is that right?'

Ah yes, just as I'd thought: short memory; mind on higher, more creative things. Any minute now I'd be producing the forgotten script from my bag.

'That's right.' I smiled and helped him out as one would help a small child. I leaned forward and spoke very slowly. 'You interviewed me last week, remember?' I smiled encouragingly and nodded.

'Yes, yes, of course I did. It's just that last week you looked, um, different . . . more sort of businesslike.' Nick coughed and adjusted his extremely businesslike navy blue tie which I could tell was never going to swivel.

Now, I'm sensitive to atmosphere, and the one we had here was not good. In fact it dawned on me that I'd cocked up. I surreptitiously slid the bubble-gum from my mouth to my hand and pulled the leather skirt down from around my knicker-line, trying to make it look less like a belt.

Nick was shifting around in his chair looking uncomfortable. 'I suppose I'd better make it clear right now that we have quite a lot of important clients coming in and out of here, and whilst some of them I'm sure are very broad-minded, they're probably not used to seeing quite such, um, unusual clothing in an office. I don't want to appear dogmatic or old-fashioned, but I was wondering if in future you could, um, well – tone it down a little?'

'Oh, it's OK,' I said quickly, 'I can explain. I know exactly what you mean about the clothes, but you see I stayed at my sister's place last night and had to borrow some of her things. She's only sixteen and going through a rather rebellious stage, hence the – well, hence the rather avant-garde style! Not me at all!'

'Oh, I see.' He wasn't totally convinced.

'Yes,' I hurried on, 'she's such a worry to my parents: thinks life is just one big party, you know; sex, drugs, rock and roll.'

'Drugs?' he looked alarmed.

'Oh well, not strong ones, no,' I laughed nervously. 'Just, you know . . . recreational.' Was that the word? Nick's eyebrows shot into his hairline. Obviously not.

'No, no, not recreational, I don't mean that, just aspirin really, oh, and the odd paracetamol or two,' I nodded sagely, 'nothing to worry about really.'

'Ah.' Thankfully his eyebrows were coming down from orbit and it seemed his alarm had turned to mere surprise.

I was desperate to change the subject and get away from my fictitious junkie sister. I slapped my thigh in true jolly-hockey-stick style. 'But don't you worry, I'll be back in my own wardrobe tomorrow.'

'Ah good, so tomorrow we can expect to see something a little more, er, restrained?'

'Back to the tweeds and the brogues!' I grinned. And so, I seem to remember, did he, which must have been a first and only.

It wasn't that I didn't like Nick, it was just that he was so bloody difficult to get to know. He was always so incredibly busy, and when I did manage to speak to him, he was invariably abrupt, off-hand, and sometimes downright rude. He would nod his thank-yous and bark out his orders.

A normal opening gambit of a Monday morning would be, 'There's a meeting in half an hour, I'd like tea, coffee and an agenda,' not, 'Good morning, Polly, how was your weekend? If you've got a moment could you possibly find time to make some coffee and then maybe type a little agenda if it's not too much trouble,' to which I would have smiled sweetly and acquiesced. As it was, I barged around in the kitchen slamming cups on to saucers and invariably breaking something.

He was still pretty young to be in his position — about thirty-three or thirty-four — and I had to admit quite good-looking, if you liked that sort of thing. Of course, I didn't. He was tall and slim but with broad shoulders, very dark hair and dark bushy eyebrows. His eyes were dark brown and deep-set and he had very striking angular features, including a rather hooked nose which somehow suited his face. Unfortunately he spoiled the effect by looking continually tired and harassed which he probably was since he was the only one in the agency who appeared to do any work.

As far as sharing conspiratorial lunches in groovy restaurants was concerned, the only thing I'd ever seen him eat was a hastily grabbed sandwich at his desk in between meetings. By all accounts he was screamingly intelligent, or so Pippa — whose brother had been up at Cambridge with him — told me, so he naturally despised the rest of us who survived on one brain cell between us.

As I inanely filled in the D of Dempster with Tipp-Ex and yawned with boredom, in he swept with a face like reinforced concrete. His old tweed coat streamed out behind him like Batman as he flew past at speed, his black eyebrows knitted together in fury.

'Good presentation?' I ventured, closing the paper and trying to look intelligent.

'Bloody client didn't pitch up!' he bawled as he charged into his office slamming the door behind him.

'Oh dear,' I said lamely.

'Happy days,' murmured Pippa, grimacing.

I was just about to grab my notebook and take his messages in, when the door opened again and he poked his head round. 'By the way, Polly, there's a chap downstairs waiting to see you.'

'A chap?' I said in surprise. 'Downstairs?'

It's a bit of a habit of mine to repeat what people say, especially when I'm nonplussed. It obviously irritated the hell out of Nick. He ground his teeth together and shut the door without replying.

Who on earth could it be? No one ever came to see me at work. Suddenly my heart leaped into my oesophagus. Of course! Harry! Harry had come to see me. He knew Pippa had spotted him last night and he'd come to explain himself, to ask my forgiveness and implore me to go out with him tonight, that was it! But why hadn't he telephoned? Why had he come all the way from his computer screen in the city just to see me? Love? Impulse? Even I was clued-up enough to realise he didn't know the meaning of either word. All the same, I jumped up from my chair with joy in my heart and a kiss ready and waiting on my lips. Just in case.

'How extraordinary, Pippa, a man downstairs to see me! Who on earth d'you think it could be?' I babbled excitedly as I brushed my hair and scrabbled around in my drawer for my lipstick.

'I don't know. But I'll tell you one thing, it's not who you think it is,' she said caustically, eyeing my preparations with suspicion.

'Oh God, you're such a killjoy, how do you know?'

'Take it from me. I just know.'

I sighed. Why couldn't any of my friends share my enthusiasm for the man I loved? Never mind. Wouldn't it just show her if it were Harry? I snapped my make-up mirror shut and bounced off down the corridor.

I leaned over the banisters and peered down to the marble hallway below. Whoever it was was sitting on the sofa, most of which was obscured from my view by the stairwell, so all I could make out was a pair of long slim male legs clad in beige trousers with a pair of Docksiders at the end of them. Not Harry's, definitely not Harry's; his Docksiders were brown, not blue; but funnily enough I thought I recognised them. I craned my neck, but couldn't see any more of the body without doing myself a serious injury.

I shrugged. Oh well, it wasn't Harry, but the legs didn't look too bad, so I bounced down the stairs in what I hoped was an attractive, skippy manner, with my blonde hair bobbing around behind me.

'Can I help you?' I inquired in my most imperious, up-market, I-just-bash-a-word-processor-for-a-lark, I-don't-need-the-money, voice.

At that moment the beige trousers uncrossed, the Docksiders hit the deck, and the legs straightened. As he stood up and turned to face me, I realised why the trousers had looked familiar. I'd seen them less than half an hour ago; sat opposite them, in fact. I gasped and my hand shot to my mouth. Good God, it was Ginger!

Chapter Two

I gasped in amazement and gripped the banister rail. Oh Christ, he'd followed me. He'd seen me giving him the glad-eye on the tube and got completely the wrong idea. Now he was going to force himself on me right here on the cold marble stairs and I was too frightened to scream. I looked around desperately. Where was Maurice? Where was Bob? Even a sex-crazed dog was preferable to this. I wasn't even carrying the rape alarm that Mummy had given me for Christmas. Ginger walked towards me. I moaned softly and backed upstairs.

'Hi,' he said.

'What do you want?' I whispered in a very small, unimperious voice.

He took another menacing giant stride in my direction and placed a large freckled hand on the banister rail. I whimpered in terror and jumped back up another step. He smiled in an extremely un-threatening way and the blue eyes crinkled.

'Hey, I'm sorry, I'm not trying to frighten you or anything, I just want to talk to you.'

Pure Ivy League. I'm very hot on accents, especially American ones. I was somewhat relieved, but keen to be totally relieved.

'But you followed me,' I squeaked. 'You followed me from the station, I saw you on the tube.'

'You're right, I did follow you, but hey –' he laughed

– 'there's a perfectly innocent reason. I'm not a mad rapist or anything; I'm certainly not after your body, if that's what you're thinking!'

'Oh.'

He made the very idea sound so absurd I was rather miffed. I drew myself up to my full five feet three inches and adopted a second-position ballet stance, which I've been told gives one poise. Dignity and composure were slowly beginning to course through my veins again.

'So what exactly do you want, only I'm rather busy. I was in a meeting,' I said haughtily.

I had to admit he didn't look like the mad axe-man and, anyway, now I'd got my breath back, I was sure I could scream the place down if I felt like it.

'Actually, I need your help,' he said. 'Look, I'm sorry I followed you, but I couldn't help noticing your scarf.'

'My scarf?' I clutched my neck. I wasn't wearing a scarf. Sometimes I wear a silk scarf under my shirt, but today I definitely wasn't. He *was* mad. A madman with a scarf fetish. Perhaps he wanted to strangle me. 'I'm not wearing a scarf!'

'Your woollen scarf,' he said patiently. 'You were wearing it on the tube this morning.'

'Oh, that one!'

'Yes, that one.'

'What about it?' Was this guy for real? He liked my old school scarf? OK, it was about the only decent legacy I'd got from St Gertrude's, a rather dashing college-style affair with bright red and green stripes, but even so, come *on*. 'It's just my old school scarf, St Gertrude's.'

'Yes I know, I recognised it, that's why I followed you.' Suddenly he reached inside the front of his jacket and went for his gun. Christ! I ducked down on the stairs, hands on head, Miami Vice-style. He pulled a wallet out of his breast pocket.

'Hey, calm down, I just want to show you something.'

He produced a rather crumpled photograph and put it under my nose as I straightened myself out with the help of the banisters. Feeling more than a tad foolish, I took the photo. It was a girl of about my age, maybe younger, with wavy fair hair and quite a sweet face. Pretty-ish, but nothing special.

'Do you know her?' He looked at me intently.

'No . . . I don't think so.' I shook my head.

'Her name's Rachel Marsden, she was at school with you,' he said with some urgency.

'Really? At St Gertrude's?' I had another look. 'Can't say I do, I'm afraid. How old is she?'

'Twenty.'

'Ah well, that's a little bit younger than me, and if she wasn't in my house, which I don't think she was, I wouldn't know her from Eve.'

'I'm pretty sure her house was called something like Finch or Fich—'

'Finches. No, well in that case she definitely wasn't in my house. Well, there you go, sorry. Can't help you, I'm afraid.' I handed back the picture.

He looked crestfallen. 'Are you absolutely sure?'

'Absolutely.'

'Perhaps you'd remember some of her friends?'

'Who were they?'

'Well, that's the problem, she was a bit of a loner really. I'm finding it pretty hard to locate anybody.'

He put the photo back in his wallet and ran his hands through his hair. He really was rather good-looking. Especially when he did that. I was intrigued.

'So um, you're looking for her, is that it?'

He sighed. 'Yeh, that's it.'

'Why, has she done something wrong?' What was he, Special Branch, MI5?

He laughed hollowly. 'No, she hasn't done anything wrong, she's my . . .' He hesitated ' . . . My fiancée.'

23

'Your fiancée!' I was flabbergasted. Some mousy nobody probably a year or so below me at school who I didn't even remember had got herself engaged to this yummy American hunk, done a bunk, and left him moving heaven and earth to find her? And how in God's name do you loose a fiancé? I know if I had one I'd have him locked in a little cage in my bedroom with a heavy padlock on the door.

'Well, if she's a missing person, why don't you go to the police?'

He sat down on the bottom step and shook his head. He looked all in. He was also getting cuter by the minute. I quickly sat down next to him and looked sympathetic, sweeping my hair back from my forehead so he could see my profile, and opening my eyes wide.

'Well, she's not a missing person exactly,' he said. 'Her father knows where she is, but he won't let me see her.' He gave a wry smile and scuffed the toe of his Docksider on the marble. 'He doesn't exactly approve.'

'Oh! Why ever not, you don't look like too much of a reprobate to me.'

He laughed. 'I'm not, he just doesn't . . . Well, let's just say we don't see eye to eye.'

I looked at him warily. Perhaps he had done something terrible after all. Walked off with the family silver, seduced the parlourmaid, made a pass at the dog — it would have to have been something in that line for my own parents to disapprove. Mummy practically tripped men like this up in the street for me, so desperate was she to shorten my shelf-life and climb into her mother-of-the-bride outfit.

'Why on earth doesn't he like you?' I asked nosily.

He hesitated and I thought he was about to tell me, but he obviously thought better of it. 'Oh, it's a long story.'

I took the hint and got to my feet briskly. 'Well, I'm sorry I can't be more helpful, but I honestly don't remember er, whatsername, Rachel thingamy.'

He stood up immediately and held out his hand. I shook it. What charming manners.

'That's OK,' he said, 'thanks a lot for trying, anyway. I really appreciate it.'

'Not at all.' I almost said, Do come again.

'Well goodbye, and thanks.' He turned to go and was walking towards the door when he suddenly swung around and stared at me intently. He looked desperate.

'Look, if you see anyone from school who remembers her or who might have seen her recently, would you please let me know? I'd be really grateful. You see, I've got nothing to go on at the moment, and to be honest I'm really at the end of my rope, I just don't know what the hell's happened to her. I mean, maybe if you rang a few people up? You know, old schoolfriends? I don't want to be a nuisance but I just . . . I just don't know what to do next. I'm staying at the Savoy till the end of the week, so you could get me there if you come up with anything. My name's Adam Buchanan, by the way. Shall I write that down?'

'No, it's OK.' Adam Buchanan. Somehow I thought I'd remember. Savoy, eh? I smiled. 'I promise I'll ring you if I hear anything.'

'Thanks. It would mean so much, really. Well, goodbye, it was good to meet you.'

'Um, you too. Bye,' I smiled.

This time he went, closing the door softly behind him. Well! I stood on the stairs for a moment, inwardly digesting. Then I walked slowly back upstairs. Poor chap, what a shame, and how horrid Rachel Thingamy's father must be not to like him. Fancy searching London for his girlfriend; he must be crazy about her. I couldn't see Harry looking under the bed if I went missing.

'Well?' asked Pippa eagerly as I wandered into the pit, chewing my thumbnail thoughtfully. 'Was it him?'

'Who?'

'Harry, you goon.'

'Oh, Harry, no, but it was quite interesting . . .' I explained at length, embellishing the story a bit here and there for her benefit. She was suitably horrified at the potential rape situation, clapping her hands over her mouth and rolling her eyes in terror, and then was almost moved to tears, as I knew she would be, by the futility of the lover's quest.

'Oh Polly, how awful! You mean he's an innocent abroad, combing the streets of London and grilling complete strangers in an effort to find her,' she said dramatically. 'God, he must have been desperate to follow you.'

'Thanks a bunch,' I said dryly, but I knew what she meant.

'Well, ring up some old schoolfriends and see if they remember her!' she said eagerly.

'Oh, come on, Pippa,' I said, eyeing the enormous pile of typing Nick had obviously just deposited on my desk, 'I have enough trouble sorting out my own life, let alone someone else's.'

'But you could really help him, Polly, someone might have seen her. Just ring a couple of people, please,' she impassioned.

'I will later, if I have time,' I lied. 'Just let me get through some of this first.'

I went on to auto-pilot and started bashing out the first contact report of the day. One of only two million, I was sure. Pippa always made me feel like such a heel. She'd help every lame dog she came across and positively went looking for them. There was an old tramp at South Ken station who should have been wearing designer labels saying, 'Clothes by Pippa Harvey', she threw so much money at him. I bashed away, taking my lack of humanity out on the typewriter. Suddenly my hands froze in mid-air.

How had he known my name? How on earth had he known who to ask for, for God's sake? Bloody hell, there was something fishy going on here! I pushed back my chair and charged into Nick's office without bothering to knock.

'Who did he ask for, Nick? Did he know my name?' I gasped.

Nick was behind his desk, and sitting opposite him was Mr Hutchinson, probably our most important client. He could have been the Queen for all I cared.

'Did he say Polly? Or Polly McLaren, or what?' I urged.

They both stared at me. Mr Hutchinson was on the edge of his seat: he liked a bit of drama because he led such a dull life. He was a little rat of a man with thin grey hair, a pale waxy face, and thick pebble glasses through which he blinked a great deal. On rare occasions he gave a tight little smile, but mostly his expression was similar to that of an undertaker's. His front teeth protruded slightly, just like a rat's, and he did a lot of slurping and sucking in an effort to cover them with his upper lip. He was a great one for giving Pippa and me the vicar's handshake, a two handed ever-so-sincere jobby, and we decided that was probably the closest he ever got to sex. A hell of a nasty thought. We always washed afterwards. He was blinking away at me now like a Belisha beacon, but the tight little smile had yet to surface.

Nick looked at me coldly, keeping his own eyelids well under control. They didn't bat once. 'If you mean the gentleman downstairs,' he said evenly, 'he simply asked for Miss McLaren. I've no idea how he knew your name.'

'But that's so spooky, isn't it, don't you see?' I was raving now. 'I mean, he must have been on to me for days, he probably knows where I *live*, for God's sake, and there I was falling for his story and even trying to *help* him when all the time—'

'*Polly*!' Nick cut in furiously and with volume. It did the trick. I'd never heard him raise his voice and I ground to a halt. He glared at me. 'I've no idea how he knew your name, nor, come to that, what the hell you are talking about. Now let's sort this out later, shall we?' It was said with about six inches of solid steel blade running through the middle of it.

My P45 fluttered briefly through my fuddled brain and I saw his point. I retreated, closing the door quietly.

Pippa looked at me with horror as I came out. 'Mr Hutchinson's in there!' she hissed.

'I know,' I whispered, 'but how did he know my name?'

'Who, Hutchinson?'

'No, idiot, scarf-spotter downstairs.'

'Oh! Did he?'

'Yes! He asked for Miss McLaren!'

'Oh!' Pippa looked almost as shaken as I did for a moment, then she suddenly swung round and grabbed my scarf from the hat stand.

'You said it yourself, he's a scarf spotter! It's got your name on it, see?' she said, waving it under my nose. 'Here, look!'

And of course there it was. P. E. McLaren, red letters on a little strip of white tape, sown on by my ever-loving mother, years before I embarked on my career as a job-wrecker.

'He'll sack me!' I wailed. 'I was like a loony in there!'

'No he won't,' said Pippa doubtfully. 'He'll just be furious.'

And so he was. Bloody furious. When Mr Hutchinson had gone he asked me, murderously, to come into his office. 'Now please!'

I slunk in meekly and sat down opposite him at his vast, leather-topped desk. I decided to get my story in quickly before he had a chance to ask, thereby deflecting the shit from the fan.

'Look, Nick, I'm terribly sorry about bursting in on you and Mr Hutchinson, but the guy downstairs followed me from the tube, can you believe it? I mean, OK, I was staring at him first, but only as a joke — you know it's this game I play every morning, which man would you fancy going to — er, well anyway — I thought he'd got the wrong idea, and that was why I was so alarmed, but in fact he's lost his fiancée and was following me because he recognised my old school scarf and the reason he knew my name is that—'

'Stop!' Nick had his hand up like a policeman stopping traffic. His eyes were tightly shut. 'Just stop!'

I stopped. He opened his eyes. Except they didn't look like eyes, more like bits of flint. I had a feeling the shit was making a detour my way. He leaned forward and folded his arms on his desk. His face was about a foot from mine. A muscle was going in his cheek and he looked deadly.

'Listen to me, Polly,' he said quietly. I listened. 'This is not a large agency: in fact it's extremely small. We have a few minor clients who provide us with a smattering of income, but we have one major client who happens to bill a great deal of money with us, namely Mr Hutchinson. He is, as you know, a total jerk but, be that as it may, he has us by the short and curlies. Because if he decides, for whatever reason, to take his revolting instant coffee away to another agency, we're sunk. Snookered. Finished. Washed up. Bankrupt. Am I making myself clear?'

'Yes,' I whispered, feeling about twelve.

'Our image is extremely important. Like it or loathe it, it sells us. It is therefore absolutely imperative that we create a good impression in front of clients. You come charging into my office, ranting and raving like a banshee, and we look like a Mickey Mouse agency. D'you get my drift?'

'Yes,' I whispered again, squirming in my seat. What did he think I was, a moron?

Nick leaned back in his seat and surveyed me, tapping the desk with a pencil. 'And another thing, Polly. If you ask me, your private life is intruding too much on your work. You just haven't got your mind on the job, have you? If you're not sitting at your desk filing your nails, you're mooning around thinking about your boyfriend and waiting for the telephone to ring. Well, that's harmless enough as long as you've done all your typing, but now I find you're picking up men on trains, bringing them into the agency, and chatting them up downstairs. I'm afraid that's just not on. I don't give a damn if you behave like that in your spare time, although frankly I'm surprised, but for God's sake don't bring these guys into the agency.'

Steam was pouring from my ears now, and I opened my mouth to speak, but the policeman's hand flew up again.

'Let me finish! It's quite simple, Polly, and we don't need to discuss it any further. I simply ask that you don't bring your men friends into the office, and that you don't burst into important client meetings raving like a lunatic. Is that clear?' The telephone rang, he picked it up instantly. 'Yes, hello? Oh, Mr Rawlings, yes, I was going to get back to you . . .'

My mouth was wide with indignation, which I was bloody well going to voice in no uncertain terms, but Nick waved me out of the office. I ignored him and sat tight. He was not getting away with this. He carried on talking, saw me still sitting there, and frowned, waving me off again. Still I sat there, determined to have my two penny-worth.

Suddenly he put his hand over the mouthpiece. 'Polly, if you don't get out of my office this minute and let me talk to Mr Rawlings, I will really lose my temper!' he hissed.

I ran. But by golly was I livid. Exactly who did he think he was talking to? Mooning about my boyfriend! Picking up men! Filing my nails! I don't even have a nail-file — come to that, I don't even have any nails! He'd just thrown that in to make me sound like a Sharon, the bastard.

Pippa tried to placate me with numerous cups of strong, sweet tea, but the steam was gushing out of every orifice now, and I gnashed my teeth in fury, waiting for my chance to set Mr Penhalligan straight.

Unfortunately, Nick shut himself away for the rest of the day to work on a presentation, giving the strict instruction that under no circumstances was he to be disturbed. I don't have that much of a death wish, so I left him alone and finally went home on the dot of five-thirty, seething with rage and plotting my revenge.

Chapter Three

I marched up the steps to our front door in Tregunter Road, slammed it behind me, and stomped up the innumerable stairs to the garret flat I share with Lottie. I was still steaming. *No one*, I repeated to myself, *no one* has *ever* spoken to me like that. *No one*. I viciously shouldered open the flat door which always sticks, flung my bag on the floor and collapsed on the sofa in a deep depression. Fine Young Cannibals assaulted my eardrums at full volume. The flat was in the most disgusting mess: dirty glasses, wine bottles and overflowing ashtrays covered every conceivable surface area, a line of bras and knickers in varying shades of sock-grey were drying on the radiator, bits of chocolate digestive had been trodden into the rug, there were dog hairs everywhere, and penicillin was sprouting from the various coffee mugs that were littered around. Why doesn't anyone ever tidy *up*? I thought savagely.

'Harry rang!' shouted Lottie from the bathroom.

I sprang to my feet, eyes shining. Suddenly the flat seemed beautifully cosy and lived in and — oh, just charmingly Bohemian, and the music was joyous and uplifting. I ran to the bathroom where Lottie was brushing her teeth in her underwear. A bath was running, bad sign, I'd have to have her water.

'When! What did he say? Is he ringing back?'

Lottie paused, her mouth full of froth. 'Ten minutes

ago, he's coming over in an hour to take you out to supper and no, he's not ringing back.'

She gargled, making sure she didn't swallow any toothpaste — we'd read somewhere that it was full of calories — and then went back for some more vigorous brushing, her D-cupped boobs bouncing up and down under the strain and her long dark hair dripping in the basin.

'Oh joy! Oh joy! Oh thank you God!' I did an ecstatic little dance and wrapped the shower curtain around me in a dramatic Grecian sweep.

Lottie put her toothbrush down and looked at me accusingly. 'So you're going,' she said grimly.

'Well of course I'm going.' I dropped the curtain in disbelief. 'I've been waiting for this phone call for six days now!'

'Exactly.' Lottie rinsed her mouth. 'If you were really cool you'd ring back and say you were busy. Look at the way he just assumes you're free!'

'Oh I know.' I felt deflated. 'But don't make me do it, Lottie. I can't, I'm mad about him,' I wailed.

She sighed. 'I know. And the worst thing is he knows it too. Rung up for his weekly bonk, I suppose.'

She peered in the mirror, looking apprehensively at potential blackhead areas. I watched her reflection as I perched on the side of the bath. Her round sweet face was framed with long dark silky hair and she had beautiful huge dark eyes that looked at me critically now. Oh dear, I was in trouble.

Lottie was my only truly sensible friend. She ran her life in an orderly, no-nonsense fashion, and boy did she get results. I once analysed the secret of Lottie's success and realised it was mind-blowingly simple. During the day, she focused her mind on the job in hand, which in her case was that of being a solicitor in a large city practice. That was what she was there to do and that was what she did. She didn't loll all over her desk nursing a hangover, eating chocolate and dreaming about men. She didn't block the office phone-lines gossiping endlessly to girlfriends, neither did she go shopping in office hours searching for that elusive little black number. No, no. Lottie did something that was anathema to me. She worked. Consequently she was well respected, well liked and well paid. A simple formula, you might think, but one that had yet to filter down to my neck of the woods.

Then there was Lottie's love life to consider. OK, she was experiencing a temporary lull at the moment, but purely at her own instigation. A particularly sweet (but rather short) antique dealer was probably at this very moment throwing himself off Blackfriars Bridge because Lottie had gently but firmly eased him out of her life. Lottie finished with men. They did not finish with her. Lottie was pursued into cupboards, behind sofas, into expensive restaurants: you name it, she'd been there.

Now admittedly she's a good-looking girl. But if I say so myself, and she would say it too, I'm not bad looking either. Granted, I'm prone to pushing the scales over nine stone, but who isn't? And I have nice blue eyes, a good complexion, a pair of rather stylish cheekbones (a rare commodity these days, I've noticed), longish, blondish hair, a thankfully unremarkable nose and pretty remarkable legs, so how do I manage to get it so wrong?

Do I have an unattractive personality? Am I perhaps lacking in humour, or a sartorial sense of style? My friends tell me no. As far as humour's concerned I like nothing better than a good laugh and, as for style, if they handed out O-levels in how to accessorise, I'm sure I'd have a shed-full.

Ah, so perhaps it's something more sinister, I hear you whisper. Perhaps there's a personal hygiene problem lurking nastily under the armpits. Again, the answer, I assure you, is no. I happen to be a rigorous pit sniffer –

just my own — and I'm also an avid, and noisy, mouthwash gargler. So what exactly is my problem?

Simple, says Lottie, I aim too high. Way, way too high. Apparently I should be aiming lower — much, much lower; underground preferably, somewhere around pit level, amongst the slugs and the worms. Lottie is actually the greatest exponent of her theory, her maxim at a party being, 'Go ugly early.' Why waste valuable time, she says, lining up behind all the other prospective female candidates to chat up the best-looking man in the room, when you know you're going to end up with that short, balding insurance broker in the corner?

All this, of course, makes huge sense, but sense and I have never made very good bedfellows. The one and only time I took Lottie's advice, sense did indeed turn out to be huge, about six feet nine inches, in fact; more of a giraffe than a human being. And hard though I tried to keep his 'good personality' to the forefront of my mind, I couldn't help being distracted by his colossal nostrils (of which I had an excellent view from my low vantage point), and his enormous expanse of smooth white forehead which seemed to go back and back in an uninterrupted fashion almost to the nape of his neck. Needless to say he had to go and, as he went, my feet went dancing off to the sunny side of the street again, where the beautiful people live.

Of course, this side of the street is harder work. Back on the sensible side I'm way up in the pecking order, but over here with the stunners, I'm only fair to middling. I had to fight my corner, and fight I did, until one day I went home with the prize. Harry. Now this should have been my moment of glory. I should have been able to dangle his delectable personage in front of Lottie's sensible nose crying, 'You see! You see! I hooked one in the end!' But no. The more I dangled, the more Lottie was able to shake her head at me and sigh. Like now. Oh-oh.

Lottie set aside her toothbrush and sat on the linen

basket facing me. She folded her arms in an ominously businesslike manner. 'Polly, let me ask you something. Do you honestly enjoy your dates with Harry?'

'Enjoy them? Of course I do! What a question! Enjoy them? I positively live for them!'

'Yes, I know that, I know you spend every waking hour dreaming about them and listening for the phone, but when you actually go out, do you relax? Is he good company? Does he make you laugh? Does he – I don't know – look after you, see that you're having a good time?'

'Lottie, don't be absurd; we never stop laughing, he's marvellous company!'

'But do you feel relaxed? I mean really? Or d'you feel that you're constantly making an effort with him? It's just that whenever I see you with him it all seems such a strain, so sort of – artificial really. I mean you never just get a video out and curl up on the sofa with him, do you? You never just have a quiet evening in. It's always night clubs and parties and restaurants; and you always have to look marvellous, and it's not as if you've just met him, you've been going out with him for ages now, and I shouldn't think he's even seen you without lipstick, let alone no make-up at all.'

'Oh Lottie, what's make-up got to do with it? You know I wear a lot anyway.'

'Not around the flat, you don't, and not when you go to your parents.'

'Oh well, that's different—'

'But why? Why aren't you more natural with him? Let him see what you're really like instead of, I don't know, always being perfect. I'm not trying to spoil things, and I know you're excited because he's phoned, but honestly Polly, it's been about nine months now and I sometimes wonder if you really know this guy at all!'

I sighed and picked my nails, feeling hemmed in. 'I

know what you mean, Lotts, but honestly, everything's fine. Harry just likes me to be like that, you know, made up and dressed up and—'

'Exactly! That's exactly what I mean!'

'I know, I know, but, well, if Harry likes it, well then I like it too . . .' I trailed off lamely. I could see from Lottie's face how pathetic that sounded, but my argumentative powers were fading fast. I rallied myself.

'The thing is, I can't explain why, but I enjoy it all. The preparation and – and the excitement, the build up. I don't want us to be mundane and boring – living on takeaways and watching telly and taking each other for granted.'

'No but surely there's a happy medium. I mean—'

'Please, Lottie. I know what you're saying, but seriously, I reckon I've nearly cracked it with Harry. A couple more weeks and he'll be eating out of my hand! In fact, I'm pretty sure he's mad about me already,' I lied.

Lottie looked totally unconvinced. I took a shifty look at my watch. Christ, quarter-past six already.

'Look, I promise, everything's fine, I couldn't be happier! And honestly, I'd love to talk about it more with you, but the thing is he'll be here in about an hour and I desperately need a bath,' I said, eyeing her water enviously. 'I couldn't possibly . . . ?'

'Yes, yes, go on, have it,' she said, caving in dramatically, 'I'll have it after you. I'm only going to the cinema with Sophie, I'm sure she won't mind if I'm covered in scum and leg shavings.'

I hugged her, grateful for the water and for her submission. 'Thanks, you're an absolute star, and I promise I'll think about what you've said.'

'Promise?' she said, knowing I wouldn't.

'Promise,' I said, knowing she knew that I wouldn't.

When she'd gone, I quickly poured half a bottle of my most expensive bubble-bath into the water, hoping it would overpower her Radox, and leaped in. Only an hour! Even less, in fact! I didn't have much time and there was so much to do! I scrubbed and shaved and plucked and washed and rinsed and sloshed around a bit, then jumped out and ran dripping to the bedroom where I emptied the entire contents of my wardrobe on to the bed.

I looked at the mountain of clothes and groaned. 'Oh God, I've got nothing to wear!' I wailed. 'Lottie, can I borrow your suede trousers?'

'They're at the cleaners,' she yelled back.

'Oh no! What else have you got?'

I ran into Lottie's bedroom where she obligingly emptied her own wardrobe on to the bed. I wriggled in and out of things like a maniac, but eventually ran back to my own mountain and settled on a short black skirt and a silky red jumper with a slashed neckline which slipped seductively off one shoulder. I clinched it all in with a black suede belt. The shoulder looked a bit anaemic, so I rubbed on some fake tan with tiny pieces of make-up sponge which Wellington, Lottie's Yorkie, had thoughtfully chewed into little bits. I ran into the sitting room where Lottie was ironing a shirt.

'What d'you think?' I said, balancing on the sofa and peering into our only decent mirror above the fireplace. I'd coaxed my hair into mad gypsy curls of the blonde variety, and completed the look with some enormous gold hoop earrings which had eaten up most of last month's salary and were so heavy that they almost made me walk with my head bowed.

'Wow!' Lottie was genuinely impressed. 'That should knock him for six.'

'Really?' I was pleased, Lottie was a tough critic. 'Not too tarty?'

'Oh well, it's tarty all right, but you can't have it both ways.'

I hoiked the jumper up a bit to cover the shoulder. 'Better?'

'Well, it'll come off later anyway, so what does it matter? I take it you're playing away tonight?'

I ignored Lottie's disapproving tone, and jumped around on the sofa with excitement. 'I expect so! Don't double-lock, but don't expect me either – and stop looking at me like an old fishwife with a rolling pin. Haven't you ever been wild and irresponsible?'

Lottie sighed and said truthfully, 'Just give me half a chance. Seriously though, Polly, don't hang on to his every monosyllable, and don't race him back to his flat when he suggests coffee, and don't iron every single shirt he possesses, and don't—'

The doorbell rang in the middle of the lecture. I leaped off the sofa, then leaped back on again, yelping with panic.

'He's early! You go, Lottie.'

'Oh sure, then he'd really think it was his lucky night.' Lottie was still in her underwear. 'A flat full of push-overs.'

She went off to dress and I buzzed Harry in, my heart beating as loud as the thump-thump-thump of his feet coming up the stairs.

I knew I'd settle down eventually, but for the first half an hour with him you'd think I was on drugs. I'd leap around like a maniac, talking in a strange high-pitched voice, breathing heavily, offering him cigarettes when he didn't smoke, and pouring him large gins when he drank whisky. Anyone else, said Lottie, would get terribly insecure and think there was a chain-smoking, gin-swilling hunk knocking around the rest of the week, but not Harry.

He came bounding into the flat like a golden retriever puppy, all long-legged and blond and floppy-haired. He looked, as usual, divine. He was tanned from a long weekend skiing, and his hair was blonder and streakier than ever from the sun. I could feel my much touched-up roots sizzling with jealousy.

'Polyester!' he yelled as he came charging through the door, rugby tackling me on to the sofa. 'How the devil are you? Hang on, we're off!'

I shrieked with laughter as the sofa got under way and we slid across the room on the coasters. Lottie wandered in wearing her dressing gown and munching a jaffa cake. She sidestepped the cruising sofa with weary indifference. She'd seen it all before.

Harry looked up as we came to a standstill next to her. 'Hi, Lottie, how's your sex life?' he said, pulling her dressing gown cord undone.

'Not as complicated as yours, I suspect,' said Lottie dryly, tying the cord up again.

Harry laughed nervously. He wasn't sure about Lottie, she was a bit too smart for him. He swept his hair back in a practised gesture. 'I see it's nice and tidy in here as usual,' he said, taking in the debris-strewn flat. 'That ironing board seems to be a permanent fixture! Modern art, is it? Ha-ha!'

'No, we're looking back in anger,' Lottie quipped, but it was lost on Harry.

He turned his cornflower-blue gaze on to me. God he was attractive. I bit my hand to stop myself from giving him the first kiss. Wait for it, Polly, wait for it . . . Ah, here it comes. He leaned down and kissed me briefly on the mouth. He always started with a little one, a teaser, then bent his head down again for the big clinch. I responded enthusiastically, considering Lottie was still in the room.

When I eventually let him go, his lazy, sexy grin spread over his face and his blue eyes roamed all over me as we lay on the sofa. He took my chin in his hand. I smiled, overwhelmed with love.

'So, young Polly,' he murmured, 'what have you been

up to all this time? I haven't seen you for absolutely ages. Been a good girl?'

He made it sound as if I'd been deliberately avoiding him instead of staring at the phone willing it to ring.

'Oh, I've been out and about,' I said as casually as I could. Harry liked independent girls. 'A couple of drinks parties, out to supper once or twice.'

'Terrific, that's what I like to hear. Got to keep your finger on the pulse.'

My own pulse was going like a bongo drum as he ran his fingers through my hair. He was making slow progress, and I leaped up as I realised he was wading through half a ton of mousse and gel. 'Must have a ciggy,' I said quickly.

He sat up and watched me as I lit a cigarette. I knew I was being appraised, so I lit it slowly, then stood with my back to the fireplace – chest out, tummy in – reclining against the marble shelf. Quite uncomfortable really, but it worked. He looked me up and down approvingly.

'You're looking extremely tasty tonight, Poll. Where shall we go to eat before I ravage you? Or shall we skip the meal and I'll ravage you here, much easier!'

'Easier on your wallet,' muttered Lottie.

Harry missed it, but I caught it and said bravely, more for sisterhood than for myself, 'Actually, I'm quite hungry.'

'Of course you are, my little pumpkin, I was only joking. Where d'you want to go?'

'Oh, I don't know. How about Giovanni's?'

'Right, Giovanni's it is. Let's go then.' He drained his glass and stood up, ready for a change of scene.

I was always staggered by his low boredom threshold. He was like a small child, constantly needing to be amused by new toys.

I jumped up too, hurriedly stubbed out my cigarette, and knocked back my drink, throwing most of it down my jumper and choking on the rest. Lottie shook her head in disbelief.

'Steady darling!' Harry patted me on the back, laughing. 'Don't choke on it! Right, we'll be off then. Packed a bag?'

'Er, no, not yet.'

I hadn't, because the last time I'd packed one he'd dropped me back at my flat at ten-thirty saying he was going on to a dance – hadn't he mentioned it? He hadn't, and I'd felt like a complete berk trudging up the stairs to the flat, overnight bag in hand.

'Won't be a minute!' I said, grabbing a pair of knickers from the radiator and stuffing them in my handbag. 'There.'

Harry raised his eyebrows. 'That's it?'

Yes, that was it, or did that look slutty?

'Er, well no, not quite, hang on a sec . . .' I ran into my bedroom.

'No rush, no rush!' he called after me, but I was too wound up to slow down now.

Nothing seemed to be clean, so I rummaged through my dirty linen basket and recycled a navy blue shirt that didn't show the dirt, and grabbed my cleanser, moisturiser and toothbrush, although I always liked to use his. I rummaged under the bed, found an old carrier bag, and shoved everything in.

When I got back to the sitting room he was standing by the door, jangling his keys and looking impatient.

'Sorry,' I panted, 'couldn't find a shirt.'

'No worries. All set now?'

'Yes – bye Lottie!'

I gave her a backward wave, not having the nerve to meet her judgemental eyes; and anyway, I had to run, because Harry seemed to be half-way down the stairs already. I pounded down the stairs after him. Funny how he's always one step ahead, I mused, as I jumped the last few and ran out on to the pavement. He was already revving up the car. I ran around to the passenger door and limbo-danced my way into his low-slung crumpet-catcher. With a good deal of throttle we set off for the restaurant.

And that's another thing, I thought as I settled back into the impossibly-difficult-to-get-out-of bucket seat, how come I never rip him off? How come I never have the nerve to say, 'Well actually, I thought we'd go to Le Gavroche tonight.'

On the other hand, I reflected, as he pulled up outside the extremely reasonable little Italian I'd picked, this was where he'd fallen for me on that first magical night, and I always hoped he'd remember and fall for me all over again.

As we ploughed our way through the only edible food on the menu – avocado, mozzarella and tomato followed by veal marsala – I had him rolling in the aisles as I recounted various anecdotes, apocryphal or otherwise, that I'd saved up and made up during the week. My efforts were rewarded handsomely.

He leaned back in his chair wiping his eyes at one of my more outrageous witticisms. 'Polly, that's hysterical. I don't know where you get these stories from!' he cried.

From my imagination, of course, was the answer to this, but why tell the boring truth when you can tell a good lie? Flushed with success, I helped myself to another glass of wine by way of celebration, although I couldn't help thinking that things were slightly arse about tit here. Wasn't he supposed to be laughing me into bed? And how come I was pouring the wine? Lottie's wise words came briefly to mind, but I banished them hastily. Utter rubbish, I was having a marvellous time.

Oh God, he was off and I hadn't been listening. I rearranged my face so that it took on an absorbed expression as we had our weekly bulletin of Stockbroking News.

I didn't understand stockbroking, but since Harry had explained it twice already, the second time in a painstaking, stockbroking-for-morons tone of voice, I didn't feel I could ask again. I just smiled knowingly and nodded a lot, and when there was a gap in the monologue, made what I thought were appropriate remarks like:

'Really, as much as that?'

'Forty-two per cent, my goodness.'

'No, of course not, that would be insider dealing.'

'Isn't that what they call a bear market?'

It was all pretty hit or miss stuff, but he never seemed to suss me. Once he'd got into his stride he was unstoppable, and he didn't really notice what I said anyway. It suited me because it gave me a chance to catch my breath and think of some more outrageous lies to amuse him with later.

'Polly?'

Harry was wiping his mouth with his napkin and looking none too pleased. Oh God, he'd come to the end of his story which I now remembered he'd prefixed with the words, 'I think you'll find this rather amusing', and I couldn't for the life of me remember what he'd been talking about. Too late for a belly laugh? Definitely. I shook my head and twisted my mouth into what I hoped was a wry little smile.

'How funny, but when you come to think about it, sad too, don't you think?'

Harry looked rather taken aback. 'Er . . . well, I suppose so, for his wife maybe. You can bet your bottom dollar the bra wasn't hers.'

It was my turn to look mystified, but before he'd had time to rearrange his brain cells, I charged off on a completely different tack and told him about my encounter with Adam Buchanan. Of course I hammed it up like mad, and had the distraught man practically crying on my shoulder, begging me to help him find his girlfriend. I naturally expected Harry to laugh like a drain and sneer at

45

such love-struck, unmanly behaviour, but not for the first time in my checkered career with him, I was wrong. Harry was on the edge of his seat; in fact, Harry was leaning forward, keen to hear more. Now this was a first. Harry always leaned back. I was the one who leaned forward. I once tried leaning back in the hope that he'd come in, but we just ended up yelling at each other across the table in an effort to make ourselves heard. But here he was now, eager for details, gripped, engrossed and, wait for it, sympathetic.

'How extraordinary. You say they're engaged?'

'Apparently.'

'And now she's just vanished?'

'That's what he says.'

'And the father thinks he's a bad influence. You can bet your life Daddy's hiding her somewhere, the bastard. And presumably this American guy doesn't know where to start looking for her; he probably doesn't know anyone in London, does he?'

'No, he doesn't, that's why he followed me, you see, because of the school scarf.'

'So what are you going to do?'

'Do?'

'Yes, to help. Didn't you say you'd try and help?'

I fidgeted a bit. 'Well, no, I didn't really.'

'Why not?'

'Well, for a start I didn't even know the girl at school; and secondly, well secondly, what on earth can I do?'

'More than he can in a strange country, that's for sure. I don't know, use your imagination!'

This stung. I smiled sweetly. 'Yes, but it's none of my business really, is it?'

'Except that he's made it your business by following you to work and asking you to help. God, Polly, aren't you intrigued? I mean, how amazing to fall in love and find the person you feel you can spend the rest of your life with, but then have her vanish into thin air! Pretty irritating, don't you think?'

I snorted with derision. 'Hardly thin air, Harry. She's probably shacked up with some hunk in Bayswater. I mean, who knows if this guy's telling the truth? Who knows what's going on?'

'Not you, obviously,' said Harry, helping himself to more wine.

I took a sharp intake of breath and reached for my wine glass. My God, he was pissed off. Pissed off because I couldn't end the story, couldn't give him the punchline. Harry's new toy had been taken away from him just when he was enjoying it. Well gosh, I'm sorry.

But my indignation was misdirected and I knew it. What had really knocked me sideways was that all-revealing sentence of his: 'to find the person you feel you can spend the rest of your life with.' Had he really said that? Harry, the happy hunter, who couldn't even commit himself to a quick drink in the pub, let alone the rest of his life with a wife? Harry, who I'd naturally assumed was an emotional cripple because he'd never come up trumps in the love and slush department?

I'd convinced myself that it all stemmed from his childhood. In fact I'd spent many happy hours fantasising about a strict and puritanical upbringing at the hands of uncompromising and no doubt brutal parents — too many smacks as a child, not enough chocolate, not enough telly — comparing it to my own cuddly, chocolatey, telly-viewing childhood. I was sure that this had soured his outlook, but that with a little patience I could show him the way, lead him up the Mills and Boon path of true romance, teach him what love was all about. But he knew! He knew about it, and what's more — and this was where I nearly gagged on my courgettes — he thought it was 'wonderful'! Harry, like the rest of the human race, was on the prowl for that elusive love match, and all along I'd

47

put his compulsive prowling down to an insatiable desire to stick his hand up girls' skirts.

I struggled womanfully with the courgettes, pushing them firmly down my throat and trying desperately to remember what had brought about this earth-shattering revelation. Oh yes, Rachel Whatsername.

'Anyway,' I said, swallowing hard, 'I don't suppose I could have helped. I mean, I didn't know the girl at school. I only know what she looks like from that photo he showed me.'

'That's it,' said Harry snidely, 'put your head in the sand as usual.'

I was furious. 'How dare you! What do you expect me to do, ring up all the old girls I can find in the phone book and quiz them rigid?'

'Wouldn't hurt,' he said. 'Give you something to do at work for a change.'

Harry was enjoying himself now. I'd worked myself up into a nice little state, and he was steadily winding me up.

Like a moron I took the bait. 'Well for your information,' I said furiously, 'I said I'd look into it for him!'

Harry threw back his head and roared with laughter. 'Oh, really? Inspector McLaren's looking into it, is she? Off to sniff the pavements, eh? Well I shall look forward to hearing how you solve the case!'

The waiter arrived to take our order for pudding. I fumed and tore my napkin into a million pieces. We sat in stony silence as Harry demolished a delicious-looking crème-brûlée which I'd petulantly refused. Just you wait, I thought. It'll take me exactly two minutes to find that girl. Just you wait. I downed the rest of my glass in one gulp, which seemed to have a calming effect. Get a grip, Polly old girl. This is ridiculous. This is no way to end the evening.

Harry was obviously thinking along the same lines. After all, it's not much fun going to bed with a grumpy girlie. He crowbarred his way back into my good books. 'So, how are your parents?' he asked with a glittering smile.

I smiled back reluctantly. I was potty about my family and, given half a chance, could bore for England about my wonderful parents and my gorgeous older brothers.

'They're really well, thanks.'

'Still living in the country?' he grinned maliciously.

He had to spoil it, didn't he? When I'd first met Harry, I'd told him I was going home to the country one weekend. He'd roared with laughter when he discovered we lived in Esher.

'Esher's not country, Polly! You might as well live in Surbiton!'

I'd blushed hotly; I'd always rather liked Esher. Harry's parents lived in Derbyshire, in 'proper country', where his father was a farmer, a gentleman farmer, of course, none of that ploughing the fields and scattering lark for him: he employed people to do that. No, Harry's father strolled around his thousands of acres doing important things like ordering fences to be put here and ditches to be dug there, shooting the odd recalcitrant pheasant; or peasant probably, if he felt like it.

My father wasn't nearly so grand, he was just a consultant at the local hospital. A humble doctor who did little more than save lives every day and bring people back from the dead, that sort of thing. His work was very mundane: a brain tumour one day, a heart attack the next; run-of-the-mill stuff. I'd always been terribly proud of Daddy, but Harry had shown me the error of my ways.

'Very middle-class, Polly, like all the professions.'

He'd once introduced me to some smart friends of his as 'the doctor's daughter from Esher', and laughed. Why? No matter, I was keen to learn. Luckily I'd learned enough already to know that one house just wasn't enough. It was with this in mind that I answered his question.

49

'Yes, they are in Esher at the moment,' I replied. 'Just back from our place in London, actually.'

'Oh really?' Harry looked surprised. 'I didn't know your parents had a house in London.'

Neither did I, but apparently I'd just invented one.

'Oh yes,' I lied, 'we've always kept a little place up here. So useful.'

'Ah,' he grinned, 'a little place. What is it, a flat?'

'No, it's not actually. I say "a little place" out of habit, but it's quite a big house.'

'Really?' He looked startled. 'How big?'

'Oh I don't know, about six or seven storeys, the usual sort of townhouse.'

'Six or seven storeys!' He was incredibly impressed. I'd obviously overdone it. 'Whereabouts?'

'Oh, um, Knightsbridge.'

'Really? Whereabouts in Knightsbridge?'

Whereabouts again? We'd just done that one, hadn't we? Wasn't he being just a touch nosy? I began to panic. Think of a street, any street, but make sure it's in Knightsbridge.

'Montpelier Street.'

'No! Montpelier Street? My aunt lives in Montpelier Street. What number?'

What number? Christ! Pick a number, any number, just don't let it be Auntie's. I hesitated, this was like Russian Roulette.

'Don't you know?' asked Harry.

'Yes, of course I know, it's number twenty-thre— four!'

'Twenty-four! But that's right next door. Aunt Rose lives at number twenty-six! How extraordinary!'

'Well, not really. I mean someone has to live next door, why not Aunt Rose?'

'But she must know your parents. I'm seeing her on Sunday, I'll ask her, she's bound to!'

'No! I mean, um, I wouldn't ask her, because she won't

necessarily know them. You see the thing is — the thing is, it's rented! It's rented on a sort of permanent basis to other people.'

'Rented? But I thought you said your parents had just come back from there?'

Ah yes, Polly, you did, you did.

'Oh! Oh yes, well, they were there for a few days last week, that's true, but that's because, um, that's because they know the people it's rented to. Old family friends, you see, known them for years, so they let my parents stay whenever they're in London.'

'What are they called?'

'My parents?'

'No, idiot, the friends, who are they? Aunt Rose will probably know them.'

Yes, Polly, who are they? These very old trusty family friends, practically your godparents, who exactly are they?

'Well, I er, I don't exactly know them myself, they're friends of my father's really. Daddy's the one who's known them for years, they're colleagues of his, you know, doctors.'

'Ah.' Harry looked more than a little confused, and who can blame him. 'So you never actually use the house yourself?'

'No, oh no, never.' It was such a relief to say something truthful that I said it with a vengeance, with gusto even. I shook my head vehemently. 'Never ever, in fact.'

'Oh. Seems a bit odd really.' God he *would* go on. Couldn't we talk about something else? His ego perhaps? Or his sex appeal? 'I mean, to have a house in London that you can't use . . .' He looked thoughtful, then he sneered. 'I suppose your parents need the money.'

I bristled furiously. 'Certainly not! Need the money? Good gracious, no. In fact these people don't even pay the rent, they just borrow it.'

'Oh!'

Oh indeed. So what do we have here now, Polly? A massively philanthropic gesture, is that it? On behalf of some poor impoverished doctors who have been close to your family for many years but whose names escape you? A nice, rent-free, six-, nay seven-storey house in the middle of Knightsbridge for which they pay not a sausage? What are your parents anyway, missionaries? Born-again Christians?

Happily, in the nick of time, the waiter arrived with a bottle of wine which, according to Harry, was corked. This took Harry's mind off things as he sent the waiter scurrying back and forth with new bottles. I blessed the hapless waiter from the bottom of my heart. But I also realised I'd done irreparable damage. It was quite obvious that Harry could never meet my parents now. I imagined him settling down to a quiet chat with Daddy after Sunday lunch in Esher. 'Polly tells me you have a house in Montpelier Street, Mr McLaren.' Oh no, that would never do. They must never meet. Oh dear, so I couldn't marry him! Or if I did my parents wouldn't be able to come to the wedding! It was too horrrific.

I'd talk to Mummy, she'd understand, if a little vaguely. I'd catch her while she was gardening; I could see her pausing for a moment as she pruned the roses. 'Yes, of course I'll pretend, darling, but I don't understand why you said we had a house in London in the first place. Whatever made you imagine we had? We haven't, have we?'

Daddy would be a different matter, glaring at me over his glasses in the study, stern and unamused. 'No, Polly, I'm sorry. If you're ashamed of our house here, that's too bad, but I will *not* become a millionaire overnight just to please your playboy friends.'

I sighed as Harry tasted the new bottle. Oh well, something would come up. Perhaps we could sell it. Yes, that was it, we'd sell it! Get rid of the sodding house once and for all. I brightened considerably. It would be sold tomorrow – but quietly. So Aunt bleeding-nosy-parker Rose didn't get to hear about it.

The new wine had obviously been deemed drinkable and was apparently on the house, so Harry was agreeable now and wanting me to be agreeable too.

'And how is that dreadful boss of yours? Still bullying you and Pippa and throwing his weight around?' he asked.

I smiled. This at least was a subject we both agreed on. As far as Harry was concerned, any man who spent his working days west of the City and certainly west of Fleet Street was either a shirt-lifter or an estate agent. Failing that, he had to be an ad-man, which was the lowest of the low. If he felt like it, Harry could put on a high moral tone and pontificate for hours about the immorality of off-loading unwanted products on to an unsuspecting, gullible public through the medium of advertising. Then he'd put the boot into spineless individuals like Nick who, failing to get a proper job, had gone into advertising to propagate this corruption and earn enormous salaries.

Of course, he'd concede, it was all right for girlies. Girlies had to work in the West End to be near the shops and to have lunch with each other and discuss their boyfriends in the City. But for a man, advertising was the pits.

I told Harry how Nick had shouted at me today when I had simply knocked on his door and very politely interrupted his meeting to ask a pertinent question.

Harry leaned across the table and took my hand. He stroked it sympathetically. 'But he's an ad-man, poppet, that's what you have to remember, he's not like the rest of us. He wouldn't have the first idea how to talk to a lady. He probably didn't even go to public school.'

Nick had gone to Harrow, but I let that pass. I liked the hand-stroking bit and I also liked the bit about the lady.

Harry ordered me a Cointreau without even asking, and I sipped it while he signed the Access slip, feeling decidedly perkier.

I even kept my cool when a drop-dead blonde in a spray-on black lycra dress walked passed us and Harry nearly knocked the table over, so desperate was he to spring to his feet and kiss her very enthusiastically on both cheeks.

'See you tomorrow at Ransome's,' he called after her swaying bottom as it undulated off to the loo like a metronome, mesmerising most of the men in the room.

I tried not to but I couldn't help it. 'What's happening at Ransome's?'

'Oh, it's just a little party. A guy I've known for donkey's years is having a birthday dinner there. He's paying for the whole bash so it's invitation only, of course. Sorry, my sweet, I'd love you to come, but there it is. Actually, it'll probably be rather boring, but I've got to go.' He drained his glass. 'Ready, darling?' He stood up and held my coat out for me.

Again, I was taken by surprise, but I obediently knocked back the Cointreau and stood up. 'Ready.'

And with that I slipped into my coat, slipped into the front seat of his car, slipped into his flat, slipped down a Rémy and slipped into bed.

Well, that's how it always was with Harry, I reflected as I lay there waiting for him to brush his teeth. I felt like a well trained poodle jumping through the hoops as he skilfully manoeuvred me round the course. From restaurant, to car, to flat, to bed. You know the rules, Polly. Not that I was complaining, of course. Perish the thought.

Harry appeared in the doorway looking like a toothpaste commercial — tall, blond, brown, and with a whiter-than-white smile. I giggled because I knew what was coming next. Harry had pinched a child's diving board from his parent's swimming pool and screwed it into the floor-boards at the end of his bed. He would bounce up and down on it before launching himself, with a blood-curdling scream, on to his victim. It always reduced me to fits of giggles, but when I'd told Lottie about it she'd looked at me with horror, her eyes like saucers, as if I'd said he dressed up as the fairy queen and cried, 'Beat me, beat me!'

The dive from the board very much set the tone for the rest of the evening, because what always ensued can only be described as a romp. Our particular form of rumpy-pumpy was punctuated with great gales of laughter from him and screams and giggles from me. Pillow fights would occur on a regular basis and even, on one memorable occasion, a water fight with squeezy bottles. Anything, basically, to stop Harry from getting bored. It was certainly fun, and I reckon I lost pounds in the process – one had to be reasonably confident figure-wise, as there was never any question of the light going off – but it was never, by any stretch of the imagination, romantic.

It would have been quite out of place, for example, for me to murmur anything more romantic than, 'Oh no, not on the chest-of-drawers again!' or, 'Come and get me!' from the top of the wardrobe.

I did once, in an extremely drunken and foolhardy moment and after a particularly passionate bout of love-making half-way out of the window, venture, 'Oh Harry, I do love you,' but it was met with such a look of mock horror and surprise that I never tried it again.

This evening was no exception. The Squire and his wench, for wenchy was how I always felt, romped and rolled and screeched and chortled until oh, two-thirty in the morning.

And that was when Harry sat up in bed and gave me a strange and questioning look. 'What would you like to do now, Polly?' he asked.

What would I like to do? Well, sleep was pretty high on my list of priorities. After all, it was two-thirty a.m. and I had to go to work in a few hours. I also felt we'd pretty much run the gamut as far as re-enacting the raunchiest of *The Canterbury Tales* was concerned but, not wishing to be a party-pooper, I opened my eyes wide and let an inquiring little smile play around my lips.

'I don't know, Harry, what would you like to do?'

'Well, how about a little shave?' he asked, innocently enough.

A shave? I sat up and stared at him. What on earth did he mean? I thought I had shaved. I felt my legs . . . fine. One or two bristles, but that was only to be expected considering the time I'd been given to get ready. I frowned. Under-arms! I gasped in alarm, had I forgotten? Was I sitting in Harry's bed like an Italian shot-putter, unmanageable pits flowing on to his whiter-than-white Conran bed linen? My hands shot under my arms. No, false alarm, smooth as a baby's bottom. So what did he mean, a shave? I looked at him quizzically, keen to learn.

'Down there Polly.' He pointed downwards.

I followed his finger and almost gagged on my tonsils. Down there? A shave down there? What, off? All of them? Surely not! He couldn't be serious. I looked up at him again, wary of falling for a practical joke which would later be relayed to a group of friends in the pub. 'Polly thought I wanted to shave her! Can you believe it?' I studied his face. I'd better believe it. A huge grin was spreading slowly from one ear to the other. Harry had thought of a new game. It was called disfiguring Polly. I gulped.

'So what d'you think?' he asked.

Yes, what d'you think, Polly, eh? Baldy? Eh? What do you think? I stalled and played for time.

'Well, I'm not really sure. I mean won't it be a bit, um, prickly, you know, afterwards? For both of us really?' I didn't want to appear selfish.

'Well, a bit maybe, but it won't take long to grow.'

'Really?'

Stupid, very stupid. Harry instantly took this mad impulsive 'Really?' as a sign of accord; in fact he obviously regarded it as being tantamount to a 'Yes please!' He jumped out of bed with alacrity.

'Great!' he cried, joyfully making for the bathroom.

With trepidation I listened to him clattering around in there; taps were running, blades were being changed, probably sharpened too. Oh Lord. I peeped under the bedclothes and gave myself a last lingering look. In a trice he was back, stark naked, armed with a large bowl of steaming water, a fluffy white towel, a razor and a mad, Jack Nicholson grin. He arranged his equipment on the bed in an unnervingly practised fashion. I half expected him to pull a pair of rubber gloves out from under the bed.

'Now hold still, Polly, there's a good girl.'

'I've changed my mind!' I squeaked.

'Don't be silly, you won't feel a thing.'

Won't I, I thought, feeling a lot of hot soapy water sloshing around my nether regions? All of a sudden I knew I'd gone past that point. The one you can return from. Harry was humming a merry tune as he went about his business, 'Tum-ti tum-ti tum-ti tum.' I dared not move. I lay there as if I'd been turned to stone, not moving a muscle, not even lifting my head from the pillow to view the operation because *what if he slipped*! Yes, dear God, what if his hand slipped a millimetre? It just didn't bear thinking about.

'More soap!' cried Harry joyfully, and I looked up to see him trotting off to the bathroom for supplies, whistling away, happy in his work.

I took a sneaky look down. Great Scott! I was receding rapidly; in fact I was half bald. I looked about eight years old on one side and twenty-two on the other. Maybe, I thought desperately, maybe if he stopped now I'd still be in with a chance. Maybe I could sweep one side across to hide the bald patch, yes, that's it! That would do the trick!

Too late. The demonic barber was back again, a razor shining in his hand and madness glinting in his eye. I thought long and hard of England as he deftly completed his task before giving me a wash and . . . no, no brush up this time.

'There you go!' he said, busily putting away his equipment. 'All finished!'

I sat up and gazed down at the alien territory below my tummy. Was that me? And if so where were my knickers − quick, it was obscene! Ah, there they were on the diving board. I grabbed them and whipped them on inside out.

'Polly, don't . . .' He pulled at them; I pulled back. I won.

I sat there in my knickers, forcing a smile.

'So what do you think?' he grinned. 'Something for the weekend, madam?'

'How about a toupee?' I said with forced jollity, rallying a brave smile.

'So you like it?'

'Oh yes, it's great, yes, thanks a lot!'

Should I tip him? I thought wildly. I mean, what does he expect? He deprives me of my womanhood with one quick flick of the wrist and wants to know what I think. I think I'm going to cry, that's what. Tears were welling. One even escaped down my cheek. Harry spotted it.

'Oh Polly, what's wrong? Don't you like it? You should have said!' He put his arm around me. 'You are an old silly!'

Yes, I am, aren't I? But then I'm in love, and love makes us do crazy things. I snuffled a bit and nuzzled into his shoulder.

'Look, don't worry. If you don't like it, it'll grow soon!' he said cheerfully.

Now where had I heard those words before? They sounded very familiar. Ah yes, that was it, about twice a year at my hairdresser's. Of course, it was all just a bad dream and in fact Harry was just Raymond in disguise, taking two inches off my split ends before I left, as usual, in tears.

'Yes, of course it will grow,' I smiled bravely. And it'll hurt like hell too, I thought grimly.

When I woke up the next morning I realised he'd made a pretty awful job of it too. I already had the makings of designer stubble. George Michael, I thought, would be proud of that. Harry wasn't.

'Oh sorry Polly, I've made a bit of a mess of that, haven't I? Tell you what, I'll have another go.'

I stood my ground very firmly this time and clutched my George Michael possessively. 'No bloody fear.'

I pulled the bedclothes around me. Harry looked slightly miffed. 'Polly, really . . .'

Don't upset him. 'I mean, no thanks. Thanks awfully, jolly kind of you to offer, but no more, thanks all the same.'

He accepted this, albeit sulkily and reluctantly, but he accepted it, and anyway he was late for work.

'Oh well, if you must go around looking like a diseased hedgehog,' he said as he jumped out of bed.

Yes, I must, I thought. It's all your fault, but I must, if I want to stand any chance of looking like a normal twenty-two-year-old again, that is. Thank God I wasn't in a rugby team or something. At least I wouldn't have to suffer the indignity of communal showers.

Harry bathed quickly, then raced around the bedroom throwing his clothes on while I dragged myself out of bed and into the bathroom. I peered blearily into the mirror and lanced a spot before it even had time to surface. Splat. Harry appeared just as I was cleaning it off the mirror.

'Must dash, darling — doing a spot of housework? Thanks so much, the washing-up needs doing if you've got a moment. See you in a day or two.' He kissed me noisily, goosing me at the same time. 'Bye Polyester!'

'Bye!' I called down the stairs after him, wishing for the millionth time I'd never told him that the 'E' in my initials stood for Esther. It had been a practical joke of my father's way back in the swinging sixties when I'd been born. A friend of his had given his daughter the singularly groovy name of Silk, so Daddy, for a laugh, had called me Polly Esther. What a wag. Stupidly I'd told Harry, who'd laughed like a drain and couldn't leave it alone. Ah well, my fault again, I suppose.

I dragged myself away from the mirror and looked at my watch. God, eight forty-five already, I didn't have much time. I had a quick shower, jumped into my clothes, and set about my weekly task of looking for 'signs'.

These 'signs' were unspecified in appearance, but could take the form of jewellery – perhaps a pair of earrings or a necklace; scent bottles; clothing – especially underwear, anything of that nature; all of which would have sent me completely ballistic. Thus far I'd never found anything, but one could never be too careful and I always had to look.

It wasn't a long job, because Harry had such a trendy minimalist flat with very few searchable places. A couple of cupboards, one or two drawers, no shelves. His walls were full of urgent white space with just one or two obscure pictures hanging in strange places, like near the skirting boards or above a window. The floor was polished and wooden and bits of twisted chrome or knotted leather were dotted about here and there making statements, about what I don't know. Occasionally you'd come across something made of both chrome and leather which could be a chair or a sofa, but was certainly uncomfortable. It wasn't my sort of flat at all but, because it was Harry's, I bullied myself into thinking it was beautiful.

Consequently, the search for 'signs' was really confined to the bedroom and the bathroom. I went through both with a fine tooth-comb, terrified of what I might find but totally unable to stop myself.

There was the usual dried-up lip gloss in the bathroom cabinet and the tarnished silver bracelet in the second drawer down in the bedside table, but they both pre-dated me, so that was OK. No letters, no earrings, no scent bottles; in fact no sign at all of any other female visitor. Good.

Feeling much perkier, I threw a cup of tea down my throat, made the bed roughly, almost washed up but just managed to stop myself, grabbed my handbag and charged off to work, putting my lipstick on as I ran downstairs.

Chapter Four

Pippa was rolling her eyes and gesticulating madly when I arrived panting like a dog at nine forty-five a.m.

'He's been waiting for you since nine-thirty!' she hissed, jabbing her finger in the direction of Nick's office.

'Oh Christ!' I wriggled out of my coat, leaving it where it fell on the floor, and dashed into his room, grabbing my shorthand book on the way.

'Sorry, Nick,' I gasped as I flopped down on his leather sofa. 'I had a bit of trouble with the tubes.'

'For someone who lives two tube stops away you seem to spend a hell of a lot of time commuting,' he said sardonically. 'Anyway, let's get on, I've got a lot to do today. Letter to Dick Appleby. Dear Mr Appleby, Further to our conversation yesterday . . .' and he was off.

He paced around the room, talking to the walls, the window, the carpet, his shoes, dictating like a steam train while I scribbled away like mad, trying to keep up.

'Slow down!' I screeched in desperation when I was at least a paragraph behind. I was fast, but I wasn't that fast.

He stopped pacing and turned, surprised. Then he grinned sheepishly. 'Sorry – getting a bit carried away.'

'Can't imagine that ever happening,' I said without thinking, and then blushed, instantly wishing I hadn't said it.

Nick raised his eyebrows. He looked at me inquiringly, a slight smile playing on his lips. 'Oh really? It's something you've thought about then, is it?'

'No, of course not.' My blush deepened and spread to my neck. I squirmed around uncomfortably on the sofa. Well really, this was most unlike Nick. Indulging in friendly banter and sexual innuendo first thing in the morning, or for that matter at any time of day. Whatever was the matter with him? I glared studiously at my notebook and let my hair fall over my flushing face.

He grinned. 'Right! Well I'll try to go a bit slower then.'

He set off again at a slightly more sedate pace, and then the telephone rang. It was our media buyer. I doodled on my pad as I waited, and drew a rather unflattering picture of him. It just showed, though, I thought, as I added a large and rather phallic nose to my portrait; when he loosened up a bit he could be almost human. I drew a pair of bushy eyebrows, Dennis Healey-style, and studied him as he sat in his big leather chair, sideways-on to the window. His profile jutted out against the skyline of tower blocks behind. It had to be said that his nose was definitely on the large side, but then again his jaw was very square, which seemed to balance it. The eyes were deep set and slightly slanted, and his hair was thick, straight and very dark. Somehow it all worked rather well if you liked a lot of angles on your man. Personally I was much more into soft, boyish good looks with melting baby-blue eyes and honey-gold hair. Funny that.

Nick was issuing instructions down the phone in a quiet, authoritative way, his voice deep and thoughtful. A lock of dark hair flopped into his eyes and he pushed it back impatiently. Suddenly he swivelled round in his chair to consult his diary and caught me staring at him. He smiled. He smiled! I mean, for God's sake, whatever next? And not just a little twitch, a dazzlingly broad grin. Good grief, perhaps he was flesh and blood after all, and not just a collection of old memo pads and documents held together with paper clips. That smile had definitely been directed at me, hadn't it? I had a quick look over my shoulder just to make sure — no, there was definitely no one else here.

Well well. Could it be that he was finally coming round to the discreet and subtle charms of one Polly McLaren? Had a beam of sunlight darted through the window and lingered becomingly on my blonde curls for a moment, making them shine like spun gold and reminding him of a cornfield in summer perhaps? Had he at last noticed my finely chiselled features, my sparkling eyes, and that attractive dusting of freckles over my pert little nose? Odd that he'd never noticed all this before, but no matter. He'd got there in the end. And if it was going to make him all smiley and agreeable, I would obviously have to draw more attention to my assets, thereby ensuring myself an easier, happier, and hopefully bollock-free working environment.

First a smile, heavens, whatever next? Intrigued, I carefully arranged myself in what I believed to be a seductive manner. I rested my elbow on the back of the sofa and balanced my chin on my hand. Then I curled my legs up beneath me in a kittenish style, failing to notice that I'd also curled some papers up with my feet. Once in position I sucked my cheeks in and stared moodily out of the window, pouting slightly as I sucked the end of my pencil. I made sure I could still see him out of the corner of my eye in order to clock his reaction and — good grief! He was doing something with his hand, flapping it around from side to side, could it be — yes, he was, he was *waving* at me. How odd! Gosh, he was really letting himself go now. Well there was nothing else for it, was there? Rude not to. I raised my hand and fluttered back, eyes wide, smiling encouragingly. Was that OK, I wondered? This waving lark was a new one on me. Winking yes, smouldering looks, fine, I could cope with all that, but waving? He barked a final order down the phone, making me jump slightly, and slammed the receiver down.

'For goodness sake, Polly, stop lolling around over those papers. I've got to sign them later.'

He flapped his hand again, gesturing for me to move. Oh Christ!

'And sit up properly, please, you're not at home now.'

Bastard! I flushed furiously and sat bolt upright. Who did he think he was, my father?

The telephone call had obviously put him in a filthy mood. His brows were knitted together now and a thundercloud settled in its usual position on his face.

'Right, let's go again. Dear Mr Hutchinson, Please find enclosed a pre-production schedule . . .'

Once again we raced off at breakneck speed, and this time I didn't have the nerve to slow him down. Luckily, I was saved by the bell again, and I scribbled away, making up lost ground as he answered the phone.

'Yes?' he shouted impatiently. God, he was charming. 'Oh it's you, sorry, darling.'

Darling? I felt like Dr Spock as my ears sprang into action. It was obviously the bird, Serena. I kept my head well down, pretending I was still writing.

'I know I said I would,' he was saying wearily, 'but honestly, I'm so snowed under here I'll probably be working till about midnight.'

I carefully studied the spiral binding in my notepad. A low profile was all-important if I was to go unnoticed.

'Well, can't you go on your own, or get Hugh to take you?' He was irritated now, and so was she, judging by the long silence at this end as he listened to the monologue. The Hugh suggestion had obviously gone down like a cup of cold sick.

'Look, I said I'd try, I can do no more. I'll ring you as soon as I know how long I'll be, but don't bank on it because I think it's highly unlikely. For one thing—' He broke off suddenly, remembering I was still in the room.

He put his hand over the mouthpiece.

'Polly, if you don't mind, we'll carry on with this later.'

I nodded, smiled sweetly, and went back to my desk, closing his door softly behind me.

'Serena saved my bacon,' I said to Pippa, who was buried in *Harpers and Queen*. 'He was going for the world shorthand speed record in there.'

'Mmmmm . . .' she murmured as she stared longingly at London's twenty most eligible men, salivating slightly as she digested the profusion of titles, bank balances and good looks assembled before her.

'I can't imagine him with a girlfriend,' I said, flicking through a pile of TV scripts that had been put on my desk for typing. 'I wonder what she's like.'

'A bit of a handful, by all accounts,' said Pippa, licking her lips greedily as she dissected one particularly affluent viscount. 'Keeps him on his toes.'

'Really? Well he certainly wasn't giving an inch on the phone. I wonder if she lives with him.'

Pippa didn't answer. She was miles away – in Dorset, in fact – walking slowly up the aisle of a private chapel on her father's arm. Resplendent in an ivory silk wedding dress, a flurry of little bridesmaids behind her in matching ivory with apricot sashes, she smiled shyly at her guests from beneath her veil. As she neared the altar, the organist reached his crescendo and her viscount turned to watch her, bursting with pride at her beauty. She smiled at him serenely . . .

'I wonder what she looks like,' I mused.

But Pippa was still walking, her head held high to Purcell's 'Trumpet Voluntary'.

'I shouldn't think she's much of a beauty,' I went on. 'Blue-stockinged I expect, with buck teeth and a smattering of acne.' I giggled.

Pippa stuck her finger firmly in the viscount's bank balance, determined to keep her place. 'You know what she looks like,' she said, tearing herself away from her future husband for a second.

'I don't. I've never met her.'

'No, but you know what she *looks* like.'

'What d'you mean?'

'Serena Montgomery, you've seen her in films, haven't you?'

'Serena Montgomery! Nick Penhalligan is going out with Serena Montgomery! I don't believe you!' I shrieked.

'Shh, he'll hear you. He's been going out with her for ages.'

'Good grief! How did he meet her? What does she see in him? Are you sure, Pippa?'

But Pippa was already in her receiving line, a countess now, standing next to her husband and graciously greeting all her friends — particularly those friends who thought themselves rather grand and who, at one stage or another, had snubbed her, left her off their drinks party lists, or failed to send a Christmas card, and who, at a later date, would no doubt be grovelling to be guests at her balls and shooting parties. She smiled at them benignly, tiara twinkling.

I left her to her dreams as I picked my jaw up from somewhere around bra level, digesting this bombshell. Serena Montgomery, no less! Miss Montgomery was a startlingly beautiful English actress who had up and come at the tender age of about twenty-five. She only appeared in frightfully tasteful arty films, usually English or continental, and had achieved her fame without getting her hands dirty with any gratuitous smut or violence. She was extremely successful and extremely sought-after, and Nick Penhalligan, my boss and cross to bear on a daily basis, was going out with her! My mind was boggling so much I thought it would boggle out of my earholes.

I simply had to drag Pippa away from her wedding

reception. 'But what on ear   does she see in him?' I repeated.

'Well, you know, he isn't bad 'ooking, Polly, and he's probably totally different out of t. e agency. I mean, you work for him, so you're bound to be jaundiced.' She looked thoughtful. 'I think he's rather cute, actually, and, you never know, he might be a demon lover.'

'Demon lover! That lump of rock-solid granite in there. He hasn't an ounce of sensibility! Are you mad?'

I shook my head in disbelief and began to bash away at my scripts. As I waded through coffee plantations in Kenya, where the highly optimistic creative team had set their commercials in the hope of wangling a trip abroad, my thoughts oscillated between Nick and Serena and, just for a change, Harry. I went over our little débâcle in the restaurant. I hadn't forgotten. I was determined to find Rachel Thingamy, just to show him. Just to show him what, I wasn't sure, but just to show him something.

Every so often I caught a glimpse of Nick through his glass door, scribbling away. I tried to imagine him in a clinch with Serena Montgomery. Hidden depths, all right. I was jolted out of my daydreams by the telephone. It was Lottie.

'Polly? It's me. Listen, I completely forgot, Caro's coming round for supper tonight and I haven't got any food. You couldn't be an angel and get something on the way home, could you? I'm up to my eyeballs here.'

'Sure, I'll go to Safeway's.'

'Great, get a lasagne and some salad stuff. How was last night?'

'Brilliant,' I lied. 'We went to—'

'Tell me later, I can't talk now.' Lottie couldn't rabbit on for hours like the rest of us.

'OK, oh Lottie – ' I suddenly remembered ' – very quickly, d'you remember someone at school called Rachel Marsden?'

'No, why?'

'Curly fair hair, bit mousy looking, a year or so below us. Have a quick think.'

'Can't say I do, but Caro might, ask her tonight. Polly, I must go. Bye.'

I put the phone down. Of course, Caro might know. She was Lottie's younger sister and would probably have been in the same year as Rachel. Caro made occasional visits to our flat, principally to view the latest collections in our wardrobes and walk off with most of them. I'd ask her.

I left the agency, as is my wont, at five-thirty on the dot — I don't believe in unpaid overtime — and made my way to Safeway's. Wednesday night is late-night shopping and, being in the middle of the King's Road, it takes on the atmosphere of a drinks party rather than a supermarket. I reapplied my lipstick at the door and grabbed a basket. True to form, the aisles were already throbbing with bright young things snapping up dinner party fodder.

A shriek of delight rang out as someone rounded a corner and bashed trollies over the dog food with a neighbour they hadn't seen for at least a day. There was lots of noisy kissing and, 'Darling! How lovely to see you!' as they compared trolley loads, exchanged gossip and threw in the Lapsang Souchong.

There were always plenty of single men sniffing around, advertising their availability with a solitary cod steak and a packet of frozen peas. Predictable chat-up lines would pop out over the freezers as lone males exclaimed, 'Oh, I see you've got Chicken Kiev. Is that good?' or some such other notable opening gambit, whereupon the lone female would reply, 'Oh, frightfully, haven't you tried it?' to which the response would come, 'Well, I'm not very good with ovens . . .' hoping that the offer of a practical demonstration would come his way.

I always reckoned you could tell a lot by what a man had in his basket — his wire basket, of course. Fillet steak and peas were fine, and a bottle of Sancerre wouldn't go amiss, but it was always a good idea to steer well clear of the Pot Noodles, Carlsberg Special and extra-strength deodorant brigade.

I threaded my way through the usual merry throng, throwing necessities into my basket along the way: avocado pears, gravadlax and quails' eggs, as well as one or two frivolous little luxuries like oven cleaner and washing powder.

Having located the lasagne and salad, I made a detour to a less fashionable part of the shop to chuck in some loo paper, which should have been a necessity but in our forgetful household was often a luxury. It always made a nice change from the *Evening Standard* or Lottie's dressmaking patterns. Maddeningly, they always put the loo paper high up on a shelf above a freezer, so that midgets like me had to stand on tiptoe and pretend to be a tree to reach it.

I was just stretching up and trying vainly to flick a couple of rolls off the shelf, when suddenly I teetered wildly, completely lost my balance and fell, with a mighty shriek, head first into the freezer. I lay there, pole-axed with shock, my nose pressed up against the Arctic Roll, my legs sticking straight up in the air behind me. The freezer was deep and relatively empty and I'd landed at a pretty acute angle; so acute, in fact, that I couldn't move. Jesus Christ, I couldn't move! And apart from anything else it was bloody cold and my jumper was sticking to the ice.

'Help! Could somebody help me?' I wailed feebly as I eyeballed the Arctic Roll. I waited a second, but didn't detect the sound of pounding feet running towards me, and no helpful hands appeared to be winging their way down, so I desperately tried to rock backwards and heave myself out. I spread my hands on the floor of the freezer and pushed hard. 'Huurmphhh!' Alas! Too much of my vast weight was freezer-bound and, strong and meaty

71

though my thighs are, they didn't have the muscle to lever me out. It was no good, I would have to climb in, turn around, and then climb out again.

I set about this task with a vengeance, curling my legs round and down into the frozen wastes – my skirt at this stage was somewhere up around my earrings. I scrambled to my feet and from here began the tricky ascent up the south face of the freezer.

By now I was aware that, far from being alone as I'd assumed, a small army of shoppers had broken off from selecting their mid-week groceries and were collecting in a gawping, open mouthed semi-circle around me.

'What's happening?' someone at the back asked.

'There's a girl in the freezer,' came the muttered response from the front.

'Oh, thanks very much, don't help, will you!' I spat furiously at no one in particular, glimpsing out of the corner of my ice-packed, bloodshot eye, an extremely attractive girl who looked terribly familiar. She was laughing her head off.

Puce with shame I brushed my wet hair out of my eyes, swung a leg over the side, and began to clamber out. Unfortunately, in my haste, I was unlucky enough to catch the heel of my shoe in a wire basket full of oven chips.

'Bugger!' I shook my foot furiously, straddled, as I now was, over the side of the freezer, but I couldn't for the life of me shake the basket free. Finally, in desperation, I leaned down and wrenched it off, pulling the heel of my shoe off with it. No matter, at least I was liberated. I swung my leg over, knickers no doubt flashing wildly, and landed, pretty unsteadily, on the other side. With shaking hands I straightened out my skirt, pulled down my jumper – which had ridden up to bra level and was covered with little bobbles of ice – and, with my head held high, I turned on my broken heel and marched, or rather hobbled, through the gawping crowd, shopping basket in one hand, broken heel in the other.

By the time I'd arrived at the check-out desk my teeth were chattering like a monkey's, my hair was dripping wet and the ice bobbles on my jumper were beginning to melt.

I slammed my groceries down on the conveyer belt, muttering oaths and obscenities under my breath. The gum-chewing check-out girl raised her eyebrows in surprise as she took in my dishevelled, damp condition. Of all the snooty, stuck-up people — what did they think I was doing in there? Stealing fish fingers? Stuffing frozen peas up my jumper? Jesus, it was unbelievable. I could have died of frostbite and no one so much as raised a finger to help!

Safely back in the flat half an hour later, I wrapped myself in a blanket, poured myself a large gin and tonic, and lit a rather shaky cigarette. When I'd consumed about half of each, I recounted my miserable expedition to Lottie and Caro.

Lottie cried with laughter. 'At least you didn't knock yourself out: you could still be there now, lying unconscious in the raspberry ripple. Imagine someone reaching in for some ice-cream and grabbing hold of your nose or something.' She wiped her eyes with her shirt. 'Oh God, Polly, you are an idiot!'

Caro smiled politely, staring at me with naked incredulity. She was so self-possessed and perfect, she'd be incapable of tripping over a rucked-up piece of carpet, let alone falling into a freezer.

Caro and Lottie were obviously sisters, with their long dark hair, hazel eyes, pale skins and sooty lashes and eyebrows, but Caro was very definitely the beauty. Lottie's eyes were big and round, but Caro's were almond-shaped with long sweeping lashes. Her mouth was a perfect little rosebud and, whereas Lottie was prone to plumpness and had a round, sweet face, Caro was reed slim with a little heart-shaped face. She had the sort of dark silky hair that looks so good spread out on pillows, and she wouldn't know a split end if it ran her over.

Like her sister, she had an enormous bust, which I didn't envy her for; but, unlike her sister who tried to disguise it with baggy T-shirts and sloppy jumpers, young Caro positively flaunted hers. Most of her tops were snug-fitting clingy numbers, and she was very fond of stretching up and locking her arms behind her head, or lying with her back on the floor, propping herself up with her elbows, chest to the fore.

She didn't have a line on her face, principally because she betrayed very little emotion. When she smiled it was a controlled, tight little smile, like the one she was giving me now. She wouldn't dream of rocking around like Lottie, who was clutching her stomach and roaring with laughter. I am quite sure that Caro has never, ever farted.

Lottie doted on her little sister and spoilt her rotten. Their mother was dead and Lottie had always felt responsible for Caro. Caro took everything Lottie had to offer and, as far as I could see, gave very little in return. Let's just say she wasn't my favourite person.

This evening, as usual, Caro had her eyes firmly on our wardrobes. 'Can I see what you've bought recently, Lottie?' she said, making a bee-line for Lottie's bedroom. I stuck to her like glue. As usual, half my wardrobe was in Lottie's room and vice versa. I didn't want her to get her thieving hands on anything precious.

'Yes, but tell me what you're borrowing,' shouted Lottie, who was glued to an old 'Dallas' repeat.

Caro was already riffling through her sister's drawers. I sat on the bed and lit a cigarette.

'Ooh, this is nice, I'll have this,' she said, pulling out the only cashmere jumper I'm ever likely to possess.

I snatched it out of her hot little hands and smiled sweetly. 'Sorry, Caro, that's mine.'

Caro pouted sulkily. 'You obviously lent it to Lottie, it was in her drawer.'

74

'Yes, but then I know that Lottie won't come home doused in red wine and aftershave.'

'Oh, all right.' She threw it back in the drawer and added cattily, 'Black's a bit old for me anyway.'

I smiled, suddenly remembering that I needed her help. 'I have got a lovely red polo neck you could borrow, though.'

'Oh?' Caro was interested. She tried it on and looked infuriatingly stunning. I stood next to her as she admired herself in the mirror, and then stepped hastily away again to avoid the comparison. My tatty old candlewick dressing gown with make-up stains down the front and holes in the bottom where Wellington had chewed it didn't really stand up against her slimming black ski pants and the red jumper stretched tight across her ample bosom. Neither, I thought, looking at her clean silky hair, did my rather dirty blonde curls, streaked with grease rather than highlights.

'Yes, I'll take this,' she said, as if she were in a shop. I gritted my teeth, thinking that a please or a thank-you wouldn't be out of place, but since I needed to pick what passed as her brain, I wisely held my tongue.

'Listen, Caro, d'you remember someone at school called Rachel Marsden?'

'Mmmm, vaguely,' said Caro, picking up a skirt of mine and holding it up against herself in the mirror.

'What was she like?'

'Very quiet, brainy, musical, not my type at all.'

That figures, I thought.

'D'you know what she's doing now?'

'Haven't the foggiest,' said Caro, slipping off her skirt and stepping into mine. I prayed it wouldn't fit. 'Why?'

'Oh, someone I know was asking after her. Who were her friends at school, can you remember?'

'She didn't really have many, she was a bit of a loner, but I suppose Sally Lomax was her closest friend. She lives in Paris now.'

'Do you know where?'

'No, but her parents live in Godalming, you could ring them and find out, I suppose.'

Well, that at least was a start. Adam could get in touch with Sally if I got her number for him, but Paris seemed awfully remote.

'Anything else? What about her family?'

Caro took off my skirt which was miles too big for her − a mixed blessing − and sighed. She was getting a bit bored by this inquisition.

'Well, her father is ghastly, I know that. He's a judge, and a pretty Victorian one at that. He doesn't agree with girls having too much education − thought needlework and a few French lessons was good enough for Rachel, can you believe it? Anyway, he dragged her out of school before her A-level year saying she didn't need to pass exams. There was a terrible row, because of course she was so bright. I remember he came up to the school and they were all locked in Miss Harper's study for ages with Rachel crying her eyes out. Anyway, he got his way and Rachel left. Whose is this?' she said, holding up a yellow shirt.

'Mine,' I said wearily. 'Yes, I suppose so, Caro.' She folded it and put it on top of the little pile she was collecting.

Well, this was getting more interesting. And now I came to think about it I vaguely remembered someone's father storming up to school and dragging his daughter out before A-level year. There was quite a row about it. Old man Marsden sounded like a complete nightmare. Not only didn't he approve of very passable boyfriends, but education too. I had one last shot.

'What about the teachers, did she get on with any of them particularly well?'

'Well she was brilliant at music, played the piano and one of those fluty things, so you might try Mr Saunders. Oh, and she was good at maths too, so that would be Mrs

Compton . . . Polly, why are you so interested in Rachel Marsden? She was bloody boring, you know.'

Caro had obviously had enough, so I left it at that and started smearing on a mud face-pack.

'Oh, no reason really, thanks Caro; oh, and can I have my red jumper back in a couple of weeks, please?' I said without much hope of success.

'Sure.' She gathered all my clothes together and went into the sitting room to catch the end of 'Dallas'. Just then the doorbell rang.

'I'll get it,' yelled Lottie.

I padded into the kitchen in my cosy old slippers, trying to keep my face still as the mud-pack began to set like a rock. I was dying to wash it off, but the packet had said ten minutes. I mulled over the information Caro had given me. Quite good for starters; at least I could give Adam a few snippets, I thought, as I shoved the frozen lasagne in the oven.

I lit a cigarette with difficulty, then spotted a rather scrummy-looking chocolate cake sitting on the side. Caro had obviously brought it. I cut a large piece and couldn't decide whether to eat that first or finish my cigarette, so I did both, trying to keep mouth movement to a minimum on account of the concrete on my face. I paddled off down the corridor back to the telly. My slippers were flopping around like boats and I had to clutch my dressing gown like a bag lady because it had long since lost its cord. As I shuffled through the sitting-room door, cake in one hand, dressing gown in the other, cigarette therefore in my rather muddy mouth, I suddenly stopped dead in my tracks. For bounding through the front door, in his own inimitable, puppy-dog style, was Harry.

Chapter Five

Understandably, Harry didn't recognise me at first, but then slowly the penny started to drop. If I hadn't been the freak show, it would have been pretty to watch. His eyes glazed over, his forehead puckered thoughtfully, his jaw fell. Then it dawned. He bent double, clutched himself with his arms, his eyes bulged, his mouth got wider and wider, and he ultimately let rip with an enormous bellow of what I supposed was laughter. So enormous, in fact, was the animal-like bellow he'd summoned up, that poor Harry had to hold on to his stomach to stop it from falling apart at the seams. As he clutched his aching belly with one hand, he grabbed the door frame for support with the other, obviously in imminent danger of losing control of his legs. Was he going to have a hernia?

'Oh God, Polly, you look like − you look like you've just stepped out of a horror movie or something! What's that muck all over your face?' he gasped between convulsions.

I felt like running into my bedroom and sobbing uncontrollably into my pillow, but I kept as cool as I could with my face burning away beneath the mud. Any minute now the bloody thing would melt with the heat. I couldn't actually speak properly but, depositing cake and cigarette in a nearby ashtray, I flashed my brave old eyes, wiggled my hands about Al Jolson style and, old pro that I am, threw myself into a spirited rendition of the opening bars of 'Maa-amie — Maa-amie!' Then I gave him a quick flash of George Michael, just for good measure. When in doubt, play it for laughs. This had him rolling in the aisles.

'Oh God, you look such a sight!' he gasped. 'What is it?'

'It's a face-pack, you berk, haven't you ever seen one before?' I mumbled in my ventriloquist's voice.

'And there was I thinking it was all natural,' he spluttered. 'I didn't realise you had a face-lift every other night, and what an incredibly sexy negligée that is!'

Once again he dissolved into a helpless heap as he took my ten-year-old candlewick on board. I did a catwalk twirl in response and he roared even louder. He was easily pleased. I turned to my flatmate.

'Perhaps you'd get Harry a drink, Lottie?' I said with as much dignity as I could muster under the circumstances. 'Meanwhile, I shall get changed into something less hysterical.'

Lottie, who'd been horror-struck when she first saw me, was now beside herself with giggles. She ran around getting ice and whisky, glad of something to do.

Right on cue, Caro sauntered in with freshly applied make-up, looking as if she'd just walked out of *Vogue*. She was still wearing my red jumper — and good grief! Weren't they my new black leggings?

Harry had collapsed in a heap on the sofa where he was still convulsing but, as she sauntered in, the bellowing ceased, and he looked up in wonder. There was a rather too meaningful silence. His eyes lit up like a pinball machine as they took in one attraction after another. The face — those eyes — that mouth — that figure — those — those boobs! Bloody hellfire, those enormous, gigantic, socking great boobs! The poor fellow tried desperately to tear himself away from the upper torso to smile at the face. Who was this divine creature?

'Caro Hamilton, Harry Lloyd-Roberts,' I said by way of

explanation, flipping my hand from one to the other and trying to keep the misery from my voice.

Caro, realising she'd made something of an entrance, milked it for all it was worth. The saunter became a swagger, a slow, bottom wiggling, undulating stroll, which finally came to rest in *my* favourite position, propped up against the mantelpiece, back to the fire, chest out, tummy in, etc, etc. She got out a cigarette, lit it slowly and, raising her chin and pursing her rosebud lips, blew the smoke seductively into the air. It was more than I could bear. She did it so much better than I did. With a strangled little yelp which I turned into a cough, I ran for the safety of the bathroom.

I slammed the door and yelped for real, adding one or two muffled wails for good measure. Oh, why had he come? I couldn't have looked more repulsive if I'd tried! I scrubbed away at the face-pack, which wasn't going to relinquish its position easily. I looked around wildly, desperate for a hammer and chisel, and hit upon a nail-file which would do just as well. I chipped and scrubbed and chipped and scrubbed until finally something vaguely resembling a face was revealed, albeit a pretty blotchy one. Oh God, I looked diseased! I frantically slapped on a bit of Polyfilla foundation, added a shaky black line under each eye, and applied the only lipstick I could find – which was Lottie's and too red for me. I whimpered in dismay at my by now trollopy little reflection, and ran a comb through my hair.

Lottie poked her head round the door. 'You'd better get in there quick,' she hissed. 'They're getting on like a bloody mansion on fire!'

'But I look so disgusting!' I wailed.

'No you don't,' said Lottie doubtfully. 'A bit of make-up might help, though.'

'I'm covered in make-up!'

'Oh. Oh well, never mind, just hurry up! You've been in

here for ages, he'll know you're upset.'

She was right. I ran into my bedroom, shed the hateful dressing gown, and pulled on a pair of jeans and a jumper.

When I eventually returned, it was quite obvious that Harry wouldn't have noticed if I'd sprung another head, let alone been a little upset. He was reclining in the corner of the sofa with his arm resting along the back, his hand within about an inch of Caro's hair. For Caro had relinquished her position by the fireplace in favour of an altogether more cosy one. She'd curled herself up into a cute little ball, not at the other end of the sofa where most newly acquainted people would sit, but in the middle, right next to Harry. So close – without actually touching, and so snug – without actually snuggling, that she was in danger of disappearing up his armpit. I was in danger of throwing up.

I fought back the bile as it rose in my throat, and forced a bright little smile on to my unwilling face. I sat down on the sofa opposite the happy couple, next to Lottie who, appalled at her sister's antics, was looking decidedly grim. We faced them across the coffee table and watched, spellbound, as the show unfolded before us. A bag of popcorn might have come in handy, but I settled instead for a lungful of nicotine.

Meanwhile, on the Harry and Caro show, the protagonists were busy unearthing mounds of mutual friends as a front for their outrageous flirtation.

'Oh the Watson-*Smith's*!' Caro was saying with lots of Sloaney random emphasis. 'Yes of *course* I know them, they're *really* good friends of mine – I simply *adore* Hugo and Amanda. Gosh, so you're a *cousin*! I'm surprised I haven't met you *before*!'

'They must have been keeping you from me,' murmured Harry, devouring her with his baby blues.

'I quite often go there for the weekend, actually, they have the *most* beautiful house, don't they?' Caro gushed on. 'I must ask them all about you!'

'Don't believe a word they say,' he flashed her his most winning smile. 'It's all lies, every word of it!'

'Ah-ha! Got a bit of a reputation, have we?' She prodded his chest playfully. 'Bit of a playboy, eh?'

I ground my teeth, still smiling broadly.

'Oh well,' he feigned modesty. 'I wouldn't say that . . .'

'I think I'm going to puke,' muttered Lottie sotto voce on my right.

Caro giggled. 'Well, I've certainly heard a lot about you from Polly!'

'Oh, really?' Harry grinned. 'Such as?'

'Oh well, I know for instance that you're a stockbroker, and you live in Flood Street, and you've got a beautiful flat all sort of minimalist and trendy, and you drive a Porsche – oh, and a motorbike, and – oh gosh, all sorts of things!'

'Well, well,' drawled Harry, 'I had no idea I was such a topic of conversation!'

I flared my nostrils most becomingly and made a sort of strangled chicken noise. Thanks, Caro. No, really, thanks a lot. I made a mental note that the red jumper was leaving this flat over my dead body. I pushed the corners of my mouth up again and tested my voice for cracks with what I thought was a surreptitious little hum.

'Hrmmm . . . so what brings you so far from Chelsea, Harry?' I sounded like Kermit the frog. 'Slightly off the beaten track for you, isn't it? I trust you've brought your barley sugars for the journey home?'

Harry pulled a little yellow pill packet out of his trouser pocket and waved it in the air. He grinned. 'Well, talking of sweeties, darling, you forgot your smarties.'

I flushed unattractively. 'I've got plenty more where those came from, thank you!' I snatched them out of his hand.

'Well we don't want any, ha-ha, cock-ups, do we? I

thought it best to be on the safe side.'

Caro giggled.

Typical, I thought, seething: the only thing that gets Harry over to my flat in a flaming hurry is a paranoiac fear of becoming a father. I composed myself with difficulty.

'Well, I'm sure I can rely on you to face up to your responsibilities should the situation ever arise, God forbid; but in the meantime I dare say you'll be wanting to get off to the dinner party at Ransome's — it is tonight, isn't it?' I said sweetly.

Harry had returned his lust-glazed eyes to my jumper, the one I wasn't wearing, but he managed to tear them away for a second. He looked at me in surprise.

'Oh yes, that.' He'd forgotten. 'Yes, I suppose I'd better go at some stage — don't suppose they'll miss me for a bit, though.'

His eyes seemed to be on a piece of elastic which was inexorably twanging them back to the red cable-stitch. And who could blame the poor boy? For the red cable-stitch was being stretched to within an inch of its life. Caro was uncurling herself languidly from her little ball, yawning widely and str-e-tching her arms up, way, way up in the air, arching her back and sticking her ample bosom out further and further — gracious, there was so much of it, it was almost obscene! She reached the climax of her stretch, gave a little moan, then relaxed her elbows and rubbed the back of her neck, thereby still keeping her assets well to the fore. It was one helluva routine.

'Ooooh, I'm so stiff!' she groaned.

'Really? Perhaps you should have a massage,' murmured Harry.

'Mmmm . . . I suppose I should really, it's sitting at a typewriter all day that does it. Oooh . . . gosh, I've got quite a crick in my neck.'

She unfurled her legs, splayed them out in front of her, pointing her bare little toes, then brought them in again to sit cross-legged on the sofa, back ramrod straight now, hands on her knees. Now what? She shut her eyes and dropped her head forward, then she rolled it around rhythmically on her swan-like neck. Round and around it went.

'Mmmm . . .' She sighed in what can only be described as an orgasmic fashion. 'That's better . . .'

By now we were all totally mesmerised. Even Lottie and I had our mouths open. Any minute now she'd slip into the lotus position, or even, I thought in wonder, that one with the ankles behind the ears. Saliva was positively dripping from Harry's mouth, and he was making no effort to hide it.

'Better?' he murmured salaciously, as his boggling eyes roamed around her gyrating figure, savouring the swaying bosom, the tiny waist, the firm thighs spread akimbo on the sofa . . .

'Mmmm . . . much . . . a little bit of yoga works wonders, you know. You should try it, it's so relaxing and really easy.'

'Really?' He leaned in, keen to receive his tuition right now if she had a moment. 'D'you, er, practise a lot?'

'Quite a lot. Keeps me supple.'

'I should say . . .' Harry drooled.

'Um, Harry, I thought you were supposed to be going out to dinner?' Lottie burst in desperately, eyeing her sister's contortions with horror.

Caro took a break from the head-rolling routine and opened her eyes wide. 'Oh, I always think dinner parties are so boring. All that talking and not enough action.'

'Well, I suppose some people might find them a little taxing if they're not used to exercising the brain!' I spat in what remained of my voice as I ground my teeth to powder.

'And there's nothing worse than turning up late, it's so incredibly rude, don't you think?' said dear Lottie, jumping up quickly. 'I'll get your jacket, Harry.'

She rushed off and returned in a flash, brandishing the jacket like a matador shaping up to a young bull. Harry drained his glass unwillingly and allowed himself to be helped into his jacket, eyes still glued to Caro. He pecked me perfunctorily on the cheek and patted my bottom.

'Bye Polyester,' he grinned. 'Keep taking the pills.' He kissed Lottie. 'Look after your little sister, Lottie, or someone else will!' He winked at Caro who squirmed and giggled; I tried to ignore the electric current that seemed to be zig-zagging between them. 'Goodbye, Miss Hamilton, it was a great pleasure to have made your acquaintance.'

Caro giggled and simpered, fluttering her hand in a dinky little wave. 'Bye, Harry!'

As soon as he was out of the front door, Lottie rounded on her sister furiously. 'Why didn't you take all your clothes off and wriggle around on the floor? You might just as well have done!'

But Caro was unmoved. 'Don't be silly, Lottie,' she said yawning widely, 'I was just doing a bit of yoga. He is rather cute, though, I'm not surprised you keep him to yourself, Polly. What's happened to your face, by the way? It looks a bit blotchy.'

I didn't trust myself to speak. I stared at her perfect face, the corners of the rosebud mouth turned up in a mocking little grin, and a wave of pure hatred swept over me. I wondered for a moment if I was perhaps about to commit murder. How interesting, I'd never killed anyone before. I looked around for a handy implement, but by the time I'd decided that the heavy china fruit bowl, hurled forcefully and accurately, was just the thing to bash her brains out with, the wave of hatred dissipated and was replaced by one of misery. Why take it out on Caro? I was the one who'd made a comprehensive laughing stock of myself. Why not just kill myself? Ah, so it was suicide, was it? Again, interesting, but not so much fun, I hazarded.

Just me, a large tub of paracetamol, and then a wafty little float through the stratosphere in a white nightie. Hang on a minute, a large tub of . . . Suddenly a think bubble appeared over my head — of course! I knew exactly what I was going to do. It was less messy, less drastic, and ultimately more satisfying than either murder or suicide could ever be.

I leaped up and strode purposefully into the kitchen, making straight for the fridge. There was something inside shouting to be let out. Lottie was after me in a trice, five years at school and two in the flat had left an impression. She raced ahead and flattened herself possessively against the fridge door, arms spread out defiantly, shielding it from the imminent onslaught. It was a spirited defence, but doomed to failure from the outset. My hand was already firmly on the handle.

'Out of my way, Lottie,' I said between clenched teeth. 'I don't want to have to hurt you.'

Lottie suppressed a giggle. 'Don't do it, Polly,' she implored, 'he's not worth it!'

'OUT OF MY WAY, LOTTIE!' She stood her ground for a moment, but only a moment. There was a dangerous glint in my eye and Lottie wasn't very brave. She hesitated, then stood aside. I flung the door open dramatically and made for the ice-box. Ahhh . . . there was my prize, nestling innocently between the frozen peas and the ice-cubes. A family sized tub of Häagen-Dazs chocolate ice-cream, ready and waiting for just such an emergency. I removed it carefully using both hands, slid a knife around the outside of the precious confection and up-ended it ceremoniously on to a large plate — plop! What a divinely decadent noise. I stood back, arms in the air as if I'd just produced a rabbit from a hat. It got a ripple of applause from Lottie and more giggles. I felt better already.

'There,' I said triumphantly, and then, in case anyone was in any doubt, 'and it's all mine!'

'Not the family-sized, Polly,' wailed Lottie, wringing her hands in mock despair. 'Look,' she delved into the ice-box and pulled out a meagre little choc bar, waving it around in front of my nose like a carrot. 'What about one of these nice big choc ices: that'll do the trick, won't it?'

I brushed it aside scornfully. 'Don't be ridiculous, I'm feeding a crisis, not a minor incident. Now for the topping, ooh look!'

A large slab of cooking chocolate had found its way like magic from the back of the fridge to the palm of my hand. I tore open the wrapper like a five-year-old on Christmas morning, and broke it savagely into little pieces, sprinkling them with greedy abandon over the ice-cream.

'Now, what next?' I murmured thoughtfully. 'Ah yes, the cream.'

I strode purposefully back to the fridge, enjoying myself hugely, and seized a carton. I was just about to pour it all over the top when – oh-oh, not so fast, Polly old girl, take a look at the label. My suspicions were confirmed, it was only single. I sniggered. Lucky I spotted that before it was too late, I thought, as I replaced it and returned with the double. Lottie was eyeing the proceedings with deep concern.

'He's not worth it, Poll!' she cried as I poured the cream from a dramatic height, making nice big swirly dollops over my feast.

'Now for the nuts!' I cried, ignoring her pleas. I tore open a large packet of roasted peanuts – I could almost see the monosodium glutamate crawling all over them as I threw them on top. I rubbed my hands with glee: that should do it! I went to sit down. But wait a minute now – I paused in mid-sit – had I got enough calories here? I eyed my plateful with suspicion. I had to have at least two thousand five hundred, it was no good going off half cocked.

I got up again and prowled slowly around the kitchen,

looking for inspiration, searching for hidden carbohydrates. There was definitely something missing, an elusive little *je ne sais quoi*. I scratched my head, what could it be? Of course! The maple syrup! I rounded on my hapless flatmate.

'Have we got any maple syrup, Lottie?'

'I, I, I'm not sure, no, I don't think—' So we *had*!

I ran to the cupboard she was so obviously shielding, threw it open, and spied a tin, glinting in the fluorescent strip-lighting. Only about a third of a tin, but no matter. I scooped away, scraping it to within an inch of its life. A little metal poisoning wouldn't go amiss either. I sat down with a spoon poised over the top of the mound. Did I need a tablespoon? I dithered.

Lottie saw my hesitation and misread it. She was beside me in an instant. 'You don't really want to do it, do you, Polly?'

I grinned demoniacally. Did I!

'A moment on the lips, a lifetime on the hips?' she ventured. I gave her a withering look. 'You'll have to do better than that.'

She tried harder. 'Remember Monica Stewart?'

I remembered, and wavered for an instant, but only an instant. Monica Stewart was far and away the largest girl we had ever known. She'd been in our year at school and we used to fight to sit next to her at lunch so as to marvel at what she put away. Half a steak-and-kidney pudding, mounds of mashed potato, saucepans full of seemingly inedible cabbage, jugs of custard, bowl after bowl full of wobbly pink blancmange: nothing was too much trouble for Monica. And as she ate one could almost see it visibly adding to her enormous bulk. A little more padding on the thighs, one more ripple on the tummy, another chin, perhaps. She, and she alone, could lay claim to the epithet, 'A legend in her own lunch-hour'.

'That was glandular,' I muttered. My spoon was

dangerously close and getting closer by the moment.

'OK, OK, your new tartan trousers from Kenzo.' The spoon wobbled like a jelly. 'The ones that cost over a hundred and fifty pounds,' she went on ruthlessly.

Oh that was cruel, very cruel. I'd hardly been able to squeeze into them in the fitting room, but I'd bought them anyway in the hope that a week or two of concentrated dieting would do the trick. I racked my brains for a way out of this one. Of course! The summer was coming, tartan trousers would be much too hot, they'd been a big mistake.

Nothing could stop me now, the green light was on as far as I was concerned. I dug in and scooped up a spoonful of mammoth proportions. Lottie put her hand on my arm as it made its way to my mouth. Good grief, what now? A last-ditch attempt? She stuck her face in front of mine and stared deep into my eyes. 'Think,' she said slowly and carefully, 'think of Caro's long . . . slim . . . legs . . .'

It was done with all the best intentions, but it was the biggest mistake she could have made. I gave a sort of blood-curdling, *Last of the Mohicans* shriek, pushed her hand away, and ladled about two hundred and fifty calories into my mouth. If anything was going to make me eat this, it was the thought of Caro's legs which, coincidentally, were at that very moment strolling nonchalantly through the kitchen door. I eyed them speculatively as they passed by, almost tempted to take a chunk out of one of them with my teeth, but I thought better of it. Not meaty enough.

I tucked in with relish as Caro sat down at the table with us. She looked at the mountain of food with disbelief, and then stared at me in horror as I shovelled it into my willing mouth by the spadeful. She turned to Lottie with eyes like saucepan lids.

'What's she doing?' she asked.

90

Lottie grimaced. 'Getting her own back.'

'I don't understand . . .' said Caro.

'You wouldn't,' I said, looking at her twenty-two-inch waist.

'It's called comfort food, Caro,' said Lottie.

'But I thought we were having lasagne . . .'

I paused between spoonfuls, ice-cream and chocolate dripping from my chops. 'Change of plan,' I said, spraying her with cream and nuts. 'Not fattening enough.'

Lottie giggled and got a couple of spoons from the drawer. She handed one to Caro and then got stuck in herself. 'If you can't beat 'em, join 'em!' she cried joyfully, tucking in with a vengeance.

'Atta-girl!' I cried back, crunching on the nuts and imagining for a moment that they were Harry's — only for a moment, mind.

Caro got up from the table in disgust. 'Honestly, this is just too silly,' she said pompously. 'I don't think I can bear to watch such a dreadful display of pigging out. That is what you're doing, isn't it? I mean, what's it all in aid of?'

'You,' I said under my breath, but she'd already left the room for the safety of 'Dallas', where she could identify with the skinny-hipped, lettuce-eating glamour pusses at her leisure.

Lottie and I ploughed on, but I'm happy to say were defeated by at least half of my calorific concoction. We chucked it in the bin then sat back in our chairs, giggling and holding our stomachs. Totally replete. Or were we?

'Lasagne?' suggested Lottie mischievously.

'Clever girl!' I replied admiringly.

She went to the oven and brought it out, a little burnt and frayed at the edges, but still eminently edible.

'Caro, supper's ready!' I called.

She appeared at the door. 'You didn't really eat all that, did you?' she said in amazement.

'Certainly we did,' I replied. 'Just a little starter, and now it's time for the main course.'

She sat down, thoroughly bemused, and we ploughed womanfully through the lasagne, which defeated us none too soon. I staggered back to the viewing room again and sank into a sofa, feeling a million times better for my binge, but knowing I'd regret it later. As I heaved my colossal legs up on to the sofa, I suddenly remembered something. Of course! There was just one other thing I needed to do to get even with Harry. I grabbed the mobile phone and took it into my bedroom.

'Who are you ringing?' asked Lottie to my disappearing back.

'I'll tell you when I've done it,' I said mysteriously.

I gathered together a glass of wine, a packet of cigarettes and an ashtray, and shut the bedroom door behind me. Then I sat cross-legged on the bed and lit a cigarette. Should I ring him? I practised a few smoke rings which I've never been able to do, and still couldn't. I took a large gulp of wine and rang the number quickly before I could change my mind. At this stage I didn't really have much to lose, did I?

After only a couple of rings a girl answered. 'Savoy Hotel.'

'Hello, could I speak to Mr Adam Buchanan, please?'

I licked my lips nervously as I heard the telephone ringing in his room.

'Hello?'

'Mr Buchanan?' I decided to keep it formal and businesslike.. 'It's Polly McLaren here. You asked me to volunteer my services yesterday.' Oh God! My attempts at formality had led me to sound like a prostitute. 'I mean, um, you asked me to help – you know, find Rachel and that sort of thing.'

From prostitute to blithering idiot. Get a grip, Poll. I took a gulp of wine.

'Hey, yes, of course!' He sounded keen and excited. 'Did you find anything?'

Ah-ha! I had him dangling on the end of my line all right. I paused, enjoying my brief moment of one-upmanship. I have so few, but I was too soft-hearted to tease him for long.

'Well, I've been speaking to a girl who was in the same year as Rachel at school and she told me a couple of things, but the thing is − ' and this had only just occurred to me − 'I thought maybe I should hear the whole story from you before I − you know divulge anything.'

What if she didn't want to be found? What if she hated his guts and was avoiding him like the plague? He saw what I was getting at immediately.

'Of course,' he said quickly, 'I totally understand. Why don't we meet and I'll tell you all about it − tell you what, have dinner with me tomorrow night.'

Tomorrow night? Dinner? I was rather thrown by this suggestion, but not displeased.

'Er, well − tomorrow might be a bit difficult.' One couldn't be too readily available, and tomorrow was Friday, rather an uncool night to be free. 'How about next week, Tuesday perhaps?'

'Tuesday would be fine. Why don't we eat here? The Grill Room's very good, shall I book a table?'

Things were looking up: the Grill Room, no less.

'Why not?' I said in an off-hand way, as if I lived in the Grill Room.

'About eight-thirty?'

'Perfect.'

'OK, I'll look forward to seeing you then. Bye now.'

As I put the phone down I felt breathless and strangely elated. It's not every day I meet strange American men for dinner at the Savoy. I leaped off the bed and ran into the kitchen to tell Lottie. She was scraping burnt lasagne into Wellington's bowl who, not surprisingly, was turning his nose up at it.

'He's a Yorkshireman, Lottie, not a bloody Italian.'

'More's the pity,' said Lottie, putting some Pedigree Chum on top to fool him. 'We could do with some hot-blooded continental talent around here.'

'How about a bit of Yankee talent?' I told her about my date on Tuesday.

'Wow!' Lottie was impressed. 'So he's employed you as his private detective, has he? Paying you in kind with a slap-up meal at the Savoy.'

'Why not? I mean if Harry's out on the tiles every night, why shouldn't I be out with a hunky rich American?'

'Why not indeed?' Lottie narrowed her eyes speculatively. 'How hunky? How rich?'

I laughed. 'If we don't find Rachel, I'll point him in your direction. He's a redhead, not my type, but quite cute, you might like him.'

'Carrots?' she said warily.

'No . . . more, more russety really, like a red setter.'

'Mmmm . . . bring him home in a doggy bag.' We both giggled as Caro drifted in.

'I think I might go home now. I've left your clothes on your bed, Polly. I thought, you know, you might need them.' She avoided my eyes. 'Anyway, they look better on you.'

Good grief, was this her conscience talking? I met her half-way.

'Have them if you like, Caro, I won't miss them for a week or two.'

'Thanks, but it's OK, I think I'll leave them. Bye Polly, bye Lottie.'

She kissed us both, looking rather ashamed of herself. Lottie went to the front door with her. I think they had a little talk. She came back, biting her thumbnail and looking thoughtful.

'Sorry about Caro,' she said gruffly. 'She asked me to

apologise. She's a bit, um, insecure at the moment.'

'S'alright,' I said. 'It's not your fault your sister's a tart.'

We giggled and spent the rest of the evening polishing off the wine.

When I went to bed that night, I was surprised to find that for the first time in ages my thoughts didn't revolve around Harry. Instead, my mind was full of Tuesday night's tête-à-tête with Adam Buchanan.

Chapter Six

The rest of the week passed uneventfully, which was pretty much par for the course in my life, and then eventually Tuesday evening arrived. A taxi dropped me off in the Strand exactly ten minutes late, and in my nervous state I overtipped wildly. I ran my hand down the back of my black dress as I got out of the cab, smoothing out the wrinkles and hoping it hadn't creased too disastrously. Linen was always a nightmare. It was also a bit tight and I probably should have taken my pants off to avoid a knicker line, but Lottie had been horrified when I'd suggested it.

'Suppose he notices!'

'He's hardly likely to, unless he crawls under the table and looks up my skirt.'

'Take it from me, Polly,' she'd said, giving me her wise old sage look. 'Some men can just tell.'

That was enough for me: the knickers stayed put. I fingered my pearls as I walked to the Savoy entrance. Should I take them off? Wasn't a little black dress and pearls just a trifle unimaginative? Probably, but they gave me something to fiddle with when I wasn't smoking. They stayed put too.

First stop was the loo. I nipped in and had a quick look in the mirror. Not too bad at all, considering. My skin was surprisingly clear and my eyes looked almost blue in this light. I put my head down and shook it around to jazz up my curls, then threw it back and gave it a blast of hairspray. I considered the effect. Hey. This could almost be called glamorous. Almost.

Feeling faintly giggly, which might have had something to do with the bottle of wine I'd shared with Lottie for Dutch courage, I pushed through the glass double doors on which 'Grill Room' was written in discreet little gold letters. I remembered the last and only time I'd been here. It was for a sixteenth birthday treat with my parents and two older brothers. I'd been wildly over-excited on that occasion too, and had my first legitimate taste of champagne, my illegitimate tastes being the dregs left behind in the glasses after my parents' drinks parties which I used to quaff with a vengeance. My expensive tastes developed at a tender age.

I strolled in, trying to look nonchalant and hoping to God he was here before me. I had a quick look round, but couldn't see him; mind you, I'm pretty myopic at the best of times. The maître-d' cruised up beside me in an instant.

'Can I help you, madam?' he murmured.

'Yes, I'm dining with Mr Buchanan, perhaps you'd show me to his table?' I murmured back, as if I had a bit part in a 1940s film and this was my big line.

Not one eyelid batted. This was obviously the way most people spoke in here. He ran a finger swiftly down a list. 'Ah yes, follow me, please.'

I followed the ramrod-straight, dinner-jacketed back through a sea of tables as we wove our way across the elegant dining room. With its panelled walls, brass fittings and green velvet seats, it could almost be a gentleman's club.

Out of the corner of my eye I spotted Roger Moore having supper with his wife and children. I resisted the temptation to stare, and, anyway, I'd spotted Adam.

He was wearing a beautifully cut charcoal-grey suit with a pale blue shirt and navy spotted tie, all of which did wonders for toning down the red of his hair and bringing out the delphinium blue in his eyes. Things were looking up. He was sitting in the far corner of the room over by the window, and he instantly stood up as I was led to the table. This was a tricky little manoeuvre, as the table had banquette seating so he couldn't push his chair back and he had to maintain a rather uncomfortable skiing position as we shook hands. I sat down quickly to ease the discomfort and he sank back, relieved.

'Hi. It's good to see you, Miss McLaren.'

Oh God, the forties movie was rolling on apace: my fault, no doubt, for being so pompous on the telephone.

'Polly's fine, really,' I said smiling.

He visibly relaxed and smiled back, eyes crinkling. 'Good. Polly it is. Champagne?'

He gestured towards a bottle cooling in a bucket by our table and, as if by magic, an obsequious little waiter appeared to pour me a glass. I lit a cigarette, the first of many. Christ, this place was so understated it was in danger of not existing at all. A little different from the South Ken wine bars I frequented, where you had to rugby tackle your way to the bar, limbo dance your way to a seat at a table, and have a voice like Pavarotti to stand any chance of being heard. I hoped I wasn't going to get loud and raucous.

Adam was obviously a professional mind-reader. He grinned. 'I know, it is a bit subdued in here, but I thought it would be easier to talk. I guess you're more used to Langan's or something?'

'Er, yes, something like that' — but cheaper, I thought — 'but this is, um, charming.' Oh stop it, Polly, when have you ever, ever, said anything was charming? I must be nervous. I hid my face in the enormous menu and guzzled the champagne greedily.

'Any idea what you're going to have?' asked Adam.

'The Dover sole's pretty good, but feel free to have anything you like.'

'Oh no, I'll have the sole,' I said, relieved that at least one major decision had been made for me. 'I love fish.'

Fish? Was that really the way to describe Dover sole meunière? We're talking bank-breaking seafood here Polly, not cod and chips wrapped in newspaper. Oh dear. I sank into the champagne refuge again.

'Two Dover soles it is then,' he said, snapping the menu shut.

The waiter seemed to sense a decision and reappeared out of thin air. Adam ordered for us both with the assurance of a man who'd ordered more meals than I'd had hot dinners. That done he turned to face me. He put his elbows squarely on the table and fixed me with his steely blues.

'Look, I was thinking, instead of making polite conversation and skirting round the subject for hours, why don't I just tell you all about me and Rachel and get it out of the way? Then we can just forget about it and enjoy the meal, how does that sound?'

I nodded enthusiastically. 'Sounds good to me.' I was all for enjoying myself, whenever, wherever and with whomever − in the nicest possible way, of course.

He sat back, folded his napkin into a neat little square and took a deep breath. 'OK. Well, I could start with how I met her, but I'm going to go back a bit, so bear with me, it'll make sense in the end, you'll see.'

'OK, fire away.'

He leaned forward again. 'Rachel, as you know, was at the same school as you − St Gertrude's, right?'

I nodded. 'Right, poor thing.'

He shrugged. 'Well, funnily enough she rather enjoyed it. Her home life was pretty non-existent, so I think she was glad to be away at boarding school, that's probably why she did so well. She buried herself in her books in the holidays too, as far as I can gather. I guess there was nothing else to do.'

'Ah well, that's obviously why I did so badly at school. My home life was far too happy by half. Too many treats, parties, outings, ponies, friends — all my parents' fault, of course. I have them and them alone to thank for my lack of O-levels.'

Adam laughed and stopped folding his napkin into squares. Good. I may not be the brightest pixie in the forest, but I can perk up an atmosphere at the drop of a joke or two and I wanted to keep this as jolly and lighthearted as possible. His eyes looked a lot less steely.

'At least it sounds as if you had a good time. Unlike Rachel. She just swotted away at school and, consequently I guess, got straight As in all her subjects. By all accounts she was brilliant at music and maths and all set to glide through her A-levels and then go on to music school. But uh, uh, no such luck.'

I grimaced. 'Enter the wicked father.'

Adam looked surprised. 'You know about this?'

I could have bitten my tongue out. I wanted his version, not mine. 'Oh, I heard vague rumblings from someone in her year, but go on.'

'Well, as you say, enter the father. Wicked is probably a little strong, but reactionary, Victorian and bloody-minded will do just as well. Anyway, right out of the blue he arrives at the school and, bold as brass, insists that she packs the whole thing in and comes home with him. Can you believe it?'

'I can't really, I mean why? It's not as if he couldn't afford the fees or something, just to drag her out for no reason seems crazy.'

'He is crazy. In fact I think he's certifiable. Apparently he had some archaic idea about her turning her hand to a little flower-arranging or needlework — crap like that, something feminine and undemanding. Said he didn't want her turning into a hardened career woman and that educating girls was a waste of time anyway because all they did in the end was get married and have babies.'

'Good grief, he's positively Dickensian.'

'Totally. Well, anyway, Rachel may be a bit timid and shy in other respects, but she's pretty passionate about her music and she wasn't going to take this lying down. By all accounts she put up a hell of a fight, as did your headmistress incidently: she was pretty horrified too.'

'I can imagine. It's not as if she had many star pupils,' I said, licking my lips as the most enormous Dover sole I've ever seen was put in front of me.

He paused for a second as silver dishes full of juicy little new potatoes and gleaming, al dente broccoli florets were flourished around. Adam seemed oblivious to the food. He pushed it dreamily around his plate, then started fiddling with his napkin again. I covered the fish's eyes with a piece of lettuce so he couldn't eyeball me, and tucked in with relish while Adam talked.

'Of course, there was no contest really. Old man Marsden was, after all, holding the purse strings, and Rachel's pleadings were like water off a duck's back as far as he was concerned. Let's face it, he's used to dealing with the criminal classes on a daily basis, so a schoolgirl was no match for him. He'd made up his mind and that was that.'

He picked up his fork again and toyed idly with his sole. I wondered if it would be terribly gauche to offer to eat what he didn't want, and decided on balance it would. 'Was she terribly upset?'

'Devastated. Cried and cried for ages, which rather disconcerted her father. I think he thought she'd sulk for a bit and then toe the line; but she shut herself in her room for days on end, refusing even to speak to him.'

'Good for her.' I was attacking bare fish bones now, and he hadn't even started. I played with my broccoli, trying to make it last a bit longer. The champagne was slipping down nicely, thank you very much, and I was beginning to feel rather lightheaded. Thus far, of course, I knew the storyline. It was the next bit I wanted to hear.

'I guess she decided that all she really wanted was to get away from him, so she asked if she could go abroad for a bit. It was the first time she'd said two words to him for days, and he was so nonplussed he just agreed on the spot, on the condition that she didn't just travel around, bumming and rucksacking, but went to stay with my family in Boston.' Adam reached for the bottle and topped up my glass.

'What's the connection?'

'Marsden and Dad were at Oxford together, they go way back and they've always kept in touch. According to Dad, he wasn't such a bad guy in those days, although it's hard to imagine him being anything other than a complete bastard.' He abandoned his sole and lit a cigarette. I watched longingly as a waiter whipped his plate away.

'So that's how you met her?' I lit one myself to keep him company.

'Right. I was staying with my folks at the time, and they asked me to pick her up at the airport.'

'You'd never met her before?'

'Never. It was her first time in America, and I'd never bothered to look her up when I'd been in England. So anyway, off I went to the airport with "Miss Rachel Marsden" written on a little placard, thinking this was all a bit of a bore and I could be getting on with some work or having a drink with the guys or something . . .'

He paused and slowly blew a long line of smoke over my head. His hand was caressing his wine glass. He seemed to be miles away. 'I'll never forget my first glimpse of her . . .' he said softly.

I smiled wryly. Now come along, Mr Buchanan, I thought, you're not going to tell me you were dazzled by her beauty or something, are you? I mean, judging by that photo you showed me she's OK looking, but she's not going to stop the traffic. Do you, perchance, carry a white stick?

If he did, his telepathic powers made up for his bad eyesight. He smiled ruefully. 'OK, OK, I know what you're thinking and you're right, she's no great beauty, but Polly – ' he leaned in earnestly – 'you should have seen her that day. Not beautiful, I grant you, but still pretty enough and so young and innocent-looking as she came through the gate with her baggage. She looked – I don't know, it sounds so corny – lost and wide-eyed, her pale, worried little face searching for a friendly face: she just looked so vulnerable. I knew it was her without even having to hold up my sign. She was wearing her school coat . . .'

I nose-dived into my champagne glass at this – Christ, her school coat? That dreadful old green thing? Did this girl have no sense of style whatsoever? Next he'd be telling me she wasn't wearing any make-up.

' . . . and that ridiculous scarf you all seem to wear. Sounds crazy, I know, but I reckon I fell for her almost immediately.'

'How romantic,' I murmured. I was totally unconvinced, but nonetheless made a mental note to dig out my old school coat and try out the vulnerable look. I couldn't help thinking it would need a good six inches off the hemline and not a lot of clothing underneath to make it anywhere near alluring, though. I was enjoying myself hugely now, lapping up the champagne and the dialogue with a vengeance.

'So you whisked her off her feet there and then?'

'Well, not exactly, but I had some time on my hands so I spent the next week or so showing her round Boston, going to concerts and museums and taking her to my folks' country place by the sea.'

Ah-ha! My ears pricked up. I know all about those

empty little cottages in the country. I had the feeling we were coming to a sexy bit.

'Well, one thing led to another, I suppose . . .' He paused, was that all he was going to say? He looked miles away, he wasn't going to go all misty eyed and withdrawn on me, was he?

'And?' I said, breathlessly and shamelessly.

' . . . and . . . within only a couple of days, we were . . . well, we were lovers.'

'A couple of days!' I squeaked. 'What, of her arriving in Boston? Gosh, you didn't waste much time!'

Adam looked alarmed. 'Hey, look, I didn't push her into it or anything, if that's what you're thinking. She was pretty willing, I assure you.'

Ah-ha. So Rachel was the instigator was she? Fast work, kid, and all achieved with a pale face, mousy hair, and an old school coat. I had to hand it to her.

Adam sighed. 'Look. I know it sounds ridiculously soft and unbelievable considering how long I'd known her, but honestly, Polly, I was already in love with her.' He was desperate for me to believe him and I did. I liked the way he said my name, too. Paully.

'Hell, no, it don't sound soft at all.' Why was I speaking with an American accent all of a sudden? And a deeply southern one at that. I cleared my throat and reverted to Queen's English. 'I think it's wonderful, actually. I only wish that sort of thing happened to me,' I added truthfully.

He grinned. 'Well, it had certainly never happened to me before.'

'So you just stayed there? I mean at the cottage? In a romantic little huddle?'

'For a while; then we went home to Boston and I talked to my mom about it. I'm pretty close to her, and she was great about the whole thing, if a little alarmed at first because Rachel was so young.'

'She can't have been more than seventeen!'

'Eighteen, actually, but I agree, still very young, and remember her father had entrusted her into my parents' care.'

'Serve him bloody well right!' I said, waving my champagne glass around. I was more than a trifle pissed. 'You didn't tell him, did you?'

He grimaced. 'Well, given his rather manic disposition, we decided to keep quiet for a while. I didn't particularly want him arriving at Boston airport bearing a meat cleaver with my name on it. Rachel wrote saying what a terrific time she was having—'

'—but not *who* she was having!' I interjected drunkenly, roaring with laughter at my own puerile wit.

He smiled. 'Quite.'

It was rather a polite little 'quite'. Simmer down, Polly old girl, I thought. Lay off the juice for a sec or you'll never get to the end of the story. I laid off for precisely one sec before hoovering up again.

'Anyway, the old boy seemed to soften slightly and wrote back saying she could stay on for a bit. Maybe he was feeling guilty about wrecking her academic career, I don't know. Meanwhile we moved back into the house by the sea in Marblehead. He was none the wiser because my parents sent her mail on.'

'Did they mind?'

'A bit, I suppose, but they knew we wanted to be together and they knew he'd come and get her if he ever found out. Mom and Dad are pretty laid back. Rachel couldn't believe them. D'you know she'd never even been allowed to have a date with a boy, even a boy of her own age. Don't you think that's weird? Maybe that's the English way, but Jeez, in the States the kids are dating at about fifteen!'

'Well, I think that's a little early, but even so . . .' I thought of my own relaxed parents who had generally let me do what I liked at that age, providing they met the boys in question and providing I came in at a reasonable hour. I couldn't begin to count the number of times I'd crept up the stairs after a late party, shoes in hand, always to be greeted by my mother's sleepy voice as I got to the landing, 'That you, darling?'

'Yes,' I'd whisper, 'go back to sleep.'

In the morning she'd come and sit on my bed and quiz me mercilessly, wanting to share it all. Who had been there? What had the girls been wearing? Had I met anyone nice? It was all part of the fun of the night before, and I couldn't imagine it any other way. I'd never had to go behind her back – although I have to say, Daddy would have gone into orbit at the thought of me shacking up with some older guy in America. I drained my glass rather conspicuously and it was instantly refilled.

'Sho you lived together?' I was dimly aware that I was slurring my words slightly.

'Yep.'

'How long for?'

'About a year or so, I guess, and then I asked her to marry me. She said yes and . . .'

'Congratulations!' I cried, swinging my champagne glass towards his own unsuspecting vessel and ricocheting off it with a loud clink. I swayed backwards into my seat rather unsteadily. 'Here's to the bride and groom! The happy couple!' I was flying now, and one or two people on the next table were turning round to look. They smiled, probably thinking we'd just got engaged.

Adam laughed, if a little nervously. 'Er, thanks – shall I go on?'

'Pleash continue!' I slurred, making a magnanimous sweeping gesture with my glass and indicating that the floor was all his.

'Well, we talked about the wedding, where it should be – in England or America, how many people we should have, bridesmaids, flowers, etc, and the more we talked, the more we realised there was no getting away from it. We'd have to tell Rachel's father eventually, so we might as well tell him straight away. We could have gone behind his back and just got married, but Rachel didn't want that, and I agreed. I was also quite prepared to wait a year or so if he thought she was too young.'

Even in my inebriated condition, I could see that Adam was looking pretty miserable now. He hadn't even touched his summer pudding, which was a dead giveaway, and he was busy picking the table decoration of rosebuds to pieces.

'So . . . I put her on a plane to England about two weeks ago. That was the last time I saw her.'

He scattered the petals over the tablecloth, rested his elbows on the table and ran his hands through his hair. I sat quietly, sensing no smart-arse remarks would be welcome.

He sighed and lifted his head. 'I thought she'd ring after a day or so and give me the low-down, and when she didn't I rang her father's place. He just put the phone down on me. I tried again and again, same response each time. I wrote a letter and got no reply. I telegraphed − still nothing. After about a week of this I got on a plane and came over. I was terrified he'd dragged her off to Australia or something.'

He leant back wearily in his seat and still, miraculously, I managed to hold my tongue. I looked down and tried to focus on my hands which, rather alarmingly, seemed to have reproduced. If I wasn't very much mistaken there were about twenty fingers on that tablecloth. I started counting them, to myself you understand, but moving my mouth a lot so I didn't lose count. One, two, three . . .

'I went to his house and he slammed the door on me. I shouted through the letter-box, threw pebbles at the windows, camped outside the house in a hired car. I even

– ' and here he looked rather abashed – 'I even tried to break in one night, but the place is wired up like Fort Knox. But that's how worried I was about her.'

He was worried, I thought, staring at my hands; what about my bloody fingers? How would he like to have twenty-two of the bloody things, or was it twenty-three? They seemed to be fluctuating all the time as they moved in and out of focus. Better have a recount just to be on the safe side. I'd got up to eighteen when the coffee arrived. I took a large gulp. It had a surprisingly dramatic effect. Hot, black and strong, it surged through my furred-up veins and made a quick dash to my brain where, miraculously, it brought a brief moment of lucidity. I took another slug. Yes, this was definitely doing the trick; lo and behold, a few bruised and battered little grey cells were surging into action and making a dramatic comeback. Now what were we talking about? Ah yes, of course, Rachel; we were looking for Rachel.

'But she could be anywhere!' I managed to articulate and, flushed with success, roared on to form yet another sentence. 'She could be, well – in the country, abroad – ' I gestured wildly round the room – 'in here even!' Should we look under the tables, I wondered thoughtfully? Might that not be a start?'

'She's not abroad and she's not in the country,' said Adam decisively. 'She's here in London.'

'She is? How d'you know?'

'Because I've seen her.'

This shock tactic worked better than any black coffee could.

'You've seen her! Where?'

'In a taxi. She was with her father in the back of a taxi in Piccadilly. I was stuck in a jam going in the other direction, so there was nothing I could do – but it was her all right.'

'Did she see you?'

'No, she was looking straight ahead. I just remember how pale and sad she looked.'

'Oh!'

God what a mess. What a complete bastard her father must be. I drank a whole cup of coffee down in one and suddenly felt tolerably sober. I looked at my hands. Ten. What a relief: the offspring had flown.

'So where else have you looked, now you know she's in London?'

'Well, apart from laying siege to their house in London, I've waited outside court to try to speak to her father; but that's impossible, he goes everywhere by chauffeur-driven car, which whisks him away before I can get to him. He never walks anywhere, so there's no chance of tripping him up in the street.'

He rubbed his eyes. He looked tired. 'Two days ago I flew to Paris.'

'To see Sally Lomax?'

'You know her?'

'I don't remember her, but I asked around and found out she was Rachel's best friend.'

'Her only friend really. I was desperate and I thought Rachel might have managed to get a message to her. She hadn't, but she'd written Sally a letter on the plane going over to London, obviously posting it at the airport. Sally gave it to me.' He smiled ruefully. 'She said it was more mine than hers anyway.'

Adam took his wallet out of his breast pocket and produced a thin sheet of paper that had obviously been smoothed out, read and re-read over and over again. I spread it out on the table and concentrated like mad. I seemed to be focusing reasonably well. It was written in a round, schoolgirlish hand.

Dear Sally,

If my writing's terrible it's because I'm scribbling this

on a rather bumpy plane journey to England, so bear with me. Fabulous news, you'll never guess — Adam's asked me to marry him! I'm so thrilled I can hardly believe it. I've been mad about him from the moment I saw him — when he picked me up at the airport, in fact — and now I'm going to be Mrs Buchanan. Isn't it fantastic? He's so divine, Sally, I know you'll adore him. He loves the same sort of music as me, a real bonus, added to which he's incredibly good looking (well, I think so, but then I'm biased!).

I couldn't help looking up at this point. He caught my eye and grinned sheepishly. I grinned back and read on.

I can't wait for you to meet him; we're actually thinking of coming to Paris for our honeymoon, but before that I want you to come to London and be my bridesmaid. Please say you will. I'll let you know when, but it'll probably be around the end of September.

The only dark cloud on the horizon is the one waiting for me at Heathrow. I'm flying home to ask Daddy for his permission, and you know what he can be like — help! We'll go ahead and get married whatever he says, but it would be so much nicer to have his blessing. Anyway, I'll let you know how it goes. Must dash, the inedible plastic lunch is on its way round. Write soon,

Masses of love, Rachel.

I folded it in half and handed it back to him. 'Well, that's one of the leads I had for you blown. I should have realised you'd know who her best friend was. The only other thing I discovered was that she got on very well with a couple of teachers at school. I could ring them up and see if either of them has heard from her, if you like?'

'If you think it might help, I'd be grateful.'

He paused and looked at me steadily for a good ten seconds. I instinctively put my hand to my face. What? Had my make-up slipped? Did I have eyeshadow on my nose? Lipstick on my teeth? A bogey? What? He leaned forward and kept those steely blues boring into my shifty greens. What! I thought desperately, what is it?

'Polly, would you do something for me?'

'How can I possibly refuse?' I burbled, relieved that he'd finally spoken and feeling decidedly giggly.

'Would you go and see her father for me?'

'What! Me!' I nearly ate my coffee cup. 'Why?'

'Because he might talk to you. You can say you're an old schoolfriend, which is half true, and ask him if he knows where she is. Say you're organising an old girl's reunion or something. He'll never suspect you're anything to do with me.'

He had a point there, but did I really want to get that involved? Up to now it had been a bit of a laugh, but I wasn't sure I wanted to do battle with a crusty old judge with a meat hook.

I hesitated and tried not to look at Adam's eyes, which were pleading with me to say yes. Damn. I looked at them. 'OK,' I said weakly, 'I'll have a go.'

His whole face creased delightedly and his mouth grinned so hugely it almost split his face in half. He gave me such a hearty slap on the back I thought my Dover sole was going to reappear on the plate in front of me.

'You're a hell of a girl, Polly!' he boomed joyfully. 'A hell of a girl!'

Well, aren't I just? He seemed so overwhelmed by my agreement that it occurred to me he probably hadn't reckoned he had a snowball's chance in hell of getting me to do it. Ah yes, but then he'd reckoned without the sucker of all suckers, Miss Polly McLaren. No job too small, no fee too low, all assignments considered. Need a secretary you can really wipe the floor with? I'm your girl. Looking for a girlfriend you can park inside your front door with 'please wipe your boots' printed on her back? Look no further. Got a little problem with an axe-man of a judge? You've come to the right place. Polly McLaren's the name and gullibility's the game.

'This is where he lives,' Adam was saying, eagerly scribbling the scene of my death on a piece of paper. 'You'll obviously stand more chance of finding him in at the weekend or in the evenings . . .' When it's nice and dark, I thought, and when my blood won't show up quite as much on the carpets. 'Just keep your head' – no chance, it'll be rolling around on the floor, severed inexorably from my neck – 'and I know you'll be fantastic. I can't tell you how grateful I am . . . Tell you what, let's celebrate. More champagne!'

God, I had made him happy, hadn't I?

'Oh no, I couldn't possibly.'

' 'Course you could!'

'No no, really, I'm sobering up nicely on this black coffee.'

'Just a couple of glasses.'

'Oh well . . .'

'Waiter!'

The deed was done. He obviously thought I doth protest too much and he was absolutely right. All that making other people happy lark had given me one hell of a thirst. The bottle arrived. The one that would pour the glass too far. The one that would send me tumbling over the edge.

We both relaxed considerably as we quaffed the champagne. He was now doing his damnedest to keep up with me, but I could tell he was an amateur and, anyway, I had a two-bottle start on him. I started to tell him about Harry – trying to make him sound like the best thing since filtered cigarettes, but somehow he ended up sounding like a bit of a jerk. Surely I wasn't experiencing a touch of in vino veritas?

'Sounds like a bit of a jerk to me,' said Adam, echoing my thoughts, which I must say I thought was a bit strong considering he was talking about the father of my unborn children.

'What about the guy you work for,' he said, 'the guy I met on the stairs. He seemed nice enough, and isn't he what you girls would call a hunk?'

'Ah, now you really *are* talking jerks.' I warmed to my favourite subject and gave Adam a thumbnail sketch of Nick, pitching it somewhere between Paul Daniels and Saddam Hussein.

'And he's the boss, is he?' asked Adam.

'Yes, he set the place up about five years ago with a chap called Hugh Waters, but Waters doesn't have much say, he's just a sleeping partner. Apparently we're doing really well, as small agencies go. Nick's pretty bright, but he will spoil it by charging around barking out orders and instructions as if he owned the bloody place.'

'I thought you said he did.'

'Oh. Yes I did, but he doesn't have to show off about it, does he?'

I fumbled for my cigarettes. My fingers had once more gone forth and multiplied, and it was hard to remember which were the ones I usually used to pick things up with.

Adam laughed. 'You English really crack me up. It's considered bad form for anyone to make money and be a success, isn't it? What accounts do you have?'

We took an appropriate commercial break here as I seemed to be hell-bent on massacring cigarettes as they came out of the packet, but third time lucky I managed to extract an unbroken one. Hand-to-mouth coordination was becoming a real problem now, as someone appeared to have moved my mouth. It certainly wasn't in its normal position. Luckily Adam came to the rescue, turning my cigarette the right way round so I didn't light the filter, sticking it in my mouth and lighting it for me. It occurred to me that he could have gone the whole way and smoked it for me too, but I guess that was asking too much. I inhaled deeply. Now what had that last Brain of Britain question been about? Our accounts? Really? At this time of night? God, he really knew how to tax a girl: was he trying to kill me with a mixture of alcohol and Mensa?

I opened my mouth, hoping the words would just come out of their own accord: these accounts were tongue-twisters at the best of times. Nothing happened, so I decided to go the whole hog and recite them in Swedish, or was it Russian?

'Well, wev got Sujuper Roztie Cwoffee, um Lemonjina Sjoft Drinkz, um . . .'

Adam magnanimously let me off the hook. 'OK, OK,' he laughed, 'some other time perhaps. Somehow I think it's time to make a move.'

'You're going to make a move?' I looked alarmed, this guy was indeed a fast worker, and a fickle one at that.

'Home, Polly,' he explained patiently. 'I think it's time we were going.'

Ah yes, going. This was the moment I'd been having mixed feelings about. What remained of my brain definitely knew it was time to leave, but I wasn't sure how my legs were going to take it or, more particularly, my knees. The table was pulled out for us, and I tested them gingerly as Adam instructed the waiter to add the bill to his room tab. The knees weren't too bad, but the top half of my body seemed to have been caught up in a hurricane: it swayed dangerously from side to side. Had someone left a window open in here? I looked around suspiciously. Adam caught me as a particularly strong gust blew me sharply to the left, nearly knocking me over. I clung on to his arm and, slowly, we began the tricky little exercise of navigating our way out of the restaurant. Some bastard had thoughtfully placed an obstacle course in my way, but I rose to the challenge and meandered through a sea of tables, chairs and fellow diners with surprising agility, although I must say Adam's arm was necessary as well as decorative.

This time I couldn't resist cocking an eyebrow at Roger Moore, who didn't cock one back, which I thought was pretty unsporting. I stuck my tongue out at him. Yeh, I can be rude too, you know, I thought.

Just as we were lurching past the penultimate table, I spotted a very familiar figure in black tie walking into the restaurant. I knew him well but couldn't quite place him; nonetheless I greeted him like the old friend he undoubtedly was.

'Hi there!' I shouted, much to my fellow diners' amusement. I waved cheerily.

'Don't tell me, no − don't tell me, it's on the tip of my tongue?' I went on, bashing my forehead for inspiration. 'You're um . . .'

'He's the maître-d',' Adam hissed in my ear.

'May Tradee? May Tradee?' I said loudly. 'No, that's not it, I'd have remembered a sissy name like that. How many men are called May, for God's sake? Don't be ridiculous, Adam.'

'He showed you to the table,' said Adam, forsaking the whisper − what was the point? The whole dining room had laid down their knives and forks with amusement and were damned if they were going to miss anything.

'He showed me a table?' I thought hard. Ah, yes, obviously an assistant from Peter Jones. I was in there so often. 'Adam tells me you once showed me a table!' I cried as I was propelled past him at speed. 'Well, I think that was very sweet of you! Adam wait, I want to thank him, I—'

Somehow I found myself approaching the front entrance. An east wind was whipping around my kidneys as I was escorted from the premises and out on to the street by this burly American. Ah-ha, this was obviously the same wind that had tried to knock me over in the restaurant. Where was it from: Siberia? Were the Russians buggering around with our weather again? Bastards. I wrapped my pearls a little more tightly round my neck for warmth and shivered. A taxi purred up alongside us and Adam swiftly poured me in the back.

'Where do you live, Polly?' he asked.

'Chunder Road.'

He looked taken aback. 'Chunder Road? Are you sure?'

I tried again. 'Chegunder Road.'

'It's all right, mate,' said the taxi driver through his partition. 'That's pissed for Tregunter Road. I'll see she gets home safely.'

Adam grinned and waved me off. I turned round to wave back as the taxi rolled away, and wished I hadn't. The cab lurched round the corner into the Strand and so did my tummy. I clutched the handrail with one hand and my mouth with another. A friend of mine had once thrown up in the back of a taxi after just such an evening, and been forced to sit watching her dinner roll from side to side in the back as the cab lurched round corners with the driver screaming blue murder at her at the top of his voice. I tried not to think about that, nor my brother's joke about a man hailing a taxi and asking the driver if he had room for eight pints of lager and a takeaway curry before throwing up in it. Oh no. I kept my lips tightly pursed as we trundled down the Fulham Road, up Hollywood Road, and finally came to rest in Tregunter Road.

I tumbled out and handed the driver my purse, trusting him not to rob me of all my worldly goods. I certainly couldn't trust myself to try and open the damn thing. He handed it back to me with a grin.

'It's OK, luv, your boyfriend paid.'

Harry? Good Lord, how extraordinary. The taxi driver

waved a cheery goodbye before disappearing over the horizon, leaving me to chew on this dramatic turn of events. Harry? Where on earth had he sprung from, and how uncharacteristically generous. I shook my head in awe and wonder as I staggered up the front steps.

Before long, however, I had an even bigger conundrum to consider. Like how to get the key in the front door. How bizarre. The keyhole was much too small for my key and it also refused to keep still, leaping around all over the place whenever I tried to stab it. Stab stab stab. Move move move. Well this was a bit of a blow to morale. I thought hard. Ah yes, Lottie had obviously changed the locks while I was out. Too many men had been laying siege again, pestering us for dates. I'd have to break in.

I failed, but made so much noise attempting it that the door flew open and Lottie appeared in her nightie brandishing a tennis racket.

'Lottie! Couldn't get in, bloody lock, bloody key . . .' I mumbled, swaying violently. 'Been playing tennis? Little late, isn't it?'

'Get in!' she yelled, dragging me forcibly by the arm. 'I thought you were a bloody burglar! I was just about to bash you over the head!'

She pulled me in, swearing like a trooper and promising all kinds of vile deaths as she pushed me up the stairs, frogmarched me through the sitting room, and propelled me into my bedroom. She deposited me unceremoniously on my bed, where I lay until morning in a deep and blissful coma, boots still firmly on my feet like all good cowboys.

Chapter Seven

When the fire alarm went off the next morning I realised, with a start, that I was dead. More than dead in fact, reincarnated. Because this sure as hell wasn't my body I was lying in. Whoever I'd come back as had got the most enormous tongue: large and furry and much too big for her mouth. At least, I hoped it was a her. All sorts of problems loomed if it wasn't, most of which were either sexual or lavatorial and didn't bear thinking about in my present condition; or, should I say, this body's present condition.

And what a head this person had: full of throbbing, hammering noises which caused the eyes to ricochet around in their sockets quite unnecessarily. I'd have to sort that out when I knew who I was: no doubt there was a little man in Harley Street who could soon put a stop to all this funny business. As for the throat, how could anyone bear to have that amount of sandpaper stuffed down their neck? Or was it birdseed? Whatever it was, it would have to go. This reincarnation lark was a real eye-opener, a real revelation as to how the other half live. The bloody fire alarm was still ringing. The body swung out a hand and knocked it on the head.

An hour later the alarm went off again. Ten past nine, said the clock through blurred vision. My blurred vision. Oh God, I was still alive!

'Jesus!'

I leaped out of bed and instantly regretted it. I groaned and clutched the head that so manifestly belonged to me and sank back down on the bed again. Any form of movement was agony, but move I would have to, unless I was planning on forsaking my present job and swelling the ranks of the unemployed.

I fumbled through to the kitchen, feeling my way along the walls and hanging on to door frames for support. I drank a pint of water, instantly regretted it, and sat down, weak with exhaustion after so much activity, and feeling sure that any second now I was going to be sharing my water with Wellington, who was sitting at my feet looking up at me quizzically, his head on one side. Perhaps he didn't recognise me in my present condition. Let's face it, I'd only just made the connection. God, my head hurt, I must have been drinking for England last night.

I made my way shakily to the bathroom, pausing en route to poke my head into Lottie's room. It looked like the *Marie Celeste*. There was no sign of life but all the lights were on, the radio was blaring, and her curling tongs, I noticed, were just about to burn a hole in the carpet. I switched everything off. She must have left in an almighty hurry; probably overslept after her disturbed night, it occurred to me guiltily.

Ah yes, Lottie. She hadn't been happy had she? Yvonne Goolagong in a winceyette. I giggled. What was it she was going to do to me? Forcibly extract the larger of my intestines − I remember she'd been most precise − string it between two trees and use it as a washing line: a variation on the guts for garters theme, no doubt.

I made it to the bathroom and ran a bath. It was all coming back to me now. Or was it? There were still some pretty huge gaps, whopping great big chasms, in fact, like what happened between seven o'clock and midnight. I remembered a large Dover sole had been involved somewhere along the line − I clutched my mouth, don't even think about Dover sole — and I vaguely remembered promising to see a judge about a daughter, but I could easily extricate myself from that one. I also remembered making very free with Mr Buchanan's champagne bottle, but had I disgraced myself in the process? I racked my addled brain trying to recall any moments of debauchery, indiscretion or indecent exposure, none of which, I hasten to add, usually feature in my repertoire — well, not all at once. I thought hard. Nah. Not a sausage. I lowered myself gingerly into the bath. I'd obviously behaved impeccably, bringing not one iota of shame upon either myself or mein host. What a relief.

The warm Radoxy waters were behaving almost as they'd promised in the advertisement, refreshing the parts I didn't even know I had, or could reach — or was that called mixing my commercials? Anyway, after a brief soak I climbed out, feeling reasonably human and strong enough to face up to clothes and make-up. I pottered into the bedroom.

But not so fast. On closer inspection every single pair of tights I possessed had a ladder in them, and both pairs of trousers were at the cleaners (I didn't count the leopard-skin ones with the chains hanging from them, as I didn't think Nick would find them as amusing as I did). It would have to be jeans. I retrieved them from the bottom of the heap on the floor, pulled them on quickly, and added a black silk shirt that wasn't too disgustingly creased. This clothing lark had taken longer than I'd envisaged. No time for make-up now: it would have to be the natural look.

I grabbed my coat and bag, but as I was running like stink down the passageway to the front door, I was unlucky enough to catch a glimpse of myself in the hall mirror en passant. I dug my heels in and skidded to a halt, almost singeing a hole in the carpet. Backtracking slowly, I reaffirmed my suspicions with another peek. Oh-oh, just as I'd thought. So natural that no one would recognise me;

in fact I might even frighten some timid soul.

I hastily applied some muck to my face, but no sooner had I put it on than it was sucked down into the parched and arid depths as my poor dehydrated skin acted like a demented sponge. No matter, it would have to do: I was seriously late now.

On the shelf next to the mirror sat the telephone, and for one crazy moment my hand hovered over the receiver. Should I pick it up and call in sick, or dead, or dead-grannyed, or something? I dithered, then happily thought better of it. Four times in three weeks might well be construed as taking the piss, and since I'd already killed off most of the geriatric members of my family, I'd have to start on the more immediate members, which I couldn't quite bring myself to do.

Instead, like a brave little soldier, I tottered stoically off to Earls Court tube, feeling incredibly virtuous and quite forgetting my delicate condition was entirely self induced. Once there, I found the nearest pillar and hugged it gratefully. I couldn't even summon up the strength to buy the *Daily Mail*. I just snuggled up to my pillar, breathing heavily and feeling slightly dazed.

As I stood there, basking in the gloomy April drizzle, I felt something soft and warm nestling against my foot. It wasn't an altogether unpleasant sensation, in fact it was rather comforting, but I thought I'd better take a look down in case it was a furry little rat that had decided to curl up and die on my foot. I was close. Because there, poking out of the end of my jeans and about to fall on to the platform, were my knickers.

They were instantly recognisable as mine because of the crumbling elastic and the uniform grey colour that all my knickers go when they've been lucky enough to join in with the sock wash. Blushing furiously, I grabbed them and stuffed them quickly into my handbag.

Thus deposited, I kept my face well down, concentrating

like mad on my shoes as I felt my blush spreading to my fingers, toes, buttocks: you name it, it spread there. Still staring platformwards, I vowed furiously that never again would I take my jeans and knickers off in one fell swoop, thereby leaving myself open to just this sort of embarrassing predicament whereby I not only take them off together but put them on again together too. Furthermore, I vowed that I would eliminate all forms of sluttish and disgusting behaviour from my life once and for all. Thus resolved, I deemed it safe to look up.

I peered under my fringe. OK left, no one seemed to have noticed. Good. I rather over-confidently swivelled my eyes to the right, only to encounter a sadistic little pinstriped chappie grinning at me from behind his *Financial Times*. Mortified, I instantly turned my back and was about to walk away when the tube came in.

I managed at least to get into a different carriage, but as I stepped on I looked down the platform and saw him winking at me. Bastard. It could have been worse, though. It could have happened at work with Nick there to witness it. I shuddered. At least I'd been lucky enough to have a premature ejaculation at Earls Court tube.

Pippa, of course, was the picture of sobriety, good health and secretarial efficiency when I finally arrived at the agency. She was in the middle of greeting a telephone caller in the correct manner – 'Good morning, Penhalligan and Waters, how can I help you?' – when I lurched in clutching the furniture. Her highly polished shoes, nails and telephone manner were almost too much to bear; but, bless her, she had the decency to put the phone down on the prospective client as she caught sight of my miserable condition.

'Coffee?' she asked anxiously, sensing my distress.

'Please,' I bleated feebly, lowering myself thankfully into position. As I did so, a mound of correspondence rose up to greet me from my in-tray. I rested my head thankfully on this thoughtfully placed, snowy-white, A4 pillow.

'Polly, can I give you a list of things I'd like done this morning, please?'

My head shot up from its resting place and I opened my eyes wide, smiling in a bright and alert manner. God it hurt.

Nick was towering above me in his coat. I'd obviously beaten him by seconds, although it was a pretty pyrrhic victory as my last venue had been bed whereas his had been a client meeting on the other side of London. With any luck he wouldn't realise I'd only just arrived.

'Have you just arrived?' he demanded.

'Er, no, I've been here ages,' I lied.

He put his hands on my desk and bent down to have a look at me. He frowned. 'Are you all right?'

'Yes, why?' I said between a smile and clenched teeth, not wanting to breathe on him.

'You look a bit sort of . . . odd, that's all.'

'Oh, do I?' He was getting closer now, peering at me under my fringe; and what's more, he looked concerned.

'Are you cold?'

'No, why?'

'Well you've still got your coat on.'

'Have I? Oh, how extraordinary. I was so busy I didn't notice.' I wriggled out of it.

'And your eyes look like something out of an Ordnance Survey map.'

'Thanks very much,' I muttered, dropping the bright and alert look. 'I've probably been overdoing it a bit lately.'

'Oh I see, it's like that, is it?' He in turn dropped the concerned look. 'Burning the midnight oil while you brush up on your shorthand, I expect,' he said dryly.

'Something like that,' I said, gritting my teeth. What the hell did it have to do with him how I spent my evenings?

'Right, well since there's obviously nothing wrong with you apart from a touch of alcohol poisoning, let's get on with some work, shall we?' he snapped. 'I'd like this document copied eight times and then bound, neatly please. All this correspondence needs typing, as you're probably aware, although I fail to see that you've made any inroads into it so far, and I'd like these two big call reports corrected. If Jason thinks that that's the budget the client agreed to, he and I were clearly in completely different meetings. Although I must confess,' he added wearily, 'sometimes I think he's just on a completely different planet.'

I giggled. Poor Jason was a young account exec, terrifically keen but very green and nervous. He couldn't even pour the coffee in meetings without scalding a couple of clients along the way.

'So change the budget from two million to two thousand, and could I have tea and coffee for six in my meeting at eleven, please? Yes?' This last bark was directed at a caller who'd been put through to him on my telephone. It was the hapless Jason phoning from a meeting at a production company, obviously completely out of his depth. As Nick patiently explained the difference between a double head and a rough cut to the poor boy, I took the opportunity to examine this man-mountain in front of me. From my low-vantage point, I had to admit he was a pretty impressive sight.

Beneath the shock of dark hair his rugged features jutted out at some pretty acute, and even cute angles, and what a gigantic scale it was on. Imagine throwing the rope around that Roman nose and scaling the rolling chest before perching on the dizzy heights of those broad shoulders. It must be quite a view from up there. I giggled. Good grief, that champagne must have been quite something to give me a hallucinogenic hangover: I'd be seeing him in psychedelic technicolour next.

Unfortunately, whilst I'd been tripping merrily, Nick had replaced the receiver and was busy issuing yet another instruction which I appeared to have missed. He hissed through his teeth as he repeated it, ending with the ominous threat, 'And if I were you I'd get this done as soon as possible. You're on thin ice, Polly, thin ice.'

With that he swept off into his office in search of something better to do than torment me, and I rattled away at the word processor feeling decidedly rough.

As soon as he'd gone, Joss and Ron, our only creative team — art director and copy writer respectively — emerged from their office. They sat on my desk to inspect my hangover, for they were, after all, the experts.

'Undercooked fried egg sandwich, Polly?' suggested Ron.

'Nice glass of dog piss?' ventured Joss.

Ron put his hand on my thigh, supposedly to test my reactions. I swept it away, giggling.

'Hmmm . . . a little slower than usual, darling,' he reflected.

Joss and Ron were a pair of ageing hippies who couldn't quite believe that the sixties had really gone forever. They were forty-three going on twenty-three, and both had long greying hair which curled over their collars, and even shoulders in Ron's case. They'd met many years ago at college in Scotland, come down to the smoke together, and twenty years on still behaved like a couple of likely lads who'd just discovered Carnaby Street. Their life-support system consisted of a series of free lunches, one-night stands and piss-ups, and they didn't give a toss about anything. Luckily, the ad racket provided them with all the ingredients they needed to live a debauched and happy life, but they led a precarious existence, treading a fine line between taking four-hour lunch breaks and doing just enough layouts, scripts and headlines to avoid a P45. If they stepped over the line once too often, which, let's face

126

it, wasn't hard, and failed to return from lunch more than, say, ten times in a month, they were invariably fired from whichever agency they happened to be freeloading on at the time.

Once unemployed, a period of austere sobriety would ensue. The boys (for that is what they were at heart) would stay sober for at least a week, carefully comb their greying locks, rearrange their portfolios, adding their latest commercials – and pinching one or two along the way – before sallying forth to seek re-employment. After a few false starts they would invariably land on their feet through an endearing mixture of charm, experience (these boys were drinking in Charlotte Street while Charles and Maurice were still barmitzvahing) and, it has to be said, talent. Once their designer trainers were firmly planted under new desks, they'd rattle off a couple of ads before, worn out and thirsty, they'd be off to check out the nearest hostelry, feeling they'd earned their money for that month.

Every so often, nervous young account executives like Jason would dare to enter their office. Pale, trembling, sweaty with fear and clutching long overdue briefs in their hot little hands, they would approach the sleeping/ drinking/hungover couple only to be told like Oliver Twist:

'*More*! You want *more* work? Fock me, laddie, it'll have to be Kettner's first!'

A table would be duly booked and Jason would have sleepless nights wondering how to explain yet another expense-account lunch to Nick. Once ensconced in their favourite watering hole, the boys would ignore Jason and greet all their creative friends – of which there were many for, remember, these boys had been around – who were also being wined and dined by anxious, timid souls in suits. Towards the end of lunch (about five p.m.) Ron and Joss, who were not unkind, would take pity on young Jason and languidly scribble a couple of layouts on the paper tablecloths so thoughtfully provided by Kettner's, which they would then rip off and hand to the young boy.

'There you go, lad. Now run along and don't lose it. That's an award-winner there if ever I saw one!' they would declare, beaming graciously at him.

Jason, flushing scarlet with relief and clutching the precious paper to his chest as if it were a signed Picasso, would thank them profusely before rushing to the loo to have a long, relaxing, well overdue pee.

Work completed, the boys would sidle off and steadily work their way through the bars of Soho in hot pursuit of chicks, as they still called them. They were childishly obvious in their methods. Joss thought nothing of accidentally spilling beer on a blouse in order to rub it off again, and Ron was forever dropping coins to look up skirts. It landed them in all sorts of trouble, and once back at the agency they were constantly ducking phone calls from irate wives/mistresses/chicks/ships-in-the-night, all of whom were demanding to know what the hell was going on. It would be at this point, when they were well and truly hemmed in, backs against the wall, chips down, that they'd look at each other, shake their old grey heads and declare, sadly, that there was no such thing as a free bonk.

Of course, once a mixture of cajoling and downright lying had been used to extricate themselves from a potentially hazardous situation, the larks would continue apace, but it was all so bad and so obvious you simply couldn't take offence. Everyone in the agency adored them, including Nick who, although he refused to be twisted round their little fingers, recognised a creative talent he couldn't begin to imitate.

On this particular morning, Ron and Joss, having completed a series of headlines and layouts the week before, were going through one of their resting periods. I typed away, trying to ignore them. This was hard, as Ron was stroking my cheek and Joss was staring deep into my eyes.

'What colour are they, darling?' he asked thoughtfully.

'Blue.'

'Really? Blue knickers? How nice.'

I giggled, it was all so predictable. Then I paused for a moment and told them about the knickers-on-the-station episode, knowing it was right up their alley. They cried with laughter.

'Oh God, Polly,' said Joss, wiping away a tear, 'I always thought you were the sort of girl who'd drop 'em at a moment's notice.'

Just then Ron's phone rang. He pressed the requisite number and picked it up at my desk. It was the wife. Her indoors. His back went rigid and he held up his hand for complete silence. We all obeyed, listening in with bated breath. Unlike Joss who was on wife number four, Ron was still married to his first wife, but only by the skin of his teeth. She was a teacher, and apparently he was terrified of her.

'Yes, my sweet? . . . no, no, never too busy . . . Oh, a PTA meeting? What a shame . . . you quite forgot. Well, not to worry . . . No, no, I'll get my own supper . . . Sausages will be fine . . . and baked beans yes . . . Apple pie in the fridge, I'll find it . . . Yes, my sweet . . . No, my sweet . . . No no, don't rush, I'll be fine . . . Have a good meeting then . . . bye bye.'

He put the phone down and looked at Joss, eyes shining with excitement. He rubbed his hands together gleefully. 'Oh joy! Joy! A PTA meeting! Ron, my boy, there'll be bevy and rooty-tooty for us tonight!'

Joss shook him warmly by the hand, and there was much back slapping and jubilation, at which point Nick's head appeared round his door as if it were on a stick. He cast his eye around the room, taking in this happy, unprofessional scene.

Pippa had her feet up on her desk, mine was occupied by Joss and Ron, and Jason, who was back from his meeting, was sitting on top of a filing cabinet, giggling away at the big boys showing off. Nick's face darkened. Jason disappeared behind the filing cabinet and Joss and Ron slipped off my desk in a trice. They tiptoed into their office and closed the door quietly. They could spot a harassed, overworked boss at fifty paces.

Nick turned to me wearily. 'Polly, if you're not too busy — ' was that sarcastic or what? — 'could you get me something to eat, please?'

'Sure, what d'you want?' I was dying to ring Adam to thank him for last night and apologise for any outrageous behaviour. At this rate I wasn't going to have a moment.

'Oh, just a couple of sandwiches, tuna and um, peanut butter will do.'

I ambled off to the sandwich bar, wondering if Harry would ring today. He sometimes did mid-week if only to tell me what a fantastic weekend he was about to have and how sorry he was not to be seeing me.

At Giovanni's takeaway café I had my usual first-form Italian lesson with my friends the proprietors — 'Ciao, bella. Come stai?' on their part and, 'Sì sì bene!' on mine — before sauntering back to the agency.

Nick was scribbling away at his desk when I delivered his lunch. 'Thanks, poppet,' he mumbled, miles away no doubt, as I put them down. You could have knocked me down with an iron girder.

He looked up and came back to reality. This was no poppet, this was the woman whose effigy he stuck pins into every night. He looked flustered. 'Oh, er, Polly, sorry, thanks a lot, what do I owe you?' he unwrapped his sandwich.

'Oh, about one-eighty, but have it on me, you can buy me one next time.' I was still staggered by the endearment, and I always throw my money around when people are nice to me.

He smiled and looked surprised. 'Thanks, I'll do that.'

Suddenly he made a face like he was going to throw up. Perhaps he was. I looked around desperately for the wastepaper bin. He stared at the sandwich in disbelief. 'What's this?'

'What you asked for, tuna and peanut butter.'

He groaned. 'Not together, Polly,' and then he went on in the voice he reserved for morons and retards. 'You see, they don't really *go* together.'

'Oh! Oh gosh, sorry, I wasn't thinking, I'll get you some more.'

He waved me out of his sight. 'No, never mind, never mind,' he said wearily, chucking the disgusting concoction in the bin. 'Just go and finish that pile of typing. I'll get something later.'

I walked out miserably. Why did I have to cock it up, just when we were making progress? Pippa was going out so she offered to get some more sandwiches. I decided to ring Adam. I needed to talk to a man who could bear the sight of me. The switchboard at the Savoy put me through in a second, and all at once I was being soothed by his dulcet, laid-back, North American tones.

'Hi, Polly, how's it going?'

'Badly. I've just been balled out by my pig of a boss.'

Nick's back stiffened behind his glass door. Christ! How much could he hear in there?

'Listen,' I went on, 'I wanted to thank you for last night. It was brilliant.'

'My pleasure, I had a ball!'

'Really? I thought I might have been a bit, you know, tipsy?'

'Hell, Polly, you were flying!'

I laughed. 'Oh dear, I'm afraid that doesn't come as too much of a surprise. Look, Adam, about this judge business . . .' I wondered how I was going to get out of this. I should have thought it through before I picked up the phone.

'The judge? Will you see him tonight?'

'Um, well no, perhaps not tonight, you see I was wondering—'

'Oh sure, sure, tomorrow will do, don't you worry.'

'Oh, well . . .'

'Yeh, yeh that's fine, it'll keep a day or two, but be sure and ring me the moment you get back to tell me how it went. I'm counting on you, OK?'

'Er, yes but—'

'Great. Listen, I gotta go, I'm meeting some guy from back home downstairs in the bar. I'll hear from you soon though, OK? And listen — look after that hangover. Hair of the dog's what you need! Bye now.' He put down the phone.

You berk. You complete and utter moron. You completely cocked it up. Now you'll just bloody well have to go, won't you?

As I sat there feeling sorry for myself, Pippa arrived back with the sandwiches, closely followed by a stunning-looking girl in the most beautiful Armani jacket. I'd clocked it in their window last week, but it was beyond even my wildest overdraft.

She had the sort of cropped, blonde, boyish hair that you can only get away with if you're very young or very beautiful. She was both. She was as slim as a piece of macaroni, had perfect, regular features, and her slanting green eyes did parallel lines with her cheekbones. Aside from the covetable Armani jacket, she was wearing — just — a tiny black lycra skirt which showed off her incredibly long slim legs, clad as they were in dark opaque tights, black suede pumps and a silky yellow polo shirt. The effect was breathtaking. She was beautiful, but also somewhat familiar.

132

'Can I help you?' I asked in awe.

'Yes, I've come to see Nick — don't I know you?' It dawned on us both at more or less the same time.

'Of course!' she cried. 'You're the girl in the freezer!' and off she went into peals of tinkly laughter.

Ah yes, and you, I thought grimly, are the girl who stood watching me. Famous film star, raving beauty, and Nick's girlfriend all rolled into one. Serena Montgomery. The incessant tinkling was getting on my nerves.

'That's right,' I said breezily, 'I was doing a spot of research for one of our clients with a frozen food product. He wanted to find out what temperature the freezers are kept at. It's to do with shelf life, that kind of thing, but I don't suppose that would mean much to you.' I smiled, but with my mouth only. 'I like to throw myself into my job, you see.'

'Yes, you certainly do, don't you!' she chortled, and went tinkling off into peals of laughter again, obviously under the mistaken impression that she'd made the pun.

Out of the corner of my eye I saw two faces squashed against a glass door. Joss and Ron had heard a mating cry and were instantly alerted, tails up, sniffing around.

I raised my eyebrows efficiently. 'Is Nick expecting you?' I asked, as if he were the chairman of ICI.

'Er, no, but I just thought I'd drop by and take him out to lunch. I just can't tell you how funny you looked in that freezer. You—'

'Then please don't try,' I interrupted smoothly. 'If you'll just wait here, please, I'll see if Nick's available. And you are?'

'Sorry?'

'Who exactly are you?' I asked, giving her a sickly smile as I walked towards Nick's door.

'Serena Montgomery,' she snapped.

'Thank you so much,' I purred. 'I won't keep you a moment.'

I went into Nick's office and leaned against the door. Bitch. But why should I hate her? I probably had looked pretty ridiculous. I sighed, feeling rather tired of life.

Nick looked up expectantly. 'Did you want me?'

'Serena's here to see you.'

He looked alarmed. 'Here?'

'Yes, she's outside, she wants to take you to lunch. Just as well you didn't have a sandwich after all.'

He put down his pen wearily. 'Ask her to come in, would you?'

I opened the door and purred in my best Miss Moneypenny voice, 'Miss Montgomery? Mr Penhalligan will see you now.'

Nick looked at me in amazement and I detected the ghost of a smile on his lips as Serena marched past, glaring at me. I smiled sweetly and shut the door.

A few minutes later she was out again, looking extremely sulky as Nick steered her gently across the room towards the stairs.

'I do think you're being a bore, Nick. I've booked a table at Bibendum, and Justin's waiting for us,' she said.

'Well, I'm sorry,' we heard him say as they clattered downstairs, 'really I am, but I'm absolutely rushed off my feet. I've got a million things to do today. Give Justin my regards and apologise but—'

The rest was out of earshot, but Pippa, Joss, Ron and I rushed to the window and looked down in time to see him guide her around a Mercedes convertible and deposit her in the driving seat with a peck on the cheek. She pouted but looked slightly mollified.

'Wow. He's quite a coolie, isn't he?' breathed Pippa, steaming up the window. 'Not many men would turn down Serena Montgomery, Bibendum and a Mercedes convertible all in one lunch hour.'

'Mmmm . . . Ice coolie,' I agreed reluctantly.

Joss and Ron were speechless with admiration and

incredulity. 'The mon's a fockin' nutcase,' Joss managed eventually, shaking his head.

Ron just looked shattered, and they retired hurt to their office, lost in wonder at a fellow man's totally inexplicable behaviour.

Suddenly I realised that Serena would undoubtedly spill the beans on the freezer episode to Nick, probably later tonight, in bed or something. I saw the two heads, one dark and one blonde, sharing a pillow, and I could imagine him roaring with laughter saying, 'But that's just so typical of Polly. She's a complete head-case!'

Footsteps could be heard on the stairs, and Pippa and I jumped back into our seats just as Nick came marching through the room.

'Polly, Pippa, I'm going to write a presentation now, so no telephone calls and no more interruptions, OK?'

'OK, Nick!' We said in unison, grinning from ear to ear like a couple of schoolgirls.

He grinned back and shut himself in his room.

'*Very* sexy when he smiles,' whispered Pippa.

'Oh, Pippa. Anything in trousers.' But I had to agree, the odd flashes of humanity in Nick were quite agreeable.

My hangover seemed to get worse and worse as the day wore on, and once or twice I reached such a low ebb that I was tempted to ring Harry.

Pippa talked me out of it. 'Once he starts treating you like a girlfriend and less like a rabid dog, I'll let you ring him.'

'But I miss him,' I wailed feebly.

'Tough,' she retorted.

I sighed. She was right, and I knew the rules. I eventually went home and crawled straight into bed with *Tatler*, a Big Mac and a hot water bottle. To be quite honest, I really don't think I could have raised the necessary energy even if Harry had crawled in next to me, added to which, George Michael was becoming unbearably prickly, and I'm not at all sure that he, or should I say she, would have thanked me for submitting to any funny business.

Chapter Eight

The next morning I got up early and rang the school. It was a Saturday, so there wouldn't be many people around, but as far as I could remember, Mrs Compton took a tutorial on a Saturday morning. Miss Arnold, the school secretary, answered, and for a moment I could have been fifteen years old again, with a too-short skirt and ten Number Six hidden in my pocket. I automatically twiddled a strand of hair around my finger, a nervous adolescent habit I'd almost grown out of, but as her belligerent, argumentative voice came resounding down the line, I instantly regressed.

'Yes? St Gertrude's school,' she barked. 'Yes? Speak up, I can't hear you!'

I hadn't said a word. 'Hello, may I speak to Mrs Compton, please?'

'MRS COMPTON!' she bellowed incredulously, as if I'd said Ark Angel Gabriel. 'Mrs Compton is taking a TUTORIAL, she can't POSSIBLY be disturbed.'

'Oh, I see, well could I leave a message for her, please? Perhaps you'd be kind enough to ask her to ring Polly McLaren? My number is 723-1982, I'm an old girl, she'll remember me.'

'Don't bank on it!' she snorted – the charm-school department of St Gertrude's had really rubbed off on her – 'we can't be expected to remember all the gels that pass through these gates, you know, especially those who didn't exactly distinguish themselves, eh?'

I smiled. She remembered me all right.

'Thank you so much, Miss Arnold, and please remember me to your charming sister.'

'Humrph!'

She put the phone down. Her sister had been the matron, an equally nasty piece of work. One icy glance from her had been enough to cut off the blood supply to your heart. She didn't believe in illness. You had to be dying from cholera before she'd grudgingly admit you to the san, and even then you'd rather just die quietly at your desk, thank you very much.

I was quietly burning some toast, mulling over old school days and wondering what one wore when one made house calls to judges, when the telephone rang. It was Mrs Compton.

Now Mrs Compton was a rare breed amongst the teachers at St Gertrude's. Not only was she a wife and a mother, but she was also totally devoid of warts, bunions, hairy legs, varicose veins, bad breath or BO. She was relatively young, most certainly pretty and God knows what she was doing there.

'Hello, Polly, I gather you rang. Don't tell me you've decided to brush up on your algebra at this late stage?'

'Not likely, I can still count to twenty with a packet of cigarettes to help me; that's enough, isn't it?'

She laughed. 'Obviously. OK, so what can I do for you?'

'Well, I was wondering if you'd heard anything from Rachel Marsden. I tried to look her up the other day but she seems to have vanished.'

'Rachel? Hardly the lipstick and disco brigade, was she?'

I laughed. 'No, I suppose not, it's just that a few of us thought we'd get together and somebody suggested Rachel . . .' I trailed off lamely.

'Well, the last I saw of her was when her father took her

out of school. Shame, such a clever girl, but no, I haven't heard a dicky bird from her since.'

'What about Mr Saunders. He taught her too, didn't he?'

'Oh, yes, they got on very well, because of course she was a brilliant musician, but he moved to another school in Sussex quite a while ago. I don't suppose he's spoken to her since, but I could give you his number if you like?'

'No, don't worry, I'm sure I'll find her through some of the other old girls. Thanks very much, anyway.'

'Not at all, give her my love when you find her, won't you? And take care of yourself, Polly, try to keep out of mischief. I seem to remember you had rather a penchant for it!'

I laughed. 'I'll try. It was nice to talk to you.' I put the receiver down.

Well, that had proved to be a dead end, as I'd rather suspected it would. There was nothing else for it. I'd have to go and face Judge Marsden. Once again the eternal question loomed large. What on earth was I going to wear?

I abandoned my toast and ransacked my drawers, hoping for a solution. Quite by chance I found one nestling in the bottom drawer. A kilt. I shook it out and held it up for inspection. How eminently suitable; I'd forgotten I even possessed one. OK, it was a bit short, and the tartan was Fiorucci rather than Black Watch, but what the hell? I put it on, adding navy blue tights and lace-up shoes, which was perhaps taking things a little too far, but I do like to look the part. I wrapped my school scarf around my neck, and tied my hair up in a pony tail. All I need now is a satchel and an apple for the judge, I thought, as I bounced down the passageway into the kitchen, singing the school song at the top of my voice.

Lottie was huddled at the kitchen table in her dressing gown, her nose oscillating between her cornflakes and the *Daily Mail*. She looked up in disbelief. 'Don't tell me.

Harry's into schoolgirls and you're going off for a good caning. He gets to wear the gown and mortar board.'

'Wrong, it's all for the judge. I'm supposed to be an old buddy of Rachel's, remember? And she is a few years younger than me. What d'you think?' I asked, giving her a twirl.

'Oh yes, very Lolita. I hope you've got your navy blue knickers on, he's bound to check.'

I laughed and ran out of the flat feeling unaccountably excited. It was obviously the underhand nature of my mission that was appealing to me and prompting all this adrenalin to whoosh around. Perhaps I should have been a spy.

Adrenalin abounded in the garden too. It was a beautiful early spring morning and the bulbs in the tiny patch at the front of the house were responding eagerly to the call. It was as if they sensed that spring had come rather late this year, and were now doing their damnedest to catch up. A dozen or so slim green tongues were pointing straight up to the sky, like a row of little green soldiers standing to attention, straining to make themselves as tall as possible on the parade ground. Up in the sky a gentle breeze was playfully buffeting a few clouds around, but other than that it was a clear, bright blue morning.

I jumped into my old Renault Five – previously known affectionately as 'Rusty' owing to his chronic problem around the wheel arches, but now just plain old 'car' since Harry had told me that giving a car a name was about the twee-est thing imaginable. And I'd had no idea! You see I was learning all the time. Going out with Harry was really quite an education.

I jammed on my seatbelt, turned the key in the ignition, and shut my eyes as I prayed fervently to God, Allah and Buddha, thus wildly hedging my bets. Miraculously it started first time. I kissed the battered old steering wheel passionately and hurtled off to Kensington, still singing the old school song at the top of my voice.

The Honourable Mr Justice Marsden lived in just the sort of house you'd imagine a man in his position would inhabit. A tall, inscrutable white number with an elegant little square of garden at the front. It was just the sort of garden I wanted to mess up, actually. I had a violent urge to rush around emptying packets of seeds all over it, planting lots of bright vulgar flowers like marigolds and nasturtiums just to break up the tedious tastefulness of it all. A few off-white daffodils were nodding their discreet little heads in the breeze, and even the carefully pruned magnolia tree placed, just so, in the centre of the lawn seemed on the brink of budding. Odd how rich people's flowers even seem to come out first. Do they have the monopoly on sunshine, do you suppose?

I stared up at the house for a moment. Naturally I was looking for clues, like any good private detective worth her free meal at the Savoy would. Ah-ha. Up on the third floor, an Austrian blind in a dotty pink Laura Ashley fabric suggested a young girl's bedroom. Was she there? And if so, was it any of my business?

I could feel my courage running off down the street, and I wanted to run after it. The school song seemed to be stuck in my throat; I warbled middle C just to keep my pecker up. What on earth was I doing here? Did I have a death wish or something?

I tiptoed up the front path, hoping my shoes weren't making too much of a mess on the immaculate gravel path, and stopped at the bottom of the marble steps which led, inexorably, up to the front door. They looked about as steep and uninviting as the ones going up the pyramids in Egypt, and at the top was a large, forbidding, black front door. There was still time to turn and run, but for some crazy reason, I didn't. I climbed those steps – although how I managed it without a few crampons and a length of heavy-duty rope, I'll never know. The air was decidedly thin at the top, but I took a deep breath, pressed the brass bell, and then feverishly rubbed off the dirty fingerprint with my sleeve.

I cleared my throat and murmured, 'Good morning' to myself a few times to see if my voice still worked. After a while, I heard the steady click-click of heels on a polished wooden floor. They came to a halt at the door, and there was a pause as someone obviously had a look through the spy-hole. I tossed my pony tail in the breeze and struck an attitude of frozen gaiety. The door opened a crack but the safety chain was still firmly in place.

'Yes?' inquired a woman's voice.

'Oh, hello,' I said brightly, 'I was wondering if Rachel could come out to pl—was at home, if she was at home.' Christ, get a grip, Polly.

'Who are you?'

'Oh, I'm just an old school chum of hers.' I resisted the temptation to verify this by doing a merry jig on the step, and wondered briefly how this 'chum' word had mysteriously entered my vocabulary.

I had a quick peek around the two-inch gap and caught a glimpse of the owner of the voice: a middle-aged woman with steely-grey hair drawn tightly back from her face in a no-nonsense bun. She had a pointy little face and a pointy little red nose which almost certainly had a dew drop hanging from it. She was wearing a white housecoat, which obviously placed her firmly in the lower orders. Ah yes, this would be Mrs Danvers, the loyal but insane housekeeper.

'Just a moment,' she said.

I grinned in a 'Bunty has fun in the Lower Fourth' sort of way, and she shut the door in my face. Charming. A moment later the door flew wide open and I stepped back in surprise, a sure sign of guilt, I thought later.

I was confronted by a very tall man, at least six foot

four, thin as a reed and with a shock of thick white hair
swept back from his forehead. His head was slightly
bowed, and he reminded me somewhat of one of his
daffodils in the garden. He was elderly without being
ancient, and was wearing a patched old cardigan over a
checked Vyella shirt, tatty old corduroys, and a pair of
carpet slippers. He was not an intimidating sight. In fact
the only thing that made him look vaguely judicial were the
half-moon spectacles perched on his nose. He smiled and
peered over them benignly.

'My housekeeper tells me you're looking for Rachel.'

'Yes, I am actually,' I said rather breathlessly.

'Won't you come in?'

'In?'

'Yes, do, come in.'

'Oh!' I nervously crossed the threshold. Even in my
most pessimistic moments I'd imagined that when I was
being bludgeoned to death with the blunt instrument I'd
still be outside on the doorstep. It never occurred to me I'd
have to go inside. I made a mental note to put my fees up
and hold out for dinner at Annabel's next time.

I followed the carpet slippers into a beautiful pale yellow
drawing room full of books and pictures and dominated by
a baby grand piano. A roaring fire was crackling away in
the grate and the mantel above it was stiff with invitations.
Well, he was obviously popular. Shafts of light were
streaming in from the large bay window at one end of the
room and the open french doors at the other. One or two
sunbeams lay across a pile of legal-looking papers and
textbooks on a desk in the corner. The wages of sin, I
thought grimly. An ancient golden retriever lay stretched
out in front of the fire. He watched my progress across the
room and thumped his heavy tail on the floor, apologising
for being too old to get up and greet me properly. There
were lots of silver-framed photographs dotted around and
quite a few of Rachel. Any minute now, I thought, she'll

walk in and I'll just yell, 'Adam's at the Savoy!' and run for my life through the french windows.

Mr Marsden motioned for me to sit down in a blue Colefax armchair. I perched nervously on the edge. He sank down in a comfortable old chair opposite me with his back to the window.

'And you are?' he asked, getting a pipe out of his cardigan pocket and stuffing it with tobacco. Hardly a murderous gesture.

'Oh, my name's Polly McLaren, I'm an old schoolfriend of Rachel's.'

'Oh really?' he smiled, patting his cardigan pockets for his matches. 'You were one of the St Gertrude gang, were you?' His eyes were friendly and encouraging; in fact I'd go so far as to say they twinkled.

I relaxed. 'That's right,' I said, gaily throwing one end of the scarf around my neck as if I never took it off, even in bed. 'Gosh, we had such fun there!'

He smiled and lit the pipe. 'Well, you know what they say: best years of your life, supposedly, although I was never totally convinced myself. All I remember from my school days are cold showers, fagging, and a great deal of unpleasant food.'

'Ah, yes. Well the food hasn't changed much, they still put putty in the custard, but you'll be pleased to hear that warming up the loo seat for the prefects has gone out of fashion.' Perhaps a little risqué, Polly? You only introduced yourself a second ago, and already you're getting lavatorial.

Luckily he threw his head back and laughed, obviously appreciating my fine line in scatological humour. Plenty more where that came from, your honour, I thought, warming to his merry eyes.

'Well I'm very glad to hear it,' he said. 'Would you like a cup of coffee? I was just going to have one.'

'I won't, thanks awfully, I can't stay long.'

'Ah. Oh well, never mind.' He looked disappointed. Poor old boy, perhaps he didn't get many visitors. After all, it probably wasn't every day he got to reminisce about his school days and engage in witty repartee with a pretty young gel like me. I was so relaxed now I felt I could almost put my feet up on the table and turn the telly on.

'I drink too much coffee anyway,' he was saying, as he puffed away at his pipe. 'Keeps me awake at night.'

The dog ambled over for a pat and he stroked his head. I eyed the impressive array of spirits and bottles on the Georgian cabinet in the corner and wondered idly what time the judiciary limbered up to Bloody Mary's of a Saturday morning. It was getting on for midday. He caught my eye, and my drift.

'What about a glass of sherry, then?' he ventured eagerly, raising his eyebrows and sensing a kindred spirit. He consulted his watch. 'I think we could declare an early drinks time, don't you?' he added naughtily.

'Oh, I don't see why not! As my father always says, it's got to be twelve o'clock somewhere in the world!' I bandied back, resisting the temptation to wink. The old rogue, that was quite a sparkle he had in his watery old eye.

He rubbed his hands together like a mischievous little boy and jumped up with alacrity. He was over to the drinks cupboard in a moment, busily picking out beautiful crystal glasses, holding them up to the light, checking for smears, etc. He turned and peered over his specs. 'Sherry all right, or would you prefer something else?'

'No no, sherry would be lovely.'

There was a satisfying glug-glug-glug noise as the golden liquid left the decanter. It wasn't strictly my tipple, but I could certainly rise to the occasion. He handed me an extremely large drink.

'Thanks, gosh, I'll have to get the bus home!' I quipped.

He laughed. 'Leave it if it's too much: I'm told I'm

rather heavy-handed when it comes to pouring sherry.' He sat down in his armchair again. 'Were you a special friend of Rachel's?' he asked in a distracted way as he wiped the rim of his glass with a rather dirty-looking spotted hanky. He held the glass up to the light, peering critically at it.

'Oh well, perhaps not special, I don't suppose she'd have mentioned me, but then she had so many friends.'

He looked surprised. Well done, Polly, first boob of the morning.

'You were in the same year?'

'Er, no, not quite. I was a couple of years above her.'

'Same house?'

'Er, no . . . but we both um — ' my eyes roved wildly round the room and lit on the baby grand — 'we both played the piano, you see.' I said, sitting firmly on my stubby, highly unmusical hands.

'Ah, another musician.' He smiled and looked at the piano. Christ, there was no way he could ask me to rattle off a little sonata to prove it was there?

'Er, yes, but I'm not in Rachel's league at all,' I said quickly.

'Oh come now, I'm sure you're very accomplished. It's just a question of practice really, isn't it? At least, that's what Rachel tells me. Can't play a note myself, I'm all fingers and thumbs. Anyway, I'm rambling on and you're probably very busy. You'd like to get in touch with her, is that it?'

'That's right,' I said brightly. 'Thought it was time we got together again, maybe play a few symphonies together or something.'

He looked surprised. 'Symphonies? You play with an orchestra?'

'Er no, not symphonies, I mean — well, you know, duets, that kind of thing. Anyway, I just thought it would be nice to see her again really,' I gabbled, desperate to get away from all this musicality.

'Ah.' He nodded, sucking hard on his pipe which had clearly gone out. He tutted with annoyance and started the pocket-patting routine again.

'Your matches are on the little table,' I said kindly. This old buffer was more like a benign and scatty professor than Hanging Judge Jeffreys.

'Ah! Thank you. Damn thing goes out all the time. Terrible habit, you know. Can't seem to give it up, though.'

'Oh, I know, I'm the same with cigarettes,' I said soothingly.

'Any particular reason?'

'Oh, just something to do with my hands, I suppose. Mind you, I'm pretty addicted to nicotine now. I gather there's a nicotine chewing gum you can buy that's supposed to make you give up, but I thought I might just buy some to chew when I'm not smoking. I rather like the idea of constant nicot—'

'No, no,' he broke in. 'Sorry, I meant any particular reason why you want to see her again?'

'Oh!' I was rather taken aback. 'Oh well yes, actually. You see I'm organising an old girl's reunion.'

'Really?' He smiled encouragingly, but the next question came zooming out of nowhere like a ballistic missile.

'Whereabouts?'

'Er, well, I'm not quite sure yet, um . . . my flat maybe, or, or, a restaurant.'

'I see, and when is it likely to be?'

'When?' I was beginning to feel a little hemmed in here as I dodged these quickfire questions. 'Well, quite soon really. Er, probably within the next couple of weeks if I can get everyone together by then.'

'Everyone? Sounds like quite a big gathering. Who have you got lined up so far?' He crossed his legs, rested his head back, and puffed away at his pipe, but it seemed to me he also fixed me with a pair of rather steely-grey eyes over some equally steely-grey bifocals.

I could feel my fringe begin to curl as it always does when it gets wet. My forehead must be getting sweaty. It was awfully hot in here, too hot for a fire. I thought hard of people Rachel might know.

'Well let me see, there's Sophie Steward-Jones, and er, Caro Hamilton and um . . . oh yes!' I cried suddenly inspired, 'Sally Lomax is coming!'

'Sally Lomax? From Paris?'

'Yes, from Paris!' I smiled happily. What a triumph!

'Really? Good Lord.'

Mr Marsden stood up and walked slowly towards his desk, then he paused, drumming his fingers thoughtfully on the blotter. He picked up a heavy leather-bound legal tome and blew some dust off the spine. He opened it and flicked through a few pages, occasionally running his finger down the margin. Evidently he'd just thought of some vital piece of law which was pertinent to his next case. Well fine, don't mind me, I thought, taking a slug of sherry from my basin.

Then he started to hum. The book was still open but, good Lord, he wasn't reading at all, he was staring into space. What on earth was he doing? I studied his profile, he seemed to have almost forgotten that I was in the room. Of course! Yes, of course, he was about to take me into his confidence, and he was wondering how to go about it. Yes, that was it. My playing the Sally Lomax card had worked a treat. He was about to tell me exactly where his daughter was: locked in the basement, living on a Kibbutz in Katmandu, dancing with the Tiller Girls – I couldn't have cared less; what mattered was that he was working himself up to tell me. Obviously he was agonising over how he should go about asking me to keep it to myself. How could he explain that it was a deadly secret and that on no account should I divulge her whereabouts to any living soul? I gripped my sherry tightly, intent on his response.

Suddenly he turned to me and smiled. 'How nice,' he murmured softly, 'I'm very fond of Sally, I had no idea she was coming over. She must of course stay here, Rachel will insist.'

'Oh well, er, yes, I expect she'd love to.'

'Unless of course she's staying with you?'

'No, no, not to my knowledge — I mean, no, she isn't.'

'Good. Then we're agreed that she stays with us.'

'Sure, no problem.' I said, nodding in agreement. I couldn't really care less about Sally's sleeping arrangements, and I was rather unsure where all this was getting us. It was getting us rather neatly over to an address book and a telephone.

'I may as well ring her now and let her know there's a bed for her here. Don't want her doing anything foolish like booking a hotel. In a couple of weeks, you say?'

The crafty old bugger. He flipped through a large flowery address book written in a feminine hand, and his wise old finger came to rest in the 'L' department. My forehead was dripping now and my fringe was frizzing with activity. He found the requisite number and reached for the telephone. He began to dial.

'No!' I jumped up in alarm and started towards him.

Slowly he replaced the receiver. Then he turned to face me. 'No? Why ever not, Polly?' This sudden, rather menacing use of my Christian name chilled me to the marrow. I tightened my grip around my bowl of sherry and stared up at him. The sweet, kindly old man had vanished for ever, and in his place was a wicked, bitter, twisted old judge with murder on his mind. He didn't take his eyes off me.

'Why ever not?' he said again.

'Well, because, um because — you were right after all, you see, she is staying with me. I'd just forgotten! Momentarily forgotten!' I jabbered.

I abandoned my drink to a little tripod table and took a

couple of steps backwards in the direction of the door. I had my eyes firmly on the judge, so I very nearly tripped over the dog who yelped and hid under the sofa. I yelped too and considered joining him.

'Miss McLaren, if that is indeed your name,' said the judge quietly, in the voice he no doubt usually reserved for terrorists and serial killers, 'I'm afraid to say that I think you've come into my house under false pretences. In fact, I would go so far as to say that I believe you to be a liar and a fraud. Now what do you have to say to that?'

'I-I say, I say, I say,' I bleated shrilly in true joke-telling music-hall style, only this wasn't funny. Oh God, no. This was bloody frightening. I didn't know what to say.

'I don't believe you know my daughter at all. Neither do I believe you went to school with her. You certainly don't have her best interests at heart. You thought you could trick me, didn't you? You thought all you needed to do was wrap a borrowed scarf around your neck, adopt a silly schoolgirl manner, reel off the names of a few old girls and I'd lead you straight to Rachel. That's what you thought, isn't it?'

The judge was advancing towards me slowly. Where were my twelve men good and true? Where was my defending counsel? This wasn't the English legal system I'd come to know and respect, was it? I kept going backwards in the direction of the front door and the free world.

The judge had finished his summing up and was about to pass sentence. 'You are an evil woman, Miss McLaren – ' Christ! Bit strong wasn't it? – 'and you're obviously in cahoots with a certain American gentleman who, as I've made perfectly clear, will simply NOT BE TOLERATED!'

This was bellowed at about twenty million decibels. The dog yelped again and tried to dig a hole in the floorboards.

I stammered something incoherent like, please don't kill me, and backed even further away, scared out of my few remaining wits. He was still bearing down on me as I backed round the drawing-room door and down the hallway, the once friendly, kindly eyes flashing angrily now. How could I ever have thought he was as mild and reassuring? He was about as mild and reassuring as a Rottweiler. All this over an unsuitable boyfriend? The man was absolutely barking.

'I want you out of my house,' he said softly but dangerously. I was whimpering like a demented kitten now, and my hair had gone completely Afro as a result of the downpour erupting from my forehead.

'I'm going, don't worry, I'm going,' I whispered, as I backed up in terror, trapping myself like a fool against the front door. I felt behind me, desperate for the door handle, frantic to twist a friendly little knob. It was at that moment that he raised his hand to deal the death blow.

'Please don't hurt me!' I screamed, covering my head with my hands and sinking to my knees like the lily-livered coward I am.

His raised hand reached beyond my cowering head and found the door knob. As he swung the door open he almost knocked me flying, and I actually had to advance towards him in order to creep out around the door. Once out, I ran like hell. I took off down those marble steps, half expecting a carpet slipper in my backside as I went, but I was spared that indignity.

'And don't come back!' he yelled after me, at which point a million neighbouring curtains, or drapes as they were probably called in this area, seemed to twitch in unison as a whimpering Afro-haired, overgrown schoolgirl hurled herself down a mountain of steps.

I scrambled to my feet at the bottom and ran down the path, leaping the garden wall and charging across the road to my car. I can run when I feel like it, and I really felt like it.

I wrenched the door open and flung myself into the

driving seat, then with a desperately shaky hand turned the key in the ignition. Nothing.

'Oh come on, come on!' I shrieked. 'Don't desert me now, Rusty!'

In my despair I reverted to his pet name, but there was zilch reaction. Not a sausage. My temperamental little car was having a siesta, and nothing in the world would stir him, except, for I know my car of old, a wait of say ten or fifteen minutes.

I bashed my head on the steering wheel two or three times. Oh God, I wanted to get out of this place so badly! I wanted to get away from that axe-man of a judge who was no doubt sharpening his weapon as I sat here trapped like a rat in a rust-heap.

'Help!' I shrieked, and looked frantically up at the house, expecting the door to fly open at any second. There was no sign of him. And he didn't even seem to be watching from the window. But he'd be out here in a minute, wouldn't he? Out here, axe in hand, demanding to know why I was still sitting in his road, practically outside his house. I wondered if I should rig up a sign or something, write a message in lipstick on my windscreen perhaps. 'I'd really love to be going, I hate you as much as you hate me, but unfortunately, my car's broken down.'

I looked at my hands. I was shaking, really shaking. As far as I was aware this had never happened to me before, and I sat watching my trembling fingers with a morbid fascination. It reminded me of an accident I'd seen when I was young. A man had been knocked over by a car in the middle of the road and was shaking so much that somebody had covered him with a blanket. My mother had propelled me past as the ambulance arrived.

'Why was he so cold?' I'd asked.

'He wasn't cold, he was in shock, darling, that's all,' she'd murmured as I stared wide-eyed.

I eyed my hands rather proudly. Oh yes, I was definitely

in shock, no doubt about it. So where was my blanket? Or my mummy, for that matter?

Experience dictated that I had to wait a bit longer before I could try the car again, so I lit a shaky cigarette which seemed to have something of a blanket/mummy effect and calmed down just enough to contemplate for a moment the awfulness of Judge Marsden.

I blew a stream of smoke at the windscreen. The man was certifiable, no doubt about it. I didn't fancy Adam's chances at all. In fact, if I were Adam I wouldn't fancy Rachel either. Who'd want to end up with a father-in-law like that? I'd have to tell Adam the whole story. There'd be no need to embellish it with additional graphic detail: it was graphic enough as it was. He wouldn't be too happy with the outcome, but after all, I'd done my best, hadn't I? I certainly wasn't bloody well doing any more, that was for sure.

The cigarette was helping enormously. I took nice long drags right down to my boots and looked at my watch. Another couple of minutes and this old heap of a wagon might just about start. I looked in my rear-view mirror. What a sight. Coils of frizzy hair stuck out like bedsprings from my pale little face. I found a lipstick on the dashboard and added shocking pink to my quivering blue lips, so that they ended up deep purple. Yuck. I rubbed it off. I looked at my watch again. One more minute and I'd try again. I bit the skin around my thumbnail and thought about Rachel. Poor, poor Rachel. Was she locked in the attic or something? Was she manacled in chains in the cellar with just a bowl of water and the rats for company?

I looked up at the house, half expecting to see a little white face at the third-floor window mouthing, 'Help me'. Instead I saw the front door opening. Jesus Christ, he was after me again! I fumbled for the key and turned it quickly. There was an initial splutter, then a rumble — it started! I looked up as I revved the engine and crunched the gears, half expecting to see him bearing down on the bonnet, but to my surprise I realised it wasn't the judge at all who was coming down the front steps, it was the housekeeper.

She was wearing an old tweed coat and a green felt hat and was half carrying, half dragging, a rather battered old suitcase. It was bulging fit to burst. Was she leaving? Had she handed in her notice in disgust after witnessing the most unpleasant scene imaginable between her bullying employer and a sweet, fresh-faced young girl?

Intrigued, I shunted back into neutral and sat and watched as she made her way slowly down the front steps. The case was small, but was obviously quite heavy, as she was clearly having problems lifting it. She dragged it along the gravel path, then bumped it down on to the pavement. All this activity was too much for the old case. It flew open and spewed its contents over the pavement. I seriously considered helping her, but was understandably wary of going anywhere near that house again, so I stayed put.

She huffed and puffed with growing irritation as she stooped to gather up her clothes, throwing them back in again and muttering away to herself. But hang on a moment. Black Levis? A leotard? Leggings? I looked at the old tweed coat and felt hat. Surely not? She reached for something that had fallen in the gutter. A Walkman? Good grief, was this woman a funky dude in disguise? Was she taking advantage of her day off to go and get on down? Or did all this groovy gear . . . belong to someone else? Of course it did. Of course. I felt a sense of excitement growing within me. It belonged to a young girl. It must belong to Rachel.

Chapter Nine

I kept my head well down as she bundled the suitcase back together again, forcing it to close and snapping it shut. She heaved it towards a battered old Mini parked right in front of the house and opened the boot. It was a strain, but she managed to haul it in. I slid right down in my seat and covered my face with my hands, peeping through my fingers as she walked around the car and got into the driver's seat. My heart was thumping with excitement. Her mission was obvious. To take a change of clothes to the prisoner. Make no mistake about it, this woman was Rachel-bound and I had to follow her.

By rights, of course, I shouldn't have witnessed this little scene. They obviously thought I was long gone, and so I would have been if it hadn't been for trusty old Rusty failing me so magnificently. I mentally patted his battered old bonnet affectionately, keeping my eyes firmly on the action on the opposite side of the road.

The aged Mini was objecting to being woken from its slumber under the trees, and there were one or two false starts before the engine grudgingly turned over and spluttered into action. Luckily my own vintage car was still quietly shuddering away, and as she pulled out in the direction of Church Street, I followed at a discreet distance.

As we trundled down the hill, I opened the glove compartment and fumbled around amongst the sweet wrappers until my hand closed upon my Ray Bans. I rammed them on my nose, pulled at my pony tail letting my hair fall over my face, and wrenched the school scarf from my neck. If she was anything like me, she wouldn't use her rear-view mirror too assiduously, but it was as well to make sure that, if she did, she didn't recognise me. To this end, as we slowly wound our way down Church Street, I had a quick look over my shoulder, surveying the back seat for further disguise. I always travel heavy, and there are usually quite a few props lying around amongst the cigarette packets, plastic bags and general debris that seems to collect there. Today most of it seemed to be seduction paraphernalia – high-heeled shoes, low-necked tops, etc – but, nestling underneath a leather skirt and an empty beer can (not guilty, incidentally), was my father's old brown felt hat. I jammed it over the wayward curls and pulled the brim down over my eyes. I looked in the mirror: shady and incognito. I didn't even recognise myself, so she didn't stand a chance.

I gripped the steering wheel hard as buckets of adrenalin whooshed around my body. I'd already used up a tankful today, and I only hoped I'd kept enough in reserve for this little escapade. We turned left and motored off towards Kensington Gardens, my nose practically pressed against the windscreen due to chronic shortsightedness and the night-time driving conditions foisted upon me by my incredibly dark glasses.

On we cruised, up the hill and on past the immensely phallic Albert Memorial which usually brings a wry smile to my lips. Victoria must have reckoned he was a helluva guy to have had that enormous great thing erected in his memory, and bang in the middle of the park, if you please, for all the world to wonder at. You'd think she'd have parked it somewhere private, like outside her bedroom window or something. This morning, however, my mind was on even weightier things than Albert's member, and I didn't give it a second glance as we swept towards a surprisingly uncongested Knightsbridge.

As we cruised through two sets of green lights together, my hands became sweaty with excitement and the old heart hammered away somewhere in the region of my oesophagus. Where on earth were we going? I had a quick look at my petrol gauge and hoped to God we weren't setting off for a day in the country. I had about a gallon at the most. I cursed my false economy of only putting in a couple of pounds-worth at a time.

We manoeuvred Hyde Park Corner, which proved to be quite a challenge as she caught the tail end of each set of lights and I had to jump a couple to stick with her. I have to say I was enjoying myself enormously now, and just wished she'd put her foot down a bit so I could really show off. We crawled along at a couple of miles an hour. This lady was no speed merchant, and I had trouble keeping down with her but I curbed my Miami Vice-like instincts and rounded every single corner in second, steadfastly resisting handbrake turns.

The Palace was crawling with tourists, and the traffic had come to a standstill as the massed bands of the Coldstream Guards strutted their stirring stuff in the middle of the road. Boom Boom Boom went the kettle drums, and Boom Boom Boom went my heart. Please God, don't let me lose her here, I thought as we waited: it wouldn't be difficult. The band played on as one guard left and another one took its place. Come on boys, hurry it up, I murmured as the soldiers marched past. I couldn't help noticing that the officer in charge looked rather attractive, as far as one could tell under that bearskin. Oh well, not now Polly. At last the guard was well and truly changed, and our little Mini and Renault convoy was waved through by a benevolent policeman. We crawled off towards Parliament Square.

By now I was almost lying on the floor. All this stopping

and starting had provoked even me to look in my mirror once or twice, and I was praying she hadn't glanced behind once too often and wondered why a dirty blue Renault was sticking to her like chewing gum on a jumper.

As we turned left along the Embankment, a rather nasty feeling stirred in my waters. We were getting closer and closer to the river entrance of the Savoy. What was going on? Was this some kind of weird, elaborate joke? It was something of a relief when we sailed past the hotel towards the city and – oh God, yes, of course – the East End! Poor Rachel was obviously holed up in some dirty little attic room above a launderette or a chip shop, chained to a rusty iron bed, no doubt, with nothing to eat or drink. Never fear, fellow old Gertrudian: help is on its way!

I wiped my by now damp hands on my skirt and felt a rousing mixture of guts, determination, and the old Dunkirk spirit stirring in my soul. In my excitement I inadvertently gave the accelerator a bit of welly which almost blew my cover: I damn nearly went up the back of her as we turned left – left? What here? – through some enormous black iron gates that I didn't even know existed. And I thought I was a girl about town. Where the hell were we?

I followed blindly as we drove under an arch and then up a narrow lane with ancient stone buildings towering above it on either side. I nearly bumped my head on the car roof as we crunched over a couple of sleeping policemen and then turned sharp right under another arch and into a courtyard.

To the right of the courtyard was a beautiful garden surrounded by iron railings. An immaculate lawn was laid out like an enormous green tablecloth, and all around it were well-tended flower beds full of mature shrubs, rose bushes, lilac and crocuses. Opposite the garden was a large brick building that looked like a hall and – hang on a minute, this all looked vaguely familiar. Wasn't this where all those barrister chappies had their offices — or chambers? My suspicions were confirmed as a couple of young men rounded the corner and ambled past. They were dressed in their weekend mufti of cord trousers and tweed jackets, but under their arms they clutched bundles of papers tied up with pink ribbons and, if I wasn't very much mistaken, those papers were otherwise known as briefs. Ah-ha, nicely deduced, Polly.

I also had a vague and distant memory of a vague and distant cousin who, having bagged herself a particularly attractive young barrister, clinched the deal in a church not a million miles from here — Temple church, that was it. And of course, if this was the Temple, as I believed it was, Marsden would undoubtedly have chambers here. Things were looking up!

Far from being deserted as one might expect on a Saturday there were quite a few cars dotted around the car park. There were also one or two tourists who were wandering around, snapping their cameras at the Dickensian backdrop complete with old-fashioned gas lamps.

I hung well back and tucked myself in behind a Range Rover as the housekeeper parked her car in the bottom right-hand corner of the courtyard. I switched my engine off.

Mrs Danvers, as she'd become in my mind, got out of the Mini, walked round to the back of the car, opened up the boot and dragged the case out. She carried it with some effort and made her way to . . . now, let's see — yes, the very last doorway on that side. Number . . . forty-one? Was that it? Yes, forty-one! I kept my eyes fixed firmly on that doorway as she disappeared inside. My eyes were watering under the strain of staring wide-eyed for so long, but after what seemed like an hour but was probably more like two minutes, she appeared again, minus the case.

She got back into the Mini and started the engine. I slid

right down on to the floor and peered over the dashboard as she performed an immaculate three-point turn and drove up towards me. She must have passed right by me, but by now my knees were in my ears and I was inspecting the brake pedal. I counted to sixty then crawled up on to the seat and looked around. All clear.

Tingling with excitement, I wondered how I should go about covering the ground between my car and number forty-one without anyone taking too much notice of me. Should I stroll casually down to the door as if I had nothing better to do than mooch around the Temple of a Saturday morning, or should I run like the blazes and get it over and done with? In the end I compromised and did the most conspicuous thing of all: an incredibly guilty running tiptoe incorporating a few deft little zig-zag turns — which I felt were important — as if I were under fire. All I needed was the Sundance Kid giving me cover from behind and I could really have drawn attention to myself.

I ran up the stone steps to the open doorway and peered inside. There was a small flagstone hallway with steps leading up to the next floor. On my right was a black door with a list of names printed on it: Mr Michael Nelson, Mr Charles Morgan-Browne, Mr Richard Solmes, and so on and so on. I gingerly turned the handle. Locked. These were obviously chambers. I ran upstairs and on the next landing found a similar black door with yet another list of names. I quickly ran through them. There was no mention of Marsden. I tried the handle — locked again. The staircase seemed to go on and on, so I followed it up to the next landing.

As I rounded the corner to the third floor, I was confronted by yet another black door, but instead of a list of names, there was just the one. Above the door in gold letters about four inches high was written: SIR EDWARD MARSDEN. If this had been a movie the gold letters would have flashed in and out of focus and the orchestral score would have risen to an almighty great crescendo. As it was I had to clap my hand over my mouth to force my own crescendo down into my throat. Sir Edward Marsden! This was *it*! I'd *found* it! There was absolutely no doubt about it, Rachel Marsden was behind that door!

But what a door. I stood back and surveyed it. Unlike the ones I'd encountered downstairs which had glass panels and brass handles, this one was completely solid and seemed to be made from half a tree. It had no handle to speak of, and no less than three large keyholes: it was like something out of the Tower of London. I couldn't begin to get her out of there on my own. I needed help. I needed a man, or preferably men and – yes, of course, I needed Adam!

There was no doubt about it, I had to get Adam over here immediately. There was no point in trying to break that door down on my own, I'd just end up in hospital. I was just about to batter on the door, shout Rachel's name and tell her I was off to telephone for help, when I suddenly had a thought. What if she weren't alone? Suppose there was someone in there with her, a guard of some sort? Yes, suppose she was being watched over by a heavy? Suppose, as I bashed on the door, he came out and boffed me over the head? Tempted though I was to reveal myself as her rescuer, I decided that the mature thing to do would be to wait until I'd collected a little more muscle in the shape of Adam and perhaps even the police.

I charged down the staircase, bubbling over with excitement. I had to find a phone-box. As I ran, I imagined myself telling Adam and hearing first the disbelief, then the astonishment, and then the joy in his voice as I broke the news. I gave a yelp of delight as I jumped the last few steps and scampered out into the sunshine.

Of course, Rachel and Adam would feel indebted to me for ever, I thought, as I ran in the direction of an exit to the courtyard. Once we'd released her and they'd done their preliminary hugs and kisses, they'd clasp hands, look at me with dewy eyes, and say things like, 'Oh Polly, how can we ever repay you?' Then they'd try to shower me with all kinds of presents — jewellery, money, blank cheques, that kind of thing — but I'd be so magnanimous. I'd smile modestly and refuse everything, saying that all I really wanted was to see them happily married.

Ah yes, the wedding. Naturally, I would be the guest of honour, mentioned in the speeches — mentioned? Good grief, there'd be a whole speech devoted to me, delivered by Adam, of course. I'd blush prettily as a hushed audience listened to him recounting tales of my tenacity, my bravery, my undiluted courage — what was the name of that film about the resistance fighter? *Carve Her Name with Pride*, that was it; that would be a good theme for the speech, wouldn't it? I'd suggest it to him, discreetly, of course.

I dashed out into one of the little sidestreets that led from the Temple and encountered a row of tatty old warehouses, a few decidedly closed pubs and not a lot else. Somewhat lost now, I tried desperately hard to remember the A-Z, and hung a left in what I imagined was the direction of Fleet Street. It was a successful gamble, and I was rewarded by a glimpse of a red bus flashing past and what looked like a shopping parade.

As I hurried on, my mind scurried back to the wedding reception. People would be clamouring to meet me and pointing me out to each other. 'That's her,' they'd say, 'that's the girl who risked her life to bring them together. Isn't she wonderful?' They'd all want to hear the story and I'd repeat it over and over again — probably embellishing it very slightly to include me dodging a few blows to the head from the mad judge — oh, and of course I'd speed up the bit about me following the housekeeper, making that more of a life-threatening car chase. Everyone would be incredibly impressed and all the good-looking men would ask for my telephone number and Harry — God yes, Harry would have to be there, I wanted him to witness all this — yes, Harry would be looking on with pride, casting furious looks at all the predatory men and I'd overhear him saying things like: 'Yes very proud . . . oh I agree, terrifically brave.'

I spotted a phone-box in Fleet Street and fairly skipped into it. I never seem to carry any change, but today God had placed a whole ten pence piece in my purse. I dialled the Savoy's number which I knew off by heart now and rammed in my coin.

'Adam Buchanan please, room twenty-four.'

'One moment please,' said a man's voice.

I heard the telephone ring in his room. I heard it ring, and ring and ring. Oh God Adam, come on, come on.

'I'm sorry, Mr Buchanan doesn't appear to be in.'

'Could you try again?' I asked desperately. 'He might be in the bathroom or something.'

We tried again. 'I'm sorry, he's still not answering. Would you like to leave a message?'

Damn! Where the bloody hell was he? He knew I was due to see the judge today; he should have been sitting by the phone waiting for me to call. My heart sank deep into my lace-ups.

'Could you please just make sure he hasn't left a message for me? He really would have been expecting me to ring. My name's Polly McLaren.'

'Just a moment please, I'll look.'

I drummed my fingers impatiently on the receiver.

'Yes, madam, there is a message for you.' My heart made a quick dash up to my blue-stockinged knees. 'It says he's just popped out for a quick lunch and will be back at about one-thirty.'

One-thirty! I looked at my watch, it was nearly one o'clock. That wasn't too bad.

'In that case, I'd like to leave him a message, and it's

very important that he receives it the moment he comes in. Do you understand?'

'Yes, madam, I understand,' said a rather tight-lipped voice.

'Please could you say that I've found Rachel.'

'You've found Rachel.'

'Yes, she's at number forty-one, Queens Bench Walk in the Temple. Oh – and please could you direct him to the Temple and tell him I'll be there waiting for him? Could you read that back to me, please?'

'She's at forty-one, Queens Bench Walk in the Temple, and you'll meet him there.'

'You'll be sure he gets it?'

'Yes, madam.'

'The moment he comes in?'

'Madam, I'll make a point of personally tripping him up the second he steps through the door,' said the voice dryly.

'Thank you so much.'

I put the receiver down and raced back to the scene of the crime. I wish I'd thought to mention that if Adam could lay his hands on an axe it would come in handy, but no doubt we'd improvise when he arrived.

I took the stone steps two at a time and arrived at the third floor panting and breathless. The big black door loomed up before me again. I looked at the name again. *Sir* Edward Marsden, no less and I'd called him Mister. Good job too. Suddenly all reserve and restraint failed me. That poor girl had been cooped up in there for weeks now, and the least I could do was let her know that help was on its way. If she was being guarded, which in retrospect I somewhat doubted, it would do the thug good to know that I was out here – probably put the wind up him a bit. Thus decided, I really let that door have it. I hammered with both fists making a terrific racket, shouting at the top of my voice:

'RACHEL! RACHEL! IT'S OK! WE'RE GOING TO

GET YOU OUT OF THERE!' I paused for a second, then pounded some more, yelling even more loudly: 'RACHEL! RACHEL! WE'VE COME TO TAKE YOU AWAY, IT'S GOING TO BE ALL RIGHT! YOU WON'T HAVE TO STAY THERE MUCH LONGER, WE'RE GOING TO GET YOU OUT OF THERE!'

Just as I was working myself up into a nice little frenzy, the door swung open and Rachel stood there staring at me in amazement. My fists were flailing around in mid-air and I damn nearly punched her in the eye.

She looked terribly pale and thin and her little heart-shaped face was drained of all colour, totally washed out. She was wearing an equally washed-out blue T-shirt over grey leggings which had gone baggy at the knees. Her mouse-blonde hair looked greasy and bedraggled: she obviously hadn't been able to wash it for weeks, poor thing. Her pale blue eyes blinked nervously, obviously unaccustomed to daylight.

I stepped back in surprise. 'Rachel!'

'Er, yes?' she said doubtfully.

'Thank God! I was so worried you might be dead or something — how did you manage to open the door? Did the housekeeper leave it unlocked by mistake or something, how extraordinary! How ironic, just think you could have *walked* out! You could have just opened the door and actually *walked out of here*!' I gabbled.

'Um . . . yes, I suppose I could.'

'Gosh, you look dreadful you poor thing, absolutely dreadful, so thin and pale, and those ghastly filthy clothes. I bet you don't even know what day it is, do you? Well, it's Sa-tur-day.' I said it slowly in case she had trouble dealing with this, she'd probably been scratching little marks on the wall to keep abreast of the days and I hoped this coincided with her calculations. 'Did you know it was Saturday?' I asked anxiously.

Rachel's mouth was hanging open and her eyes were

wide with wonder, 'I'm . . . I'm sorry, do I know you?'

'Oh!' I whipped off my hat and glasses. 'Of course, you wouldn't have recognised me, but you see I had to wear a heavy disguise just to be on the safe side. Good, isn't it?'

She blinked. 'Er, yes, very good, I'm sorry I still don't . . .'

'Polly McLaren, at your service, I was at school with you, remember? St Gertrude's?'

'Well . . . yes, vaguely.'

Vaguely? She vaguely remembered me — a bit of a schoolgirl legend if I say so myself — or she vaguely remembered St Gertrude's? Either way it was worrying. I peered at her anxiously, scanning her face for evidence of cuts or bruising, bumps on the head and suchlike. None were apparent, but she looked decidedly vacant. Drugged perhaps?

'Are you all right?' I asked anxiously.

'Yes, very well thanks, and you? Would you like to come in?'

Would I like to come in? Do you ask the Seventh Cavalry if they'd like to come in? Or the SAS? Or Bodie and Doyle? Very well thanks, and you? Is that what the Scarlet Pimpernel had to contend with when he flung open the cell doors for the French aristocracy? Oh, hi there, Pimpernel. Yes, very well thanks, and you? I admired her sang-froid, but really.

I shook my head in disbelief and followed her dumbly into the drawing room. The drawing room? Hang on a minute, this was supposed to be some sort of chambers, and yet here we were in a beautiful eau-de-Nil room with large shuttered windows overlooking the courtyard. The neck-rickingly high ceiling sported an enormous chandelier and on Persian carpet level there were quite a few spindly-legged antiques dotted around, plus two enormous powder-blue sofas that looked as if they'd swallow you up whole if you so much as perched on the edge of them.

Hardly what you might call cell-like. More what you might call lap of luxury-like.

'What's this?' I said, not bothering to close my mouth when I'd finished my utterance.

'What's what?' she asked politely.

'This place, I mean it looks like a flat or something.'

'It is,' she said patiently. 'It belongs to my father: quite a few judges have them.'

'Bet they don't keep their daughters locked up in them, though, eh? Boy, I bet you're glad to see me, aren't you!'

She didn't seem to know quite what to say to this, and instead of throwing herself on my bosom and sobbing out her heartfelt gratitude, she perched on the edge of a powder-blue sofa and narrowed her eyes at me in a confused manner. Then it came to me. Oh God, had they brainwashed her or something? Was that it?

'Rachel . . .' I knelt down in front of her and peered earnestly into her pale blue eyes. She looked even more confused at this; in fact she looked downright bloody bewildered, poor kid. I spoke very slowly and carefully.

' . . . Rachel, can you hear me?'

'Er . . . yes.'

'Listen to me, Rachel, have they hurt you in any way? The housekeeper? Your father? Did they swing gold watches in front of your nose? Try to hypnotise you or anything? Can you remember?'

She frowned and looked annoyed. 'Now look here—'

'All right, it's OK.' I took her hand and spoke soothingly. 'We don't have to talk about it now if you don't want to. Some other time. Have you had anything to eat at all?'

She wriggled her hand away from mine and moved nervously along the sofa. 'Yes, I've just had lunch, actually. Look here, what's this all about?'

'About? What's it about? I've come to get you out of here, of course!' Christ, talk about ingratitude, but then, I thought kindly, she's probably still in shock. I sat down next to her and put my arm around her, resting my hand reassuringly on her shoulder. She sat bolt upright and looked at the hand on her shoulder in disbelief, then she looked up at me, her eyes like saucers.

I gave her a bit of a squeeze. 'Rachel, I've been looking for you for a while now,' I said quietly.

'Christ!' She leaped off the sofa in alarm, holding her arm where I'd touched her as if I'd singed her with a cigarette. 'You have? But I don't even know you, why?' Her eyes were flying saucers now.

'Oh, not just me, of course!' OK, I thought, I'll sock it to her now; watch her face light up like a Belisha beacon. I licked my lips with anticipation. 'Your boyfriend's been looking for you too!'

'My boyfriend?' Her face, if anything, darkened.

'Yes, your boyfriend,' I said impatiently. I was getting rather tired of all this playing hard-to-get nonsense. I also had the distinct impression that, far from showering me with jewellery and presents, even a simple thank-you might be out of the question. 'Adam of course, Adam Buchanan.'

I waited for the hug, the tears, the emotion. Instead she backed away from me, her face ashen. Her hand leaped to her mouth. 'Adam? Adam's coming here?' she whispered.

'Yes, Adam's coming here.' Why did she have to repeat everything I said? It made conversation so long-winded, and she'd got me doing it now.

'Oh my God!' Her voice cracked. 'When?'

I consulted my watch. 'Oh, in about ten minutes I should think!' I said jauntily. 'You've just got time to put a spot of make-up on,' I added, eyeing her peaky little face. She wouldn't want him to see her looking like that. I rummaged in my handbag and produced a leaky mascara and my favourite hot pink lipstick. I wasn't entirely sure her face could take hot pink, but it was better than nothing.

'Here, borrow mine,' I said, offering them up generously.

'Oh God!' This came out as a sort of strangled cry, as if someone had got her by the throat, and she rushed out of the room, one hand still clasped to her mouth.

I sat on the sofa, still proffering my make-up and feeling more than a little confused. I frowned and put the lipstick away. Somehow this scenario wasn't going quite as I'd envisaged it would. I bit my lip and wondered where I'd gone wrong. Had it all been too much of a surprise for her? Too much of a shock? She did play the piano, after all, and they were terribly sensitive these artistic types. Perhaps I should have broken the news a little more gently?

An awful lot of banging around was coming from a room down the hall. I cocked an ear in the direction of the noise and then got up, wondering what on earth I should do. There was certainly a lot of frenzied activity going on in that room. Was she doing some kind of happy-clappy dance to celebrate Adam's return? As I've said before, she was very musical.

I crept tentatively down the passageway and poked my head around the bedroom door. Rachel was opening drawers and cupboards, grabbing armfuls of clothes and throwing them on the bed. Ah-ha! Now this was a scene I recognised, this was straight out of Tregunter Road! Of course — she was wondering what on earth to wear for this momentous occasion. I stepped forward eagerly, wondering if I could be of assistance — convinced, in fact, that I could: this was after all my specialised subject. I was just about to offer my services when I noticed that the clothes on the bed were now being stuffed into a red hold-all. I frowned. They were going to get awfully creased in there, and what was the point? Skirts and jumpers were flying in,

169

vests, vests? So small? A teddy, another teddy – Good Lord, how many teddies did a girl need – and, heavens, what on earth was that dreadful wailing noise?

I followed the wail to the end of the bed and there, lying in a carry-cot and peeping out from beneath a pale blue blanket was a little ginger head. A baby! A real live baby.

Everything on my face was as open as it could be now: eyes, mouth, even my nostrils gaped.

'It's a baby!' I cried moronically.

Rachel carried on stuffing the bag as if I didn't exist. Still slack-jawed with disbelief, I watched as Rachel grabbed the carry-cot by the handles and barged past me into the kitchen. I followed blindly. She grabbed bottles from shelves and jars of baby food from cupboards and rammed them in the bag, hissing and snarling as she went. As she flung yet another lorry-load of bottles in, she swung around to face me. Her face was white with loathing and her mouth had curled up into a terrifying snarl.

'You stupid cow,' she hissed. 'You stupid, interfering cow!'

My jaw was still hanging from its hinges, and I tried to form a sentence or two, but could find neither wind nor words. One thing was becoming remarkably clear though. I'd made a major miscalculation somewhere along the line. Rachel was kind enough to fill me in on what it was.

'He wants the baby, you dickhead!' Her voice was rising to an hysterical level. 'Don't you understand? HE WANTS MY BABY!' She screamed straight into my face, her nose about two inches from mine.

In retrospect I'm glad she pitched it thus, because somehow the proximity of her distorted face and the volume at which this staggering piece of news was imparted did actually have the effect of passing through my thick skull and into my brain. I recoiled from her in shock. Adam wanted the baby. He didn't want the girl, he wanted the baby. I'd led him to the girl, therefore

I'd led him to the baby. I felt sick.

'Oh my God!' Now it was my turn to rise to fever pitch. 'He'll be here any minute, you've got to hurry, *hurry!*'

I grabbed her bag but, not very surprisingly, she grabbed it back and pushed me forcibly back against the wall. Flattened against the eau-de-Nil, I watched in despair as she hauled the bag over her shoulder and picked up the carry-cot which was equally heavy. Puffing and panting, she heaved her load out of the front door and began the tricky matter of descending the stone stairs with half a hundredweight of layette in her hands. It would take for ever. Ignoring her snarls and protests, I snatched the red bag from her and lugged it down the steps ahead of her.

'You've got to believe me!' I shrieked as I pulled the bag down on its bottom, my head swivelling back like a periscope as I pleaded with her, 'I had no idea! Absolutely no idea! He used me; he told me this long story about how you wanted to marry him and your father wouldn't let you. He said he was devastated, he said *you* were devastated, he never even *mentioned* a baby, I swear it. Honestly, Rachel, I had no idea. Please, *please* believe me!'

She staggered down behind me, tight-lipped and word-less, concentrating like mad on not tipping up the baby.

'I know I'm a stupid, interfering fool, I know I am, but I'll make it up to you, I swear I will. Honestly, I would never have got involved had I known, but — but he seemed so honest, so believable — well, you must know what he's like, how persuasive he can be, I just had no idea!'

She didn't look in the least convinced, but some of my hysterical ranting must have had some effect, because when we eventually arrived at the bottom, blinking and sweating in the sunlight, she looked one way, then the other, and then, in sheer desperation, at me.

'You absolutely swear it?' she hissed. 'You didn't know?'

171

Almost on my knees I swore on my life, my mother's life, my grandmother's grave, my dog – I thought desperately of other precious things – Harry, Harry's parents who I'd never met but who were obviously precious to him and therefore precious to me, Harry's dog – but she interrupted me.

'*Shut up, will you!*' I shut. 'Quick, where's your car?'

'Over here!'

We ran to the car, sharing the burden of the carry-cot. The little redhead looked up in surprise as we raced him over the cobblestones. Rachel's breath was coming in hysterical sobs now as we flung the carry-cot on the back seat and leaped in the front. I fumbled with the keys, terrified that any minute now Adam's face would appear at the window and a large freckled hand would reach in and close firmly over mine. The car started first time and I made a mental note to treat it to a service one day as a mark of my eternal gratitude.

We shot out of that car park in true Hollywood style, and flew over the ramps in Middle Temple Lane like Freebie and the Bean before coming to a screeching halt at the Embankment. The traffic was roaring in both directions, but at the merest hint of a gap I shut my eyes and put my foot down. A lorry swerved violently and slipped behind my tail, missing me by millimetres, honking his horn and shaking his fist. I swung into the stream of traffic on the other side of the road amidst more honking and fist-shaking and various allusions to my anatomy, but I cared not. We revved and roared and lane-hopped and light-jumped our way towards central London.

Neither of us spoke for a while. Out of the corner of my eye I noticed that Rachel's face was the same colour as her leggings and she was doing a great deal of blinking and lip-quivering out of the window.

I dug deep and found a very small voice. 'I'm so sorry, Rachel, I really am.'

Her chin began to tremble and a tear trickled down the side of her nose. She brushed it away furiously. 'Why couldn't you just mind your own bloody business?' she hissed savagely.

Yes, why couldn't I? I'd never felt so awful in my life. Apart from that time at junior school when I'd trodden on the school hamster in front of the whole class. By mistake, of course: he escaped and I went to catch him. Yes, quite dead. But this was all my fault, I'd screwed up quite comprehensively. I'd fallen for everything Adam had said without even considering Rachel's position. Off I'd shot like an unguided missile, tearing round to her father's house, who, I now realised, had simply been protecting his daughter and grandson and then, not satisfied with upsetting him, I'd charged off again and exposed her quite brilliant hiding place. It had been brilliant, too. How many people would have the faintest idea that those flats existed? Not many Londoners, and certainly not an American.

I still couldn't quite get my mind round all this, though. Rachel had a baby. Adam had a baby. They both had a baby and they both wanted it. What they didn't want — yes, yes, I was getting there slowly — what they *didn't* want was each other. Brilliant Polly. I would have liked to have known why, why they'd fallen out, what had gone wrong in the idyllic house by the sea in America, but I had a shrewd suspicion that now was not the time to ask.

I took another sideways glance and assessed the damage to her face. She seemed to be under control now. In a second or two we might have a bash at a conversation and try to determine the best place for her to go. But then of course she wouldn't have any idea, why should she? I'd only ousted her from her flat ten minutes ago, and she was hardly likely to have yet another brilliant hidey hole up her sleeve. I had to come up with something, and fast. I called upon my under-worked brain to perform some kind of miracle for me. Let me see, let me see, we couldn't go to her father's — God, what a nasty piece of work he must have thought me, I'd dwell on that later — and we couldn't go to my flat because Adam knew where I lived. Did she perhaps have any friends in London?

'Do you have any friends in London?' I ventured timidly.

She shook her head, and either this sad admission or the violence of the shake provoked another fresh trickle of tears down her nose. God I felt a heel. I plunged into my mental file of my two hundred closest friends and went straight to the top. There was really very little competition for this job. It was a position that had to be filled by someone with a big enough heart and a big enough flat to house a distressed girl and a baby. There was only one person who was unlucky enough to qualify, and that was Pippa. Big heart, even bigger house. Pippa it was.

By now, Rachel seemed to have abdicated all responsibility, and didn't even bat an eyelid as we did a U-turn in the middle of the road and headed off to Kensington. She did look up as we approached the bottom of Church Street though.

'Not to my father's,' she said in alarm, 'that's the first place he'll look!'

'I know, I know, don't worry. We're going to a friend's house.'

We dodgemed our way down Kensington High Street, turned left by the cinema and then right into Pippa's road. We came to an abrupt halt outside her house and my head dropped like a stone on to the steering wheel. Thank God that journey was over, I'd aged about a year in ten minutes. My hands, released from their position on the wheel, now began to shake like a couple of pink blancmanges. They'd been getting a lot of exercise in that respect today.

I raised my head and looked at Rachel squarely. It was an effort because her eyes were still understandably hostile, but I felt it was the least I could do.

'I'm so sorry, but believe me, you'll be all right. I promise I'm going to look after you and see that he doesn't find you. I absolutely promise.'

She nodded dumbly. What else could she do? She was in my extremely incapable hands. But I meant what I said. One way or another, I'd see this one through until she and the baby were safe, and well away from the clutches of Adam Buchanan. For once in my life, I, Polly McLaren, would not screw up.

Chapter Ten

When Pippa eventually answered the door it was obvious she wasn't alone. Her usually sleek blonde hair was somewhat tousled, her face was flushed and her eyes were far too bright. She was wearing a short white towelling dressing gown and not a lot else. She pulled the dressing gown closer around her as she peered round the door at her visitors, brushing the hair out of her eyes. 'Polly! What a lovely surprise!'

It clearly wasn't, but I was desperate. 'Pippa, this is Rachel,' I said, pushing a wordless Rachel ahead of me into the house.

'Oh, hi Rachel, um, come in.'

She was in, I'd seen to that, and I was right behind her with the carry-cot. This didn't escape Pippa.

'You've got a baby!'

'He's Rachel's,' I replied, staggering in. God, what did she feed him on?

'Well, I'm glad to hear he's not yours. He's lovely though, isn't he?' she said, bending down to do a bit of cooing. 'How old is he?'

'Five months,' muttered Rachel.

'Oh, he's divine. Is he really yours? You lucky thing.' She straightened up and peered at Rachel. 'Oh gosh, hang on — you're not *the* Rachel, are you?'

'How d'you mean?'

Pippa turned to me. 'The Rachel you've been looking for? Adam's Rachel?'

'Er, yes, but you see the thing is, Pippa, she didn't actually want—'

'Oh! Oh, how exciting!' She turned to Rachel and gripped her arm enthusiastically. 'But that's brilliant, isn't it! She found you, the clever old thing found you! Aren't you thrilled? You must be! Gosh, you look worn out, you poor thing. Have you been hidden away for ages? Yes — yes, how silly of me, I can see that you have, you look simply ghastly. I expect you're dying to have a wash and get out of those filthy clothes, aren't you? I can lend you some things if—'

'I'm perfectly all right, thank you. I had a wash this morning, my clothes are quite clean and no, I'm not remotely thrilled she found me!' Rachel hissed, shaking her arm free. She grabbed the carry-cot and stalked into the sitting room.

Pippa looked bewildered. She raised her eyebrows at me. 'What did I say?' she whispered.

'I'll tell you in a minute. Oh, it's awful, Pippa, you've *got* to help us!' My voice cracked; I was on the verge of tears.

'Yes, but Polly, the thing is I've got—'

'In a minute, Pippa, I'll explain in a minute, come on.'

I grabbed her arm and pushed her into her own drawing room. For a moment I thought she'd been burgled. Every conceivable square inch of carpet was covered in debris, mostly of the clothing kind, but there was also quite a lot of pizza around. The coffee table was on its side, all the large sofa cushions were on the floor, and full ashtrays and empty bottles abounded. Even Pippa looked slightly nonplussed, she obviously hadn't ventured downstairs since the night before.

'Oh, er — sorry about the mess, we had a bit of a raucous evening last night.' She jerked her head meaningfully in the direction of the stairs and rolled her eyes dramatically. I got her drift but pretended I hadn't: I needed her much more than he did, whoever he was.

Rachel was picking her way across the room to a chair. She turned it the right way up, and with forefinger and thumb removed a rather dirty bra before sitting down with the baby in her arms. She turned away from us and stared out of the window into the garden as if she'd temporarily vacated her body.

'I was um, just about to make some coffee,' said Pippa. 'Would you like a cup?' Rachel didn't respond.

'I'd love some,' I said quickly, 'I'll help you make it.'

We escaped to the kitchen and she shut the door. 'What the hell's going on?' she said in a hoarse whisper. 'Is she demented or something? Few sandwiches short of a picnic? She doesn't look all there.' She wiggled her finger around on her temple.

'I'll explain in a minute, Pippa, but listen, promise you'll help us. We're in real trouble.'

'Polly, do you have any idea who I've got upstairs?' hissed Pippa as if she'd trapped a wild animal.

'Who?'

'Only Charles Stanley!'

'No! Charles Stanley? Really?' In spite of my predicament I gasped in admiration. I'd never met the man, but I'd heard him talked of in hushed and hallowed tones by Pippa and various other girlfriends of mine, and was clued up enough to know that in terms of finds he was something of a Holy Grail.

'Exactly, Charles Stanley. I've been after him for *months*, Polly, as you well know. You just can't *do* this to me, in fact you're not going to do this to me, so why don't you just quickly tell me what the bloody hell's going on so I can tell you to bog off and get back to him.'

I groaned. 'Oh no, Pippa, please don't do that, I really need you. Couldn't you just have a tiny word with him and say — say something earth-shatteringly important's come up and you'll see him very soon? Please do, please,' I begged.

Pippa gasped. 'Get rid of him? Now?'

'Oh, I'm sorry, I know I shouldn't ask you, but I'm desperate, really *desperate*!'

'Polly, you must be mad!'

I certainly must have looked it, because she stared at me for a few seconds then shrugged her shoulders in despair. She threw a few mugs on a tray and threw in the towel at the same time.

'All right. But it had better be good. Bloody good. You make the coffee and I'll go and have a word with Charles.' She rammed the Nescafé into my hand and made to go upstairs.

I fell on her arm with relief. 'Oh thank you, Pippa, thank you! Listen — you could meet him later, it's just we must talk to you now, and um — borrow a bit of your house.'

'Oh really?' Her eyebrows shot into her fringe. 'Oh yes, well, please feel free. Which bit would you like: my bedroom perhaps?'

I didn't laugh, in fact I was just about to cry. She sensed it and gave my arm a squeeze. 'Look, don't panic, Polly. Just make the coffee and I'll go and square it with Charles. Tell me all about it in a moment, OK?'

'OK,' I whispered shakily as she ran off up the stairs, dressing gown flapping.

I wondered if my blancmange-like fingers were capable of getting boiling water from the kettle to mugs without giving myself third-degree burns. I just about managed it, and was on my way back to the drawing room with the tray when Pippa reappeared down the stairs followed by one of the most beautiful men I've ever seen. He was tall and long-legged with dark wavy hair which was currently attractively tousled, slanty green eyes, and a huge, lazy, sexy grin which I had the feeling was pretty permanent. He extended the grin even further towards his ears when he saw me.

'Hi, you must be the desperate friend,' he said, tucking his shirt into his jeans.

'I'm terribly sorry—' I began, but he'd already turned to Pippa, taken her in his arms, and was in the midst of giving her the most thorough kissing I've ever seen outside the cinema. I stood there like an usherette with my tray of coffee as he finished the scene.

'Bye, angel,' he whispered as he held her face in his hands. 'I'll see you later.' Pippa whispered something back and opened the door for him. I was impressed. I'd never seen Pippa in action before.

'Right! In here,' said Pippa in a businesslike manner when she'd shut the door. She shepherded me into the drawing room. I put the coffee down and flopped on to the sofa. The white-faced girl in the corner didn't appear to have moved an inch.

'Now, what's this all about?' said Pippa, looking at me. 'I am right, aren't I? This is the Rachel that chap Adam whatshisname was looking for? The guy who took you to the Savoy for din—'

'Yes, yes,' I said, interrupting her hurriedly. I didn't want my free meal at the Savoy to feature too heavily in my tale of courageous — albeit misguided — fortitude. 'This is Rachel, only — oh well . . .' I took a deep breath and dived in, gabbling away about judges, housekeepers, disguises and car chases, but trailing off miserably when I got to the bit about bursting into Rachel's sanctuary.

Pippa turned to Rachel. 'So that's how she found you?' Rachel didn't respond. Pippa turned to me. 'So that's how you found her? She was in the flat all the time?'

'Yes, but you see—'

'Well, so what's the problem then?' said Pippa staunchly. 'It seems to me you've been absolutely brilliant!

I mean, you went to all that trouble just to unite a couple of complete strangers. You've been absolutely marvellous.' She turned to Rachel sternly. 'You've got a lot to thank Polly for, you know. There aren't many people who'd put themselves out to that extent, most people wouldn't have bothered to do anything. I think she's been tremendous, absolutely tremendous. Selfless, spirited, enterprising and—'

'Er, hang on, Pippa' I interrupted nervously. 'I haven't finished yet. You see, the thing is—'

'The thing is,' Rachel's head suddenly turned one hundred and eighty degrees to face us. It was a bit like something out of the *Exorcist*; any minute now we'd be in for a bit of projectile vomiting. Her face was grim, and her eyes almost disappeared into her face they were so screwed up with bitterness. 'The thing is that I didn't want her to find me at all. She's just a stupid, interfering old cow.'

'Oh now, look here!' said Pippa warmly. 'Talk about ungrateful. I mean—'

'No, Pippa. Listen to me,' I burst in. 'Adam wasn't looking for Rachel at all, he was looking for Jamie.'

'For Jamie?'

'Yes, for Jamie, the baby — this baby.' I jabbed my finger babywards. '*Their* baby.'

Pippa's eyes grew wide. 'Oh!'

I sighed. 'Exactly.'

'Oh! Oh gosh, how awful! You mean he just pretended . . . You mean he tricked you into . . . Oh!' She turned back to Rachel. 'So you didn't want to be found at all!'

Rachel declined to answer this, and gave her a look of such withering magnitude that most people would have been silenced for life, but Pippa was determined to get things straight in her head. 'So — so hang on a minute,' she persisted. 'This is like a tug-of-love thing, is it? You know, with the baby in the middle? The kind of thing you read about in the papers, is that it?'

Again this was deemed to be unworthy of response, and Rachel resumed her contemplation of the cherry tree in the garden.

Pippa looked at me, all rolling eyes and raised eyebrows. Oh my God, she mouthed. I nodded back miserably, agreeing wholeheartedly. Yes, oh my God.

'What are you going to do?' she whispered to me.

'I don't know,' I whispered back.

There was a profound silence. I looked at Jamie, who was sleeping peacefully in his carry-cot, oblivious to all the fuss and confusion surrounding him. He really was quite divine: all pink and white and chubby-cheeked with lovely little creases round his neck. Shame about the red hair, but if he turned out to be as good looking as his father, he'd be all right.

As for the mother – I sneaked a quick look at her grim profile – well, I had to say I still didn't remember her. She had a fluffy cloud of fair hair which not only needed a wash but, to my practised eye, could have done with about forty pounds-worth of highlights; a pale, heart-shaped face with pointed features; and small, bluey-grey eyes with those rather unattractive blonde eyelashes. She was, I decided charitably, sweetly pretty in a little-girl-lost sort of way, but next to Pippa, who admittedly had a head start with the just-got-out-of-a-hot-bed-of-lust-look, she scored about minus six on sex appeal. The big grey cardigan didn't help, because you couldn't really tell what sort of a figure she had, but I supposed she had a certain helpless attraction and would appeal to men of the caring and protecting persuasion. I had a sneaky suspicion she was pretty damn tough underneath that oversized cardigan, though: she was certainly toughing this silence out.

'So what's your sto . . . I mean, what's the real story then?' I said as sympathetically as I could. I was beginning to feel a trifle irritated. After all, I'd tried my damnedest to help her. OK, I'd got it completely wrapped round my neck, but the least she could do was shed a bit of light on things instead of sitting there in supercilious silence like something out of a Botticelli madonna and child portrait.

'Rachel?' I raised my voice slightly. Still nothing.

Pippa coughed nervously. 'Well, of course you're welcome to stay here for a bit if that's what you'd like. I mean, I know it's not ideal but, um . . .'

Rachel continued to stare at the cherry tree and the tongue stayed hinged. Pippa looked at me and raised her eyebrows. I licked my incredibly dry lips.

'Well, Pippa, that's terribly kind. I think we'll say yes please, if that's all right with you and if, um, Rachel agrees . . .'

Suddenly Rachel turned towards us, she opened her mouth and – yes – she appeared to be contemplating a sentence. I for one was on the edge of my seat.

'Do you have anything stronger to drink besides coffee?' she asked. Wow! Not just a sentence, but a show-stopper of a sentence.

Pippa leaped up off her chair as if she'd been goosed, and was instantly hospitality itself. 'Gosh yes, of course. What would you like?'

'Could I have a gin and tonic?' It was getting better and better. In fact it was the first sensible thing she'd said since I'd met her.

Pippa raced off to the fridge and came back brandishing a frozen ice-tray, which she banged on the upturned coffee table spraying ice everywhere. Meanwhile, I poured three whopping great gins, adding a soupçon of tonic. We gulped them down thankfully and lit cigarettes. All at once a slightly less frosty, more conspiratorial atmosphere seemed to prevail.

Rachel put the sleeping Jamie in his carry-cot, crossed her legs and rested her chin in her hand. She sighed. 'OK.

I'll tell you how I got into this mess.' Pippa and I leant forwards in unison, anxious not to miss a syllable.

'As you probably know, my father dragged me out of school just before my A-levels.'

'Gosh, how awful, why did he—' began Pippa.

'Sshhh.' I nudged her. For God's sake, she'd started, let her finish. 'Go on, Rachel.'

'Well, I was desperately upset, in fact when we got home I couldn't even bring myself to talk to him. I just locked myself in my room and refused to come out. I think that really shook him, so much so that when I asked if I could go abroad for a bit, amazingly he agreed, on the condition that I stayed with some friends of his in Boston. Well I went, and that's how I met Adam, their son.'

So far so good, I thought.

She hesitated and took a long drag of her cigarette. 'Adam was — is, ten years older than me, good looking and very charming. I was incredibly unhappy, still rather shell-shocked, I suppose, and in dire need of a shoulder to cry on.' She shrugged. 'His was the obvious one: he offered it and I took it.' She paused for a moment and took another glug of gin. 'He was kind and sympathetic and, actually, great fun to be with. He made me feel a hell of a lot better, and we began to see each other practically all the time. Inevitably, of course, we ended up in bed.' She shook her head. 'God, when I look back now . . . you see I was so ridiculously innocent, he was the first person I'd ever slept with, and I was so clueless that I didn't even think about contraception. I mean, I knew all about it, but I just didn't think.' She sighed. 'I got pregnant almost immediately.'

Let that be a lesson to you, Polly my girl, I thought. Keep taking those pills.

Rachel took another huge gulp of gin and continued. 'I didn't tell him for a while because I was frightened of what he might say, but when I really couldn't squeeze into my jeans any longer, I did. He couldn't have been nicer. At one time I'd thought about having an abortion but was too much of a coward to go through with it, and Adam was appalled that I'd even considered it. To tell you the truth, he was thrilled about the baby, and determined we should keep it and get married.'

'Well, that's not so terrible!' I said. I imagined Harry's reaction to fatherhood would be to frogmarch me off to Harley Street where he no doubt knew of an obliging little clinic.

'No, I agree, and for a while things were great. We lived in his parents' house in Marblehead and I got bigger and bigger and felt reasonably happy about it. When I was about seven months pregnant, we rang my father and broke the news.'

'What!' I gasped. 'Didn't he go ballistic?'

Rachel smiled. 'He's not nearly as bad as you seem to think, you know.'

You could have fooled me, I thought.

'I mean sure, he wasn't exactly thrilled to bits, but he came round eventually and, anyway, what could he do? I was due to have the baby in two months. Anyway, he came out to see me in America, met Adam properly, and everyone agreed that we should get married. Everyone, that is, except me.'

'Why on earth not?' said Pippa.

'Because – ' Rachel struggled to explain – 'because I wasn't really in love with him.' She bit her lip and stared beyond us, almost as if she were thinking the whole thing through again as she spoke. 'I'd fallen for Adam when I was at a very low ebb, you see. I was depressed, miserable and lonely. I needed someone to turn to, and he just happened to be that someone. Looking back, I suppose it could have been anyone, within reason of course. D'you know, I think that even then, even right at the beginning when I was sleeping with him, in the back of my mind, I

186

knew that I wasn't in love with him.' She looked up. 'Does that sound terrible?'

Pippa and I shook our heads vigorously.

'No, of course not!'

'God no.'

Oh yes, we'd both been there. We'd both had a few — ahem — liaisons shall we say, with individuals who didn't altogether make our hearts beat faster.

'So you can see why I couldn't marry him?'

We nodded, but less vigorously this time. This was slightly trickier, since neither Pippa nor I had ever been on the receiving end of a marriage proposal. We would have liked to have been, but somehow those four little words had never cropped up in our earshot, and it was hard to say what our response would have been. Nonetheless, we agreed wholeheartedly with the sentiment.

'Oh absolutely,' said Pippa.

'Oh God, I agree. Couldn't marry someone I didn't love,' I added. Unless, I thought privately, he was very *very* rich.

'Anyway,' Rachel went on, 'I prevaricated for a bit and said I'd rather wait for the baby to be born. After all, I was pretty enormous, and I pretended I wanted a proper white wedding.'

'Just playing for time,' said Pippa.

'Exactly. So two months later Jamie arrived, and actually we were OK for a while; I remember feeling reasonably happy. Then Adam started pestering me to marry him again. I put him off and put him off and we began to argue quite a bit. I was also desperate to get back to my music, I wanted to study some more — go back to college and get a nanny for Jamie. Adam was horrified — he thought I should stay at home; but eventually I persuaded him and in fact in the end he stayed and looked after Jamie because he could work from home. But things got worse and worse.'

Rachel rubbed her eyes with the back of her hand. She looked all in. 'Adam became incredibly possessive, questioning me endlessly about the boys at college, refusing to let me go for a quick drink after school with anyone; in fact he took to waiting at the college gates in the car just to make sure I didn't. I even caught him reading my diary once. It was ghastly. I began to really resent him, and then of course, I began to hate him.' She smiled sardonically. 'You know what it's like. A little irritation can easily turn into full-blooded hatred.'

'Perhaps you should have gone on holiday together or something, just the two of you, without Jamie, tried to fall in love again?' said Pippa, who read lots of agony columns.

'But you see I never really *was* in love with him, that was the root of the problem.' Rachel sighed and ground her cigarette out in the ashtray. 'One night we had an absolutely furious row, a real hum-dinger, and the next morning I decided I'd just had enough. Adam had gone to Boston for a meeting, so I booked myself on a flight to London, packed a bag, left a note and went, taking Jamie with me.'

Pippa and I looked rather shocked.

'I *had* to do it like that,' she said emphatically, 'or I'd never have got away. You don't know Adam, he's just so determined.'

I did know Adam, vaguely, and I took her point. If she'd so much as suggested a separation she'd never have got across the doormat, let alone to the airport. I looked across at Pippa who was gripped, her mouth hanging open and about two inches of ash hanging from the cigarette in her hand. I grabbed an ashtray and held it underneath. Too late.

'So you went home to your father's?' she said, ignoring the pile of ash on the carpet.

'I had nowhere else to go. He was pretty shocked and

tried to make me go back and patch things up, but once I'd sat down and talked it through with him, he came round, and in fact he said that in retrospect it was a good thing we'd never got married. The next day Adam telephoned, extremely drunk and extremely belligerent.' She sighed and took out another cigarette. 'He called me all sorts of names, threatened me with all kinds of hideous things, and said he'd never let me have Jamie. That happened about three times. He also threatened my father and said he was coming over to take Jamie back. I didn't consider it an idle threat either, because I know what he's like when he wants something. That's when Daddy and I decided I should go and live at his flat in the Temple. He's had that place for years, but he hardly ever uses it, and I don't suppose anyone even knows he's got it.' She lit her cigarette, blew the match out and crushed it in her hand. 'I liked it there. I felt safe.'

I looked down at my shoes and wondered which part of my body she'd imagined she was breaking into little bits when she savaged the matchstick. I had the feeling another apology might be in order at this point.

'I'm really sorry, Rachel,' I began. 'I had no idea—' but she interrupted me.

'It's OK. I dare say I was living in a fool's paradise anyway. He probably would have found me sooner or later.' I privately rather agreed with this, especially since her father's name was written in six-inch gold letters above the door.

'But surely,' said Pippa, 'surely with your father being a judge and everything, you could have held on to Jamie legally. I mean, couldn't you have got a court order or something?'

'Oh yes, legally, and that's what I intend to do; but that still doesn't stop Adam snatching him back and just getting on a plane to the States, does it?'

'Well what about,' Pippa went on, feeling her way

carefully, 'what about if you had some kind of custody agreement, you know: you have him for a while, and then Adam has him for a bit?'

'What, so Jamie spends his whole time to-ing and fro-ing across the Atlantic?' snorted Rachel. 'No thanks. Anyway, once Adam had him out there he'd never give him back, I know him too well.'

I couldn't think of anything to say. I'd been well and truly hoodwinked. And yet he'd seemed so straightforward, so . . . in love. Suddenly I plucked a thought from my brain.

'But there was a letter! A letter to Sally Lomax from you, saying what a terrific guy he was and how mad about him you were. Where did that come from?'

'Oh, come on,' scoffed Rachel, 'pretty easy to forge something like that, isn't it? I mean, do you know what my handwriting looks like?'

'No. No, I suppose not.'

Was I stupid or what? I'd sat at the Savoy making a complete prat of myself. I dug my nails into my hands in embarrassment. What a fool I'd been, and what a con man he was. I couldn't help remembering that bit in the letter about him being so good looking: he'd got quite a nerve to write that about himself, hadn't he? Quite a nerve. I stared into space, contemplating the magnitude of his gall.

Just then, Jamie decided it was time to wake up and exercise his vocal chords. He gave us the benefit of his extremely healthy lungs and – SCREAMED. I had no idea babies could cry quite so loudly. Pippa and I clustered round and bent down for a closer look as Rachel gathered him up in her arms. He stopped crying and Pippa held her arms out for a hold, but Rachel pretended not to notice. She obviously wasn't letting him out of her arms, let alone her sight.

Pippa straightened up and tied her minuscule dressing gown around her in a businesslike manner. 'You'd better stay here for a while, Rachel.' I could have hugged her. 'He's hardly likely to come looking for you here, I mean I don't know him from – oh well, you know.' She giggled, Rachel didn't. 'So you can have the whole of the top floor if you like: there are two tiny bedrooms and a bathroom. It's not particularly spacious, but it's clean and reasonably tidy and, er, oh!'

Whilst Pippa had still been in mid-flow, Rachel had walked straight past us, into the hall and up the stairs. I felt hot with embarrassment. She was beginning to annoy me, a small thank-you here and there wouldn't go amiss. I waited until she was out of earshot.

'Thanks so much, Pippa, you're an angel. Sorry about that ungrateful cow. I mean, honestly, she's probably safer here than she was in the Temple.'

'It's OK. She's probably still upset,' said the ultra-tolerant Pippa, picking up the sofa cushions from the floor and gathering together what looked like a crateful of empty bottles. 'Oh, and you'd better stay too, of course.'

'Me? Why?' I said in surprise, gathering clothes from the floor and folding them up on a chair.

'Because, dick brain, what's the first thing Adam's going to do?'

I turned a pair of jeans the right way out and gave it some thought. 'Go to Judge Marsden's flat?'

'Right, and then?'

I dropped a full ashtray on the floor in horror. 'Go to my flat!'

'Exactly, employing whatever bully-boy tactics he feels are appropriate to pick your brains.'

'Oh my God!' I felt like Salman Rushdie. I was being persecuted – I needed police protection! I reached for my felt hat and pulled it down over my eyes, ramming my Ray Bans on my nose with my other trembling hand. I was not a very brave girl.

'What shall I do?' I whispered, sliding down into a

chair. My knees felt rather weak.

'Just stay here and lie low for a bit.'

Oh, I would. I would lie very low. I would lie under that sofa if necessary, or, or down in the cellar where it was very low, I'd be so low you'd have to rip up the floorboards to find me.

I ran off to the hall to telephone Lottie. I told her the whole horrendous story and explained that she might have a visitor in the shape of one large ginger-haired Adam Buchanan ready and willing to wrench out teeth, hair and entrails in his search for his son. Lottie was totally unfazed by all this: her streak of yellow wasn't nearly as wide as mine. She said she'd pop over later with some clothes for me. All at once I knew who my friends were.

'Oh, and Lottie!' I screamed as she was about to put the phone down. 'Don't drop them all over the pavement, will you? Don't use a case, use a black binliner or something and — and look behind you to make sure you're not being followed. Remember whoever it is could be in disguise and, and — just be bloody careful!' I squeaked into the receiver, thinking of my own skin of course rather than hers.

When Pippa and I had tidied up and she'd shed her dressing gown for something more suitable, we all trooped off for a rather strange and subdued lunch in the Scarsdale. We were an unlikely bunch in the pub that afternoon: Pippa, Charles Stanley, Rachel — with Jamie asleep in a sling — and me.

We couldn't possibly tell Charles the whole story, but you could see his brain was working overtime as he wondered what this dolly mixture of girls was all about. Who was that white-faced one in the corner with the baby? And why did she and the one in the brown hat and dark glasses leap up and down every time someone came into the pub? Were they being followed? These and other unanswered questions clearly ran through his mind, but

Charles, who was a good chap, said nothing and coped wonderfully – entertaining us, feeding us, plying us with drinks, and resisting all offers of payment.

It was rather as if Pippa had suddenly sprung a large and motley family upon him which he was expected to provide for, no questions asked. And wasn't he just taking it all in his giant stride, I thought, as I watched this long-legged hunk of man gaze adoringly at Pippa over his Guinness.

How would Harry have reacted, I wondered? He always enjoyed Pippa's company because she was so pretty, but I wasn't quite sure how he'd have coped with the anaemic waif and baby. I realised with a jolt that I hadn't thought about Harry for at least a day. Seeing Pippa and Charles so happy together made me miss him with an almighty great pang. I'd ring him later. Yes I would. Bet you anything he was wondering how I was. I was almost as good at lying to myself as I was to other people. Had he been trying to ring me, I wondered? At least he could reach me at the agency. I went cold. So could Adam.

'Pippa!' I squeaked, rudely interrupting Charles who was deep in the finer nuances of the latest French film at the Curzon, 'Pippa, he knows where I work! He'll be bashing down the agency door on Monday!' Pools of blood were swimming before my eyes as I imagined the nasty stains on the agency carpet.

'Yes, I was wondering about that,' said the altogether unflappable Pippa, obviously alive to the possibility before it had even filtered through my own fuddled brain. 'You'd better take the day off tomorrow and stay at home with Rachel. If he puts in an appearance, we'll say you've taken some leave: gone to stay with friends in the country for a couple of weeks or something.'

'Suppose he doesn't believe you!' I wailed.

'So what? What can he do? He might well believe it anyway; I mean it's quite likely really, considering he's after you.'

After me! Great Scott, someone was after me! I sank back in my chair in despair, nursing my gin and tonic. Perhaps I should change my identity completely, steal a passport, become a nun or something, emigrate to Australia perhaps.

Out of the corner of my eye I could see that Charles was looking more and more mystified. This latest outburst from the maniac in the hat had really got the cogs whirring in his brain. Ah yes, I was obviously on the run from my drunken, wife-beating husband — he looked at the empty ring finger on my left hand — common-law husband. He switched his gaze to Pippa. Pippa was obviously sheltering me, perhaps she ran a home for battered wives or something, or perhaps — yes — that was it, she was working for the Samaritans. He took her hand tenderly. That would explain the white-faced single parent in the corner. Perhaps white face was also a drug addict or a prostitute and Pippa had generously taken us all under her wing. He stroked her hand and his eyes shone with love and admiration. I drained my glass. Well, one good thing had come out of this saga. We were obviously doing wonders for Pippa's big-hearted image.

That evening, back at Pippa's, I weakened and rang Harry.

'Hi Polyester, how's it going? I've been looking for you everywhere, where have you been hiding?'

My knees buckled and I sat down very hard on the wooden chair by the telephone. A vase of flowers on the table next to it wobbled perilously. Harry had been looking for me?

'Well, I'm staying at Pippa's for a few days,' I replied in a somewhat dazed voice.

'Ah, so that's where you've been. I tried to ring you at lunchtime to see if you wanted a drink, but there was no answer from the flat.'

This time I had difficulty staying on the chair, in fact I

had to grab hold of the banisters. 'You did?'

'Yes, I fancied a pint.'

'Oh! Well, what about tonight?'

'Oh God, I'd love to, darling – ' Darling? – 'but I'm tied up now, I've got to work.'

It didn't matter, nothing mattered, he'd wanted to have lunch with me, he'd actively looked for me, no – no, he'd *searched* for me, oh joy!

'Listen,' he went on, 'I'm up to my eyeballs revising for this bloody stockbroking exam on Monday. I'll ring you in the week, shall I?'

Was he asking my permission? 'Yes, yes, fine!' I said, unable to keep the ecstasy from my voice.

'OK, take care.'

'And you . . .' I hesitated, dug deep for courage, and chanced it ' . . . darling.'

I waited for the snort of derision; none came. 'Bye then.'

'Bye!'

I replaced the receiver and leaned weakly against the front door. Harry had actually phoned me on a normal, common-or-garden Saturday. He'd picked up the telephone and dialled my number because he wanted to see me. No, no, correction. He'd *missed* me. I salivated and tried to recreate the scene – yes, yes, that was it. First he'd missed me (Oh Polly, oh miss miss miss, oh where are you, Polly? Oh, I miss you so), and then, *then* he'd picked up the telephone (rush to telephone, must see Polly, must see Polly now) in order to ask me, to *ask* me (please Polly, please? If you're not too busy?) to meet him for lunch. Nothing mattered now, nothing at all. The whole ghastly Rachel and Adam business faded into insignificance.

With a shriek of joy I leaped two feet off the ground and skipped off down the hall, whooping and thumping the air as if I'd just won an Olympic gold. I ran slap-bang into Rachel who'd been changing Jamie's nappy in the downstairs loo.

'Oops, sorry Rachel! Didn't see you there!' I couldn't wipe the silly grin from my face.

She ignored me and pushed past, taking Jamie upstairs for his bath. Oh God, she must think me a complete cold-hearted bitch, messing up her life and then whooping with pleasure. I went in search of Pippa who was in the kitchen. She was pleased for me, but not as impressed.

'Well, he damn well should ring you at weekends,' she said, shaking a wet lettuce round the kitchen. 'He should ring you every day, come to that.'

But nothing could dampen my spirits now. After a jolly supper with Pippa, minus Rachel who said she wasn't hungry, I went to bed feeling absurdly happy and hugging my happiness to myself.

Later on that night I was awakened by Jamie crying for a bottle, and much much later on I was woken again. Only this time it wasn't Jamie's crying I could hear, it was Rachel's.

Chapter Eleven

When Monday morning arrived it was beautifully sunny. I drew the curtains and hopped back into bed, pulling the duvet up around my chin. I lay there, staring out of the window at the Kensington chimney pots set against a bright blue sky, and watched the plane trees swaying in the breeze. I could hear Pippa banging around in her bedroom next door getting ready for work, and for the first time in my life I actually felt jealous. What the hell was I going to do all day alone in the house with Rachel? Sit next to her in uncompanionable silence?

I would have helped her with Jamie, but she rejected all offers, and in fact positively discouraged me from having any sort of contact with him, which was irritating as well as insulting. It wasn't often I had the chance to get my hands on a real live baby, and I was just getting to the stage in my life when they were becoming vaguely interesting. Only vaguely. I had an idea that it would be rather pleasant to bounce one or two Harry look-alikes around on my knee, help them with their finger painting (or did that come later on?), and watch the little darlings in the nursery school nativity, dressed up as angels or shepherds (later still perhaps?).

Anyway, I liked the whole concept of babies; what I wasn't so sure about was the having of them. This worried me. I'd even taken to prowling round Sainsbury's, browsing around amongst the frozen turkeys looking at the eight- or nine-pounders. They were big bastards those nine-pounders, I can tell you. And that was the size of an average baby? And that had to come out of — well. It took my breath away just thinking about it; no wonder you had to go to classes and learn to breathe all over again. I really took my hat off to my mother and all the other mothers I knew. Talk about the camel going through the eye of the needle: knowing my luck, I'd probably have something about the size of a camel.

I'd read in a magazine somewhere that one of the Mitford sisters had been plagued by similar misgivings, and had asked her mother what it had felt like to give birth. 'Well,' her mother had said, frowning with concentration as she tried to remember, 'it was rather like having an orange pulled out of your nostril.' This awesome simile had stayed with me for a long time afterwards, and I crossed my legs and winced every time I thought of it.

I would have liked to have asked Rachel for her views on the subject, since she had first-hand experience, but she wasn't really the sort of girl you could sit down with for a cosy labour and contractions chat. She wasn't actually the sort of girl you could sit down with for a cosy anything chat, I thought, as she stomped moodily into the kitchen in a full-length vyella nightie to give Jamie his breakfast.

'Morning!' I ventured cheerily, clocking the vyella with amazement.

'Oh, uh, morning,' she mumbled back, as one might mumble to a slug.

'AY AY AY AAAAAY!' chirped Jamie, giving me a great big beaming smile. Now that was more like it!

'Woo Woo, Jamie!' I waved back and made a funny face; he laughed delightedly. Shame he seemed to be on permanent send at both ends though, I thought, as a rather unpleasant smell began to pervade the kitchen. How could a baby as small as that produce smells so monumentally vile? Rachel shovelled Weetabix into his mouth, but he seemed more concerned with spitting it out than getting it in and — oh God, what was he doing now? Pushing it up his nose? Perhaps I'd take a rain check on babies, or maybe I'd adopt one when it had got past this rather messy stage. Pop down to the orphanage and pick out a clean one. When did they become clean I wondered; round about three? Or more like ten, perhaps?

Pippa appeared dressed for work and began spooning what looked like sawdust and milk into her mouth in her latest desperate bid to open up the bowels, an on-going problem that occupied most of her waking hours.

'Still no luck?' I asked. Like most constipation sufferers, she liked to talk about it.

'It's been five sodding days now,' she mumbled back through the sawdust.

'Oh well, never mind, it's probably all that sex.'

'What d'you mean?' she spluttered, spraying me with milk.

'Well, it's bound to bung you up, isn't it?'

'Is it? Christ, so celibacy's the only answer, is it? The only way I'm going to get regular is to make sure I don't get it regularly?'

I giggled. 'Exactly, and the reason you have to eat so much bran is that you get too much oats.'

'God, imagine being a nun, you'd be on the bog all day, wouldn't you?'

We giggled. Rachel looked totally unamused.

'What will you tell Nick?' I asked, as another megaton of fibre found its way in.

'I'll just say you're sick,' she munched.

'Oh, OK. Just hope he doesn't ring the flat, that's all.'

'He won't — why should he? And if he does you can just say you were asleep and didn't hear the phone, I mean, that's what you normally say when you skive, isn't it? Anyway, must go, bye.' She flung her spoon down and replaced it with her handbag.

'Bye,' I said dismally. 'Have a good day at the office.' I felt like the bored housewife already.

It wasn't as if it was high summer and I could lie in the sun all day, and it wasn't as if I had any money to go and play with. I shoved some toast in the toaster. Window shopping was no good. I just ended up feeling poor and envious, and then I had to indulge in a spot of retail therapy to make me feel better. That meant buying something cheap and cheerful and then realising on the bus on the way home that a purple mini-skirt was a big mistake and wouldn't go with any of my other clothes. Then, of course, I'd have to spend the whole of the following lunch hour taking the wretched garment back to the shop. That involved endless imaginative lies about how I'd been high on valium at the time of purchase on account of severe depression following a close relative's death and therefore not in my right mind, or else I'd go through the rigmarole of putting a curtain ring on my finger and saying my husband didn't like me in purple (actually I got a vicarious kick out of this one), and then I'd have to spout out the same stories all over again when the dreary shop assistant called the manager.

'I'm not really supposed to do refunds, you'll have to speak to Mrs Meekins. Mrs Meekins, there's a lady here who says her husband's got a thing about purple . . .'

Some boot-faced old bat would appear and, together with dreary, she'd inspect the garment thoroughly amid loud cries of, 'I hope it hasn't been worn, madam, only it seems rather *soiled*. I see a little stain here!'

'No, no, I think you'll find that's just the sheen of the cloth,' I'd say and − oh God, so it went on. An exhausting waste of time that could easily take up two whole days with absolutely nothing to show for it at the end.

No, shopping was definitely out. I'd just have to watch soap operas all day. I was on my way to the viewing room, wondering if nine-thirty wasn't perhaps a little previous for even the most bored of housewives, when the telephone rang.

'Hello?' I said gloomily into the mouthpiece en passant.

'Hi, Polly? It's Lottie.'

'Lottie! Hi, how are you getting on without me?'

'Oh I'll manage. Listen, I rang the agency and gathered from Pippa you were lolling around doing nothing, so are you free for lunch?'

'Free? I've never been so free in my life, that's a brilliant idea! I'll come to the City shall I?'

'Why not. I'll meet you in Corks at about twelve-thirty. OK?'

'Great! See you then, bye.'

I put down the phone. Things were looking decidedly upward. In fact, when I saw Rachel's stony face advancing towards me down the corridor, I felt as if I'd discovered the wooden horse. My escape was taking shape. Freedom was on the cards. I gave my face a look of friendly concern.

'Will you be all right on your own here if I pop out for a while at lunchtime?' I asked her.

'Of course.'

'Sure? Only I don't want to leave you if you feel nervous. I should lock all the doors, oh, and probably best not to answer the door, or even the phone.'

She didn't bother to reply and gave me a look of utter contempt. Who was I to tell her about safety?

I ran out of the house at eleven-thirty, and leaped the little wall at the front of the garden as if it were Colditz barbed wire. It was ridiculously early, but if I caught a bus it would take ages to get there, and I liked sitting on the top deck at the front. There's nothing nicer than taking a bus through London if you've got bags of time and nothing worse if you're late and desperate to get somewhere.

The number eleven chugged and spluttered its way

slowly through the West End and out towards the City. As we trundled past the Bank of England and then rounded the corner, we passed Harry's office, as I knew we would. I peered in through the dark grey smoky windows on the off-chance that I might get a glimpse. Poor Harry. He was probably scribbling away at his exam at this very moment.

I arrived at Corks at bang on twelve-thirty, and sauntered down the stone steps to the cellar. The place was packed already, heaving with bankers and brokers braying loudly at each other and 'haw-hawing' with laughter. I began pushing my way past a million pinstriped backs, knowing Lottie would be late and arrive looking hot and bothered with tales of ghastly clients wanting advice who had kept her talking on the phone. I peered around the gloom of the dark cellar bar looking hopefully for a table that didn't already have a dozen city types jostling for position around it, and was surprised to see Lottie over in the corner, already in possession of this very rare commodity. What's more, she had a full bottle of wine in front of her. She looked pale and utterly worn out. Overworked and underpaid, I thought sympathetically: she should have stuck to shorthand and short hours like me.

'Hi! What's with the bottle of wine? I thought you people with proper jobs didn't drink at lunchtime?'

'I don't normally, but I thought we might need it under the circumstances,' she said a trifle grimly.

'Oh really?' I kissed her and sat down. Gosh, she really did look all in. Whatever was the matter? Lottie only cracked under the severest of pressure, unlike me, who needed a drink after a typing error. I peered at her through the candlelight.

'Are you OK? You look terrible, if you don't mind me saying so.'

'Had a bit of bad news,' she said, taking a swig of wine. Oh poor Lottie, whatever could it be? Her home life minus a mother wasn't the happiest of places anyway. I hoped nothing had happened to her father, or Caro perhaps?

'What is it, Lottie, what's happened? Is something wrong?'

'Yes, it is actually, and in the absence of anyone else coming forward to tell you about it, it seems to have fallen to me to be messenger boy.'

I felt an Arctic chill pass through my shoulderblades and down my spine. I knew at once that it wasn't her, it was me. I sat very still.

Lottie looked me in the eyes for the first time. She took a drag of her cigarette. 'Pour yourself a drink, Polly,' she said gently.

'In a minute. Go on, Lottie, just tell me.'

Lottie sighed. 'OK. Harry is seeing Caro.'

I let this bombshell of a sentence whistle through my ears, cruise into my brain, and crash into my heart. It exploded on impact and all my blood seemed to drain downwards into my feet. I found my tongue and licked my lips, except they didn't feel like my lips.

'He can't be,' I whispered.

'He is,' said Lottie brutally, knowing full well that brutal was what she would have to be.

'I don't believe it.'

She put her hand over mine and moved her face closer. 'Believe it, Polly, he is, I know he is.'

'But — but, he phoned me yesterday, he called me darling, he wanted to see me, he *asked* if he could ring me later — he *can't* be, Lottie, he just *can't* be!'

'Guilt?' said Lottie simply. Suddenly I knew she was right.

Lottie let me get used to the idea for a second. She poured me a glass of wine. I took a large gulp.

'Define seeing,' I whispered.

She looked down at the red-and-white checked tablecloth and picked a bit of candlewax off it with her fingernail. 'She spent Saturday night there and she was there last night too.'

I gasped in amazement. Somehow, what struck me more than anything was the luxury of two nights in a row. I'd never been afforded that privilege, not even in the early days. Harry was seeing Caro. Harry was *sleeping* with Caro. My guts seemed to be knotting themselves into a fierce ball of anguish. I clenched my fists and tried not to scream. It was a small wine bar and Lottie's local: it wouldn't look good. Try as I might I couldn't resist imagining the scene. It was vivid. I saw Harry launching himself in all his golden glory from the diving board; I saw a giggling, squirming Caro, her perfect body naked on the Conran sheets, her perfect hair spread all over the pillow. My sheets. My pillow. My hand flew to my mouth. I wasn't going to scream, I was going to be sick. I gulped down the nausea and took deep breaths of musty, smoky air. He'd only met her in the flat about a week ago and already . . . I moaned softly.

'How long have you known?' I asked, keeping my sentences to the minimum. A certain amount of puke might well escape if I kept my mouth open for too long.

'Not long.'

'How long?'

'A couple of days.'

'How did you find out?' Details were important.

Lottie sighed. She looked wretched. 'Harry phoned me at work on Thursday for Caro's number.'

I stared at her, dumb with disbelief.

She squirmed and continued bravely. 'It's true Polly, that's how much of a bastard he is. He telephoned *me*, your *best friend* for Caro's *number*.' She spoke slowly, using TV presenter *emphasis* to try to ram the idea home.

'What did you say?'

'I told him to sod off. And I didn't tell you in case he'd

just had one too many at lunchtime and thought better of it later. I rang Caro this morning. I wasn't going to mention Harry but I wondered if she would. She did. She was full of it, bubbling over, couldn't tell me quickly enough in fact,' she said bitterly.

I felt a brief pang for Lottie. Divided loyalties were awful, and she must be feeling ghastly, but it was only a very brief pang. Most of all I felt sorry for me because I was hurting like hell. If someone had whacked me round the head with a cricket bat I couldn't be more stunned. This must be how a man felt when he'd been kicked in the balls. I wouldn't mind kicking some at this very moment, actually. I looked around murderously for a spare pair of wandering balls; any pair would do, as long as they were male and firmly attached. I wondered if it would be possible to kill someone like that. I hoped so. I returned slowly from my homicidal depths and emerged with a raging thirst. I wanted more wine and I wanted it *now* and I wanted more details too. I wanted to cram my head full to bursting with Harry and Caro's indecent exposure and as many nasty, sordid facts as my head had room for, and then I wanted to take a deep breath and explode with self-pity. And boy, would I explode. I drained my full glass and filled it up again, hoping the cellars here could cope with my sudden insatiable thirst.

'I want to know everything, Lottie.'

She sighed. 'Not much to tell, really. Apparently he eventually got her number from those friends they were discussing the other day, the people in Hampshire. Then he rang her up, took her out to supper—'

'Where?' It was important.

'Er, well, Le Caprice, I think,' said poor Lottie.

'*Le Caprice*!' Ouch! I caught that one right in the stomach. It fair doubled me up with pain. Never in my wildest dreams, and let me tell you, there had been some pretty wild ones – including holidays in Mustique, a

clothing allowance at Chanel, and sapphire eternity rings
– but never, *never*, had I ever dreamed that Harry might
take me to Le Caprice. He'd always been dead against
fancy – or should I say expensive – restaurants on
principle. All that money for a carrot cut into a flower?
And all those ridiculous service charges just because we're
sitting in Mayfair? Of course I'd been right behind him,
thinking there were much more important things for us to
spend his money on – like diamonds, for instance. Le
Caprice! I recovered from the body blow and lit a shaky
cigarette.

'Go on,' I gasped.

'Oh Polly, you don't want to know. I mean, it's obvious
really, isn't it? Dinner, coffee, back to his place . . .' She
tailed off miserably.

'But they definitely did it?'

'Of course they did it,' she said crossly. 'What, you
think they might have played Scrabble until dawn or
something? Of course they did it.'

All at once a little ray of hope scuttled across the dark
horizon. 'Well – well, maybe it's just a quick fling?
Perhaps he just fancied her rotten and felt like a spot of
how's-your-father? Because – because of course I haven't
been around much recently, you know, Lottie, I've been
very busy. In fact he tried to ring me at the flat yesterday,
but I wasn't there, but perhaps – perhaps now I'm back
he'll drop her like a cup of cold sick and – and come
running back to me? Maybe he just couldn't help himself?
Some men are like that, aren't they? What d'you think?'

Lottie narrowed her eyes as she blew smoke across the
table. 'Maybe.'

'You don't think so.'

She ground her cigarette out and sighed. She leaned
forward, perhaps imagining that the closer she got to me
the easier it would be to drum some sense into my skull.

'Look Polly, did he ever treat *you* as anything more

than a quick fling? I mean, I know you wasted nearly a year of your life on him, but how many times did you see him? About twenty? Thirty? Think about it, did you ever see him at weekends? Did you ever meet his parents? Did you ever go away together, even for a day or two, let alone a holiday? Did he ever give you anything – flowers, a birthday present, security, happiness, love, anything?'

I was shrinking down in my seat under this rain of bullets, each one hitting the spot. She saw my tortured face and stopped, although there was more.

'I'm sorry, Polly, I don't want to make it worse, but you've *got* to believe it. You can't keep hanging on to someone who was never even there in the first place and hope that this nobody is going to come back in order to give you precisely nothing. Think about it, please.'

I couldn't. All I could think about was Harry and how much I loved him, had always loved him, in fact, from the moment I'd first set eyes on him. I vaguely remembered someone else saying that to me recently. Of course, it was Adam, waxing lyrical on the grim-faced Rachel at Boston airport. My heart went out to him for a millisecond. I drained my glass again and tried to get my head round this nightmare. Harry and I were no more. Harry was seeing someone else. I'd been dumped. His future no longer contained me.

We drank the bottle and ordered another, Lottie drinking much less than me. An hour later I swayed out into the sunshine, blinking hard against the bright light, hoping I'd dulled the pain but knowing I hadn't. Lottie hugged me and shepherded me to a bus stop. She waited until a bus came along then hugged me again and put me on it, handing me sixty pence for my fare as if I were a child. I clutched the coins and walked shakily up to the top deck. I walked down the aisle very carefully, holding myself together like a piece of broken china. If I let go I might spill out all over the place. I made my way to the front and sat down.

London was still bathed in sunshine as we headed back West. Once again we passed Harry's office. I wondered how the exam had gone, and then remembered that it had been a lie. He'd been in bed with Caro. I got out my purse to pay my fare, forgetting that I was already clutching it. Harry's photograph stared at me from the credit card section. I took it out and rubbed some dust off with my finger. It wasn't even one that I'd taken: I'd found it lying around in a drawer in his flat and stolen it. He was lying on his tummy on a Greek beach, squinting slightly from the sun, laughing into the camera, brown and sandy and beautiful.

The tears began to fall. They started slowly at first, just a few trickles down the nose brushed hastily away with the back of my hand, and the odd catch in the throat that could be contained and might well be passed off as a touch of hay fever. But then the tears stopped being individual and became continuous rivers which flowed and flowed. I couldn't stop them, they got faster and faster and my hay fever got louder and louder until there was nothing I could do to control it. I was doing proper shoulder-shaking sobs now, heaving and gasping as I limbered up to reach fever pitch.

'Ooooooohhhhhh . . . hagh-hagh-hagh . . . oooohhhh-hoooo . . . hagh-hagh-hagh . . . ohohooooooooo . . .'

The top deck was full, but I didn't care. I let them have it, every single anguish-ridden decibel. The conductor avoided taking my fare, and I kept on shaking and sobbing all the way to Hyde Park Corner. Eventually a fat lady in a furry hat and tweed coat could bear it no longer. She came bustling down the gangway and plonked herself down next to me in the seat that no one else wanted. People were sitting on each other's laps, heads, feet — anything to avoid that seat.

She patted my hand and passed me a tissue. 'There, there, dear, it's all right, it's all right. You have a good cry.'

That's what I was doing, wasn't it? Christ, I was positively in overdrive, what on earth did she call a good cry? I was also at the talking-through-the-sobs stage now, wanting to share my grief with complete strangers, that kind of thing. It was lucky she'd volunteered to sit next to me, actually, otherwise I might have grabbed just anyone, like that terrified-looking teenager in the seat opposite, or the man next to him with his face hidden studiously in the newspaper. They could have been innocent victims.

'I-I-It's – hu hu, my bo-o-y frie – nd – hu hu, he's – hu hu hu hu hu he's—' I sobbed to tweedy lady, wondering if she could possibly stay on as far as my stop and then come home for tea.

'Your boyfriend, is it? There, there, dear, don't worry. He'll be all right, don't take on so,' said the lady, no doubt imagining horrific motorbike accidents or worse. 'Really now, he'll be fine, they can do marvellous things these days, what with medical science and that, don't you worry.'

Oh yes, he'd be fine, he'd be fine and dandy. But it wasn't him we had to worry about, was it? It was me. Would I make tomorrow? She rummaged in her oversized handbag and pulled out a crumpled paper bag.

'Here now, have one of these.'

She passed me a rather sticky peardrop. I took it, and as I sucked, my sobs seemed to subside slightly, rather like Jamie's did when he got to grips with his dummy. It was strangely soothing. I stared out of the window and she patted my hand saying, 'There, there, it's all right,' every now and then, which again was very comforting. They should employ ladies like this to tour the hospitals with their peardrops and their tweedy coats, patting the hands of people with real problems, like relatives of accident victims, girls whose boyfriends really had come off their motorbikes. Women like this should be available on the National Health.

When we reached my stop I stumbled blindly down the aisle to the steps and realised that about forty pairs of eyes were trained eagerly upon me. This must be a little like getting married. A little. Except that this particular congregation were craning their necks to get a better look at the girl who'd had the screaming heeby-jeebies on the bus. I imagined the scenes all over London tonight, in pubs with friends, at home with mum and dad, in the kitchen with hubby. 'Cor, bloody hell, there was this girl on our bus today who had a *fit*, a real *fit*, she did, all shoulder shaking and 'ysterical-like. Ooooh, it was *awful*.' I reckoned I'd done my bit for street theatre.

As I walked home I realised I was heading for Tregunter Road by mistake. So what? I simply turned round and headed for Kensington. It would take about an hour but what the hell? I had the rest of my life to fill, didn't I? The rest of my life without Harry. I looked at my watch, it was only three o'clock. I'd be hard pressed to make it through the rest of the afternoon, let alone a lifetime.

I walked up the Fulham Road, looking at the shops but not seeing anything. On and on I walked, until the shops gave way to tree-lined avenues, the sort of avenues Harry and I were to have lived in. How crazy I'd been, living on dreams. How idiotic of me, and how presumptuous to think that I could have held him. As I walked past a garden square, I noticed the gate was open. I went in and walked around it three or four times. The wind rustled through the trees overhead, and the sun was streaming down through the leaves making a dappled pattern on the grass. I thought of all the times we'd had together; they seemed to be illuminated by the sunlight. I'd never hear his footsteps pounding up the stairs to the flat again, I'd never roar off to supper in his car, I'd never feel that excitement, that passion. But I'd hear about him. Oh yes, I was sure of that. I'd hear about his exploits with Caro, or whoever came after Caro. I'd hear about the parties he'd been to, the fun he'd been having, and I'd want to hear because that way I'd feel I was still a part of his life. I'd want to torture myself.

I walked round the garden one more time, then headed off to Kensington. It was a warm spring day and I'd walked for miles but I felt very cold.

When I reached Pippa's house, I realised I didn't have a key. I rang the bell and Rachel opened the door. She stared at my ashen, tear-stained face in astonishment. I ignored her and walked slowly upstairs. I lay on my bed with my jacket on for about an hour, not really thinking about anything in particular, just staring at the ceiling. I heard the clock down the road strike four o'clock; a few seconds later another one struck. Odd how church clocks could never seem to get it together.

After a while there was a tentative knock on the door. It was Rachel with a cup of tea. She didn't say anything, didn't even ask what the matter was. She just sat on my bed while I drank it and then took the cup downstairs again. People could be kind, I thought, as I turned my face to the wall. The wallpaper was cream with a light green trellis pattern around which roses grew. I stared at the roses winding themselves around the trellis. My eyelids felt heavy. I didn't think I'd sleep, but I dropped off almost immediately, absolutely exhausted.

Chapter Twelve

I arrived for work the next morning looking like I'd just gone fifteen rounds with Mike Tyson. My eyes were like a couple of jam doughnuts — little red holes in bloated puffs, my lips had swollen out of all proportion, and my cheekbones had risen a good three inches. Pippa marched me in like a boxing manager with a prize fighter, glaring at everyone and daring them to comment. She needn't have bothered, it was rather like the parting of the Red Sea the way everyone ran for cover — disappearing behind doors, filing cabinets and photocopiers like frightened rabbits, anxious not to get involved. Of course, as the morning wore on their curiosity got the better of them, and they crept out, sidling up to my desk to borrow a paperclip or a stapler, bending low and sneaking what they imagined was a surreptitious look at my distorted face. I felt like the bearded lady at the fairground, and rummaged in my bag for the trusty sunglasses.

Joss and Ron were among the first to slide their bottoms on to my desk. They could smell boy trouble at fifty paces.

Joss took my hand and stroked it. 'Poor Polly.'

Ron found my knee and stroked that. 'Poor poor Polly,' he echoed, 'but we did warn you, darling, didn't we?'

'Oh indeed we did,' agreed the other half, 'we warned you time and again. We said, whatever you do, Polly, don't play with boys, they're very dangerous. We did say that, didn't we?'

I nodded miserably.

'And do you know why they're so dangerous, my darling?' persisted Ron.

I shook my head wearily.

'Well, I'll tell you. It's on account of the one-eyed trouser snake. Are you with me, Poll?'

I sighed and smiled weakly.

'Ay yes, I think you are, and I think you've been playing with one, haven't you? And we all know what happens to little girls who play with trouser snakes, don't we?'

Joss nodded sagely. 'They get bitten.'

'How right you are, Joss my boy, they get bitten. Best to leave well alone.'

'Become a nun,' suggested Joss. 'I like you in black.'

'Or a lesbian?' ventured Ron eagerly, seeing himself perhaps in the role of managing voyeur.

'Either will do,' agreed Joss, 'but that's all by the by. What you need right now, of course, is some nice casual sex with no strings attached.'

'In a hotel of your choice.'

'My choice,' corrected Joss.

'Not Sussex Gardens again?'

'Why not? Very discreet, sheets are clean, a Teasmade in the bedroom, what more could a girl ask for?'

'A little bit of style, Ronnie boy, that's what! Dear oh dear, we're not talking about one of your regular scrubbers, you know. Polly's got class, she's probably even been finished off at one of those flower-arranging places in Switzerland – Mummy does good works you know, Daddy plays bridge; she's not going to drop her drawers just anywhere!'

Ron held my other hand as I eventually shook him off my knee. 'Don't you listen to him, darling. He's got no idea, and you'd never get your rocks off anyway, you'd be up all night waiting for the earth to move and it wouldn't even shudder. He's all gong and no dinner, that one. No, no, you come with me. Ronnie boy knows the ropes. We'll sneak off after lunch for a bit of afternoon delight — I know a nice little flat in Tregunter Road, actually. About four o'clock suit you?'

I smiled weakly; they were doing their best to cheer me up. 'Thanks boys, some other time perhaps.'

'I've never had any complaints, you know,' said Joss in a mock injured tone. 'I may not be as young as your Harry, but I'm just as athletic, and I can always be relied on to rise to the occasion.'

My face crumpled slightly at the mention of his name. Joss noticed and quickly lit a cigarette for me before putting it in my mouth. 'Breathe deeply,' he commanded. I sucked gratefully. 'Drink?' he offered, taking a hip-flask out of his pocket. I shook my head, that really was the slippery slope.

'Bit of a lad, that Harry, wasn't he?' mused Joss, lighting one for himself and taking a quick swig of whisky. He had a faraway look in his eye and I detected a touch of admiration in his voice. 'Still, bit rotten of him to roger your flatmate. Too close to home.' I could tell he was deeply impressed. I sighed, Chinese whispers had started already.

'Not my flatmate, her sister.'

'Really? Oh, well that's all right then.' He sounded disappointed. 'Fair dinkum. What's she like?'

'Oh, you know, pretty, young, sexy, glamorous, big tits, nothing special,' I said bitterly.

Their eyes lit up. 'Really?' said Joss. Ron whistled softly. I looked up sharply. 'What a bastard,' he added quickly, shaking his head.

Nick strode through on his way to his office. 'James Hutchinson's coming in at twelve o'clock, so clear this place up, please. It looks like a pigsty.'

Joss and Ron raised their arms in Nazi-style salutes and goose-stepped back into their office. Nick reached his own door, then paused and came back to my desk. He took my sunglasses off and peered into the jam doughnuts.

'Jesus, not again, Polly. What have you been up to this time?'

'Gastric flu,' I said, snuffling hard and hastily replacing my glasses.

'Really? Gastric flu? Not alcohol-induced?'

I shook my head. My face wobbled violently: it seemed to be full of liquid. 'No,' I whispered.

'Well, shouldn't you be in bed then?' His voice was soft now, his face kind. Oh God, don't be nice to me, please don't be nice to me, I thought desperately.

'I'll struggle on,' I said bravely, digging my nails into my hand to stop myself from crying and wishing he'd revert to his usual SS tactics.

'I really think you should go home, you look awful. Shall I order a taxi?'

I couldn't reply to this without sobbing loudly and doing the nose trick all over the document in front of me, so I shook my head violently and hoped he wouldn't notice the tear, goddamnit, that had somehow escaped and was even now peeking out from behind my glasses and travelling down my cheek.

He noticed it. 'Harry?' he said simply.

I nodded briefly, surprised that he even knew his name, and not really feeling up to any more lying. I also hoped this would put an end to all the kindly concern and cause a few fuses to blow. It didn't. Instead he did something that reduced me to a shivering mass of jelly. He took a lovely clean white hanky out of his pocket, and wiped my tear away before handing it to me. 'Here.'

This sweet touch of humanity damn nearly did for me. I breathed deeply but it was no good: the inhaling part of the exercise was too shuddery. Great shaking sobs were building up in my breast and I clutched the side of the desk in horror. I must not break down, I must not break down!

I thought hard about unemotional things like the Chancellor of the Exchequer and the Hanger Lane Gyratory System and — and the Middle Ages; anything, in fact, that would help to keep the waterworks at bay. Nick began to look rather alarmed at the prospect himself: the odd tear, fine, but a full-scale flood was clearly a different matter.

He straightened up quickly and sensibly wiped the concern off his face. 'All I really need today is a working lunch for my meeting. D'you think you're up to arranging that?' he asked briskly.

'Oh yes, of course,' I gasped between shudders, glad to be back to normal office-speak and glad to have something to do. 'I'm um, feeling much better already actually.' I managed a wobbly smile. I'd feel even better if he could see his way clear to calling me a lazy good-for-nothing slut, but I supposed that was out of the question in his present mood.

'Good.' He nodded briefly and turned to go back to his office. He paused, and swept his hand around the room. 'Oh, and don't forget to do something about this hell hole.'

I breathed a sigh of relief. That was more like it, although a few more expletives here and there wouldn't have gone amiss. It was as if the hanky episode had never happened. This was the Nick I knew and — I hesitated. For some reason, 'hated' was too strong a word. I buried myself in my typing, wishing I'd never grown out of the dolls and ponies stage. Men were still such a mystery.

Mr Hutchinson arrived dead on twelve, looking even more rat-like than usual. He was panting slightly from climbing the stairs, but as I watched his mousy little chest palpitating up and down, I couldn't help wondering if he hadn't in fact just been for a nice little pedal in his wheel. His beady eyes darted around taking everything in, especially, it seemed, my battered face. His whiskery nose twitched with excitement, and he actually stood on tiptoe

217

to peer over my glasses. I straightened up to my full five foot three inches, which seemed to be more than he had to offer, and he lowered his heels admitting defeat.

'You're looking very mysterious today, Polly. Not trying to hide from me, are you?'

'Of course not, Mr Hutchinson,' I said, taking his paw which he'd held out for a shake. 'I'm just getting over the flu and my eyes are still a bit sensitive.'

Did one's eyes get sensitive? I always enjoyed such rude health I could never quite remember which symptoms went with what ailment, but Ratty didn't seem to want to query this. I relieved him of his grey coat, grey scarf and grey umbrella, and wondered briefly if his underpants were grey too. At least I didn't have to relieve him of those. Suddenly I felt a bit peculiar and wished I hadn't thought about that. I showed him into Nick's office.

'Would you like some tea?' I asked as the two men shook hands.

'Naughty, naughty Polly!' he remonstrated, waving a little claw in my face. 'You know I only drink coffee, don't you!'

'Oh yes, sorry. I'm afraid we're out of filter, though. We've only got instant muck at the moment. Is that OK?'

Mr Hutchinson's face froze. Behind him, Nick shook his head in despair before putting it in his hands. The rat's eyes were narrowing.

'Well I'd better have some instant muck then, hadn't I?' he said nastily.

I groaned and clutched my mouth. 'Oh gosh! No, sorry – um, no – I didn't mean Special Roasty, that's not muck, that's delicious, no – I – I meant something else, something really horrid that's been sitting in the cupboard for ages – I'll get you some Special Roasty right now.'

I disappeared in confusion. When I returned with the tray I didn't look at either of them. I set it down on the desk and scurried away. After all, I didn't really have to look: I could feel Nick's icy glare freezing into the very marrow of my bones.

'Well, I've lost my boyfriend, I might as well lose my job,' I said gloomily to Pippa as we arranged the cold roast beef for lunch on a plate in the tiny galley kitchen.

'Never. He's much too fond of you,' said Pippa, throwing a salad together.

'Fond of me? Don't be ridiculous,' I scoffed, although a white linen hanky did make a brief, fluttery appearance in my mind's eye.

'It's true, he thinks you're wild and wacky.'

'Oh terrific.'

'What's wrong with that? It probably makes a refreshing change from all those sophisticated models and actresses he usually hangs around with.'

'Thanks very much,' I said dryly. 'You mean he thinks I'm gauche and stupid.'

'Something like that . . . Where's the knife to cut this cheesecake with?'

I rummaged in the drawer. 'We've got about a million spoons and forks and no knives – here, use this.' I handed her Ron's scalpel which he used for cutting up layouts.

'Polly, that's hardly hygienic—'

'Oh don't be silly.' I ran it under the tap. 'Here, give it to me.'

She handed me the cake and I cut it into slices.

We deposited the lunch in Nick's office amid deep and turgid discussions about brand shares and meal figures, whatever they were. Once again I thanked my lucky stars that I hadn't been born bright enough to be a career girl. I perched on Pippa's desk and cut the split ends off my hair, wondering if I'd ever be happy again.

'Oh, by the way, Adam was here yesterday,' said Pippa absent-mindedly as she typed away.

I gasped and dropped the scissors. 'No! Was he? What here, in the agency? Pippa, why didn't you tell me?'

'I'm telling you now. You've been a bit preoccupied, you know.'

'What happened? Where was he, was he waiting outside? Pippa, stop typing and bloody well tell me what happened. It's all right for you; it's not your blood he's after!'

Pippa paused and swivelled round in her chair. 'Yes, he was waiting outside; well, pacing actually, stomping up and down like a caged animal, shaking that mane of red hair – incidentally, he's not my type at all, you know, you always get much redder pubes than you think you're going to with—'

'Go *on*, Pippa,' I urged. God, she always got so sidetracked.

'Anyway, he was pacing up and down, and – and shaking his head about like this –' she shook violently all over her word processor – 'like a rabid dog, in fact, and mouthing obscenities – well, what I assumed were obscenities. Honestly, Polly, if you ask me he's seriously disturbed. In fact he reminded me of a friend of my brother's who went really loopy when he came to stay with us one summer, started talking to himself and—'

'Pippa! What happened?'

'Oh well, eventually Mummy rang the hospital and the little men in white coats came to—'

'*No*! With Adam?'

'Oh. Oh, well the moment I arrived he pounced. He'd obviously pounced on everyone else as well, but he grabbed my arm like this –' she demonstrated with a sharp pincer grip on my arm; I suppressed a scream – 'and asked me if I worked with you. I said I did and funnily enough I'd spoken to you only last night. I said you'd telephoned to say that you wouldn't be in for a couple of weeks because you'd gone to stay with friends in the country.'

'Good girl. What did he say to that?'

'He grabbed my other arm like this — ' more demonstrations — 'and asked me who the friends were and where they lived. When I said I didn't know, he said perhaps I was lying and secretly shielding you. I tell you, it wasn't very pleasant. Anyway, just as he was about to draw the silken cord from his pocket and wrap it around my throat, Nick came flying to my rescue.'

'Seriously, was Adam getting aggressive?'

'Well, maybe not aggressive,' said Pippa grudgingly, 'but I must admit I was jolly glad when Nick appeared. Adam had a pretty loony look in his eye — that guy is definitely barking, Polly. Nick thought so too.'

'OK, OK,' I waved aside Pippa's amateur psychoanalysis. 'So what did Nick say?'

'Well of course he was slightly taken aback when he heard about your sudden departure to the country leaving him secretary-less.'

I groaned. 'Oh no!'

'But it was OK, he rose to the occasion beautifully and said how he wasn't really surprised because you'd been looking so tired recently and you probably needed a break—'

'Knowing it was a pack of lies?'

'I suppose so. I mean he didn't look surprised to see you this morning, did he? Anyway, he was brilliant, he even said Adam could sit in reception and wait for you if he liked, but he'd be waiting there for a couple of weeks. Of course Adam lapped it all up, coming as it did from a fellow man in a suit with a proper job rather than a mere secretary. I mean, talk about gullible. Anyway, he came up here just to make sure, had a good poke around, in fact,' she giggled, 'he even looked under your desk. Then eventually he sloped off, probably to slit his wrists; he looked capable of it.'

'Poor Adam. Did you tell Nick what it was all about?'

'Not really, I just said this guy was hounding you

because he thought you were hiding his girlfriend.'

'What did he say?'

'He shook his head and sighed and said, "You know, it really wouldn't surprise me," in a kind of resigned voice.'

'Oh God. He thinks I'm mad,' I said miserably, tapping Ron's scalpel on the desk.

'Probably, anyway then—'

'Pippa, look at this.'

'What?'

'The scalpel, look!'

She looked and grabbed it from me. 'The blade's missing!'

'Exactly.'

We stared at each other for a few seconds.

'It must have fallen off when you cut up the cheesecake,' she said slowly.

'So where is it now?'

I jumped off the desk and bolted to the kitchen. I ran my hand over the work surface looking for a small, but potentially lethal, razor-sharp blade.

Pippa peered into the sink. 'It could have gone down the plughole, couldn't it?'

'Unlikely,' I said, feverishly shaking out tea towels and dish cloths. We faced each other again, at the same time facing the awful truth.

'It must be in the cake!' I gasped.

We ran as one, as if we were tied together in a three-legged race, to Nick's door, and pressed our noses up against the small square of glass. Luckily Mr Hutchinson had his back to us. Nick spotted us and frowned but carried on talking, no doubt trying to pretend that it was quite normal for us to take such a keen interest in client meetings.

The roast beef had been demolished, as had the salad, but the cheesecake was still mercifully intact. But not for long. Still talking, Nick handed Mr Hutchinson a side plate, and then pushed the cheesecake towards him.

'Say no, say no,' I breathed. But how silly, of course he'd want some, after all, it was cheese, wasn't it? The little claw came shooting out cake-wards, but then, miraculously, paused in mid-plunge. It waggled around a bit as Mr Hutchinson no doubt decided it was time to put Nick straight on some highly important point, like how he was the client and it was his money so what he said went. Nick conceded, making a Prince Charles gesture with his hands and nodding his head. Mr Hutchinson sat back in his chair, pleased with his point, probably believing it was his superior intellect that had secured his victory rather than his dosh; at any rate, the cake was forgotten.

We breathed again, steaming up the glass somewhat. But too soon! Seconds later those ratty little taste-buds were reasserting themselves and, with a swift dart of the paw, Mr Hutchinson lunged forward and helped himself to the largest slice of the cake. It was too much for me. I flung open the door and in an equally swift movement removed both the cake from the table and the slice from Mr Hutchinson's hand. It was the work of a moment. Both men stared at me in astonishment, the client blinking away as if his life depended on it.

I laughed nervously. 'I'm so sorry, but it's off.'

'Off?' said Nick.

'Yes, it's bad, you know, gone off. Just had a call from the cake shop.'

Nick looked deadly. 'Polly, what on earth is going on?'

'It's past its sell-by date, you see — way past, in fact — months, years past. They forgot to tell me when I bought it, but they rang just now to let me know. So sorry! I'll take it back.'

'It can't be . . .' began Mr Hutchinson.

'It is, though. Weird, isn't it?' I gave him a synthetic little smile and fled, cake in hand.

Mr Hutchinson's voice trailed me. 'But it looks so delicious . . .'

I closed the door on him. OK, Nick was furious, but I'd rather incur his wrath than kill a client — just. I could see the headlines in *Campaign* next week. 'Secretary kills client — razor in cake.' I shuddered and ran into the kitchen, where Pippa and I inspected each slice like a couple of forensic scientists. We picked them over one by one and, sure enough, the last slice yielded a small, sharp, deadly blade.

'Thank God!' I cried, holding up Exhibit A in my fingers.

Just then the kitchen went dark. I looked up to see Nick's large frame filling the doorway. I instantly dropped the blade in the sink.

'Have you gone quite mad?' he barked, striding over to me. I pressed the cake back into his hands, thus keeping a cake plate's distance between us. It was still too close for comfort. The glare from those eyes was enough to make me want to reach for my sunglasses again.

'Oh Nick, it was all a terrible mistake!' I blurted out. 'The cake shop just rang to say it wasn't our cake that was stale at all, it was somebody else's! They'd got it wrong, isn't that marvellous? So we can eat it after all!' I grabbed a piece and crammed it into my mouth. 'MMmmmmmmm, oh yesh, mmmmm, delishious!' I said, spitting crumbs all over the place and rolling my eyes to demonstrate its delectability.

Nick stared at me in disbelief, but I did wonder if around the mouth region there wasn't just the hint of a flicker of a ghost of a — no, perhaps not.

'I'll speak to you later, Polly,' he snapped. He turned on his heel, cake in hand, and marched back into his office closing the door very firmly behind him.

I staggered back into the pit and fell reeling into my seat. I felt like I'd gone through a mangle. This was all I needed, today of all days. I hadn't even had much time to indulge in some serious self-pity it had been so chaotic. Maybe I should take advantage of Nick's earlier suggestion and go home, stopping off en route to jump in the Thames. At least if I were dead he'd have to think of some nice things to say about me to my parents at the funeral. I sighed. I didn't really want to die, I just wanted to press a fast forward button and be about two months, or two years, hence. I couldn't really go home, anyway: Nick was going away for two weeks on Thursday and there was still masses to do before he went. At least then I could have a break.

I switched on to autopilot and bashed away at the keyboard, wishing it was Caro's face. Perhaps I should have kept my suntan going? Had a few sunbeds? I'd been so brown when I'd met Harry, he'd liked that. Did Caro have an all-over tan, perhaps? I bet she did. I snarled and thumped the keys viciously, well on the way to giving her severe brain damage. I tried to look on the bright side. No need to have my hair highlighted quite so often, ease up on the leg waxing too, I thought. At least I'd be marginally richer — and marginally darker haired and hairier legged too. Yes, really attractive, Polly, just the right combination to catch a new man. But whatever was I thinking of? New man? Good Lord, no, I was in mourning. Odd though, how in the very, very back of my mind — and we're talking archives here — there was just the remotest, almost non-existent feeling of, how shall I put it — relief? Now why was that? Because I didn't have to jump every time the telephone went? Because I didn't have to arrange my life in such a way that everything could be cancelled at the last minute in case he called? No, surely not, it was — good grief, what on earth was that noise?

I looked up from the battering I was giving Caro and cocked my ear in the direction of reception. There was the most almighty commotion going on out there. Probably Josie the receptionist arguing with yet another salesman, I thought. I thought wrong. Because at that moment the door flew open and in strode Adam, looking, as Pippa had so rightly put it, seriously disturbed.

Josie appeared behind him, red in the face and flustered, her glasses slipping off her nose. 'I'm sorry, Polly, I couldn't stop him!'

Adam was terribly pale and hollow-eyed and his lips were thin and bloodless. It made quite a contrast with the red hair. He was almost unrecognisable as the healthy, sparkly-eyed, all-American jock of a week or so ago. A muscle in his cheek was pulsating away at an alarming rate, and I instinctively rose from my chair, realising that a little fast running might well be in order.

He was over to my desk in a second. 'Where is she?' he said in a dangerously quiet voice.

'I – I don't know.' I whispered back, equally quietly, but not in a dangerous way, more in a bloody terrified way.

Adam slammed two large, freckled hands the size of meat plates down on my desk. It seemed to me that on the back of one hand was written the word 'Polly's' and on the other 'neck'. The fingernails were white with pressure, the same pressure which would soon, no doubt, be transferred to my swan-like. He was just limbering up. Pressure applied, my head would come popping off like an easy blackhead – one of those really ripe ones that's been brewing up nicely for a couple of days – just a little bit of a squeeze and – pop! Off it would come, highlights and all, and over the desk it would fly before landing neatly in that conveniently open filing cabinet over there – plop!

I sensibly backed away, self-preservation high on my list of priorities now, all previous ideas about throwing myself in the Thames long forgotten. I wanted to live. I forced my eyes up from the freckly, murderous hands to the cold bloodless lips.

'You bitch,' he breathed.

'Now don't be like that, Adam,' I muttered.

'You're going to tell me where she is, Polly. I know you know, and you're damn well going to tell me, because if you don't I'm going to break your fucking *neck*!'

I knew it, I just knew it would be my neck. I was frightened, bloody frightened. He had a clenched calmness about him that terrified me. I was also dimly aware that I should try and talk him out of anything untoward, that was the received wisdom on dealing with rapists and murderers, wasn't it?

'Now look here,' I squeaked, 'killing me won't solve anything you know. It's — it's pointless and futile and — and totally counter-productive, it's been proved many times and, and — well, it just won't get you anywhere!'

Adam's eyes glazed over. The thought had obviously not occurred to him as yet, but now it was right up there amongst the grey cells where I'd so thoughtfully lobbed it. Hmmm . . . murder, yes of course, that was undoubtedly the answer; thanks, Polly. To this end, one of the freckled meat plates inched forward on the desk and closed slowly round a rather sharp-looking paper-knife that I'd been careless enough to leave lying around. I whimpered. Oh God, yes — that was for my heart. Any minute now he'd raise it above his head and then plunge it into my breast with a Tomahawk screech — HAYACK!! I wondered how far the blood would spurt, over to the photocopier perhaps? As far as the window? And who would clear it up afterwards, Pippa? Josie? Probably Pippa I decided, sobbing wildly.

Knife in hand, Adam took two slow steps to the left, advancing round the desk. I mimicked him perfectly, but cannily took my two steps in the opposite direction, thereby keeping the desk well and truly between us. He took another to the left, I jumped to the right. We occupied diagonal corners now. He paused, then — three to the right! Off I went to the left! Then two to the left! I hopped to the right! Left! Right! Right! Left! I was squeaking with terror but keeping in step like a sort of manic Ginger Rogers. He was dancing up a storm, but I was with him every step of the way, my heart banging away like a demented dinner gong.

A small corner of my terrified mind wondered how the rest of the agency were taking this drama. A quick peek was enough to ascertain that they were taking it 'from behind'. Pippa and Josie were 'behind' the photocopier, Jason was 'behind' a large potted cheeseplant, and Ron and Joss were peering out from 'behind' their door. They could smell the blood all right but, understandably, didn't particularly want to get it on their hands. Thanks, guys, I thought grimly.

Adam and I paused briefly as we once again occupied diagonal corners of the desk. I licked my lips and addressed myself bravely to his steely stare, totally devoid of any of the old Savoy sparkle.

'Look Adam, can't we talk about this sensibly? I mean, it's crazy to behave like wild animals, anyone would think we were— Aaaah!'

I screamed as a mighty great hand came crashing down on the desk, sending papers flying and my fellow members of staff running for even more cover.

'CUT THE CRAP POLLY AND JUST TELL ME WHERE SHE IS! OK? JUST TELL ME!' he bellowed at the top of his voice.

'I – I don't know, I really don't,' I yelped, experiencing a curious loss of confidence in the leg department: they were decidedly wobbly and I hoped fervently that all the dancing was over for today. I was also acutely aware that my deodorant wasn't all it was cracked up to be.

Adam leaned across the desk. 'You do know,' he said, softly now – I infinitely preferred the bellowing – 'and you're damn well going to tell me, because if you don't, I'm going to kill you. Do you understand?'

'She's — she's at her father's,' I lied.

'DON'T LIE!' Christ, he was quick, but then I've never claimed to be a good liar, just a prolific one.

'Well, OK, yes — yes, you're right. I just sort of said that really, she's not at her father's at all, she's er, she's er . . .' Yes, that was it, I'd just carry on saying 'she's er' and something would eventually crop up. He'd get bored, it would be time to go home, the phone would ring, the police would arrive, the building would collapse. 'She's er, she's er,' I muttered — and something did happen. He lunged across the desk towards me and grabbed hold of my hair, yanking my face towards him.

'AAAAAAHHHHHHH!!' I screamed with terror, loud and shrill, and as I did so, Nick's door flew open. There he stood, a veritable God of War in a Savile Row suit. If anything he looked even more terrifying than Adam. I fervently hoped I'd die of shock and wouldn't have to experience the next ten minutes.

'WHAT THE HELL IS GOING ON?' he thundered.

Adam dropped my hair for a split second, but it was just split enough for me. I seized my chance and legged it, scuttling off in the direction of Nick's broad back. I just wanted to run up those grey flannelled legs, duck under the jacket, and scurry across the blue-and-white striped shirt until I got to the armpit where I would adopt the foetal position and snuggle down with my thumb in my mouth for the next hour or so. Instead I shot around the un-Adamed side of him and cowered behind his beautiful, broad, oh so welcome, grey suited back. And there I stayed not glued, but welded.

'Please leave,' he said to Adam, in what would appear to an innocent bystander to be a reasonable voice, but which was in fact his most lethal. He walked forward. I walked too, shadowing his every move, although why we were going forwards rather than backwards was a mystery to me. He clenched his fists, I clenched mine — you see I'd lost my identity. We were one and the same now, Nick and Polly. A Nolly.

'Come on,' he said, jerking his head towards the door, 'out you go.'

'Not until I've talked to Polly,' said Adam, advancing towards us.

'PLEASE LEAVE THE BUILDING NOW OR I'LL CALL THE POLICE!' Nick strode towards the telephone, I strode too, it was poetry in motion, and as I went I admired the exquisite tailoring at the back of his jacket; anything to keep my eyes off Adam. I was riveted, never have I seen such stitching. Nick had his hand on the phone. There was an eerie silence. Eventually I dragged my eyes away from the grey flannel and took a peek at Adam.

His face was crumpled and wretched. He caught my eye. 'Polly, please!' he said, stretching out a hand and changing tactics dramatically. 'Please, just let me talk to you for a minute, just for a minute. I promise I won't hurt you,' he pleaded.

I felt for him, really I did, but what could I do? I had to stand by Rachel and, besides, I was yellow through and through. I averted my eyes, and in doing so caught a glimpse of the rat, peering out of Nick's office. His little nose was twitching away and his glasses were steaming up with excitement. This was probably the closest he'd ever got to a thrill in his whole life.

Nick picked up the receiver. 'I'm going to give you ten seconds to leave this office and then I'm calling the police. One, two, three, four—'

'OK, OK.' Adam raised his hands in defeat. 'I'm going. But you haven't heard the last of this, oh God no. I'll be back, Polly, you can be sure of that. I'll find my son, don't you worry, I'll find him whatever it takes!' His voice cracked with emotion.

He turned to go, raising his hands again in a despairing gesture. They fell limply to his sides. He looked utterly destroyed. I counted to ten before looking again, and was just in time to see his back disappearing out of the door. It slammed behind him.

A tense silence fell. Nick eventually broke it. He turned to Mr Hutchinson and smiled. 'I'm sorry about that, James. As you can see, Polly has an extremely persistent suitor on her hands, but I'm sure he's got the message now. Shall we continue?' he said, motioning him back into his office with his hand.

Mr Hutchinson reluctantly sidled back into the room looking hugely disappointed. No rape, no blood, no murder – shame. He'd have to revert to slowing down on motorways to view the accidents.

The two men disappeared but, as the door was about to close, Nick stuck his head around it and gave me a meaningful look. 'When I've finished my meeting, Polly, I want to talk to you.' With that he shut the door.

I clutched my desk, lowering myself carefully into my chair. Oh God, that was awful, truly awful. I felt positively ill.

My colleagues gathered around me now, like bees at a honey pot: exclaiming, commiserating, wondering, shrieking, gabbling; glad of a chance to tell me now how they'd been right behind me all the way, straining to hold themselves back from leaping to my defence. Indeed, it was a mystery to most of them how they'd managed to control themselves. I listened to their excited chatter in silence, taking the occasional swig of whisky from a hip flask and dragging a whole cigarette down in one. I wondered if I'd ever be the same again.

Josie was the first to mention the unmentionable. 'Do you think he'll sack you now, Polly?' she said, wide-eyed behind her specs. 'Do you think you've really done it this time?'

'I'd say it's probably a safe bet, Josie,' I said weakly. 'I wouldn't open a book on it, put it, that way.'

'I mean, this is probably the worst thing that's ever happened to you here, isn't it?' she persisted, eyeing my desk somewhat covetously, 'and in front of Mr Hutchinson too!'

I sighed. 'Yes, Josie, I think you're probably right — and rest assured, you'll be the first to hear about it should my position become vacant.'

Eventually they drifted away and I sat out the rest of the afternoon in a daze while Pippa did all my typing for me in silence. It was bad news when she couldn't think of anything comforting to say.

At about four-thirty I showed Mr Hutchinson to the door, dressing him up once again in the grey ensemble. He lingered, keen to discuss the afternoon's events, but I shook him firmly by the paw and practically bundled him down the stairs. Then I walked meekly into Nick's office, head bowed, poised thus for the guillotine to fall.

Through the glass in the door I could see the gang assembling at my desk as they waited for the verdict. Ron had even rustled up a few bottles of red wine. Presumably this bevy was intended to soften the blow, but they appeared to be cracking into it already. Josie had brought her knitting along; she sat in my chair, legs crossed, glasses slipping down her nose, clicking away like a true tricoteuse.

I sat down on one end of the sofa and stared at my shoes. Nick got up from his usual position behind his desk and sat down next to me, obviously favouring the softly-softly approach. He scratched his head and sighed, no doubt wondering how to phrase this without provoking a fresh flood of tears. He looked at his watch. 'Look, Polly, I haven't really got time to talk to you now because I'm supposed to be in a meeting outside the agency in a few minutes, but I'll tell you what. Book a table for lunch somewhere tomorrow and we'll talk about it then, OK?'

I looked up in surprise. 'Oh no, it's OK, that's not

necessary, really. Just do it now and I'll go, really, it's no problem.'

'Do what?'

'Well, you know, aren't you going to fire me?'

He looked exasperated. 'No, I'm not going to fire you. Not yet, anyway — don't tempt me. But what I would like to know is why you arrive at work looking like you've been beaten up, tell our most important client his product is shit, try to kill him with a razor blade in a cake, and then encourage some bulging biceped American to throw his weight around in here, frightening the life out of my staff, not to mention my clients!'

I opened my mouth to begin some form of convoluted explanation (oh God, he'd spotted the scalpel blade), but he held his hand up and shut his eyes firmly, staunching the inevitable flow.

'Not now! Not now. Please, Polly.' He opened one eye cautiously. 'Not now. Tomorrow, at lunch. Book a table somewhere.'

'But Nick—'

'Just do it, will you?' he said desperately, getting to his feet. 'For once in your life could you please just do as I say?'

I stared at him, totally at a loss. A table? Lunch? Was this a stay of execution? And was the interview truly over? Had I somehow survived? I obviously had. Nick raced around the room grabbing documents, files, a pen, his coat, then he departed in a flurry of tweed, briefcase flying, leaving me sitting there to ponder my good fortune.

We were to have lunch tomorrow. Just the two of us, me and the man who loathed taking clients out to expense-account lunches, let alone members of staff. To talk things over, he had said, not to hand me my P45. I breathed again and, in a fit of gratitude, slipped off the black leather sofa and went down on my knees on the grey flecked carpet. I shut my eyes tight.

'Oh please God,' I whispered passionately, hoping He remembered me, 'please don't let me cock it up. Please let me get my story straight, don't let me get it all arse about tit as usual. I've lost my boyfriend — that's Harry,' I added quickly, in case He'd missed his brief appearances — 'but please, oh please, don't let me lose my job too. It's all I've got!'

There was a loud click as the door handle went down and I looked up from my position on my knees to see Nick's startled face peering round the door. He slipped his hand in, grabbed his umbrella from the hat stand, clocked the born-again Christian but, wisely, made no comment. Then he disappeared, shutting the door quietly behind him.

I sighed, got to my feet, and went in search of some communion wine.

Chapter Thirteen

That night I paid a brief visit to my own flat and gathered together everything Harry had ever given me. Needless to say, it didn't take long. Theoretically I was going to throw everything associated with Harry straight in the bin, thereby exorcising him from my heart for ever – a cathartic exercise. Practically, of course, I didn't quite have the guts to go through with it, so instead I decided to parcel everything up, hide it away somewhere and completely forget about it. Then, one day in the far distant future, I'd be turning the flat upside down looking for something like my birth certificate – I'd probably need it to get married or something – and while I was searching I'd chance upon the Harry bundle and have a good old chuckle as I recalled my silly, love-struck, misspent youth. That would be in about one hundred and fifty years' time. Right now, before I hid it away, I was going to have a good old blub over my pathetic little pile of memorabilia, and even I had to admit that 'little' was the word.

First, I dripped copious tears over the two paperbacks he'd given me for Christmas, stroking their covers and marvelling at the vast number of pages – he really could be quite generous. One was called *Cookery for Morons* which I'd thought a huge joke, but which Lottie had insisted was about as subtle as an air-raid and the other was *The Vogue Book of Beauty Tips*, which on reflection wasn't much better, especially since he'd inscribed the inside front cover with, 'Happy Christmas, Polly, Read, learn and have a go, especially Chapter Eleven! Love Harry xxx.' Chapter Eleven was entitled, 'Say Goodbye to Cellulite'. Charming. I sighed, placed the books neatly in the cardboard shoebox I'd enlisted to act as the coffin, and turned my attention to my one and only love letter.

This treasured missive had been hastily scrawled on a scrap of paper and slipped under the flat door one evening when I was out. It was short, but very sweet. It read: 'Called round on the off chance, sorry to have missed you, love Harry.' Now I have to admit that, as love letters go, it wouldn't stand up to too much scrutiny in an Oxford anthology, if there is such a thing, but as with most pieces of literature, there were two ways of looking at it. Oh yes. On the one hand you could read it straight, as I have just demonstrated; but the subtle, more imaginative way, was to fold it in half, thus eliminating the first nine words. This revealed something altogether more romantic, namely, 'missed you, love Harry', and since this was of course the deep, implicit meaning behind the note anyway, it really wasn't cheating at all. Funnily enough, this was my favourite interpretation, so much so that the note was in danger of falling apart, so often had I creased it down the middle.

I smoothed it out now and placed it on top of the books, remembering how Lottie had snorted with laughter when I'd seized it on our way in from the pub, jumping around the flat with excitement, the evidence of my man's love waving around in my hot little hand.

'On the off-chance of what?' she'd scoffed. 'On the off-chance that you might be on for a quick one?'

I sighed. Poor Lottie. She really did have a very cynical outlook. It must be something to do with being a solicitor.

I turned to my next piece of correspondence from Harry – golly, I'd quite forgotten what a prolific letter writer he'd been – a carefully chosen scenic postcard featuring a mountain range complete with chairlift. It read: 'Pissed again on the piste, chalet girls are brilliant . . . cooks! Love Harry.' Gosh he was funny. How I'd laughed when I'd received that. I placed it a trifle grimly on my motley pile, deciding on balance that the letter under the door was far more touching and much more — well much more *Harry* really.

Then I turned to the jewellery collection. Surprised? Oh yes, Harry had given me jewels. The choice had been a little unfortunate, I admit, since the silver (hallmarked, I checked) earrings had in fact been designed to go through pierced ears, which I do not possess. Tainting the earrings even more was the faintly disturbing but highly unreliable piece of gossip that these very same baubles had once dangled from the pierced lobes of a previous girlfriend, which suggested to some people — but not to me — that the ex had left them behind in Harry's flat and he'd simply recycled them. The very idea! More unbridled cynicism. No, no, these earrings had been chosen for me, by Harry, with me and me alone in mind. OK, I couldn't wear them, but I could polish them, couldn't I? I gave them a quick rub on my jumper to prove it and placed them carefully in the box.

To this now burgeoning treasure trove I added the butt of the cigarette he'd smoked when we'd first made love — I'd retrieved it from the ashtray the next morning — and a cutting from his Busy Lizzie plant, which unfortunately had failed to re-root. OK, it had died, only I'd never liked to think of it in such bald terms before, in case it had been symbolic in some way; but what did it matter now? It had been lovingly pressed for posterity, and I laid it like a wreath on top of the correspondence.

Now there was, I'm ashamed to say, one last memento to add to this collection. A pickled kidney stone. Harry had passed it in acute agony in the loo at his flat about two months ago, amid rather a lot of unmanly screaming. I hadn't really thought about it at the time, but I thought about it now and, my God, he'd screamed. Anyway, once he'd passed it, he'd fished it out, washed it, and together we'd inspected it, marvelling at how such a small thing could cause such pain. He'd been about to throw it down the loo again when I'd piped up with the idea of keeping it, well – actually with the idea of *me* keeping it. He'd found the concept hugely amusing, but had graciously handed it over, and even gone to the lengths of providing me with an old jam jar and some vinegar to pickle it in. Unfortunately, within a matter of days it had gone rather a funny colour, what you might call diarrhoea yellow, and had disintegrated slightly. Perhaps I should have held out on the pickling front until I'd got home and used white wine vinegar instead of Sarson's malt. I hadn't liked to suggest it at the time for fear of sounding like a vinegar snob. I placed the jar carefully in the box.

Now that the collection was complete, I put the lid on and tied a red ribbon around it, sobbing quietly. Actually, my tears made a rather nice effect on the cardboard, and I squeezed out a few more, admiring the distressed – literally – look I'd achieved. Eat your heart out Jocasta Innes, I thought as I placed it tenderly at the very back of my wardrobe under a pile of dirty washing. I was quite sure I wouldn't stumble upon it there for a very long time.

Now for the gallery. This consisted of five, or was it six? Yes, six enlarged photographs of guess who, arranged in a haphazard manner on the ceiling above my bed – it had been my way of kidding myself that I woke up with him every morning. There was Harry smiling, Harry pouting, Harry laughing, Harry working, Harry frowning (sexily), and Harry looking moody. I ruthlessly dragged them down, taking care not to damage any part of his gorgeous anatomy, and shoved them unceremoniously under the bed. I also removed the large black-and-white portrait photo from my bedside table and, devil that I am, even managed to flick a rather half-hearted two fingers at it before hurling it under the bed. I instantly regretted it and dragged it back out, pressing my face ardently to his and whispering – didn't mean it, didn't mean it, didn't mean it – before pushing it back under the bed again.

Safely back at Pippa's an hour later, I crawled into bed feeling exhausted. I'm ashamed to report that, during the night, I was ambushed by tears yet again. I tried to beat them back and failed, but at the end of the day it was no bad thing, because I woke up feeling so ghastly I resolved never to shed a tear over a man ever again. So when Jamie had a sobbing fit at the breakfast table and threw his marmite fingers around the room, I sympathised, but didn't automatically feel like joining in as I had yesterday. A major step forward.

Buoyed up by my new attitude, I set off for work feeling a weeny bit tougher. Positive thinking was definitely the answer. One just had to think happy. Mind over matter.

Unfortunately, I was so engrossed in my positive thoughts that I clean forgot to book a table for lunch. It wasn't until twelve o'clock that I remembered and spent a frantic ten minutes ringing round all the local watering holes, desperate for a table. The only place that would agree grudgingly to squeeze us in was San Frediano's in the Fulham Road. Great fun though this teeming joint is, it's hardly conducive to impressing one's boss and hanging on to one's job, but it was the last resort, so I took it.

'What's this place like?' asked Nick as we walked down the Fulham Road twenty minutes later.

'Oh it's great, the food's good and it's got plenty of, um – ' I groped for the right word – 'atmosphere.'

In fact the atmosphere greeted us right around the next bend, before we'd even set foot in the place. A taxi screeched to a halt outside and the driver flung open the door with a flourish, glad to be shot of his cargo of four or five half-cut secretaries, who tumbled out on to the pavement, shrieking with laughter. They pushed past us and poured through the restaurant door. Nick stood aside and raised his eyebrows, but didn't say a word.

He held the door open for me and a terrific barrage of noise hit us full in the face. 'Are you sure you booked, Polly?' he shouted, pitting his voice against the braying and shouting. 'This place looks full to bursting.'

'Oh, definitely,' I yelled back, grabbing the nearest laughing cavalier waiter, complete with whiskers, by the arm.

'McLaren,' I yelled, 'table for two!'

He knew better than to waste his breath and compete with the noise level, but nodded and grinned widely before showing us to a table about the size of a postage stamp, right next to the very same typing-pool party we'd encountered in the street.

Nick lost his patience. 'Don't you have anything quieter?' he barked.

The cavalier grinned even more widely, and threw his arm demonstratively around the gobbling, gabbling throng, as if we might somehow have overlooked the crowd scene. 'So sorry, signor, fully booked!' he beamed, glowing with pride, lira signs shining in his eyes. 'But,' he added, tapping his nose conspiratorially, 'for young lovers – ' I cringed deeply – 'I find more room. I find somewhere more private!'

With that he took a firm hold on our postage stamp and moved it a good nine inches away from the hen party. 'There!' he said, standing back and admiring his handiwork as if he'd miraculously discovered a private room. 'Now you have plenny room to tell her how much you love her!'

I cringed some more and Nick sat down, resigned. 'Really, Polly, couldn't you have booked somewhere a little less "atmospheric", or do you have to live your life in a permanent disco?'

240

'Sorry,' I mumbled. 'I left it a bit late.'

I crunched maniacally on a bread stick like a demented rabbit. Not a very auspicious start. I also realised that I was unaccountably nervous, sitting here in what one might call a social setting, with my knees about a millimetre away from my incredibly anti-social boss's. I tried to remember if we'd ever had a conversation that didn't begin with something like, 'Dear Sir, Please find enclosed . . .'

Nick's face was only about a foot away from mine, and suddenly I wished I was looking a bit more presentable. I bore a startling resemblance to Chairman Mao, what with the slitty eyes, puffy cheeks and greasy hair plastered attractively to my head: I hadn't washed it since Black Monday – what was the point?

I ran my hand through the limp curls, trying to fluff a bit of life into them, and knocked over our table arrangement with my elbow. A glass vase containing a solitary carnation smashed noisily on the floor. The hen party freeze-framed for a second, then burst into hysterical giggles, pointing and whispering.

The cavalier arrived and brushed it away, instantly replacing it with another. 'You nervous!' he whispered in my ear. 'Ees OK, he love you!'

I blushed hotly and made a mental note never to patronise this restaurant again. Luckily Nick had missed this little aside, but he was beginning to look irritated. 'Polly, just relax, will you? What on earth's wrong with you? You're jumping around like a frog in a bucket.'

'Sorry.'

'And stop apologising all the time.'

'Sorry.'

He shook his head in bewilderment and addressed himself to the menu as the waiter arrived. I ordered the cheapest salad available, not wanting to look like a lunch tart.

'Are you sure that's all you want? Just a salad?'

'Yes, thank you.'

'Well, I'll have a rare fillet steak please, with french fries, and we'll have a bottle of house red.' He handed back the menu.

'Now then.' He folded his arms on the table and leaned forward, which wasn't easy given the limited surface area. His brown eyes bore into mine, but they were kind and encouraging. 'Suppose you tell me what's been going on recently?'

I was afraid we might get around to this, but hadn't envisaged getting around to it quite so quickly. Couldn't we limber up with a bit of friendly repartee first, just to remind ourselves how it was done? Christ, I hadn't even got a glass of wine to slurp on.

'Oh, nothing really,' I said, shifting around miserably in my seat and doing a spot of origami with the paper napkin. What did he want to hear? And in my view that was all that mattered. It was no good getting all honest if it was going to backfire me down to the dole queue.

'Come on, Polly, I'm not that much of an ogre, am I?' I looked up from the shredded napkin and thought I hadn't seen a kinder face in a good long time. But it was no good. He was my boss, and we'd never enjoyed a think-of-me-as-a-normal-human-being sort of relationship, so how the hell did he expect me to start now? I shifted about a bit more, but the brown eyes held their unwavering beam and I knew he wouldn't be easily deterred. I reached for my comfort pack, lit one, and took a deep breath of nicotine.

'OK, where would you like me to start?' I ventured, thinking birth might not be a bad idea if he wanted a catalogue of disasters.

'How about starting with the obsessive redhead?'

Oh yes, him. Nick was obviously still under the impression that Adam was hounding me for my body. I suppose he was, in a way, except that he wanted to cut it up into little pieces and scatter them around the countryside. I could at least put him straight on that score.

I embarked on the Rachel and Adam saga, telling it exactly how is was with no exaggerations or embellishments or what other people call lies.

Nick listened intently, chewing thoughtfully on his steak. When I'd finished he paused and pushed a few peas around before looking up at me. 'That's quite a story, Polly.'

'But it's true!' I said indignantly.

'Oh, I believe you, don't worry.' He wiped his mouth with his napkin. 'Not even a consummate liar like yourself could make up something as outrageous as that. And don't look so miserable, it's not totally your fault, you acted with the best intentions. How were you to know there was a baby involved?'

'Exactly!' Whew. One tiny Brownie point.

'Bloody stupid to get mixed up in all this in the first place, though.' He had to spoil it, didn't he? 'Why couldn't you have left him to sort his love life out for himself? Did you fancy him or something?'

'Certainly not!' I said, bristling. 'I felt sorry for him, he struck me as − as an innocent abroad,' I added piously.

Nick threw back his head and roared with laughter. 'Oh God, Polly, you're so theatrical! An innocent abroad? That guy looked about as innocent as Crippen. Didn't you notice the murderous glint in his eye or the mean and twisted mouth? I suppose those little details escaped you at the time: no doubt you were quaffing buckets of champagne down at the Savoy, were you?'

'The champagne had nothing to do with it!' I said hotly. 'If you must know I hardly touched a drop. I − I just helped him out of the goodness of my heart.'

'Ah I see, just another of your philanthropic gestures.' He grinned. 'OK, Polly, don't get in a bate, I'm just mobbing you up. So what are you going to do now?'

'Do? What d'you mean?' Was there still *more* I had to

243

do? Why was it always *me* who had to do the doing? Couldn't someone else do something for a change?

'Well, she can't stay at Pippa's for ever, and neither can you. How long do you imagine that arrangement can tick along for?'

I sighed. 'I don't know, really. As long as Pippa will put up with us, I suppose. She's being very good about it, but it's playing havoc with her love life.' I thought of poor Charles.

'Doesn't Rachel have any plans?'

'Well, her latest idea is to go and live in Paris.'

'Why Paris?'

'Because that's where her friend Sally Lomax lives, the one I was telling you about who was supposed to have written the letter. Of course, she can't actually stay with Sally, because Adam knows where she lives, but she's asked her to find a flat for her.'

'That sounds like quite a good plan, but who would finance all this? Has she got money?'

'Oh, that's no problem, her father's loaded and she's an only child. Thing is, though, finding a spare flat in Paris takes time; people kill for accommodation over there. I could have her on my hands for weeks.'

'And the idea is to stay at Pippa's till then?'

'It's not ideal, I agree.'

'It certainly isn't. He's only got to follow you home one night, and you've had it.'

I didn't care for the macabre way this was put. Did he mean 'had it' in the sense that dead meat has had it?

'Have you got any better suggestions?' I snapped, irritated that all he'd done so far was put the fear of God into me.

Nick wiped his mouth with his napkin and stared into space, well, not space actually, more like the top of my head where I'm sure my dark roots were flourishing wildly, springing wantonly from my head, untouched by human hairdresser's hands for many a long month.

'Hmmm . . . I'm not sure,' he mused thoughtfully. I waited meekly for the oracle to speak. I fidgeted a bit. He was taking his time and I can only be meek for so long.

'Look, Nick, it's nice of you to take an interest, but the fact is it's my problem and I'll have to deal with it. I'm sure I—'

'Hang on, hang on, you're always so bloody impatient. If you must know, I do have an idea. I'm just trying to work out how to orchestrate it.'

'Oh, really? What is it then?'

Nick finally dragged his eyes away from my roots and fixed me with his piercing beam.

'You know I have a house in Cornwall, don't you?'

Christ, what did this have to do with anything – and no, I didn't know actually, was I supposed to? Was it in my job description or something: always keep a tally of the number of houses your employer owns. How the hell *should* I know, when he played his cards so close to his chest?

'Oh yes,' I mumbled, nodding inanely.

He went a bit misty-eyed. 'I grew up there, it's been in my family for years. It's nothing special really, just a rambling old farmhouse by the sea, probably in imminent danger of falling into the sea it's so run-down, but I love it . . .'

He stared into his wine and I shifted about again. I mean, I was very pleased for him and all that, but what the hell did his idyllic Cornish childhood have to do with keeping wolf-man from the door?

'Tim, my brother, lives there during the week with his girlfriend, and I go down at weekends to make sure the farm's ticking over.'

'The farm?'

'Yes, I said it was a farmhouse, didn't I?'

'Yes, but I thought you meant a sort of converted one. I

didn't imagine it had a proper farm attached.'

'Oh yes, in full working order. In fact, you're looking at the farmer.'

I gagged on my lettuce. 'You! A farmer? You must be joking!' Nick was about the most unlikely farmer I'd ever seen. I tried to imagine him leaning over five-barred gates sizing up the cattle, straw in mouth, briefcase in hand . . . I stuffed my napkin in my mouth to stifle a guffaw.

He grinned. 'I suppose that is quite hard to believe, seeing as you've only ever seen me in a suit at work; but I can assure you, I'm far more at home delivering a calf than I am sweet-talking old rat-face Hutchinson.'

I grinned. So Nick thought he was a rat too, eh? That was promising. 'But — but what's all this got to do with Rachel?'

Nick looked surprised. 'Oh, didn't I say? I thought she could go down there for a while. As I said, it's a big place, she'd have plenty of room and still be out of Tim's way, and this Adam character wouldn't dream of going down to Cornwall to look for her so she'd be perfectly safe. What d'you think?' he calmly folded his napkin.

I sat there, bug-eyed with amazement. Nick would accommodate Rachel in Cornwall? In his house? I struggled to find my voice.

'Bloody hell, Nick, that's a marvellous idea, but we couldn't possibly, it's — it's much too much of an imposition. I mean, you don't know her or anything.'

'You didn't know Adam, but you got involved — and who knows,' he grinned, 'she might even be my type.'

'Highly unlikely, but Nick, why should you? I mean, it's terribly kind, but I just feel it's too much to ask.'

'You didn't ask, I offered.'

'Yes but—'

'Look, Polly,' Nick leaned forward. Suddenly he looked remarkably serious. 'I've been joking about this, but the fact is you're in a hell of a mess, to put it mildly. I saw that

246

guy's face yesterday, and he's not going to stop hounding you until he finds his child. So far he's gone slightly mad in the process. You and Pippa are protecting the mother, which is all very fine and laudable but, frankly, dangerous. For one thing he knows where you work, and is quite likely to turn up every day to terrorise you and pick fights with anyone else who gets in his way. Paris is a good idea but, as you say, it could take a few weeks to get it together. Now, it's no skin off my nose to have her to stay in Cornwall. It's a big house, so I probably won't even see much of her. I'm planning to go down for a couple of weeks as from Thursday, so I can at least keep an eye on her. Now, what I suggest is that you come down with her and stay the weekend so she's not completely fazed by a crowd of strangers, help her to settle in, and then, when she's found her feet, just leave her to have a peaceful few weeks by the sea until the flat in Paris is organised. Now, does that sound reasonable?'

He drained his glass of wine, sat back and lit a cigarette. My eyes and mouth were wide. Reasonable? It was the sanest thing I'd heard in days; it made complete sense. It was also incredibly kind. As for me going too, the idea of staying with Nick at his house initially filled me with horror, but on reflection, as I studied my employer over the table, I almost warmed to the idea. What bliss to get away from all the horrors London held for me – Adam, Harry, everything. I'd been to Cornwall before in the spring and it had been heavenly – brimming over with primroses and early daffodils. I turned the idea over in my mind, and the more I turned it, the more attractive it became.

'Will the daffodils be out yet?' I asked dreamily.

He laughed. 'Would you like me to ring and check before you make a decision?'

I grinned. 'No. No, the more I think about it, the more I think it's an absolutely brilliant idea. I just don't know how to thank you enough, really it's—'

'Not at all,' he said briskly, cutting me off in mid-gush. 'Of course Rachel will have to agree.'

I groaned. 'That's a point, grumpy old cow, I'd forgotten about her.' I had. I'd been skipping through the daffodil fields singing a happy tune, not a sulky face in sight.

'Well, give me a ring at home tonight and let me know,' Nick was saying, filling up my glass, 'because if she agrees, I suggest we set off tomorrow morning instead of waiting for Thursday. No point in hanging around waiting for the mad axe-man to strike.'

'But what about work, haven't you got meetings tomorrow?'

'Only one, and Jason can handle that. It's about time he earned his keep.'

I giggled. Poor Jason was wildly intelligent in the academic sense, but totally useless in any other sense. Client meetings would send him into paroxysms of fear, his glasses would steam up with embarrassment, and he became paralysed with shyness, visibly palpitating whenever it was his turn to utter a few words. Occasionally a sentence would emerge, but when it did it would take him completely by surprise and he'd almost jump out of his skin, looking around wildly as if he half expected someone else to take the credit for saying it. Nick despaired, but was too soft to fire him.

'He'll cope better without you there. You frighten people.' By now my tongue was totally unhinged by alcohol.

Nick raised his eyebrows in surprise. 'Me? Frighten people? Don't be ridiculous; I don't frighten you, do I?'

'Well, no,' I said, thinking well, yes, and we're talking living daylights actually, 'no, not frighten exactly.' I wriggled uncomfortably and felt my colour rising. 'But you can be rather, you know, intimidating.'

'I'm sorry.' He looked genuinely surprised and even a little hurt. 'I don't mean to be.'

'Oh no, it doesn't matter,' I said quickly. 'It's quite nice really in a — in a forceful sort of way.' Christ, what was I saying? Forceful? I'd be on to thrusting next.

Nick looked even more surprised but hugely amused. I went about the colour of the tomato on my plate.

'Forceful, eh?' he said, grinning. 'Is that how you like your men?'

Now in my normal line of work I can take any amount of sexy banter and always come back with a witty riposte, but this was different, this was Nick, for God's sake. What on earth was he playing at? I squirmed about on my seat, gushing from every conceivable pore and wishing I was somewhere else, like in the Ladies'.

He watched me wriggle, then laughed and let me off the hook. 'All right, we won't go into your love life. I have a feeling that's an even bigger can of worms.'

No, just the one, I thought miserably, and even he's buggered off to a new mate. Happily the waiter appeared with the coffee, so I was spared making a reply. As I stirred my cappuccino it occurred to me that Nick had his own love life too.

'What about Serena, won't she be coming down?'

'No, she won't,' he said shortly. Too shortly. I was intrigued as well as relieved; I didn't particularly want to look at her gorgeous face all weekend.

I ploughed on nosily. 'Doesn't she normally go to Cornwall with you at the weekend?'

It was his turn to shift about a bit. He lit another cigarette. 'She's not mad about the place, to tell you the truth; more of a London girl, I suppose. Anyway she's filming this weekend.'

'She must be quite busy — I mean, as an actress?'

'Yes, quite.'

'So I suppose if you go to Cornwall every weekend,

you don't see that much of her?'

'I suppose.'

'And of course you work so late during the week, that must put a strain on—'

'Polly, shall we just stick to sorting your life out for the time being?'

I grinned, mentally notching up marks for trying. Still, it was odd. They obviously didn't see a great deal of each other; perhaps he was still playing hard to get. She was quite a catch, after all.

Nick paid the bill and we left the still throbbing restaurant. Of course I'd drunk too much as usual, and the cold air hit me like a fridge door in the face. I felt a bit unsteady on my feet, and had a sudden desire to put my arm through Nick's strong, dependable tweedy one. I giggled and resisted it. Instead I shivered and pulled my ineffectual bum-freezer of a leather jacket around me. It was pretty damn cool in both senses of the word.

Nick regarded me dubiously as we started up the Fulham Road. 'D'you want my coat?'

'No, it's OK thanks,' I said between chattering teeth. Meanwhile he'd flagged down a passing taxi and I found myself being bundled, protesting, into the back.

'But we're only going up the road!'

'Never mind. I don't particularly want an invalid with pneumonia on my hands in Cornwall.' He pressed the heater button. 'And why don't you eat more? That rabbit food you eat won't warm you up. You're not dieting or something stupid, are you?'

'No.' I sulked in the corner. God, he was such a bully. What business was it of his whether I froze or starved to death? As it happened, for once in my life I wasn't dieting. I just didn't feel much like eating and my clothes were falling off me. It was the only compensation for having a broken heart, I thought wretchedly.

That night, I tackled Rachel on the subject of Cornwall.

I picked my moment, waiting until she'd bathed Jamie, read him a story, put him to bed, made up his bottles for the following day, and eventually had a firm grip on a gin and tonic and normality. I topped the gin up for her and sat down beside her on the sofa. I explained about Nick's house, phrasing the plan carefully so she wouldn't think I was pushing her into it.

'Oh Polly, that's a marvellous idea, but won't he mind?' She turned to me with such eagerness it made me jump.

'Not at all, in fact he suggested we go tomorrow, if you don't think that's too much of a rush?'

'Of course not, the sooner the better, I can't wait to get out of London.' She leaped up from the sofa with hitherto unimagined alacrity. 'I'd better ring my father and let him know, then I'll pack a few things. Thanks, Polly!'

Thanks, Polly! Good Lord, had I found favour? Suddenly I felt a sharp stab of pity for her. I'd been so busy with my own private tragedies I'd forgotten about hers, which were, after all, on a much grander scale. Perhaps she'd been scared stiff on her own here every day, just waiting for Adam to swing through an upstairs window with a knife in his teeth. How awful not to have anyone at all to turn to. There were plenty of friends in the country to whom I could have escaped, but she didn't seem to have access to any. Some uncharitable little notions about how, if she made herself a tad more pleasant and accommodating she might have more friends, were bubbling under in my brain, but I hastened them back down again.

I listened to Rachel's excited voice coming from the hall. ' . . . It'll take a little while to get the court injunction served, won't it? And you know I've always loved Cornwall. It'll be so good for Jamie to get a breath of fresh air, and now I know Adam's in London I can't wait to get away!'

Perhaps the judge didn't feel so murderously inclined to

me now. Well for once, Polly old girl, I thought, you've hit the jackpot. You've actually managed to get something right – or rather, I conceded magnanimously, Nick had. I waited until Rachel had finished and then dialled his number. I'd never spoken to him at home before, and the thought filled me with ridiculous nervous dread.

I practised a bit while it rang. Don't say hi, say hello; remember not to say, 'It's me'; try to sound intelligent. A girl answered, which completely floored me.

'Hello?'

Serena.

'Oh, um hi – er, is Nick there, please?'

'Who is it?' She sounded cross.

'Um, it's Polly – from work,' I said quickly, nearly adding, 'just a boring little secretary with dark roots; no competition at all.'

'Hold on,' she said tersely. Charming telephone manner, suppose I'd been Franco Zeffirelli in disguise, ringing up to offer her a part in his new film?

A second later Nick came to the phone and I told him we'd love to come. We agreed he'd pick us up in the morning at about nine a.m.

I put the phone down slowly and wondered what they were like together. Did they snuggle up on the sofa and watch TV? Did he run his fingers through her white-blonde hair and kiss her pert little nose? Did she trace his rugged features with her finger, a tantalising little smile playing about her luscious lips? Did they walk upstairs together, arm in arm, giggling and kissing the while? Did they get undressed first, or did they still rip each other's clothes off and fall in a tangled shrieking heap on to the bed? Did they gaze into each other's eyes as they lay there, dark and blonde on the pillow before he reached out and gently stroked her – Polly, stop it! I thought, alarmed at the pornographic lengths my imagination could stretch to: what business is it of yours?

That night I dreamed I was drifting through a daffodil field, one hand brushing lightly against the nodding yellow heads, the other clasped tightly in darling Harry's hand. He smiled tenderly and bent down to pick me a flower, but when he straightened up, I realised it wasn't Harry at all, it was Nick. He raised the flower above his head and I looked up, just in time to see the daffodil turn into a meat cleaver. I glanced down at him in surprise but the eyes I encountered were not brown but blue, blue with cold and blue with hate. Adam. The meat cleaver was being raised higher and higher, the music from the shower scene in *Psycho* was screeching in the background, and with an Anthony Perkins' maniacal smile on his face, he plunged it downwards, homing in on the small square inch of brow between my eyes.

I sat bolt upright in bed, shrieking like a Banshee and soaking wet. Christ Almighty, what the hell was happening to me! I flopped down on the pillow, my heart hammering around in my quivering ribcage. For God's sake, I thought miserably, reality was bad enough, couldn't I at least have some pleasant dreams?

Chapter Fourteen

The next morning, at nine a.m. sharp, the doorbell rang, piercing its way through my slumbering eardrums. I shot out of bed like a lunatic and ran, stark naked, to the open window. Without thinking, and still half asleep, I leaned out and peered down just as Nick was peering up. Our eyes met and he hastily averted his: more, I decided, backing away and looking in the dressing-table mirror, out of horror than decency. My hair was standing on end and my face was a riot of blotches and bags. Faced with such an obvious paper-bag job, he'd clearly been put off examining the bodywork.

As I slunk behind the curtain, I watched him on the pavement below, his hands thrust deep into his trouser pockets, his foot tapping away on the pavement as he gave his shoes a great deal of embarrassed consideration.

I dragged my dressing gown around me and stumbled out on to the landing in time to see Rachel appearing from her bedroom looking smug. She was not only washed and dressed, but packed – suitcase in one hand, baby in the other – and ready for the off. Why the hell couldn't she have given me a shout? Pippa put a tousled head round her bedroom door. She was wearing a T-shirt that just about covered the basics, but only just.

She rubbed her eyes and yawned. 'Nick's here,' she said sleepily. 'We overslept.'

Through the gap in the door I caught a glimpse of a

naked Charles, stumbling round the room, picking up bras and pink knickers and dropping them again, in a vain attempt to find his own underpants.

'I know, tell him I'm just coming, will you?' I said as she stumbled downstairs to answer the door.

I raced around the bedroom, throwing on a skirt and a jumper and raking a comb through my knotted hair. There wasn't time for a shower, so I doused myself in Diorissimo instead, hoping it would drown, or at the very least compete, with any unpleasant odours. It had been a stressful night.

I thundered downstairs, rubbing blusher on my pale, wan cheeks, feeling late and foolish as usual. In the kitchen, Pippa was cooking bacon for Charles and Nick, and you could clearly see two inches of bum sticking out at the bottom of her T-shirt as she stood with her back to them at the stove, frying away. Every so often she'd give the pan a vigorous little shake, which had the knock-on effect of making other things shake vigorously too. The boys were chatting away amiably enough over mugs of coffee, but without ever looking at each other: both had their eyes firmly on the chef's behind, and Charles seemed to have no qualms about sharing the spectacle with Nick.

Rachel wandered in and declined breakfast on the grounds that she'd had hers much, much earlier – one got the impression we were talking dawn here. She went to sit in the drawing room, her case at her feet as if she were merely killing time as she waited for her chauffeur to finish his breakfast in the servants' quarters.

I grabbed a piece of bacon from the pan and sandwiched it between some stale Mother's Pride, then sat down and munched away, trying desperately to wake up. Every so often I shot a sneaky glance at Nick, who was laughing and joking with Charles and Pippa.

He looked a different man in mufti. His faded cords and baggy navy sweater gave him an altogether softer, younger look. His dark hair flopped into his eyes from time to time, and he pushed it away as he threw back his head and laughed at Charles's jokes. Without the granite grey suit to augment them, his craggy features looked blunter somehow, as if he'd taken a file to them, rubbing off the sharp edges. He was all smiles this morning, too, quite different from the snarling workaholic I usually encountered first thing in the morning.

He caught me staring and flashed a smile. I flushed unattractively and started clearing up the breakfast things to cover my confusion. What the bloody hell was he up to, smiling at me like that? Anyone would think he was human. But then, perhaps he was, I thought miserably, as I stood at the sink rinsing bacon grease off my plate; perhaps it was me. Pippa certainly didn't have any hangups about him, I reflected, as I watched her larking around, pulling blonde hairs off his jumper and holding them up in evidence. They were all shrieking with laughter now.

It must be me, I thought, as I dried my plate, stacking it in the cupboard above. I obviously took this employer-employee thing far too seriously. But we weren't at work now, were we? Hell no, this was supposed to be a break — a holiday even. I'd have to stop running around, doffing my cap at every conceivable opportunity, like some sort of secretarial Uriah Heep, if we were going to spend the weekend together. Yes, I'd be my own person, call a few shots even.

I turned round from the sink, put my hands on my hips and smiled confidently. 'Right, let's go then, shall we?' I said briskly, in my new, assertive voice.

Too assertive. The others broke off from their friendly chatter and looked up in surprise. Nick hurriedly shoved half a bacon sandwich in his mouth and stood up, abandoning his mug of coffee.

'Sure,' he said agreeably from the corner of a bulging

mouth, 'I'm ready. Sorry, I hadn't realised you were waiting.'

Oh God, now I was just being a bossy old cow. What was the matter with me?

I traipsed miserably down the hall after him as he strode off to the car. We loaded it up together as Rachel stood watching. Most of the luggage seemed to consist of baby paraphernalia, which she was keen to have aboard but not too keen to touch.

As we drove away, Charles and Pippa stood at the front door with their arms around each other. They waved us off looking like something out of a soap opera, except that Pippa still didn't have any knickers on, and when she raised her hand to wave, her T-shirt rose a good six inches. Nick swivelled his head around one hundred and eighty degrees to get a better look, and narrowly missed colliding with the milkman.

When we'd negotiated most of London and were heading out to the motorway, Nick looked at Rachel in his rear-view mirror and smiled. 'So how old is Jamie, Rachel?' he asked.

'Just over five months,' she mumbled inaudibly.

'Sorry? Did you say five months?'

'Mmmm.'

'Ah. And, is he – you know, good? Is he a good baby?'

'Yes, quite.'

'Doesn't cry too much?'

'Not really.'

'Oh well, that's a relief, he won't keep us up all night then!'

'No.'

'Good, good . . . I must say, he's a nice looking little chap; solid, too: he'll be playing rugby for England soon, by the look of him – what d'you reckon, full back?'

'Sorry?'

'Full back – it's a rugby position!'

'Oh . . . oh right.'

At this point Nick gave up. A lesser man would have baled out sentences ago. Rachel's No Entry sign was firmly in position, and she sat in the back staring out of the window, pretending she couldn't really hear. It must take a certain self-confidence, I thought, to care so little about what people thought of you.

As we negotiated the final roundabout and roared off on to the motorway, I took over the role of question master.

'So how long have you had this house, then?'

'Oh, about three hundred years.'

I gasped. 'How come?'

He laughed. 'That's how long it's been in the family. Various generations of increasingly penniless Penhalligans have lived there since about 1790.'

'And now it belongs to you?'

'Yes, although my younger brother lives there at the moment while I'm in London.'

'So what about your parents, where do they live?'

'Well my father's dead and Mum moved out when he died. Said it was much too big for her to live there on her own, and I think she found it rather spooky without Dad. Too many memories and that sort of thing.'

'Oh I can imagine, how sad. So where does she live now?'

'Just outside a village called Gweek, which is about four miles away. She's converted an old barn there: we'll go and see her if you like. You'd like her,' he laughed. 'She's pretty batty!'

I gave this some thought. 'And is that why you think I'll like her? Because I'm batty too?'

He took his eyes off the road for a moment and grinned at me. 'I'd say you've got a lot of potential, although women only go truly batty at about forty. There's always a chance you'll be a bit previous though — say thirty-five?'

I grinned back, but secretly made up my mind to be a

very late developer in the bats department. I thought of Serena. Serene Serena. That's how I would be all weekend. Very sophisticated, very elegant, very cool. If I had to laugh I would tinkle rather than guffaw, and if I smiled it would be with the minimum of teeth and gum.

I crossed my legs, which were splayed out in front of me at an oafishly obtuse angle, and surreptitiously spat my chewing gum into my hand, noticing as I did so that I had a rather dirty plaster on my thumb which must have been there for at least a week. I deftly pulled it off and wrapped it round the chewing gum before depositing the nasty little bundle in . . . now, where on earth should I put it – ashtray? No, he might find it – ah yes, my handbag. As I snapped the bag shut, I looked up to encounter Nick looking hugely amused, having witnessed the whole operation. Bugger. Better laugh it off. I tried out my new tinkle.

'Cut myself while I was making supper last night – lobster thermidor actually! He-ya! He-ya!'

'What's the matter?'

'Sorry?'

'What was that noise?'

'What noise?'

'Just then, like a horse.'

'Oh! I was just laughing.'

'Really? Sounded very odd, like you had a pain in the tubes or something.'

I groaned inwardly. Christ, I couldn't win. I swiftly changed the subject. 'So who looks after the farm while you're away?'

'Oh, I've got a brilliant farm manager who runs the whole show, he's got a cottage on the estate.'

Estate! Bloody hell where was I going, Balmoral?

He saw my look and smiled. 'Oh, don't worry, it's not smart at all, very much a working farm.'

I wasn't worried. I liked the idea of Balmoral. I mentally

unpacked my suitcase — did I have the right gear? I thought on balance, yes, although I might need to do a little bit of light-fingering in Balmoral's cloakroom; a Barbour here, a pair of green wellies there — all country houses seemed to have enough to camouflage an army.

'But why keep it if you're never going to live there?'

'Who says I'm never going to live there?'

'Well, surely if you carry on running Penhalligan and Waters, you'll never actually live in Cornwall, will you?'

'Which is precisely why I'm selling the agency.'

My jaw hit my chest and my monosyllable was loaded with incredulity. '*No*!'

'Oh yes, definitely.'

'But why? Why on earth would you want to sell, it's going so well!'

'Exactly, and because it's going so well I should get quite a bit of money for it. It was only ever a means to an end, Polly. I needed the money to sort the house out and get the farm running smoothly. You've no idea how expensive it is to run a big house — the roof's caving in; we've got galloping dry rot, and wet rot too I shouldn't wonder; the heating system is archaic; the windows are all falling apart — it takes a lot of dosh to put these things right, you know. I'm just making a fast buck so I can pay for it all.'

'But — but you're so good at it!' I gasped. 'Won't you miss it? Don't you enjoy it?'

Nick threw his head back and laughed. 'Enjoy it? You must be mad. Enjoy entertaining revolting, slimy little toads like James Hutchinson, smarming up to him to make him feel important for five minutes, helping him to off-load his rotten coffee beans on to an unsuspecting public? No, I don't enjoy it, in fact the more I consider what we do every day, the more I hate it. Think about it, Polly: we spend our time filling people's television screens with false images full of happy loving couples and perfect children, we make people believe that's how the other half live, with

261

their big houses and their cars and their holidays, and we hold our hands up in horror when someone breaks into the local hi-fi shop and steals a video because they've seen it on the telly and think they have a perfect right to own one. Advertising stinks, Polly, and the more I see of it, the more I want to get out.'

'But – but what will happen to the agency?' I stammered. 'I mean, you run the place, it'll fall apart if you leave.'

'Course it won't,' scoffed Nick. 'And anyway, I'm not going to sell you all down the river; you'll all keep your jobs. I'm just going to sell out to Waters. I daresay he'll just employ another managing director to lick you all into shape.' He grinned. 'Who knows, he might take you to a few shoots, maybe even treat you to expense account lunches!'

I smiled weakly. For some reason I felt unaccountably sick. 'So – when will all this happen?' I asked in a rather small voice.

'Oh, in about six months, I should think. Hopefully we'll win that dog food pitch, which will add about half a million to our billings, and then I'll be off.'

He flashed his lights at a slow moving truck in the fast lane; it moved over to let him by and he sped past.

I stared at the rather clean bit of thumb where my plaster had been and picked miserably at the few remaining bits of dirty, sticky thread with my fingernail. Whatever he said, the place just wouldn't be the same without him. He was the whole energy behind it, the driving force. If he went, everyone else would just go to the pub. As it was, I shouldn't think many people had gone to work today. Pippa had certainly looked as if she was heading straight back to the bedroom with Charles, and Joss and Ron were no doubt already stalking their prey in a South Ken wine bar.

I looked at the combination of square jaw, Roman nose,

and straightforward eyes sitting beside me. It was all very well saying we'd be OK, but not everyone had that sort of determination or strength of character. Mention a drink, or a day off, or a long lunch, and we were anybody's. He was deserting us, leaving us to our own loose morals and weak characters. I felt absurdly upset.

'Well if you think advertising's so immoral and the people so ghastly, why did you decide to make your millions in it?' I snapped petulantly.

'I haven't made millions, and I didn't say all the people were ghastly: just James Hutchinson and one or two others like him. I know I sound like a hypocrite, and it's easy to take the high moral ground now I'm leaving, but I promise you, when I joined I didn't realise quite how much I'd hate it.' He turned and grinned. 'Which might explain why I'm so bad tempered in the office.'

'Oh I wouldn't say—'

'Polly, I'm well aware that I'm a complete bastard to work for, and I apologise, but it's because I loathe what I'm doing. I've only stayed this long because I realised how much money I could make from it, and I'm not so high-minded that I wasn't going to turn down the money for my new roof, or all the farm equipment we so badly need. All I'm saying is, I don't want to do it for ever.'

I sat in sullen silence. Well, for that matter neither did I, but what choice did I have? I didn't have a convenient farm to inherit. Everyone seemed to have plans except me – what about my life? What was I supposed to do? Hadn't anybody thought of that? I choked down the lump in my throat and tried not to feel too sorry for myself. I tried a different tack.

'Won't you miss London?'

'Not a bit. What should I miss – the traffic? The crowds? The underground? The carbon monoxide? The stress? The ultimate ulcer? Or are you perhaps referring to the gay social whirl?'

'Well, something like that,' I said uncomfortably. 'Yes, I suppose I am.'

Nick paused for a minute as he pulled over to let a Porsche go steaming by us at a million miles an hour. 'I honestly wouldn't care if I never went to another London drinks party ever again. All that tedious standing around, clutching a glass of fizzy white wine, talking to complete strangers about their dreary lives when you really couldn't care less because you know you'll never see them again. No thanks.'

'Surely there are people you like in London? Don't you have any friends?' I added maliciously.

'Oh sure, plenty, and I like seeing them for a drink after work or for supper, but what I don't like is spending an hour in a traffic jam trying to get to their bloody houses, and then coming out a few hours later to find my car's been broken into. Wait till you see what I'm swapping it all for, Polly: it might even make a city slicker like yourself want to head for the wide open spaces.'

'I doubt it,' I snapped. 'I don't suppose Armani has opened a branch in Helford yet.'

He roared with laughter. 'No, but then I don't have much use for Armani — I'd look pretty silly wading through the manure in a designer suit.'

I stared sulkily out of the window thinking life was a bitch. Speaking of which . . . 'What about Serena?'

Nick didn't answer, he stared straight ahead and a little muscle twitched in his cheek. Aha! I'd got him at last! Not so self-assured on that little point, eh, Mr Cool Dude? Mr I-Know-Where-I'm-Going?

'You said she doesn't like Cornwall!' I persisted eagerly.

'No, she's not too keen.' He narrowed his eyes and put his foot down somewhat.

'So will you stay together, d'you think?' Still no answer, but that didn't deter me. 'What d'you think?'

He laughed. 'God, you're like a battering ram. Quiz me

on something else, Polly, this isn't really my best subject.'

Now what the hell did that mean? He wasn't good at talking about it or it wasn't going very well?

I stared out of the window and watched the fields and hedges flash by. Cows and sheep, cows and sheep. We ate up the miles and Phil Collins ate his heart out on the cassette recorder. 'And now we're living, se-ep-arate lives', he crooned. I gulped again. Separate lives. Me and Harry. Another gulp and a blink too. I was definitely upset. About Harry? Perhaps, or about Nick leaving? Perhaps it was just the general feeling of rejection? Yes, maybe I didn't like being deserted on such a regular basis by one and all. I felt about five years old and back in the playground again – quick, run away, Polly's coming!

Nick's voice broke into my misery. 'I know it's a little late, but I thought we might stop somewhere for lunch. Is that OK?'

'Sure.'

It had been a good few hours since that bacon sandwich, and my tummy was doing a sensational job at accompanying Phil on the drum rolls.

We turned off the main road at Wincanton and tootled down a country lane, which led in turn to a series of increasingly smaller lanes until we seemed to be almost on a dirt track. I looked at Nick in surprise.

'I hope you know where you're going.'

'Don't worry, I've been here masses of times.'

The bumpy track, which was producing grunts of indignation from Jamie in the back, eventually came to a completely dead end. As I peered out of the window, I saw that we'd come to rest outside a very ancient-looking pub. It was thatched with pretty bay windows and, surprisingly enough – seeing as it was in the middle of nowhere – there were quite a few cars parked outside.

'Where are we?' I opened the door dubiously and looked around nervously for cow pats and puddles before I ventured forth in my oh so casual, but oh so expensive, navy blue loafers.

'Welcome to the Dog and Duck. It belongs to a friend of mine.' And so saying he whipped round to open Rachel's door. She yawned and stretched as Nick wrestled with the baby's car-seat.

As we ducked our heads to avoid the low-slung beam over the main entrance – yes, myself included – Nick turned to the left and led the way into a cosy little bar with dark, mahogany-panelled walls and an enormous fire roaring away in the inglenook fireplace.

Rachel and I made for it immediately, and stood toasting our bottoms while we looked around the room. The carpets and curtains were a lovely old rose pink, and the panelled walls were dotted with sporting prints. There was a comfortable old chintz sofa, and one or two ancient leather chairs which were sprouting horsehair at the seams, plus a few wooden tables and chairs. It was an effortlessly comfortable room, and looked as if it had been this way for ever, but I had a shrewd suspicion that a great deal of thought and consideration had gone into its well-worn antiquity. As I stared out of the leaded windows to the fields beyond, a shriek went up from my left.

'Nick!'

I swung round to see a ravishingly pretty girl framed in the doorway. She was small and as slim as a blade, with dark shiny hair cut in a bob, large almond-shaped eyes, and a wide sexy mouth which almost split her face in half as it spread into a smile of true pleasure. She squealed with delight and threw herself with gusto into Nick's welcoming arms. He swung her round in a massive bear hug, lifting her clean off her feet. Why did I feel just the tiniest bit proprietorial as she gave him a series of resounding kisses, two – no three on his cheeks – followed by a severe hair ruffle? He held on to her, laughing as she squealed to be put down, before eventually setting her back on her feet again.

'Nick!' she spluttered breathlessly, 'you old goat, what the hell are you doing here!'

'Thought I'd surprise you — catch you out and see what mischief you've been up to. I must say you're looking pretty damn fit Pen. Being a country bumpkin obviously suits you!'

'You're looking pretty tasty yourself for an advertising executive — but why the hell didn't you tell me you were coming? It might have been my day off, and I'd have killed you if I'd missed you.'

'Well I had a feeling you'd be here — you know, watching for my car, waiting by the door . . .'

She squealed with mock rage and went to hit him as he ducked and pinned her arm down. He turned to us, laughing. 'This is Penny the publican! She runs this place with irritating efficiency and alarming success. Penny, meet Polly, Rachel and Jamie.'

We all smiled and said hi, it was impossible not to take to her immediately, she was so full of fun and life. I instantly recognised a kindred spirit, with her merry eyes and naughty smile; just the sort of girl who would go down extremely well in my neck of the woods.

Penny bent down to coo over Jamie, breaking off now and again to throw questions out to Nick. How was so-and-so? What were they doing now? Who was doing what to whom? How was the agency going? They obviously knew each other extremely well. How well, I wondered?

After we'd toasted our bums a bit and they'd done the preliminary chat, we followed her through into a pretty olive-green dining room, streaky with sunlight which streamed in from the bay windows. It was surprisingly crowded, and as we sat down at the only remaining table, I was surprised to see a fair amount of silver and a crisp linen tablecloth. This was no ordinary pub.

Penny declined to eat with us on the grounds that she was far too busy, but served us herself, pausing to chat as she piled our plates high with rare roast beef, baby sweetcorn, mange tout and the tiniest, sweetest little new potatoes I'd ever tasted. It was all absolutely delicious and I told her so.

She smiled. 'Well that's all down to Tim, Nick's brother. He grows organic vegetables and delivers them here whenever he can. I must say I adore them, they really do taste quite different, don't they?'

They certainly did, and so did the summer pudding with great dollops of clotted cream which followed. I sat back, full to bursting, as she brought our coffee and pulled up a chair to join us.

I studied her carefully as I sipped the piping hot coffee. This was no country bumpkin. What on earth was a beautiful girl like this doing running a little country restaurant, albeit a very attractive and obviously successful restaurant, in the middle of nowhere? Shouldn't she be charging down Sloane Street looking for that elusive but crucial little black number to wear to some crumpet-filled Chelsea drinks party tonight?

Nick and Penny chatted about old friends and old times, all of which meant nothing to me, but I listened carefully, waiting for interesting snippets to fall by the wayside.

'So how are you and Serena?' asked Penny, dropping me the very snippet I was looking for. 'Still throwing plates and gin bottles at each other?'

I tried to look casual as I stirred my coffee, but my ears felt like Mr Spock's, pricked to distraction.

Nick smiled, lit a cigarette — funny how the mention of her name made him do that — and blew the smoke out thoughtfully. 'Well, let's just say we've reached a stage of armed neutrality.'

Curiouser and curiouser, what the hell did that mean?

'You mean you're both standing by your guns but you're not using them?'

'Something like that.'

'So whose guns are the biggest?'

Nick laughed. 'Ah well, that would be telling!'

Well, we wouldn't want to do that, would we? Hell, no. Would someone please tell me what they were talking about? I love gossip — thrive on it actually — especially, I thought, looking at Nick, in this case.

Nick expertly manoeuvred the conversation away from his love life and round to the restaurant, giving advice when she asked for it, and praising her for everything she'd done. Rachel and I joined in with equally effusive praise. When lunch was over, we wandered back through the rickety corridor and out under the low beam of the front door into the sunshine.

Nick and Penny kissed each other goodbye with, to my practised eye, a great deal of unnecessary hugging, and we all piled back into the car. She stood at the door, smiling and waving until we were out of sight.

I was burning with curiosity, but managed to hold myself back until we'd at least negotiated the bumpy track and were whizzing down the country lanes again.

'So how d'you know Penny?' I asked casually.

'Oh, she's just an old friend.'

'Looked like a pretty good one to me.'

He grinned. 'OK, a pretty good, old friend.'

'Why on earth is she running a pub out here in the middle of nowhere?'

'She likes it, I suppose.'

'But it's so . . . quiet.'

He smiled. 'That's why she likes it.' He turned on the cassette recorder but I wasn't dissuaded that easily.

'Have you known her long?' I persisted.

Nick caved in. 'Penny's an old girlfriend. We went out together, years ago. It was just after I came down from

Cambridge. I was living in Cornwall at the time, and she lived there with me. When we split up, she went back to London and found she couldn't bear living in the city any more; she really missed the country. I scouted around in this area and helped her find the pub. She'd been left a bit of money, and the rest she borrowed, and she's been here ever since making a very decent living. Her boyfriend owns the antique shop in the village and, as far as I know, she's extremely happy — is that so strange?'

It was to me. 'No, no, not at all!' I lied, thinking I'd go stark raving mad stuck out here in the country, miles from anywhere. So Penny was an ex-girlfriend, eh? That explained all the kissing and cuddling.

'Are you on such good terms with all your exes?'

He laughed. 'I suppose I am, although there haven't really been that many, only Penny and—' He broke off and pretended to look at a signpost, although he must have known the way blindfolded. And who? Who couldn't he bring himself to talk about? God, he was mysterious.

I resigned myself to the fact that no more blood was going to come out of this particular stone at present, and contented myself with staring out of the window, watching the countryside slip by.

Little by little the scenery was changing. The fields seemed to be getting smaller, the hedges taller, the hills steeper and the lanes narrower. The hedgerows at the side of these tiny lanes had gone quite berserk; primroses and bluebells were jockeying for position on the steep banks, and all the flowers seemed to have the same death wish as their heads were inevitably knocked off by cars as they swept past.

The lanes were so thin that there came a point when we seemed to go backwards more than forwards, as we reversed to let other cars, or more often tractors, pass in the opposite direction. It was impossible to see into some of the fields now, the hedges were so high, but every so often I caught a glimpse of a beautiful lush green meadow, or saw a flash of yellow as a field full of glorious daffodils shot by.

I sat up eagerly, like a child waiting to see the sea. Now and again a village – or perhaps even a hamlet, they were so small it was hard to tell – would whizz by. If you blinked you'd miss the irregular smattering of low, whitewashed cottages, their heavy thatched eyebrows frowning over tiny latticed windows, all clustered around a small, mouse-grey church. I opened the window and leaned right out, shutting my eyes and letting the wind sweep through my hair.

Nick laughed. 'What are you doing?'

'Giving my diseased lungs a taste of this wonderful country air – you're right, it is lovely here.'

A broad grin spread across his face. I'd pleased him. How touching to be so proud of a little patch of England. I couldn't quite imagine feeling the same way about Esher. Even Rachel, who'd been asleep, was now sitting up in the back, pointing out cows and sheep to Jamie who was gurgling appreciatively. Suddenly I felt almost happy. There was a definite holiday atmosphere in the car, a real sense of adventure and camaraderie – any minute now I'd break into a spirited rendition of 'Green Grow the Rushes Oh'.

As we hurtled down a particularly narrow lane at breakneck speed, with Rachel and I squealing in mock terror, Nick suddenly changed dramatically from fourth to second gear and swung the car left through some crumbling white gates. We trundled over a cattle grid and down a narrow, pitted drive. It was long and windy with woods on either side, through which the sun flashed intermittently, as if someone were shining an almighty great flashlight at us. Seconds later, the woods parted, and a sweep of lawn rose up before us. Straight ahead, looking out proprietorially on to this sylvan scene, was a large and ancient grey stone house.

It was long and low, with large sash windows at the front and an imposing arched front door surrounded by a sweep of grey stone. Covering almost half of the house was a giant wistaria, which looked about as old as the house itself and, as we drew nearer, I could see what looked like a stable block behind, with a bell tower peeping out over the rooftops.

I caught my breath with delight. 'Oh Nick,' I breathed. 'It's beautiful!'

'Isn't it just!' echoed Rachel.

Nick beamed with pleasure, looking like the Cheshire Cat. 'It is rather a decent-looking place but, unfortunately, as you'll see on closer inspection, it's falling to bits.'

We got out of the car and wandered up — and I did see. The brickwork was literally crumbling to the touch in places, and most of the windows were rotten, hanging in their frames at precarious angles.

Nick strode ahead and pushed through the giant wooden door, leading us into a large creamy hall which looked remarkably like the National Gallery. The walls were crawling with ancestors, and a very gloomy crowd they looked too. Most had piggy brown eyes and big noses, and were swathed in what looked like velvet and ermine. They also appeared to be sporting quite a few sizeable baubles, notably around the head and neck region. What was going on here: was Nick related to royalty or something? Was I in fact in the presence of a young pretender, the last of the Cornish Plantagenets, perhaps? One of the old codgers on the wall certainly bore an unnerving resemblance to that king with the hunchback and the dodgy leg who does a lot of Shakespeare. He gave me the creeps and I decided to keep well clear of him. I could do without being followed around by those piercing, judgemental eyes.

'Tim? Where are you!' yelled Nick. 'It's me!'

I heard voices coming from behind the double doors

opposite, and a shout of recognition went up. Nick pushed open the doors and, as he strode through, a smaller, thinner version of Nick leaped up from an armchair, scattering pieces of *The Independent*, and sending an ashtray flying.

'Nick!' he vaulted over a sofa to get to us. 'What the devil are you doing here? I didn't expect you till tomorrow!'

He slapped Nick on the back, who slapped him back, grinning, and then they slapped each other a bit more, as men seem to do.

While the Morris Dancing was going on, I noticed a pretty girl with curly brown hair and freckles get up from a chair in the corner. She put down her book and took her glasses off, smiling shyly. Nick took two giant strides to get to her and kissed her smartly on both cheeks.

'Sarah! It's good to see you. How are the stables? Still up to your knees in it?'

She laughed. 'They're fine, thank you, and you'll be pleased to hear I change my jeans when I come over here, so no more manure jokes, please.'

'Glad to hear it, especially if you're sitting on my chairs . . . Oh, this is Polly, and Rachel, and Jamie. Sarah Mansfield, Tim's — revolting word — fiancée.'

She grimaced. 'Isn't it just, but I suppose that's what I am. Hello.' She turned to Rachel. 'What a beautiful baby, can I hold him?'

Jamie was duly bundled into her arms with a smile from Rachel. Sarah cooed and tickled him, and I wondered if she'd been briefed — be nice to the scared-looking one with the baby who looks like she's just got out of Belsen. Jamie took hold of her finger and squeezed it in his fierce little grip.

'Oh! Aren't you sweet!' she cooed. 'I've got a little nephew just like you, but not nearly so good looking!'

Rachel looked proud, and they knelt down by the fire

talking babies. Rachel looked positively happy. I supposed this must feel rather like reaching Switzerland after escaping from Colditz. Nick offered to show me the house and, as we were on our way out, Rachel turned to him, eyes shining.

'Thanks, Nick!' she blushed. 'I mean for driving me here, and – and everything.'

'No problem,' said Nick, 'just make yourself at home. I thought you and Jamie could have the pink room at the top. It's got its own bathroom. Tim will show you where it is.'

Tim nodded, 'Sure.' He was staring at her intently as she sat huddled by the fire in her outsized grey cardigan, thinking, I'm sure, what most people think when they meet her for the first time: how small and lost and vulnerable she looked. He poured her a large drink, and Nick and I disappeared to look around the house.

As we wandered from one vast, high-ceilinged room to the next, I realised why Nick was so desperate to keep it. It was just as pretty inside as it was out, but again, in a precarious way. I felt that a sudden gust of wind breezing through an open window could sweep all the fragile pieces of china off their shelves, whisk the soft silky curtains from their few remaining threads, and break the legs on all the spindly little pieces of antique furniture. Everything was beautifully pale and washed out, too, rather as if someone had turned down the colour on the telly. The floors were very pale oak, the Persian carpets were so faded you could hardly see the pattern, and the walls had lost most of their original colour and were those lovely soft, muted shades that paint manufacturers would kill to recreate. It was indeed beautiful, and it occurred to me, as I ran my amateurish, *Antiques Roadshow* viewer's eye over it, that it all looked rather valuable too.

I casually picked up a pretty blue and white plate which weighed about half an ounce, and put it down hastily as I realised how eminently breakable it was.

'Couldn't you sell some of this?' I ventured timidly, gesturing around at the treasures. 'I mean, if the house is costing so much to repair, surely you could get quite a bit for the furniture and, um – china?' Was china the right word? Somehow it sounded too much like the ground floor of Peter Jones.

'I could, I suppose. I daresay the porcelain – ' the very word I'd been groping for – 'would fetch quite a bit at auction, but I don't want to. I grew up with all these things – they're like family to me. Anyway,' he grimaced, 'it wouldn't be enough. Holes in roofs make pretty enormous holes in pockets.'

We wandered into the dining room and encountered a vast mahogany table, heaving with silver. An enormous candelabra stood in the middle, surrounded by lots of little silver animals: pheasants, foxes, ducks . . . I picked up a little hare and turned it over in my hand.

'Oh! How pretty!' I exclaimed. 'Where did you get them from?'

'I'm not sure,' said Nick, scratching his head. 'They've always been here. I suppose Mum would know, but they were probably here when she arrived on the scene too.'

Of course, how stupid of me, people like Nick didn't buy their own silver. I wondered how many more cringe-makingly naff remarks would fall from my lips during the course of the weekend. Any minute now I'd be demanding to know why there wasn't a fluffy little mat on the loo seat, or how come the front door bell didn't play 'Jingle Bells' when you pressed it.

Nick showed me the rest of the house. I smiled a lot and nodded admiringly whenever I deemed it appropriate, but said little. Surely smiling and nodding couldn't be wrong?

As we went back through the hall, though, I couldn't help enthusing about a dear little walnut table which stood at the foot of the stairs. It was terribly delicate and intricately inlaid, just the sort of thing I'd kill to have by my bed one day. On it stood a tiny bowl of primroses which were just dropping a few of their petals on to its smooth walnut veneer.

'Oh look!' I breathed. 'Isn't it divine? What a beautiful little table!' I ran my finger over its smooth, highly polished surface.

'It's pretty, isn't it? It was a Christmas present, actually.'

'Really? How incredibly generous. Who from?'

Nick looked slightly uncomfortable. 'From Serena.'

'Serena? Gosh!' I recalled my own, I'd thought, incredibly generous Christmas present to Harry – one navy blue cashmere scarf – and realised I was well out of my depth here.

'How kind,' I muttered.

'Wasn't it?' agreed Nick. He stooped and picked up a few rose petals that had fallen just by my feet. His hand accidentally brushed my shoe. He straightened up and smiled. 'Nice legs.'

I flushed with pleasure, thrilled that he'd noticed one of my undoubted assets, set off, rather attractively today, by black lycra tights. I lowered my eyelids and smiled coquettishly.

'Yes, I love the way they bow, ever so slightly, at the bottom,' he went on.

I gasped with horror. Who was he calling bow-legged! Bloody hell! I intercepted his gaze and followed it back to the walnut table – oh! Oh, yes I see, OK. I nodded vigorously, hoping he hadn't noticed my flaming face.

'Oh I agree, I um – I like them like that, sort of – curvy.' I followed him meekly back into the drawing room, feeling decidedly disappointed. Tim and Rachel were sitting by the fire, chatting away in what I have to admit was quite an animated fashion. I even heard Rachel laugh once or twice, and at one stage I could have sworn she came close to completing a paragraph.

Tim was listening intently, egging her on and encouraging her to reveal yet more of her wildly attractive personality. He seemed intrigued by her, willing to spend time and energy coaxing words to flow from her mouth. And flow they did, albeit in a somewhat jerky fashion. Perhaps a combination of these kind, friendly people and the country air was getting to her, and perhaps now, finally, we could all relax a bit, I thought, flopping down thankfully into a nice squashy sofa.

Sarah had gone back to the local riding stables which, I gathered from Tim, she ran practically single-handed. It sounded like a pretty labour-intensive job, and not one I particularly envied. I always like to slip into a nice tight pair of breeches and some black leather boots if there's anyone around to admire the effect, but I'm damned if I want to get near the beastly creatures, and as for working in a stables – imagine the pong! But Sarah returned a couple of hours later looking flushed and happy, and reeking, not of manure, but of job satisfaction.

'Two new pupils today!' she said cheerfully, helping herself to a glass of wine. 'And they've both signed on for a course of ten lessons!'

'Excellent!' beamed Tim. 'If you keep going at this rate, I can retire! Keep at it, work harder!' he cried, cracking an imaginary whip. 'What's for supper, by the way?'

She threw a cushion at him, laughing. 'You'll be getting it yourself if you're not careful, but since you ask, beef bourguignonne. I'll just go and see how it's doing.'

And so saying, this capable girl whizzed off to the kitchen to put the finishing touches to her dish, wisely waving aside my feeble offers of help – for feeble is what they would have been. Beef bourguignonne was the sort of thing I ordered in restaurants: I'd certainly never attempt to recreate it.

Supper that night was a happy and relaxed affair. After

Tim and Nick had dispensed with the preliminary farm chat, with Nick asking questions about crop yields and lambing, and Tim prefixing his answers with words like 'high', 'excellent', and 'bloody good considering', all of which made Nick beam with pleasure, we got down to the interesting bits, like me asking who owned what – surreptitiously, of course.

The house and most of the land apparently belonged to Nick, who had obviously inherited the lion's share, but Tim owned a certain amount of acreage adjacent to Nick's estate, which he also farmed, but in a purely organic way. There was apparently a cottage on the land, too, which Tim and Sarah were painstakingly restoring so they could eventually live there.

'Probably in about the year 2000 at the rate we're going!' said Sarah, laughing; but she looked pretty happy about it, and Tim blew her a kiss over the table.

'Don't you worry, I'll be struggling over the threshold with you long before that!'

'Oh!' I said breathlessly, seizing on a subject that was close to my heart. 'When are you getting married?'

'Next year,' said Sarah happily, 'at the church in Manaccan. It's so pretty, you must come and have a look at it.'

'I'd love to!' I said, jumping at the chance to talk flowers and bridesmaids' dresses and wedding lists. I wondered if the London stores would take on a wedding list this far away? No doubt it was a problem she'd already wrestled with, but I supposed there were obvious compensations attached to a country wedding: a picturesque setting; off to the reception in a pony and trap; perhaps a dance in a marquee in the evening . . . I sighed wistfully.

We laughed a lot that night. The beef bourguignonne was ambrosial, the claret flowed, and Nick showed the sort of form I wouldn't previously have thought possible. He and Tim had us in stitches as they played a couple of

Cornish yokels, affecting deep country burrs and clowning around in a ridiculous manner, egged on by the shrieks of laughter from us girls. As I watched him larking around with his brother, he turned suddenly and caught my eye, smiling, and raising his eyebrows inquiringly. 'All right?' he mouthed. I nodded and smiled back, hoping he wouldn't notice that there were tears in my eyes. Recently I wasn't used to anyone bothering to find out if I were happy or not.

That night, I left the curtains open and pulled the bedclothes high up under my chin as I stared out at the vast black sky. An owl hooted way off in the distance. A lamb bleated for its mother, then there was quiet. I breathed deeply, savouring the cool night air. I smiled. How comforting it was to know that in the morning I'd wake up – not to an alarm clock, followed by a rushed breakfast, followed by the underground – but to those enormous oak trees swaying in the breeze outside my window, and a field full of sheep with their spring lambs. I snuggled down further in the bed and closed my eyes, letting the dark night wash over me. This was the nearest I'd come to happiness in a good many days.

Chapter Fifteen

At breakfast the next morning, over great platefuls of bacon and eggs, expertly cooked by Tim, Nick suggested we all had a look at the farm. My heart sank deep into my Docksiders. I had visions of myself, up to my designer-jeaned knees in cow pats and manure, miserably swatting flies with my handbag.

'Sorry, I'm far too busy, got to get the beans in today,' said Tim, helping himself to more toast and mopping up his fried egg. He grinned at his brother. 'Some of us have to work, you know!'

'Well, you're lucky you can do it down here rather than in London. How about the wife-to-be, or are you keeping her nose to the grindstone, too?'

''Fraid so,' said Sarah. 'I've got a new pony arriving at about ten o'clock. Maybe I'll catch up with you later, though.'

'Rachel?'

She sighed. 'I'd love to, but unfortunately Jamie will have to have another sleep in about an hour, so I'd better stay here with him.'

Nick made a face. 'God, I'd no idea this mothering lark was such hard work. Having you and Jamie around certainly makes me think twice about throwing myself into parenthood.'

'Ah yes, but you'd only be a father, wouldn't you? That doesn't come with quite so many occupational hazards,' said Rachel darkly.

That's pretty rich, I thought, considering Adam's moving heaven and earth to take on those hazards, but I wisely held my tongue.

Nick turned to me with a smile. 'Looks like we're on our own, then — how about it?'

For some reason, my heart stopped lurking sulkily in my shoes and rocketed swiftly back into position again. 'Yes, I'd love to see the farm.'

'Sure? You don't have to be polite, you know, you can do what you like.'

'I should think the last thing she wants to do is trail round a smelly old farm,' said Tim. 'If I were you, Polly, I'd catch a bus into town and check out the only boutique in Helston.'

'Don't be silly, there's nothing in that ghastly little shop that would interest Polly. Why don't you come to the stables with me?' suggested Sarah. 'I'm only doing half a day today, we could go and have some lunch in a pub when I've finished.'

'Oh no, that's very kind, but I'm not desperately fond of horses and, anyway, I'd really like to go with Nick!' I said eagerly. Far too eagerly. The phrase 'really like to go with Nick!' seemed to hang, echoing in the air. I felt it needed a little explaining. 'You see,' I stammered, 'I'm . . . I'm terribly interested in farming!'

'Really?' Nick looked up from his bacon and eggs in surprise. 'Polly, I had no idea!'

No, neither did I, and hopefully he'd forget I'd said that, but he showed no signs of doing so just yet.

'Which particular areas are you interested in?' he asked.

'Um, d'you mean — which particular areas, in particular?' I faltered, playing with some crumbs on the tablecloth.

Nick looked confused. 'Well, yes, I suppose I do mean that.'

'Oh. Oh well, all sorts really.'

'All sorts?'

'Yes, but, um, if you want to get specific, I'd say particularly animal, vegetable and, er – mineral.'

By now Tim, Sarah and Rachel had all put their knives and forks down and were looking at me in astonishment.

'Animal, vegetable and mineral?' inquired Nick, his mouth twitching slightly.

'Yes, you know, cows, sheep, er – hay, straw . . .' I racked my brains. What else did they have in these bloody places? One of Jamie's animal books sprung helpfully to mind. 'Oh yes, and chickens, horses, zebras—'

'Zebras!' cried Sarah in astonishment.

'Oh, er – did I say zebras? Oh well, perhaps not in this country, but certainly in Africa. Yes, there are a hell of a lot of zebras out there, and of course I'm interested in farming on a very global scale – you know, global farming.' I seized this concept gratefully.

Tim snorted with derision. 'But zebras are wild, they charge around on game reserves. People don't farm them!'

'Oh you'd be surprised, Tim,' I said, nodding sagely and wishing I too was safely charging around on a game reserve in darkest Africa. 'Some of those tribesmen will stop at nothing.'

'Have you spent a lot of time in Africa then?' asked Sarah in wonder.

'Well, perhaps not a lot, but certainly a bit, yes, I'd say a fair bit.'

'Really? Whereabouts?'

'Whereabouts? Oh, all over really, but mostly – mostly East, you know, East Africa.'

'What – Tanzania? Kenya? Or further up?'

'Mmmm . . . yes, mostly – I say, I love that jumper. Did you buy it locally?' I snatched desperately at the first handy distraction to catch my eye.

'What, this old thing?' said Sarah dubiously, staring

down at what indeed was a very old thing, a sort of dirty grey Shetland wool affair with bobbles of wool where it had been rubbed and patches on the elbows. She gazed at me incredulously. 'This is the one I wear to the stables. D'you like it?'

'Very much.' I nodded vigorously, chewing hard on my bacon and staring at the truly repulsive jumper which had absolutely nothing to recommend it. I waved my fork in its general direction. 'Everyone's wearing them like that in London. It's quite the thing this season, especially with the elbows patched. Goes with the ripped jeans, you see. Rachel's got one, haven't you?'

'Have I?' asked Rachel, wide-eyed.

'Yes, except it's not quite a jumper is it? More of a cardigan, really, that lovely baggy grey thing you wear all the — quite a lot.'

'Oh that! God, I wasn't aware it was fashionable.'

'Oh, very, very,' I said, still nodding furiously, lips pursed, and I have to admit, warming wickedly to my theme. 'I know girls who'd kill for a cardigan like that — kill. You can't move for them in the King's Road at the moment.'

Out of the corner of my eye I caught a glimpse of Nick, who seemed to be stuffing the tablecloth into his mouth and making strange hiccuppy noises.

'Really?' Sarah looked dumbfounded. 'I had no idea that sort of thing was trendy, but then it's so long since I've been to London — oh well, I've got hundreds more like this. In fact there's a mauve one upstairs which is so threadbare it's unreal. You can borrow it if you like. I'll run and get it.' She put down her napkin and made to go upstairs.

'Oh er, no, Sarah, it's OK,' I said, polishing off my bacon and eggs in one huge mouthful and jumping down from the table. 'I don't think I'll wear a jumper today. I find it frightfully warm for the time of year, don't you?'

I fanned my face with my napkin, which was suitably flushed with the exertion of so many verbal gymnastics, and beat a hasty retreat upstairs to the safety of my bedroom and my beautifully smooth, unbobbly lambswool jumpers.

I threw myself thankfully on the bed. I felt exhausted already, and it was only half-past nine. Why did I have such a propensity to dig whopping great holes for myself and then proceed to clamber inexpertly out of them in front of a vast audience? Ah well, never mind, at least the agenda for today was looking good. A whole day on the farm with Nick – now why was that such a treat? I declined to answer, afraid of all the mighty implications it could throw up.

'Don't think about it,' I instructed myself, jumping off the bed. I opened my suitcase and pulled out a whole heap of clothes, throwing them into a huge colourful pile on the bed.

Now, for someone who's more at home in South Ken than South Cornwall, 'A Day on the Farm' was a tricky brief, but I rose gleefully to the challenge. What it called for, I decided, was something that would ease me gently into the part without looking too contrived. In the end I settled on a pair of brown corduroy jodphurs, a yellow and red checked shirt which leant on the lumberjack side, and a pair of brown leather riding boots which were serious but sexy. I studied the overall effect in the mirror. Hmmm. Whilst not exactly looking at one with nature, at least I didn't look as if I'd been born in a wine bar.

As I bounced downstairs in a jaunty, country girl manner, I saw Nick waiting patiently for me at the bottom. He was leaning against the hall table reading an old copy of *Country Life*. He looked up and smiled as I came down. I smiled winningly back and skipped on down; then, warming to my jaunty theme, decided to jump the last few steps to display a certain amount of fresh-faced athleticism. A huge error. As I took off I realised – too late – that five steps and a shiny wooden floor as a landing pad was, to say the least, ambitious. As I plummeted through the air, I had just enough time to catch the look of alarm on Nick's face as I hurtled towards him. Nine-and-a-half stone of blonde lumberjack cannoned into him and sent him crashing to the ground.

'Oooof!'

'Sorry!' I gasped.

'Christ, steady!' he cried in alarm, as he was sent sliding towards the front door, pinned to his ancestral floorboards by my tremendous weight. As we shuddered to a halt, perilously close to Serena's fragile little table, he struggled desperately – too desperately, I felt – to free himself from my bone-crushing bulk.

'Sorry!' I gasped again, as I clambered to my knees. 'Lost my balance!'

Nick was on his feet before I was and he pulled me up. 'So it seems. What were you trying to do, kill yourself? Or kill me, perhaps. Are you OK?'

'Fine,' I lied, wincing from a shooting pain in my ankle and the embarrassment of it all. What must he think of me? Did he think I was being incredibly forward or something? Did he imagine I was literally flinging myself at him? I blushed to my dyed roots.

'Sure you're all right?' he asked with concern, still holding my arm as I gingerly tried my ankle. 'Can you walk on it?'

I hobbled around. 'Yes, honestly, I'm fine, sorry about that.'

'It's OK. Just warn me next time you're feeling energetic, and I'll lay on some trampolines or something . . . Christ – what's that terrible pong?' He sniffed the air suspiciously.

'What pong?'

'That funny smell, like rotting cabbages or something.'

'Oh that,' I cringed deeply. 'It's called Country Girl.

Just something I put on to make the cows feel at home.'

'You mean you bought it? In a bottle?'

'It didn't smell too bad in Boots,' I muttered.

'Jesus. Well let's hope it doesn't knock the cows out. Come on, let's go.'

He marched off, farmyard bound, and I hobbled along after him, nursing my pride and my ankle.

As it turned out, the farm was immaculate: hardly a cow pat to be seen, and certainly not a pebble out of place in the cobbled yard. The barns were spotless, and everything that could shine did, in fact the milking equipment looked like it had been on the receiving end of a passionate love affair between Mrs Mopp and Mr Sheen. I half expected doormats as we inspected the outbuildings.

'Hope my shoes are clean,' I muttered as we entered a huge Dutch barn, 'I had no idea farmers were so houseproud.'

Nick laughed. 'It's just been cleaned up, actually, but I agree, we keep the farm in better nick than the house. Sometimes I think it would be more comfortable to sleep in the haybarn than in my bedroom, where the windows don't fit and the plaster's falling off the walls. The thing is, though, the farm's always got to come first. It's our livelihood.'

Our livelihood? I wondered who he was planning on sharing it with.

We looked in on the cows in their five-star accommodation. It was cool and dark in the shed, and the cows stood in a long row, pulling at hay nets and stamping their feet. They turned their heads briefly and stared at me insolently before going back to their rhythmical munching, swaying their heads and rotating their jaws. I felt as if I'd interrupted some kind of religious sect chanting a mantra. I patted one gingerly on the bottom. She stamped her foot and swished her tail around in irritation. I backed off smartly.

'Sorry,' I muttered.

'They're waiting to be milked,' explained Nick. 'They get a bit jumpy with strangers.'

One of Nick's farm hands appeared and started to fix them up to milking machines, so we left him to it, emerging out into the sunshine again, blinking against the bright light.

Just then a hearty male voice hailed us. 'Hello, hello! I can't believe you're the new cow girl, but if you are, things are looking up!'

I swung around to see a rather attractive man smiling at me from the other side of the post and rail fence. Although he was the wrong side of forty, he had obviously been extremely good looking once, but was now steadily going to seed. His bright blue eyes sported terrific bags, and his handsome face was lined and ruddy; the result, I suspected, of a combination of fresh air and too much alcohol.

'Good Lord, Nick, how did you manage to entice such a delightful creature into your barns. D'you think she'd like to look at mine too?'

Nick grinned. 'Polly, this is Jack Crawley: neighbour, stud farmer, womaniser and piss artist.'

'Come now, dear boy — "bon viveur" is much more to my liking . . . Enchanted, my dear!'

He grasped my hand and put it to his lips. I smiled delightedly, keen to make the acquaintance of someone who would flatter me rotten in front of Nick. He ran his rather sexy, bloodshot eyes over me appraisingly, and held on to my hand for a second longer than was absolutely necessary.

'Been showing you the equivalent of his etchings, has he? Want to see mine?'

I grinned. 'Are they up to scratch?'

Jack roared with laughter and, as he opened a gate to let us through, took my arm and whispered in my ear, 'So I've been led to believe, but who am I to say? Women tell such terrible whoppers. Come and see the horses anyway and then we might find time for a little mid-morning tipple . . . Got time, Nick, or shall I take her myself?'

'I think I can spare a couple of minutes,' said Nick with a grin. 'You're incorrigible, Jack.'

We followed the delightful Jack through his lush green fields towards the stable block in the distance. Over by the far gate were a few brood mares with their foals. The foals frolicked around in the sun, bucking and kicking, trying out their spindly new legs. Every so often they would return to their mothers for a reassuring nuzzle before shying off to test-drive their legs again. The mares, meanwhile, munched contentedly at the grass, or just stood staring into space, basking in the early spring sunshine, resting a back leg and swishing the occasional fly away with their tails. It looked a peaceful sort of life.

One elegant bay mare trotted over, and I stroked her velvety nose as she blew warm, sweet air into my face. She seemed to like me, so it was with a new enthusiasm for horses that I went to the yard to meet Sorcha, Jack's prize stallion.

There were quite a few boxes in the yard, most of which were unoccupied, but there was a great deal of stamping and snorting coming from the one in the corner. I wandered over and leaned over the stable door, peering in to see what all the fuss was about. Suddenly Sorcha's enormous chestnut head came looming out of the darkness, eyes rolling, teeth bared, like Jaws emerging from the depths.

I yelped and jumped backwards, dodging the teeth as they went to take a chunk out of my nose. He'd obviously got a whiff of Country Girl and couldn't believe his nostrils, but I must say I was mildly insulted.

'Jesus, he's a bit wild, isn't he?'

'It's nothing personal,' laughed Jack, 'he's just a

dreadful old misogynist, I'm afraid.' He patted his nose, and Sorcha nuzzled his hand like a pussycat.

'Doesn't bode well for the brood mares, does it?' I said doubtfully.

'Oh, he's keen enough when it comes to sex, he just can't be doing with the social niceties.'

'Hmmm, I've known a few like that,' I muttered darkly.

Jack laughed. 'Oh, the mares don't mind, they've been so revved up by the teaser he could pick his nose while he was on the job for all they cared.'

'What's the teaser?' I asked, wondering if it was some kind of sexual aid for horses, an Anne Summers equine tickler perhaps.

'Here's the teaser,' said Jack, indicating a small and rather scruffy looking grey in a nearby stable. He was circling round and round, neighing his head off in a demented manner. 'Meet Roger.'

'Poor old thing,' said Nick, patting his neck. 'His only role in life is to sniff around the mares and make sure they're in season. He gets them thoroughly sexed up and, just when he thinks he's going to get his wicked way, the mare will be led away for the likes of Sorcha or one of the other stallions to service.'

'So he never actually gets to do the business himself?'

' 'Fraid not, poor old Roger.'

'That's a singularly inappropriate name, isn't it?'

Nick laughed. 'It's Jack's warped sense of humour, I'm afraid.'

I watched, fascinated, as Roger was indeed led out to inspect a mare. He sniffed and snorted and rolled his eyes, prancing around her in a provocative manner and evidently pronouncing her to be not only in season but ready for anything. After a great deal of flirting and circling and, just as the poor old boy thought he was getting somewhere, the by now thoroughly over-excited mare was abruptly led away to the covering yard for bigger and better things.

At this point Sorcha was led out of his box by a stable boy. He strolled casually over to the covering yard, looking, I have to admit, devastatingly attractive: tall, dark, and not a hair out of place on his gleaming chestnut coat. His muscles rippled, he tossed his arrogant head, and the poor, mystified grey mare went weak at the knees, all thoughts of Randy Roger completely forgotten.

It reminded me of a haunt of mine in the King's Road, a nightclub where quite a few pretty girls go to dance round their handbags and get picked up. Invariably some spotty no-hoper of a guy would do just that. Having made contact with a girl, he'd ply her with drinks, dance his little socks off, shouting above the disco to make himself heard and, just as he'd be about to pounce, lo and behold, his good looking coolie friend – six foot two and not a spot on his chiselled, smouldering face – would stroll up and take over. Coolie would claim just one dance – usually a slow one – before disappearing into the night with her, leaving spotty no-hoper to gnash his teeth and chew the dashboard of his second-hand Mini.

Like a lot of these cool Chelsea guys, Sorcha had no manners whatsoever and didn't know the meaning of foreplay. He walked nonchalantly around the back of the mare, and heaved himself on board without so much as a friendly neigh in her general direction. Having said that, I have to admit he did his stuff with one of the most impressive pieces of kit I've ever seen. It was enough to make your eyes water, and the little grey mare looked pretty impressed too, if her eyes bulging out of their sockets were anything to go by.

'Make sure it's in deep, for God's sake!' yelled Jack to the stable boy, who had the mammoth task of guiding Sorcha in.

At this point I had a violent attack of schoolgirl giggles, and had to move away, stuffing a hankie in my mouth to muffle the snorts. The whole thing was titillating enough

291

anyway, but somehow, standing next to Nick made it even worse. I felt ridiculously embarrassed.

I went off to comfort Roger, who was thrashing around in his stable looking thoroughly pissed off, chewing anything he could get his teeth into: stable door, bucket, manger — anything to relieve the frustration. I hastily moved away, just in case he decided it was time to bury those enormous yellow teeth into harmless human flesh.

When Sorcha had finished and the mare had been led away to recover and ponder her good fortune, Nick and Jack wandered over.

Jack rubbed his hands together. 'Well, hopefully that's another prize winning foal in the bag. Where did you get to, Polly, you missed the best bit!'

'Didn't want to put him off his stride. I thought he might perform better without too much of a gallery.'

'Don't you believe it, old Sorcha likes an audience. Got time for a swift one back at the house, you two?'

'Some other time, Jack,' said Nick. 'I promised to show Polly the rest of the farm, and then I really must get down to some work.'

'Ah, that's your excuse, is it? Fair enough, I know a couple of love birds when I see them. Run along and frolic in the cornfields then. See if I care!'

Nick laughed. 'You've got a one-track mind, Jack. See you tomorrow, possibly — come up to the house.'

'Will do. Bye, Polly.' He winked. 'Watch him now, he's one hundred per cent pure beef, like the rest of his herd!'

By now my face was puce pink, but I laughed gaily and shook hands, rather unaccountably at a loss to know how to react to this sexy banter. The natural thing would be to tell Jack he'd got the wrong end of the stick, but on the other hand . . .

Nick and I climbed the fence and strolled back towards his farm again. It has to be said there was rather a telling silence. I'm not very good at silences, telling or otherwise.

'He seems like a nice chap,' I said lamely.

'Jack? Oh he's great fun. Got a brain the size of a pea, though and he keeps it between his legs.'

I laughed. 'Yes, he did seem a little — obsessed.'

Nick opened the gate to his yard. 'Well, let's face it, he runs a stud farm, so it's all he ever thinks about. He lives and breathes sex, does Jack . . . Jump in, I'm just going to check on the cows.' He indicated an open-topped Land Rover standing in the corner of the yard.

I obeyed, quietly relieved. My shiny brown boots were already caked with mud, and my legs were beginning to ache from all this exertion. A minute later, Nick jumped in beside me. Now you're talking, I thought, as we zoomed off, my hair streaming away from my face like corn in the breeze, or so I liked to think. This was much more my scene.

As we charged around the farm, Nick pointed out his woods and fields and, in the very, very far-flung distance, boundaries where neighbouring farms began. He seemed to own half of Cornwall, and it occurred to me to wonder whether he wasn't in fact Prince Charles in disguise. That would certainly explain all the regal looking portraits in the hall.

We roared off down a particularly bumpy track, which seemed to be going nowhere. All I could see in the distance was bright blue sky. The bumps were getting larger, and I folded my arms protectively across my chest, fervently wishing I'd had the nous to invest in a sports bra before embarking on an all-action weekend like this. All of a sudden, Nick slowed right down and we came to a shuddering halt. He turned the engine off.

I wondered why we'd stopped, there didn't seem a great deal to see, but I got out obligingly. We were at the very edge of a cornfield and, as I walked to the edge, I caught my breath. The cornfield sloped away to green fields below, and below that, to what I'd originally perceived to be the sky, but which was in fact a great expanse of sea. I stared down at the sparkling chasm that had opened up in front of me. It was dotted with tiny boats which bobbed jauntily around, their sails fluttering in the breeze. The water was as smooth as a mirror, just tilting now and then to offer up a different angle for the sun to reflect. Far away, on the opposite shore, I could make out a cluster of tiny white cottages basking in the sunshine.

I turned to Nick in amazement. 'This is absolutely beautiful. I had no idea we were by the sea!'

He laughed. 'Really? Well, I suppose technically we're not. This is a river, actually. It runs up to Gweek which is a few miles in that direction, and out to sea the other way. Over there is Frenchman's Creek — see?' He pointed out a dark and narrow inlet overhung with trees and heavy foliage.

'Oh yes — is it really? How romantic!' It was one of the few books I'd read, and I could quite imagine the dashing young Frenchman snaking up there in his boat to treat his aristocratic lady friend to a bit of *je ne sais quoi* behind some ancient oak tree.

'The village you can see over there is Helford,' said Nick pointing to the white cluster in the distance. 'If you like we'll take the boat over there tomorrow and I'll show you around. It's really pretty.'

'You have a boat?' Was there anything this man didn't have?

He laughed. 'Well, it would be pretty silly to live here and not have one. Do you sail?'

Now I don't actually 'do' anything that one is supposed to do, like ride, ski, sail, hunt, or even cook, and the only time I can answer a 'do you?' question in the affirmative is when the next word is either drink or smoke; but having come up against quite a few of these tricky little inquiries in my time, I go armed with a set of stock replies. I smiled up at him.'No, but I'm very good at lying around in a bikini waiting for the sun to pass over the yard-arm.'

He laughed. 'I bet you are, but I'm afraid there's no deck to speak of on this little dinghy. It's more of a ropes and reef-knots affair. What are your knots like?'

'Oh I do a lovely sheep shag,' I said with a smile, and then realised that wasn't quite what I'd meant at all.

Nick roared with laughter. 'Well you've come to the right place for that. There's a whole flock in the next field who'd be only to pleased to oblige! Perhaps I'd better let you off the actual sailing part, though. You can just sit at the back and look decorative. I must say I like the sound of the bikini.'

He gazed down at me speculatively from his dizzy heights. I met his eye fleetingly, but instantly looked down and dug up an ear of corn with my toe. Good Lord, was he flirting with me? Surely not. I looked up again and saw the brown eyes still twinkling away in my direction. A smile played around at the corners of his mouth. I immediately returned to my ear of corn. Christ, he was, and what's more the shock had completely taken the wind out of my normally flirty little sails. This was most out of character for both parties. Surely he should have warned me? Sent me a memo or something?

To Polly: Just to inform you that on Saturday 12 April there may be a brief and uncharacteristic flirtation on my part in the large cornfield overlooking the Helford River. Please be ready to anticipate just such an eventuality and respond accordingly. Nick.

Yes, that would have been much more in keeping. As it was, I was struggling to remember just one of the well-honed lines that would normally trip straight off my tongue in this sort of situation, and which had ensnared the likes of Harry Lloyd-Roberts and plenty more before him. I bit my lip.

'Wind . . . that's your problem,' Nick muttered.

I gasped with horror, wind? Christ! Had I, in my nervous confusion, inadvertently expelled some vile and evil-smelling gases? How unspeakably ghastly!

I looked up in alarm, but he wasn't looking at me any more. In fact he seemed to have totally forgotten about my existence. I followed his gaze out to sea. He was watching an unfortunate windsurfer who was struggling to stay on his board, collapsing repeatedly into the water.

'You've got to have a bit of wind to keep the thing upright,' he went on, shading his eyes against the sun and monitoring the sailor's progress. 'It's absolutely hopeless in this sort of weather, can't think why he's even bothering.'

'Oh! Oh yes, crazy . . . on a day like this,' I managed.

I tried to pull myself together. I realised now of course that Nick's reference to the delights of my bikini had just been small-talk. Yes, that was it. A casual pleasantry designed to please and perhaps even flatter, but nothing more than that. I, of course, had overreacted as usual, and had taken it to mean that he couldn't wait to take me in his arms and bowl me over in the cornfield.

I breathed deeply. How hugely disappointing. Hang on a minute — hugely what? Disappointing? Good grief, whatever was happening to me! Wasn't I supposed to be heartbroken? Hadn't I more or less decided that, since I couldn't have Harry, I was through with men and would probably remain celibate for the rest of my life? What on earth was I thinking of? I had a quick mental flick through my file of Harry pictures and found the pre-launch diving board one, an old favourite. I studied it carefully. Good gracious. How extraordinary. Surely his eyes hadn't always been that close together? And wasn't that mouth just a tad on the pinched side, and was it possible that his hairline was — heavens above — receding?

Shocked to the core, I filed the picture away again and

looked up at the one beside me. Wide-apart eyes, generous mouth, plenty of hair. Oh no. This could not be happening to me. My toes twitched nervously in my boots.

Of course, I reasoned, it's bloody hard to be cool and objective when you're up to your knees in corn, gazing out at just about the most beautiful sylvan scene in Christendom, and standing next to the dashing young owner of all that the eye can see. Confused? Who wouldn't be?

The windsurfer eventually called it a day, and swam back to shore dragging his board behind him. The sun disappeared behind a cloud. I shivered. Suddenly the sylvan scene didn't seem quite so peaceful and serene. In fact it seemed full of danger.

'Cold?' asked Nick, noticing my shiver.

'Mm, a bit chilly.'

Nick looked at the sky. 'I have a feeling it's going to rain, actually, which would be no bad thing. We could do with the water. Come on, let's go back, I could do with something to eat, apart from anything else.'

We climbed back into the jeep and sped off across country again. As we bumped along by the side of the field, I surreptitiously studied Mr Many-Acres sitting beside me. One arm was resting on the door, the other was casually guiding the wheel, his shirtsleeves rolled up to the elbows exposing already brown, muscly forearms. He hadn't shaved that morning, but that did nothing to detract from the strong chin and the classic jawline.

I looked away, wondering how many other girls had fallen for his rural charms down here: not that I had of course − yet − I mean at all, and nor would I, but I just wondered. It was, after all, interesting to muse, wasn't it? How many others, exactly? According to him, not many. Penny I discounted on the grounds that she was a historical figure and very much a mate now, but Serena. Ah Serena, she was a different matter. She was not only very current but very beautiful. I bet she looked great, flat on her back in a cornfield. For some reason my teeth seemed to grind together when I thought of this, and my top lip curled in an unattractive manner.

Where was she at the moment? Ah yes, filming. Dangerous job filming. All sorts of accidents occur, so I'm told; falling lights, masonry, scaffolding, that kind of thing. I wondered if anything untoward would befall her this weekend. Not that I wanted it to – dear me, no, nothing serious anyway. But perhaps if a piece of scenery did collapse – not too heavy mind, just a tree or something – and if she were to suffer, not a permanent injury, but something that would put her out of action for a while, briefly incapacitating her for, say, a couple of months? A broken leg maybe? And perhaps an arm too? Oh, and a touch of facial bruising, I added quickly, thinking she'd still look darned attractive lying in a hospital bed in plaster unless the face was, temporarily of course, disfigured. Well then, that would clear the way a bit, wouldn't it? Give me a bit of time. For what, Polly? What exactly did you have in mind? Goodness, I thought, shaking myself, sometimes I even managed to shock myself.

Chapter Sixteen

As Nick had promised, we spent the following day in true Enid Blyton style. Five Go Sailing on the Helford River: Nick, Tim, Rachel, Jamie and me. It was a fine, blustery morning, and we seemed to rocket across the river in record time. I'd always imagined sailing was a slow, rather sedate form of travel, but both Nick and Tim seemed to be speed merchants when it came to boating, doing their damnedest to get as much wind into the sail, and leaning right out over the side on a frighteningly dangerous rope affair, appropriately called a trapeze. I forced a jolly smile on to my rather green face, but was secretly extremely glad when we hit terra firma. I had a feeling it would take me a while to find my sea legs; if, indeed, I had any to be found.

We tied up the boat − or moored, as I'd come to call it, by the jetty on the Helford side and strolled up to the conveniently placed pub which overlooked the water. We laughed and chatted as we went, and I relished the prospect of crab sandwiches and ice-cold lager. This place was having a curious effect on me: I seemed to be permanently hungry. As we walked in, we greedily surveyed the list of goodies chalked up on the blackboard, licking our lips at the prospect of a boozy, slap-up lunch − at least, three of us did. Once we'd secured a table outside and sat down, Rachel declared that she wasn't in the least bit hungry, and was going for a walk with Jamie. 'Sometimes,' she announced, with more than a touch of the Greta Garbo's,

'I just want to be on my own – you know, to think things through a bit.'

She bit her lip and stared wistfully out to sea. Greta was now playing *The French Lieutenant's Woman*; all she needed was a hooded black cloak.

She sighed mournfully and turned back to us, 'I don't want to be rude, it's just – well, I've got so much on my mind at the moment. I just need a little time alone.'

Don't we all, darling, don't we all? But we don't make a big song and dance about it, do we? We don't sell tickets. We just creep off when no one's looking and lick our wounds in private, and when we return to the fold, we fervently hope that nobody noticed our absence, and if they did, we pretend we got stuck in the loo or something. But not our Rachel.

'It's just that – well, it all gets a bit much sometimes, and I have to get away,' she whispered, clutching Jamie to her breast, a pained expression on her peaky little face.

'Of course you do,' said Nick, looking concerned. He stood up and put a protective hand on her shoulder. 'You've been through a hell of a lot recently. I don't know how you've coped.'

Rachel sniffed a bit.

'Poor you, it must be awful,' agreed Tim. 'Shall we look after Jamie for you?'

'No, no,' she clung to him, chin up now, a brave little soldier look on her face. 'I'll carry him in his sling. I – I hope you don't mind, though, me going off like this?' Her eyes were wide and anxious.

'Not at all, not at all!' I chirped. 'Bye!'

'But will you be all right on your own?' asked Tim.

Would she be all right? For Christ's sake, she was going for a walk, not a bungee jump off the nearest suspension bridge – more's the pity. Of course she'd be all right.

Rachel bit her lip and nodded furiously, as if she didn't quite trust herself to speak.

I certainly didn't trust myself. Over the last couple of days it hadn't escaped my notice that, in her own quiet way, Rachel Marsden was one hell of a drama queen. She spent most of her time having long and meaningful discussions with Tim, the majority of which were conducted in huddled whispers by the drawing-room fire. He would gently prod and probe, asking her questions about Jamie, Adam, her father, and she would stare into space, twiddling a piece of hair around her finger before eventually muttering a monosyllable which you needed a hearing aid to catch.

This scintillating repartee would come to an abrupt halt if anyone was foolish enough to also want to sit by the only fire in this large and freezing-cold house. She would break off in the middle of one of her riveting replies such as, 'Um, I'm not sure,' or, 'Yes, perhaps,' and stare moodily into the flames, until the offending intruder got the hint and tiptoed off into another, colder room, at which point she would resume the halting discussion, pausing now and then to look up at Tim shyly from beneath her eyelashes.

It made me want to run to the nearest loo and stick my fingers down my throat, it all seemed so unbelievably phoney, but I wisely kept my counsel, not wanting to appear the arch bitch.

Tim found her fascinating and delighted in 'bringing her out of her shell', as he called it. He was patience itself, and regarded every muttered utterance on her part as a major breakthrough. Nick told me that Tim had always been brilliant in this respect, particularly with animals. I'd guffawed at the time, thinking this was a bit rich even with regard to Rachel, but I knew what he meant. He had a way of coaxing the timid and the shy, and Rachel certainly seemed to be opening up to him, but it occurred to me to wonder what Sarah thought about all this opening up while she slogged her guts out at the stables.

So here was our tragic heroine once again, standing on

the sea front, baby clasped to bosom. 'See you a bit later,' she whispered, and off she drooped, cardigan flapping in the breeze, hair straggling down her shoulders, head bowed against the elements.

'Bye-ee!' I trilled.

'Poor little thing,' muttered Nick.

'She just seems so . . .' Tim struggled for the right word. If it turned out to be 'vulnerable', I decided I'd have the screaming heebie-jeebies and throw myself headlong into the river, tearing my hair out en route. ' . . . defenceless,' he finished.

This was almost as bad. I ground my teeth together to stop them from seizing Tim's arm and shaking it like a dog.

'Hardly defenceless,' I said in what I hoped was a cool and level voice, but which I suspected had a touch of madness in it, 'I mean she's got you two socking great lads running round in circles, ready to defend her at a moment's notice.'

'Well, if she needed us of course we'd be there,' Tim agreed staunchly, failing to notice the shovel-load of irony I thought I'd piled on.

He folded his arms and leaned towards me over his pint. 'I must admit I find her fascinating. How well d'you know her, Polly?'

I sighed. 'Not well at all, she wasn't a friend of mine at school or anything.'

'So you only got to know her because of all this Adam and Jamie business?'

'Yes, and I'm quite sure our paths wouldn't have crossed otherwise,' I said with feeling.

Tim shook his head and looked thoughtful. 'You know, I get the feeling there's a lot more to Rachel than meets the eye. She's obviously extremely intelligent and very highly strung. I'd like to find out more about her, but it's so difficult to get her to talk, although I must say she's certainly started to chat a bit more since — Jack!'

He broke off in mid sentence to jump up and slap Jack Crawley on the back. Jack, by some miraculous stroke of good fortune, had appeared at our table, grinning from ear to ear and swaying violently. He was definitely the worse for a gin and tonic or six. I'd been groaning inwardly as Tim had opened up yet more discussion on the topic of the fascinating Rachel, so I was immensely pleased to see him.

'Hello there, one and all!' he boomed, clutching the table for support.

'Jack! What the devil are you doing here!' Nick quickly slipped a chair beneath his bottom as it headed floorwards.

Jack sat down heavily. 'Oops! Thanks, old man — just been to a drinks party at the yacht club, hell of a good do, you know, can't think why you weren't there. Christ, they make a mean Bloody Mary, though; nearly blew my socks off. Thought I'd pop in here on the way home and see if you reprobates were propping up the bar as usual, and here you are! I say, it's the gorgeous Polly again!'

He slipped a lecherous hand on to my knee, and leered into my eyes. I giggled and brushed him off.

'Been showing you round the haybarns again, has he?' he asked with a grin, winking towards Nick. 'Can't see what a sophisticated girl like you sees in a chap like that. You'd be much better off with me, you know!'

The hand reappeared on my knee, and the other one went around my shoulder. 'How about a little drinkie over at my place tonight? Slip into something a bit more comfortable, preferably diaph-, diaphan-, diaphanous — oops! Bit of a tongue-twister that one, when you've had a few. Anyway, you know what I mean, black netting, or chiffon or something, and come round at about, ooh, nine o'clock? That suit you?'

I giggled. 'That's way past my bedtime, Jack.'

'Splendid, splendid! Couldn't be better! S'way past mine, too, so that's where I'll be, in the bedroom — you can't miss it, top of the stairs, second on the left. I'll be the wildly attractive one lying on the square flat thing in the corner with not a lot on, now what d'you say? Eh?'

And so he went on, flirting outrageously, falling over his words and making us scream with laughter as he recounted what I suspected were mostly apocryphal tales of his love affairs with what seemed like the entire female population of Helford.

It only took Nick or Tim to prompt him with, 'And what about that blonde one, Jack?' or, 'Whatever happened to Sue?' and Jack would be weeping with laughter into his pint as he recounted yet another romp in the hay, the back of the Land Rover, the stable, or even — so he claimed — the covering yard.

We spent an entirely happy hour or so, laughing and joking and trying unsuccessfully to stop Jack pouring yet more drink down his throat. Eventually he admitted defeat and got unsteadily to his feet.

'S'no good, y'know, I can't sit here all day chatting to the likes of you lot. Some of us have got work to do. Some of us have got mares to service!'

Just then Rachel appeared around the corner.

'And speaking of mares, here's another pretty filly!'

Tim got up quickly and gave her his seat. 'Rachel, this is Jack Crawley, a neighbour of ours. Jack, Rachel.'

Jack took Rachel's hand and held it to his lips, as was his wont. 'Enchanted,' he murmured in his practised manner.

Rachel frowned and pulled her hand away as soon as was politely possible.

'Rachel's staying with us for a while, with young Jamie here,' Tim explained as she sat down.

Jack chivalrously pushed her chair in for her and made an exaggerated sweeping bow. He lost his balance and staggered slightly on the way up. 'Delighted to hear it. The more girls the merrier, I always say!'

Not in this case, I thought grimly.

Rachel smiled thinly, looking at his bloodshot eyes with distaste, clearly deciding he wasn't worth even the briefest of hellos.

'So this must be young Jamie!' Jack roared, undeterred by the chilly reception he was getting. 'I say, what a fine-looking chap, look at those rosy little cheeks! How are you, young fella?'

He leaned, or even lurched across the table to tickle his face, and no doubt poor Jamie got covered in an entire brewery's worth of fumes, but Rachel's reaction was, nonetheless, unforgivable.

She swept Jamie away out of Jack's reach and turned to him with a look of utter loathing. 'Keep your hands off my baby, you disgusting old drunk!' she hissed.

Jack drew back in alarm, retrieving his hand as if he'd been burned, his mouth wide with disbelief.

There was a moment's shocked silence as this gratuitous attack was digested. Rachel, pink with fury, stared defiantly at Jack, who was rooted to the spot. It was probably the stillest he'd managed to stand all lunchtime.

Nick leaped in quickly and put his arm round Rachel's shoulder. 'Jack didn't mean any harm, Rachel, he's a friend of ours, he wouldn't hurt Jamie!'

' 'Course he bloody wouldn't!' I added staunchly, rage pouring from my nostrils.

'I say, certainly not,' muttered Jack, puce with embarrassment. 'Most awfully sorry and all that, didn't mean to frighten you or anything.'

Tim looked at her kindly. 'I'll get you a drink, shall I? You're just a bit overwrought, that's all.'

Rachel looked at the shocked faces assembled around the table and burst into tears. 'I'm sorry,' she sobbed. 'It's just − I have to be so careful, I hate anyone coming near him, I'm so sorry!'

'There now, it's all right,' soothed Tim. His hand

covered hers on the table. 'Of course you feel like that, it's only natural after what you've been through, but old Jack here wouldn't hurt a fly, you know.'

Old Jack was doing a good job at catching them, though, as he stood facing her, wide-mouthed and incredulous. 'Lord, no, 'course not!' he mumbled.

'I know, and I'm so sorry, I do apologise, I totally overreacted,' managed Rachel at last, between sniffles. She looked up at him. 'I'm — I'm just a bit nervous about anyone touching my baby at the moment, you see.' She blew her nose noisily into a hankie.

'Quite understand, quite understand,' said Jack, who clearly didn't. He shook his head vigorously. 'Can't be too careful these days, can you? Best forgotten now though, eh?'

Rachel nodded and smiled briefly. 'Yes, absolutely.' She turned to Tim. 'I think I will have that drink now, Tim, if you don't mind.'

'Sure,' he got to his feet. 'Gin and tonic?'

'Please. I'll just go and wash my face. Rachel got up and headed towards the Ladies'.

Jack turned to me and raised his eyebrows. 'I say, what about that?' he said quietly. 'I don't mind drunk, or even disgusting, but old!' He looked at me in horror and I giggled.

Jack polished off his pint. 'Might just slip off, though. Don't want to catch the sharp end of that one's tongue again. One always knows the women one can and can't charm, and I couldn't charm the shoes off that one, let alone the pants. Bye all!' and with that he donned his flat cap and hastily withdrew.

Rachel returned looking composed but, I was pleased to see, slightly shamefaced. As she sat down there was an awkward silence, and I for one was determined not to break it. I hoped it was killing her.

Tim took pity and smiled, handing her her drink.

'Before Jack arrived, I was about to ask Polly how you two knew each other. I gather you didn't bump into each other much at school?'

Rachel took a sip of her gin and visibly relaxed. 'No, Polly was a few years above me, but I knew of her of course. Everyone at school had heard of Polly, she had quite a reputation!' She smiled at me and I tried not to fall off my stool.

Heavens! Could this be for real? Was Rachel paying me a compliment? I beamed graciously at her. Ah yes, it was true, of course, I had been a bit of a lad. A bit of a one for the dastardly deeds – shimmying down knotted sheets from dormitory windows, putting salt in the headmistress's tea – all pretty mundane stuff in retrospect, but jolly daring at the time.

'Oh yes,' Rachel went on, warming to her theme, 'there are so many stories about Polly I hardly know where to begin!'

I was keen for her to begin wherever she felt like it, if it was going to make me look terrific.

'Most of them apocryphal, I'm sure,' I said bashfully, lowering my eyes and playing with a beer mat to keep me from rubbing my hands together with glee, 'or, at least, exaggerated,' I added quickly, lest anyone should think the daredevil stunts Rachel was about to recount were entirely make-believe.

'What sort of things?' asked Nick, intrigued.

Yes, what sort of things Rachel? I was on the edge of my seat. I was vaguely aware that I'd been regarded as a bit of a coolie by the lower forms, but I'd no idea I'd gone down in the annals of schoolgirl history as some kind of wild and abandoned folk heroine. A sort of Joan of Arc of the Upper Fifth.

'Well, let me think now . . .' Rachel frowned as she tried to remember some of the more hilarious anecdotes.

I leaned forward eagerly, wishing I could prompt her,

but realising that might look a bit keen.

'Oh yes, I know!' she said.

Oh goodie!

'What about that time you were caught handing out drugs to everyone. D'you remember that, Polly?' Rachel turned to me with wide, innocent eyes.

Drugs! The word hit me hard in the face and seemed to stick there, slap in the middle of my forehead, written up in red. I caught Nick's rather shocked face out of the corner of my eye, and nearly gagged on a slice of gin-soaked lemon as my elbow went into overdrive, chucking it down my throat. Christ! What the bloody hell was she up to? I retrieved the lemon from my tonsils and brushed the gin off my chin in what I hoped was a nonchalant manner.

'Oh well, hardly drugs eh, Rachel?' I said lightly, cranking up a smile. 'I mean a few magic mushrooms mixed with the leaves of what I thought was a marijuana plant, but which in fact turned out to be an Aspidistra – I mean that hardly constitutes hard drugs does it? No one's going to mainline on Aspidistra leaves and mushrooms, are they?'

Nick and Tim roared with laughter. Phew. What a relief.

'Oh God, Polly,' said Nick. 'I can just see you chopping up Aspidistra leaves and cramming them furtively into little plastic bags!'

'Was that all it was?' Rachel looked disappointed. 'Oh, I'd heard there was more to it than that. I thought the police were called in and—'

'Good Lord, no!' I cut in hastily, 'No, no – nothing like that!'

There had, admittedly, been a brief interview with the headmistress in her study on account of the wooziness of one or two faint hearts in my dorm, and yes, this particular interview had in fact taken place in the presence of one Police Constable Moore from the local constabulary, but one piddly little village constable hardly amounts to calling in the police, does it? I mean, come on, Miss Marsden, we're not talking Miami Vice here, are we? And anyway, once I'd explained that I'd merely been attempting to make some herbal tea and had distributed it around the dorm on the grounds that it might be a soothing bedtime relaxant, all had been forgiven and forgotten, as I sincerely hoped it would be now.

'You see, that's how these little stories get exaggerated!' I cried, laughing nervously and taking a slug more gin: my throat was inexplicably dry. Come on, Rachel, get off the subject of drugs and police and on to some of my more amusing escapades, like the time I streaked naked through the village for a bet, or what about when I—

'Oh yes!' she announced, raising her index finger.

Oh good, I thought with relief. But it was oh bad.

'What about that dreadful business when you were caught cheating in your history O-level – looking at someone else's paper or something. D'you remember that, Polly?'

I did, and I didn't like the taste of sawdust in my mouth or the nasty glint in her eye. This was most definitely below the belt; so far below that I felt my knees sag in my leggings.

Of course I hadn't cheated. The very idea. No, it was all perfectly simple. Sophie Maxwell, sitting next to me, had dropped her paper and I'd merely picked it up, pausing, of course, to glance at it and to check that – well, to check that her name was at the top of the paper and that it was in fact hers, before handing it back to her. Wouldn't anyone? Anyone, it appeared, except the ghastly invigilator who hauled me out of the exam room and accused me of nicking Sophie's dates. The historical kind of course.

I narrowed my eyes at my new accuser. 'That was all a big misunderstanding,' I said slowly, sounding, I hoped, rather like Margaret Thatcher, 'a total misunderstanding which was cleared up very quickly. There was a full inquiry, and I'm pleased to say I was fully vindicated.'

'Ah,' said Rachel thoughtfully, 'I wondered. I mean, after all, you didn't pass, did you? So it wasn't as if you even benefited. Am I right in thinking you were the only girl to leave St Gertrude's with absolutely no qualifications whatsoever? What a scream!'

Not nearly as much of a scream as you'll make when I get my hands round your throat, I thought savagely.

'But am I right?' persisted Rachel. 'Did you get any?'

I ground my fingernails into my rather damp palms, thinking that it must surely be time Rachel went for another walk, along the clifftops perhaps, perilously close to the edge.

Nick looked confused. 'Oh no, no, that can't be right, can it, Polly? Because on your CV it says you got six O-levels, I distinctly remember.'

Which in turn distinctly reminded me of something I'd temporarily forgotten. This was my boss we were talking to, or rather, Rachel was talking to. Surely there were rules about this sort of thing? Unions to complain to, punishments to hand out. Surely she couldn't get away with it without a life sentence to contend with?

'It was six, wasn't it?' repeated Nick.

My eyes glazed over and my mouth opened bravely. What on earth would come out of it? I marvelled at its courage. What form of words would it deem appropriate? I sat waiting, as they did too, for my lips and tongue to surge into action.

'That's right, six. I took them at a Crammer,' I spluttered. Brilliant! Absolutely bloody brilliant! Who needs O-levels when your mouth can say things like that, eh?

'Which one?' piped up Rachel, but she was fighting a losing battle. No one was terribly interested in which Crammer I'd gone to.

'Which one? Oh, one in Oxford,' I said vaguely, 'can't remember the name of it. Would anyone like another drink?'

'No thanks,' said Tim, draining his glass. 'We'd better be getting back, I've got work to do.'

And so have I, I thought savagely as we sailed across the river ten minutes later. It was called murdering a fellow house-guest in cold blood without anyone noticing. If only I'd read more Agatha Christie. Perhaps I could just slip her over the side? I peered into the water. It looked pretty deep and cold, eminently suitable, but this was a very small boat and I didn't think I could subtly up-end her into the murky depths without drawing attention to my actions and ending up in deep water myself. I would bide my time, I thought, grinding my teeth to pulp. Revenge, they say, is a meal best eaten cold.

I was still quietly seething when we got back to the house. Nick disappeared to tend to his sheep, so I made for the only warm chair in the house, the one Rachel usually bagged by the fire. I found a little footstool for my feet, and arranged the intelligent bits of the Sunday papers decoratively around me, although of course in reality I was shaping up to an hour or two's uninterrupted kip.

Rachel curled up on the rug by my feet. I shut my eyes and thought how amusing it would be if my leg had one of those involuntary spasms that sometimes occur when you're almost dropping off to sleep, and I inadvertently kicked her in the teeth. My foot twitched eagerly but I held it back. It might, after all, look a little too obvious.

I drifted off into a glorious dream in which I was quite the heroine of the hour as I singlehandedly delivered twin lambs. It was late at night and Nick was in the Dutch barn, where he'd been struggling for hours with a heavily pregnant ewe who was groaning in agony as she tried to give birth. Alerted by all the noise, I appeared in a rather fetching little nightie, and because my arm was thinner

311

than his, was about to stick it up the sheep's whatsit and deliver the lambs. (I knew, of course, that in reality this would have been absolutely impossible because at the merest hint of blood I'd have been heaving and chucking all over the place, but happily, of course, in dreams, one can ride roughshod over little details like that.) Anyway, suffice to say, Nick was absolutely delighted, beaming at me and showering me with compliments and praises, in fact — yes, that's right, he was hugging me, giving me a great big bear hug when, all of a sudden, Tim's voice piped up in the distance.

'Come on, Rachel!'

I opened one eye. He was over by the grand piano, patting the stool in an encouraging manner. 'Come on, come and give us a tune, it's about time we heard you play!'

I groaned softly. Oh God, we were bringing out Rachel again. I shut the eye and snored softly, hoping to suggest that I for one did not relish the prospect of being hauled from the Land of Nod by Rachel doing her party piece.

'Oh no, I couldn't,' said Rachel.

I couldn't resist a peep. She was huddled by the fire, smiling shyly and twiddling her hair.

'Oh come on,' urged Tim. 'We'd all love to hear you!'

Speak for yourself, I thought grimly.

'Oh no, really, not now . . .'

'Oh please do,' said Sarah, who had just arrived back from the stables. 'No one ever plays that piano unless it's to bash out "chopsticks" or something.'

'Oh no, I don't think I could.'

'Oh, please.'

'No, really.'

Just as I was about to rise up from my chair like a woman possessed, charge across the room and single-handedly ram the entire grand piano into her mouth, she demurred.

'Oh well, OK. I'll just play a bit of Bach.'

She shuffled over to the piano and sat down. I braced myself. She flexed her fingers around a bit, and then she played. And I have to say it brought a lump even to my cynical throat. As the music filled the room, full of sadness and heartbreak and loss, I listened and stared, mesmerised. She certainly had a gift, a real talent. It was almost as if she'd become a different person. I blinked. That surely wasn't Rachel Marsden over there, venting all that passion and emotion, was it?

It was a long piece, but we were all on the edge of our seats, and when she finished, there was a moment's silence. Then we all clapped like mad, even me, which I thought was big of me.

'Bravo! Bravo!' shouted Tim.

Rachel smiled shyly. 'Thanks,' she whispered, looking down at her hands. 'It really wasn't awfully good, you know.'

She slipped off the stool and slunk over to the fire again to resume her hunched, gnome-like position once again. All emotion had gone, all passion was spent. Rachel, the tight-lipped little mouse was back *in situ* again.

Tim was in raptures, falling over himself to praise her. 'But that was fantastic, Rachel! I've never heard anyone play like that and, honestly, I may strike you as a philistine, but I have been to quite a few piano recitals. You really should take it up professionally, you know, I'm quite sure you're good enough. I honestly think you could be a concert pianist or something.'

'Oh well, one day maybe,' murmured Rachel.

'You really should try, you know, you've got so much talent. Don't you think so, Polly?'

'Definitely,' I muttered.

After this, of course, there was no stopping her, and with more encouragement from Tim, she performed for Nick when he arrived back from the farm. All the pieces

313

she played were serious and melancholy, and marvellous though it all was, I felt ready to slit my wrists at the end of it. I also realised, with a dull thud of my heart, that it was time to go home.

I sighed and pulled a train timetable out of the bookcase, flipping through it miserably. I looked at the clock. God, at this rate I'd be back in London at about three a.m; I really must go and pack and get someone to take me to the station. The idea of leaving Cornwall filled me with doom and gloom. Who would have thought I'd want to swap the bright lights for cow pats so quickly? Of course, that wasn't the whole story, it had more to do with finding a different set of bright lights, namely the ones shining in those dark eyes over there. They met mine as I looked up from the timetable, and advanced towards me. I gulped as Nick sat on the sofa beside me and instinctively lifted my thighs up a bit to make them look thinner.

He took the book from my hands and snapped it shut. 'Is there any real need to go back tonight?'

Oh heavens, he was going to be all masterful. My knees began to wobble with excitement, and I had to abandon the raised thigh position.

'Well, no, I suppose I could go back in the morning – but I'd be a bit late for work.'

'And who would be there to care?'

I took his point, but wanted to appear conscientious. I frowned. 'There's quite a lot to do you know,' I said piously, 'all the scripts for the Din-Din's Dog Food pitch have to be typed up, not to mention the entire presentation.'

'Well, I've yet to write it, so it can hardly be typed.'

'Even so, the work will be piling up.'

'Rubbish. I'm not there so why should you be? You might just as well stay here for a while.'

For a while? My heart did a backward flip-flap and danced merrily around in my ribcage. He wanted me to stay! He really wanted me to stay − or, to put it another way, he simply didn't want me to leave him! Of course. Yes, it was obvious. Over the last two days he'd become totally besotted with me, and whereas previously he couldn't bear to have me *in* his sight, he now couldn't bear to have me *out* of it. What a funny old world. I tried my voice.

'I'd − I'd love to . . .' too high. I coughed and tried again. 'I'd really love to stay, I − I really would, I just love it here, it's all so beautiful − the countryside, the house, the animals and oh − just everything. I haven't been as happy as this for ages!' I gushed.

Steady Polly steady, don't overdo it. I took a few deep breaths and tried to calm myself.

'Good!' He tossed the timetable over the back of the sofa. 'That settles it, then. To be honest I really can't be fagged to drive you to the station.' He grinned.

I winced, but managed to smile back as I caught the body blow. Ouch. It had hurt quite a bit actually, but not enough to entirely dampen my spirits. If you really wanted someone to leave you'd move heaven and earth to get them to the station, wouldn't you? I mean, if someone was really getting on your tits, a little forty minute car ride would be a breeze, wouldn't it? Absolutely. I realised, though, that I might have to review his besottedness in the light of this comment. Later. Much later. For the moment I was happy just sitting here on the sofa, close to him − really quite close to him indeed. I'd say there was no less than, what − three inches between our respective buttocks?

He flung his arm along the back of the sofa, fixed me with his liquid brown's and talked about the farm. I sighed happily and thought about the farmer. Blissikins.

'Sorry, am I boring you?'

'What? No of course not! Why?'

'I thought you yawned.'

'Did I? Oh! No just a sigh. I was just thinking – well, I was just thinking how nice it is to be staying on, um, for a bit – not long of course, just a bit.'

'Stay as long as you want,' he replied with a dazzling smile.

'Thank you,' I whispered, staring into his glorious deep brown eyes and wondering if we were talking weeks, or months or even . . . No, don't be silly, Polly. I gave myself a little shake and listened attentively as he spoke of crop yields and lambing figures, nodding intelligently and asking pertinent questions, as any good farmer's wife, I mean, secretary should.

Chapter Seventeen

The next few days flew past. Rachel and Jamie stayed mostly at the house, and Tim and Sarah went back to work, which left Nick and me. We walked for miles, sat in quiet little pubs eating crab sandwiches and treacle tart and talked endlessly. When we weren't walking, talking or eating, we were either rowing or sailing – depending on the wind – up and down the river.

On one particularly sunny morning, as we drifted slowly up Frenchman's Creek, I lay back in the boat and pulled my straw hat down over my face. Through the holes in the straw I could peer at Nick without being observed. His black hair was tousled and his face, if not brown, was certainly ruddy after just a few days in this early April sunshine. All week his increasingly tanned forearms had stuck out of an array of denim shirts and baggy jumpers, and today it was the turn of a rather countrified checked number to expose him to the elbows.

I stared at his strong hands as they gripped the oars tightly, expertly guiding the boat around rocks and overhanging branches, and tried to remember what they'd looked like when they'd held documents and files and protruded from the sleeves of a pinstriped suit in an office in South Kensington. Then I tried to imagine all of him back in South Kensington. Funny, it seemed like another world, and one that he didn't belong to at all. Did I belong? Where was my world?

I shut my eyes and imagined for a moment that it was here. And not just in a small way, but in a mighty big way — so big, in fact, that within a twinkling I was mistress of Trewarren, wife to Mr Nicholas Penhalligan and mother of his — ooh, let's see, five, no — six children. It was the work of a moment. And within another moment, I'd pictured myself in Trewarren's kitchen, up to my elbows in cake mixture, singing away tunefully as I baked a cake for tea.

Now and again I'd smile down indulgently as my black-haired, brown-eyed babies frolicked around at my feet, happy with their finger paints and their Play-doh, and with none of that unnecessary shouting and screaming that seems to accompany most children's games. They were certainly the most angelic of babies, and one or two of them — or perhaps even all of them — were capable of changing their own nappies, had done so since birth, in fact; and they'd never been sick in their lives. But I digress.

As I poured my Victoria Sponge mixture into a baking tin, the kitchen door opened, and who should appear, fresh from the fields, with the smell of corn in his hair and a special kind of wife-hungry light in his eyes, but my husband, the farmer. I wiped my floury hands on my apron, and greeted him with a tender kiss. Filled with a passion that hadn't wavered for a moment during four wonderful years of marriage — hang on, how many children did I say? Well some of them were obviously twins, er — yes, all of them, actually, three sets of twins — anyway, filled with this passion, he seized me firmly around the waist and pulled me, quite roughly really, towards him.

Under his coarse, tweed jacket which tickled my face, I could feel his hard, muscly body rippling against me, simply aching to take me upstairs, or perhaps — yes, that was it, what he really wanted to do was to ravish me right here and now on the kitchen table.

'How about it?' his eyes seemed to say. I glanced down at the children. 'Not now,' my own eyes seemed to say, a smile playing around my luscious lips, 'later.'

Panting hard, but somehow managing to control himself, he gazed deep into my sapphire eyes and planted a long lingering kiss on my full, rosy lips, marvelling, for the umpteenth time, at his supreme good fortune in finding himself such a terrific wife, who was not only effortlessly capable and ran the house with sizzling efficiency, but was also devastatingly attractive and downright saucy in the bedroom.

I frowned under my hat. Would the capable and efficient bit be a problem? I scratched my chin thoughtfully. I dare say I could learn, but − wait a minute, why bother? Why on earth should I be immersed in cake mixture? Surely I'd have a cook? Yes, of course. I wouldn't be in the kitchen at all, I'd be in the morning room!

Quick as a flash there was a speedy scene change and I was transported to the morning room, seated at my writing desk with the sun streaming in behind me through the huge bay window. Now what was I doing? Ah yes, planning the menu for a forthcoming dinner party. Such a bore, but one must entertain the locals occasionally: the Master of the Hunt, the neighbouring farmers etc; they expected it, and of course I did it so well.

I took off my diamond bracelet − a wedding present from my husband, but so incredibly heavy it made writing difficult − and jotted down the courses: watercress soup, followed by salmon en croute, followed by raspberries and cream. There, that should do it. Oh, and I must remind Jenkins to get the appropriate wine from the cellar − or would Nick do that? I wasn't sure.

Anyway, I got up from my desk, pausing only to smooth a few wrinkles out of the wonderfully understated navy blue Armani dress I was wearing, and adjusted my pearl choker — another wedding, no, anniversary present from my husband. I caught a glimpse of myself in the mirror. The pearls looked so good around my throat, gleaming away against my Christmas-in-the-Caribbean suntan.

As I passed by the window I spotted my delicious children being either pushed in prams or carried around the immaculate gardens by a tribe of uniformed Norland nannies. I opened the window and blew them all a kiss — 'Co-ee darlings!' They waved back adoringly.

I drifted on into the kitchen in search of my cook, Mrs Bridges — no all right, too obvious — Mrs, um, Smith.

'Ah, Mrs Smith there you are. You'll be pleased to hear I've finally decided on tomorrow night's menu.' And so saying, I'd sink languidly into the large wheelback chair by the Aga and cross my slim, silk-stockinged legs.

'Very good, M'am,' she'd say, wiping her floury hands on her apron (*her* floury hands, note — not mine), and giving me her undivided attention. Would she curtsey? No, of course not, don't be stupid, Polly.

I leaned forward and fixed her with my capable, efficient eye. 'Now, as you know, Mr Penhalligan is very partial to watercress soup so I thought—' Just then, just as I was in the middle of briefing my cook, the door flew open and in strode my husband — fresh from the fields, smell of corn in hair, wife-hungry look in eye, etc, etc. Without pausing for a moment, he strode over to the chair, took me in his arms and — oh, just *before* he took me in his arms, Mrs Smith suddenly got an urgent telephone call from the butchers, saying the joint she'd ordered was ready and would she please come and pick it up *immediately* because, um — because otherwise it would go off. So off she rushed, and as soon as the door had closed behind her, he strode over to the chair, corn in hair, wife-hungry look, and took me in his arms. His breath was roaring away in my ears. 'Oh my darling!' he murmured, 'I want you so badly!' He kissed me hungrily, then he lifted me into his arms and strode to the table where he set me down, and roughly but gently, but firmly but roughly, he—

'What on earth are you doing?' My hat flew off my face at the very best bit and I looked up to see Nick, my boss — friend at most, but certainly not my husband — staring down at me, a puzzled look on his face.

'Are you all right?'

I sat up guiltily. 'What? Yes, of course. Sorry what was I doing?'

'Well, you've been muttering and sort of squirming and wriggling. At one point you started moaning, quite loudly actually, about watercress. I thought perhaps you were having a nightmare, except you seemed to be rather enjoying it.'

'Ah! Yes — well, you're right, you see I was dreaming! I fell asleep and — and had this awful feeling that great clumps of watercress were bearing down on me, like — like the Triffids. It all came rising up out of the river and got me round the neck, like this!' I demonstrated, clasping my throat hard. I shivered. 'Phew, lucky you woke me when you did. That was no joke, I can tell you!'

'You look rather hot, your face is terribly red.'

'Is it?' I fanned my flaming face with my hat. 'That's probably because I thought I was being strangled, all the blood probably went to my face.'

'Are they always so vivid?'

'What?'

'Your dreams.'

'Oh! Oh yes, always. God, sometimes I cry out and . . . and thrash around. Once I even got up and walked downstairs. I've got such a terrific imagination you see, and it all seems so real. I'm hell to sleep with.'

'Really?' Nick raised his eyebrows.

I fanned my face even harder as it got hotter and hotter. 'Well, no, having said that, no I'm not, I'm pretty easy to

321

sleep with actually — easy in the sense that, well in the sense that I'm not difficult . . . I mean, no one's actually ever complained — not that there have been many who would — complain I mean, simply because there really haven't been that many, if you see what I mean.' Things were getting decidedly out of hand here.

Nick roared with laughter. 'Polly, you are hysterical. I really couldn't care less how many people you've slept with or whether or not they've complained. It's none of my business.'

'Well I haven't,' I said crossly, indignant now, and keen to set the record straight, 'slept with many, that is, and the few that I have haven't complained either, so there.'

I childishly turned my back on him and stared down into the water, furious with myself for behaving like an idiot, and furious with him for not wanting it to be any of his business. I could feel my face heating up the river. God I was a moron.

Nick rowed on, and I couldn't see his face but I was sure he was laughing at me. Determined not to turn around, I let my hand drift along in the water, grabbing at reeds and bulrushes and pretending I was thoroughly absorbed by the ripples.

The silence was deafening but I wasn't going to break it, he would just jolly well have to be nice to me for a change, and he'd have to make a real effort. How dare he laugh at me like that and — and how dare he be so rude? He needn't think he could get round me with a couple of glasses of cider and a ploughman's lunch either, oh no, he'd have to do better than that.

'Polly?' said Nick after a while.

'Hmm?' I responded sulkily. Whatever he wanted, the answer was no.

'I thought I might go to Gweek this afternoon. It's about time I looked in on Mum; she'll think I'm avoiding her. D'you want to come?'

'Oh yes please!' I spun around eagerly. 'I'd love to come!'

'Good. I'll give her a ring when we get back.'

Sulk? What sulk. It was high time I met my mother-in-law.

And so it was that a few hours later I found myself being driven off to meet Mrs Penhalligan. I mean surely. Come on. He could quite easily have gone on his own, couldn't he? It would have been much more natural to say, 'Hope you don't mind, but I must go and see my mother, can you amuse yourself this afternoon?' But no. No, it was important that I came too.

As we whizzed along in the Land Rover, I unclenched my nervous hands and smoothed out the skirt of my Laura Ashley dress.

Nick had looked highly amused when I'd waltzed down the stairs in this particular number, but there was no doubt in my mind that it was absolutely perfect. To capture the essence of this dress, one really has to refer to it as a 'frock', a sort of spriggy cotton muslin affair with daisies and an itsy-bitsy collar and a flouncy skirt. Twee, I grant you, but it's only ever worn on 'meet the parents' outings, and it's never failed me yet. Eminently suitable.

I tucked a little lace hanky into the sleeve for good measure, and gave Country Girl just one more chance, restricting it this time to wrists only and not backs of knees, neck, or other assorted pulse points.

Now. Chocolates? Flowers? Daffodils would be a little like coals to Newcastle, I decided, so I settled for chocolates and ordered Nick to stop at the village shop. He obeyed, and looked even more amused when I reappeared bearing a large box of fudge.

'Who's that for?'

'Your mother, of course.'

He exploded with laughter at the wheel.

'What's so funny?'

'Nothing, it's just that that's what all the plebby tourists buy to take back to Purley or Dagenham. Look at the label.'

I turned it over and saw, 'A present from Cornwall' in olde-worlde writing surrounded by gnomes and fairies. I sighed and tossed it into the back seat. I knew I should have gone for the clotted cream.

As we rounded the corner into Gweek, I was pleasantly surprised to see that it had a rather refreshing, businesslike air about it. Helford was undoubtedly prettier, but it was very much a holiday homes and cream teas village. Gweek, on the other hand, was a village where real people lived and worked. No cutesy cottages here; in fact the only one I saw was right on the edge of the village, perched on the top of a hill. It was whitewashed and thatched with honeysuckle rampaging around the front door and clematis winding its way around the windows. A large tabby cat sat sunning herself on the doorstep.

'That's Mum's place,' said Nick as we sped past.

'Oh! How pretty!' I nearly twisted my head off in an effort to catch a glimpse. 'But why aren't we stopping?'

An icy hand gripped my heart. Had he got cold feet? Had second thoughts? Couldn't bring himself to introduce someone as gauche and stupid as me to his undoubtedly highly sophisticated, elegant mother?

'Because she won't be there, she'll be in here.'

We rounded a corner and scrunched to a halt on the gravel drive of a pub just outside the village.

'Oh!' I was deeply shocked. You wouldn't catch my mother in the Fox and Hounds in Esher High Street on a Thursday afternoon. The Conservative Party Bring-and-Buy sale, perhaps, but not the Fox and Hounds.

'Has she got a problem?'

My vision of the immaculate Mrs Penhalligan, dressed in twinset and pearls and deftly arranging chrysanthemums in a crystal vase in her drawing room, was plummeting fast in the direction of a whisky swilling bag lady, pub-crawling her way round southern Cornwall.

Nick laughed. 'Good God, no, I mean she certainly likes a drink, but it's not a problem.' He held open the door for me.

'So what's she doing in here in the middle of the afternoon?' I asked suspiciously as I ducked to avoid a low beam.

'This is where she gets her inspiration.'

'Inspiration? For what?'

'You'll see.'

My eyes took a while to adjust from the bright sunshine outside to the near darkness of the saloon bar, but when they did, Hetty Penhalligan was the very first person I saw.

She was sitting in the corner by an open window which shot the only beam of light into the gloomy room, surrounding her in a faint halo-like gleam and lighting up the unmistakable Penhalligan features.

Although I recognised her instantly, she was totally unexpected. I'd somehow assumed that the boys had inherited the Roman nose and square, determined jaw from their father, but in fact they sat very well on her strong, chiselled face. Her black hair, now streaked with grey, was cut in a sharp, geometric bob which complemented her striking features. She was a handsome woman.

I fluffed up my skirt and set my face in a sweet girlie smile as I followed Nick over to her but, as we got closer, my sweet smile froze and I had a violent urge to tear my frock from my back and run to the nearest Oxfam shop.

For that is undoubtedly where Mrs Penhalligan bought her clothes. Over a pair of baggy blue mechanic's overalls – or was it a boiler suit? Yes, it was a boiler suit – anyway, over this she was sporting a man's tweed jacket with the sleeves rolled up to her elbows. Around her neck was a spotty red handkerchief and on her feet were a pair of what looked like hobnailed Doc Marten boots. The whole ensemble was splattered with paint as if someone had systematically flicked the entire contents of a Dulux factory at her.

She didn't look up as we approached, but kept her eyes firmly on an old man sitting opposite her, staring at him in a peculiarly penetrating way. His eyes were staring equally fixedly into his pint.

As the penny dropped it activated my jaw which swung open with surprise. A painter! Propped up in front of her was a canvas, to which she added a couple of quick daubs, and, to her left, a glass of white wine which was rather an odd colour. It became apparent why, when she absentmindedly dipped her paint brush in it, mistaking it for the water.

'Damn!' she bellowed, 'I keep *doing* that! Barney, get me another drink, will you? This one's gone Prussian blue again.'

She waved the offending glass at the barman, and then caught sight of Nick. 'Darling!' she cried, in a crackly, gin-soaked voice, 'what a lovely surprise!'

Nick kissed her. 'Hi Mum, thought I might find you in here.'

He settled himself down next to her.

'And who's this charming little flower?' she asked, her eyes roaming over the itsy-bitsy frock.

'Oh this is Polly McLaren, a friend of mine.'

'Hello Mrs Penhalligan,' I said, holding out my hand and smiling.

'You must call me Hetty, everybody does,' she said, taking my hand. 'Oh look, how silly of me, now you've got paint all over you. Here,' she handed me a piece of oily rag and I wiped my hand.

I felt absurdly self-conscious in my frock, and faintly irritated that Nick hadn't warned me. It wasn't as if I couldn't have looked the part, too: I had a whole collection of arty-farty clothes back at the house just aching for an outing. There was that lovely French peasant's smock and the pedal-pushers and, oh, all manner of bohemian gear. I whipped the lace hanky out of my sleeve and hitched the ghastly skirt up a bit when I sat down.

'Barney, for Christ's sake!' she roared, making me jump out of my skin. 'It's like the bloody Gobi desert in here. Line up three gin and tonics, will you, there's a love.'

Barney grinned good humouredly from behind the bar, put down the glass he'd been wiping, and hastened to oblige his customer. It had to be worth his while, she was a pretty colourful asset for any pub – cheaper than buying a fruit machine, I thought to myself.

'So how's it going, then?' asked Nick, straddling a stool next to his mother and peering over her shoulder at the picture. 'Been discovered yet?'

' 'Course I bloody haven't,' she boomed – this seemed to be the only volume her voice could manage – 'the philistines around here wouldn't know a decent canvas if they stuck their heads through it. All they want is chocolate-boxy pastoral scenes or little children with tears running down their cheeks. Ugh. No, I'm afraid I'm just going to have to kill myself. Nothing like a dead artist to send prices soaring through the roof.'

'Or cut your ear off?' I suggested tentatively.

'Might work,' she agreed, 'bit messy though.'

I looked at the painting. It was a riot of blotches and blobs and I could quite see why the locals weren't too enamoured. I thought it was dreadful. But I also knew, from my experiences at private views in London, that what I thought were unspeakably bad pictures were usually deemed to be extremely good.

'It's awfully good,' I lied creepily.

Nick guffawed loudly. 'Looks like someone's been sick!'

Hetty ignored her son and addressed herself to me

327

instead. 'Thank you, my dear. Yes, it is rather, isn't it?' she agreed calmly. 'But then it helps to have a sitter as ugly as Arthur here. Bags of character.'

I glanced quickly at poor Arthur and hoped he was deaf as well as ugly. Hetty's voice had a certain resonance about it which made it hard to miss. Luckily he appeared to be not only deaf but brain dead too, as he sank further and further into his pint.

'Thank you, Arthur!' she yelled at the top of her voice, prodding him in the arm. 'That will be all for today!'

He waggled a bony hand in acknowledgement and raised his watery old eyes briefly from his beer.

I smiled at him. Sweet old man. It took me a few seconds to realise that he wasn't a sweet old man at all. He leered nastily at me and, rolling over on to his left buttock, let rip with a fart of such asphyxiating intensity it left me positively reeling. I gasped. Something had obviously crawled up and died inside him.

Hetty fixed him with her steely glare. 'I said thank you, Arthur, that will be all.'

But Arthur seemed unwilling to leave the cosy little gathering and join the rest of his cronies in the public bar. He sat resolutely still, leering into his pint.

Hetty sighed and got to her feet. 'Let's go and sit in the garden. It's much too stuffy in here anyway.'

Stuffy was the mildest possible way to describe the putrefied atmosphere that prevailed, courtesy of Arthur, and I followed her with alacrity as she headed off through the back door.

She stuck her head round the bar as we left. 'Oh, and Barney, we'll have three rounds of sandwiches and some of Mabel's lovely bread-and-butter pudding, please, when you've got a moment!'

This command was greeted with much mock forelock-touching amongst the bar staff, and one of them caught my eye and winked. I giggled.

'Your mother's very imperious,' I whispered as Hetty strode on ahead.

Nick grinned. 'That's nothing, you should see her when she's feeling bossy!'

We walked through the garden carrying our drinks. It was no more than a field really, the grass was long and full of wild flowers, and strewn here and there were one or two rugs for the customers to sit on. We found a sunny spot and sank down happily amongst the flowers.

Hetty sat next to me. 'Aah . . . that's better, I can't bear being inside that smelly old pub for too long. Have to get out in the fresh air.' She turned to me. 'Are you a country girl, Polly?'

'Oh yes! Well, I mean, at heart I am. I live in London but my parents live in Esh . . . in the country.' I knew from experience that not a lot of people considered Esher to be the country.

Hetty took hold of my chin and turned my face at an angle. 'Hmm . . . you've certainly got a fresh, country look about you.'

I wasn't quite sure how to take this. Did she mean in the bumpkin sense, I wondered?

But Hetty was nodding appreciatively now as she turned my head this way and that. 'Marvellous profile . . .' she muttered. 'Love to paint you some day.'

Thrilled to bits, I sucked my chin in and lowered my eyelids. This was definitely to be encouraged. I let her manhandle my face for a while, hoping it would give Nick a chance to stare long and hard and realise just what it was I'd got that Serena hadn't. And just what was that? I wondered, recalling Serena's Helen of Troy-like perfection. I also recalled that Hetty had found Arthur's profile pretty marvellous too. Laughing nervously, I rescued my face from her vice-like grip on the pretext of lighting a cigarette.

'Terrible habit,' said Hetty, getting one out herself.

'You'll end up with lungs like mine, shot to bits I shouldn't wonder. I keep telling the boys to lay off the ciggies but they won't listen to me: they don't listen to anything I say these days.' She turned to Nick. 'How's the farm going? Did you interview that chappie I told you about? The one I said would make a good farm manager? I suppose you didn't take my advice on that score either.'

'Tony? Oh no, I hired him. You were right, actually, he seems pretty good. I had a long chat with him the other day and we appear to be doing much better than we were this time last year. I think he's quite shrewd, but time will tell.'

'You see!' Hetty was pleased. 'I told you he was all right. Old Bob Hawkins said he was a marvellous manager. So you do listen to your old mother occasionally! Got to keep an eye on him though, it's no good letting him have his head too much. Remember all the trouble Dad had with that dreadful chap – whatsisname – Reg Parker – remember?'

She reached out suddenly and touched my arm. 'Sorry, farm talk. Boring for you, I know, but I do like to keep in touch.'

I smiled. 'Oh no, don't worry about me, I'm perfectly happy.' I lay back on the rug. 'I'll catch up on my suntan while you catch up on the farm.'

I shut my eyes and they chattered on. Every so often I'd catch a sentence or two, but it wasn't long before I was back playing dinner parties in the blue Armani dress. Except that I'd progressed to a rather beautiful pink silk Versace number now, and I wasn't hosting a dinner party I was opening the local fête, or – yes, agricultural show. Well, they were bound to ask me, weren't they? I was, after all, the modern equivalent of the squire's wife.

I frowned. If I had to cut a ribbon or two I would probably need quite a selection of hats, and hats were always a problem. I had quite a big head and they never seemed to fit properly. Ah yes, of course, I'd have them specially made; silly of me not to think of it before. I'd whisk up to Herbert Johnson to be measured or – no, I'd go to Paris! Yes, one or two trips to Paris every year would be a very good idea. I mean the country is undoubtedly lovely, but one wouldn't want to take root, would one?

Yes, I'd spend a couple of weeks every year viewing the collections. I rather fancied the idea of perching on one of those spindly little gilt chairs in the front row of a fashion show, with – oh, I don't know, Princess Caroline on one side and Jackie Onassis on the other? I'd probably saunter in a bit late, and of course a million heads would turn and then the whole place would be buzzing.

'Who's that?' they'd whisper.

'Don't you know? It's Nicholas Penhalligan's wife.'

'Ah . . . I'd heard she was a beauty, but I had no idea . . .'

'They say he's absolutely besotted, hates to let her out of his sight for even a moment.'

'Well, I can imagine . . .'

And so it went on, getting more and more outrageous and out of hand. I was just agonising over what I was going to wear to dinner at Kensington Palace, and wondering how I would manage without a cigarette between courses because of course Diana is very anti, when I heard a snippet of real-life conversation that made me open my eyes and sit up.

'How's Tim, married Sarah yet?' Hetty was asking.

Ah ha. Cows and sheep were off the agenda and marriage was on. This was just my tipple.

Nick laughed. 'Don't you think the news might have filtered down your way if he had? I mean, I know he plays his cards close to his chest, but I think he might tell his own mother.'

'Can't think why he's hanging around till next year,'

grumbled Hetty. 'Why not do it now? Seize the moment, go for it. He's so bloody prudent it's ridiculous. All this talk about money and where they're going to live − what does it matter? Why don't they just go and shack up in a rented flat or something? A lovely girl like Sarah will be pinched from right under his nose if he's not careful.'

Atta-girl, Hetty! I mentally applauded like mad. This was fighting talk and I was right behind her. Why pussyfoot around when you're in love? This woman certainly had her heart in the right place. She obviously wasn't the sort of mother who couldn't bear for her sons to let go of her apron strings either. All of this boded well for the future.

'Well, you tell him, then. It's no good talking to me about it!' laughed Nick.

'I will,' promised Hetty, 'and while we're on the subject, what about that uppity little actress bit you were seeing. I hope the emergence of young Polly here means that that's all over and done with.'

She put a friendly arm around my shoulders and raised her eyebrows quizzically at Nick. 'Am I, perhaps, sitting next to your latest girlfriend?'

I sat bolt upright, rigid with delight, hardly daring to breath, and the little bit of breath that did escape was well bated, I can tell you. Yes, Hetty, I thought gleefully, are you perhaps? I resisted the temptation to raise my eyebrows too.

He laughed, obviously quite used to her blatant nosiness. 'Mind your own bloody business, Hetty,' was his disappointing answer.

Hetty sighed. 'They're both the same, I'm afraid, these boys of mine. They won't tell me a thing. I should have had a daughter, they're much more forthcoming.'

It was on the tip of my tongue to venture that a daughter-in-law might do just as well, but decided that, even with Hetty's obvious penchant for straight talking, it might be considered a little previous.

'So tell me, my dear,' asked Hetty turning her beady brown eyes on me. 'What do you do? You don't throw yourself about half naked on film sets do you?'

'Certainly not,' I said priggishly. 'I'm a production assistant.'

Nick's eyebrows shot into orbit. 'You're a what?'

I was so used to lying about my job I'd forgotten for a moment just who was listening in. 'Oh, er – I mean a personal assistant,' I said quickly. Nick's eyebrows lowered very slightly.

'Well actually,' I said humbly, coming completely clean. 'I suppose I'm just a secretary really.'

'Oh no, I'd say you were definitely a personal assistant,' said Nick, grinning.

I grinned back. Just then a young girl walked through the field towards us armed with great platefuls of sandwiches and bread-and-butter pudding. She set them down in front of us; my mouth watered greedily.

'A secretary, eh? So what's your boss like?' asked Hetty, passing me a sandwich.

'A bastard to work for, but totally divine out of the office.' I gave Nick a huge smile, what did I have to lose? He had the grace to blush.

'Just like you, I bet!' said Hetty, prodding Nick's arm with a bony finger. 'I'd hate to have to work for you, I bet you're thoroughly bad tempered.'

'He is,' I said truthfully. 'You see, it's Nick I work for.'

'There you are, what did I say!' She threw back her head and roared with laughter. 'So I was spot on! How hysterical. Well, don't you take any nonsense from him, Polly. Lick him into shape. He needs a firm hand, you know.'

'I'll see that he gets it!' I said gleefully.

'Must be difficult, though,' said Hetty, tucking into an enormous roast beef sandwich. 'I mean, with the baby. I suppose you have a nanny, do you, or does it go to a childminder or something?'

She sounded so sure of herself that for a moment I wondered if perhaps I did have a baby and had temporarily forgotten about it, tucked it away in a drawer or something. I am incredibly absent-minded, but not normally on such a mammoth scale. I was pretty sure I'd remember giving birth, too. It was, by all accounts, pretty bloody painful. I racked my brains. No, I definitely hadn't given birth.

'I don't have a baby,' I said carefully.

'You don't?'

'No.'

'Oh.' Hetty frowned and looked perplexed. Was this a problem, I wondered? Did she like her future daughters-in-law to come complete with babies? Was there a breeding problem with the Penhalligans?

She turned to Nick, winking broadly. 'Darling!' she drawled, 'What a hectic life you lead.'

'Come on, Mum,' said Nick, getting cross. 'What the bloody hell are you babbling on about?'

Hetty finished her sandwich and got out a cigarette. She lit it and puffed the smoke out thoughtfully. 'Well, I thought Polly here was someone else, you see, another of your female friends.'

'Who?' he said impatiently.

'I don't know, do I? I've obviously never met her, whoever she is.'

'Christ, Mum, what are you on about?'

'Well you see, yesterday I was sitting in the pub painting, when this chap came in and asked at the bar for Mrs Penhalligan. I popped up my hand and he came over. We chatted away for a bit, he said he'd seen one of my pictures in London and had really liked it and because he was on holiday down here, thought he'd seek me out — load of bullshit, of course, but you know me,

I'm a sucker for compliments.'

'Oh, do you show your paintings in London then?' I asked.

'Er, well, no, I don't actually, not yet anyway.'

'Exactly,' said Nick grimly, 'go on.'

'Anyway, he bought me a drink and said he knew you,' she nodded at Nick, 'said he saw quite a lot of you in London, and that he was in advertising too and that's how you'd met. Then he asked if you were down here at the moment, and if so did you have a girl with you, with a baby. I said I had no idea, because if you were here you certainly hadn't managed to stagger down to Gweek to see your old mum and, anyway, I never really knew whether you were in London or Cornwall. Well, that's why, when you walked in here with Polly, I assumed she was the girl he was talking about.'

She put her hand on my shoulder, 'Especially in that dress, my dear. It's the sort of thing you wear when you've just had a baby.' She smiled kindly and patted her tummy. 'Hides the paunch.'

I tried to answer, but my mouth was so dry it felt as if someone had just given it the once over with a hairdryer.

'Who was this friend, exactly?' said Nick quietly. 'Did he say?'

'Oh no, I've no idea what his name was, darling. He might have said, but you know me and names. He was quite a big chap, though, burly, with red hair. American, I think, rather cute actually.'

Chapter Eighteen

My first reaction was one of horror. Nick and I exchanged shell-shocked glances in the wake of this exploding missile. Christ Almighty, he'd found us already! I reached for my tongue, but it was sensibly staying put on the roof of my mouth, glued on with a mixture of terror and bread-and-butter pudding. I left it there and abandoned myself to my second reaction which was, I'm ashamed to say, fury. Bloody Adam and bloody Rachel — damn them! Here I was having a half decent holiday for the first time in months, with a thoroughly decent man, and they were doing their best to ruin it for me. I was tempted to suggest we simply reunite the surly mother with the aggressive father and push them out to sea in a leaky boat, hoping they'd sink without trace, but I could see that Nick was determined to take a more conscientious line.

He was questioning his mother closely. 'When exactly did you see him?'

'I told you, yesterday.'

'Yes, but what time of day?'

'Around lunchtime, I suppose, yes, about twelve o'clock. He said he'd been over to the house earlier and there was no one there.'

'We were all out yesterday, thank goodness, but you didn't actually say I was in Cornwall?'

'No darling, why should I? I didn't know you were here, you never let me know what your movements are. In fact I

337

distinctly remember telling him that, since I hadn't heard from you, I imagined you were probably in London.'

I relaxed slightly. That was something, surely? Maybe Adam had somehow heard that Nick had a house in Cornwall and had come down purely on the off-chance, just to check it out? And, on finding it empty, he'd headed back to London? But how on earth had he rumbled the fact that Nick was even remotely involved? Just a hunch? Or was he slightly better informed? None of this boded well.

Nick chewed his bottom lip thoughtfully. 'I don't suppose you have any idea where he's staying, Mum?'

'I do actually, he's renting one of Mrs Green's cottages in Manaccan, that little white terraced one in the middle of the village, I think. I've got her telephone number in my address book if you want it.'

Oh Christ, renting. That sounded a bit too permanent for my liking, but there weren't, I supposed, too many five-star hotels around these parts, and a bed and breakfast would be a bit infra dig for our Adam.

'So you definitely didn't say we were here, or were expected down soon, or anything like that?' persisted Nick.

'Darling, do stop banging on, I told you, I simply said I had absolutely no idea where you were,' said Hetty petulantly, her eyes wandering somewhat: she'd got rather bored with this interrogation. 'Oh look there's Arthur!'

Sure enough, out of the back door came Arthur, roaring along on his Zimmer frame.

'Darlings, may I leave you to fend for yourselves now? Only I must finish Arthur this afternoon, I fear he's not long for this world. Arthur! Co-ee! Arthur, you're not going home yet, are you? Where are you off to?'

Arthur pointed to the outside loo and made an obscene gesture to indicate his intention on reaching it.

Hetty sighed. 'He's quite repulsive, of course, but what

can I do? He's such a marvellous sitter, so still and corpse-like. Honestly, the sacrifices I make for art's sake. I'll intercept him on his way out — must fly!' She gathered her cigarettes and lighter together and got up to go.

Nick grabbed her arm. 'OK, Mum, but listen, if you see this guy again, don't mention you've seen us, will you? Oh, and hang on, the phone number.' Nick pushed a scrap of paper and a pencil under her nose and she jotted it down.

'Bye, my darlings!' She blew us a kiss. 'Have fun — oh, and if you fancy another little drinky-poo, just tell Barney to put it on my slate, all right?' And with that she disappeared.

I felt my insides curdling. 'Will we have to go back to London?' I whispered miserably, selfishly thinking of my own happiness as usual.

Nick was staring into space, eyes narrowed. He didn't answer for a moment. 'No . . .' he eventually said, slowly, 'I don't think so. In fact, the more I think about it, the more I think we'll just stay exactly where we are. In fact . . . yes, I want him to know that we're down here.'

'But you just told Hetty not to say anything if—'

'I know,' he said impatiently, 'but I've changed my mind. We'll face him head on this time. I'm not being ousted from my own house by one lousy American, nor am I going to run around England like a fox with the bloody hounds behind me.'

'What — so we just stay put and wait for him to pay us a visit? I mean, he will find us Nick, there's no doubt about that, and he's not going to politely knock at the front door either. He'll probably smash his way through the french windows — or, or through my bedroom window most likely!' I gabbled, frightened out of my cowardly little mind. It was all very well, but Adam definitely hated me more than anyone else in the whole world. I was number one on his hit list without a shadow of a doubt. Nick was silent.

'Well?' I squeaked.

'Hang on, Polly, I'm thinking.'

'But you've seen what he's like, he's a nutter! In fact he's probably clinically insane by now, he'll stop at nothing – and – and anyway, what about Rachel and Jamie?' I added charitably but desperately.

'Don't worry, I'm not abandoning them at this stage, although God knows, sometimes I think Rachel deserves all she gets. No, we'll just have to think of a way around this.'

'But what if—'

'Polly, for God's sake shut up, will you? I'm trying to think!' he snapped.

Ah. I pursed my lips and sat back, folding my arms. I recognised a flash of the old Nick there: hadn't taken long to surface, had it? Nevertheless, I obediently shut up and waited for my next order. I didn't wait long.

'Come on, hurry up.' Nick got to his feet and drained his pint.

'Where are we going?' I scrambled around, looking for my handbag.

'Back to the house, of course. Thank God Tim and Rachel have gone into Helston this afternoon.' He strode off.

'Oh! Right, hang on, just coming.' I drained my glass, scooped the last of the bread-and-butter pudding into my mouth, and ran after him.

Nick was already half-way across the garden. 'Bring the glasses will you, Polly?' he yelled over his shoulder.

I dashed back meekly to pick them up. Odd how in a crisis we'd suddenly reverted to our more usual roles of servant and master.

I panted back down the garden after him. 'In a couple of weeks we'd have been shot of her, she'd have been in Paris

340

and we could have told him to sod off. Oh, why did he have to come now?' I grumbled breathlessly, running to keep up as he strode round the side of the pub to the car park.

He didn't answer but, without pausing to open the door, vaulted neatly into the open-topped Land Rover and revved up the engine. It was a cool, effortless move straight out of the movies.

Suddenly I felt a little twinge of excitement. After all, here we were, bang in the middle of what the tabloids would call a tug-of-love scenario, protecting the mother, and ducking and weaving from the vengeful father: we were a team, a duo – yes, we were partners. We moved as one, we thought as one, we stood up for justice, we protected the weak, we leaped into jeeps – I took a little run up, grabbed the top of the door and jumped – about two inches off the ground. Nowhere near. I tried again, run and – hup! Gosh, how on earth did he do it? Panting with exertion, but determined to crack it, I stepped back for another try. I charged towards the door just as he, simultaneously, leaned across and swung it open to let me in. It caught me full in the stomach.

'Oooofffff . . .' With a loud, yob-like moan I fell back on to the gravel, bent double and clutching myself like a footballer who's been kneed in the privates. As I lay there, moaning and rolling around in a heap of Laura Ashley, he came running round to retrieve me.

'Gosh, I'm really sorry, I had no idea you were still leaping around out there. Are you OK?' He helped me up.

'Sure,' I croaked, staggering to my feet and clutching what was left of my stomach. 'My fault, really, showing off as usual.'

Would I ever be able to have all those babies now, I wondered? Wasn't that where all the important tubes were? I nursed what remained of my abdomen, wincing and gingerly feeling around for signs of blood. None, unfortunately.

Nick heaved me bodily into the jeep, slammed the door and ran round the other side. With a screech of tyres and a great deal of flying gravel, we shot out of the drive.

We sped off in silence, and I was loathe to break it, knowing from experience that whatever I said would be wrong. He was either hatching a master plan, or so pissed off he couldn't speak. At last he did.

'Right . . .' he said slowly, 'now listen, Polly, this is what we're going to do.'

'Yes?' I whispered. Surely yes couldn't be wrong?

'First of all, we're going to send Rachel and Jamie away, get them as far away as possible from the action, somewhere safe.'

'Like where?'

'Like Penny's. Tim can take them, he often goes to deliver vegetables anyway. He's pretty quiet on the farm at the moment, so he could probably stay a few days and surreptitiously play bodyguard, make sure they're OK. There's no way Adam will find them there.'

Don't be too sure, I thought grimly, he found us here; but I had to agree, it wasn't a bad plan.

'Will Penny mind?'

'Not a bit, she's got bags of room at this time of year, and she's always glad of some company.'

'OK, and meanwhile?'

'Meanwhile, I'll telephone Adam and invite him over for a drink.'

'You'll what!'

'I'll ask him over for a drink.'

I was bug-eyed with amazement. 'Well, don't mind me, but I'll just be down at the nearest travel agent negotiating a one-way ticket to Australia!'

'Listen, Polly, if we seize the initiative we might just get away with it. I'm not prepared to sit around and wait for him, and I think it makes sense to catch him off-guard. The last thing he'll expect is a friendly telephone call.'

'Well I'm not crazy about being a sitting duck, either, but what happens when he accepts our offer and turns up keen to stage the Cornish Chainsaw Massacre?'

Nick paused as he slammed down a gear and negotiated a tricky hairpin bend. 'We tell him a little story,' he said softly.

'Oh really? And what might that be?'

'We tell him that the strain of being caught in the middle of this ghastly situation — you know, looking after Rachel, leaving your flat, and not being able to come to work, not to mention splitting up with your boyfriend — left you feeling absolutely exhausted.'

'Too right,' I said with feeling.

'You were totally drained, emotionally and physically, so much so that you almost became ill — basically you were in dire need of a break.'

'Dire. Dire need.' I nodded emphatically.

'So, I suggested that a little holiday in Cornwall might do the trick. You agreed, and here we are.'

'What, just the two of us?'

'Why not? After all,' he took his eyes off the road for a second and gave me a most dazzling smile, 'we are having an affair, aren't we?'

I gulped, getting my oesophagus in a serious twist. 'An — an affair?' I stammered, through twisted tubes.

He grinned. 'Yes, an office romance — you know, dipping the pen in the company ink and all that. Goes on all the time. But of course, it couldn't be conducted in London for all the agency to witness, so we came down here for a bit of peace and quiet.'

'I — I see,' I faltered, recognising a somewhat familiar fantasy here, 'and what about Rachel?'

'We have absolutely no idea where she is now, neither do we care. The last we saw of her was when we dropped her off at her father's house.'

'Oh come on, that's very weak. Adam will have been

watching the house in Kensington like a hawk. He'll know she's not there.'

'Exactly, he'll know we're lying, and he'll pounce on that immediately. That's when we deliver the red herring. Under extreme pressure — and I mean extreme pressure, let him stamp around a bit and flex his muscles, maybe even exert a few bully-boy tactics — you eventually admit that you heard her on the telephone inquiring about homes for unmarried mothers.'

'Christ, we'll have him breaking down every hostel door in London!'

'So what? They're quite used to lunatic fathers raising merry hell, they'll just get the police on to him. Good thing too.'

'Suppose he doesn't believe us?' I quaked.

'Well, what does it matter? He won't find them if he decides to search the house, and then what can he do — kill us? He a frustrated father, Polly, not a mass murderer.'

'Don't be so sure,' I muttered nervously, recalling those giant freckled paws, which in my mind's eye had already grown Mr Hyde-like claws. 'So do we tell Rachel all this?'

'Christ no, she'll be terrified if she knows he's down here, we don't want her panicking all over the place. I'll have a quiet word with Tim, explain the whole story, and get him to ask her if she'd like to go up to Penny's for a few days.'

'She'll smell a rat though, won't she? I mean, why should she go to Penny's?'

'Because Tim will tell her we want to be alone to conduct our illicit affair in private.'

'Oh God, you mean she's going to get the story about us having a ding-dong too?'

'Why not? He'll tell her we're both feeling rather self-conscious and we'd like a little time to ourselves, just a couple of days, of course. Once we've seen Adam and we think the coast is relatively clear, they can come back,' he grinned, 'to the hotbed of lust and passion!' He threw his head back and laughed, no doubt at the sheer outrageousness of it all.

'Oh yes, I see, very good!' I said faintly. I threw back my own head and added a merry little chuckle of my own, but it was awfully hollow, principally because I couldn't quite see the joke. What was so side-splittingly funny about us being lovers, I wondered? He was still guffawing loudly. Was he going to be sick?

As he coughed and spluttered over the steering wheel, I considered the joke from Nick's point of view. Good-looking, successful, loaded young blade, with beautiful, highly desirable actress girlfriend, risks all to nip down to Cornwall for a bit of how's your father with gauche, dyed blonde, overweight secretary. I squirmed uncomfortably. Yes, well, put like that I could see wherein lay the mirth.

I stared miserably out of the window. The hedgerows reared up and waved at me as we flew past; grasses and flowers waggled their heads knowingly: it was as if they were laughing, mocking me, and who could blame them? I'd been living in a dream world these last few days. Nick would no more fall in love with me than sell the farm and become managing director of ICI. And why should he? He had a perfectly good girlfriend back in London. I stared out of the window. Yes, she was all the way . . . back in London.

I was feeling low, very low, but not low enough for this last, indisputable fact to escape me. The girlfriend was, indeed, a long way away, and I was, indeed, right here. She was three hundred miles up the M4, while I was all of three inches. She was over six hours from his presence, while I was half a moment. What's more, we were to be alone.

A small window of opportunity presented itself. It was about the size of a cat-flap with about as much visibility, but still, it was there. I mean, there's a great deal to be said for being on the spot, isn't there? If only in the sense that it's better than not being on the spot. I gave myself a little inward shake. Atta-girl, Polly, where's that famous McLaren spirit? Rally it fast, please.

It wasn't as if I'd really turned on the charm yet either — OK, yes, I'd been trying, but not very hard, not as hard as I could. I hadn't, for example, fixed him to any of my smouldering hot looks, I hadn't got as far as the come-hither eyes or the sexy suggestive smiles, and I hadn't even begun to turn him on with my wardrobe. And my golly, I had some pretty lethal gear with me one way and another: the leather mini-skirt, the clinging cross-over top, the blue silk shirt with most of the buttons undone, the tight black leggings — he didn't stand a chance. And of course, once I'd hooked him, winding him in would be the work of a moment. I smiled smugly, secure in the knowledge that I may be a talentless little secretary, but at least my snogs were up to scratch.

As we turned the corner and swept through the gates of Trewarren, I felt a little better. So you think it's all a big joke do you, Mr Penhalligan? Well, we'll soon see about that.

As soon as we got back to the house, Nick buttonholed Tim in the cow shed. I left him to it, unwilling to be deafened by the bellows of laughter, or to witness the side-holding and thigh-slapping that would undoubtedly occur when the incredible Nick-and-Polly fantasy was raised.

It had already been decided that Tim, of the famous animals-and-oddballs touch, would speak to Rachel but, until he'd done so, I couldn't let her out of my sight. Odd, I thought, that I could be so allergic to Rachel but still not want to see her baby wrenched from her arms. I shadowed her around to the extent of following her into the tiny downstairs loo while she changed Jamie's nappy.

She frowned up at me as she knelt on the floor, a half-dressed baby wriggling around between her knees. 'Did you want something, Polly?'

'Noo, noo nothing,' I laughed nervously, 'just interested really. Oh, I see, those disposable things just have sticky tape at the front, do they? No pins?'

'Polly, you've seen me do this millions of times.'

'Have I? Oh well, I must have forgotten. Anyway, I might have a baby of my own one day, so I need all the practical demonstrations I can get.'

'What, you look after a baby? Do me a favour.' She snorted with derision.

'And why not?' I said hotly. 'I'll have you know I'm extremely maternal; I'd be a brilliant mother.'

'You might be maternal, but you're hardly responsible, are you? Babies are one hell of a commitment, you know, you can't just look after number one all the time.'

I fumed silently, steam pouring from all orifices. Ungrateful cow, if only she knew. She was one hell of a responsibility, and I was shouldering her pretty well at the moment. I waited until most of the steam had subsided. No point having a row with her now.

I shrugged. 'I suppose I'm just a bit bored, really.'

'Well d'you think you could move slightly to the right, only I need to spread this plastic mat out?'

'Oh yes, right.'

There wasn't much room, so I put the lid down on the loo and stood on that instead.

Rachel looked up at me in alarm. 'Are you sure you're OK?'

'Fine, fine . . .' I gave my face a vacant expression and stared up at the cracks on the ceiling, biting my thumbnail, swaying slightly and humming to myself. Hopefully she'd just think I'd gone a bit mad and ignore me. I was making Jamie laugh, anyway. I rolled my eyes and pulled faces as he gurgled up at me.

'Rachel?' Tim shouted from the corridor.

'In here! Come in, everyone else has.'

Tim poked his head around the door. He looked up at

me in wonder. 'Don't tell me — number of people in a downstairs loo? *Guinness Book of Records*?' He leaped up beside me. 'Three! Four with Jamie!'

I giggled and jumped down, closing the door behind me. No, I thought grimly, bodyguard to the sulky and undeserving. I wandered off to the kitchen in search of calories. Instead I found Nick, prowling around, locking doors and windows.

'Don't do that!' he snapped, as I opened the larder and made for the light switch. I jumped and snatched my hand back.

'Sorry!' Was he possessive about his chocolate biscuits? I knew the feeling. 'Just felt a bit peckish,' I stammered guiltily.

'Fine, go ahead, but don't turn the light on!' He came over and put a hand on my shoulder. 'Sorry, didn't mean to snap, it's just that while Rachel and Jamie are still here we've got to be so careful. If Adam is prowling around outside, we don't want him to think there's anyone here. When they've gone, which hopefully will be soon, it doesn't matter, but just for the moment let's keep all the doors and windows locked, turn the lights off and keep away from the windows, OK?'

'OK,' I whispered. Anything was OK if he kept his hand on my shoulder like that. I'd creep around on all fours if he liked.

'Did you speak to Tim?' I asked, trying to keep him talking, trying to keep the hand on the shoulder and prolong the ecstasy.

'Yes I did, he's talking to her now. I hope they're going to leave as soon as possible. Tim was planning on delivering some vegetables tomorrow, anyway, so it's worked out quite well.'

Footsteps approached the kitchen. The hand disappeared like lightning.

'Well!' said Tim, rubbing his hands together and smiling

as he came in. 'Rachel thinks it's a great idea, don't you?'

Rachel was right behind him. 'Yes, I'd love to go. It'll be a nice change and, of course, it'll give you a break, Polly.'

Her mouth twisted into an unattractive little smirk as our eyes met. Ah yes, of course, she'd heard about the Polly-and-Nick affair, the one that was so unspeakably sordid it needed acres of space in which to be conducted. It couldn't come within miles of another living soul, so shameful was it. She obviously thought I was a right little tart, too. Only a few days ago she'd dished out tea and sympathy as I'd lain prostrate on my bed, distraught at Harry's desertion, and now here I was throwing myself at Nick.

Well for your information, *dear*, I thought glaring at her, it's all an elaborate hoax laid on for your benefit, purely to save your anaemic little skin. I conveniently forgot that it would be fine by me if the fantasy we'd cooked up turned into reality; for the moment I was concerned only with her deeply hypocritical smugness. I mean, didn't she just take the biscuit? It was only because of her little indiscretion with a man she didn't love that we were all running round in circles now. Oh yes, it's all very well taking the high moral ground with me, Miss Marsden, but if you hadn't jumped into bed with Adam, we wouldn't be going through with this idiotic charade now. I glared back at her.

'Er, good!' beamed Nick, ignoring the sparks that were so obviously flying between the women. 'That's settled then. You'll enjoy staying with Penny, Rachel, the food's infinitely better than it is here, and you get room service thrown in too. I must say I envy you, I could do with a few days of being waited on hand and foot!'

'Oh, I'm sure you'll survive,' purred Rachel. 'After all, you've got Polly to look after you.'

Nick blushed. 'Oh, er – yes, well of course. Um – tell you what, let's all have a quick drink before you go. It had

349

better be a quick one, though, because I expect you'll want to get off while it's still light.'

'Oh there's no rush is there?' said Rachel. 'I thought we might go after supper. It only takes a couple of hours to get there, doesn't it?'

'Er, yes, but Penny might be expecting you for supper — oh God, that's a point, I'd better ring and tell her you're coming!'

Rachel looked puzzled. 'She doesn't know? But I thought she invited us?'

'Oh! Yes, she did! Rang this morning actually. No, what I meant was, I'll just let her know when you're leaving.'

'So she can have some supper ready,' I added soothingly.

'But — but I thought you said she was expecting us for supper?'

'Oh she is, she is!' said Tim quickly. 'But it's always as well to remind Penny, she's so absent-minded, we don't want to turn up and find she's closed the restaurant, do we!'

'It's hardly likely, it's only five o'clock now!'

God, she would go on, wouldn't she?

'Is that all!' Tim looked at his watch. 'I had no idea it was so early — to tell you the truth, Rachel, I'm absolutely starving, and I just want to get to Penny's as soon as possible so I can get stuck into some decent food! A man could die of starvation in this place.'

'Oh, right.' She looked reasonably convinced. 'Oh well, I'll just go and pack. I won't have a drink thanks, I'll just get my things and organise Jamie.'

She shuffled off to her room and the three of us headed thirstily for the drawing room where the gin bottle beckoned.

'Christ!' Nick flopped down on to a sofa nursing his drink. 'All this lying is really taking it out of me. I didn't

350

realise it was such hard work. I must say, you're awfully good at it, Polly.'

'Years of practise,' I said without thinking. 'Er — well, you know, I've been in one or two tight spots before.'

'I can believe it.' He twinkled knowingly at me.

I squirmed uneasily. Now what was that supposed to mean? As I sipped my drink I brooded on its implications.

A few minutes later, Rachel reappeared laden down with baby gear. The boys sprang up to help her. Tim drove the car round to the back door where there was more privacy. They loaded the car, sat Jamie in his car seat, Tim and Rachel climbed in the front, and with a scrunch of tyres on the gravel, the Wincanton party sped off.

Nick and I watched from the window, peering out from behind a curtain. I for one heaved a huge sigh of relief. Thank God. I'd just about had it up to here with that ungrateful little hussy, and was very much in need of a sabbatical.

As the car reached the end of the back drive and turned the corner out of sight, I gazed out at the view. It was a beautiful afternoon. The sun was still bright but it was quite low on the horizon, and the countryside was bathed in a golden, soupy glow. The trees that lined the drive cast long skinny shadows across it at intervals, like an erratic railway track. Up in the sky, a few clouds raced along in the blue, as if they'd been separated from the rest and were dashing to catch up. Just outside the window, the daffodils were bobbing around like billy-o, trying to keep their heads up in the breeze. I sighed dreamily. This was England at its very best, at its most beautiful. And I was alone with Nick.

He was standing next to me by the window, holding the curtain open a crack. Our shoulders were close. I turned to him and gave him one of my most turning-on smiles.

'So what shall we do now they've gone?' I murmured. 'It's such a beautiful evening, why don't we take the boat out on the river? Or go for a walk along the cliffs?'

'We'll do neither,' he said grimly. 'We'll ring Adam Buchanan.' He turned on his heel and made for the telephone in the hall.

'Oh.' My heart sank down into my espadrilles. 'Yes, I'd forgotten about that.'

He turned and looked at me in amazement. He shook his head. 'Sometimes, Polly, I wonder what planet you're on.'

He marched on, telephone-bound. I trudged meekly after him. Well, I thought gloomily, I'd like to be on a wildly uplifting planet, or even over the moon perhaps, but unfortunately someone keeps bringing me right back down to earth.

Chapter Nineteen

I sat down at the bottom of the stairs, hunched up and hugging my knees like a little gnome. Any minute now, Adam would be on the other end of that telephone. I shivered. Suddenly there seemed to be a nasty east wind whistling through the very marrow of my bones, and yet it was such a beautifully warm day. These old houses were unbelievably draughty. I pulled my jumper right down over my hunched-up knees as Nick picked up the telephone.

'Shall I go away?' I asked. 'Would you be better on your own?'

'No, stay,' he licked his lips nervously, 'I need moral support.'

Any time, I thought dreamily, studying his Docksiders as I sat at his feet; moral support, physical support – my eye was roving up his blue-jeaned legs – surgical support . . .

Nick took a crumpled piece of paper out of his back pocket. He telephoned Mrs Green and got the number of the cottage in Manaccan.

'Right,' he said replacing the receiver, 'ready?'

'As ready as I'll ever be to invite a mad-man for a drink.'

He grinned. 'Courage, Polly, courage!'

He dialled the number. There was a long pause as it rang at the other end. Please God, please let him be out – my huge yellow streak was well to the fore as usual — please let him be out and I promise I'll go to church when I get back to London; Matins, Evensong, confession, happy-clappy tambourine time — you name it, I'll be there. God had heard it all before. Adam was in.

'Mr Buchanan?' Nick raised his eyebrows, I held my breath. 'It's Nicholas Penhalligan here, I saw my mother this afternoon, she said you were looking for me, is that right . . . ? Yes, of course, no problem, but I can't help you much, I'm afraid. I gather you're looking for Rachel and Jamie . . . No, no, they're not . . . No, I've no idea where they are, I'm afraid . . . Polly? Well no, she's not in London, she's down here with me . . . Yes, staying here. She's sitting right next to me, actually.'

He glanced down and winked. My hands started to sweat, I dug my nails into my palms.

'Well, let's not go into that right now, shall we? Why don't you come over for a drink, then we can all have a civilised chat about it . . . Yes, why not? . . . Seven o'clock? . . . Fine, we'll see you then . . . Goodbye.'

He replaced the receiver. I wiped my sweaty hands on the stair carpet and looked up anxiously. 'Well?'

'That's it. He took the bait, and he's coming over.'

'How did he sound?'

'Perfectly normal.'

Perfectly normal. That's how people always sound when they're about to do something perfectly atrocious. Everyone always says so afterwards: the neighbours, the greengrocer, the stunned and weeping mother. 'Oh, he seemed perfectly normal that day, right as rain. He was always such a good boy, such a comfort to me, I can't think why he suddenly took it into his head to let loose with a Kalishnikov and mow down two innocent people in cold blood.' Yes, it was always thus. Suddenly I felt awfully scared.

'Could I perhaps stay in another room while you speak

to him?' I ventured timidly. 'I mean there's no need for me to see him, is there? Three's rather a crowd, isn't it? You could tell him our little story and I could be getting on with something useful upstairs. Maybe I could clean out the attic or something? Would that be a help?'

He laughed and kicked his shoes off, changing into one of the many pairs of wellingtons that lay in a jumble in the hall. 'Polly, it's all going to be fine, stop worrying. He's just coming for a friendly chat.'

'But – but I might say the wrong thing, cramp your style, you know.'

'I wasn't aware that I had a style. Anyway, you don't have to say anything much if you don't want to.'

'But – but what are you going to tell him? Shouldn't we get our story straight? Synchronise watches? That kind of thing?'

'Don't worry about me, I'll just wing it!' He grinned, grabbed his Barbour from the banisters and headed for the front door. Where the hell did he think he was going? I grabbed his arm in alarm.

'Where are you going?' I squeaked, hanging on like a limpet, feet almost off the floor. 'Take me with you!'

'I'm just going to check on the cows.'

'I'll come with you,' I gasped. 'The dear, darling cows, haven't seen them for ages!'

'Don't be silly, it's getting dark so you won't see much, and anyway they don't like to be disturbed. I won't be long. Pour yourself a nice big drink and turn on the telly. This will all be over before you know it.'

He patted my hand abstractedly, then prised the fingers one by one from his arm before wandering off to the relative calm and comfort of the cow shed.

It's all very well for you, I thought miserably, dragging my feet back to the drawing room; you've got your ruddy cows, what have I got?

I curled up on the sofa and tried to watch the television,

maniacally switching from channel to channel and staring blindly at the flickering cathode rays. I seemed to be sucking a cushion. I started to play 'what if?' with myself. What if he didn't believe us? What if he turned nasty? What if he had a knife? I stuffed the cushion further into my mouth and nearly gagged on the tassel. It was quite conceivable though, wasn't it? I mean, OK, I had Nick to protect me, but what if Adam was armed: there wasn't an awful lot Nick could do against a sub-machine gun, for instance, was there? And Americans carried guns as a matter of course these days, didn't they; it was in the constitution or something. In fact, I had a feeling it was compulsory for all American males over the age of twenty-one to carry a gun.

Suddenly I knew what I had to do. I reached for my handbag, pulled out a pencil and rummaged around for a piece of paper. I found my bank statement, which I never open and which therefore always serves as a handy notepad. On the back I began, in a shaky hand, to pen my final instructions.

Dear Lottie,
In case I never see you again, I want you to know that I leave you my compact-disc machine and all the cassettes. Please also take whichever clothes you fancy and offer the rest to Pippa. I'd be grateful if you didn't give any to Caro. My legit jewellery had better go back to my parents, but by all means make free with the Butler and Wilson. I want you to know that you've always been a terrific friend and ally over the years, please think of me fondly from time to time, your dear, most probably dead friend, Polly.
    PS. Please ensure that Harry hears of my demise and gets an invite to the funeral.

Ah yes, the funeral. Death does have its compensations

doesn't it? I sucked my pencil thoughtfully. I wondered where it would be. Probably in that nice little church off Pont Street, yes, that would be quite smart, quite – you know, social. Handy for a wake in the Admiral Codderington afterwards. Funny how my fantasies always seemed to revolve around churches. I'd been up and down this particular aisle on a number of occasions – vertical, of course, and dressed in white. This time I'd be horizontal and dressed in, well, in a shroud, I supposed. Were they white too?

I could see my coffin, laden with flowers as it proceeded slowly down the aisle. The church was packed – naturally – so much so that some people had to stand outside. Harry was a pall-bearer, as was Nick (if he wasn't dead too, of course), and there they stood, side by side in their dark suits, heads bowed, breasts heaving with emotion, united in their grief. They stared down at my coffin which lay at the front of the church.

'There'll never be anyone quite like Polly,' whispered Harry between sobs, hanky dabbing wet eyes. 'How could I have been such a fool? My own little Polyester – gone for ever!'

Nick simply couldn't speak, his face was contorted with emotion, he wrestled with pent-up tears. Eventually, of course, his grief got the better of him and he broke down, flinging himself at my coffin, beating on the lid with his fists and crying, no – better still, shrieking – 'Polly, Polly! My only true love, come back to me, don't leave me! I can't bear to go on without you! I just can't bear it!' I sucked my pencil thoughtfully. Was that too over the top? Too – you know, nancy-boyish? I hesitated. Nah, for God's sake, I was dead, wasn't I? He was entitled to be over the top.

Anyway, eventually he was prised from the mahogany by other mourners who tried to calm him, but he pushed them all away and stumbled outside, blinded by tears, unable to face the rest of the service; unable, in fact, to face the rest of his life.

At the bottom of the church steps was Serena, looking remarkably unattractive for her, actually: greasy hair, one or two spots, bags under the eyes. 'Nick – darling!' she called out, but Nick brushed her aside, quite roughly, before staggering off under the weight of so much emotion, to be alone with his memories. Or, wait a minute – yes, perhaps Serena should look absolutely stunning and *still* he brushes her aside. Yes, that would be even better.

I doodled on the envelope. Should I jot down a couple of hymns in case Lottie didn't know any real tear-jerkers? I wanted nice dreary ones to set the mood and get the weeping under way. I was just wavering between 'The Lord's My Shepherd' and 'I Vow to Thee My Country', when Nick walked in. I stuffed the letter in my handbag. No doubt the police would find it there later and pass it on to Lottie, and I dare say I could trust her with the order of service. She had, after all, been to a convent.

Nick looked calm and relaxed. 'OK?' he queried, raising his eyebrows.

'Sure, fine actually,' I bleated, with a brave little smile. 'Much better in fact.'

'Good girl.' God he was gullible. He sank down in front of the television with a sigh. 'God, I'm knackered.' Then he sat up a bit. 'Oh great, "Dad's Army" – it still makes me laugh, even after all these years.'

And laugh he did, quite a lot actually, was this man human? I had a go, just to show willing, but it sounded like a pregnant hen being strangled. He looked at me in alarm.

'It's going to be fine Polly, really. Don't worry about it.'

I nodded dumbly, feeling very sick all of a sudden. My tummy was churning and rather a lot of bile was rising up from it en route to my throat. Just at that moment the doorbell went. Coincidentally I completely lost my bottle. I shrieked and ran out of the room.

'I really don't think I can cope with this, Nick, please don't make me!' I pleaded from behind the door. 'I've got this terrible pain in my tummy, I really think I ought to go and lie down, I've had it before and if I don't lie down I'm generally sick all over the carpet!'

'Don't be silly.' Nick dragged me out from behind the door. I dug my heels in but he was too strong for me. I slid along the shiny floorboards.

'Would you just sit down and relax? Here.' He steered me, like a professional ice-skater with a beginner for a partner, towards the sofa. 'Now stay there while I let him in.'

I looked doubtfully at the sofa. He gave me a little push. 'Sit.'

My knees creaked as they bent unwillingly into it, my buttocks clenched with terror as they sank down towards it.

'It'll be an absolute breeze, I promise,' he lied, and with that he sallied forth to answer the door.

'I whimpered quietly as I heard Adam's unmistakable trans-Atlantic drawl getting closer and closer. A moment later, Nick was ushering him into the room. He seemed to fill it. Everywhere I looked there was a piece of Adam — an arm here, a leg there; I'd forgotten how big he was, and how red. I cowered back in terror, watching his enormous shadow lurk along the curtains.

'Hello, Polly,' he said in a strained but civil voice.

'Hello,' I whispered.

'Drink?' asked Nick.

'Please. Whisky and soda, if you've got one.'

He sat down at the other end of the sofa, but I felt as if he'd sat on my lap. Christ, there were plenty of other chairs in the room, weren't there? I scrambled right into the corner, holding on tight to the arm. Adam crossed his legs and leaned back, flinging his arm along the back of the sofa. I flinched as his freckly hand landed inches from my head. Bastard. He grinned, rather menacingly I thought.

'Don't worry, Polly, I'm not going to bite you.'

'That's what I keep telling her,' said Nick over his shoulder from the drinks cupboard, 'but she won't have it. She thinks you've come round to bump her off.'

Adam grinned. 'Not unless I'm severely provoked!'

'Don't provoke him, Polly,' warned Nick. 'I don't want to have to pick up the pieces. Ice?' he asked Adam.

'Please.'

Oh terrific, I thought grimly, glaring at Nick. Gang up on me now, won't you? Be Adam's buddy boy, laugh at silly old Polly. Well wait till he chases you round the table with six inches of cold steel at your throat, because he undoubtedly will: see how funny you find that. I looked furtively at Adam's jacket, looking for bulges that might indicate a jack-knife or a gun. Nothing was glaringly obvious. Perhaps in his socks; people often kept knives in their socks, didn't they . . . I dropped my cigarette packet and bent down to pick it up, meanwhile scrutinising his footwear.

'I'm not armed, if that's what you're wondering,' said a sarcastic voice in my ear.

I breathed in sharply and jerked upright to find ice-cool blue eyes boring into mine. Of course, he was telepathic, I'd quite forgotten. Somehow this was more frightening than any arsenal he might have secreted in his socks. I scrambled back to the relative safety of my corner again, bringing my knees up to deflect any body blows.

'Just dropped my cigarettes,' I mumbled, taking one out of the pack with a shaky hand.

A gold Cartier lighter flicked silently into action under my nose. The flame was bright and steady. I dipped my trembling cigarette into it and sucked hard.

'Thanks,' I muttered.

'How are you finding Cornwall?' asked Nick as he handed Adam a whisky.

Adam's eyes narrowed. 'Look, I'm not about to beat the shit out of anyone, but let's cut the crap, shall we? Cornwall's fine, but I didn't come here to pick wild flowers, I came to get my son.'

'Well, in that case I'm sorry, but I'm afraid you've come all this way on a wild goose chase. It seems you had too much faith in Polly's sense of responsibility. Jamie's in London with Rachel, we left them up there. They're fending for themselves now.'

'So you said on the telephone,' said Adam grimly, 'but I'm not entirely convinced, I'm afraid.'

'Look.' Nick sat down opposite Adam. 'D'you mind if we look at this from our point of view for a minute? Get things into perspective a little?'

'Sure, if you must.'

'I must, because you don't seem to realise that you're not the only one in a tight spot here. Polly feels very guilty about the mess she got Rachel into—'

'You mean the mess she got *me* into,' interrupted Adam fiercely, jabbing his chest with his finger, no doubt to indicate the size of his massive pectorals which were soon to partake in the dismembering of my body. He glared at me. I whimpered and threw more gin down my throat and, oddly enough, my jumper.

'All right, all right, the mess she got you into, have it your own way,' sighed Nick. 'I'm not prepared to go into whose side she should have been on, because the point is that she shouldn't have been put in the position of having to pick sides in the first place. I mean, none of this whole ridiculous business had anything to do with her, did it?' He turned to me. 'In fact, it still beats me why you ever got involved in all this in the first place.' He shook his head with genuine incredulity. I hung mine in shame.

'Anyway,' he went on, 'that's another story, and we

361

won't go into Polly's inability to mind her own business right now; but believe me, when she told me all about it my immediate reaction was one of absolute horror. I couldn't believe she'd got mixed up in all this. I told her in no uncertain terms that she should extricate herself from the whole affair, tell the pair of you to bugger off, and let you fight it out between yourselves. As far as I was concerned, there was no reason why she should dig herself in any deeper − I mean, it's not as if she even knew either of you, for God's sake. It's one thing to help out old friends, but complete strangers? Come on. She'd done more than enough.'

Too right. I rather enjoyed that little speech, it had a nice protective ring about it. Adam looked thoughtful. He cradled his whisky in his fingers and swirled it around a bit. He didn't say anything.

Nick leaned forward. 'The whole situation was becoming totally absurd. She couldn't go home to her own flat in case you were waiting for her there, she couldn't come to work in case you followed her and attacked her—'

'Oh come on!' said Adam. 'You make me sound like an animal. I had no intention of attacking her—'

'Oh really? Well that wasn't the impression we got. You come charging into our office, brandishing knives and scaring the pants off everyone − what are we supposed to think?'

Adam shrugged, he looked a little shame-faced. 'OK, OK, I admit I acted a little crazy that day, but I was − well, I was desperate. I'm sorry, I apologise for all that, it's totally unlike me, I hate violence − really, but I've been under a hell of a lot of strain lately, as you can probably imagine. I guess I just lost my rag.'

Nick shrugged. 'Well, fair enough, it happens, but you can see my point. We weren't to know that you'd just temporarily "lost your rag". Polly really thought her number was up.'

Adam shook his head and sighed. 'This is crazy, you know. I'm not trying to hurt anyone, or even frighten anyone. I just want to find my son.'

'Fine, I realise that, but all I'm saying is that, at the time, we weren't to know that your threats were idle. Polly was scared out of her wits, and I was pretty worried myself, I can tell you. Anyway, that's why I suggested – ' he paused and let a hint of a smile play around his lips – 'with, I have to admit, something of an ulterior motive, that she come down here and stay with me for a while. To get away from it all and to – well, to have a holiday.' He grinned. 'I've been trying to drag her down here for some time, actually. In a way this was the perfect excuse.' He shot Adam a quick, half embarrassed, half cocky look, and then turned to look out of the window, letting this sink in.

I was impressed. Talk about the gifted amateur, this was the work of a seasoned liar, not a total beginner. Perhaps he'd been taking notes from me.

Faced with Nick's back, Adam swung round to me for confirmation. I'd done nothing but look permanently shifty for the last five minutes, and it was a demeanour which suited this revelation right down to the ground. I shifted some more.

Adam's top lip curled into a knowing sneer. 'Well, well, what do you know? Looks like I've stumbled in on a bit of a love nest here, doesn't it? Well congratulations, you guys, I hope you'll be very happy together,' he drawled.

'Thanks very much,' said Nick with a grin. 'I'm sure we will.' He got up to pour himself another drink, and paused en route to take my hand. He gave it a quick squeeze; it instantly broke out into a muck sweat. He looked casually at Adam. 'Another drink?'

'Sure, why not?'

'Polly?'

'Mmmm!' I nodded furiously, and gulped hard, hoping

nobody was expecting me to say anything more than that. Just breathing and drinking were proving to be enough of a struggle at the moment.

'Well, Polly,' smirked Adam, 'you've certainly changed your tune, haven't you?'

'What d'you mean?' I said quickly. Too quickly. As usual my mouth had responded before my brain had had time to engage. I didn't want him to tell me what he meant at all.

'Well, as I recall, a little over a week ago, Nick here was not exactly your favourite guy. And certainly not what you might call dream-boat material. In fact, if I remember rightly, you went so far as to write him off as a total jerk, am I right?'

I tried hard to erect a dam at the top of my neck to stop the red hot blush from spreading on to my face, but it was no good. 'Don't be ridiculous!' I spluttered. 'I would never say anything so − so absurd!'

'Ah, but you did!' said Adam, enjoying himself. 'In fact, I remember your very words. You called him − not a jerk, but that marvellously English insult − a git!'

Nick threw back his head and hooted with laughter. 'Well, thank you, my darling. A git, eh? That's not what you said last night!' He tapped me playfully on the nose as he handed me my drink.

I fumed at Adam, puce with embarrassment. What must Nick think? 'How dare you! It − it's outrageous of you to repeat a private conversation. I remember now that I'd had a bad day at work and was feeling a bit miffed with Nick over something silly, I don't remember what, and − and I might have said something to you in the heat of the moment about how I was a bit, um, irritated with him, but I certainly wouldn't have called him a git!' I gabbled.

Adam and Nick were both grinning widely. Nick sat on the arm of the sofa, threw an arm around my shoulders and hugged me towards him.

'Don't worry, darling, he's teasing you. Anyway, I know what you used to say about me, I dare say I've said a few uncharitable things about you in the past, too, but that's all forgotten now, isn't it? And of course you know what they say: there's a very thin line between love and hate!'

'Yes — yes, they do say that, don't they? D-darling,' I stammered. I was positively dripping with perspiration, and we hadn't even got to the difficult bit. Perhaps I could go and clean the attic now? The only consolation was that Adam had loosened up a bit, obviously enjoying my discomfort.

He smiled sadistically. 'Well, hey, I'm sorry if I've put a spanner in the works. I guess you'll have fun kissing and making up when I've gone, though. I must say it's fascinating to hear yet another chapter in Polly's some-what chequered love life.'

'Chequered?' I spluttered. 'There's nothing chequered about it. I'll have you know it's always been extremely straightforward!'

He laughed and held up his hands. 'OK, OK, I'll take your word for it. Anyway. We digress. Let's not get too sidetracked by your incredibly "straightforward" love life, shall we? We don't want to lose sight of the point of my little visit.'

He swilled his whisky around in his glass. For a moment I'd completely forgotten what the point was. He hadn't.

'Polly, where's Rachel?' he asked, in a soft but deadly voice, raising his eyebrows at me.

I shrank back. Did I say he'd loosened up? I felt the blood drain away from my face. Victoria plum to sheet white in less than five seconds; quite an achievement, really. My eyes caught on his like Velcro.

'I really don't know,' I whispered.

Nick strengthened his grip on my shoulders. 'Look, Adam, we haven't a clue where she is now, but there's no

365

harm in telling you that we dropped Rachel off at her father's house before we came down here.'

'Oh, come on, d'you really expect me to believe that? There's no one at that house except the judge and the housekeeper. D'you think I haven't been watching?'

'Well, maybe she's not there now, but I can tell you, we dropped her off there last Wednesday morning, plus Jamie and half a ton of baby gear. That's the last we saw of them, and we haven't heard from Rachel since.'

Adam shook his head. 'No way.'

'Take it from me, it's true. Maybe they were only there for an hour or so, perhaps they moved on almost immediately, I don't know. I'm just telling you that that's where we bow out of the story. That's where we left them.'

Nick looked Adam straight in the eye. Adam hesitated. My toes were creaking with suspense. He must have heard them, he turned to me.

'You spent a few days with Rachel, Polly, you must have talked to her. Did she give any clues as to what she was going to do? You must have discussed it with her. What were her plans?'

'I really don't know, she didn't say.'

'Oh come on, she must have said something!'

'She didn't – really, she kept very much to herself.'

'You know, you really shouldn't tell lies, Polly.'

'But it's true! Honestly, it's true, she – she didn't say a word!' I stammered nervously, no acting required.

Adam stared at me for a moment, then he rubbed his eyes and sighed deeply. He scratched his head. He didn't look in the least bit menacing now, he just looked tired.

'Look. I can quite understand why you don't want anything more to do with this business, but just listen to me for a minute, the pair of you, will you?'

I nodded dumbly. Did we have any choice?

'I'm not going to try to snatch Jamie away from Rachel.'

I looked at him suspiciously. 'You're not?'

He shook his head. 'No. Now I admit that originally I was so incensed that all I wanted to do was to find the pair of them, grab Jamie, and take him back to the States with me; but I've had a lot of time to think recently.' He leaned forward and rested his forehead in his hands, staring at his shoes. 'I've sat in quite a few hotel rooms, or rented houses, staring at walls trying to get things straight in my mind, and I've come to the conclusion that in the long run, it wouldn't get me very far. Rachel and her old man would have the police on to me in seconds. I'd just spend the whole time running and hiding. It would be pretty horrific for Jamie, too.'

'It certainly would,' agreed Nick.

'Yeh, yeh, I know, don't worry, I've worked it all through now. I know I'm on a hiding to nothing. All I want to do is find Rachel, talk to her, and see if we can't sort something out like a couple of sensible adults. There must be some kind of custodial agreement we can come to without going through the courts.'

'But she's too frightened to see you now, she won't speak to you,' I said.

Adam held out his hands in despair. 'But why? For God's sake, why won't she speak to me? There's no rhyme or reason why she should be scared. OK, in the heat of the moment when I was absolutely furious − and blind drunk incidentally − I made a couple of stupid telephone calls to her father's house, but she knows me well enough to know that I'd never hurt her, or Jamie. She's making out that I'm some kind of maniac, some kind of homicidal nut-case − it's crazy! What have I ever done to her, apart from love her, have a child with her, and ask her to marry me? Is that so terrible? Well, apparently it is, because d'you know what she did? Without any warning whatsoever, without even giving me an inkling of what was on her mind, she just up and left one day taking our son with her. She left a little itsy-bitsy note — about three lines long, it was — on the kitchen table and, cool as anything, walked out. Can you believe that? She just packed a bag, tucked Jamie under her arm, and got on a plane to England. And now she won't even speak to me — don't you think that's a little strange after all we've been through together? Wouldn't it drive you a little crazy if you were in my position? My whole world has collapsed and everyone's acting like I'm the lunatic, like I'm the one who's acting irrationally!' He shook his head in disbelief.

'Look, Adam . . .' began Nick softly, but Adam went on as if he hadn't even heard him. It was as if we weren't even in the room.

'But you know what? D'you want to know the craziest thing of all? In spite of all she's done, I still love her. I'd marry her tomorrow if she'd have me. We had a child together, my son, who I love more than anything in the world. That's what's important. That's what I keep hanging on to.'

He paused and ran his fingers through his hair. He looked terribly tired. Nobody spoke for a moment. At length, Adam continued. His voice had a crack in it.

'Now, I realise she doesn't feel the same way about me. I'm coming to terms with that, and I daresay one day I'll even accept it. People fall out of love all the time, and I just happen to be the injured party, that's all. OK, fine, but Christ, she owes me some sort of an explanation, doesn't she? Jesus, just to get on a plane and take off to another country like that without a word, taking Jamie with her.' His voice all but collapsed here; he fought to control it. 'I mean, whatever you think of me, you've got to admit, she owes me some kind of access to my son. She owes me the right to see him from time to time, doesn't she? Am I asking so much of her?'

I stared out of the window. I was surprised to discover I had tears in my eyes. I blinked. The curtains hadn't been drawn, and while we'd been talking it had got quite dark. A black, starless sky hung over us. The wind had dropped completely and all was still and quiet. There wasn't even a rustle in the trees, or a distant bleat of a lamb.

Of course he wasn't asking too much. She did owe it to him, and she owed him a lot more besides. I tried to imagine what it must be like to come home from work one day and find that your family has disappeared. We were well and truly caught in the middle here, and more and more I realised where my sympathies lay. I wanted to tell him where she was. I wanted to blurt it out – say that he'd find her holed up at a little pub called the Dog and Duck just off the Wincanton Road. All the same, I knew I couldn't. I was supposed to be feeding him the unmarried mothers line. I looked in desperation at Nick. He too looked pained, and shifted about uncomfortably on the arm of the chair. I wondered if he was thinking the same thing as me.

'Nick?' I whispered.

Adam pounced, misinterpreting my appeal. 'Nick, is there anything you can tell me? Something you know?'

Nick hesitated. 'No – no, not really . . .'

'For pity's sake, please!' Adam urged him.

'Well – well, actually she did mention something . . .'

'Yes! Yes – go on.'

'No Nick, don't,' I said softly.

He put a hand on my arm, 'I think we should, Polly.' I gulped and stared at the carpet. This was going to be more convincing than we could have possibly imagined, and I couldn't bear it. I couldn't look at Adam's eager face.

'Go on?' he leaned forward eagerly.

Nick sighed. 'Well, it's just that, while the girls were staying with Pippa, before they came down here, Polly overheard Rachel on the telephone.'

'Yes?'

'Well, she got through to one of those hostels, a

369

home for unmarried mothers . . .'

A light seemed to go on inside Adam's tired, dull eyes. I turned away. 'A home? You mean like a shelter, that kind of thing?'

'That's it. I don't suppose she was thinking of staying there on a permanent basis, perhaps for a week or two, I don't know, and I'm afraid I've no idea which one.'

Adam shot me a look. I shook my head vigorously. 'No,' I whispered, 'no, she didn't say.'

He stood up slowly. 'An unmarried mothers' home. Yeh, we have those in the States, I know what you mean.' He walked to the window and looked out at the black night.

'You won't get in,' I said quickly — somehow I couldn't bear to think of him beating his way into these places to no avail — 'and — and they'll just get the police on to you if you try.'

Unwittingly I'd managed to seal it. He drained his whisky. 'Will they indeed?' he said grimly. 'Just let them try.'

He turned to face us. His freckles stood out harshly on his pale, determined face. His eyes were wide and staring now. He put his glass down on a table.

'Thanks for the drink,' he said curtly. He nodded to us and turned to go. As he got to the door, he hesitated, his hand on the handle. He turned back. 'Thanks. I realise you didn't have to tell me that. I'm grateful. Thanks, Nick. I guess you can understand a little of how I feel.' With that he opened the door and walked out.

Nick and I sat in silence. I heard the front door close behind him, then I heard a car door slam. An engine turned over and roared into life. There was a crunch of gravel as the tyres spun on the drive, a familiar rattle as the car crossed over the cattle grid, and finally a distant roar as it sped off, no doubt heading for the London road. Still neither of us spoke.

Chapter Twenty

Eventually Nick sighed heavily and got to his feet. He crossed over to the fire and kicked one of the logs savagely, sending sparks flying on to the hearth. I felt like kicking something myself, but I'd had so much to drink I didn't think I was capable of standing up, let alone raising one leg off the ground and taking aim. Instead I sat in a booze-sodden heap feeling seriously depressed. Nick threw a couple more logs on the fire, and stood brooding down into the flames. Then he turned, warming the backs of his legs. He saw my dejected face and shook his head.

'It's no good looking like that, Polly. We did what we had to do.'

I sighed. 'I know. It just seems so unfair, though. Why do we have to take her side?'

Nick shrugged. 'Why do we have to take any side? It's a bloody ridiculous situation. Here we are, being forced to manipulate the lives of two people we hardly know, sending one off on a wild goose chase, and playing bodyguard to the other.' He shook his head grimly. 'I tell you, the sooner this is all over, the better.'

He turned back to the fire. We watched the flames for a while.

'Poor Adam,' I said eventually. 'He'll be banging on all the hostel doors in London tonight.'

Nick turned on me angrily. 'Well, that was what you

371

wanted, wasn't it? It's no good saying "poor Adam" now!'

'I know, I know, but – well, I just feel so awful, I almost wish we'd told him where she is!' I blurted out, feeling close to tears.

Nick looked at me, exasperated. 'God, Polly, sometimes I just don't believe you! What did you expect me to do, for God's sake? Dig out a road-map and trace a route for him from here to the Dog and Duck? Wave him on his way and let him charge up the motorway and go storming into the pub without giving Tim, Penny or Rachel any warning? Is that what you wanted?'

'No but—'

'Well, what then? And anyway, who's to say that he's telling the truth? Who's to say that he wouldn't just grab Jamie and take him back to America: how would you feel then? You'd be saying "poor Rachel" then, wouldn't you? Well, wouldn't you?' he demanded angrily.

'Yes, I suppose so,' I whispered.

I blinked hard. It had been a tough evening, and I really didn't think I could cope with anyone else having a go at me. Tears were literally poised on the precipice. I bit a very wobbly lip and looked away, but he saw the wobble and immediately sat down next to me, contrite and full of remorse.

'Oh Polly, I'm sorry, don't cry. It's not your fault, I'm just letting off steam. I know I shouldn't take it out on you, but to tell you the truth, I'm fed up with being in such a bloody awful position. It's really beginning to get me down.'

My chin wiggled dramatically as I fought with the waterworks. He sighed and ran his fingers through his hair.

'And I know why I'm angry. Because for what it's worth I feel the same way you do now. The more I hear about this saga, the more I think that Rachel acted abysmally, but that's not the point, is it? The point is, we promised we'd look after her, and we can't just abandon her now. You do see that, don't you?'

I gulped. 'Yes, I do, and I know you're right but − but it just seems so rough on Adam. He's not such a bad chap really, is he? A little impulsive, I grant you, but who wouldn't be under the circumstances?'

He laughed dryly. 'I must say you've changed your tune. Half an hour ago he was public enemy number one.'

'I know, but everything looks different now. He's been so hurt, and for what? I mean, as he says, all he's ever been guilty of is falling in love with a girl, getting her pregnant, wanting to marry her, and wanting to look after her and the baby. That's not so terrible, is it?' I gritted my teeth and clenched my fists. 'If you ask me, Rachel Marsden is a complete and utter bitch!'

Nick grinned. 'Feel better for that, do you?'

'I do, actually.'

'Polly, I agree with you, and the whole thing is very frustrating, but there's nothing we can do about it. Let's just try and forget it. We've got rid of Adam, and in a few days we'll get rid of Rachel, too. Then it'll all be over and you can relax. OK?'

I smiled weakly. 'OK.'

'In the meantime,' his voice softened considerably, 'why don't we just forget the pair of them and try to enjoy what's left of this little holiday?'

Now I know a seductive tone of voice when I hear one, in fact I can detect one at twenty paces, and I could have sworn I'd just heard one. I looked up in surprise. Nick smiled, and − good gracious, yes − the brown eyes were most definitely soft and encouraging. Like two deliciously gooey chocolates, they seemed to be beckoning me on.

'Oh yes, please,' I whispered greedily. 'I mean, yes please, let's enjoy ourselves. I'm all for enjoyment, aren't you?'

I gave him what I hoped was my most smouldering, sexy smile, but which could well have been taken for a pissed leer. He smiled back. Suddenly everything was so still, I could hear my heart beating. I waited, rigid with excitement. *Something* was definitely going on here, *something* was about to happen. I held my breath and sat quietly. Nick's smile turned into a steady gaze which seemed to envelope me completely. I bathed in it wantonly, not daring to move.

Overhead, a lone seagull wailed mournfully as it circled the house; the long case clock ticked away steadily in the corner; the fire crackled cosily in the grate. Other than that, there was just a highly charged silence. It was killing me, and so, for that matter, was my head. An intoxicating mixture of gin and desire was sending it into something more usually associated with the final spin-dry of a washing machine. How maddeningly inconvenient. I shut my eyes briefly in an attempt to arrest the cycle. A fatal mistake. Even though I was sitting down, I swayed violently. I opened them immediately.

'Are you all right?' asked Nick, whose come-hither gaze had turned to one of concern.

'Fine, fine, really. What were we saying?'

He smiled warmly. 'Something about enjoying ourselves.'

'Ah yes,' I murmured, and smiled back, even more warmly.

The washing machine abated slightly as every conceivable nook and cranny in my body tingled with anticipation. My heart went into overdrive, thumping away as it sent red-hot blood steaming around my body, pumping it into places that didn't normally require it. Even my toenails seemed to be throbbing, charged up to the cuticles with the stuff. Please hurry, I willed him silently, please hurry *up*!

But still he sat there, silent and watchful. Eventually,

after what seemed like a century but was probably three seconds, he turned his body in towards me slightly and rested his hand on the sofa behind my head. Yes, yes, *yes*, I urged silently, go for it. GO FOR IT! He didn't take his eyes off me. His hand rested softly on the back of my head. He stroked my hair gently and smiled.

I met his gaze, but was aware that my nostrils were flaring dramatically. I seemed to have far too much breath, I didn't know what to do with it. Out it came in short, chuggy bursts, and then in went gallons more. Where did it all come from? The more I tried to disguise it, the more I chugged and snorted. Now his hand was on the back of my neck, stroking it gently, making my hair stand up on end, making goose pimples break out in the oddest places, and all the while, he fixed me with those deep brown eyes.

I wasn't used to such slick, subtle moves. Most of the men I'd had close encounters of the sexy kind with would have had their tongue round my tonsils by now and be grappling with my bra strap. This hair-stroking lark was a new one on me, but it certainly sent the pulse rate soaring.

I chugged and snorted a bit more. We were close, but not that close. About twelve to eighteen inches of Colefax and Fowler chintz upholstery was still most definitely between us. There was no doubt that either a quick lunge or a surreptitious sidle would have to be made by somebody. But not you, I told myself sternly. Don't be fast and vulgar. For once in your life, be slow and tasteful. Just concentrate on sitting very still and he'll do the rest.

But when? He stroked and smiled, and stroked and smiled, and suddenly I could bear it no longer. Slow and tasteful be damned, I'd be dead soon. In one swift, jet-propelled move, I launched myself across the eighteen inches of sofa and flew into his arms.

He ricocheted slightly on impact, and out of the corner of my eye I caught a hint of a raised eyebrow, but no matter. Hating myself for my highly previous nature, but unable to control it, I lifted my face and − yes, he was lowering his. In an instant we were locked in the most divine, the most passionate, the most, oh so exquisite kiss I'd ever experienced. On and on it went, getting sweeter and sweeter, and deeper and deeper by the moment. I could have stayed there for ever, but breathing difficulties were becoming apparent on his part, and so at last, like a couple of deep-sea divers, we came up for air. Locked in his arms, I gazed up to see what effect all this passion was having on the geometric features. They'd softened considerably. He looked pleased, if a little surprised.

'Well, well, well,' he said softly, gently tracing my mouth with his finger. 'Who would have thought . . .'

'Yes, who would have thought!' I whispered back breathlessly.

Who would have thought what? That I could be such a brazen hussy? That he could have lowered himself to the depths of snogging his secretary? Or that it could all be so deeply wonderful? Who would have thought what? I longed to know but, more than that, I longed for more. Unfortunately my head was against it. Once more it had switched into spin-dry mode, and I had to steady myself on his shoulder to stop the room from spinning round.

I held on tight and breathed deeply. It was important to take very deep breaths and on no account to shut my eyes. I concentrated like mad on the fire, I watched the flames as they licked greedily around the logs, and then, when I deemed it safe to move my head, I looked up. Nick frowned down at me as I span.

'All right?' he inquired.

All right? What − the kiss? Was he asking me? 'Oh yes! Fantastic! One of the best − the best in fact!'

Nick seemed to find this a puzzling response. He frowned some more. What a thoroughly sexy frown, I thought dreamily as it swam in and out of focus. What can he be thinking about? Whatever it was obviously required a great deal of thought. Ah yes! I know, he's wondering where we should go from here! Only literally, of course, we know in theory where we're going, but where should the action take place?

Was he the kind of man who had to do it in a bed? Or would that mouth-wateringly appetising Persian rug in front of the fire do just as well? Still he frowned. The location was obviously not to be chosen lightly. Of course! He was probably considering the hay barn! Hadn't he mentioned only the other day that he'd like to sleep in it? Now if that isn't a broad hint, I don't know what is! I helped him along.

'Are you thinking about the barn?' I whispered.

'Sorry?'

'The barn, is that what you're thinking about? Because if you are, I want you to know that I think it's a very good idea, very – you know, rustic!' I gently nudged his gloriously hunky shoulder with my head and winked in a knowing fashion.

Nick looked even more puzzled. Then suddenly he disentangled himself and got up. He went over to the fire, crouched down and poked it thoughtfully. I sat up. Gracious, this seemed to me to be an entirely retrograde step, what on earth was going on? It didn't take that much thought, did it?

'Only joking about the barn,' I mumbled. 'I'm easy.' God, that sounded awful. 'About – about where we go, I mean.' Even worse. I flushed and looked down at my hands.

More frowning, and more fire maintenance followed these brazen confessions. I bit my lip. I felt decidedly out of my depth here. These decorous periods of inactivity might be highly civilised, but they puzzled the hell out of me. After all, the first kiss had been planted, intent had been established, action should be taking place. Shouldn't we even now be thundering upstairs, tearing each other's clothes off, and launching ourselves at the double bed in a frenzy of excitement? Even the restrained hair-stroking was preferable to this malarkey. I thought hard. No Polly, no, you're wrong as usual. This was obviously how civilised people made love. Of course! How silly of me: fire-poking was probably the ultimate in erotic symbolism. After all, he had been to Cambridge, hadn't he? And I hadn't been exposed to such high-minded love-making before. Up to now it had all been very – well, very red-brick. Even polytechnic at times.

I watched eagerly as he rooted away in the grate, excitement growing within me – oh yes, I see, I see! The more he poked, the more excited I got, I was really catching on now – God, this was thrilling! But how should I respond? Join him at the fireside? Throw on a lump of coal? This was all new to me; how taxing it was!

I racked my brains. Come on, Polly, think, think. Suddenly it came to me. I would dance towards him. Yes, of course, a dance – what could be more erotically symbolic than that? And I was a good dancer too.

'Nick?' I whispered eagerly.

'Yes?' he turned around.

'Ready?'

'Er . . . yes.'

I got unsteadily to my feet, pulled a lock of hair over one eye, and fixed him with a sexy, penetrating gaze. I put my hands on my hips and wiggled them seductively. Then I rotated my shoulders, slowly. Next I concentrated on the wrists, twirling them around, seven veils-fashion, stretching out the fingers – oops, there went an ashtray, crashing to the floor, spilling ash everywhere – no matter, I was well away now. I really began to move. I swayed towards him, flashing my eyes from under their lashes, and giving the sexy smouldering smile yet another outing. Atta-girl, I thought to myself, atta-girl! This will rock his socks off.

He watched, in wonder and in a little too much amazement, as I shimmied towards him, hips snaking, arms twisting. The more I shimmied, the wider his eyes grew: he was totally captivated. I was right above him now as he sat crouched, a trifle nervously perhaps, by the fireside. I really let him have it. I threw back my head and twirled and snaked and twisted and writhed and –

'Oops!' – tripped over the rug, toppling headlong towards the fire.

'Watch out!' yelled Nick as he grabbed me, rugby-tackling me away from the flames.

'Oof, sorry!' I landed, rather heavily it has to be said, in his arms. OK, so it wasn't the most graceful of landings, but there I was, where I most wanted to be. I smiled up at him dreamily as both of his rather fuzzy heads separated for a moment and then came together again. All I had to do was lie here and wait. Any minute now he'd pull me roughly towards him, and envelope me in the most passionate embrace, kissing me madly the while. I shut my eyes in an ecstasy of anticipation.

Nick cleared his throat. 'Right. Bedtime I think.'

He just couldn't wait, could he? 'Oooh, yes please!' I wriggled gleefully, then reached up and pulled his head down towards mine, lips parted, eyes shut – one for the road, eh?

Lip contact was never made. I opened my eyes. Nick seemed to be disentangling my arms from around his neck. 'No, Polly, separate bedtime.'

He stood up, hoisted me to my feet, turned me around and pointed me in the direction of the door. 'Go on,' he said softly. 'I'll see you in the morning.'

I stood there, swaying incredulously. My mouth opened wide, my eyes boggled. I turned back. 'Separate beds?' I echoed dumbly.

'Separate,' he affirmed decisively.

My insides curdled, my jaw slackened. I was amazed,

incredulous, uncomprehending. Separate beds? That's what he'd said all right, but was he serious? And if so, what did it mean? That I'd got it all wrong? That I'd read his signs wrong? Surely not.

I frowned, pondering the mighty implications of it all. Then, quite suddenly, it dawned on me, crashing over me in a tidal wave of shame and embarrassment. Oh my God. Of course! I'd failed the kiss test.

Now, I freely admit to having failed a lot of tests in my time. Scores of O-levels, a smattering of A-levels, Grade Three piano, cycling proficiency and life saving, to name but a few, but never, *never*, have I failed the kiss test. Let's face it, I've had too much practice. In fact, without wishing to sound immodest, I generally pass with flying colours and leave the lucky recipient begging for more. But to fail! I hung my head and felt my face flame. How deeply shameful.

What could it be, I wondered? Galloping halitosis? Or something more sinister like a nasty little cold sore at the corner of the mouth? I put up a tentative hand and felt around gingerly. Nothing seemed to be glaringly apparent; it must be lurking nastily beneath the surface.

But, on the other hand, maybe it wasn't that at all. Maybe – and this was a real shaker – maybe he just didn't fancy me. Perhaps he'd thought it might be quite fun, a bit of a laugh, but when it came to the crunch he'd found it – well – rather nauseous; repulsive even. After all, he already had a girlfriend, didn't he? And a jolly pretty one at that: why should he mess around with the likes of me? I was mortified. How could I have been such a fool? I felt a bit of a lip tremble coming on. I stiffened it instantly. Bear up, Polly, bear up. We'll have none of that, thank you.

I raised my head and met his eye. 'Right-o then!' I said in a cracked little voice, desperately trying to force a hockey stick into it. 'I'll be off to bed. You're right, I am rather tired actually — cheerio! See you in the morning!'

Smiling bravely, I turned and crossed the room in a reasonably straight line, although I have to admit, I lurched the final yard or two and had to grab hold of the door frame to steady myself. Every moment in this room was unbearable now.

I was aware that he was following me. I could feel his eyes on my back as I made it through the hall to the bottom of the stairs, albeit with a bit of wall-hanging along the way.

'Are you OK?' he asked anxiously as I began, gingerly, to mount the stairs.

'Sure!' I croaked, raising my hand in a backward wave to reassure him, and quickly replacing it on the banister as I nearly lost my balance. Sure. Only about eighteen inches tall now and getting smaller by the minute, but other than that, fine, just dandy.

The stairs seemed to go up and up for ever; higher and higher they went, like something out of a 1940s Hollywood musical set, and all the time he would keep standing at the bottom watching my unsteady progress. I looked back. Yes, he was still there — Christ, what a long way down! I grabbed the banister as I stumbled: how extraordinary, I seemed to be suffering from vertigo.

I bit my quivering lip. Don't cry, I thought with rising panic. Don't cry yet. Not yet. And don't, whatever you do, look down. I climbed the last step, turned left, realised my mistake in an instant — lightning reflexes — and turned right instead. I stumbled blindly down the dark passageway, feeling my way in the dark.

At last I reached the right door. Now you can cry, I thought as I stumbled in. I shut the bedroom door behind me and leaned heavily against it. Now you can cry all you like. I threw myself on my bed and buried my face in my pillow. The floodgates opened. I sobbed and sobbed, for about — oh, a couple of minutes probably. Because after that the strangest thing happened. Instead of sobbing long and hard, and on and on, into the small hours, as I'd rather imagined I would, almost immediately, I fell fast asleep.

Chapter Twenty-one

When I awoke the next morning I was almost blinded by the light. The window and the curtains were wide open and a sixty-watt bulb was glaring down at me above my head. I blinked and rubbed my eyes. How very odd. Why on earth was the light on? Had it been on all night? I raised myself up on to my elbows. A huge mistake. A wave of fresh spring air surged through the open window and hit me full in the face. I moaned low and sank down on to the pillow again.

I felt awful, really awful. I lay still for a minute as I tried to get the measure of this. Something deeply unpleasant was going on here, mostly in the head region. My brain seemed to have expanded overnight and was fighting for accommodation, bashing away against my skull in a painful, frenzied fashion. My tongue had swollen out of all proportion and had grown fur, like some ghastly Caliban festering in its cave. What on earth had I been up to last night to surface in this sorry condition?

I frowned and cast my mind back a few hours. Slowly, the penny started to drop. It landed with a resounding clatter and the whole horror of the night before slotted into place. I stuffed the sheet into my mouth. Oh my God! I'd tried to seduce him! I'd leaped into his arms! I'd – I'd, oh horror of horrors, I'd danced! Had I really? Yes I had! I pulled the sheet right over my head and groaned. Suddenly I went cold. Had I – and here I had trouble even suggesting the notion to myself – had I, perchance, danced naked?

I sat up, terror-struck, and had a swift glance round the room. Happily, most of my clothes could be accounted for. There was my skirt on the lampshade, my shirt on the bookcase, my jumper hanging out of the window, my bra – where was my bra? I glanced down. Oh. How odd. I frowned at my chest. I seemed to be wearing it. Oh well, at least it hadn't come off; but what other face-flushing atrocities had I committed?

With a heavy sigh I lay down again and turned on to my side. As I did so, I realised there was something wrong with my feet. I couldn't move my toes. I tried to wiggle them, it was quite an effort. Ah yes, of course, I was obviously paralysed. I'd heard of people being paralysed with embarrassment before; clearly it had happened to me. Paralysed from the – let me see, I tried an unsuccessful ankle wiggle – yes, from the knees downwards. What a shame, I was rather fond of walking. I peeped warily under the bedclothes and spotted my cowboy boots still clinging to my person. Ah. That explained it. How peculiar, I usually remembered to take my shoes off.

At least that was all of my clothing accounted for, except – except my knickers! Where the hell were they? Draped over a lampshade in the drawing room? Hanging over an ancestral portrait in the hall? Decorating the banisters perhaps?

I jumped out of bed, clad fetchingly in a bra and cowboy boots like something out of a Soho sleaze joint, and stared wildly round the room. Ah! Thank goodness. There they were in the washbasin. I fell on them gratefully and hugged them to my bosom. At this point I experienced a certain amount of head rush and had to steady myself on the washbasin. I shouldn't have leaped out of bed so quickly. I took a deep breath, counted to ten, then crawled back to bed and shut my eyes tight.

After about half an hour I realised, with a glance at my clock, that it was already ten o'clock and if I left it any longer *someone* might breeze in full of pity and find me in this hideously unattractive state. Some sort of repair job would have to be done on the face before such an eventuality. Apart from that, a raging thirst was beginning to get the better of me. I had to get up.

I staggered to the washbasin and glugged desperately at a running tap, wet hair streaming down the plughole, but it was no good. A hosepipe turned on full blast was needed to quench this sort of thirst.

I gazed in the mirror above the basin. How strange. Someone rather like me but much uglier was gazing back. Same shaped face and same hair, but with tiny, slitty little eyes which were only being kept open by the weight of a huge pair of pendulous bags which dragged the bottom lids down. The complexion was pasty and pallid and the mouth enormously swollen. Swollen heart, too, I thought mournfully as I brushed two inches of fur off my teeth. That was the worst of it, and something I could only just bring myself to contemplate. He didn't want me. He'd rejected me. If I was the last woman on this earth he'd emigrate to Mars. And I loved him.

It hit me full in the face like a runaway train. I loved him. The ugly face in the mirror began to quiver perilously and the piggy little eyes looked alarmingly moist. Don't cry! I commanded the face sternly. It shuddered obediently to a halt and the eyes blinked back their tears. For God's sake. You're ugly enough as it is, don't make things worse.

I showered long and hard and dressed slowly. Then I spent about half an hour on my make-up, to no avail. It was quite clear that on this particular morning I had the choice of looking like a prostitute or a battered wife. Initially I went for the prostitute look, then got half-way down stairs and ran back to wash it all off again. If I looked like a tart it might remind him that I was one. No.

Bare-faced cheek was the order of the day.

With freshly scrubbed cheeks I crept down into the kitchen. There was no one about. Nick had obviously breakfasted long ago, up at five with the cows, no doubt. I opened the fridge and greeted the orange juice like a long-lost friend. The muesli was a different matter. I toyed with it limply and stared out of the window. Where was he? Hiding in a barn? Ringing Tim and Rachel, begging them to come back and rescue him from the hands of a nymphomaniac who'd taken the whole charade seriously and had tried — unsuccessfully, mind — to get into his jeans? I groaned. Oh, the shame.

The muesli was making me retch so I poured it down the sink, clogging up the plughole. Suddenly I looked up — I could hear footsteps on the path outside. Oh God, it was him, and before I even had time to decide what sort of an expression I would have on my face, he was opening the back door.

'Hi!' he greeted me cheerily, looking fresh-faced and windswept. His hair was tousled, his eyes were shining, and he looked utterly divine. How could I ever have thought he'd be mine?

'Hi!' I managed to gasp in response. The expression my face had chosen for me was of the timid, cowering, puke-making variety. I hovered by the Aga; should I stay? It would be too rude to leave immediately, and yet I couldn't bear to make small-talk with him.

'Had some breakfast?' he asked conversationally as he sat down and pulled his boots off.

'Oh, yes thanks.'

There was a silence. I cast around desperately for something interesting to say.

'Have you?' Pathetic, Polly. Truly pathetic.

'Yes, I had mine hours ago. Been up since six.'

'Ah.'

It was so hard to talk, and yet recently it had been so

easy. I stared miserably at the kitchen floor.

'What have you – um, been doing then? I mean this morning?' I faltered.

'Oh this and that, been out with the sheep mostly. Oh, incidentally, I telephoned Mrs Green.'

'Oh yes?' I tried to sound interested, but really I couldn't have cared less. I was fed up with other people's lives.

'And she said that Adam left last night. Just paid the rent, packed his bags and shot off, saying he was going back to London. He was in quite a hurry apparently.'

'Oh well, that's good. Gosh, that's good. What a relief!' I said unconvincingly. I stared at my fingernails. I must go on saying ordinary things.

'Everything – um, all right on the farm front, then?'

'Yes, fine, one of the ewes had twins which is always a bonus. I'd got her down as a singleton, but she popped two little ones out first thing this morning.'

'Oh good.'

'Yup, and they both seem to be doing well. Oh, and the lamb whose mother died seems to have been fairly successfully adopted by another ewe who lost a lamb, so things are looking up.'

'Great!'

A silence ensued. It had to be filled. I felt myself blushing. The whole room seemed hot.

'And – and the cows?' I faltered.

He grinned. 'The cows are fine, thank you, and I'm sure they'll be pleased to hear you've been asking after them. Shall I give them your best?'

He was laughing at me. I bit my lip. I could feel tears gathering behind my eyes. I turned away and lifted the top of the Aga, putting the kettle on to boil. It boiled almost immediately and I poured myself a coffee. Still I couldn't bear the silence. I had to fill it, however clumsily, however stupidly. I must seize new, harmless topics.

'I wonder how — how they're getting on back at the agency! Without us, I mean — well, without you.'

Nick looked at his watch. 'Oh, I should think they're probably all in the pub by now, don't you? I mean it is ten-thirty. That's where you all normally congregate when I'm away, isn't it?'

'Er, well, not always, now and again, I suppose. Yes, we do have the odd drink.'

He grinned, 'Well, why not? It's different when you're working for yourself, of course. Time spent in the pub is money lost as far as I'm concerned.'

'Yes, yes, I suppose it is.'

Another silence. This was gruesome, truly gruesome, I'd never felt so uncomfortable with anyone in my whole life. I had to get away. I sidled towards the door clutching my coffee. Nick struggled to pull his second boot off, threw it on the floor and grinned up at me just as I'd reached the door.

'So how are you feeling?'

I turned. 'Me? Oh fine, fine.'

'Really?'

'Really. Well, no all right, ghastly actually. Got a bit of a headache.'

He laughed. 'I'm not surprised! You were drinking for England last night!'

'Was I? Oh, yes, well perhaps I did have a bit too much.'

'A bit? Polly, you could hardly stand!'

Really, this was hardly chivalrous, was it? To remind a girl the following morning of a totally uncharacteristic over-indulgence the night before?

'Well, yes, perhaps I didn't — you know, pace myself very well.'

Nick got up and went to the sink to wash his hands, but it was full of muesli. Without a word, he scooped it out by the handful and threw it in the bin. I stared at his back as he rinsed his hands. It was no good. At some point I would have to make reference to last night, and I might as well do it now while I had the advantage of addressing his back rather than his face.

I took a deep breath. 'Nick, I'm sorry about last night,' I burst out.

He grabbed a towel to dry his hands and turned to face me. 'What d'you mean?'

Oh God, this was too much. What did he want me to do, rewind last night's spool and run through it again for him?

I blushed. 'Oh well, you know. Throwing myself at you and all that. Can't think what got into me.'

'A litre of gin, perhaps?'

I grinned. 'You're right, I was a bit pickled.'

He sat down at the kitchen table and looked at me as I hovered by the door. 'Polly?'

I met his eyes.

He held out his hand. 'Come here,' he said softly.

'What?'

He beckoned me over. 'Come over here.'

I sidled gingerly across to the table. 'What, right over here?'

He grabbed my arm and pulled me down on to his lap. 'Yes, right over here!'

'No, I'm too heavy!' I squeaked. I kept one foot firmly on the floor, hoping it would take most of the weight. What was this – corporal punishment time? Was he going to put me over his knee and spank me for my outrageous behaviour last night?

'Now listen to me. There's no need to apologise for anything you did last night. I loved it.' He grinned. 'Especially the dance!'

I hung my head in shame.

'But you were so pissed, so unbelievably steaming, I just had to send you up to bed on your own. I honestly think you would have passed out if we'd risked any funny business, either that or thrown up. I mean, you probably

389

don't remember this, Polly, but at one stage you were rambling on about barns. You kept talking about wanting to go to a barn, d'you remember that?'

'Um, vaguely,' I muttered. I flushed to my toes.

'At that point I thought you'd got serious alcohol poisoning.'

'Sorry,' I mumbled.

'Don't be sorry, it doesn't matter. God, we've all been in that state. I just didn't want to respond too eagerly in case I got my face slapped in the morning.'

I struggled to make sense of this earth-shattering turn of events. 'Oh! So you mean − you weren't necessarily that adverse to my, um − you know, advances?'

He smiled. 'Not necessarily that adverse, no.'

'Oh! So, so − oh. So . . .' I stumbled on, vainly trying to get my dehydrated grey matter around this revelation, and wondering what it signified. 'So, what you're saying is, that in a way, you almost liked them. My advances, I mean.'

He threw back his head and roared with laughter. 'Yes, I think we could safely say that I almost liked them, most certainly, Polly, yes.' He stopped laughing and just smiled, rather tenderly in fact. 'To tell you the truth, I've been thinking about them for some time now.'

I gulped. He looked utterly serious.

'Really?' I breathed.

'Really.'

I wanted to say I'd spent every waking moment thinking about his advances too, but that would have sounded silly. I sat as still as I possibly could on his knee. A silence enveloped us, but I couldn't fill the gaps any more, couldn't think of any words. I just felt dumb with longing.

In the event, no words were necessary. Nick gazed into my red-rimmed eyes which must have looked remarkably like road maps. I held my breath. He cupped my face in his hand and tilted it towards him. And then he kissed me.

Softly and gently. At length, we parted, and as I breathed again I realised I'd been kissed like that once before. Of course, last night. As he held me tightly against him, I was relieved to hear his breath roaring in my ear. At least this time I wasn't the only one with respiratory problems.

'So,' he whispered, puffing a bit, 'shall we go upstairs?'

I opened my mouth to answer, thought better of it, and nodded. Surely if I just stuck to nodding I couldn't cock it up too comprehensively?

We climbed the stairs hand in hand. Those stairs had seen a lot of action one way and another. Twelve hours ago they'd borne me up in the depths of despair, now they bore me up in ecstasy. I felt as if any minute now someone might appear from behind a curtain, snap a clapperboard in front of my nose and cry, 'Right! Take three, Miss McLaren, let's try those stairs one more time, but this time we'll do the despair again, shall we?'

But no. We reached the top and walked hand in hand down the passageway that led inevitably to his bedroom.

But once inside I hesitated. I felt suddenly shy and awkward. My face was a mess and I had none of the gung-ho, alcohol-induced courage of the night before. I looked at him apprehensively. I did hope he wasn't just being kind. Charitable even.

'Nick, I do hope we're doing the right thing. I mean, it would be a shame to spoil our — you know — our friendship and everything, shouldn't we—'

But my heart wasn't in it, and anyway, whatever else I'd been going to say was lost as he took me in his arms and kissed me very firmly on the mouth.

'For once in your life, would you just shut up?' he asked reasonably.

What was a girl to do? I demurred, and let him kiss me again.

We were just inside the bedroom door. Still we kissed. Filled with a sudden desperate greed, and impatient as ever, it occurred to me that we still had a lot of floor space to cover before we were to make contact with the double bed and enjoy the pleasures of the horizontal, but I needn't have worried, Nick was alive to this. He wisely rejected carrying me, but steered me gently towards the bed. Still locked in each other's arms, and indulging in yet more passionate lip contact, we sank down on to the duvet with awesome choreography. This was obviously meant to be. As he went on to address my ear, my mouth and my neck and ultimately of course, my buttons, he whispered tenderly in my ear.

'Sorry if I smell of cow shit.'

I giggled, delighted that someone else was feeling disadvantaged on account of their slovenly ways.

'Couldn't matter less. Sorry about the bloodshot eyes, the dog breath, the sweaty palms . . .'

'I love it . . . all of it,' he muttered back.

It was quite some time before we muttered again. When we did, he was lying on his back, one arm around my shoulder, and I was nestled up against him, my head resting on his bare chest and my arm thrown across it.

'Happy?' he murmured.

'Delirious,' I muttered back.

He smiled and stroked my hair. I studied his chest as it rose gently up and down, centimetres from my eyeballs. It was a pale, biscuity-brown colour with a discreet little smattering of dark hairs growing in a clump in the middle. I wondered how well I would get to know that clump. My eyes travelled up along his neck, and came to rest on his chin, which jutted out dramatically above me. It looked like the Rock of Gibraltar from my vantage point. I traced round it with my finger and smiled, 'Well, who would have thought.'

'Who would have thought what?'

'Exactly.' I grinned and shifted up on to my elbow to look at him. 'You don't remember, do you? That's what you said to me last night and that was exactly my reaction. Who would have thought what?'

He laughed. 'I suppose I must have meant, who would have thought this could finally happen.'

'Are you happy about it?' I asked tentatively, not wanting to spoil anything, but needing to know that it hadn't been a horrible mistake on his part and that he wasn't even now plotting how to get me on the next train to London.

He reached up and pulled me down towards him. 'You bet I am.' He kissed my nose. 'You're beautiful, Polly.'

I smiled, hugging the words to myself. I wasn't beautiful. I was rather overweight, my features were not desperately regular, and this morning did not find me at my best, but if he said it, I could feel it. He went on staring at me and, oddly enough, instead of squirming away and hiding behind my hair, the more he looked, the better I felt.

We lay there, locked in each other's arms, and would no doubt have embarked on a stream of tender pillow-talk for the next hour or two if my tummy hadn't decided it was time to register a protest. It had, of course, rejected the muesli some time earlier on the grounds that it might not have stayed put, but now it was rumbling noisily and clamouring to be given a second chance.

Nick laughed. 'Something tells me you need some blotting paper to mop up last night's excesses.'

I smiled ruefully. 'I suppose I am a bit hungry, but I'll survive.'

There was no way food was coming between me and pillow-talk. I snuggled up to him. My tummy had other ideas. Mount Vesuvius eat your heart out, I thought, as it rumbled again.

Nick laughed. 'Bloody hell, you'll erupt in a minute . . . Come on, let's eat, you're in danger of wasting away.'

'That'll be the day. I always used to wish for anorexia at

Christmas when I got the wishbone.' I sighed. 'But you're right, I'm starving. I'll get up and get us some breakfast – or lunch even.' I glanced at his bedside clock. It seemed to be twelve-thirty.

He kissed my shoulder. 'Let's have it in bed.'

'Oh yes, let's!'

How unlike Harry he was, who had always wanted to get up as quickly as possible and get on with the important things in life, which had never included me.

I threw back the covers and climbed out of bed. He pulled me back down again. 'I'll get it, you stay here. I want to come back and find you exactly as you are.'

I sank back down on to the pillows again. My whole body seemed to be wreathed in smiles. Oh joy! A man who actually wanted to do things for me! I was totally unused to this; it was a long time since I'd been out with anyone who wasn't a complete and utter bastard.

Nick got up and I was treated to a quick glimpse of his broad brown back before he pulled on his jeans and a shirt. He smiled down at me as he tucked the shirt into his jeans.

'You look fabulously wild and dishevelled. Don't move an inch. Just stay exactly like that and I'll be back in five minutes complete with tea and toast.'

'I won't move a muscle,' I said in a ventriloquist's voice, without moving my lips.

He grinned and leaned down to plant a kiss on my forehead. 'Peanut butter or Marmite?' he murmured.

'Peanut butter.'

And off he went, thundering noisily down the stone stairs. I heard him singing along to the radio as he clattered around in the kitchen, getting out mugs, boiling the kettle, making toast. I stretched luxuriously, feeling like the cat who's not only got the cream but the whole dairy too. I couldn't have been happier. He thought I was beautiful. Wild and dishevelled, eh? If only he knew how easy it was to look like that; it was sophisticated and elegant that caused the problems.

How wild, I wondered? I nipped out of bed and stole across to the oval mirror propped up on a chest of drawers. My face was quite attractively flushed and my eyes had widened considerably; there was a definite sparkle about them, too. Not bad, I thought appraisingly, not too bad at all considering the very raw material of first thing this morning. My hair was all over the place, but that apparently was no bad thing, and thank God I'd washed all that make-up off. It would be decorating his pillows by now.

I hopped back into bed and drew the sheets up under my chin. My feet took it upon themselves to do a little jig of joy under the duvet. So. Here I was at last. In Nick's bedroom. I took a good look around the room. It was perfect. Not like Harry's with its silly futon and oh-so-tasteful minimalist bits and pieces, but cluttered and lived in and – yes, welcoming.

The walls were Wedgwood blue with an indistinct criss-cross pattern, and the carpet a darker blue and very worn, with a series of reddish Persian rugs strewn over it, probably hiding a few holes. The bookcase underneath the window was crammed with books, which jostled each other for space and spewed out on to the floor, and the drawers in the huge chest on which the mirror sat were mostly open, with clothes falling out of them. A series of hunting prints covered one wall, and on another there were a few old maps. Above the bed was a rather modern, and quite good, painting of the house.

The room was untidy, but not massively so. Of course it had nothing on my sluttish tendencies, but it definitely showed promise. The bedside table, for instance, was covered with a thin film of dust, and in one corner of the room a pair of dirty jeans, some old socks, and a jumper lay festering in a heap. A nice touch, I thought. There were no photos either. Good. I liked a man who didn't wear his heart in his picture frames.

Balancing on top of the curtain pelmet were a few old Airfix planes. They brought a lump to my throat. He really had grown up in here. I wondered if he'd made the planes with his father. I wondered what he'd been like. Suddenly I wanted to know everything about him, about his parents, his childhood – everything. That was the joy of it all. We were at the beginning, with so much to find out about each other. I smiled to myself. Happiness flooded through every vein.

I plumped up the pillows and arranged myself decoratively upon them, with my hair spread out like a fan around my face. Then I set about my cleavage with a vengeance, draping the duvet seductively so it just covered my boobs but left quite a lot protruding voluptuously over the top. I positioned my arms to wedge the duvet in position, but made sure they didn't actually touch my sides or they'd look fat. I looked down. All was in order. Thus arranged, I waited. He'd been gone at least five minutes now, hadn't he? What was he doing, making the bread? Picking the tea? I smiled to myself. No. He was probably doing something terribly sweet like picking flowers for the tray. I'd pretend to be really surprised. 'Nick! Daffodils, how gorgeous!' I'd cry as he pressed a large bunch into my arms.

But wait a minute? What was that? Was that Nick's voice? Yes, it was, who on earth was he talking to? I frowned. There was another voice down there too. Female at that. Rachel? Surely she wasn't back already! No, it couldn't be Rachel, it must be – yes, of course, it must be Sarah! Sarah, over from the stables for a break and a cup of coffee. Of course. Hopefully Nick would get rid of her, tactfully. We could always ring her later of course, ask her over for a cup of tea. If we weren't indulging in a spot of afternoon delight, that is. I allowed myself a quiet little squeak of excitement — eeeeek! It really was all too thrilling!

The next minute I heard heavy footsteps bounding up the stairs. Goody-goody! I gave the duvet a last-minute adjustment and smiled eagerly. The door flew open and Nick came in. He stood in the doorway. His face was pale and drawn and the muscle in his cheek was bobbing up and down. The sweet, tender look of ten minutes ago was nowhere to be seen. He didn't say anything for a moment.

'What is it? What's happened?' I whispered in alarm.

Nick came over and sat down on the edge of the bed. He ran his hands through his hair. He looked shattered. 'I'm afraid we'll have to postpone our lunch, Polly, we've got a visitor.'

'Why? Who is it?'

He looked down at the duvet. There was a terrible silence. I felt my heart pause in mid-beat, then it started hammering away somewhere in the vicinity of my mouth. What on earth was going on?

'Nick, who is it? Who's downstairs?'

Funnily enough I knew the moment I'd said it. Nick merely confirmed my fears. He looked up and met my eyes.

'It's Serena,' he said quietly.

Chapter Twenty-two

'Serena!' I sat bolt upright.

Nick looked wretched. 'She's just arrived, I'm afraid. Look, Polly, I'll try and explain—'

'Darling? Darling, are you upstairs?' A strange bird-like trill interrupted us, warbling up from below, shrieking down the passageway, careering round the bedroom door, and hitting me full in the face like a runaway train. Those were Serena's dulcet tones, all right.

'You'd better go,' I whispered, suddenly filled with panic at the thought of her venturing upstairs and appearing at the door in all her Armani glory to witness this sordid little scene. 'Go on, quick. She might come up!'

Nick looked at my stricken face and took my hand, giving it a reassuring little squeeze. 'I'll explain everything later, Polly. It's just that − well, she's terribly vulnerable at the moment, and I really don't want to hurt her if it's at all possible. You do understand, don't you?'

He looked at me beseechingly and I nodded bravely, understanding precisely nothing. Hurt her? How about hurting me? Vulnerable, eh? Yes well, if you must know, I felt about as vulnerable as an open wound. An open wound that's just been on the receiving end of a Bruce Lee Kung-Fu kick, one of those flashy sideways ones that comes at you out of nowhere − ha-ya-ho! − and leaves you doubled up on the floor, spluttering and gasping for breath.

'Dar-*ling*!' There it was again, that voice; shrill, clear and confident, ricocheting off the bedroom walls.

Nick dropped my hand hurriedly and disappeared.

I lay there for a second feeling numb. Then I crawled slowly out of bed and fumbled around for my jeans and jumper. A tear dropped on to the Persian rug as I sat down to pull on my socks. I blinked hard. You silly little fool, I thought savagely, did you really think you were meant to be that happy? Don't you know the story of your life by now? What made you think you could start rewriting it at this late stage?

I found a comb and pulled it through my hair, looking in the mirror. The same mirror that moments earlier had revealed a flushed, excited, happy Polly. Now it revealed a white-faced, scared little creature with wet eyes and a trembling jaw.

I faced my reflection and addressed it sternly in a stage whisper. 'Pull yourself together, will you? OK, so the girlfriend who you'd both conveniently forgotten has arrived – it had to happen some time, didn't it? And just remember this, he's very, very fond of you. No one, *no one*, could have pretended like that back there – I eyed the crumpled sheets meaningfully – without being very, very, well, fond.' Ghastly word. One could be fond of a hamster, but one wouldn't necessarily want to spend the rest of one's life with it. I revised my adjective. 'Special, then. You're very special, OK?' I commanded my reflection. Somehow it didn't look convinced. What seemed to me to be more convincing was the blatant truth, but could I take it?

I eyed myself menacingly. 'OK, try this one for size, wobble-jaw. Nick Penhalligan is madly in love with the extraordinarily beautiful actress Serena Montgomery, who, unfortunately, is too busy attending to her glittering career to be with him for much of the time, so out of sheer frustration, and on the spur of a mad and lecherous moment, he bonks his secretary, Polly McLaren, of whom he is reasonably fond.'

I gulped hard. It certainly rang true. My reflection nodded back dumbly. Yes, that seemed to be much more like it. In which case, where did that leave me now? I felt panic rising within me. What was I doing upstairs? Tidying the airing cupboard? Dusting the bedrooms? Just making myself useful? What did concubines do, I wondered?

I buried my face in my hands, but only for a second. Then I shook myself. No, there was no doubt about it, she had to be faced, but this time − I flew out of Nick's room and ran down the passageway to mine − with war paint on and guns blazing.

Feverishly, I slapped on a protective coating of blusher, eyeliner, mascara and lipstick, then, suitably masked, I marched downstairs, summoning up as much of the old Dunkirk spirit as I could possibly muster. OK, I was going down, of that there was no doubt, but I wasn't going down without a fight.

However, all ideas of fighting Serena on the beaches disappeared in a little puff of smoke as I walked into the drawing room. My guns gave a brief splutter, a windy little fart, and died. She was sitting, or should I say, reclining, on the sofa, armed up to the eyeballs with beauty, poise and, what's more, a glass of white wine and a cigarette. Here she had me at an immediate disadvantage − what I wouldn't do for a cigarette, I thought, eyeing her pack enviously − but it was her staggering beauty that had me disadvantaged in a much more serious manner. We're talking crippled, actually.

How could her eyes be as green and sparkling as that? And did those cheekbones seriously shoot off into her temples in such a breathtaking manner? And was her complexion really so clear and peachy? What the devil was Nick up to, playing around with a flaky old yobbo like me when he had this devastating creature in tow? Was he insane? Or blind? Or perhaps her beauty intimidated him? It certainly intimidated the hell out of me.

As I came in, she ran a hand through her ash-blonde hair and stood up; not, you understand, out of any sense of politeness, but purely to give me the benefit of her devastating figure. The long, long legs seemed to take an eternity to unfurl and straighten and, as they sauntered towards me, clad in brown suede and topped with a cream silk shirt, I realised that, whereas I in my pancake make-up and tight jeans looked just wrong, she, on the other hand, looked just right. Not too glamorous for the country, but stunning enough to put anyone else to shame. In fact, come to think of it, she reminded me of a beautiful young filly: long-limbed, beautifully groomed, and gleaming to perfection, even down to her shiny little feet, shod as they were in expensive Italian leather and gleaming like newly oiled hooves.

There was simply no competition. I know when I'm beaten. This was Nick's girlfriend all right, she had it written all over her.

I shuffled towards her, forcing a smile and feeling like somebody's mother. 'Hi,' was all I could manage.

'Well, hello,' she said, raising her eyebrows as she extended an icy white hand complete with immaculate red nails.

I took it gingerly, then dropped it hurriedly as Nick appeared in the doorway with a tray full of coffee. I wasn't standing next to her for comparison, no siree. I shuffled off to my basket in the corner and curled up on a cushion. I knew my place, and it was low, very low. Definitely floor level.

Serena evidently knew her place, too, and it seemed to be reclining on the arm of the sofa, head back, legs crossed, arm flung out along the back of the sofa with all her assets to the fore. If truth be told it was an old trick of mine, but one she did with a lot more style.

Nick set the coffee down and had the grace to look sheepish. He turned to Serena. 'You remember Polly, don't you?'

'Of course I do.' She swivelled the green headlamps in my direction and smiled benignly. 'Goodness only knows where you'll turn up next, though! One minute you're behind a typewriter, then you're floundering around in a freezer, and now you're lolling around down here! I mean, really, whatever next?' She gave her silly, tinkly little laugh.

'Yes, that's me,' I muttered darkly. 'Ubiquitous.'

She frowned. 'What did you call me?'

'When?'

'Just then, you said you — something-or-other, what was it?' she sounded angry.

'Ubiquitous. It's a noun, not an insult.'

'Oh.' She frowned again and I saw Nick suppress a smile.

Actually, an insult was what I really would have liked to have hurled at her, along with some incredibly heavy pieces of furniture, like that mahogany chest over there, or those thumping great fire irons in the grate. I didn't like her sneering manner, nor did I like the freezer reference or the secretary tag. I flexed my not so much bitten as tapered nails, feeling well out of practice, and looked searchingly at her as if her face temporarily escaped me.

' . . . and it's um, Selina, isn't it?'

She looked taken aback for a moment, then her eyes narrowed and the lips tightened. 'Serena,' she hissed. 'Serena Montgomery!'

'Ah yes, of course, sorry.'

I smiled sweetly and wondered what my next mode of attack should be, but my heart wasn't in it and I felt weary already. Cat fights weren't really my scene; I didn't have the nails for it. Anyway, let's face it, why shouldn't she be angry, if not livid? She was, after all, the incumbent girlfriend — although let's not mention that: she might think I was suggesting she had bandy legs — and here was I, a usurper, lolling around, as she so eloquently put it, her boyfriend's house. Sorry, seat. Well, yes, that too.

'So how long will you be with us for, Polly?' she inquired, neatly ramming home the fact that she and Nick were very much an 'us', a couple, and since three was surely a crowd, should I not perhaps be thinking about boarding the very next train back to London?

'Oh, I don't know really, not very long. Haven't really thought,' I muttered miserably, thinking — just as soon as I've stolen your cigarettes.

'Sweet of Nick to ask you down; he said you needed a break. I do hope you're feeling better?'

I glanced at Nick, but he had his back to me as he poured the coffee. So that's what he'd said by way of explanation. The benevolent employer was treating one of his menials from the workhouse to a holiday. Some poor deserving wretch, who did nothing but bash away at a word processor all day until her hands were red and raw, and who had eventually fallen on her screen in a state of nervous exhaustion, had been magnanimously rescued by her big-hearted boss, who'd whisked her away to breathe some clean, country air at his stately home. Services to shorthand no doubt. I glanced beseechingly at the back of Nick's head. Couldn't he just turn around for a second? Give me a little look to say, Don't worry, Polly, everything's going to be OK? Apparently not.

'Yes,' I sighed. 'Very good of him.'

At that moment there was a tap on the window. One of Nick's farm hands was standing outside. Nick went over and opened it.

'Sorry to disturb you, Nick,' he said, sticking his head through, 'but there's a ewe out here I'd like you to have a look at. She's cut herself quite badly on some wire. It's a pretty nasty wound, we might need the vet.'

404

'Damn.' Nick set his coffee down. 'There's too much of that bloody wire around; I thought I'd asked you to clear it all. All right, Larry, I'm coming.' He took a cigarette from Serena's pack and swept out through the french doors.

I watched him go. He strode purposefully through the garden, smartly vaulted the fence, and marched off towards his sheep in the far field. Well, thanks a bunch, I thought bitterly. When the going gets tough, the tough go shepherding. It briefly crossed my mind to follow suit and head for the wide open spaces myself, leaving Serena to bitch away to the fireplace on her own, but as usual my nerve failed and I stayed rooted to the floorboards, looking up at her expectantly like a subservient first former waiting to see if the head girl would be handing out detention today.

'You're bound to feel better soon,' she tinkled on. 'This place is such a marvellous tonic. I always come down when I'm feeling a bit – you know, rough.'

What was I supposed to be, a drug addict going through cold turkey? A drying-out alcoholic? What sort of garbage had Nick been feeding her?

'Actually, I'm perfectly all right,' I said in a level voice, adding, with an uncharacteristic show of spirit, 'in fact, there's nothing wrong with me at all, never has been. Nick just invited me down for a holiday.'

She ignored me and carried on as if I hadn't spoken. 'The sea air will do wonders for your complexion, of course. You must get Nick to take you sailing: he has a darling little boat, and Frenchman's Creek is absolutely magical at this time of year.'

All my complexion needed was a day or two off the juice and eight or nine hours uninterrupted sleep, thank you very much, and anyway, on closer inspection I decided that a great deal of hers was out of a bottle. I also realised that she wasn't quite as young as I'd originally supposed; she definitely had three or four years on me. I revised my previous description from filly to mare and felt about a millimetre better.

I wondered if I could slip away now, run upstairs to my bedroom and hide under the duvet, or slink off to the stables for a chat with Sarah, but as I tentatively tried to raise myself up from the floor, Serena fixed me with her beady eye and warbled off in her stagey voice again. I fell, winded, pinned, and gasping beneath the weight of her mighty RADA monologue.

' . . . Yes, I come down here whenever I can, I simply love it, it makes me feel human again. People just don't realise how bloody hard acting is, they really don't. The hours are simply appalling for a start, up at dawn for make-up, and then shooting all day, usually in the blistering heat of some sub-tropical jungle or desert. I mean, people think it's glamorous, but it really isn't. They see us scampering around in foreign locations and think, Wow! What a fantastic life; but what they don't realise is that I'm sweltering away under the weight of some ghastly seventeenth-century costume and positively dripping under my make-up and those hellish lights. And the people! Ugh, I can't tell you. Sometimes I'm convinced I'm doomed to be surrounded by morons, you know.' (Here she gave me a searching look and I wondered if perhaps I'd just become chief moron, a walk-on part only, of course; chief, spear-carrying moron.) ' . . . If it's not some idiot of a director telling me how to read my lines, it's some goon of a lighting cameraman – usually foreign because our ridiculous union rules dictate that we have to employ a certain amount of natives – telling me where he wants me to stand, as if I don't know by now. Some of them don't even speak English, you know! I can't tell you how frustrating that is. It happened to me in Delhi just the other day. Some cretin of a native tried to tell me my job, and he couldn't even speak the lingo! I mean, really. They say travel broadens the mind, but as far as I'm concerned it just reinforces prejudices, d'you know what I mean?'

I'd been staring fixedly at a matchstick that was wedged between a gap in the floorboards. I pushed it down with my fingernail and it slipped through, down to the bowels of the earth. I longed to slip down with it, but I managed to raise my aching eyes and murmur, 'Oh, yes, quite, absolutely.'

'No no, give me good old England any day,' she warbled on gaily. 'You know, sometimes I literally have to just close my eyes and – as the expression goes – think of England. I do, really I do. I'll be playing some ghastly love scene with some revolting ham actor with bad breath, and I try to imagine I'm back here on the farm with Nick. I imagine I'm helping with the baby lambs, or – or that we're drifting up the river together, lying back in the boat in the sunshine, my hand skimming along in the water as we row quietly up and down. It's my way of preserving my sanity, do you see?'

I nodded. I was wilting steadily and I had a nasty sicky feeling in my stomach. I had a shrewd idea she was playing a very clever game.

'I picture we're gently floating up Frenchman's Creek. I see the glistening water, the overhanging willow trees, I hear the sound of the seagulls circling overhead—'

'Yes, I've been actually.' I said, with a sudden flash of bravado.

'Oh, really?'

'With – with Tim and Sarah,' I added, coward that I am.

'Ah yes, you'll know all about it then. It is utterly divine, isn't it?'

'Oh yes, utterly,' I mumbled, this RADA lark was catching, but I couldn't help wondering where the eulogy on Frenchman's Creek was getting us. She didn't keep me in suspense for long, bless her.

'I simply adore it, it's quite my most special place.' She

put her head on one side and gave me what I can only describe as a Dame Edna smile. 'Of course, you know why, don't you?'

'Er, no.' I felt like a rat in a trap.

The eyebrows shot up. 'You mean, he didn't tell you?'

'Tell me what?'

'That that's where he proposed to me, of course! In Frenchman's Creek!'

I gasped audibly. 'Proposed!'

'Yes, didn't you know?' There was a nasty glint in her eye and she glowed with triumph. 'In his dear little boat. Down on one knee he went. God, I remember it so clearly, we were wobbling around all over the place, in fact we nearly capsized – I promise you it was priceless!'

Her tinkly laugh homed in on my nerve centre and it seemed to me that I was being slowly but surely electrocuted.

'He was so sweet, I'll never forget how he asked me. He didn't say, "Will you marry me", or anything boring like that, he said, "Serena, would you do me the honour of becoming my wife?" – isn't that just too divine? Of course I spoiled the dignity of the whole occasion by leaping up and crying, "Yes! Yes! Yes!" I was so excited! Then I just fell on him, simply covering him with kisses, and then of course the whole thing got totally out of hand and we ended up in a tangled heap at the bottom of the boat, giggling hysterically as the boat rocked perilously from side to side – I tell you, we were lucky not to go in!'

I wondered if I could just quietly be sick in that potted begonia without her noticing – or perhaps, yes, perhaps the coal bucket by the fire would stand up to my projections a little better. There might be rather a lot of it. I nodded, biting back the bile.

'Anyway, when we'd, you know, straightened ourselves out a bit – because actually the river isn't *all* that private and you never know *who's* going to cruise up beside you;

there are all kinds of nosy parkers around — anyway, that's when he produced the most darling little ring from his pocket — look!'

She thrust her hand under my nose and wiggled her finger around. A very pretty antique gold ring with a jade stone winked up at me.

I gulped. 'V-very pretty.'

'Of course, it's only a makeshift ring, until I find something more suitable — you know, diamonds or sapphires maybe, but I think I'll always wear it anyway. It's charming, isn't it?'

'It certainly is,' I managed.

'He said he bought it because it matched my eyes.'

'Yes, yes it does,' I whispered, clutching a handy Queen Anne chair leg for support.

'Lord knows when we'll find time to get married, though. We're both just so busy. I've got this new film coming up, and Nick's got to tie up the agency — you know he's selling out, don't you?'

'Yes, yes I know.' This at least was one piece of news that didn't come as a total shock.

'So anyway, it could be a while, but at least we've made the commitment. I think that's so important, don't you? So many people these days don't make that commitment, and I think it's a mistake, I really do.'

I mumbled a suitable response. I'd collapsed in a little heap now, and the more I paled and wilted, the more Serena seemed to exult and billow and triumph.

She lit yet another precious cigarette, put her gleaming blonde head on one side, and smiled that caring little smile again. 'I do hope you won't take this the wrong way, Polly?'

I gulped. All sorts of things seemed to be going down the wrong way, one more surely wouldn't make much difference.

'Fire away,' I said bravely, and didn't she just.

'It's just that, well, I met Jack Crawley on the way over here, and he said you'd been making a bit of a fool of yourself, one way and another.'

I gasped. 'What d'you mean?'

Serena held up her hand to stop me. 'Now, there's no need to explain, really. I can quite understand how it happened. I know that Nick is a very attractive man, and I don't blame you for falling for him, but the point is that – well, he's finding it all just a teensy bit embarrassing.'

'That's not true!' I could feel myself going scarlet.

'Oh, I can assure you it is,' she said in a steely voice. 'Why d'you think he rushed off to deal with his sheep like that? Larry was quite capable of sorting out that little problem, but Nick was just glad of an excuse to get away. He's fearfully embarrassed about the whole thing. You really do moon around after him, you know.'

'I do not moon around!' I flushed angrily.

'Oh, but you do, everyone's noticed it. Why, Jack told me you follow Nick around like a little dog. Honestly, Polly, I'm only telling you this so you don't make a complete idiot of yourself. It was wrong of Nick not to tell you we're engaged, but perhaps he thought you wouldn't be able to take it.'

I stared down at my shoes, wishing I was a million miles away. I wanted to tell her where we'd been when she'd arrived, what we'd been doing, but I hadn't the nerve.

I licked my lips. 'Has Nick said anything?'

'I'm afraid he has. Of course he blames himself, he knows he should never have been so weak, but I am away an awful lot and it's terribly difficult for a man when a girl – well, when she throws herself at him, d'you know what I mean? Especially when he's been – well, doing without it for a while. One can understand how he might just – you know, go for it.'

I caught my breath. The bastard, how could he? I didn't trust myself to speak, and carried on staring at the fascinating top stitching on my shoes.

'Now, Polly, don't look so glum. You know as well as I do that boys will be boys. The poor dears find it so frightfully difficult to control themselves, and when the cat's away — ' she shrugged — 'well, look what happens. Now, I'm not suggesting he's totally blameless, but I think you'll admit that most men would find it pretty hard to resist when it's handed to them on a plate like that.'

Please, could I just die quietly now? Don't let me live any longer God, please! Had he really told her? Or was she just guessing wildly? I daren't look up. There was a long pause. My face was flaming as it faced the carpet. Any minute now it would surely just melt and drip steadily through that rug into the floorboards.

'Anyway,' she said at length, ' I don't want to make a big thing of it, I just want you to know that I'm not a fool and I know what you're up to, OK?'

My eyes remained glued to my shoes.

'And I don't want to be brutal, but you must realise that hanging around here is doing you no good at all. You're just making everyone feel uncomfortable: Nick, me, all of us. You do see that, don't you?'

I nodded miserably.

'The trains to London are pretty frequent, you know. I could give you a lift to the station if you just wanted to slip off quietly? There's no rush, of course.'

I met her eye with difficulty. 'Don't worry. I won't be hanging around making things uncomfortable for you. I'll be off just as soon as I've packed — and I'd rather walk to the station, thank you very much.'

She smirked, 'You'll find it's rather a long way, I'm afraid, but as you wish.'

She ground her cigarette out in an ashtray, and brushed her hands together lightly as if that little piece of business had been successfully concluded. Having made mincemeat of me, she turned her attention to the house. She got up and glided round the room, pausing here and there to wipe dust from a picture frame or rearrange a piece of china. Her eye swept around proprietorially.

'I really must do something about this room. Honestly, when I'm not here the place just goes to rack and ruin. These ghastly covers are finally falling to bits: a blessing in disguise, I think; perhaps Nick will finally get some new ones.' She fingered the lovely faded old chintz on the sofa. 'And as for these dirty old rugs, they've been here for ever.'

I was tempted to suggest that this was entirely their charm, but decided against it as she kicked the beautiful Persian rug with her expensive Italian boot. I didn't want to be on the receiving end of that toe-cap. No doubt in her mind's eye she already had the whole place carpeted wall to-wall in off-white shag-pile.

She strolled towards me and I shrank back in terror, wondering what adjustments she had in mind − a biff on the nose perhaps, or a nice black eye − but no, she was making for the begonia. She fingered the soil in the pot and I fervently wished that I'd stuck to plan A and thrown up in it. She shook her head, tutting loudly.

'You see, no one even bothers to water the plants. If I'm not here to do it, they just keel over and die. I must talk to Nick about getting someone to help out here: a daily or, even better, someone to live in. This place needs a good seeing-to. If we're going to live here when we're married, I won't be able to see to it all on my own; I'm simply not used to that sort of thing. I must have some staff.'

She looked down at me, curled up as I was in a pathetic, squirming little bundle at her feet. She put her head on one side and eyed me speculatively. Good grief, was she sizing me up as a potential cleaner? Was she wondering if I wouldn't in fact do nicely? Why not? I was already on the pay roll, I could just change my position. From secretary to char in one swift little demotion. I had a sudden, powerful urge to grab her elegant little ankles, rugby tackle her to the floor and kick her smartly in the teeth. Unfortunately I controlled it and, instead, in a totally shameless manner, blurted out my most overpowering need.

'D'you think I could possibly have one of your cigarettes?' It couldn't be helped. Unless I got some nicotine into these gasping lungs, they'd seize up.

She was all concern and benevolence. 'Of course!' she purred, pressing the packet into my hand like Maundy money. 'Take the packet. Goodness, your hand's shaking, you poor thing.'

'I don't want the packet,' I said petulantly. 'I've got some somewhere, I just can't remember where I've put them, that's all.'

'Of course you can't,' she said consolingly, 'you must be in a terrible muddle at the moment. I bet you don't know if you're coming or going!'

'Oh, I've got a pretty shrewd idea I'm going,' I muttered darkly, 'but don't worry about me. I'm fine,' I said, grabbing a box of matches and lighting the cigarette. It wasn't easy, as the match wobbled alarmingly in my hand. I sucked the nectar down to my boots.

'Really? Are you sure you're all right?' She glided over and sat down next to me in the Queen Anne, crossing her elegant ankles. 'Only, I hope you don't mind me mentioning it, but I hear Nick's not the only man you've fallen for recently. You've got rather a tangled love life at the moment, haven't you? Mmmm?'

'What d'you mean!' What on earth did she have up her sleeve now? A jack-knife? An anaconda? An Exocet missile? I kept a tight hold on my cigarette in case I needed to jab her in the eye with it.

'Well, I hear your last boyfriend gave you a rather rough ride. It was Harry Lloyd-Roberts, wasn't it?'

413

My jaw dropped. 'How on earth did you know about that?'

'Oh, everyone in London knows Harry, he's part of the scene. In fact I even had a bit of a dalliance with him myself once, but he bored me after a while. He was frightfully upset when I dropped him, kept turning up at the studios uninvited making a fool of himself; then he used to sit outside my flat in his car for days on end, just waiting for me to come out. He's dreamy looking, of course, but there's absolutely nothing at all between the ears. No substance whatsoever. You're much better off without him, you know.'

Was there no end to her charm? Would she just go on and on like this until someone put a bullet through her brain? Please could it be me? I'd heard about girls like this, read about them in the problem pages of women's magazines, real live bitches who took pleasure in pouring salt in wounds. Well, now I'd met one. Only this time, I thought with a small degree of satisfaction, she was wasting her time. She wasn't hurting me at all. I couldn't give a damn if she and Harry had bonked for Britain. The very thought was registering absolutely zero on my Richter scale of pain. Not a pang, not a twinge, not a sausage. Sorry Serena.

I felt just a weeny bit stronger, but not enough to stand up, so when the telephone rang it was Serena who strolled off to answer it. Well anyway, it was her phone, wasn't it? I lay down on the floor and gasped, glad of the chance to catch my breath. When she came back she looked rather annoyed.

'It's Tim. He wants to speak to you or Nick.'

'I'll take it,' I said, sprinting past her, desperate to talk to a normal human being. I grabbed the telephone.

'Tim?'

'Hi, Polly, how are you?'

'Oh er, OK. You?'

'Yes, I suppose so.'

'What's wrong? You sound a bit down.'

'So do you, come to that.'

'Well . . . I s'pose I am a bit.' Riveting stuff, eh?

'Listen . . .' he said, coming slowly to the point. 'Rachel and I thought we might come back, if the coast's clear, that is.'

'Oh yes, well clear. We saw Adam last night – ' was it only last night? It felt about a year ago – 'and he swallowed the whole story. We did it rather well, actually. Nick checked with Mrs Green yesterday, and apparently he shot off back to London pretty sharpish.'

'Oh good, we'll come back then.' He sounded relieved. Was there a problem? Had Svengali and his pupil fallen out already? It wouldn't be hard, I admit, her sulky moods would try the patience of a saint; but Tim really was a bit of a saint on the quiet, and he'd been so keen to bring her out. Perhaps he'd just discovered there was nothing worth exposing.

'See you later then.'

'Yeh, see you, bye.'

I took the scenic route back to the drawing room, pausing en route to spend a couple of hours lying down on my bed. I was too upset to cry. Despair overwhelmed me. I just lay there looking at the ceiling, listening to my clock ticking. He was engaged to her. Engaged to be married, and I'd had no idea. I'd done it again, picked another bastard, and once more it was too late to do anything about it, I was head over heels in love with him. Oh God, what was I going to do? Go home pretty damn quick, that was for sure, either to London or to my parents, as long as it was far away. As soon as I'd got my strength up. I shut my eyes. To think I'd been presumptuous enough to imagine anyone in Nick's class could fall for someone as gauche and stupid as me when he had Serena – first-class bitch, granted, but beautiful and famous nonetheless –

hanging on to his arm. How could I have been so ludicrous?

Chapter Twenty-three

I lay like that for an hour or more. Not crying, just staring into space, looking at the cracks in the ceiling. I could feel myself shaking a bit, so I pulled the duvet over me and hugged the pillow for comfort, burying my face in it. In actual fact I felt rather numb. I couldn't quite believe it was all true. I shut my eyes to block out the misery, and I suppose I must have dropped off, God knows I was tired enough, because the next thing I knew, I was opening my eyes and someone was knocking loudly on the door.

I reached out my hand and grabbed the clock by the bed. Ten past three. I must have been up here for ages. Who was at the door? Was it Nick? Had he come to find me? I sat up eagerly.

'Come in!'

Tim's head appeared around the door, followed by his body.

'Oh hi, Tim, you're back.' I tried not to sound disappointed.

'Yep, just arrived. I came to tell you lunch is ready. It's gone three o'clock, but no one seems to have eaten, so Sarah's rustled up a fish pie.'

'Thanks, I'll come down.'

Damn, I couldn't escape now. I'd have to put in an appearance at what would undoubtedly be one of the most grisly meals of my life. Tim turned to go, but lingered at the door, fiddling with the handle. He didn't look quite right somehow, his normally jolly, open face was pinched and haggard. He turned back. We both spoke at once.

'Are you all right?' we said in unison.

He laughed and I mustered a smile. He came over and sat on the side of the bed. I sat up and hugged my knees.

'What's wrong?' he said, peering into my face. 'You look absolutely terrible.'

Men never seem to learn that, even if we girls feel like death, we don't like to be told we look like it.

I grimaced. 'Oh, nothing.'

'Come on, what is it?'

Could I tell him? Right now I needed a friend extremely badly, but Nick's brother? And for all I knew he might be Serena's number one fan.

'I've just got a horrendous hangover, that's all. Totally self-inflicted. How about you?'

'Oh, er – well, yes the same.' He looked shifty.

'Really? But you don't even drink, not properly, anyway.'

'Well, perhaps that's why I got so plastered, not used to it, you see.' He avoided my eyes and studied the wallpaper. Being such an accomplished liar myself, I can spot a porky pie a mile off. I reached out and put a hand on his arm.

'Tim? What is it? Is it Rachel?'

His face puckered up when I said her name, and I knew I'd hit the spot. They'd obviously fallen out in a big way.

'Have you had a row? Is that it?'

'Oh no,' he shook his head, 'nothing like that. Quite the . . . quite the reverse, really.'

The reverse? Quite the reverse of having a row? Well, what the devil was that then? They'd got on too well? Impossible. They'd got on so well that something untoward had happened? They'd got on so well that they'd ended up . . .

'Oh my goodness, Tim!'

Tim's shoulders sagged. He ran his hands through his

hair and put his head in his hands. A guilty man if ever I saw one. I was staggered.

'Tim, you mean?'

Tim nodded into his hands, still avoiding my eye.

'Oh my God. You and Rachel? I just don't believe it!'

'Neither do I, now,' he whispered. 'I really can't believe it happened. But I promise you, Polly, at the time I felt absolutely powerless. I simply couldn't resist her. She was so . . .' he shook his head as he struggled to find the words, as well he might. 'Well, she was just so – so captivating, so, I don't know – irresistible, I suppose. And it all happened so quickly. One minute we were sitting downstairs chatting, and the next minute – the next minute we were in my bedroom. It was extraordinary, I just – I just couldn't help myself.'

Rachel? Captivating? Irresistible? Hang on a moment, did we have the same girl in mind here? Frumpy old, miserable old, bag lady Rachel? I struggled to get my mind around this one. Was he trying to tell me that that grumpy little heap of mouse droppings had, in the space of just one night, lured him away from his lovely, sparky, pretty girlfriend and succeeded in bewitching him to such an extent that he'd – had he?

'Did you?'

'What?'

'You know . . .'

He ran his hands through his hair and nodded. 'Yes, of course.' He'd ended up compromising himself wildly. Well, blow me, you had to hand it to her, didn't you? And here he was now, this handsome hunk of a man, reduced to a shivering pulp, eaten up with what I fervently hoped was remorse and not more desire.

'Do you regret it now?'

He wrenched his head out of his hands and groaned. 'Of course I bloody do, it was a stupid, irresponsible, idiotic thing to do, but I promise you, Polly, I just didn't stand a

419

chance! I was putty in her hands, you can't imagine how — well, how downright sexy she was!'

I tried. I tried really hard, but no, he was right, I just couldn't imagine. It made you think though, didn't it? I mean, all these years I'd been dousing myself in Chanel, pulling my necklines down, hitching my skirts up, endlessly crossing and uncrossing my legs, throwing back my hair, pulling it over one eye, practising smouldering looks in the mirror, cultivating a sexy voice, and do you know what I should really have been doing? I should have been taking piano lessons, twiddling my hair round my finger, sitting in a heap in a nasty grey cardigan and occasionally, for extra sensuality, donning a pair of tortoiseshell National Health spectacles. And there was I thinking that those spectacles were just another form of birth control, along with acne and bad breath. Ah well, we live and learn.

I was woken from this mind-boggling reverie by Tim, who was up to his elbows in confession. Once he'd started, he was determined to finish, as Magnus would say. He was over by the window, staring out at the fields, frantically unburdening himself to the sheep, the cows, the trees — anyone and anything that would listen.

'And yes, OK, I suppose I'd had a couple of glasses of wine, three maybe, which is more than I'd normally have, but that's no excuse, I certainly wasn't pissed. It just seemed so right, so natural. There we were, having supper in Penny's candlelit dining room which, as you can imagine, is pretty conducive to a little dinner à deux . . .'

Now this I could imagine. Penny's dining room would be magical in the evening, with its dark green walls smothered with oil paintings, and its cosy little alcove tables laden with silver; little hideaway places where two people could sit in relative privacy, their faces flickering in the candlelight, a cosy log fire crackling away in the grate beside them . . . Yes, I could imagine it would make quite a seduction scene. In fact, I made a mental note to reserve a table the next time an eligible young man wanted to take me out to a little country — oh well, forget that. There was never going to be a next time. It was the nunnery for me.

'Are you listening to me, Polly, because I can tell you this isn't the easiest story to tell.'

'Sorry, go on.'

'Over dinner, she started to tell me a bit about herself. I was really pleased, because you know how shy and withdrawn she can be, don't you?'

I ground my teeth together, dug my nails hard into the palm of my hand and nodded.

'She told me all about her mother dying when she was young, and how she grew up with just a father and a housekeeper, not even any brothers and sisters, and d'you know she wasn't even allowed to go out or have friends round?' Tim shook his head. 'Terrible. Then, of course, this Adam chap appeared on the scene. Just what she didn't need; I mean, he just sounds like a complete head-case. As far as I can gather the man's completely barking. He was incredibly possessive, followed her around the whole time, wouldn't let her make her own friends — rather like her father actually. You know, one way and another, she's had a really hard time, Polly.'

'I know, I know, just get to the point,' I said quickly. 'Then what happened?'

I wanted to move this monologue on apace, I really didn't think I could stomach any more of Rachel's hard times on top of my own heartache and hangover.

'Well, we chatted on and on for ages. It's a long time since I've had a good chinwag, I'm always so bloody busy. She seemed really interested in me, asked lots of questions, and I told her all about Dad dying, something I realised I hadn't talked about for years. She was really sweet and sympathetic; well, she'd lost her mother, of course, so she knew how I felt. Then I told her all about the farm, and how I was determined to make it work, even though everyone assures me that organic farming is an economic disaster area, and she didn't say that. She was really supportive and encouraging.'

Well, she would be, wouldn't she? And come to that, wasn't Sarah too, who slogged away on his farm at the weekends after a gruelling week at the stables? Or was it only candlelit support that mattered? I bit my tongue.

Tim sighed. 'Well I suppose after a while we'd exhausted nearly every channel of conversation, and we just ended up looking at each other. You know how it is, Polly.'

I nodded, a woman of the world of wine bars. 'You exchanged a few meaningful looks?'

He sighed, 'Yes.'

'She looked down shyly, then up into your eyes again?'

'Well, yes.'

'She put her hand on the table?'

'Er, yes.'

'You covered it with yours?'

He looked surprised. 'Yes.'

'Your eyes met again, and this time you both held the gaze for a fraction longer than was absolutely necessary?'

'How on earth did you know that?'

I sighed. God he was naîve. 'Let's just say I recognise the signs. Then you paid the bill in silence while Rachel sat gazing at you, elbows on the table, her face cupped in her hands. You both got up slowly from the table, she took your hand, you walked out of the restaurant and, without another word, went upstairs?'

Tim looked miserable. 'I had no idea it was all so predictable.'

'Only thus far. It's the next bit that intrigues me. I mean, it could all have ended with a reasonably chaste, albeit lingering kiss on the lips at her bedroom door, after which she smiles sweetly, thanks you for a lovely evening, and slips into her room and then into her winceyette. On the other hand . . .'

'Er, yes, on the other hand?'

'You tell me, Tim.'

'Must I? You do it so well.' He sighed. 'OK, we did go upstairs, and we did, you know, pause at her bedroom door because – well – I wanted to give her the opportunity to get rid of me if she wanted to. I even said goodnight.'

I nodded.

'And she didn't. Get rid of me I mean. She just strode on past, still holding my hand, until we got to my door. Then she took the key out of my trouser pocket – which was a hell of a turn on in itself, I can tell you – opened the door, and, well, naturally, in we went.'

I raised my eyebrows. 'Naturally.'

'Oh no, Polly, she wasn't pushy at all, it was so obviously going to happen anyway.'

'Maybe, but notice how it's Rachel who takes not only the initiative, but your hand, and the key to the door.'

My goodness she was a smart cookie. She'd had her eye on him right from the word go, and nobody, certainly not Tim, had even suspected it. She'd had him for breakfast.

'How d'you feel about her now?' I asked.

He shrugged. 'Oh, I'm fond of her, of course,' I flinched at that word, 'but if truth be told it was just a one-night stand really, probably from her point of view, too. Don't get me wrong, it was great at the time; yes, it was really – ' his eyes glazed over – 'great.'

I coughed.

'Oh, er, sorry, what I mean is, it was fun, but it didn't really mean anything, not in the heart department anyway. For goodness' sake, let's be grown-up about this, these things happen, don't they? Well, you'd know all about that, wouldn't you, Polly?'

'Thanks,' I said grimly

'Oh God, I didn't mean it like that, what I meant was, you're not stupid. You know as well as I do that it's easy to get carried away, or rather, you know how easy it is for men to get carried away.'

Don't I just? I tried to banish his equally errant brother from my mind and listen to what he was saying.

'The problem is, I feel so wretched about Sarah. I wouldn't dream of hurting her, and there's no way anyone could ever take her place.'

'Well, that's a relief. Look Tim, the best thing you can do now is just forget it ever happened. Don't, for God's sake, decide to purge yourself and run off confessing to Sarah. Believe me, she may not be quite so reasonable about it.'

Tim scratched his head. 'The only problem is, Sarah might find out.'

'Why?'

'Because Penny came into my room the next morning with a cup of tea. '

'Oh no! What did she do?'

'Well, she looked pretty shocked and left, of course, but she slammed the door behind her. She and Sarah are very close.'

'How did Rachel react?'

'Pretty calmly. I leaped out of bed in a complete panic and started throwing my clothes into a bag, but she just sort of lay there smiling to herself.'

I bet she did.

'Well, then I rang you to say we were coming back. I couldn't bear to stay there a moment longer. I didn't see Penny again, not that I actively tried to find her. She was probably avoiding me, too. Polly, d'you think she'll tell Sarah?'

I sighed. 'Hard to say really, Tim. Female loyalty's a funny thing. Whereas boys probably wouldn't dream of spilling the beans, we girls tend to think it wouldn't be fair to let a friend go on believing that her man is whiter than white. Stupid really. On the other hand . . .' I hesitated. Lottie had told me about Harry's indiscretion, and in the long run I was glad she had, but then Harry was a louse. Tim, on the other hand, wasn't, and it would certainly be better if Sarah wasn't told.

'I think you should ring Penny and ask her not to say anything. Tell her you were drunk out of your mind, it was a huge mistake, and you're still absolutely bonkers about Sarah.'

Tim brightened considerably. 'D'you think that would work?'

'It might. On the other hand, it might not. She might insist you tell Sarah yourself.'

Tim banged his fist on the bedside table in fury. 'Women! Christ, you're all so bloody smug, aren't you? Do this, do that, don't do anything naughty because if you do we'll tie you up in knots before you can even apologise. It's almost like they're lying in wait for you. I mean, it was just a quick bonk, for Christ's sake, can't we leave it at that? Apparently not, no, we have to pick it all over, examine my motives, make me feel a complete and utter bastard, and where does that get us? I mean, what is the point?'

He was feeling nice and sorry for himself. A quick bonk, eh? This, from the lips of sensitive, caring, organically and politically correct Tim. Perhaps he'd thought a quick bonk would bring her out? Perhaps he'd thought he was behaving in a social, caring manner? Ah yes, that must be it.

'Well, I can't help you then, Tim,' I said quietly. 'I've told you what I think you should do. If you don't want to take my advice, you can sort it out for yourself.'

Tim blushed and looked at his shoes, instantly contrite. 'Sorry, Polly. That was infantile of me. It's all this guilt creeping out, I'm afraid.'

I looked at his shoes, too, half expecting to see the guilt seeping out all over the carpet. I wondered if Nick was leaking as well. As we watched his shoes glumly, both lost in our own private misery, Serena threw her best operatic voice upstairs.

'Lunch-is-rea-d-y!'

Neither of us moved.

Up it came again. 'Yoo-hoo, lunch-is-rea-dy!'

Tim sighed. 'We'd better go down. Thanks for listening, Polly, sorry I've been such a pig. I do feel a bit better actually.'

Terrific, I thought gloomily, as I dragged myself out from under the covers. I'm glad somebody does.

Chapter Twenty-four

It goes without saying that lunch was an unmitigated disaster. Sarah was the only one in high spirits, which in itself was unbearable. She'd heard that Tim had come back early, and had immediately dropped everything and raced over from the stables. In the space of about ten minutes, she'd thrown together a delicious lunch for us all and was obviously hoping for a jolly reunion party. She smelled outrageous, and I was longing to shower her in Dior to overcome the horsy fumes, but she couldn't have cared less. As she rushed around, helping us all to enormous platefuls of fish pie, she positively bubbled over with enthusiasm and happiness, chattering away, and not seeming to notice that no one really uttered back.

I couldn't bear to look at her, and I couldn't bear to look at Tim. Come to that, I couldn't bear to look at Rachel, and I certainly wasn't going to look at Nick. As for Serena, she was totally out of the question. That left Jamie. Luckily I was next to him. This was generally regarded as a bad seat, but today I was thankful. I gave him my undivided attention and concentrated on catering to his every whim; picking up his spoon whenever he dropped it; smiling gamely when he poked his sticky little fingers in my eyes, and indulging in fascinating lunch party repartee which involved lots of enthusiastic nods and smiles on my part and lots of shrieking and food-spitting on his.

Only Serena and Sarah were capable of eating the fish pie; the rest of us pushed it round our plates in a desultory manner. I toyed limply with a prawn, and Rachel stared dreamily into space. Occasionally she would flash a knowing look at Tim, who would flush guiltily and look away before shredding his napkin, apparently unaware that it was cotton and not paper.

Nick glowered into his wine glass, as if the answer to all his problems were somehow floating in a sea of Frascati.

Only Serena seemed equal to the situation. She sat at the head of the table and presided over lunch like the officious table monitor she had once so obviously been. She suffocated any attempts anyone else might have had at conversation by regurgitating a ceaseless flow of drivel about her latest film. It appeared to have a cast of thousands, and all concerned had their names dropped at regular intervals.

' . . . and as I said to Anthony when we were in make-up the other day—'

'Anthony who?' asked Sarah, right on cue.

'Andrews, darling,' came back the delighted reply, and then, in case anyone had failed to link up the Christian name with the surname, 'Anthony Andrews,' and then, in case anyone had been living in a cave in Outer Mongolia for the last ten years, 'he was in "Brideshead", remember?'

'Yes, yes, we know who you mean,' said Tim, 'get on with it.'

'Well, it's just that he was saying how glad he was that he still had a base in England, and I couldn't agree more. You see, it's terribly tempting just to up sticks and go and live in Hollywood. I mean, let's face it, that's where all the work is, so that's where all the money is, but is it worth it? I mean, OK, it's great fun, what with the parties and the fantastic weather and everyone paying you so much attention all the time; but really, there's more to life than that, isn't there? I mean, yes, sure, I've been tempted to stay: I remember one particular occasion when an absolutely divine director offered me the most amazing part — God I was tempted — but it was a long TV series which would have taken for ever to film, and at the end of the day I just had to turn him down. No, I said, no, Roman, I'm sorry, but I'm going home, right? England is my home and home, as they say, is where the heart is, right? Well, of course he was flabbergasted, but what could he do? I mean, after all, it's my life, isn't it? I'm the one that's got to live it, right?'

She finished this string of platitudes with a triumphant flourish of the fork, and looked around expectantly as if awaiting applause. Most people appeared to be contemplating the table-mats, but someone must have raised their aching eyes for a moment and murmured an assent, because she ploughed on.

'I mean, sure, yes, LA is very exciting — it's fast, it's glamorous — but you know what? It's artificial. No, really, it is.' She nodded sagely as if perhaps we didn't believe her. 'Whereas,' she went on, waving her fork, 'whereas here, in dear old England, everything is — well, it's so *real*, isn't it? D'you know what I mean?' She cocked her head on one side. 'Hmmm? And you know, there's so much I miss when I'm in the States. Oh, I could bang on for ever about the countryside and the history and everything, but you know what I really miss? Hmmm? People. Because when all's said and done, it's people that count, isn't it? And there are so many characters here. In LA everyone seems to be out of the same mould, they're all — well, they're plastic, right? Yes, lots of little plastic people!'

Her tinkly laugh rang around the dining room, and then her green eyes fell proprietorially on Nick, who was sitting next to her looking slightly mad about the eyes. He was maniacally smearing fish pie around his plate.

She leaned in close and ruffled his hair. 'I know what you're thinking, darling, and no, I haven't forgotten you. It goes without saying that when I'm away I miss you most of all,' she purred. She took his chin in her hand and turned his face towards her, going on in a baby voice, 'and I don't think you'd have been very happy in LA, would you Pusskins?' she murmured, rubbing a bright red nail down his cheek. 'Hmmm? Not your scene at all really, is it?'

'Hardly,' said Nick grimly, jerking his head away and resuming his contemplation of his fish-smeared plate.

She turned back to her audience. 'Let's face it,' she said, as if some of us had been having difficulty, 'it's a fantastic place, but only in small doses, right? I know it's hard to believe, but one can get terribly bored with the rather self-indulgent lifestyle.'

'I don't find it hard to believe at all. I think it sounds a perfectly dreadful place and I know I'd be terribly homesick,' said Sarah defiantly, desperately attempting to embark on some sort of discussion to rescue us all from this weighty, oppressive, cliché-ridden, minor-movie-star monologue. Alas, to no avail.

'Oh it's not *dreadful*, darling, it's great fun! But it is rather fast, and yes, if all you want to do is muck out stables, then you'd probably hate it. But I will say one thing,' she said, waving her fork around again and not entirely shutting her mouth as she masticated the fish pie. 'If you're not careful, you can end up losing your identity, d'you know what I mean?'

'Not entirely.' Sarah looked puzzled, as well she might.

'Well, you know how it is, darling, one's constantly being entertained and fêted and flattered, but some people make the great mistake of believing all that crap. You mustn't. You must stand still for a second, stand back from the whole scene and say – hey, now hang on a minute, what's going on here? Who am I – you know? I

430

mean, what's it all about? Who are all these people? Are they for real?'

Well you certainly aren't, I thought, pushing half a ton of potato around my plate. I'd never met anyone so utterly phoney in my whole life.

'Don't you agree, darling?' She nudged Nick, who'd got bored long ago and was discussing crop rotation with Tim who was on his left.

'What? Oh yes, definitely.' He turned back to his brother.

'So that's why I decided to come home,' she concluded with a triumphant smile, as if anyone had been wondering. 'I just got fed up. I woke up one morning, packed my bags, and got a taxi to the airport.' She scraped her plate clean, put down her fork, and delicately patted her perfect cherry lips with a napkin. 'And here I am.' She turned to Sarah. 'Incidentally, Sarah, that fish pie was very good, but just a teensy word of advice. I always put a bit of parsley in mine: it makes all the difference. And perhaps a little less milk in the potato, it was slightly on the mushy side, wasn't it? I know you won't mind me mentioning it, because if you're anything like me, you'll welcome constructive criticism, right?'

Not only phoney, but poisonous too, I thought, almost with relief. What on earth does he see in her?

She leaned towards Nick and rested her head on his shoulder, although actually it was more like his back, because he'd almost completely turned around to talk to Tim.

She nuzzled into him as best she could. 'You couldn't believe it when I rang to say I was getting on the next plane back, could you, darling? Darling?'

'What?' Nick broke off his conversation.

'Honey, when I'm talking to you, you might at least listen. I can't talk to your back.'

'Sorry.' He resumed his discussion with Tim.

431

Serena turned back to address the rest of her equally unwilling audience. 'Anyway, apart from anything else, I just knew I had to come back to sort this place out. It needs so much attention. The roof is full of holes, for a start, and that's going to cost a fortune. Darling, did you speak to anyone about the roof? Darling? *Nick!*'

'Sorry, what?' He sounded irritated.

'I said,' began Serena, hissing through her teeth, 'did you talk to anyone about mending the roof?'

'No, I didn't, I'll get round to that when I've got some more money, all right? Sorry Tim, what did you say?'

'Well, you know, that might just be too late; those holes aren't going to get any smaller. You really must get someone to give you an estimate. Apparently there's quite a good chap in Helston. He's just started up, so he might be glad of the work and give you a good price. And the windows are a disgrace, they're just falling off their hinges. I mean look at that one!'

She flung her arm dramatically towards the dining-room window. We all turned our heads obediently, except Nick and Tim who were drawing diagrams on the back of an envelope now, their dark heads bent together.

'I mean, that just isn't going to survive another winter, is it? It's completely rotten, and if we get any more rain, it'll just crumble. We'll have water coming in and the carpets will be ruined. Not that there's much to ruin — look at this old thing — but Nick, you must get hold of a carpenter, really you must. Nick? Nick?'

She stared at the broad back that faced her. Still the brothers conferred. There was a terrible pause.

'NICK!' Serena flung down her napkin, scraped back her chair, and stood up. Everyone looked up at her; even Nick and Tim paused from their calculations.

'WILL YOU LISTEN TO ME!' she shrieked. Her face was white and she was shaking slightly. Suddenly she picked up her empty plate, raised her arm, and sent it crashing to the ground where it broke into a thousand tiny pieces. Then, with a stifled sob, she ran from the room.

There was a startled silence. Eventually Nick sighed, got up from the table, and with a look of resignation went after her.

We all looked down at our laps. I fiddled with my napkin. Rachel sniggered nastily.

At length, Sarah spoke up hesitantly. 'Don't take her too seriously. She can be — well, rather theatrical at times, I'm afraid.'

'Artistic temperament and all that,' muttered Tim, looking embarrassed.

'And I think,' went on Sarah, 'well, I think she's rather unhappy at the moment.' She looked at me briefly, not in an accusing way, but I flushed to my dyed roots nonetheless.

'Ah well, that gives her a perfect right to behave badly, doesn't it?' said Rachel sarcastically.

There was an embarrassed silence.

'I really must get back to the stables,' said Sarah, slipping down from her chair. 'I'm late already.'

'I'll come with you,' said Tim, throwing down his napkin and following her hastily. That left Rachel and me.

'Acting, of course,' said Rachel, licking her fork. 'She's just a spoilt little brat.'

It's hard to believe, but at that moment I felt a certain amount of sympathy for Serena, mainly because I felt such loathing for Rachel. I looked at her smug, self-righteous little face and felt myself coming up to the boil.

'And who are you to talk about behaving badly, Rachel?' I asked quietly.

She looked surprised. 'What do you mean?'

'Well, who exactly is behaving badly around here, eh? Answer me that one.'

'What are you driving at, Polly?' She narrowed her eyes warily.

'Tell me, do you feel even the slightest twinge of guilt when you sit next to Sarah? I mean, you are boffing her boyfriend, aren't you? So do you feel just the slightest bit uneasy about passing the time of day with her and eating her food, or does that hypocritical stuff come naturally to you? I assume you know they're getting married? How easy is the old adultery lark, do tell?'

She narrowed her eyes even more until they were just two little grey slits. 'I don't know, Polly, you tell me. You're the expert.'

I sat back in surprise. 'What d'you mean?'

'Well, how easy do you find it to sit next to dear Serena? After all, you're "boffing" — as you so elegantly put it — her fiancé, aren't you?'

I gasped in horror.

Rachel smiled. 'Spot on. Well, that was a shrewd guess, wasn't it?'

I gulped.

'Oh, don't look so surprised, it's quite obvious to anyone with half a brain cell. You haven't been able to take your eyes off him all lunchtime and he looks absolutely racked with guilt and remorse. So tell me, how do *you* sleep at night? When you're not with him, I mean?'

I bit my lip and looked away.

'Nothing to say, Polly?' she said quietly. 'Try taking the plank out of your own eye before you start complaining about the splinters in other people's.'

I took a large slug of wine and lit a cigarette with a shaking hand. Of course, to anyone but the educationally subnormal, the similarities between Rachel and myself would have been obvious long ago. But recognising the obvious, especially the painfully obvious, has never been my forte, and when my brain is addled up with wine, lack of sleep and heartache, it's even more difficult. However, Rachel's acute observation pierced through the fog and left me reeling.

I licked my lips and tried to think of something to say. But what was there to say? She was right. I was no better than her, no better than Caro, and no better than any other cheap little slimeball who went around stealing other people's men. Serena and Nick were engaged to be married. I listened to her sobs coming from the kitchen and, not for the first time that day, felt sick. But this time with myself. Why shouldn't she rush down here to warn me off, waving her little green ring under my nose? Why shouldn't she point out the structural changes which were to occur under the forthcoming Mrs Serena Penhalligan regime? Of course she wanted to know when I was going: she wanted my claws out of Nick and back in London as soon as possible.

And what, after all, did I mean to Nick? Much the same as Rachel meant to his brother? A one-night stand? It was becoming more and more apparent that our one and only morning of passion had been a rather amusing indiscretion − perhaps even a charitable act − on his part.

I heard Nick's voice coming from the kitchen, soothing her, comforting her. Gradually her sobs subsided and there was quiet. No doubt he was kissing the tears away.

Not before time, I too slipped down from the table. I didn't look at Rachel, because I knew the sort of smile she'd have on her face. I just ran. At least I could do that. I could run away.

Upstairs, I tore around the bedroom like a lunatic, throwing things into a suitcase. Red shirt, leather skirt, little black dress, riding boots − all those well thought-out outfits had done the trick all right, but where had the trick got me? In one hell of a mess, that's where.

The tears were streaming down my face by now, and I made no effort to check them, I just bunged on my sunglasses. I loved him so much, but I mustn't think about that because I'd go mad. The best thing I could do would be to slip away quietly and let him breathe a huge sigh of relief when he discovered the empty bedroom.

The only problem was, I couldn't do my case up. As always, I seemed to have twice as many clothes as when I'd arrived. I sat on the blasted thing and bounced up and down, but even my colossal weight couldn't close it. Eventually, in desperation, I took out a couple of jumpers and a pair of shoes and shoved them under the bed. I just had to get away.

I stole downstairs as quietly as one can steal with a two-ton case in tow, looking around feverishly for any sign of life. No one seemed to be about. Nick and Serena were probably still in the kitchen at the back of the house, Rachel and Jamie were no doubt up in her bedroom by now, and Sarah and Tim were at the stables.

I tiptoed quietly across the great hall, dragging my case, which luckily had those nifty little wheels at the back. I was just about to heave the solid oak front door open, when the telephone rang.

Christ! I dropped my case and ran to it in a frenzy, terrified that someone else would hear and come running. I managed to grab the receiver just after the first ring. I put my hand over my mouth to muffle my voice.

'Yes?' I whispered.

'Hello?'

'Yes, hello, who is it?' I hissed rudely.

'Oh, er, sorry to disturb you. I was just wondering, is Polly McLaren staying with you by any chance?'

I sat down heavily on the bottom step. I'd know that voice anywhere.

'This is Polly,' I said quietly.

'Is it? Polly! God, it didn't sound like you at all. It's Harry!'

'I know.'

'You sound a bit odd, are you all right?'

'I'm fine. Fine. Hang on a minute.' Harry! It was no good, I had to have a cigarette. I dropped the receiver for a second, ran to the door, dragged my case back and punched it open. I rummaged desperately, flinging clothes out all over the parquet floor, found my ciggies, lit one, and inhaled deeply. Harry. Harry ringing here, looking for me. No wonder my hand was shaking. I picked up the receiver again. 'Hello?'

'You still there? I thought you'd done a bunk!'

'Er, no, I'm still here. What d'you want, Harry?'

'I rang to apologise, Poll.'

'Oh yes?'

'Yes, and to, well, to tell you I miss you.'

'Oh!' I was shocked to the core. I took another drag of nicotine and found my voice. 'But what about Caro, Harry? Isn't she keeping you company?'

'Oh Polly, don't be like that, I can explain, really I can. I just – well, I just got carried away, and I didn't think you'd find out, which I know is an awful thing to say and no excuse at all but – honestly, Poll, Caro was just a flash in the pan; ships in the night and all that, you know? I can't tell you how much I regret it now. When I heard you'd buggered off like that, I just didn't know what to do. Honestly I was tearing my hair out. Please forgive me, darling, please!'

My mouth was open. I didn't know what to say. I didn't know what to think.

'Say something, please Polly!'

'I . . . don't know what to say, Harry.'

'Oh, Polly, don't be like that, you sound so cold and hostile. Please don't go all hostile on me, just tell me you understand, I promise you it'll never happen again.'

'Oh, really?'

'Oh God, you're really pissed off, aren't you? Are you pissed off?'

I sighed. 'I honestly don't know.'

'Don't be, please don't be. It was such a mistake, such a ghastly, never-to-be repeated mistake. For what it's worth, it only happened once. She's so childish, she drove me up the pole after just one day. I know that doesn't make it any better, but I promise I've been regretting it ever since. I'm sorry, really I am, I can't tell you how awful I feel about it now. I've been all this time trying to trace you, none of your friends would tell me where you were.'

'So — so how did you find me?' I stuttered in disbelief.

'I worked on Pippa and she cracked eventually. Polly, I've got something very important to say to you.'

'Oh yes,' I croaked.

'It's not easy, because to be honest I've never said it before, but I've done a lot of thinking while you've been away, and I've come to a pretty staggering conclusion. You see, I reckon I'm in love with you.'

I gasped and reeled back against the stairs, grabbing the banisters for support. The receiver slipped from my nervous grasp. I fumbled to retrieve it.

'Hello? Hello? Polly, are you still there?'

'Y-yes, I'm here.'

'Look, I know this must come as a bit of a surprise. I mean, I know I wasn't exactly the model boyfriend, and I didn't treat you particularly well, but — well, I just took you for granted in London. You were always there. It was only when you went tearing off to Cornwall that I really began to miss you. And once I'd started I couldn't stop. Please come back. I really need to see you.'

I couldn't believe this was happening. Harry missed me? Harry needed to see me? Harry — hang on, brace yourself for this one girls — Harry *loved* me? I gaped into the receiver.

'Polly . . . ? Polly . . . ? This must be a really bad line, I can hardly hear you.'

'It's OK, Harry, I can hear you. Look, the thing is, I'm on my way back right now actually.'

'You are? Great! That's terrific! What train are you catching, shall I meet you?'

'Er, no, it's OK, I'll get a taxi. I'm not sure what time the trains are.'

'Oh, OK. Well, when you get to London, why don't you get the taxi straight round here.'

'Straight round where?' I said stupidly.

'Here, to my place. We could grab something to eat and then well, you know,' he laughed. 'Get to know each other again!'

I stared into the mouthpiece. He shouldn't have said that. He really should not have said that. It was a big mistake. It not only made my skin creep, it made my toes curl up in their boots. Get to know each other again? Me and Harry? The diving board and futon nonsense all over again? In bed? With no clothes on? Embarking on a sexual marathon? With perhaps a little short back and sides thrown in for good measure? The very idea repulsed me. Oh no, I couldn't go back to that, not when I'd tasted the real thing. I thought of Nick. No, I could never go back to Harry.

I leaned back on the stairs, relief flooding over me. A colossal weight seemed to be lifting from my shoulders. I was shaking off my chains, I was free, and it was the most wonderful feeling. He meant nothing to me. Harry Lloyd-Roberts was history. Hoo-bleeding-ray.

'Polly, I think I'd better ring you back, I can't hear a word you're saying.'

'That's because I'm not saying anything, but I'm going to say something now, Harry. Are you ready?'

'Er, ready,' he said uncertainly.

'You're absolutely right.'

'I am?'

'Absolutely. You did take me for granted in London, and you're right, there is no excuse. Not only weren't you the model boyfriend, you weren't even a boyfriend. Far from it. If you really want to know, you were a pig. And I've been doing some thinking too. I've been thinking that

I've actually got along quite well without you down here. I'm sorry, Harry, but our few days apart have obviously brought us to entirely different conclusions. You see, I'm over you. I hate to be brutal, but I'm afraid you're just too late. Sorry and all that.'

I heard a few distant splutterings at the end of the line. Without waiting for a reply, I gently replaced the receiver. Then I gathered my clothes up from the parquet floor, stuffed them back into my case, sat on it, snapped it shut, and dragged it over to the door again. With an almighty heave, I lugged my belongings over the threshold and staggered off down the drive towards the Helford Road.

Chapter Twenty-five

As I panted down the sweep of gravel to the gate, dragging my case behind me, I went over the extraordinary conversation again in my mind. It was incredible, what on earth had brought about this sudden change of heart? A little over a week ago he'd been indifference itself, now he was all over me. Did people change their minds as dramatically as that? I suppose they did. I mean, look at me, a couple of weeks ago I'd have flown back into his arms and been the happiest girl in the world, but not now. Not after Nick.

Nick. He'd changed too, hadn't he? And even more rapidly, come to that. Only this morning he'd told me – well, what had he told me, after all? Nothing very much when I came to think about it – that I was beautiful, yes, but that was just pillow-talk; he hadn't said anything truly heartfelt, had he? My own heart lurched as I thought of what he was telling Serena now. That he loved her? That he wanted to marry her more than anything in the world? That I'd been nothing more than a – what had Harry said about Caro – a ghastly mistake?

I sobbed audibly, and dragged the wretched case over the cattle grid at the gate, tears streaming down my face. It didn't help matters that I had three-inch heels on: I'd changed my shoes before lunch in a desperate attempt to make myself look a bit taller and perhaps even to come up to Serena's tummy button. I cursed my black crumpetcatchers now as I wobbled around precariously on them, tottering off in the direction of the river.

I had to get the ferry across to Helford before I could even begin the epic journey to Helston, and I had no idea when there'd be a boat. Did one just sit and wait, or did I have to hail one like a taxi? I struggled along the bumpy road feeling none too dry under the arms, and then turned off left and lugged the case down the bumpy track to the river. It bounced along behind me, steadily gaining momentum down the steep slope, forcing me to go faster and faster, so that when we eventually arrived at the bottom I was running pretty fast and very much out of control. Luckily I careered into some white railings on the jetty, which saved me from going in the water, and I sank down gratefully in a crumpled heap to wait for the boat, glad of a chance to get my breath back.

'You hopping on luv, or what?' said a voice.

I looked up. A little boat was bobbing around in front of me, packed full of people. They all seemed to be staring at me.

'Sorry?'

'I said are you hopping on?' said the voice again. It appeared to belong to a man with a blue cap and a wide grin. ' 'Cos if you are, you'd better get a move on, we're leaving any minute.'

I stared at the little boat. 'Oh! Is this the ferry?' Somehow I'd been expecting something much bigger, something more like the cross-channel jobbies that go over to France. This was just a little dinghy.

He grinned again. ' 'Tis as far as I know — and I should, I've been ferryin' it there and back for more 'un twenty years now!'

I jumped up with alacrity. 'Oh! Oh well, yes please, don't go without me.'

'Give me that, luv.' He reached over and took my case. Someone else stretched out a friendly hand and helped me aboard. I sank down gratefully into the last available seat and, with a shrill whistle and a little blast of steam, we chugged off.

We were packed in like sardines, and I was jammed between two large women with enormous tweedy bottoms that cushioned me nicely on either side. It was really quite comfortable. I studied my fellow travellers. They were mostly sensible-looking women with empty shopping bags, off to do the weekly shop, no doubt. Their brown, wrinkled faces viewed me with interest and their kindly eyes twinkled. I tried hard to twinkle back but my face seemed to be locked into the forces of gravity which continually pulled it downwards. I'd twinkle later, I decided, when I needed to ask them the quickest way into town.

By now my feet were killing me. I decided to risk it and swap the ridiculous heels for a pair of espadrilles. My case was at my feet and I snapped it open, threw in the accursed shoes, and pulled on some heavenly flat ones. I crammed the lid down again, but of course once opened, the damn case wouldn't shut again, at least not with a pair of bulky high heels inside it. I got up from my seat and sat on the case. I bounced up and down, but it would hardly close, let alone shut. Tears of rage and self-pity were welling up in my eyes now.

'It's not goin' to shut, is it lover!' ventured the tweedy woman next to me. She cackled in a friendly manner. 'Reckon you've got too much in there, you see!'

'Certainly looks like it, doesn't it,' I mumbled back, aware that my voice had a wobble in it.

I had one last bounce, but to no avail. Suddenly I could bear it no longer. With a squeal of rage I grabbed the stilettos and threw them overboard. They hit the water with a satisfying plop! and then sank slowly down into the murky depths, never to be seen again. With a gleeful little shriek, I jumped on the case and snapped it shut.

I heaved a sigh of relief and grinned around at my neighbours. 'I never liked those shoes anyway!' I said to one and all.

Eight or nine horrified pairs of eyes met mine. Their good, honest, hard-working faces were aghast. No one smiled, no one spoke. They just stared. There was a terrible silence. Yes, in one reckless flick of the wrist I'd succeeded in alienating the good folk of Helford and Manaccan. The very people on whom I'd hoped one day to bestow prizes graciously at the village fête were open-mouthed with horror and disbelief. One by one they turned away, and a whispered muttering rose up around me. I caught the eye of the friendly captain. He looked away. I stared at the floor, hot-blooded shame filling my face.

How could I have been so stupid? Those shoes probably cost, oh, let's see, about as much as it took to feed a family for a week − God, a month even! Most of these people probably thought themselves lucky even to own one pair of shoes; their children probably ran around barefoot. I mean, they did in the country, didn't they?

I stared down miserably, not daring to look up. Eight or nine pairs of shoes met my gaze. That confirmed it. All the shoes looked like museum pieces. They were at least a hundred years old, no doubt handed down from generation to generation, from grandmother to mother to daughter, lovingly cared-for and restored − no, cobbled, that was it − over the years.

As we chugged across the water and then into the quay on the Helford side, I braced myself to look up. It was true, my fears were confirmed. Distrust and suspicion had replaced any kindly interest that might previously have helped me to secure a lift into Helston. Take those labourers, for example. Now normally I have a good working relationship with labourers. I saunter past, they whistle, I look coy, they make obscene gestures, I toss my head − everyone's satisfied. But not today, oh no. I tried a timid smile as they got off the ferry, but they instantly looked away, jumping into a waiting Land Rover and speeding off without so much as a, 'Cor, 'ello darlin'!' in my general direction.

As everyone else scattered, I realised I was the only one left standing on the quay. Feeling nice and sorry for myself, I took hold of my case, put my head down, and trudged down the lane in search of a bus. Get real, Polly, a bus? It took me half an hour before I could find anything that even remotely resembled a bus stop, and even then I wasn't sure. The little red symbol looked remarkably like a cattle truck to me. Oh well, I could hardly walk all the way to Helston. I sat down heavily on my evil case and waited. And waited. And waited.

After what must have been a good half-hour, I decided to take my life in my hands and hitch a lift. I rummaged around in my handbag and, right at the bottom, my hand closed gratefully on an enormous pearl that was stuck in the lining. I pulled it out. Ah yes, there it was, my giant-sized hat-pin. On the odd occasion when I'm forced to hitch a lift, I like to keep it to hand. Lord knows where I imagine I'm going to stick it: somewhere soft, certainly, but I've never got more specific than that, it just comforts me to know it's there. I stood up and struck a pose at the side of the road. I stuck my thumb out purposefully; it was erect and jaunty.

Twenty minutes later, my thumb was wilting sadly. Alas, word had spread about, above and beyond. The good people of Helford had clearly been forewarned: do not, on any account, pick up an overweight blonde girl dragging a case. She's a profligate hussy with more shoes than sense. Not one car even slowed down, let alone stopped.

Eventually though, a little old lady came waddling towards me with an empty basket. Now she must be going into town, I thought, and surely someone of her age and stature — she was wider than she was tall — wouldn't walk all that way, now would they? I watched her approach with mounting excitement. It was like something out of Monty Python. Any minute now I expected a bus to career round the corner, whereupon she'd stick out her foot and trip it up. No such luck. She waddled straight past me.

'Excuse me!' I shouted desperately.

She stopped, turned around, and stared at me with curiosity. 'D'you happen to know if there's a bus into Helston today?'

She cackled with laughter. 'Oh, so that's what you're waiting for, is it? No, not today, lover. Tuesdays and Thursdays, yes, but not today.'

She cackled a bit more and made as if to walk on. Not so fast, Grandma, I thought. I persisted, somewhat nosily.

'Well, how are you getting into town then?'

'Me? Oh I've got a lift comin', don't you worry about me!'

Her use of the personal pronoun was distressing enough, but just as I was about to disregard it and suggest I shared her transport, sure enough, it appeared around the corner. A milk float. With room enough for one.

'Af'ernoon, Dolly!' hailed the cheery milkman.

' 'Tis for some!' she cackled back as he heaved her aboard by the arm. She plumped herself down beside him and, with a cheery backward wave, they rattled off into the distance.

Well, that did it. That really did it. Without any more ado, I put my head in my hands and sobbed. And not just the whining, snuffling nonsense that I'd been doing for the last couple of hours, oh no, this was a good, honest-to-goodness sob.

I worked my way through a repertoire of gasping, spluttering, moaning and case-kicking, and was just building up to a nice shoulder-shaking crescendo, when I became aware of a car engine purring away in front of me.

Pausing for a moment from my gasps and heaves, I peered through the deluge and made out an orange Golf convertible, fully converted. It had stopped right in front of me and was humming away quietly. An electric window slid silently down.

'I thought it was you!' A familiar voice foghorned out. 'What on earth are you doing sitting there in the road?'

As the mist and rain clouding my vision cleared slightly, I made out the shadowy figure of Hetty Penhalligan at the wheel. I banged on my Ray-Bans and sprang to my feet, relief and alarm alternating within me. She might at least take me into Helston, but what on earth was I going to say to her by way of explanation?

'Are you trying to get to Helston?' she asked.

'Yes!' I yelped joyfully.

'Well that's where I'm going. Hop in, and throw your case in the boot.'

I had the suitcase in the boot and my seatbelt clunk-clicked before she'd even blinked.

'Are you all right, my dear?' She peered anxiously over my glasses. 'Only you look absolutely terrible. Why on earth were you sitting by the side of the road like a little gnome?'

'I was trying to get to Helston and I thought there might be a bus, you see. I didn't realise they only ran about once a year down here.'

'D'you mean to say you've walked all this way with that heavy case? How perfectly ghastly!'

She crunched into first gear and we shot off, achieving nought to sixty in about ten seconds. I caught my breath, recovering from what felt like whiplash in my neck, and hung on for dear life as we hurtled round the lanes at a spectacular speed.

'Why on earth didn't Nick bring you?' she shouted above the roar of the engine.

'It was an emergency and Nick wasn't at the house!' I shouted back.

'Oh? Where is he?'

'He's um – he's gone to market!' Wasn't that where farmers went?

'Market? Today? How extraordinary,' she mused. 'It's usually on a Monday.'

'Er, yes, that's right, so he said, but apparently they changed the day because, um, a lot of the farmers couldn't make it last Monday.'

She looked at me as if I had two heads. 'What on earth do you mean, couldn't make it?'

Yes, what on earth did I mean? I struggled to make sense of myself. 'Well, you see a lot of them were away last Monday, on holiday – well, long weekends. You know, because of the good weather and all that. They took an extra day. So the people who organise the market, the, the er, market organisers, decided that since so many of them had missed it, they'd have it today instead!'

Hetty threw her head back and roared with laughter. 'Is that what he told you! Good Lord, that's a good one. Long weekends, eh? Ha ha! Polly, I'm afraid you've been had; he's obviously up to no good. Farmers don't even have weekends, let alone long ones!'

'Oh, really? Yes, well I must say I thought it was a bit odd, I expect it was a little white lie then – ha ha!' It made a nice change to blame my lies on someone else, I don't know why I hadn't thought of it before.

'So what's the emergency?' she yelled, as we took another bend at death-defying speed. I hung on to the door handle and shut my eyes hoping to God it was locked.

'What?' I yelled back, playing for time.

'The emergency, why are you rushing back?'

'Oh! Oh well, I've just heard that my mother's ill.'

'Oh dear, I'm so sorry, what's wrong with her?'

I gripped the dashboard as we shot over a humpbacked

bridge, taking off from all four wheels and landing with a smack on the tarmac. Hetty obviously thought we were in Monaco rather than Manaccan. She also had an unnerving habit of leaning over to one side as she took her corners, as if she were on a motorbike. For some reason I felt myself leaning with her. It was quite hard to concentrate on my poor mother when I'd become the indispensable second half of a bobsleigh team.

'What's wrong with her?' she shrieked again.

'Malaria!' I shrieked back wildly.

Suddenly a traffic light loomed. It was red. I shut my eyes and offered my soul to the Almighty, plus anything else he considered worth taking. We screeched to a halt.

Hetty peered at me, full of concern. 'Malaria? How perfectly dreadful, has she been abroad lately?'

'Er, no, I don't think so, why?'

'Well, because one doesn't usually catch it in England.'

'Oh, abroad! Sorry, I wasn't quite with you. Yes, yes, she has been abroad. She went to, let me see – yes, France! She was in France last week, only you see she goes so often I sort of forget that it's abroad really. We've got a house out there, so it's rather like a second home.'

Hetty raised her eyebrows. 'She caught malaria in France? How frightfully unlucky. Especially in April.' She looked doubtful. 'Surely not mosquitoes?'

Damn. Of course, how stupid of me. Malaria was one of those nasty tropical diseases, wasn't it? You could only pick it up if you were spearing crocodiles in the Congo, or going native down the Nile. Why hadn't I picked something average, something close to home, something you could pick up in your local supermarket if you felt like it? Flu, for example, that would have done very nicely. Why did I have to be so ambitious?

'Er, no, you're right, it wasn't mosquitoes. The doctor thought perhaps it was something in the water. She was, after all, very deep in the deep South of France.'

449

I lowered my voice dramatically in an effort to suggest that my intrepid mother had ventured where perhaps no white man had gone before; certainly no white, middle-aged housewife.

'I mean,' I went on desperately, 'to be honest, we're talking Spain really.'

Happily, this struck a chord with Hetty, who obviously thought anything south of Paris was third world.

'Ah well, that explains it. Spain. Yes, of course. Never trust the Spics.' She shook her head violently. 'Never! The sneaky bastards, I wouldn't put it past them at all!'

I leaned back with relief as we sped off from the lights. At least we'd sorted that one out, but I was nonetheless confused. Was Hetty suggesting that these untrustworthy Spics had actually put something in my mother's water? I'd always imagined the water just became contaminated naturally, from the archaic water system, or the sewers perhaps. I had no idea that the locals actually went around slipping evil potions into glasses of aqua con gas which were then served up to unsuspecting tourists. How appalling! Someone should be told! I shuddered, and it was with some relief that I realised that my mother was not, in fact, lying prostrate in a hospital bed, but was safely at home in Esher, and probably even now absent-mindedly putting Pedigree Chum into the shepherd's pie and giving half a pound of minced beef to the dog.

We hurtled around another hairpin bend, and I once more adopted the obligatory Barry Sheen position. A lorry swung away from us in alarm as we occupied far more of our share of the road than was strictly fair, and the driver shook his fist at us as we passed. Hetty waved back cheerily. Another bend and yet another lorry loomed, this time with two tons of hay on its back. My knuckles were white with fear as they gripped the dashboard, and my foot pumped away at an imaginary brake.

'Look out!' I screeched, as it missed us by inches.

Hetty looked at me in surprise. 'Am I making you nervous, my dear?'

'No, no, not at all!' I lied, as we roared dangerously into a village and slithered to a halt at another welcome set of lights. My heart was pounding wildly. 'I'm just not used to these twisty little lanes, that's all.'

'Oh don't worry, I know them like the back of my hand. You're quite safe.' She patted my rather sweaty hand.

I smiled but doubted it. In fact I was convinced I was going to die in this car. But on the other hand, I thought brightly, as I looked around at the little village we'd stopped in, if I was so concerned about dying, I must feel I had something to live for, right? Otherwise it wouldn't bother me, right? Right. But what?

I stared dreamily out of the window at the row of cottages we'd pulled up next to. They were all thatched, but each one was different and achingly pretty in its own way. Their pink, blue and white faces basked peacefully in the afternoon sun, their leaded windows sparkling as they caught the light. They were heaven. Crawling with honeysuckle and early roses which were already trying to bud, they had tiny cottage gardens at the front, and were flanked at the back by long stretches of lawn which swept up the hill beyond. The gardens backed on to fields where clusters of little creamy lambs danced and played, butting their patient mothers and snatching at the bright spring grass. I sighed. How beautiful it all was, and how unfortunate for me that I'd not only fallen in love with Nick, but also with Cornwall.

I bit my lip as the eyes welled. That way madness lies, I told myself fiercely, don't even think about it. Instead I stared out of the window fixedly, and concentrated like billy-o on a green Volvo that had just drawn up in front of one of the cottages. I studied the hub caps fiercely. Don't think about Nick and don't think about Cornwall, or you'll flood the car, and then what will Hetty say? I suppose I could have blamed the sudden emotion on my mother's malaria, but I didn't really want to get embroiled in that little malarkey again.

I blinked hard and concentrated on the Volvo. The door was opening and a cloth cap was emerging. It belonged to a young man who was getting out of the driving seat. He slammed the door behind him, not bothering to lock it. Well, why should he? We weren't in thieving Fulham now, were we? I sighed despondently as I realised that I very soon would be. The young man strode up the path towards the pink cottage, taking a key out of his hip pocket as he went. What an idyllic place to live, I thought, as he put the key in the door. I bet it was full of quarry tiles and oak beams.

The lights began to change. Hetty, keen as mustard for a Le Mans start, slammed into first and revved up the engine. The young man opened his front door and made to go in. Funnily enough, although I hadn't seen his face, he struck me as being rather familiar. He had a certain gait which reminded me of someone . . . Yes, it was definitely the way he walked, and, yes, something about those broad shoulders, that hair sticking out from under his cap . . . that . . . red hair.

My hand flew to my mouth. 'Oh my God!' I shrieked from the open-topped car.

He swung around instantly. Our eyes met. I ducked down, and at that moment Hetty saw green and roared off, but it was too late.

'What?' she yelled at me over the engine. 'Oh my God, what?'

'It's him!' I wailed, wringing my hands. 'It's bloody him again, isn't it!'

Chapter Twenty-six

I swivelled round in my seat. Adam was standing stock-still, half-way up the garden path, staring after us. We hadn't fooled him at all, he was still here! Not in Mannacan, of course — having an iota of intelligence, he'd probably realised we'd check that out — no, he'd simply switched villages. How stupid of us to be so sure of ourselves, so arrogant, so complacent! I swung back into my seat again, panic rising within me.

Think, Polly, think. I thought. I gripped the upholstery. Oh my God, if he had any sense he'd act fast! Let's face it, he didn't have much choice now that he knew I'd seen him. In fact, at this very moment he was probably sprinting down the path to his car, revving it up and speeding off to Trewarren to snatch Jamie back before I raised the alarm. Then he'd whisk him off to the nearest port and from there, back to America. I imagined little Jamie, wide-eyed and trusting, bundled up in his blue blanket, hurried on to boats, planes, through customs. My heart lurched. Oh poor little baby! I bit my lip. It was no good. I couldn't possibly go to London now. There was only one thing to do.

'Stop the car!' I yelled at the top of my voice.

Even though we were at that precise moment negotiating an immensely tricky hairpin bend, Hetty accepted the challenge. She shot me a quick sideways glance, just to ascertain that I was serious, and, having satisfied herself, slammed on the brakes and executed a surprisingly immaculate emergency stop.

'Quick, quick! Turn around!' I urged.

'But why?' she began, 'Why have we—'

'Never mind, never mind, I'll explain in a minute, but please hurry, we must be quick!'

Wide-eyed but unprotesting, she acquiesced, throwing herself into this impromptu driving test with gusto. With a great deal of revving up and sheep-frightening, we performed a five- or six-point turn in the middle of the snake-like lane. Hetty was enjoying herself now. She was keen to please. She leaned forward, gripping the wheel, looking up at me expectantly, eagerly awaiting her next instruction. What she really wanted to hear was, 'Follow that tractor!' or some such other Miami Vice-like instruction, suitably adapted to our rural surroundings.

'Quick, quick!' I squeaked. 'Back to Trewarren!'

Crouched over the wheel like a bird of prey and with her mouth set in a determined line, she rose gleefully to the occasion. I had the distinct impression she'd been waiting for this moment for years. With a little whoop of pleasure, she let out the clutch and we shot off in the direction of Trewarren.

My mind was in overdrive now. Of course he hadn't believed us, what fools we'd been to think he would! As we hurtled back past the row of pretty cottages in the other direction, I noticed that the green Volvo had gone. He hadn't wasted any time, but if we hurried, we might just catch up with him.

'Hurry, hurry,' I muttered softly under my breath, but not softly enough for Hetty's keen ears. Her eyes widened and glinted with pleasure as she caught the magic words and the accelerator hit the floor. I gripped the dashboard and prayed hard as an amber light greeted us around the next bend. We screeched through on red, a cloud of dust shimmering in our wake.

Only now, as we zipped along a fairly open stretch of road, did Hetty allow herself to question the abrupt curtailment of her weekly shopping trip to Helston.

'Why the hell are we going to Trewarren?' she yelled above the roar of the engine.

'Because of the baby!' I shrieked back, forgetting for a moment that she didn't know the full story.

'The baby?' she looked at me quizzically.

She was one of those drivers who has to look at you while she's talking to you, unnerving for any passenger, but especially a nervous one travelling at the speed of light. I had to think quickly. The Rachel/Jamie/Adam story was much too long and complicated to go into right now, and Hetty would feel obliged to look at me throughout, which was not conducive to staying alive. I rooted around for a suitable lie.

Hetty helped me out. 'You mean we're going back for the baby?'

'Yes, that's it!' I agreed, grateful to her for providing me with such a marvellous explanation, and so simple a one too. 'I've forgotten the baby!'

'Oh!' Hetty's eyes were off the road and on my face in an instant.

'Yes, you see you were quite right. He is my baby, after all, I was just a bit embarrassed about it when you asked me before. I thought you'd disapprove, you know, unmarried mothers and all that − but he really is mine and the awful thing is, I've forgotten to bring him with me! I only realised, just back there, that he's probably still lying in his cot in Trewarren. I completely forgot about him, can you believe it!'

Hetty obviously couldn't, and was staring at me in a rather horrified manner. We were also slowing down quite dramatically. I licked my lips and realised − too late − that this story wasn't as simple as I'd hoped, and I had quite a lot of explaining to do. Hetty looked scatty enough, and was no doubt capable of leaving all sorts of things lying around – her purse, her car keys, her glasses – but a baby? Who forgets a baby? The speedometer was dropping by the second. Forty, thirty, twenty – she wasn't happy. I struggled to defend myself.

'It's – it's this damn post-natal depression, you see!'

'Ah!'

Was that a look of sympathy? Had I struck a chord?

'Yes,' I went on. 'I went into a complete decline after he was born: couldn't eat, couldn't sleep, and couldn't really believe I'd had a baby at all! I kept thinking he must be someone else's. And – and the terrible thing is that, even though I'm much better now, I still forget occasionally that I'm a mother, and I leave him lying around in the most awful places!'

'My poor child!' She put her hand on my arm in consternation.

Buoyed up by her concern, I warmed to my subject. 'Yes, I left him in Peter Jones once.'

Hetty shook her head and tutted sympathetically. 'Easily done,' she muttered. 'China and glassware?'

' 'Fraid so. Oh, and once I left him outside the post office, and in the greengrocer's, and the cinema—'

'You take him to the cinema?' Hetty looked alarmed.

Oh Christ, didn't babies go to the cinema? Probably not – wouldn't it have been easier to go into the Adam and Rachel saga? Too late. I struggled valiantly on.

'Oh well, it helps him go to sleep, you see, and I don't take him to see anything sexy or violent, just love stories and that sort of thing, or nature films, you know, anything soporific.'

'Oh, right.' Hetty still looked dubious. 'Was it a terrible birth then?'

'Oooh shocking, shocking! Went on for weeks!'

'Weeks!' Hetty gaped at me and we almost came to a

standstill, she was rooting in the glove compartment for a cigarette.

Oh, hell! If only I knew more about birth. What a pity Rachel hadn't been more forthcoming, but surely I'd heard that some women were in labour for ages?

'Er – well, no, not weeks, it just felt like weeks, but certainly days, about, um four or five anyway.'

Hetty looked horrified. 'You poor thing!'

'I know, it was ghastly, all the doctors said it was quite the most appalling birth they'd ever come across. It took five of them to deliver me: they needed forceps, ropes, pulleys, all sorts of things. I made medical history, there's a bit in a textbook about it now. It crops up in exams, and someone even wrote a thesis on it. Anyway, that's why I get so depressed and, well, you know, forget about him occasionally.'

'Well of course, of course.' Hetty shook her head. 'Goodness me, we must get you some help,' she muttered, looking grave.

Happily though, she seemed satisfied with my bizarre explanation, and the speedometer climbed again. I watched it like a hawk. Within seconds we were well into the fifties. It occurred to me that Hetty might consider popping me into the local police station for some routine questioning on child abuse, or stopping at a telephone box to report me to the NSPCC or the Esther Rantzen Childline, but no. Thankfully she was obviously of the opinion that a child's place was with its mother, no matter how hopelessly deranged that mother happened to be.

No more was said, and eventually we rounded the bend that led to Trewarren. We swung through the gates, fairly flew over the cattle grid and, with a spray of gravel, came to an abrupt halt in front of the house.

I was out of that car and leaping up the stone steps to the front door in a trice. Knowing what superhuman strength it took to force the door open, I ran at it, ramming it with my shoulder. Unfortunately it was already deceptively ajar, so I burst in a little faster than I'd anticipated. I careered across the hall like an unguided missile, and cannoned into Nick who was coming out of the drawing room.

'Hey! Whoa, steady on!' he said, grabbing my shoulders as I headbutted him in the chest. 'Ooof! Polly, it's you!'

He obviously recognised me by my entrance. I thought he looked slightly relieved, if a little winded. However, if it was relief, it was very momentary, and it very soon turned to anger.

'Where the bloody hell have you been? I've been looking everywhere for you, why did you just take off like that?' He spotted Hetty behind me. 'Mum! What are you doing here?'

Hetty was still glowing from the after-effects of having just broken the land speed record. She fanned her rather flushed face.

'Hello darling, isn't this a surprise? I simply must have a large drinky. I'm absolutely pooped! We've just had the most terrifically exciting car journey, and Polly's been simply fascinating company. Honestly, the things she's been through, you just wouldn't believe it. First the baby, and now her poor mother . . .' She collapsed on a chair in the hall. 'Darling, hurry up with that gin, I'll expire in a minute.'

Nick jerked his head towards the drawing room. 'Help yourself, Mum, would you? Usual place.'

Hetty got up, and thankfully disappeared in the direction of the drinks cupboard before she had time to elucidate further on my fascinating career.

Nick still had my shoulders in a vice-like grip. 'Polly, just what the hell is going on here?'

'Where are Rachel and Jamie?' I blurted out.

'As far as I know, Rachel's reading in the garden, and I think Jamie's asleep upstairs. Why?'

I wriggled out of his hands, pushed past him, and leaped up the stairs two at a time. As I reached the landing, I heard Rachel's voice coming up from the hall below. I glanced down quickly. She was wandering in from the kitchen, book in hand. No Jamie.

She frowned. 'What's going on?' she asked, as she watched me scramble up the stairs like a neurotic mountain goat.

Nick shrugged and leaped up the stairs after me. 'Search me. Polly, what are you up to?'

'Jamie,' I muttered as I flew down the corridor to his bedroom.

The door was open. I raced over to the cot and looked down. A much-sucked teddy bear looked back at me with beady black eyes. The pale blue blanket was pushed back to reveal a white sheet sprinkled with yellow buttercups. A little blue rabbit was half squashed through the bars. Other than that the cot was empty. Somehow, although I'd been expecting it, I wasn't prepared for the reality.

My hand flew to my mouth. 'Oh Nick, he's gone!'

Nick raced in behind me. 'Oh well, hang on a minute, I may be wrong. He may have been in the garden with Rachel, or—'

Rachel was in the room in an instant. She rushed, white-faced, to the cot and looked down. Then she screamed. She gripped the side of the cot and just screamed and screamed as if she would never stop. It wasn't a sound I'd ever heard a human being make before: it sounded more like the shriek of a snared animal, an eerie, primeval sound that tore at the heart and froze the blood.

'He's gone! My baby's gone! He's taken my baby – oh my GOD!' She covered her face with her hands and screamed again.

Then she turned on me, her face drained and bloodless. 'Where is he? Where is he! You saw him, didn't you, you saw him! Tell me where he is!'

She ran at me, beating me with her fists, shaking my shoulders, her white, distorted face inches from mine.

'This is all your fault!' she shrieked. 'Tell me where he is!'

I was terrified. Nick was over in an instant, pulling her off. She gave a moan and collapsed on to him. He held her tightly as she shook violently in his arms.

'It's Adam!' I gasped, shaking quite a bit myself. 'I saw him coming out of that little row of cottages in New Town, he didn't go to London at all – and he knew I'd seen him, so he obviously rushed over here and – and just took him while he still had the chance!'

Rachel moaned again and put her head in her hands.

'Shit!' hissed Nick through clenched teeth. He sat Rachel down on a chair and knelt beside her. She was sobbing and shaking uncontrollably. He took her hands.

'Now listen to me Rachel. It's OK, it's going to be all right. We'll get him back in no time, don't you worry, he can't be far away – minutes at the most. Everything's going to be fine.' He straightened up and shot me a look. 'Look after her,' he muttered, as he rushed from the room.

'Where are you going?' I ran after him.

'To ring the police.'

I bounded downstairs behind him. By the time I'd got to the bottom he was already dialling the number.

'Green Volvo!' I breathed.

'Good. Anything else? Registration?'

'Didn't see, but it was a big one, an estate.'

He got hold of the local police and briefed them in a controlled and lucid manner. A baby had been snatched from its mother at Trewarren. A tall, red-headed American, about thirty, driving a green Volvo. Could well be making for the London road, or possibly a port. Hurry.

'Wearing a cap!' I prompted.

Nick gave me a withering look and refrained from imparting this vital piece of evidence. Then he slammed the receiver down and made for the door, grabbing his car keys from the hall table.

'Where are you going now?' I cried, running after him.

'He can't be far away, I'm going to look for him.'

'I'm coming with you!'

'No, stay with Rachel,' he ordered.

'Not likely,' I muttered, throwing myself down the front steps after him.

He jumped into the Land Rover. 'For God's sake, who's going to look after her?' he growled as I jumped in beside him.

'Your mother,' I said, slamming the door, 'she's brilliant with distraught young mothers, I know that from experience. Now come on!'

We reversed, and the tyres spun on the gravel drive as we took off. Nick swung the Land Rover around the side of the house, and we sped off down the back drive, bouncing all over the place on the un-made-up, rock-strewn road.

'Where are we going?' I gasped, steadying myself on the window as we roller-coasted down towards the back gate.

'We'll head for the London road,' said Nick. 'We'll just have to take a chance on him going that way. He obviously didn't go back towards Helston or you'd have seen him. I know a short-cut to the main road so we might be able to cut him off.'

'If he's smart he'll ditch the car, he knows I've seen it.'

'What, and charge about on foot? Come on, Polly, a redheaded man carrying a baby for miles is pretty conspicuous, and it would take him for ever to get to the main road and hitch a lift.'

'He might get a train.'

'The police will be on the look-out at Helston station, and that's the only main line around here.'

We paused for a second at the bottom of the drive, before swinging round left into the lane. He flashed

461

me a look. 'What the hell were you doing in New Town anyway?'

I stared out of the window. 'Going back to London.'

'Idiot,' he muttered, but made no further comment, as we tore off down the road.

We raced around a sharp bend, taking half the hedge with us, and I hastily withdrew my elbow from the open window. Nick had obviously learned to drive at his mother's knee, I recognised the style. If I wasn't very much mistaken, this was a former pupil of the Hetty Penhalligan Kamikaze School of Motoring. At least I'd been on a trial run once already today, so I knew the ropes. I planted my feet firmly on the dashboard to act as shock absorbers, and gripped the upholstery with my nails. The tyres screeched around on the tarmac, reminding me abruptly of Rachel's screams. I shivered.

'D'you think we'll find him?'

'I just don't know.'

'How far away d'you think he is by now?'

Nick, thankfully, didn't have his mother's penchant for eyeball contact. He stared straight ahead. 'Hard to say, a mile maybe, perhaps two if he's really motoring.'

He obviously wasn't feeling chatty so I kept quiet. Well, at least for a couple of seconds, anyway.

'What are we going to do if we do see him?' I ventured timidly.

'Follow him of course.'

We lurched sideways as we swerved to avoid an old man on a quivering bicycle.

'Yes, but then what?'

In my mind's eye, I saw us drawing up alongside the Volvo and gesturing for Adam to pull in, whereupon he'd shoot us a villainous sideways glance, snarl, and go even faster — but he'd be no match for us. We'd be right by his side, tearing along through the twisty-turny lanes, neck and neck, until eventually we'd ram him and force him

462

into a ditch. Nick would leap out, drag him from the car, and spreadeagle him over the bonnet in a half-nelson, and I'd be right beside him, frisking him and reading him his rights: 'You have the right to remain silent, but anything you do say . . .'

'Use the car phone to telephone the police and give them his exact position. They'll have a squad of cars after him in no time,' answered Nick calmly.

'Oh. Oh yes, of course, good idea.' I was rather disappointed.

As we rounded the next bend, we nearly went straight up the back of a little red post office van which was tootling along at a leisurely thirty miles per hour. Nick sat on the horn, but the van stood its ground, which happened to be most of the road.

'Oh, come on, you berk! Move over!' I cried, banging the dashboard in frustration and willing Postman Pat into the nearest ditch. He was damned if he was moving over, but eventually the lane widened slightly, albeit on a horrifically blind corner, and Nick shunted down a gear and roared up beside him, forcing him into the hedge. As we shot past I caught a glimpse of a little purple-faced man, waving his fist and shouting obscenities. Blood pressure was clearly a problem, and a heart attack looked imminent, but I had no sympathy. He'd cost us vital seconds.

The next thing I knew, we'd hung a sharp left into a ploughed field and were bouncing along down the side of it. All four wheels seemed to be leaving the ground at regular intervals. Thank goodness I hadn't managed to make much headway with the fish pie, I thought, as my bottom left the seat and my tummy shot into my oesophagus. I gritted my teeth and clutched my bosoms as we took off from a particularly deep rivet. God, I was getting some exercise on this holiday.

At last the dark furrows came to an end, and we swerved

into another field, this time, thankfully, of the green and pleasant variety. My organs slipped back into their rightful slots and I managed to speak, or squeak, 'Where the hell are we going?'

'Short-cut!'

'But won't the farmer mind?' I asked, as hordes of terrified sheep scattered in all directions.

'I am the farmer.'

He slammed on the brakes and we screeched to a halt in front of a huge fence. Oh no! What now? Through it? Over it?

'Open it!' he barked.

Oh Christ, it was a gate! I hurriedly scrambled out and fell flat on my face in some very dubious business.

'Oh God, yucky poo! Sheep shit, all up my nose!' I wailed in disgust as I got slowly to my feet.

'Get on with it!' bellowed Nick, banging the steering wheel.

Nausea was rising within me, but I hurriedly wiped my nose and addressed myself to the gate. It had one of those really complicated catches, with bits of wire and binder-twine all over it − the sort of thing you need a degree from Cirencester to open. My fingers were like sausages as I fumbled nervously around.

'I can't do it!' I wailed pathetically.

'Jesus!' a voice hissed in my ear. Nick was beside me. He swept my inept fingers away and muttered something under his breath, but I couldn't quite catch what he said except it sounded like 'hopeless', 'fucking', and 'prat', but I probably misheard.

He had it open in an instant, then he ran back to the car, revved up, and shot through.

'Now shut it!' he barked from the driving seat.

It was bloody heavy, but I prayed to God and luckily He provided me with some superhuman strength. I rammed it shut.

As I ran back to the car, I suddenly glimpsed a long flash of green through the hedge on the opposite side of the field. The green streak was travelling at speed down the lane at right angles to ours.

'There he is!' I shrieked, 'that's him!' and almost before I was back in my seat, Nick was after him.

We roared up to the crossroads, swung left without stopping to see what was coming, and raced up the lane. There was no sign of the Volvo now, but at least we knew we were on the right road.

'After him! After him!' I squealed, bouncing up and down in my seat with excitement.

'Put your seatbelt on!' ordered Nick as I bounced a bit too hard and nearly cracked my head on the roof. I dragged it across and snapped it into place.

An uncharacteristically long stretch of road opened before us and, right at the very end, just as it was about to disappear over the brow of the hill, we saw the green Volvo.

Nick opened up the throttle and we fairly flew along, all thoughts of ringing the police forgotten in the chase. As we reached the same brow, the road twisted suddenly − then again − and again − and again. Each time we rounded a bend, I saw a tantalising flash of green appear and disappear, all in the space of a millisecond.

'Quick, quick! Faster, faster!'

Nick didn't utter, but his mouth was set in a grim line and his knuckles were white on the steering wheel. We were definitely gaining on him. Nick had the advantage of knowing the lanes backwards, so he anticipated every bend and cornered expertly. I tried the motorbike lean so favoured by his mother, but obviously went a touch too far when I ended up with my nose in his lap.

'For God's sake sit still, will you!' he yelled, and I scrambled dutifully back into my corner, hanging on to the strap above the door as the speedometer approached eighty m.p.h. I'd always wondered what that strap was for, and now I knew. Life-threatening situations. They don't mention that in the glossy brochures though, do they? Added extra – one handy strap for hanging on to when you're looking death in the face.

'D'you think he knows we're behind him?' I yelled above the roar of the engine.

'Doubt it, I shouldn't think he's looked behind him once, he's just driving like a maniac to get the hell out of here!'

We seemed to be gaining on him all the time, but then so, unbeknown to us, was a tractor. Only the tractor was travelling in the opposite direction. It had recently emerged from some fields a mile or two hence, and was trundling back to the farm that bordered on Nick's, just over the hill. It was a large, red, uncompromising vehicle, the old-fashioned variety with huge protruding wheels at the front and a trailer at the back. It was making slow but steady progress down the lane, just as Adam was making fast and unsteady progress up it.

We were far enough behind not to witness the inevitable meeting, but the sickening crunch of metal was unmistakable.

I shrieked and covered my face with my hands. Nick hit the brakes. Within seconds we were skidding around a corner, and then another, before coming to a precarious halt, inches away from a horrifically concertina-ed Volvo.

Its back end was jutting out at right angles to the road. The front was almost totally embedded in the tractor. I couldn't see Adam or the tractor driver.

Nick was out and running before I'd even come to my senses. I stumbled out and raced after him, but as I approached I stopped dead in my tracks and shrank back in horror. Adam's twisted body was draped upside down over the front of the tractor. He'd obviously gone straight through the windscreen and somersaulted down on to his

466

back. Blood was gushing down on to his face, over his eyes, and into his open mouth. His head was slumped forward at a peculiar angle to his crumpled body, and I couldn't see his legs at all. They seemed to be embedded somewhere in the tractor.

Vomit rose up in my throat and I turned away. I threw up on the verge several times. By the time I looked up, which was a good minute or so later, I could see that Nick was crawling precariously over the tangled heap, slowly inching his way towards Adam's immobile body.

'Oh God, he's dead! He's dead, isn't he?' I shrieked.

By now Nick had reached him. 'No he's not, he's still alive — just!' He yelled back. 'For Christ's sake, get Jamie out!'

'Jamie! Oh my God!'

I ran like stink to the back of the car and peered in, bracing myself for what I might find. At first I couldn't see him at all, there was nothing on the back seat. Then I saw him. The carry-cot was on the floor in the back, wedged in between the front and back seats. Jamie's big blue eyes stared up at me. His little mouth was open and getting wider by the minute. The eyes disappeared as they screwed up tight; he took a deep breath.

'WHHAAAAAaaaaaa!'

Thank goodness! That sounded healthy. I yanked the door open and dragged the carry-cot out. It was the old-fashioned sturdy sort with rigid sides, and it was completely unharmed; and so, as far as my totally inexpert eye could see, was Jamie. He was bloody cross though. He bellowed in indignation as I grabbed him roughly and held him close, stroking his little back and feeling his warm, comforting weight, heavy against my shoulder.

'Whaaaa . . . whah, whah! Hu, hu, hu . . . whaaa, whaaa, whaaaahhh . . . !'

'Sshhh, shush Jamie, you're all right now, I've got you, you're all right.'

467

His cries gradually subsided, and after a while he made little snuffling sounds as he snuggled happily into my neck, grabbing at my hair and shoving it into his mouth, suddenly oblivious to the drama surrounding him. I was shaking like a wet puppy, but he didn't seem to mind.

I turned back to the mangled car. Nick was perched precariously on the bonnet, crouching down over Adam.

'He's all right!' I yelled, 'Jamie's perfectly all right, not hurt at all!'

'Thank God. Adam's in a pretty bad way, though. Quick, Polly, ring for an ambulance on my car phone.'

'Right!'

I grabbed the carry-cot from the car and, clutching Jamie, raced back to the Land Rover. I put him in his carry-cot on the back seat, then I jumped into the front.

'Car phone, car phone . . .' I muttered as I scrambled around looking for something with familiar dials or buttons on it. I don't even own a portable phone, let alone a car phone, so I was a bit out of my depth here. Where do people keep these things – on the dashboard? Under the seat?

'Oh please let me find it, please . . .' I muttered desperately as I feverishly rooted around in the glove compartment. 'Please, don't let me be a complete and utter moron!'

I emptied every compartment I could find and threw everything on the floor; torches, maps, barley sugars, but no telephone – where the hell was it! I dived down on to the floor and thrust my hand under the seat. Was this where it was kept? Under here?

'Oh where is it, Jamie, help me!'

The door flew open and Nick was behind me.

'I can't find it!' I wailed, wringing my hands from my cringing position on the floor.

'Christ, Polly, you're just the person to rely on in an emergency, aren't you?'

I thought this was a bit rich considering all I'd been through, but I kept mum as he leaned over and wrenched open a catch by the handbrake, pulling out a handpiece with buttons on it. He punched out 999.

'I thought that was part of the handbrake!' I whispered.

Without bothering to answer, he barked out instructions to the ambulance service.

I looked in the back seat. Jamie's eyelids were getting heavy. I watched as they closed, his little mouth opened, and his clenched fist unfurled. A second later he was fast asleep. I tiptoed away. Retching violently, I forced myself to go back towards Adam. I crept down the lane with my hand to my mouth. As I tentatively inched closer to the wreckage, I thought I saw his eyelids flicker.

'Adam?' I whispered, from a good ten yards away.

This time the mouth twitched too. I inched a mite closer.

'Adam?'

'What the bloody hell happened?' said a voice out of nowhere.

I jumped about a foot in the air and swung round to see the tractor driver staggering around in the road holding his head. Oh Christ! We'd forgotten about him. He was about seven foot tall and built like an all-in wrestler, a great bear of a man. He looked as if he was pretty much intact, but he was swaying violently, like a tree in a gale, as if he'd completely lost his sense of balance. I ran to steady him.

'Sit down, sit down!' I cried, lugging him towards the grass verge. As I lugged I realised he had the most spectacular BO. I wondered whether it was due to fear, or whether he was always so highly perfumed.

He sat obediently. I sat down next to him, then inched away as the odour shot straight up my nostrils. 'What happened?' he muttered.

'There was a crash, you're obviously in shock,' I informed him at arm's length.

469

He looked at me with bleary eyes. 'And who the hell are you, Florence Nightingale?'

I ignored this smart remark, and peered into his face which was florid and jowly. He had a little cut above his right eye, and a terrific bruise appearing on his chin, but other than that there wasn't a scratch. The tractor was completely open to the elements, so he'd obviously been thrown clear without the added complication of going through a windscreen.

'You don't look too bad,' I ventured. 'Are you all right?'

'No, I'm not sodding all right. I feel bloody awful! I've got a sodding great lump on my head and a pain in my back and my leg's killing me. Who the fuck was that idiot in the Volvo? What the bloody hell was he up to, he must have been doing about ninety miles an hour — ooh, my bloody head!' He swooned a bit.

'Put it between your knees,' I ordered, grabbing hold of the back of his bull-like neck and shoving his face downwards.

'Geddoff, will you?' he protested, pushing away my hand and making as if to scramble to his feet. I couldn't cope with a lumbering man-mountain on the loose.

'Just shut up and sit still,' I ordered. 'I'm a nurse.'

This seemed to do the trick. He looked doubtful for a moment, then lowered his head obediently until his nose was about two inches from the tarmac.

We sat in silence. I looked across at the tangled heap of machinery in front of us. Nick had climbed back to be with Adam again. Adam looked larger than ever, his huge bulk plastered over the front of the tractor like an enormous insect splattered flat by the impact. Blood was pouring out of his head and his shirt was scarlet now as it trickled down his neck to his collar. He was totally motionless. Nick reached out and took his hand. I shivered, hugging my knees to my chest and resting my head on them.

'Oh, please God,' I whispered, 'let Adam be all right. Let him live. I know I haven't prayed for ages, but this isn't for me, it's for Adam and Jamie. I mean, he only wanted his baby, didn't he? Please don't let him die for it.'

I prayed on and on, mumbling into my knees for what seemed like an eternity. I couldn't look at the wreck any more. A great stillness seemed to descend on the scene. After a while I heard voices in the background. Other cars had evidently accumulated behind us: car doors were slamming, people were whispering hoarsely to one another, 'What happened?' 'Is he dead?' Still I didn't look up.

Eventually I heard the distant wail of a siren. I lifted my head from my knees. Flashing lights were appearing around the corner.

A small crowd of concerned but goggle-eyed motorists had gathered, and the police, who had arrived simultaneously, had to organise them all out of the way before the ambulance could even begin to nose its way through. It seemed to take for ever. At last they managed to clear a path. The ambulance pushed its way through, the back door swung open, and a stretcher appeared. A couple of ambulance men inched their way gingerly over the stunted Volvo towards Adam's twisted body. With Nick's help they managed to prise him from the wreckage and lift him on to the stretcher. They covered him in a red blanket and tucked it in around him. At least he looks more comfortable now, I thought, as he was loaded into the ambulance. The tractor driver was also ushered in, grumbling and blaspheming, and the doors slammed behind him.

Nick approached the driver. 'We'd like to follow, if that's all right.'

'You know him?'

'Yes, and we've got his baby here with us. He was in the

car. He seems fine, but he should be checked over at the hospital.'

The driver nodded. 'OK.'

In silence we got back into the car, and for the third time that day I sped off down the lanes. We trailed the solid white ambulance with its siren blaring and lights flashing for about a mile and a half and then, suddenly, without warning, it slowed right down, indicated left, and came to an abrupt halt in a lay-by. The siren and the flashing light stopped. We drew in behind it.

The driver opened his door and jumped down. Nick wound down his window. With head bowed the driver walked back to us and crouched down at the open window. He took his cap off and scratched his head.

'I'm sorry, sir, I thought I ought to stop and tell you. His injuries were just too severe and he'd lost too much blood. There was nothing we could do. I'm afraid he's dead.'

Chapter Twenty-seven

There were forms to be filled in at the hospital and questions to be answered by the police who arrived to grill us, but eventually, after a gruelling hour and a half, we were allowed to go home. I'd telephoned Rachel from the hospital to let her know Jamie was safe and well. I didn't mention Adam and she didn't ask.

We drove home in silence and, as we rounded the corner to Trewarren and swept up the drive, I saw a little hunched figure in a grey cardigan sitting on the top of the steps by the front door. She stood up as we scrunched to a halt and ran down to meet us.

I was holding Jamie in the back seat. Rachel opened the door and I passed him to her. She buried her face in his tiny body, tears streaming down her cheeks.

'He's OK,' I said wearily. 'They checked him over at the hospital. Luckily his carry-cot was wedged on the floor in the back of the car and that saved him.'

She nodded, but couldn't speak. I put my arm around her shoulders, but she shook it off violently and turned on her heel.

I sighed and slowly climbed up the steps behind her into the house. She disappeared into the kitchen. I made for the drawing room, helped myself to a stiff gin, and flopped down into the nearest armchair. There was no sign of Hetty; perhaps she'd gone home, or resumed her shopping trip in Helston.

I was exhausted. I felt as if I'd aged dramatically in the last few hours. But then death did have that effect on one, didn't it? It was rather a sobering experience, watching someone die; made you grow up a bit. And Adam was definitely dead. I still couldn't quite get used to that fact, but he was.

Nick appeared and sank down on the sofa opposite me. He rubbed his eyes vigorously with the heels of his hands as only men do, girls being too aware of smudgeable mascara, and yawned widely. I wondered if I looked as tired as he did. His face was drawn and haggard.

There was something I had to ask him. I leaned forward. 'Nick, you don't think,' I began timidly, 'you don't think we chased him into that tractor, do you? It's just I'd hate to think that we somehow caused him to speed up or—'

Nick shook his head. 'Polly, don't even think about it. As I said to you at the time, he probably wasn't even aware that there was someone on his tail. He had to go at that speed because he must have known the first thing we'd do would be to alert the police. He had to put his foot down whether he knew we were there or not. No, it wasn't our fault, although God knows, that doesn't make it any better.' He rubbed his weary eyes again. 'I just wish there was something we could have done to save him. I felt so helpless, I just didn't know what to do apart from be with him, hold his hand, talk to him. I was so terrified of moving him . . .'

'You did all you could,' I said soothingly. 'God, I was hopeless, I couldn't get within inches of him. You did plenty.'

'Well, it wasn't enough, was it?'

He slumped forward and stared miserably at the carpet. I wanted to reach out and touch him, in fact my hand ventured forth in his direction for a moment, then I remembered Serena and I snatched it back.

It occurred to me briefly that there was no sign of the

474

lovely Serena. In fact, now I came to think about it more than briefly, she hadn't been around when I'd arrived back with Hetty. Probably down in Helston choosing curtain material for the dining room, I thought bitterly. I didn't like to ask. For once my own problems seemed somewhat eclipsed by recent events. I'd never experienced death before and it made me feel mighty peculiar. I shivered.

Nick noticed. He leaned forward. 'Are you OK, Polly?' he asked gently.

'Yes, fine,' I said, 'just a bit cold.'

'It's probably the shock — here, have this.' He whipped off his jumper and threw it over to me. I put it on and snuggled into its woolly warmth. It smelled delicious. I wondered if he'd notice if I stole it.

Rachel appeared from the kitchen with a bottle in one hand and Jamie astride her hip. She sat down on the rug in front of the fire and propped him up on her knee. She offered him the teat and he latched on to it enthusiastically, sucking greedily. We sat in silence, watching him drink, his eyes half shut, his podgy little hands clutching the bottle eagerly as he gulped away. So small and vulnerable, thank goodness he was all right. He drained the bottle in minutes. Rachel sat him up and rubbed his back to wind him. He let rip with the most enormous belch. We all laughed, breaking the silence.

Then Nick got up and stood by the fire next to Rachel. He licked his lips. 'Rachel?'

It seemed as if she'd never be able to tear her eyes from her baby, but eventually she looked up at him.

'Yes?'

'Adam died in the car crash.'

She stared at him for a second, then a ghost of a smile flickered on her lips. I felt sick.

'Yes,' she said, 'I thought as much.' She quickly looked down at Jamie again.

Nick was taken aback. 'I'd um — I'd like to be able to

tell you he didn't suffer much, but I'm not too sure about that . . . I'm pretty sure he was unconscious most of the time though . . .'

Rachel didn't even look up.

Nick soldiered on, braving her stony silence. 'Look, I was thinking, we'll have to contact his parents . . .'

Rachel raised her head. 'I'll deal with that,' she said coolly.

There was a silence. I stared at her. On the one hand I rather admired her lack of hypocrisy – at least she wasn't pretending to be upset – but, none the less, her cold-blooded attitude unnerved me. She had, after all, been in love with the guy at one time – about to marry him, in fact, and he was also Jamie's father.

I suddenly felt an urge to speak up for Adam. 'Don't you feel anything at all, Rachel?' I blurted out.

She slowly lifted her head and looked at me. Her eyes narrowed. 'Why should I?'

'Oh, er, well I don't know really,' I faltered, back-tracking like mad; Rachel rather frightened me these days. 'It's just that, well I can't help thinking—'

'What can't you help thinking?'

'I don't know . . . I can't help thinking you're being very calm about all this, that's all.'

'Really?' she sneered. 'And what did you expect, tears? Hysterics?'

I had a feeling I was well out of my depth here, but I dug deep for courage and ploughed on regardless. 'No, of course not, but – I mean, you were going to marry him at one time and, after all, he was Jamie's father and all he really wanted—'

'Was he?' she cut in, silencing me.

I frowned, puzzled. 'Was he what?'

'Jamie's father?' she said in a cold, flat voice.

'Well – well, yes, of course he was, well, wasn't he?' I blustered.

She looked me straight in the eye and her thin little mouth all but disappeared. 'No, he wasn't,' she said shortly.

I gasped. Nick and I exchanged shell-shocked looks.

'Well, for Christ's sake!' blustered Nick. 'What's this all been about then? Why was he so obsessed with taking Jamie? Why have we been chasing him all over Cornwall? What the hell are you talking about, Rachel?'

Rachel tied a bib around Jamie's neck and took a jar of baby food out of a bag. She unscrewed it and, without a word, calmly began feeding him as if Nick hadn't even uttered. Nick wasn't having that. He crouched down on the rug next to her and took her chin in his hand, jerking her head towards him, forcing her to look at him.

'Rachel, a man has died today. Come to that, Polly and I damn nearly died trying to get your baby back. Now what's going on here? If Adam isn't the father, who the hell is?'

Rachel stared at Nick for a second, her face inches from his, then she brushed his hand away contemptuously. She drew herself up and took a deep breath as if she were about to make a speech.

'If you must know,' she said briskly, 'and to be honest I can't see that it's any of your business, Jamie's father is a man called David Saunders.' She turned to me, 'You'd probably remember him better as Mr Saunders.'

I stared at her. I hadn't the vaguest idea what she was talking about.

'Mr Saunders?' I echoed dumbly.

'From school.'

From school. My God. It came to me. It hit me like a flying grand piano. My jaw dropped, my eyes boggled, I spat the dummy. Jesus Christ, Mr Saunders the music teacher!

'Mr Saunders the music teacher?' I gasped in disbelief.

'That's right,' she affirmed calmly.

Then I remembered. Of course. Mrs Compton had mentioned him when I'd telephoned the school; said Rachel had got on particularly well with him. I'd thought nothing of it, why should I? Jesus. Mr Saunders. Mr Saunders with the . . . ginger hair. I looked at Jamie's red tufts, which had previously made him so obviously Adam's son. But Adam didn't have the monopoly on carrots, and Rachel clearly just had a penchant for it. Well, would you believe it: Rachel Marsden, the brilliant music student with her mind on more than treble clefs. Base clefs, more like. But of all people, Mr Saunders . . . Nausea rose within me. It wasn't the fact that he was a teacher that stunned me — although that in itself was pretty breathtaking — it was more the physical attributes of the teacher in question that had me reaching for the sick bag. We're talking yuck-a-roony here. I gagged quietly.

'Now just hang on a minute,' said Nick. 'This chap Saunders is Jamie's father? Not Adam? Did Adam know that?'

Rachel sighed. 'I tried to tell him, but he wouldn't believe me. Look, Nick, if you don't mind, I really don't want to go into all this right now. It's personal, I'm very tired, and it's a long story.'

She tucked Jamie under her arm, got to her feet, and made as if to go. Nick grabbed her arm and pulled her down on the floor. I've seen him look pretty furious in my time, but nothing like as incensed as this.

'Tell it, Rachel,' he hissed grimly. 'Tell the story in all its sordid personal details because, believe me, we need to know. Polly and I really need to know.'

Even Rachel looked taken aback. She looked warily at Nick's grim, determined face and bit her lip. She sat down again.

'Well, all right, if you must know, I'll tell you,' she said sullenly. 'It's just hard to know where to begin.'

478

'The beginning will do nicely,' said Nick, still staring grimly at her, 'try starting there.'

Rachel sighed. 'All right,' she said at length. She held Jamie in one arm and twiddled her hair with her other hand. 'David was a teacher at our school. You remember him, don't you, Polly?'

I cast my mind back a few years. Sure. I remembered him all right. Mr Saunders. I could see him now, with his thin white face, his wispy ginger hair, his John Lennon glasses and his goaty little beard which he'd twiddle round his finger whenever he was nervous, which was most of the time. He was totally unsuited to teaching, and had no idea how to control a class full of bored sixteen-year-olds, whose minds were always on boys and pop music and never on Debussy.

I could hear him now. 'Girls! Girls, settle down please!' he'd plead in his thin reedy voice, visibly palpitating behind his glasses. 'Let's have a little hush, shall we?'

This pathetic appeal would only serve to augment the noise, and more desk-banging, rubber-throwing and shrieking would ensue, whereupon, in desperation, he'd put Beethoven's Fifth on at full volume in an attempt to drown the noise and to make it appear to any casual passing teacher that he was in full control. Then he'd slump down at his desk in a deep depression, miserably aware he was an unmitigated disaster.

His shoulders were constantly hunched: weighed down, no doubt, by his sense of failure; but also, I suspected, by the constant avalanche of dandruff which landed in drifts on his musty tweed jacket. Little white flakes would float down, gather, and be brushed off surreptitiously, only for more to land not a moment later. As a bored-out-of-my-skull teenager, it made fascinating viewing.

But dandruff was the least of Mr Saunders' personal problems. The biggest cross this unfortunate man had to bear was undoubtedly his dampness. His nose and forehead were permanently wet and, try as he would to wipe the beads of sweat away with a variety of spotted hankies, the drips would automatically reappear. His hands were obviously in the same state, as he was constantly wiping them on his trousers, and his little horn-rimmed glasses steamed up on a regular basis. Again, it made compulsive viewing, and we girls did a lot of sniggering and mock puking behind his back as we speculated on the probable state of his armpits. In fact, 'snuggling up to Saunders' gushing pits', was one of our 'Fates Worse Than Death', alongside licking Matron's corns and squeezing Dorothy McAlistair's spots. We would dream up these revolting forfeits in the dorm at night, and then stuff our duvets in our mouths and squeal with horror at the thought of executing them. And to think Rachel had done more than snuggle . . . I drifted out of my reverie and stared at her in disbelief.

'Yes – yes, I remember him,' I whispered.

Rachel laughed. 'You probably fancied him yourself, didn't you, Polly!'

I stared at her in horror, choking down the bile. I shook my head dumbly. 'Er, no, not as such, no.'

'Oh come on, we all fancied at least one of the male teachers. Who did you have your eye on then?'

Now this was perfectly true. It has to be said that most of us girls had formidable crushes on the very few men who flitted in and out of our sheltered lives at school. Monsieur Ferout, French master and ultra-smooth froggy dude, had reputedly received no less than fifty-two valentine cards one year, and I'm ashamed to say mine was amongst them. Clive, the gardener, was constantly finding bunches of half-dead wild flowers placed lovingly in his potting shed, and even Billy, the odd-job boy, had apparently been propositioned behind the guinea-pig hutches by a desperate fifth former, but never, *never* Mr Saunders.

I licked my lips and stared at her glassy-eyed. How could she? 'Oh well, you know, er, no one in particular. I kept an open mind.'

'I bet you did! Kept your options open, eh?' she smiled nastily.

I was about to rise furiously to the bait, when Nick interrupted sarcastically. 'Fascinating though this tale of unrequited schoolgirl passion is, can we get back to the point? You had an affair with this Saunders chappie, then?' he asked Rachel.

'David and I were in love,' she said simply.

I had a bit of trouble taking this concept on board, but somehow managed to turn an incredulous guffaw into a hacking cough. She looked at me suspiciously as I snorted into a hankie.

'How long had it been going on for?' asked Nick.

Rachel stared into the fire. 'About three months, I suppose. It all started when he organised a trip to a concert at the Festival Hall. He put a notice up on the board in the common room, and I was the only one to put my name down. It was all strictly above board, of course, in fact he even press-ganged another girl into coming too, but she didn't turn up. Anyway, because it was just the two of us, we went for something to eat afterwards. Nothing happened then, of course, but we talked for hours and hours, we got on so well. I felt as if he was the first person in my life who'd ever understood me.'

The flames lit up her face as she remembered. For a moment she looked quite pretty, quite transformed. She smiled. 'We just couldn't find out enough about each other, in fact I remember now we very nearly missed the last train back, we were so absorbed. I think we both knew then that this was the start of something. That there was no going back.'

She turned away from the fire and back to us. The soft, dreamy look suddenly disappeared. 'Anyway, that's how it all started. After that, we'd meet in the town whenever I could slip out of school. Our so-called affair was really just an endless and frustrating stream of cups of coffee or walks in the park; all pretty tame, really.'

'But how did you manage to keep it so quiet?' I felt a certain grudging admiration. If I so much as put a toe out of bounds, I was invariably hauled back by the scruff of the neck and severely punished. The idea of conducting a clandestine affair, tame or otherwise, with a member of staff, filled me with horror.

'We were very careful. It meant a hell of a lot to both of us, and we were determined not to be found out. Occasionally we'd get daring and go to an evening concert or a play together, but that was about it. Until of course — well, until we just couldn't bear it any longer, couldn't control it.' She smiled wryly. 'And naturally, that was the one time we were discovered.'

'What — you mean . . . Where were you?' I faltered.

'In bed, of course. Well, not literally, but certainly figuratively.'

I gasped. 'Good grief, you mean you were actually — you know, doing it — when someone . . . Who found you?'

Rachel gave a wry smile. 'Miss Fisher.'

'Miss Fisher!' I gagged on my tonsils. It couldn't have been worse. Miss Fisher, the deputy head, of the razor-sharp tongue, the biting wit and the fine line in sneering sarcasm. Even now, years later, I cringed at the thought of her.

Nick grinned. 'So where were you when she found you, his place or your dorm?'

'Actually, we were in a deserted boat-house by the river,' she turned to me. 'Remember that funny old place by the broken bridge?'

I gulped again and nodded; by now grudging admiration had developed into unreserved hero-worship. The boat-house had been so totally and categorically out of bounds, it was considered dangerous to come within feet of it unless you had an overwhelming desire to be expelled. It was a beautiful old weather-boarded place, surrounded by reeds and bulrushes and flanked by an enormous old weeping willow which wept all over the roof. It was apparently falling down, and its collapse was always said by the staff to be imminent, but countless girls had dreamed of a romantic tryst in there; it was the perfect setting. It was permanently locked, but I imagined 'David' would have had access to a key. I tried to imagine Miss Fisher's face at finding them there.

'Was she furious?'

Rachel grinned. 'Speechless, literally. She appeared in the doorway, a vision in red flannel and rollers, flashing a torch around. We were lying on a pile of rugs in the corner without a stitch on. We just looked at her and she kept opening and shutting her mouth and nothing came out.'

I gaped. 'God, I wish I'd been a fly on the wall. What did she do?'

'Well, of course it was the middle of the night, and anyone with any sense would have left it until the morning, but oh no, she insisted on marching us back to the school and parading us in front of Miss Harper there and then. She telephoned Harpie, and we sat in the study for ages waiting for her to come down, whilst Miss Fisher breathed fire and paced up and down. Eventually, poor old Harpie appeared in her dressing gown looking bleary-eyed and pissed off, and told us to go back to bed, saying she'd deal with it in the morning.'

I grinned. I could imagine our laid-back headmistress being more than a little irritated at being woken up in the middle of the night.

'Anyway, the next morning I filed back in to see her, and after a brief discussion was unceremoniously expelled. Daddy was summoned to take me away.'

I nodded. 'I remember that. Everyone thought he was dragging you out of school for no good reason. We thought it was terribly bad form just before your A-levels.'

'That was the story that was put around to keep you lot off the scent.'

I had to hand it to old Rachel. There was I, thinking I was a real Jack the Lass for organising the occasional cider knees-up in the dorm, and discussing what 'doing it' might be like with my virginal comrades, and grilling Rebecca Crocker over and over again because she'd come close to 'doing it' on a skiing holiday, and all the time Rachel, the quiet, mousy scholar was shagging the life out of one of the teachers in the strictly out-of-bounds boat house. Impressed? I was prostrate at her feet in awe and wonder.

'So what happened to David?' asked Nick.

Rachel looked sad. 'I never saw him again. He wrote to me from a school in Kent where he'd managed to get a position. Evidently Miss Harper had told him that if he left without a fuss his family wouldn't be told.'

'Family?'

'He had a wife and two children,' said Rachel calmly. 'Apparently he told his wife he'd been dismissed due to musical differences with Miss Harper. Ridiculous really. Harpie wouldn't know F sharp from B flat, but anyway, she swallowed the story and off they went to Kent.'

'But why was it all kept so quiet?' asked Nick. 'Surely he should have been hauled over the coals by the board of governors and all that sort of thing, made an example of?'

'Very probably, but you see my father was one of the governors and he had a lot of sway. In his position as a judge he just didn't want the publicity – I mean, you can just see the tabloids, can't you: "Teacher in Love Nest with High Court Judge's Daughter".' Rachel smiled wryly. 'Oh yes, Daddy made sure it was all hushed up.'

'So then what, he packed you off to America?' I asked.

'Yep, Daddy arranged it all. He was terrified I might try

to get in touch with David, which of course I would have done, so he arranged for me to go and stay with friends of his in Boston. I didn't know at the time that I was pregnant, had no idea. For what it's worth, David and I had only slept together that one time, so I really didn't even consider it. Anyway, by the time I'd missed two periods, Adam was well on the scene, both as a shoulder to cry on and – well, as a lover, to take my mind off things. I was just so miserable. I knew I didn't love him, but I allowed myself to go along with it, hoping a steamy affair would cure me of David. Of course it didn't. Anyway, by the time I was obviously pregnant, everyone naturally assumed it was Adam's, including Adam.'

'But couldn't it have been his after all?' asked Nick.

Rachel shook her head. 'Definitely not. I know that for a fact, because my dates worked out exactly to that one night with David. I'm glad too.' Rachel held Jamie close. 'I wanted his child. I wouldn't have wanted Adam's.'

'So as far as everyone else was concerned, Jamie was just a bit earlier than expected?' said Nick

'Exactly. Jamie arrived a month early and I pretended to be as surprised as anyone.'

'And they all believed you?'

'Why shouldn't they? No one knew about David.'

'Except your father,' I said.

'Yes, except Daddy, and I dare say he had his suspicions when he found out I was pregnant; but of course when Jamie arrived with red hair, he promptly breathed a sigh of relief. He'd never met David, so he wasn't to know there was another source.'

Nick straightened up from where he'd been crouching beside her and looked down at her thoughtfully. 'OK fine, that all makes sense, but just tell me one thing, Rachel. When you realised you didn't love Adam, and you wanted to get away and bring Jamie to England, why in heaven's name didn't you tell him he wasn't the father? I know it's brutal, but you could have avoided all this aggro.'

Rachel smiled up at him and shook her head sadly. 'D'you think I didn't try? Of course I did. I told him the day before I got on that plane. We had a fearful row, but he just wouldn't believe me. Then when I got to England I wrote to him, spelling it all out, telling him the whole story about me and David. He still didn't believe it, and he categorically refused to have a blood test, saying it was ridiculous to have to go to such lengths to prove Jamie was his son when it was so palpably obvious. You see, he didn't want to believe it. Yet there must have been a smidgen of doubt in his mind, don't you think? Otherwise, why not do the test?'

'So he just decided to come over here and snatch him back,' said Nick.

Rachel nodded. 'Exactly. He obviously decided not to try to gain access through the courts because he'd have to do a blood test to prove he was the father, so he just planned to grab him. And I knew how single-minded he'd be about it, too. He'd stop at nothing. I'd have spent my whole life looking over my shoulder, always running and hiding and shielding Jamie, never knowing whether he was trailing us or watching us, waiting to snatch him away.'

She stroked Jamie's downy red head, smoothing down his wispy curls. She turned to me. 'You asked me if I felt anything about Adam's death. Well, I do. I feel relief. I feel as if an enormous great boulder has been lifted off my shoulders, because now Jamie and I can relax and try to have a normal life.' She looked at me earnestly. 'You can understand that, can't you? I mean, in my position, you'd feel the same way, wouldn't you?'

It was almost a plea, an entreaty, the first time she'd ever shown a truly vulnerable side, a need to be understood and vindicated − liked, even. I looked at Jamie, asleep in her arms now, traces of milk still on his little pink lips, his head thrown back, one pudgy hand still wrapped around her finger. Yes, I understood. I could never like her, but I understood.

I nodded. 'Yes.'

Rachel gave the tiniest of grateful smiles.

A silence enveloped us all. I looked outside. The window was full of inky black night now. One or two stars were winking away up there. I shivered and turned back to the fire which crackled away in the grate. I stared into the embers.

At length, Rachel spoke. She looked down at her baby. 'Bedtime for you, little boy,' she whispered. 'You've had rather a busy day, one way and another.'

She gathered him up in her arms and slowly got to her feet. Nick picked up his favourite blue blanket, which was lying on the sofa, and draped it over him.

'Sleep well, Jamie,' he said, stroking his hand. 'At least you haven't got the faintest idea what's been going on here.'

Rachel turned to go but, before she got to door, she stopped and turned back to us. 'Oh, I almost forgot,' she said sheepishly. 'I meant to say thank you. Thanks for getting him back, that is.'

Nick nodded and gave a half smile. 'I'd like to say, "It was nothing", but that wouldn't be quite true.'

She smiled briefly and nodded. 'I'll be going back to London first thing in the morning and I won't be troubling any of you ever again. Say goodbye to Tim for me, would you?' With that, she disappeared upstairs.

Chapter Twenty-eight

I sank back on the sofa and shut my eyes, more than a little tired. So it was all over. Adam was dead, and he hadn't even been the father. Perhaps he'd known all along, as Rachel had said. It hadn't stopped him loving Jamie, though, had it? It hadn't stopped him wanting him. And what of Jamie? I wondered which parent he would have been better off with. I wondered what sort of a mother Rachel would turn out to be. How would all this affect the way she brought Jamie up? What would she say to him when he was old enough to ask about his father? Would she tell him the truth, I wondered? Somehow I doubted it.

I opened my eyes and gave myself a little inward shake. What business was it of mine what she told him? It was about time I stopped interfering in other people's lives. The only reason I'd got involved at all in the first place was because I couldn't mind my own business. Well, it was time I learned.

Goodness, what was this, a smidgen of wisdom creeping into my soul? It was more like weariness, actually. And a growing awareness that there were some things that just couldn't be changed, and it was foolish and time-consuming even to try. All I could do was live my own life and forget about everyone else's.

I looked up and saw Nick, in a by now familiar position, standing with his back to me looking out of the window. My heart, from its already sunken position somewhere in my nether regions, plummeted even further down into my boots. The trouble with living my own life, I reflected, was that it categorically refused to go according to plan. Here, for example, was the man who held the key to my future happiness. The man on whom my hopes depended and my dreams pivoted. And what was he doing? He was counting his sheep.

I sighed and got to my feet. Of course. It was time I left. Silly of me to have stayed so long. For a moment I'd almost forgotten I didn't belong here. Another minute more and I'd have been swinging my legs over the arm of the chair, picking up the telly guide, sinking my teeth into an apple, and asking my boyfriend if he could possibly throw an omelette together because I was too knackered to get supper tonight. Wasn't it lucky I remembered my boyfriend was actually engaged to be married to someone else? He was clearly waiting for me to leave, and politely turning his back in order to let me slip away in a seemly fashion. No fuss, Polly, no hysterics, his back seemed to say. What a gent. Well, leave I would. I got up and crept towards the door. Nick swung round as a floorboard creaked.

'Where are you going?'

I froze in mid-creep, like a child playing grandmother's footsteps. 'Oh, er, well home again, actually,' I faltered guiltily. 'You know, because I was actually on my way when all this — when all this happened.'

He stared at me. Then at length he said, 'Polly, you really do amaze me. After all we've just been through — Adam's death, this whole ghastly business — it's had absolutely no effect on you whatsoever, has it? You just carry on as normal, don't you? Pick up where you left off before you were so rudely interrupted by a snatched baby, a distraught mother, a car chase and a dead man. That's about it, isn't it?'

'No, of course not! I'm absolutely shattered by what's

happened, but I've still got to go, haven't I? I mean it doesn't change anything!'

'So what were you going to do – sneak off without saying goodbye again?' He shook his head wearily. 'Go on then, off you go. Back to Harry, no doubt.'

I gaped at him in amazement. At length I found my voice. 'Back to Harry? Don't be ridiculous, of course not!'

He didn't answer, but he gave me a strange, penetrating look before turning back to the window. I stared at his back. For a moment I felt chastened. Guilt-ridden even. Then I bridled. Why? Why should I feel guilty? How dare he? How dare he talk to me like that! I was only going to make things easier for him! Suddenly all guilt and humility left me and I felt my colour rising. I rounded on him, pink with indignation. 'You've got a sodding nerve!' I blurted out.

He turned back, raising his eyebrows. 'Oh? And why's that? For pointing out your propensity to bugger off when the going gets a little tough?'

'A little tough? *A little tough*? You call what happened this morning a little tough?' I squeaked.

'Look, if you're talking about Serena pitching up here, as I said at the time, I'm sorry, but there was nothing I could do about it, I had no idea she was coming. I also said everything would be all right if you could just be patient, but patience isn't in your repertoire, is it, Polly? You like everything to be tickety-boo instantly and if it isn't, if there are one or two slight complications, then you really can't cope, can you? You just wait until my back is turned and sneak off like – like some sort of criminal.'

'How dare you!' I exploded. I marched over to him and prodded him in the chest with my finger. 'How dare you speak to me like that! *You're* the one who goes limping off across the fields to see your sheep the moment your girlfriend arrives on the scene, leaving me at the mercy of her unfortunate personality disorder! *You're* the one who refuses to acknowledge me in her presence and lets her prattle on to me about living here as lady muck of the manor!'

'Now just a minute!' Nick grabbed my finger as I prodded away, but I shook him off, well and truly unstoppable now.

'LET ME FINISH!' I bellowed, punctuating each word with more piercing prods to his chest. 'And *you're* the one who led me to believe you even vaguely fancied me, so that against my better judgement — and totally out of character for me I might say — I allowed myself to submit to some *very* amateur love-making on your part! And all the time — yes, all the time that shameful act was taking place, *you* were thinking how safe you were because of course the *real* love of your life, girl of your dreams, bitch in a million, call her what you will, was waiting patiently for you in London!'

'Polly, wait—'

'Oh yes, you thought it was quite all right to give good old Polly a quick bonk, didn't think there was any question of being found out, did you? Thought knobbing the secretary was an acceptable perk of the job! But you got a bit rattled when the wife-to-be arrived on the scene, didn't you? That was a little inconvenient, wasn't it? And yes, that's what *really* bugs me, if you must know, the fact that you didn't even have the *guts* to tell me you were engaged! And now you have the — the, *nerve* to tell me — to tell me-ee . . .'

I ground to a shuddering halt as I realised my head was in danger of wobbling off my neck. My shoulders were being shaken really quite hard.

'Polly, will you shut up a minute!' Nick was yelling into my face. 'For Christ's sake, shut up!'

I shut, panting with the exertion of stringing so many words together in one go.

Nick stared at me. 'What are you talking about? Wife?

Engaged? What the hell are you banging on about, for Christ's sake?'

'Oh, don't try and pretend!' I spat with renewed vigour, now I'd shaken off his hands and reclaimed my neck and head. 'Don't come the innocent with me. I know all about it, even down to the dear little boat you proposed in. I was even lucky enough to have the dear little ring stuffed up my nose − or down my throat − as she outlined her wedding plans to me, which will of course be carried out just as soon as you've both compared Filofaxes and found a gap in your oh-so-busy schedules.'

Nick stared at me incredulously. His mouth was open but he didn't utter. I stood panting up at him, face flushed, hands clenched, well fired up now and ready to embark on any number of new accusations at a moment's notice. Just let him try and defend himself, just let him try!

At length he ran his hands through his hair and groaned. 'Oh Christ. God, I had no idea!' He shook his head despairingly. 'But I suppose I should have known.'

He turned away and sat down slowly on the arm of the sofa. He looked shattered. All of a sudden I felt as if I were floundering around in the dark again, a feeling I really should have been getting used to, as it was not uncommon these days. This wasn't quite the reaction I'd had in mind.

'What? Known what?'

He looked up at me. 'What she was capable of.' He stood up and took my shoulders again. 'Polly, listen to me. The whole thing is a fabrication.'

I felt more than a little confused. 'A fabri— A what?' For some extraordinary reason a roll of chintzy curtain material sprang to my fuddled mind.

He gave my shoulders a little shake. 'A lie, a load of rubbish, a figment of her imagination. Crap, if you will. I've never asked Serena to marry me, never did, never would, never shall.'

I stared at him in disbelief. 'Are you sure?'

'What d'you mean, am I sure − of course I'm sure! Proposing marriage is not the sort of thing you forget about in a hurry, is it! It's not the sort of thing you run around doing every day!' He sighed and shook his head. 'I suppose I should have guessed she might do something like this . . .'

'So − so what's going on? She's still your girlfriend, but you're not getting married? Or − or she thinks you're getting married, but you're not sure, or − or what?' Any number of alarming permutations ran through my crazed mind.

Nick sighed. 'Oh God, what an idiot I've been.'

I was inclined to agree, but I let it pass, if he would just tell me what was going on. 'Nick, please . . .'

He shook his head. 'She really is quite unbelievable. Quite unbelievable. Sit down, Polly. I think I'd better tell you a little bit about Serena.'

He motioned me into the sofa and I sat, dumbly. Nick perched on the arm. He licked his lips thoughtfully and stared into space somewhere above my head.

'When I first met Serena,' he said slowly, 'I don't mind telling you I was absolutely knocked out by her. I thought she was the most stunningly attractive girl I'd ever seen.' He paused and looked down at me. 'Well, you've got to admit, she's bloody pretty.'

I ground my teeth, grimaced, and admitted it. 'Bloody pretty,' I muttered. The first word was easier than the second.

Nick looked back over my head towards the fire. He narrowed his eyes. 'I remember I was at this ghastly drinks party, hiding in the kitchen nursing a glass of warm champagne and wondering when I could conceivably escape, when she came in to get a drink. She asked me if there was any orange juice because she was driving, and I remember, I could hardly answer. I just gaped and stuttered something about there possibly being some in the fridge, I was so floored by her. Anyway, she found the orange juice and wandered off again, but later on, I was in the bedroom rooting around for my coat, and she came in for hers. We laughed, and whispered something about it being an awful party and how we couldn't wait to leave, and we got chatting. We talked in the bedroom for a bit, and then of course we both walked downstairs together and out into the street. I was about to say goodbye and walk off when I thought better of it. I found myself asking her what she was doing, if she wanted to get something to eat. I couldn't believe it when she said she'd love to.'

'Fast work for a country boy,' I said dryly.

'Well, why not? I didn't have much to lose. If she'd blown me out, it would have hurt my pride, but that would have been about it. Anyway, we went out for dinner, and over the next few weeks I took her out quite a lot, feeling pretty pleased with myself, I might tell you. We'd walk into one restaurant after another, and a million heads would turn and I'd feel about ten feet tall. Pathetic really, but totally intoxicating.'

I could imagine how good they'd look together. I tried not to, but I could imagine.

'I was mad about her,' he went on, 'absolutely infatuated. The whole film-star bit, the looks — everything. I freely admit I fell for the glamour. Anyway, she seemed to feel the same way about me, and before I knew where I was she'd moved in with me.'

'Really? Just like that? How long had you known her?'

'A couple of months, I suppose.'

'Wow. Not long.'

'No, I know, but I really thought this was it. I actually remember thinking this would be for ever.'

My insides knotted a bit at this. 'Go on.' (Quickly, please.) I was anxious to pass over this lovey-dovey phase and move smartly on to the bit where hopefully it all went wrong.

He sighed. 'Anyway, that's when it all started to go wrong.'

Ah, good.

'At first it was fine, we were still in the first flush of – well, call it what you will – love, passion, I don't know. But then, everything calmed down a bit and we got down to the business of living together. You know – give and take, and who squeezes the toothpaste where and who does the washing up and all that sort of thing. It was a complete disaster. It was quite obvious that Serena had never had to think about anybody but herself in her entire life. She'd been spoilt rotten by everyone up to now – her parents, her boyfriends, her friends; she'd never had to do anything for herself or consider anybody else's feelings. Life had just fallen into her lap; she'd got by solely on her good looks and superficial charm. And that's what she was, superficial. Shallow, even.'

He turned his eyes away from the fire and back on to me. 'I'm sorry if this sounds cruel, Polly, but I want to try and explain exactly what she's like.'

'Noo, nooo, not cruel at all!' I shook my head vigorously, lapping it up. The more cruelty the better, as far as I was concerned.

'Well, to begin with I suppose I let her wipe the floor with me. Honestly, I ran around after her like a bloody servant: cooking meals, tidying up after her, taking her clothes to the cleaners, picking her up from rehearsals, dropping her off at the hairdresser's or the beauty salon – it was ridiculous. Then one day I just stopped. Said I was busy and I couldn't take her shopping at Harrods because I had to work. She was absolutely furious, I don't think anyone had ever crossed her before in her entire life. Well, that was the beginning of the end, really. We had a major row and that set the scene for the next few months. We began to argue quite a bit, like every other day, and to be honest, after a few solid weeks of her petulant, spoilt behaviour, I got to the end of my rope. I seriously began to — sounds awful I know — well, to dislike her.'

'Not awful at all,' I murmured. 'Go on.'

'I'd stay at work later and later, partly because I had to, but partly because I couldn't bear the thought of going home. Then when I did get home, she'd go absolutely berserk. She'd usually downed a couple of bottles of wine by then, and she'd fly at me as I came through the door, ranting and raving about how I avoided her and demanding that I spent more time with her.'

'She sounds like the archetypal bored housewife.'

Nick shrugged. 'Perhaps that's it, perhaps she just didn't have enough to do. Actresses spend a hell of a lot of time "resting" as they call it. Anyway, she'd fly into the most incredible rages, throwing things round the room, cutting my clothes up, chucking the crockery out of the window, and then she'd throw herself on the bed sobbing violently, so I'd have to comfort her and tell her everything was all right, although I was pretty damn certain everything wasn't all right at all. I tell you, it was really getting me down.'

I was surprised. This didn't fit in with my image of the icy-cool, controlled Serena. I frowned. 'But she's so — so cool when you meet her.'

'I know, but remember she's an actress, she can be whoever she wants to be. In reality she's completely mixed up. You saw her at lunch today: she just suddenly snaps and goes bananas.'

'She sounds like a bit of a head-case.'

Nick sighed and shook his head. 'Either that or just incredibly theatrical, I was never really sure. She's so tenacious, too; gets her teeth into something and just won't let go. It was when she started ringing me all day at the agency — you wouldn't have noticed because she had my private number — that's when I knew I had to do something. If I told her I was in a meeting, which I usually was, she'd just ring again two minutes later. It was incredibly embarrassing with clients sitting there listening. Then she started turning up out of the blue to drag me out to lunch.'

'I remember that, Pippa and I were amazed when you turned down a famous film star, a convertible Mercedes and lunch at Bibendum, all in the space of one lunch hour.'

'Well, now you know why.'

'Why didn't you just finish it? Tell her it was over?'

Nick groaned. 'I tried, I tried to end it loads of times, but she just wouldn't listen and she categorically refused to leave the flat. I hadn't the heart to physically throw her out and change the locks, although I had the feeling it would probably come to that one day. The thing is, Polly, she knew it was over months ago but she just couldn't face it. I'm not even convinced she was in love with me, I think she just couldn't bear being dropped.'

I was amazed. 'You mean she just wouldn't go? Even though you said it was over?'

'She just refused. In the end I told her I was going to Cornwall, and I expected her to be gone by the time I got back.'

'That was just before you came down here with me.'

'That's right, the day before. I have to say I didn't think even Serena would have the gall to follow me, and when she turned up I was absolutely flabbergasted. I wanted to keep her from finding out about you and me, because for one thing I didn't want to rub her nose in it, and I also had a shrewd suspicion she'd tear your hair out. It would seem to her as if I'd jumped straight from her bed to yours in the space of a few days, even though, if the truth be told, Serena and I were washed up a long time ago and I'd felt strongly about you for . . . Well, that's another story.'

He broke off here and pulled at a thread in his jumper. I gulped hard and somehow overcame a burning desire to

498

say — oh please, *please* let's get on to the other story! Much as I was enjoying this one, I had an inkling the other one, with me as the heroine, was going to be even better. I was jolly glad he'd asked me to sit down now: my knees were shaking so much from ill-concealed excitement that I doubted if they'd have supported me. I was also dying for a cigarette, but I had an idea that this perhaps wasn't the moment for ashtray breath.

He abandoned his jumper and looked down at me. 'She obviously spun the phantom engagement story when I was out with Larry.'

'Yes, that's right, you were seeing to the sheep. Oh, but hang on,' I thought back, 'what about the ring?'

'What ring?'

'The little green one.'

'Oh that! Yes I did give her that, about two weeks after I'd met her, at the height of my infatuation. It was an impulse buy, I saw it in an antique shop. It reminded me of her eyes.'

'That's what she said,' I said slowly, as everything began to fall into place. 'So — so where is she now?' I looked around nervously, half expecting her to pop up from behind the sofa, machete in hand.

'She's gone. When I found out you'd disappeared, I was livid. I couldn't continue the charade of pretending you meant nothing to me, and I couldn't bear to have her in the house anymore. I went berserk. No more softly-softly, let's tiptoe round Serena's feelings. I let her have it. Should have done it ages ago, it was bloody effective, the only language she understands. And, would you believe it, just as I was getting to the well-worn bit about never wanting to see her again as long as I lived, she gave me a resounding slap round the face, spat in my eye, told me I was a complete and utter jerk and she didn't know what she'd seen in me in the first place. Then she jumped into her Porsche and roared back off to London. Off to snare some other poor bastard, no doubt.'

Relief flooded over me. She'd gone. Thank Christ for that. I leaned back in the cushions. Bliss. Utter bliss. He wasn't going to marry her, he didn't even love her, by all accounts he didn't even like her. And surely, surely he'd more or less hinted that − well, that he liked me quite a lot, hadn't he?

I was suddenly very aware of his presence. He was perched on the arm of the sofa, his leg warm against my arm, close to me. I could feel his eyes upon me, melting over my face. I leaned my head back, half closed my eyes, and parted my lips very slightly. This was surely our moment. The most monumental touchy-feely moment of all time. I could feel the excitement tingling all over me, right down to my toenails. I waited in an ecstasy of anticipation. I waited for what seemed like an inordinate length of time. Nothing seemed to be happening. Eventually I couldn't keep the half closed eyes bit going any longer, my eyelashes were beginning to bat maniacally. I opened them.

He was watching me. 'Polly?'

Jesus. He wasn't looking remotely touchy-feely. 'Er, yes?'

'What about Harry?'

I jumped. 'What about him?'

'Well . . .' He hesitated. 'I need to know how you feel about him. I mean, you were pretty hung up on him in London and − well, I'm almost sure he got in touch with you down here.'

I sat bolt upright. 'How did you know that? Did you hear me on the phone to him?'

He looked uncomfortable. 'No, no I, er, I heard Serena on the phone to him.'

'Serena?'

'Yes, she knows him, you know.'

'Yes, I know, but why on earth would she be ringing him from down here?'

Nick shifted about a bit on the arm of the sofa. 'Well, she asked him to give you a ring.'

'SHE WHAT!'

'She asked him to — well, to lure you back to London. Said you were in her way down here — I heard it all, I was in the bathroom and she was using the phone in my bedroom. He seemed pretty flattered that she'd called him — most people are, of course. From what I could gather, he said he'd do what he could. I'm sorry, Polly, I wouldn't have told you, only I need to know if that's why you went.'

'Nick, what are you saying! Do you mean to tell me Serena actually *asked* Harry to ring up and pretend he was missing me and that he still loved me and all that crap about being the only girl he'd ever — *bloody hell*! Is that what you're saying?'

'I know, I know it's a little hard to believe, but you see she's quite capable—'

'Hard to believe! Hard to believe! It's bloody monstrous! Bloody hell! I mean, who does she think she is? Did she really think she'd get away with it? I mean, did she really think I'd go panting off back to London to see him! Christ!'

I was seething. Seething with fury at her audacity and seething also with hurt pride. So it had all been a ruse, a hoax to get me out of the way! Thank God I hadn't fallen for it.

'So you didn't,' said Nick.

'Didn't what?'

'Go panting off back to London to see him.'

I stared at him, incredulous. 'No, of course not! I told him to get stuffed, if you must know.'

Nick looked relieved. 'Oh! Oh good. Sorry, I had to ask. You see, I knew you'd dashed off out of the blue, and I was pretty sure it was because of Serena, but on the other hand I knew Harry had probably spoken to you, and I wasn't sure — well, to be honest, Polly, I wasn't entirely sure that you weren't still in love with him. And if you were, I wasn't sure that I could handle it.' He looked at me anxiously. 'You're not still in love with him, are you? I hate to be pushy, but I just sort of need to know.'

I looked up at his kind, honest face, his brown eyes searching mine, looking for clues. I smiled. All my anger drifted away. What did it matter? What did Harry matter, what did Serena matter? They were the losers, after all. The winners were sitting right here. My smile seemed to be spreading all over my body, I was positively wreathed in smiles. I felt unbelievably happy. I wanted him to kiss me quite badly now, but at the same time I felt something even more overwhelming than desire sweeping over me.

'No, I'm not in love with him,' I said softly. The feeling seemed to be getting stronger and stronger, surging from my heart, through my body, until eventually it found its way to my lips. 'Actually, I'm in love with you.'

His anxious look disappeared, his face seemed to clear, and he smiled gently. He leaned down, and the kiss that I'd been longing for dropped onto my mouth at last, soft and full.

'I'm surprised,' he murmured at length.

'Why?' I felt alarmed. Oh horrors, what had I done now? Scared him off already?

He slid off the arm of the sofa and knelt down in front of me, his arms around me felt huge and warm and strong. My heart thumped madly as he kissed me on the neck, working his way slowly and beautifully round to my ear. 'Because you don't strike me as the sort of girl who would fall for an amateur love-maker.'

I gasped and sat bold upright, gripping his shoulders hard. 'Oh no, you don't understand!' I pleaded earnestly into his face. 'I just said that to make you angry! I didn't mean it, I — I just said it to get my own back! I didn't think you were amateur at all, in fact I thought — I still think — you're, you're a true professional! Oh no! I mean, not in any awful sense of having been around, but you know, you know what to do and — oh God, I just think you're wonderful!'

He threw back his head and roared with laughter, holding me tightly against him. 'Oh God,' he gasped at length, 'I must say I think you're pretty wonderful too, Polly, but I've never known anyone with quite the propensity to get themselves in such a comprehensive mess!'

I grinned ruefully. 'Well, this is one comprehensive mess I don't mind in the least.'

'I agree,' he said softly. 'In fact, I don't mind it at all, because I believe I'm in love with you too.'

I gasped, which was lucky really, because it meant I took in a great lungful of air which kept me going as he kissed the breath out of me. When we surfaced, moments later, we clung to each other, and I could hear our hearts racing away in tandem. His breath was coming in fast and furious bursts, and I could almost see his ear flapping in the breeze as I hurricaned into his. Love, lust, excitement, and God knows what else, were all contriving to get the better of our breathing apparatuses.

'Now where were we,' he whispered, as he manoeuvred me skilfully down on to the Persian rug, deftly immobilising me beneath him, 'before we were so rudely interrupted some time earlier this morning?'

My tummy, furious at having missed at least three meals by now, rumbled ominously as I lay back on the rug. We giggled. I reached up and took his face in my hands, drawing it down towards me.

'You were making toast,' I murmured.

'I've got other plans now,' he murmured back.

Going Too Far

Chapter One

'...so if everyone would just keep their seats for a moment,' boomed the voice over the loudspeaker, 'Mrs Penhalligan will present the prizes for the best-turned-out pony and rider.'

There was a faint ripple of applause and Nick nudged me hard in the ribs. 'Go on,' he whispered, 'you're on!'

'Eh? What?' I looked around. People seemed to be nodding and smiling at me encouragingly. Oh Lord, was this it, was this me? I'd been miles away, actually, at a different, rather grander horse show. The Horse of the Year Show, in fact. Yes, there I'd been in the middle of the great Wembley Arena, pinning a red rosette on to Harvey Smith's mount, smiling graciously as I presented him with a huge silver cup, the applause of the vast stadium ringing in my ears, when all of a sudden here I was being hauled out of my reverie and on to my feet by my husband.

'Go on!' he urged.

'B-but, where do I go?' I blustered. 'Where's my hat?'

'You're sitting on it!'

'Oh no!' I retrieved the flower-strewn concoction from under my bottom and punched out the crown, feeling flustered and confused. The applause from the tiny Helston Gymkhana crowd was beginning to sound a little tired.

1

'For God's sake, get going,' hissed Nick, propelling me towards the white tape of the collecting ring. 'Everyone's waiting!'

'But which one do I give the cup to?' I hissed back, desperately scrambling around to find my shoes which I'd kicked off in the heat and which now seemed to be under everyone else's seat but my own.

'The bay gelding on the end, you idiot,' he muttered. 'It's already been judged, all you have to do is present the prizes!'

He yanked up the white tape and shoved me under. Still cramming my hot, swollen feet into shoes I'd bought a size too small on the grounds that they might make my feet look petite, I shot underneath it, losing my hat again on the way. I grabbed it, rammed it down hard on my head and turned back.

'Yes, but what the hell is a bay gelding when it's at—'

'Ah, Mrs Penhalligan,' purred an extremely agitated voice in my ear as my arm was seized in a vicelike grip. 'Come along, my dear, we've been looking everywhere for you!'

The grip on my arm tightened as I was frogmarched away by a very determined gentleman who'd materialised at my left elbow. He was dressed from head to toe in Harris tweed and came complete with white whiskers, a brown felt hat and a large red 'official' badge on his left lapel. We appeared to be heading towards a line of horses in the middle of the ring.

'Just give out the rosettes, my dear, the riders will pin them on to the bridles themselves,' he murmured, hastily thrusting four rosettes and a cup into my hands. 'Start at one end of the line and move slowly along to the other. Off you go now!'

'Er, yes, but which end of the line do I—'

'Marvellous,' he muttered, 'marvellous result for Clarissa!' and with that he burst into noisy applause and scurried back into the crowd.

I clutched the rosettes. Clarissa? Who the devil was Clarissa? I peered at the fiercely intimidating quartet of fourteen-year-old pigtailed girls astride their fat little ponies. They looked like something out of a St Trinian's film and could all quite easily be Clarissas. I took a tentative step in their general direction and smiled nervously, peering intently at their grim little faces. Totally impassive, except – hang on, suddenly I noticed that something akin to a reaction was flickering on the face of the one at the far end. Surely she was – yes, she was nodding and smiling at me in an encouraging sort of way. That must be Clarissa!

I took a deep breath and marched smartly over. Well, I thought as I got closer and noticed her bright-green eye shadow, at least this one didn't look like her horse for a change, and she was really rather nicely turned out, which, after all, was the whole point of the competition, wasn't it? Instead of having one of those boring black jackets with the velvet collars, she had on a natty tweed affair. Admittedly it was a bit on the big side and had patches on the elbows, but she'd rolled the sleeves up for a touch of trendiness, rather like I do when I borrow Nick's.

I gave her a dazzling smile and handed over the red rosette, even going so far as to pat her beast's neck. I instantly wished I hadn't, as it was disgustingly hot and sweaty.

'Well done,' I beamed, wiping my wet hand on my skirt, 'jolly *jolly* well done.' I was pretty sure that 'jolly' was a word that was bandied about with abandon in horsy circles. 'Frightfully well turned out!'

'Ta!'

She seized the red rosette in a twinkling and her eyes lit up with delight.

I frowned. Ta! Clarissa? Surely not. Within another twinkling she'd rammed the rosette on to her pony's bridle and whisked the cup out of my hands, and before you could say 'congratulations' she was standing up in her stirrups, waving both arms delightedly to her family in the crowd. At least, I thought, turning to look, I *assumed* it was her family. There certainly seemed to be an awful lot of them, and they seemed equally ecstatic, standing up in their seats and doing an extravagant kind of Mexican wave in response.

Ah well, I thought, smiling benignly at Clarissa, much as I'd done to Harvey, what it is to make people happy. I wafted gracefully along the line to present the second prize to a girl who looked equally chuffed.

'I say, *frightfully* well done,' I brayed, well into my horsy stride now. 'Terribly well turned out and what a *delightful* pony you've—' Suddenly I stopped in mid-bray as an anguished wail broke out from the other end of the line.

'That's not fair!' bawled a blonde with heavy braces on her teeth, astride a fat brown pony. 'She's given it to Kimberly and they said I was the best! Why did Kimberly get the cup, Mummy, it's not fair!' and she promptly burst into floods of very noisy tears.

'Well, it's too late now, innit?' snapped back the girl at

my end who I now saw was clearly very much a Kimberly and not a Clarissa. 'I've got it now 'cos the judge gave it to me, didn't you?' she demanded, giving me a defiant stare and clinging like billyo to the cup. Oh crikey.

'Er, oh dear,' I muttered, feeling myself flushing deep puce. 'I'm most awfully sorry, I seem to have made a bit of a—'

'You give that cup back right now, Kimberly Masters!' boomed a dragon's voice behind me, making me jump out of my skin. 'Give it straight back to my Clarissa! She won that cup and you know it, now hand it over!'

I turned to see an enormous tweedy woman, purple in the face with fury and with a matching purple hat squashed on to her Grecian 2000 curls, emerging from the crowd. She reached us in a matter of giant strides and bore down on the quite undaunted Kimberly, quivering with rage and shaking her fist in her face.

'Go on, hand it over right now!'

'Shan't,' pouted Kimberly, hugging the silver.

'You jolly well will, my girl, you see if I don't come and make you! And as for you,' she stormed, suddenly rounding on me, 'my Clarissa was far and away the best-turned-out gel here, any fool can see that, you ought to be sacked! Handing out cups to all and sundry – just look at the state of this one!' she cried, indicating the petulant Kimberly. 'Her jacket's a disgrace, a hand-me-down if ever I saw one, and she hacked six miles to get here from the council estate so her pony's up to his hocks in mud and sweating like a pig, *and* she hasn't even plaited his mane. Best turned out? She couldn't win a fancy-dress prize at a cattle market! You give that cup back right now, Kimberly Masters, or I'll damn well come and take it from you!'

'You'll do nothing of the bleedin' kind, Daphne 'Eggerty!' roared another, equally furious, but decidedly less fruity female voice. 'My Kimberly won that fair and square and the judge's decision is final, in't that right?' demanded an angry peroxide-blonde woman in a lime-green shell suit who had joined the happy gathering. I recognised her as one of the enthusiastic Mexican wavers.

'Er, yes, you're quite right,' I quavered nervously. 'Usually the judge's decision *is* final, but you see, I'm not actually here in, um, a judgemental capacity, I'm just sort of presenting the prizes.' I inched nervously away from these warring mothers. 'But you're right,' I added, nodding enthusiastically as the tweedy woman's face darkened, 'there certainly seems to have been some sort of a mix-up here, all my fault, I'm sure. Er, maybe if I took all the rosettes back and started again, we could—'

'No bleedin' way!' screeched Lime-green Shell Suit, waving a bright-pink fingernail in my face. 'No way! My Kimberly won that cup and we're gonna get her name put on it and 'ave it on the sideboard in the lounge and that's that!'

'Oh! Oh well, yes, of course, I'm sure it would look lovely but – oh look! Here's one of the judges! We'll let him sort it out, shall we?'

It was with intense relief that I caught sight of the official who was bustling furiously over. About time too, I thought, beginning to feel decidedly damp under the arms.

'Now now, ladies,' he soothed, as he eased his way between the irate mothers and stroked his moustache nervously, 'no need to get excited. I'm quite certain we can sort this out. I think perhaps Mrs Penhalligan got just a

6

teeny bit confused, so perhaps if we started again, and maybe if I were to present the prizes we could—'

'Oh, what an absolutely marvellous idea,' I breathed, hastily thrusting the remaining rosettes into his hands, 'yes, terrific! If you would be so kind as to take over,' I was already scuttling backwards, 'that would be marvellous, because you see, apart from anything else,' I clutched my head dramatically, 'I've got the most appalling migraine coming on. Must be the heat.' I fanned my face energetically. 'Bye then, and so sorry about the mix-up, all my fault I'm sure, thanks ever-so!'

With that I rammed my hat firmly down over my by now puce face, put my head down and hastened towards the edge of the ring and the gawping crowd beyond. I ducked underneath the white tape and without looking left or right, but aware that a million eyes were upon me, scurried through the murmuring masses which parted for me like the Red Sea. Scarlet with shame, I didn't even have the nerve to look around for Nick, but just headed doggedly for the exit gate. What a nightmare, what a complete and utter nightmare, just get me out of here!

I flew through the gate, rounded the corner and was just scampering off down the lane in the direction of home and sanctuary when I heard footsteps pounding along behind me. I dared not look round – please God, don't let it be one of the mothers, please God! A moment later Nick drew level with me and grabbed me by the arm.

'Hey, slow down, will you,' he panted between bouts of convulsive laughter. 'Oh God, Polly, you've no idea the mayhem you've caused back there, you really are unbelievable!' He clutched his stomach, doubled up with laughter. I shook him off and marched on down the lane.

'Oh yes, go ahead, laugh,' I snapped, feeling a bit of eye water coming on, 'very funny, I'm sure, but it's not you that's going to be the laughing stock of the village for the next six months, is it?'

'Oh, don't be silly, no one's going to laugh at you,' he said, trotting to keep up with me and trying hard to keep a straight face. 'It was just a simple mistake, that's all. I mean, let's face it, anyone could have thought that Kimberly Masters, up to her eyeballs in mud and mascara and in an old tweed jacket that clearly belonged to her father, was the best-turned-out pony and rider, anyone, Polly!' More helpless mirth followed this unkind observation.

'Well, she obviously came fourth, didn't she?' I snapped. 'I mean, she can't have been that bad!'

'There were only four riders in the competition, Poll,' he spluttered. 'She came last, actually.'

'Well, how was I supposed to know who to give the blasted cup to? I mean, I *asked* you, didn't I? Fat lot of good you were.'

'I said the bay gelding, remember? The bay gelding, not the black mare!'

'And just what exactly is a bay gelding? Eh? I mean, why didn't you say the blonde girl on the end with a mouth full of wire?'

'Bay is brown and gelding means it's had its balls off, you must know that by now!'

'No, I don't, actually,' I gulped, grabbing my beastly hat as it flew off towards a ditch, 'and anyway, what was I supposed to do, crawl around on all fours checking out its genital arrangement or something? What a ridiculous way to describe an animal! You wouldn't describe a man as having brown hair and being circumcised, would you?'

'Not quite the same thing, Poll,' chortled Nick, who was clearly finding this whole affair highly amusing. 'It's a bit more drastic than being circumcised – hey, slow down, will you, and stop sulking. It doesn't matter, everyone thought it was hysterically funny. We haven't had a good row in the county for ages. Those two families will be at each other's throats for the next ten years now, it livens things up no end!'

I sighed gloomily but slowed down a bit. 'And trust me to be the one to liven things up,' I said, kicking a pebble viciously. 'Good old Polly, you can always rely on her to cock things up and give everyone a good laugh. Why can't I ever get anything right in this blasted village?'

Nick grinned, and put his arm round me as we walked along. 'Getting the Helston Gymkhana prizes muddled up is not exactly the end of the world, you know.' He gave my shoulder a squeeze.

'I know,' I said ruefully, 'but all the same, I wish I was a bit more . . .' I bit my lip and gazed wistfully over the hedge to the field beyond us.

'What?'

'Well, you know, a bit more, sort of . . . county. And capable. I mean, don't you ever wish that you'd married someone with a name like Lucinda Raffetty-Bagshot or – or Camilla Ponsonby-Bunkup? Someone who knew her hocks from her elbows and could ride to hounds with one hand, milk a cow with the other, and build a dry-stone wall with her eyes shut?'

Nick pulled me abruptly to a halt in the middle of the road.

'What d'you mean?'

'Well, you know, I'm not exactly country-house material, am I? Don't you ever think you'd have been better off with one of Daphne Heggerty's girls, for instance?'

'What, you think perhaps the oldest one might have suited me, do you? Henrietta with the buck teeth who sprays you with water every time she opens her mouth? Or perhaps the next one down, Matilda, isn't it, whose voice has been known to smash glasses at dinner parties? God, I'd run a mile from girls like that, you know I would, they frighten the pants off me. You're all I've ever wanted, Poll, and don't pretend you don't know it.'

I gazed up at him and gulped. Yes, I thought, as I looked into his serious dark-brown eyes, yes I *did* know it, but by God it was nice to be reminded now and again, especially by this most taciturn and undemonstrative of husbands. Talk about an uncharacteristic display of affection. My eyes watered briefly, but this time it was nothing to do with cocking up the prizegiving. I gave him a watery smile.

'You're all I've ever wanted too, you know,' I whispered.

'You're so unoriginal, aren't you?' he muttered as he bent down to kiss me. 'Can't you even think of your own sweet nothings? D'you have to nick mine all the time?'

I giggled. 'What d'you mean, "all the time"? They only occur about once in a blue moon or when England win a test match, which is even less.'

'Well, I don't want to overdo it, got to be economical with my pleasantries, you know. It wouldn't do to let you get a big head, got to keep you on your toes!'

Suddenly a speeding car turned the corner and came hurtling towards us, nearly knocking us flying as we stood laughing and hugging in the middle of the lane.

'Look out!' yelled Nick, as he pulled me on to the grass verge.

'OUT OF THE WAY!' roared an irate Daphne Heggerty as she thundered towards us in her open-topped Range Rover, grey curls blowing in the wind and a horse box rattling around behind her. 'Stop bloody snogging and get out of the road!'

We flattened ourselves into the hedge as she roared past, leaning heavily on her horn. She was still purple with fury and a boot-faced Clarissa was sitting beside her, totally devoid of a red rosette or a silver cup, I noticed. So Lime-green Shell Suit had won the day after all.

'Try brushing up on your prizegiving rather than your sexual prowess!' was her parting shot to us as she flew over the brow of the hill and out of sight. The horse box nearly took off as it bounced around behind her, a surprised-looking pony nodding out of the back. We watched her go and giggled.

'She just can't believe Clarissa hasn't won the cup for the fourth year running, can she?' said Nick with a grin. 'Still, she's given me a marvellous idea. Come on!'

He seized my hand and pulled me towards the stile in the hedge. We climbed over into the field and he hurried me along, down towards the copse that marked the very edge of our land by the Helford River.

'Where are we going?' I panted, hobbling in my heels and rather unused to so much exertion.

'For a walk, and then perhaps a rest. It is, after all, a very hot afternoon, isn't it? Don't you think a little relaxation is in order? And then, as Daphne said, there's our prowess to brush up on, what d'you think?' He grinned and squeezed my hand.

11

I laughed, suddenly feeling decidedly happy. As I hobbled along I marvelled at how quickly and dramatically my moods could change. Odd, wasn't it, how one minute I could quite cheerfully slit my throat and the next I could skip happily through a meadow with my husband, on my way to an alfresco assignation?

We made our way through the long spring grass, already lush and sprinkled with cow parsley, across to the valley on the opposite side of the field, and beyond that to the gravel path that led to the river. We wound our way down, hand in hand, and reached the little copse that edged the bank. It was cool and secluded and we lay down on the mossy grass together with a sigh.

'A siesta?' I muttered, as Nick's arm curled around me.

'Absolutely,' agreed Nick, 'or rather,' he added with a smile, as he removed my crushed hat from my head and tossed it into the river, 'what I like to call a siesta *complet*.'

Chapter Two

The next morning I opened my eyes and lay in bed, listening to the birds singing outside my window and watching as a shaft of sunlight fell in a small bright square on my duvet cover. I stretched out a hand to check if Nick was beside me. He wasn't, of course, been up for hours no doubt, but I always liked to check.

I languished there for a while, thinking back to the events of the previous day. I smiled. So I'd mucked up the prizegiving, so what? What did a piffling little thing like a prizegiving matter when I had the most unpredictably sexy husband in the world? When was the last time Daphne Heggerty was seduced by her old man in a secluded copse down by the river bank, eh?

I swung my legs over the side of the bed and grinned to myself as I wandered down to the kitchen in search of calories. The sunlight was streaming in through the kitchen windows. I pushed open the back door, stuck my head out and was immediately ambushed by the sweet Cornish air. I inhaled deeply, held it a moment, then let it out with a contented sigh. Ahhh ... pure nectar. You don't get air like that in London, you know, not much carbon monoxide in that little lungful. Someone really ought to bottle it and send it up to the poor old townies to waft over their cornflakes. I stuck my chest out and took another bracing snort, but it was a snort too far; my twenty-a-day lungs objected wildly to this sudden onslaught of purity and I had a major coughing fit. Gasping and wheezing, I reached hastily for my cigarettes on the Welsh dresser, desperate for my more usual morning fix.

With fumbling fingers I lit the first of many over the gas ring and predictably singed my fringe at the same time. When I'd pulled all the burned bits out and sworn sufficiently, I tugged my T-shirt-cum-nightie down over my bottom and settled down on the back doorstep, determined to enrich at least one of my senses. It wasn't difficult. I might have comprehensively fouled up the smell of the morning air with burned hair and low-to-middle-tar tobacco, but nothing could foul up the perfect pastoral scene that greeted my eyes. As I rested my chin on my knees and gazed out at the patchwork of fields and woods in the distance, I blew smoke rings in the hazy blue air and counted my seemingly endless blessings.

You're a lucky girl, Polly Penhalligan, I told myself sternly, a very lucky girl indeed, and don't you forget it – just look at this place! The sweeping, majestic lawn, the meadow beyond dotted with sheep and spring lambs, and even further away – I squinted my rather myopic eyes – the glassy Helford River shimmering in the distance. Magic. And here you sit, on this well-worn manor-house step, mistress of all you survey. I frowned and tapped some ash on to the grass. Well, no, all right, perhaps not the river, perhaps I wasn't mistress of that – I had a feeling, English laws being what they were, that that probably belonged to everyone – but certainly, this particular *view* of it was mine, wasn't it?

I leaned back on the door frame happily, then frowned again. Try not to be too smug, Polly, it's not very attractive. But then again, I mused, plucking at a daisy, it was so terribly hard *not* to be smug. And it wasn't as if I didn't appreciate it all – God no, on the contrary, it still made my eyes boggle just to think about it. I let them boggle quietly for a moment as I sat and quietly savoured the joys of being Mrs Nicholas Penhalligan.

I smiled. It had, let's face it, been pretty convenient of me to fall in love with a man who owned quite a sizeable chunk of Cornwall, hadn't it? Not that I'd have minded if he'd been a pauper or anything, an estate agent even – Lord no, I'd have had him anyway, he was my idea of heaven with or without the lucrative trappings, but it did somewhat *cushion* life, didn't it? It was, shall we say, a nice little bonus, to get not only a handsome (very), intelligent (screamingly), sensitive (sometimes), loving (at unpredictable moments like yesterday) husband, but also Trewarren House and a thousand acres of Cornish countryside thrown into the matrimonial contract just for good measure.

Ah yes, the countryside. I sighed and stretched my legs out into the dewy grass, aware that there was no holding the smugness now. It really was such bliss. How could I ever have been happy in London? God, the noise, the traffic, the pollution, the crime! Whereas down here, well, none of that, and all the good things were just so – well, so *abundant*, weren't they? Look at that grass, for instance – I tugged at a clump with my toes – have you ever seen such luxuriant growth? My eye snagged suddenly on my bare legs, and I frowned and tucked them up beneath me. Well, yes, OK, there was some pretty luxuriant growth on those too, and perhaps they were a trifle fatter than they'd been in the past, but what did it matter? I wasn't about to pour them into ten-denier tights and excruciatingly uncomfortable four-inch heels and totter off to work for my living, was I? No, I was simply going to squeeze them into my oldest jeans and take a leisurely stroll round the farm. When I felt up to it, of course, in an hour or so perhaps. No rush.

I rested my head lazily against the door frame, feeling the sun on my face. Yes, in an hour or so I'd probably amble off and check out the cow sheds, pass the time of day with the farm hands, chew on a straw, lean on a gate, that kind of thing – nothing too taxing for a Monday. Then I might pick a few flowers for the house and ask Mrs Bradshaw, my daily, to arrange them attractively in a crystal vase, and then when Pippa arrived I'd pretend I'd done them myself and – Christ! I sat bolt upright with a jolt. Pippa! I'd almost forgotten she was coming – what time had she said? Mid-morning? I turned round and craned my neck to see the kitchen clock. Ten-thirty. Phew, relax, Polly, bags of time. Mid-morning was about one o'clock in ad-man speak, she wouldn't be here for ages.

I shook my head and sighed. Poor Pippa, it would be lovely to see her again, but what a shame it wasn't a purely social call, what a shame she was down here on business. Couldn't stop long, she'd said, too much to do. Looking for a location, she'd said, to film yet another grotty commercial, no doubt. I plucked a dandelion and frowned, twirling it in my fingers like a parasol. Yes, poor old Pippa, still stuck in the ad-racket. When I'd bailed out two years ago to marry Nick, the Penhalligan part of Penhalligan and

Waters, Pippa had wrung her hands in dismay, claiming the typing pool would never be quite the same without the other half of the dastardly secretarial duo. She'd stuck it out solo for a bit, but when Nick finally sold his half of the agency to Waters and we decamped down here to his farm on a permanent basis, Pippa had decided that that was definitely the moment to throw in the Tipp-Ex and go.

And off she'd gone, surprisingly – considering her secretarial background of answering the telephone only on the twentieth ring, reading *Harpers & Queen* whilst typing memos and only taking a letter when severely bullied into it – to become really quite something of a high-flier in a film production company.

She raved about it of course, but then she would. It sounded like bloody hard work to me. Whenever I rang her for a two-hour long-distance gossip she always seemed to be dashing off to a shoot or a meeting or some such other ghastly corporate event. It made her tetchy too – why, I remember once I'd had to drag her out of a meeting to ask her something absolutely crucial – like whether I should pick out the pink or the green in the drawing-room curtains when I re-covered the cushions – and she'd been absolutely livid.

'Polly, have you seriously dragged me out of that presentation to ask me about your sodding cushions?' she'd hissed down the phone. Most huffy, and quite unlike her usual do-the-bare-minimum-and-piss-off-on-the-dot-of-five-thirty self.

I bit my lip thoughtfully as I twiddled my toes in the long grass. I did hope she wasn't turning into a career girl or something dreadful. Work really was so terribly overrated. What she needed, of course, was a husband, preferably a

17

rich one. I'd tackle her about it when she arrived, find out more about this chap she'd been seeing, Josh, or something. She'd gone awfully coy about her love life recently and I suspected it was going downhill fast.

Still, I mused, as I reached up to the shelf by the back door and flicked the biscuit tin down in a practised manner, I really ought to get dressed before she arrived or she'd be under the mistaken impression that all I did as a married woman was sit around in my nightie eating biscuits when nothing, actually, could be further from the truth.

I prised the lid open eagerly and my hand hovered nervously as I braced myself for the biggest decision of the day. I dithered. Hobnob or WI flapjack? I mustn't be greedy, and to have both would be just that. In the end I plumped for one of the larger flapjacks and wondered, as I masticated idly, just how long it actually took to get to one's hips. Were we talking hours? Days? Weeks? Or was it, in fact, almost instantaneous? I glanced down thoughtfully, but not too censoriously, at my increasingly generous hip, bottom and thigh lines. Something really had to be done about all that. Tomorrow. Yes, tomorrow I'd start a new regime. I'd go into Helston and buy some bigger clothes. I sighed. I did what I could with leggings and baggy jumpers of course, I'm nothing if not imaginative, but there was no denying the fact that two years of doing little more than reaching for the biscuit tin was beginning to take its toll on my sartorial style.

Yes, it was two years now since Nick and I had finally, and blissfully, tied the knot in that heavenly little church in Manaccan. Clutching my posy of orange blossom and white lilies I'd floated up the aisle in a sea of raw silk, followed by a flurry of darling little bridesmaids whom I'd never seen in my life before. In a state of pre-match nerves I'd sobbed to Mummy that I simply must have some tiddly attendants and why the hell didn't I have any handy nephews and nieces we could wheel out like everyone else did, so that finally in desperation I think she'd resorted to Central Casting, or an agency or something. Anyway, they'd all looked divine and the whole thing had gone off tremendously smoothly and everyone said it hadn't mattered a bit that I'd passed out cold on the wedding cake just as Nick and I had been about to cut it. I'd obviously slightly misjudged the amount of champagne needed to steady my nerves and numbed them instead, but as I said, it hadn't mattered, and Nick had just been thankful he hadn't cut my head off with the bogus regimental sword Mummy had also rustled up for the occasion. The cake had been surreptitiously scraped off the floor straight on to plates, my dress had sponged beautifully and I'd come round in an alcoholic haze, headdress askew, just in time to articulate my goodbyes to a few remaining guests before being whisked away to the most romantic honeymoon imaginable in Antigua.

I helped myself to a Hobnob and settled down to bask in the memory of that idyllic little hotel on the sun-drenched beach, where the only minor inconveniences had been the wrong socket for my hair dryer and the Spanish honeymooners in the next room who'd insisted on shouting '*Arriva! Arriva!*' – rather competitively we thought – through the thin rush-matting walls.

I smiled and crunched my way nostalgically through a few more calories, but as I did so, I heard a crunch of an altogether different kind coming from the other side of the house. My mouth froze in mid flapjack. I listened. Christ! That sounded suspiciously like tyres on gravel. Pippa couldn't be here already, could she?

I jumped up in alarm, ran through the house to the large sash window in the hall at the front and peered out. Sure enough, a very sexy little red Alfa Romeo was cruising to a halt in my front drive. Groovy car, I marvelled enviously, could that really be Pippa's? What on earth were they paying her these days? I watched as the car door swung open and one long, slim, sheerly stockinged leg appeared, followed by another. They straightened to reveal the rest of Pippa's most elegant self, immaculately clad in the most prohibitively expensive-looking drop-dead Chanel suit I've ever seen.

'Pippa!' I squeaked, bursting forth through the open window in a flurry of excitement and chocolate-stained T-shirt. 'You're early! Hang on, I'll come to the front door.'

She waved back, but looked rather dubiously at the craters in the drive that she was apparently required to cross in order to gain access to the house. I shut the window and ran to the door. When I flung it open she was still poised nervously by the car, clutching her quilted handbag and surveying the puddles, a vision in pale pink with black trimming, her shiny blonde hair blowing out behind her like a silk fan.

'What's happened to your drive?' she wailed. 'It's like a bloody assault course!'

'We ran out of money,' I shouted. 'Had to put a new roof on the cow shed instead!'

'Well, I'm glad the cows are all right, but what about my heels?'

'Oh, come on, Pippa,' I grinned, rather enjoying her

townie predicament. 'Just get a move on and stop making such a fuss!'

'Oh, all right,' she grumbled, nervously picking her way through the mud. 'Come on, Bruce,' she threw back over her shoulder. 'Wake up, for God's sake, we're here!'

A blond head suddenly popped into view above the dashboard in the passenger seat and a pair of bleary blue eyes were rubbed sleepily. Bruce? Who the hell was Bruce? She'd brought a man with her and I wasn't even dressed? I pulled my T-shirt down over my bottom and hid behind the door.

'You didn't say you were bringing anyone!' I hissed, as Pippa finally made it across the threshold.

'Oh, it's only Bruce,' she said airily, hugging me enthusiastically and thrusting a bunch of tulips up my nose. 'He's the location-finder, had to come with me to check out the venues, you see. Gosh, it's good to see you, Polly – come *on*, Bruce!' she yelled back at the car.

Bruce opened his door but appeared to be equally put out by the drive.

'Couldn't you have got a bit closer?' he wailed plaintively. 'I've got my Gucci loafers on!'

'Oh, stop being such a pansy and hurry up, I want you to meet Polly.'

'You're cruel, darling,' muttered the gorgeous, suntanned blond creature who stepped gingerly from the car, 'very cruel. But luckily, Brucey Boy's used to it.'

I instinctively pulled in my tummy muscles and sucked in my cheeks as he tiptoed across clutching a little black bag, but I couldn't help thinking I'd never seen such a fuss over a little bit of mud, especially from a man. Of course, as he reached us, it took less than a nanosecond to realise that

Bruce was not your average man, at least, not one of the red-blooded heterosexual variety I'm so fond of.

'Bruce, this is Polly, Polly, Bruce,' announced Pippa as he climbed shakily up the front steps, looking back over his shoulder like someone who's just scaled the north face of the Eiger.

'Terrible drive,' he muttered, taking my hand, 'terrible. But none the less, enchanted, my dear, positively dazzled, by both the house and your good self, and dying to take a peek inside.'

Hoping fervently that he was referring to the house and not my good self I ushered them in.

'Bruce is a professional nosy parker,' explained Pippa as I led them through the vast hall smothered in ancestral portraits. 'He gets away with it by calling himself a location-finder but it's really just an excuse to poke around other people's houses.'

'Oh, but this is divine!' squeaked Bruce, clasping his tiny hands together with joy and twirling round the hall. 'Oh please, no further! Let me linger a moment and savour!'

We lingered and he savoured, prowling excitedly around the portraits, touching frames, peering at signatures.

'Oh yes!' he breathed. 'Yes! Utter magic, utter, utter magic!'

He tore himself away from the pictures and stood back to survey the whole hall, taking in the ancient banisters, the flagstone floor and the huge chandelier hanging from the heavily corniced ceiling.

'Absolutely sublime,' he pronounced, 'especially, my dear, after the simply hideous places we've seen today.'

He gave a quick shudder of revulsion and raised a plucked eyebrow in my direction.

'I mean, wouldn't you think a picturesque period farmhouse with attractive grounds would be an easy enough brief in rural Cornwall? Wouldn't you?' he enquired urgently.

'Er, yes, I suppose I would.'

'Of course you would! But you'd be wrong. Shall I tell you why?'

I opened my mouth to invite him to do just that, but before I'd drawn breath he'd rushed on indignantly.

'Because just when you think you've found the perfect *grande maison*, the perfect country pile, you look a little closer and discover' – he gasped and clutched his mouth dramatically – '*quelle horreur*! It's got a pylon in the front garden, or there is an assortment of satellite dishes hanging from the roof, or they've got a circular washing line twirling around in the back garden set in rock-solid concrete, I mean, imagine! Imagine the *taste* someone's got to have to *do* that to their house!'

He gazed at me in horror, feigned a swoon, then quickly seized my arm. 'You haven't got a twirly washing line or a satellite dish, have you?' he asked anxiously.

I assured him we hadn't and he recovered enough composure to raise an immaculately manicured finger to his temple and massage it gently. I swear his bottom lip wobbled.

'I'm delighted to hear it, my dear, but of course it doesn't help me in my quest for a suitable house for the Doggy Chocs commercial. I tell you frankly, I'm distressed, most distressed,' he murmured. 'What on earth am I to tell Sam?'

'Who's Sam?' I asked, suppressing a giggle. I'd forgotten people like Bruce existed.

'The director,' explained Pippa.

'Too divine,' purred Bruce, eyes shining. 'Married, of course,' he added petulantly.

He sighed and turned away, resuming his survey of the portraits. Suddenly he gasped and clapped his hands.

'Heavens! What an unbelievably noble nose! Who's that?' He peered at one of the more imposing males in the collection.

'One of my husband's ancestors,' I explained. 'I'm not sure who it is but Nick comes from a long line of big-nosed bigots. You'll meet him later and, er, probably see what I mean.'

I couldn't quite imagine Nick instantly taking Bruce to his heart, so I thought it only fair to warn him of impending rejection.

'Can't wait,' breathed Bruce, 'I *adore* bigots.'

'Big mistake,' muttered Pippa, taking my arm as we went through into the kitchen. 'You should have said he was a sensitive little flower. Bruce is very into macho men, the butcher the better, in fact.'

'Christ. Nick will run a mile,' I murmured.

I filled the kettle while Bruce minced joyfully round the kitchen, exclaiming at all he saw.

'Oh, the beams, the *beams*, and – oh God, is that a range? Is it real?'

I assured him it was.

'And the floor! Proper flagstones, none of your imitation Battersea lark, ooh, aren't you clever to have a house like this and a bigoted husband to go with it?'

I grinned, thinking they'd been my exact same thoughts not a few moments ago.

'Where is the husband, by the way?' asked Pippa, sinking

elegantly into the wheel-backed chair by the range and crossing her incredibly slim legs. I tried not to feel envious.

'With the sheep as usual. He knows you're coming, though, so he'll be in soon. It's ages since he set eyes on anyone in a skirt; he'll be delighted to see you but it'll play havoc with his blood pressure.'

I absent-mindedly flicked the biscuit tin down again as I spooned out the Nescafé, and, without thinking, helped myself to a flapjack. Pippa jumped up and was beside me in an instant. She grabbed my arm in a vicelike grip, eyes shining.

'I knew it!' she squealed. 'I just knew it! Didn't I say so in the car, Bruce? She is! You are, aren't you?' she asked urgently. 'Look at you, you can't keep your hands off the biscuit tin, and look at the size of you already! You old dog, why didn't you tell me? How many months are you?'

I stared at her in bewilderment. 'What? What are you talking about?'

'Pregnant! I knew it! Why didn't you tell me on the phone? How many months are you – four? Five? Funny how it shows on the face and neck, isn't it?' she observed, surveying me critically with narrowed eyes. 'And the legs, of course, but everyone always piles it on there. Can I be godmother?'

'Shut up, Pippa,' I said crossly, snapping the biscuit tin shut. 'What on earth are you banging on about? Of course I'm not pregnant, I'd have told you if I was.'

'You're not?' Pippa stepped back in amazement. 'I could have sworn – are you sure?'

'Of course I'm sure, don't be ridiculous, don't you think I'd know?'

'But how come you look so – how come your face is all . . .' Pippa trailed off in confusion.

'Fat?'

'Well . . . yes.'

'Oh, thanks very much,' I said tartly. 'You always did have a sublime sense of tact, Pippa, but this is ridiculous!'

'Well, you said it!'

'Because you so obviously meant it!'

'But you must admit, Polly, you have put on quite a bit of weight and you are wearing that baggy maternity thing, and I knew you wanted to get pregnant so I naturally assumed—'

'Well, you assumed wrong,' I snapped, 'and this is a T-shirt, actually, don't they sell them in London any more?'

'But you've been trying for ages, haven't you?' she persisted. 'Surely you should be – you know, sort of – pregnant by now?'

'Pippa, could we talk about this some other time?' I hissed, jerking my head meaningfully in the direction of Bruce, who was leaning against the dresser inspecting his nails with studied indifference.

'Oh, don't worry about Bruce,' said Pippa, dismissing him airily. 'He likes girl talk.'

'No, don't mind me,' said Bruce, as if it were *his* feelings I was concerned about. 'Treat me as an honorary girlie. I love all the chat, although I must say I could probably skip the pregnancy debate, not having a vested interest, if you know what I mean. Mind if I take a look around the rest of the house?'

'Please do,' I said, relieved to be shot of him. 'Here, take your coffee.' I handed him a mug.

'Thanks. And take no notice of this anorexic stick insect, I think you look lovely, very Rubenesque. Ta-ra!'

He wiggled off in the direction of the dining room, pert little bottom tucked well in, hand stuck out to one side holding imaginary cigarette. I watched him go, gnashing my teeth at his covetable bottom.

'Rubenesque,' I muttered darkly, splashing milk into mugs, 'marvellous, isn't it? My best friend tells me I'm so fat I could be pregnant and a perfect stranger tells me I look like an overblown tart in a picture. Anything else you'd like to get off your chest while you're down here?' I banged the empty kettle down viciously on the hob.

'Oh, don't be like that, Polly,' said Pippa soothingly. 'I wasn't trying to upset you or anything, I was just excited for you because I knew you wanted to be pregnant.'

'Well, I'm not,' I said shortly. 'So that's that.'

I curled up on the old chintz sofa in the corner, usually occupied by Badger, our black lab, and sulked into my coffee. Pippa slunk furtively over, kicked off her shoes and curled up beside me.

'But ... there's nothing wrong, is there?' she asked anxiously. 'I mean, you haven't got your tubes crossed or anything like that, have you?'

'No, of course not, it just takes time, that's all. These things don't happen overnight, you know, Pippa!'

'Don't they?' Pippa looked surprised. 'God, I always thought they did. I thought the moment you came off the pill, that was it – wallop, up the duff, in the club, off to the gorgeous gynie and before you knew where you were you had baby sick all down your jumper.'

'That's what I thought too, but it's simply not true. It's just a load of propaganda put about by our mothers who were clearly terrified we were going to get pregnant at the drop of a pair of trousers and flaunt the love child in front of the neighbours, but let me tell you, Pippa, it's much more complicated than that, there's a lot more to it than we've been led to believe.' I nodded sagely.

'Like what?' Pippa looked confused. 'I thought you just sort of . . . did it?'

I shook my head and smiled benignly at her. 'Oh Pippa, you're woefully misinformed, very much behind the times. In the old days, yes, I'm sure they did just "do it", but these days, what with modern science and everything, well, it's much more technical, much more advanced.' I pursed my lips knowledgeably.

'It is? In what way?'

'Well, first you've got to read all the books, then you've got to take your temperature every morning, then you buy the egg-detecting kit and set up a sort of mini chemistry lab in your bathroom, complete with foaming test tubes and dipsticks and—'

'Egg-detecting kit?' Pippa's eyes were like dinner plates. 'What are you, a hen or something?'

'Pippa, one has to know when one's eggs are being dropped,' I explained patiently.

'Blimey, now you sound like a Wellington bomber. I had no idea it was so complicated.'

'Oh yes,' I went on airily, 'it's really quite intellectually demanding, and there's an awful lot of background reading to do too.' I sighed wearily. 'Terribly time-consuming.'

'Really?'

'Absolutely, it's essential. First you've got to raid the local library for all its infertility manuals just to convince yourself you've got knots in your tubes, fibroids in your whatsits, or a husband who's firing blanks, then you've got to get hold of that *Horizon* video about the voyage of the sperm to the egg to realise there's actually only one millisecond a month when you can possibly conceive anyway and that unless you set the alarm clock for three in the morning and get bonking that very second you haven't a snowball's chance in hell of getting the timing right, then—'

'Christ! First the book, then the film—' Pippa's eyes gleamed dangerously. 'Well, at least you've got the T-shirt!' she guffawed noisily into her mug.

I viewed her icily. 'This is an extremely serious and sensitive subject, Pippa, it's no laughing matter, you know.'

'Sorry,' she said, composing herself with difficulty, 'but you know, if I were you, Polly, I'd throw all the books and paraphernalia away and just get down to it. It all sounds a bit ridiculous to me.'

'I can assure you,' I said primly, 'we "get down to it", as you so charmingly put it, at the slightest opportunity, but as I said, it's not quite as simple as that.'

'Doesn't it help if you stand on your head? I'm sure I've read that somewhere.'

I sighed. 'Believe me, I'd stand on my head and do cartwheels round the room if I thought it would do any good, but it doesn't.'

She frowned. 'But you're not worried, are you? I mean, you've only been married a couple of years and you're still jolly young.'

'No, I'm not bloody worried and I wouldn't have mentioned it at all if you hadn't brought it up in the first place!' I snapped.

'Sorry.'

'Still,' I mused, 'it would be nice. I must say, I'm looking forward to fridge magnets.'

'Can't you have those without children?'

'Not really. Looks a bit naff if you haven't got the finger paintings to go with them.'

'Oh. Right,' conceded Pippa, 'and of course, it would give you an interest, give you something to do.'

'What d'you mean?' I said, bridling instantly. 'I've got plenty to do, God, I'm rushed off my feet down here!'

'Really?' Pippa looked surprised.

'Really? Really? Pippa, I never stop, I'm at it all day long!'

'At what?'

'Well,' I blustered, 'being bloody busy, that's what!'

'Yes, but what d'you do?'

'Well, you know, I – well, this house for instance!' I swung my arm round expansively to indicate its size. 'It's *incredibly* time-consuming!'

'But I thought you had a daily, a wench from the village or something?'

'Well, yes, I do, but even so—'

'Even so what?'

'Well, God, Pippa, I practically had to redecorate the whole place when we moved in, you know, it was in a terrible mess!'

'Really? Redecorate?' Pippa looked around at the rustic kitchen with its oak beams, flagstone floor and plain whitewashed walls. 'Looks as if it's been like this since the Middle Ages.'

'Oh, well, yes, the *kitchen* has, sure, but various other rooms had to be *completely* redesigned.'

'Which ones?'

God, she would go on, wouldn't she?

'Which ones?' I echoed, playing for time.

'Yes, come on, I want to see.' Pippa jumped up, seized my arm and pulled me to my feet. 'I want to see what you've done!'

'Well . . .' I faltered, dragging my feet literally and figuratively across the kitchen, 'the um, the downstairs loo took forever, of course.'

'Really? Show me.'

I led her tentatively down the back passage and pushed open the door. She gasped, as well she might. For the walls of this very small room were painted the retina-searing yellow usually reserved for the tennis balls at Wimbledon or perhaps the armbands of midnight cyclists. On completing the job I'd realised of course that the colour chart had lied through its teeth and Morning Primrose was in fact more of a Morning Chuck-up, and in a panic I'd then tried to draw the eye away by madly stencilling fruit and flowers around the borders. Unfortunately the purple and green flora and fauna fought furiously with the acidic walls and the blue and red tiled floor. Busy was kind. Frantic was much more like it.

'Blimey,' said Pippa in awe. 'Not afraid to mix your colours, are you?'

'It didn't quite come off, actually,' I admitted. 'I think I was a mite ambitious.'

'Never mind,' said Pippa, blinking, as we turned and wandered back to the kitchen, 'it was worth a try. What else though? You said on the phone you were up to your eyes in decorating.'

'Oh, I was, it took ages to do that, you know.'

31

Pippa stared at me with wide eyes as she lowered herself into the sofa again. 'So that's it? The downstairs loo?'

'Yes, that's it,' I said tetchily, curling up at the other end. Christ, what did she expect? A reproduction of the ceiling of the Sistine Chapel? Sicilian murals all up the stairs? Franciscan angels winding their way down the banisters?

She frowned. 'But you work on the farm a lot, don't you?' she persisted. 'I mean, you help with the animals and that kind of thing?'

'Oh, not really,' I said airily. 'You see, Nick does most of it, and of course we have Larry and Mick and Jim.'

'So what do you do then?' She fixed me with a beady eye.

'Oh God, loads,' I said hastily, suddenly smelling danger and realising what she was up to. 'There's – there's the garden, of course,' I said wildly.

'I thought you said on the phone you didn't know a phlox from a fuchsia and you were going to get a man in to do it?'

'Ah, well – yes, OK, perhaps I did but – oh I know! Yes, of course, there's my cooking!'

'Cooking! You? Like what?'

'Well, like—'

'Yes?'

'God, don't be so aggressive, Pippa, I'm just trying to think what I do particularly well – oh yes, I know, my baking!' I finished happily.

Pippa eyed me suspiciously, as well she might. 'What, like cakes and things?'

'Er, yes, that's it.'

Not a lie at all, because in fact 'things' described my baking remarkably accurately. My particular 'things' were jam tarts. A circle of frozen pastry with a blob of jam in the middle. I had, of course, meant to master the oven and get down to some *serious* baking at some stage, and I'd even gone so far as to prop Delia up over the Aga and salivate greedily over her suggestions, but somehow, instead of my greed making me reach for the scales and the caster sugar, it seemed to lead inexorably to the biscuit tin again, so Delia was put back on the shelf to collect yet more dust and the rows of plump, golden scones and fluffy Victoria sponges continued to evade me. And Nick too, of course. Because, to be honest, he felt the deprivation much more keenly than me.

In the beginning he'd praised my efforts, keen to encourage me, but let's face it, there are only so many tarts a man can take – so to speak – and when he came in starving hungry from the fields, having packed more physical exertion into one day than most men manage in a week, dying for a juicy fat slab of Dundee cake with his tea, I'd come to dread his weak pronouncement of simulated joy – 'Ah! Jam tarts again!' – as his eye lit nervously upon my sticky morsels cringing by the Aga. But of course, as I told myself regularly, there was still plenty of time, and one of these days I was going to get down to some *serious* baking.

'OK, baking,' conceded Pippa warily, only marginally placated. 'All right, but you can't do that all day, can you? And the thing is, Polly, I know it's beautiful down here, but I can't help thinking I'd go out of my mind with boredom after a while, either that or turn to drink. You're not drinking, are you?' Her eyes pinned me to the wall.

'No, of course I'm not drinking, and listen, Pippa, not everyone wants to run around being a high-powered executive, you know. Don't you ever feel the urge to rip off your tights and your Chanel suit and run around the fields barefoot?'

Pippa looked doubtfully at her immaculate pink concoction. 'Not really, and even if I did,' she regarded me penetratingly, 'I'd make damn sure I'd shaved my legs first.'

I flushed. 'Pippa!' I pulled my legs up sharply and sat on them.

'Well, it's true, look at you!' I tugged my T-shirt down desperately as she hoicked it up with a manicured nail. 'There are some things only your best friend can tell you, Polly, so I'm telling you. I suspected as much the last time I came down, but now I'm convinced. You've gone all fat and complacent because you've got your man, haven't you?'

'Pippa! I have not!' I was pink with indignation now, this was outrageous.

'Well, what's with the hairy legs then?' she persisted. 'And,' she added, peering with naked incredulity at the top of my head, 'bloody hell, look at this, what about these dark roots? You wouldn't have been seen dead walking around London like that in the good old days. Come on, Polly, it's not like you to take your eye off the ball, what's occurring?'

'Don't be silly,' I spluttered. 'I haven't taken my eye off the ball at all, it's just that, well, in the country people don't worry about things like shaving their legs and touching up their roots. It's all sort of back-to-nature here.'

'Oh, so it's the country's fault, is it? You can't live in the country and shave your legs at the same time, is that it? What utter drivel. The two aren't mutually exclusive, you know, I'm sure the village shop would run to a razor, or even a tube of Immac, and what's all this back-to-nature rubbish? You always struck me as more of a back-to-the-wine-bar type.'

'Oh, OK, OK,' I said, caving in dramatically and reaching for a cigarette. 'So I haven't shaved my legs for a while, OK, Pippa, you win.'

I was getting bored with this lecture and my argumentative powers were flagging.

'No, it's *not* OK!' said Pippa sharply, suddenly thumping the arm of the sofa with her fist.

I jumped in surprise. She glared at me.

'If you must know, I'm really worried about you, Polly!'

My mouth gaped in amazement. She ... was worried about me? Wasn't I supposed to be the one who was worried about—

'I know exactly what you're doing here,' she snapped, 'you're sitting around on your bum all day, doing bugger all except eating chocolate, watching telly and waiting to get pregnant, aren't you?'

'No, of course not,' I spluttered. 'I'm incredibly busy, and anyway, since when have you been so keen on the puritanical work ethic?'

'I'm not puritanical, I'm just living my life, which is more than you're doing, and it's a crime. You're a beautiful girl, Polly, you've got it all and you're wasting it. You're piling on the pounds and going to ground down here, now why?'

'If you must know,' I snapped, 'I have to eat as many calories as I possibly can, it's part of my pre-conception diet. If I don't keep my weight up I won't conceive, it's a well-known fact. Haven't you ever heard of child-bearing hips?' I added wildly.

'Balls,' scoffed Pippa. 'You're eating out of boredom

and you know it. You've got nothing to do and no way of occupying your mind. You're bored out of your skull here.'

I felt my fists clenching. 'That's not true!'

'Of course it is, it's written all over you – I've got my man so I don't have to work and I don't care what I look like – it's as clear as day.'

I felt my face flame. We stared at each other.

'Well, if you think I'm so fat and boring why don't you just go?' I snapped suddenly.

There was a terrible silence. She gazed at me. I watched her face grow pale. Then she got shakily to her feet, gathering up her handbag from the table.

'Right,' she whispered hoarsely, 'I will.'

Chapter Three

She walked unsteadily towards the door but didn't make it through it. I was up in an instant, pulling her back, hanging on to her arm.

'Oh God, Pippa, I'm so sorry, please don't go, I – I didn't mean it, really I didn't!' I cried.

She hesitated, but only for a second. In a twinkling we were hugging each other and sniffing and snorting into each other's hair.

'Sorry,' mumbled Pippa gruffly, 'didn't mean all that.'

'No, you're right, you're right!' I wailed. 'I'm a fat slob! I'm a failure!'

'No you're not.'

'I am!'

'Of course you're not a failure,' she said, not disputing, I noticed, the fat slob element, 'but I'm so fond of you, Polly, and it upsets me to see you wasting yourself like this.'

'I know, I know!' I hiccuped into her sleek, recently highlighted hair. 'I'm a mess, a bag lady!'

'But it's all superficial,' she said, gently taking my shoulders and holding me away. 'It's all so easily rectified, just get yourself down to the hairdresser, have a few highlights, book an appointment at the leg-wax place and—'

'No,' I sniffed, shaking my head energetically, 'it's more than that, it's deeper, I'm rotten, rotten to the core!'

'Don't be silly.'

'I am!'

'No you're not.'

'Yes I am!'

And thus Bruce found us as he wandered in, clinging to each other, arguing, shrieking and crying simultaneously.

'Lordy-be,' he muttered, raising his eyebrows to heaven as he tiptoed past, 'I'm glad I'm a man sometimes.'

'Sorry,' I snuffled, grabbing a tissue from the dresser. 'Pippa was just telling me some basic home truths, had to be done.' I blew my nose hard. 'God, what's that?' I wiped my nose and stared with astonishment at the bundle of skin and bone under Bruce's arm, complete with red ribbon and mad staring eyes.

'This is Munchkin,' announced Bruce proudly, stroking the pimple that passed as the chihuahua's head. 'I hope you don't mind me bringing her in but she was crying her little eyes out in the car.'

'I don't mind at all, she can join in the waterworks in here, but I can't vouch for Badger. He eats things that size for breakfast.'

Right on cue, Badger miraculously appeared as if from nowhere, all thoughts of whiling away the morning rabbiting apparently quite forgotten. He stood to attention at Bruce's feet, nose twitching, tail erect, quivering with excitement and shooting beseeching glances in my direction. *Can I kill it?* his brown eyes seemed to say, *Can I kill it now?*

'Basket, Badge,' I ordered sternly. He dithered. 'Now!'

He slunk away to his corner, giving me a reproachful look, but still keeping a careful eye out lest Bruce should accidentally let the bundle slip, in which case he'd be only too pleased to retrieve it. It would be the work of a moment.

Bruce kept the terrified Munchkin clasped tightly to his chest and eyed Badger warily as he sat down at the kitchen table.

'Marvellous house,' he breathed, 'simply marvellous. Would make a fabulous location.' He eyed Pippa meaningfully.

'Don't even think about it,' said Pippa. 'Nick would never agree, would he, Polly?'

'Not in a million years,' I said, blowing my nose again noisily.

I could just see Nick's face if I so much as suggested a film crew run riot all over the house and garden; trampling the flowers, frightening the sheep and being all luvvie and artistic over his little patch of paradise.

'We'd pay you,' ventured Bruce hopefully. 'Quite well, actually, and we'd only need to use the outside of the house and perhaps a soupçon of the kitchen . . . ?'

I shook my head firmly. 'No way.'

Bruce sighed heavily. 'Shame. Great shame. The client would love this place, he'd go weak at the knees.'

'Yes, well, forget it, the farmer would go ballistic.'

'What would I go ballistic about?' enquired Nick, breezing in through the back door, grinning from ear to ear.

I swung round in delight. He looked divine as usual, his striking, angular face with its jutting chin and decidedly

Roman nose already nut brown from the early sun, his straight dark hair slightly tousled and his brown eyes gleaming with health and the great outdoors. He was tall, broad, and mine, I thought happily as he rumpled Pippa's perfect hair.

'Nick!' she squealed, jumping up and throwing her arms round his neck.

'Pippa, you're looking as delectable as ever,' he declared, kissing her mightily on the cheek. 'Hang on a minute, I'll just pop this in the oven.'

He untangled himself and stooped down to deposit a new-born lamb in the bottom oven of the Aga. He stood up and smiled.

'There!'

Pippa and Bruce stared at him in horror. Bruce clutched Munchkin to his chest, his eyes wide with fear, Pippa gulped and backed away.

'Jesus,' she murmured, 'that's a bit primitive even for you, isn't it? Aren't you going to kill it first?'

'Oh, I'm not cooking it,' said Nick, washing his hands at the sink, 'just warming it up. Don't panic, I'm not going to shut the door, but I've got to keep it warm. It's a sock lamb. Its mother died and it got a bit wet and cold in the field. When it's warmed up I'll give it a bottle.'

'Bit late in the year, isn't it?' I said, peering at the little thing shivering away in the oven.

'A bit, but these things happen. A late arrival.'

'And an orphan already!' Pippa looked stricken. 'What will happen to it?'

'Oh, it'll grow big and strong, lark around in the fields for a few months, and then I'll transfer it to the top oven and surround it with roast potatoes.' Nick grinned wickedly.

Pippa and Bruce did a collective gasp.

'The brute!' murmured Bruce with a touch of awe.

'Nick, how can you?' wailed Pippa.

'But you like roast lamb, don't you?'

'Yes, but—' Pippa looked seriously upset.

Nick took pity. 'OK, just for you, Pipps, I'll spare this one and let it skip in the fields indefinitely – Christ, what's that?' he said, spotting the mess under Bruce's arm and simultaneously holding out his hand to Bruce. 'Nick Penhalligan,' he muttered, keeping an incredulous eye on the dog.

'Oh, sorry, Nick,' I said quickly, 'this is Bruce, he works with Pippa, they're location-hunting, and this is Munchkin.'

'Is it indeed?' Nick looked at Munchkin as if he'd like nothing better than to pop it in the top oven right now and close the door firmly.

He smiled at Bruce, who was gazing at Nick with wide eyes, the power of speech having apparently completely deserted him.

'Been boring you with girl talk, have they? Polly's rather starved of female company down here so she's probably got verbal diarrhoea already. Anyone offered you a drink? Beer?' He opened the fridge door, pulled out a can of lager and waggled it in Bruce's direction.

Bruce, looking thoroughly bigot-struck now, simpered a negative response before backing away and draping himself decoratively over the Welsh dresser. There he posed, arms outstretched, head flung back and cocked to one side to display his profile, smouldering away at Nick through his lashes.

Nick looked momentarily alarmed, then recovered

himself quickly. He'd been in advertising long enough to recognise the Bruces of this world, and also the devastating effect he seemed to have on them. He kept the beer for himself and backed hastily in the opposite direction, positioning himself firmly in the girls' camp next to Pippa, who was perching on the back of a chair.

'Let's have a look at you then!' he said, hauling her to her feet.

She grinned and gave a twirl.

'I must say, the world of film production seems to be suiting you down to the ground,' he said, marvelling. 'You look fantastic! Gosh, you're slim, look at that for a figure, Polly!'

'I know,' I said enviously, 'you're going to have to let me in on the secret, Pippa.'

'Stress,' said Pippa proudly, smoothing her minuscule skirt down over her pencil-thin thighs. 'Having a proper job with real worries is the best diet in the world, you know. I had no idea it could be so effective.'

'Tell me about it,' groaned Nick, running his hands through his hair. 'I wondered why I was becoming a shadow of my former self. This place is obviously taking pounds off me, not to mention years.'

'But I thought it was going really well? I thought when you sold the agency you had bags of money to pour into this place?'

Nick sighed wearily and flopped down into a chair. 'I did, but unfortunately it got swallowed up by a series of disasters. Too much rain last year so we lost a lot of the hay, bad lambing the year before that, then there was that storm which took the roofs off most of the outbuildings – I tell you, I could do with a couple more advertising agencies to sell; I need miles of new fencing and every day some piece of badly made farm machinery seems to conk out on me.'

'It's not as bad as all that,' I said soothingly. 'Nick's exaggerating.'

Nick shook his head grimly. 'I wish I was, darling, but I tell you, unless something happens pretty damn quickly, next quarter's farm accounts aren't going to look too attractive.'

'You'll have to send your wife out to work again,' said Pippa with a mischievous grin.

'Ha! That'll be the day. I think Polly's retired for life, haven't you?' He leaned back in his chair and tugged teasingly at my T-shirt. 'I must say, you're looking particularly fetching today. Will we have the pleasure of seeing you in that little number for lunch as usual?'

'Oh Nick, that's not true! You know jolly well I normally get dressed by lunch time!'

'Nip and tuck some days though, isn't it?' he said with a grin. 'Not that I mind, of course, I like to see you wafting round in that sexy négligé all ready for action, makes me feel like the milkman.'

I aimed a sharp cuff to his head and he caught my hand, laughing. 'Careful! Mind my curls! What's for lunch, by the way? I'm starving.'

God, Attila the Hungry was back in my kitchen being all forceful and demanding again. For better, for worse, but not for lunch, I decided grimly for the umpteenth time.

'Lunch?' I shrieked. 'What, now? Don't be silly, I've only just had breakfast!'

'Well, I had mine six hours ago and it's damn nearly twelve o'clock.'

'Is it?' I swung round in amazement and looked at the clock. 'Gosh, so it is.'

'What were you planning on giving Bruce and Pippa then?' went on my spouse, who was getting less adorable by the minute.

'Well, let me see . . .' I said, flinging open the fridge door and improvising wildly. 'There's some bread, and – and some cheese . . . at least I think it's cheese,' I said doubtfully, picking up a piece of extremely sweaty Cheddar. Damn. I'd planned to go into Helston before they arrived and pick up some cold meat. How on earth had it slipped my mind?

'Oh, we're not staying for lunch,' said Pippa quickly. 'We really must get back and report our findings to Sam. We spent the whole of yesterday down here and we said we'd be back by tea time today.'

'Don't want to get our botties spanked,' agreed Bruce, looking as if nothing would please him more.

'Oh Pipps, I thought you were staying a while!' I wailed. 'Don't go yet, I want to hear all the news, I want to know what Lottie's been up to, who's been doing what to whom. Please stay, I'll rustle something up, really I will, I'm sure I could do something with this,' I ventured brightly, holding up the sad piece of Cheddar, 'make a pie or something, I'm quite big on pies.'

A stunned and disbelieving silence greeted this little announcement.

'Only porkie ones,' muttered Nick, rather disloyally I thought. I glared. At least Pippa had the grace to turn her incredulous guffaw into a massive coughing fit. I was beginning to feel more than a little inadequate here.

Pippa jumped up. 'Don't bother about food,' she said,

slipping her arm through mine, 'Bruce and I had an enormous breakfast at the hotel this morning. Tell you what, let's just grab that bottle of wine I spotted in the fridge and take it out to the garden. We can leave the boys to man-talk in here.'

With a wicked glance at Nick, who looked horrified, she seized the wine and a couple of glasses, and with a wink at Bruce, who flushed with pleasure at the thought of being left alone with Nick, steered me outside.

We wandered arm in arm to a sunny spot in the middle of the lawn and sat down on the grass. I lit a cigarette.

'Still smoking then?' enquired Pippa with a wry smile.

'Pippa! You haven't given up . . . ?'

'You bet I have. It's too expensive now, and I'm damned if I'm going to kill myself. It's a vice, Polly.'

Somehow this piece of news shook me more than anything. Pippa and I had chain-smoked our way through the last seven years together. As we'd skipped our way through parties, jobs, love affairs and trouble, we'd always had our trusty packets of twenty by our sides. She was changing. For the better, of course, but it depressed the hell out of me.

'It may be a vice to you, but it's a hobby to me,' I said grimly, 'and you must admit it's got staying power. I've been doing it since I was sixteen. All my other hobbies turned out to be nine-day wonders – brass-rubbing, tapestry, they all ended in tears. Except sunbathing, of course, that's always stayed the course, but now the bloody sunbathing police are out to ruin that for me too. Why can't people just mind their own business? If I want to smoke and tan myself to death I will, at least I'll look good in the coffin against all that white satin.'

I took a huge, defiant drag of nicotine, right down to my bootstraps. 'And anyway,' I said with an uncharacteristic glimmer of perception, 'I bet the only reason you've given up is because Josh doesn't like it.'

'Well, there is that,' admitted Pippa grudgingly. 'He's very anti.'

'You see! God, you must be smitten to give up for a man! It's never happened before, has it? Charles hated it and you wouldn't give up for him.'

Pippa said nothing. She pursed her lips and decapitated a daisy. I studied her closely.

'And when am I going to meet this boss of yours, eh? And how come you're not living with him yet? I thought you'd be well ensconced by now. How come you haven't got your bras hanging over his bath tub?'

Pippa shifted position and looked uncomfortable. 'Well, it's a bit tricky, actually,' she mumbled.

'In what way?'

'It just is.'

'Why? He's not married or anything, is he?'

Pippa flushed and bit her lip.

'He is! Bull's-eye! God, Pippa, you old dog, why didn't you tell me? You're having an affair with a married man, aren't you?'

Pippa squirmed.

'Come on, admit it!' I bullied. 'He's married, isn't he?'

'Only a little bit.'

'Only a little bit!' I shrieked. 'Married is married, Pippa. I'm shocked, shocked to the core.' I stared at her. 'What's it like?'

'What's what like?'

'Well, you know, doing it with a married man.'

'Exactly the same as doing it with a single man but with more logistic difficulties, and anyway, it's not that shocking, it happens all the time.'

'Not to you, it doesn't,' I retorted. 'You've always been dead against that sort of thing. A dirty little slut is what you called Miranda Baxter when she went off with that bit of rough from Rumbelows – remember? You came over very high and mighty about all that!' I was enjoying myself immensely now. For the first time that day a little bit of moral superiority was creeping my way.

Pippa squirmed some more. 'That was different, Polly, that chap from Rumbelows had been married for years and had about ten children. Josh has only been married a year and he hasn't got any kids.'

'So why doesn't he leave his wife, then?'

'Well, he feels so guilty. He knows it was a big mistake to marry her but he thinks that to walk out after only a year would be a bit rough. He feels he ought to give it a bit longer, and I can understand that.'

'You can? Crikey, you're more gullible than I thought! Get real, Pippa, he's having his cake and eating it and licking the bloody mixing bowl too!'

'What a distasteful analogy,' said Pippa, looking prim.

'Well, it's true, any fool can see that. He's got wifey at home cooking his dinner and ironing his shirts, and then he's got you at work running around in your Chanel suit being all sexy and provocative—'

'I am his assistant—'

'Doesn't mean you have to sleep with him!' I snorted. 'It's not part of your job description, is it? Come on, Pippa, he's got it made, but what's in it for you?'

'It's not as simple as that.'

'Course it is,' I scoffed, 'you're just a bit on the side as far as he's concerned.'

'How can you say that! You haven't even met him. He's mad about me, if you must know, and he's definitely going to leave his wife, it's just a question of time.'

Even as she said it I think she realised how empty and naïve the words sounded. Her eyes slithered past me and I detected a glimmer of a tear. She was smitten all right. I sighed, moral superiority forgotten.

'Oh dear. How unlike you to get yourself into this sort of mess.'

'I know,' she said miserably, pulling at the grass, 'and there's not a damn thing I can do about it.'

One or two practical suggestions along the lines of binning him occurred to me, but I decided not to voice them.

'Does everyone at work know?'

She shrugged. 'I'm not really sure. We keep it as quiet as possible but I've a feeling some people have guessed, Sam in particular.'

The back door clicked opened behind us. We turned in unison and saw Nick and Bruce slowly making their way towards us across the lawn, their heads bowed, deep in conversation.

'Don't tell Nick,' muttered Pippa quickly. 'He'll be horrified. You know what he's like about that sort of thing.'

I nodded. 'I won't,' I promised, and meant it. Nick had some pretty uncompromising views about the sanctity of marriage and I didn't think he'd find Pippa's predicament very amusing.

Bruce's eyes were shining as he reached us.

'Nick's been showing me the antiques!' he beamed.

'Pippa, you should see some of the things he's got in there, the porcelain collection is out of this world, and the pictures – God, there's even a little Renoir drawing in the bathroom! You really must see it, Pippa, it's quite superb!'

'I have,' she smiled, 'but I'm afraid it's rather wasted on me. Makes a nice change to have an appreciative audience, eh, Nick?'

'It certainly does, and Bruce really knows his stuff. I've got one piece of porcelain which is incredibly difficult to date. I'd eventually pinned it down to being mid-eighteenth century but Bruce here assures me it's late seventeenth.' He turned to Bruce. 'You must come and have a proper look around when there's more time. I know you've got to get back to London now but if you're ever in the area, drop by, there are some things in the safe I'd like you to cast your eye over.'

Bruce flushed with pleasure. 'I – I'd love to,' he stammered. 'I'd be absolutely delighted! My mother's in hospital in Truro so I come down here quite a lot, actually.'

'Oh, I'm sorry, anything—'

'Cancer, I'm afraid, and she's very old now too, so I come down about once a fortnight, I could easily pop in.'

'Great.' Nick smiled. 'Don't forget. Come and see us whenever you like.'

He held out his hand and Bruce pumped it up and down enthusiastically, his camp, mincing manners momentarily evaporated. 'I certainly will!'

Pippa got to her feet and brushed the grass off her bottom. 'Come on then, Bruce, let's hit the road and let these people get back to their muck-spreading.'

She gave me a hug. 'Ring me soon,' she whispered, 'we'll talk more.'

I hugged her back, sorry to see her go. She turned to Nick and took his arm as we wandered back to the house.

'You've made his day,' she murmured. 'Most people write him off as a big joke but you took him seriously.'

'Well, he knows what he's talking about,' said Nick. 'I was genuinely impressed, I wasn't flattering him.'

'I know, but thanks anyway.'

We walked back through the house and waved them off from the front steps. With the flick of a switch Pippa converted her covetable car into a sex machine and they roared off down the drive; Pippa's long blonde hair streaming out behind her, Bruce's hand fluttering back to us, Munchkin's red ribbon blowing in the breeze.

Nick put his arm round me as we watched them turn through the stone gateposts into the road and disappear around the corner.

'Good to see Pippa,' he murmured, 'but I couldn't live that sort of life any more, could you? The whole London scene, the social life, the ad-racket, thank God we were able to escape down here.'

'Mmmmm . . . thank God,' I murmured.

Nick gave my shoulder a squeeze. 'Must dash, I've got some fences to put up in the far field. I'll see you around tea time.' He strode off.

I turned and walked slowly back through the house. No, I mused, I certainly couldn't live like that any more, I'd gladly left it all behind me, and I'd gladly swapped it for this, but all the same . . . I made myself a cup of coffee and wandered upstairs. I paused on the landing and stared out of the window at the fields stretching far away into the distance. It was certainly beautiful, but . . . quiet. I frowned down into my coffee mug. What was this, Polly? What was the meaning of this sense of dissatisfaction that was slowly but surely seeping through me?

Chapter Four

I sat down and eyed my reflection in the dressing-table mirror. Damn, it was true, it was written all over my face, look – there, dissatisfaction – now why? Why, when only a couple of hours ago I'd been counting my blessings in the sunshine, secure in the knowledge that life couldn't possibly get any better? It was Pippa's fault of course, she'd come down and put the wind up me, jolted me out of my complacency with the earth-shattering revelation that I'd been living a boring life – me! The luckiest girl in the world!

I picked up my hairbrush and frowned, pulling some hair out of it. OK, granted, the last couple of years had been rather quiet, but never dull, never. Why, the gymkhana had only been yesterday and there was so much else to look forward to. The village fête for instance, that was only six weeks away, quite the social event of the county, and I'd been promoted to Tombola this year rather than Guess the Weight of the Cake like last year. I dragged my brush grimly through my hair as I recalled that fiasco. God, what a disaster. Some goon had forgotten to bring the cake along, so some other goon had suggested they guess the weight of me instead. I'd spent the whole afternoon with steam pouring out of my nostrils, roaring, 'What! Don't be so bloody ridiculous, I'm nowhere *near* eleven stone!'

Still, this year would be more fun, and of course there was the hunt ball to look forward to at Christmas, that was always an absolute riot. Yes, all right, eight months away. One village fête and one hunt ball. I put down my brush and gazed at my sorrowful reflection. Suddenly I scowled – oh, for goodness' sake, Polly, don't be ridiculous. You have a terrific time down here, you know you do! My eyes in the mirror looked shifty, they could spot a lie at twenty paces. I sighed.

It was true of course, country life was rather quiet. When I'd married Nick I'd willingly settled down to become a devoted, home-loving farmer's wife, determined to put my wild-child days of nightclubbing and partying behind me, but I couldn't help feeling slightly peeved that the opportunity to resist any form of social whirling had failed to even present itself. The closest I got to a night on the town was supper at the sea-food restaurant in Helford, with Nick yawning into his prawns at nine o'clock because he had to get up and milk the cows at dawn.

Then there was the holiday question. The fact that farmers tended to summer where they wintered had come as quite a shock to me. Why, even as an impoverished secretary I'd managed two weeks horizontal and motionless in the sun, and I would even have been prepared to traipse around monasteries or peer at lumps of stone in the sweltering heat as men are wont to do, but no. Apparently we had to continue to traipse around the corn fields and peer at the sheep. Terrific.

My chin quivered momentarily in the mirror. I steadied it fiercely, horrified at my audacity. Bloody hell, Polly, don't be so wet! Don't sit here in your enormous pile of a house moaning about lack of entertainment, don't gaze out at your thousand acres complaining that life's a bitch, you're the luckiest girl in the world, remember? Get a grip!

I tried. I tried really hard. Then I thought of Pippa. Pippa, rushing back to London, swinging into her Soho office, laughing with the girls, flirting with the boys, rushing to the loo to touch up her make-up, bouncing into Josh's office to report her findings, sitting down opposite him and feeling the electric current surge between them – did I miss all that? A small, remote corner of my mind admitted that I did. Not the work, of course, but the fun, the excitement, the camaraderie.

I sighed, picked up my brush again and wondered idly if perhaps Pippa and her gang could pop in here for lunch, or a drink, when they came down to shoot their commercial, *en route* to whichever location they eventually chose. My brush froze in mid stroke and I gazed steadily at my reflection. Whichever ... location ... they eventually ... chose. I watched my cheeks grow pink with excitement. My heart began to thump.

Why not? Why on earth not? It wasn't out of the question at all, why shouldn't they shoot it here? I'd dismissed it out of hand when Bruce had suggested it earlier, but if I could get round Nick – and I was sure I could – why ever not? It was perfect! Absolutely perfect!

I jumped off the stool and danced around the room, hugging myself gleefully. Oh Polly, you clever girl, you clever, clever girl! It was a brilliant idea! I stopped twirling for a second and gazed out of the window. Imagine – a film crew in my house, shooting in my grounds!

I could see it all now, and I could see me in the thick of it – not this me of course, a different me, a pencil-thin, leg-waxed, highlighted me, clad in a succession of different outfits – Jasper Conran one day, Armani the next – smiling and laughing, dispensing tea to the crew, chilled white wine to the director, largesse to one and all. Oh, and the actors of course. I'd chat like mad to them – famous ones probably, they were all so hard up these days they practically all did commercials. God, it would be terrific fun!

My imagination went into furious overdrive as I saw us all having lunch together, out on the lawn probably. I'd cook a fabulous stew – well, buy some ham perhaps – and we'd sit at those long trestle tables like something out of *Far from the Madding Crowd*. I'd be at one end dispensing the stew – ham – and Nick would be at the other being all handsome and witty, and we'd have huge carafes of red wine and everyone would get incredibly merry and the really attractive actors would flirt like mad with me.

Then after lunch I'd wander over to watch the shoot and sit in one of those director's chairs with the canvas backs, looking elegant in something beige and tailored. No – no, I wouldn't, I'd wear black jeans and a waistcoat and look dead trendy and efficient with a pencil behind my ear and a clipboard to take notes, because of course as a local girl I'd become invaluable in some terribly technical kind of way, something to do with understanding the vagaries of the Cornish light, perhaps. Anyway, whatever it was, there I'd be, part of the crew practically, watching the shoot, which – yes – which would be going rather badly that day due to the fact that the leading lady kept forgetting her lines. The director would look a bit worried, he'd raise his eyebrows to heaven, then look over and give me a grim smile. I'd smile back, raising my eyebrows too – sympathetically of course, not bitchily – and then suddenly, that's right, *suddenly*, he'd stare at me in a more piercing, professional kind of way. He'd walk over slowly, scratch his chin thoughtfully and say something like, 'Tell me, Polly, have you ever done any acting?'

I gasped with excitement, threw myself on my bed in a fit of giggles and stuffed the duvet in my mouth.

Yes, yes, yes! This was it! This was the answer to all my problems! Not that I needed an answer, I thought hastily, and not that I had much of a problem, but having a film crew around would – well, it would certainly razz things up a bit, wouldn't it? Put something of a bomb under rural life?

I flipped over on to my back and stared at the ceiling. There was no doubt about it, it had to happen. But how? How would I ever get round Nick? How could I ever get him to agree?

Suddenly I sat bolt upright. Money. Of course, that was it. Hadn't he just said we were really strapped for cash, and hadn't Bruce also said we'd be generously reimbursed for our trouble? I'd make damn sure we were. I'd make sure Pippa got us such an unbelievably generous deal that Nick would find it impossible to refuse – we'd get hundreds, thousands, hundreds of thousands. I hadn't a clue how much actually, but we'd trouser a hell of a wedge, enough for a new tractor anyway, or – or a few miles of fencing. Nick would be delighted! But how to persuade him first of his impending delight?

I sucked the duvet and thought hard. This called for tact and diplomacy. No good charging in feet first as usual and simply demanding it should happen. I had to be clever, subtle even, catch him at a good moment, when his defences were down, and if not his defences then certainly his . . . trousers.

I leaped off the bed, ran to my wardrobe and rifled feverishly through my clothes. Yes, of course, I'd seduce him. He liked nothing more than to feel I'd made an effort – these days that ran along the lines of washing under my arms and ironing a T-shirt – but this time I'd pull out all the stops, wear something low, something sexy, something outrageous, something – my hand froze on a hanger. I pulled it out and stared at the garment it suspended.

It was a basque. The one I'd worn under my wedding dress, in fact. It was white, lacy, boned for maximum figure hug and boob uplift and utterly beautiful and sexy. Sadly Nick had never seen it because of course after the wedding I'd taken off all my finery and changed into my going-away kit. Could this be his big chance? I fingered the lace. Why not? Naturally I'd wear my normal clothes on top so he wouldn't suspect a thing, but halfway through supper in the kitchen or – no, a candlelit dinner in the dining room – yes, halfway through that, just when he was feeling all relaxed and mellow and full of *boeuf en croute* and claret and was stroking my hand and murmuring, 'That was delicious, darling, what's for pudding?' Just at that moment, I'd whip off my T-shirt and say, 'I am!'

A trifle obvious? So what! He'd either find it hysterically funny or a massive turn-on, and either way we were bound to end up in a frantic heap on the floor, laughing like drains and tearing each other's clothes off. Then just as he was getting really carried away, just as he seriously couldn't control himself any longer and his breath was hurricaning into my ear, I'd hit him with the big plan. How could he refuse? Softened up by wine, good food, candlelight and tantalised beyond belief by my delectable, lace-encased body, he'd have no option but to pant, 'Yes, my darling, do whatever you want, of course your friends can shoot their commercial on my land, just let me get that bloody basque off you!'

I clutched the garment to my chest in delight, did a quick twirl of exultation around the room, and then abruptly stopped. I swung around to the mirror, holding the basque up against me. I peered more closely. It looked as if it might be a bit on the small side, I had been jolly slim on my wedding day. I frowned. Oh well, I'd just have to diet like crazy. Cut out all the biscuits. Simple.

Now! I threw the basque on the floor and set my hands decisively on my hips. The first thing I had to do was ring Pippa and arrange it all before she booked another location.

I raced downstairs and rang her at work. Her secretary answered – her *secretary*, for God's sake.

'Pippa Hamilton's office.'

'Oh, hello, I know Pippa's not there but could you ask her to call me, please?'

'Yes, of course. She's on her way back from Cornwall, but I'll get her to give you a ring later.'

'Thank you so much, the *moment* she comes through the door, please. My name's Polly Penhalligan. Please could you tell her it's very important, it's regarding the location of the forthcoming shoot,' I said importantly.

'I certainly will,' she replied respectfully.

I replaced the receiver and walked slowly upstairs again, chewing my thumbnail and smiling to myself. How uplifting it was to have something to look forward to, to have a plan. I was a great one for plans, but when the biggest and most ambitious one of my career had miraculously come off and I'd become Mrs Penhalligan I'd collapsed in a heap, flummoxed by my own success, all planned out, so to speak.

But not any longer. No, this plan was equally ambitious and far-sighted and would really put Trewarren on the map. Oh yes, this commercial was just the beginning. When it was over I'd register the house with loads of other film companies and they'd all be clamouring to use it. Remakes of *Pride and Prejudice*, *Rebecca*, *Wuthering Heights* – they'd all be made here. It would become a local tourist attraction, people would come from miles around to peer over the walls. I might even open it to the public, give guided tours, have a tea shop, sell souvenirs – a touch of the Raine Spencers – God, there'd be no end to the money-making schemes I'd dream up. I'd be an entrepreneur – more like Richard Branson than Raine Spencer, actually – it would give me a sense of purpose.

I sat down decisively at my dressing table and began to cleanse my face vigorously. I grinned at my reflection. Gosh, life was easy once you got a grip on it. I reached for a cigarette and wondered what else I could do to improve my lot. I dropped the cigarette. Yes. Absolutely. If Pippa could do it so could I. I'd give up right now.

Pulling open my dressing-table drawer, I rooted around amongst the empty deodorant bottles and chewed-up lipsticks and found an ancient packet of Nicorette patches, bought on a whim with an excruciating hangover and an overwhelming desire never to smoke again. I'd obviously opened them because the instructions appeared to be missing, but I'd certainly never used them.

Now what did one do, I wondered – stick them on the arm? Like this? I slapped one on my wrist and waited. Nothing seemed to be happening. If anything my need for a fag was increasing. I eyed the packet of Silk Cut and my hand twitched nervously. No, I mustn't. My hand twitched again. I shook more patches out and slapped one on the other arm – oh, and one on my cheek too, because perhaps it helped if it went near the mouth? I slapped one on the other cheek just for good measure. Well, that was four and I was still dying for a cigarette. In fact I seemed to have got hold of one, how odd. My other hand crept towards the lighter. Perhaps if I put a patch actually on my mouth it would have more of a chance to ward off the cigarette when it approached? It would certainly make it jolly hard to get it in. I was just plastering one over my lips with one hand and simultaneously trying to cram a cigarette in with the other, when I heard the door handle turn behind me.

I swung around to see Mrs Bradshaw, my daily, standing in the doorway. We stared at each other for a moment, then I ripped the patch off my lips.

'Oh! Er, Mrs Bradshaw, I didn't hear you arrive, I was just – just tidying up my drawers!'

Mrs Bradshaw cast a cold eye around the room, taking in the unmade bed, the still-drawn curtains, the piles of dirty washing on the floor, the clothes spilling out of the chest of drawers, and, in the midst of all this chaos, the lady of the house, in a chocolate-stained T-shirt and covered in patches. She folded her arms and pursed her lips.

I caught sight of my reflection. 'Oh! Oh, yes, these plasters, cut myself slicing the bread this morning, so silly. Now, wh-what exactly are you – we doing this morning?' I twittered nervously.

Mrs Bradshaw frightened the life out of me but I'd inherited her with the house and had kept her on out of a sense of loyalty Can't think why, she certainly didn't feel any loyalty to me. In fact, word had filtered back to me via the village that she'd fervently hoped Nick would marry his previous girlfriend, the glamorous actress Serena Montgomery, so she could swank that she worked for a film star. According to my sister-in-law Sarah, who lived on the adjacent farm, during Serena's brief occupation at Trewarren she and Mrs Bradshaw had been as thick as thieves, so it must have been a severe blow when he'd eventually plumped (an appropriate verb) for me instead. Not much kudos attached to charring for an erstwhile secretary with dyed roots, I imagined, a suspicion that was confirmed the day I overheard her on the telephone referring to me as 'that jumped-up fancy piece wot married my boss'.

Of course I should have fired her there and then, but I didn't. I had some crazy, misguided notion that I could charm her. I went for the egalitarian I-was-a-worker-too-once approach, but unfortunately overdid it to such an extent that sometimes I wondered who was working for whom. I was forever suggesting tea breaks lest I should be accused of overworking her, the result being that she took complete advantage of me and spent most of the morning sitting on her backside eating me out of chocolate biscuits and watching me with disdain as I made nervous small talk. Like now.

'Another beautiful day, Mrs Bradshaw!' I gabbled.

Mrs Bradshaw eyed me with a mixture of distrust and incredulity. 'If you like rain it is,' she growled eventually, in her deep Cornish brogue.

'Oh, er, has it been raining? Silly me, I hadn't noticed,

only it was so beautiful earlier on, and of course I've got the curtains drawn so I can't see – not that I haven't opened them yet, I have, been up for hours, in fact. No, I was trying on some clothes, you see, didn't want anyone peeking in!'

I think it occurred to both of us to wonder who, apart from the sheep, might be lurking in the open country desperate for a peek at my untoned body, but we let it pass.

Mrs Bradshaw pursed her lips, waiting for her orders. What she probably would have liked to hear was, 'Right, Mrs B, clean the floors, do the windows, polish the silver and when you've finished all that I'll see what else there is,' to which she would have doubtless responded, 'Right you are, Mrs Penhalligan,' and scurried about her business, mop in hand.

Instead, I tended to fidget awkwardly, scratch my chin and say things like, 'Well, gosh, you probably know this place better than I do, why don't you just sort of see what needs doing and, um, have a quick flick round with a duster and maybe a Hoover if it's not too much trouble,' to which she'd sneer and move slowly towards the broom cupboard, before moving even more slowly into another room, probably to put her feet up. Mrs Bradshaw had a lot of sit-down-and-stop when it came to cleaning my house.

This morning, however, I'd had orders from above to get her to do something specific.

'Can't you get that bloody woman to clean the loos? Anyone would think it was beneath her,' Nick had stormed.

It was true. Someone was going to have to get to grips with some rather unattractive limescale and I was damned if it was going to be me. On the other hand I had the feeling she was damned if it was going to be her either. I braced myself, took a deep breath, and took the plunge, loowards, so to speak.

'Um, Mrs Bradshaw, there is actually something I'd like, or rather Nick and I' – I shamelessly dragged him into this for moral support – 'would like you to do this morning.'

I paused. Now most normal people would have taken advantage of this gap in the dialogue to say something like, 'Oh yes?' or 'Really?' but Mrs Bradshaw stayed silent. She just stared unblinkingly at me, like something out of a horror movie. I was rapidly losing my nerve.

'It's – it's the loos,' I managed.

The silence prevailed.

'Yes,' I went on courageously, 'I'd like you to clean them.'

There. It was out. I gulped, waiting. She eyed me contemptuously.

'There's nothing I can do about them toilets,' she growled. 'They're too old. You got limescale in them, they need replacin'. Them toilets have had too much use, that's their problem!'

I nodded vigorously. 'Ah, ah, right. Too much use, how right you are, we do use them an awful lot, too much probably, in fact, we're always using them, I am anyway, all the time!'

She regarded me more with pity than contempt now.

'Oh! Oh, no, not that I use them any more than the next person,' I gabbled, 'no more than is usual – I mean, I don't have, you know, a problem, or anything like that!'

Still the stony silence and the icy glare.

'But how clever of you!' I continued desperately. 'Yes, yes of course, new loos, that's what we need.'

She nodded briefly as if to illustrate that she'd won hands

down, and turned to go, but not before she'd stooped to recover my basque from the floor, holding it between thumb and fingertip as if it were something revolting that Badger had brought in. She deposited it gingerly on a chair, gave me one last disdainful glare, and left.

I sighed and slumped exhausted on the dressing table. Thank God she'd gone. I ripped my patches off and lit a shaky fag, taking it right down to my toenails. Then I pulled on my clothes and went out to find Nick.

He was in the cow shed, kneeling down, fixing one of the partitions between the stalls. I leaned over, resting my chin on the top.

'Mrs Bradshaw says we need new loos,' I reported gloomily. 'She says ours have had it.'

'Balls,' retorted Nick without even looking up. 'They just need a damn good clean, tell her to pull her finger out.'

'Don't be silly, I couldn't possibly! I'm terrified of her!'

Nick paused. He wiped his mouth with the back of his hand and looked up at me. 'Are you? Well, sack her then, for God's sake.'

I looked at him in horror. 'Oh, I couldn't do that either, it would be all round the village in minutes.' I had an idea. 'I know, you sack her!'

'Don't be silly, Polly, you'll have to do it, otherwise it'll be all round the village that you didn't have the nerve and you got your husband to do it.'

I sighed and wandered back to the house. He was right, of course, so I was stuck with her. Too much of a woolly-minded liberal to tell her to buck her ideas up or I'd dock her wages, and too much of a lily-livered coward to send her packing. We'd just have to carry on as normal with her munching her way through my biscuit tin, despising me the while, and me pussyfooting around trying to keep out of her way. I slunk down to the village for an hour or two with this very aim in mind, and when I came back through the front door was relieved to hear her slam simultaneously out of the back, bang on four o'clock and not a moment later.

Later that afternoon I rang Pippa. Finally, at six-thirty, just when I thought she must have gone straight home, she answered.

'Pippa Hamilton.'

'Pippa, it's me, did you get my message?'

'Yes, I was going to ring you, but I've literally just sat down. I need to go through some papers, make a few calls, see my boss, and generally sort myself—'

'Well, never mind about all that, this is important. Listen, I've decided to do it.'

'Do what?'

'The location thing. Lend you the house, the grounds, whatever you like.'

'Really? Are you sure? What did Nick say?'

'Oh, er, don't worry about Nick, I'll get round him later.'

'You mean you haven't asked him?'

'Well, not exactly, but I'll ask him soon, I know he'll agree.'

'Will he? I should have thought he'd hate the very idea.'

'Pippa,' I said a trifle crossly, 'believe me, I know my own husband, he'll be thrilled, absolutely thrilled. Especially when I tell him how much we're going to make from it.'

'Well, I'll have to talk to Bruce about that, I'm not sure what sort of figure he had in mind, but if you're sure, I'll put it forward at the next meeting as a suggestion.'

'A suggestion? You mean it's not definite? I thought you said this place was ideal?'

'It is, but I can't possibly just say yes over the phone, I'll have to talk to Sam and we'll have to show the client some pictures and that sort of thing.'

'OK, OK, I'll pop some photos in the post to you.'

'Fine, but I have to tell you we saw quite a good place in Devon on the way back, so don't get your hopes up too much.'

'What?' I was aghast. 'In Devon? But it wasn't as nice, surely?'

'Well, it was quite pretty, and closer to London, of course.'

'Well – well, pretend you didn't see it!'

'What?'

'Pretend you didn't go there, they'll never know.'

'Polly, I can't do that!'

'Course you can! Pippa, think of all the fun we'll have, it'll be just like old times! You can stay here at the house and we'll stay up late drinking and smoking – well, drinking anyway, and we'll—'

'Polly, I can't possibly stay at the house, I have to stay with the crew.'

'Do you? Oh. Oh, but surely—'

'Listen, I've got to run, my other phone's going. I'll talk to Sam and Bruce and ring you back, OK? But don't bank on it, it's by no means certain, bye.'

She hung up. I stared at the receiver incredulously. By no means certain? What on earth was she talking about? Surely she could wangle it? Didn't she know my happiness depended on it? What did it matter if the house in Devon was better? I shook my head in amazement. Goodness, what on earth had got into poor old Pippa, she was sounding so cross and businesslike these days.

I spent the next few days loitering by the telephone, willing it to ring. I was terrified Nick would get to it first to be casually informed that a film crew would be descending on him shortly, so I craftily unplugged the phone in the bedroom and set up camp by the one in the hall. I sat for hours on the really uncomfortable wooden chair at the bottom of the stairs pretending to do my tapestry. I'd started it when I first got married, thinking it was the sort of thing ladies who lived in large houses probably did, but I'd only managed about two square inches in as many years. It was predominantly a revolting shade of mauve and I loathed the very sight of it, but it was serving an awfully useful purpose now.

'Still doing that delightful cushion cover?' grinned Nick as he passed by for the fourth time that day. 'Why on earth d'you do it here? Surely the light's better in the drawing room?'

'I like it here. I think I shall cover this chair with it when I've finished, so it sort of puts me in the mood sitting here.'

Nick eyed me suspiciously. Unfortunately he knew me too well these days.

'You're up to something, Polly, I can tell.'

'Me?' I enquired, eyebrows raised innocently. 'Up to something? Don't be ridiculous, of course I'm not, I just like sitting here, that's all.'

'All right, have it your way, but I smell a rat.'

'Oh Nick, just because I fancy a change of scene you automatically assume that – I'LL GET IT!' I screeched as the telephone rang.

I almost broke his fingers, wrenching it from his hand as he went to pick it up. Nick backed away in surprise.

'Yes? Hello?' I gasped. 'Pippa!'

I swung around to him, flushed and triumphant. 'It's for me! It's Pippa!'

'So I gathered,' he murmured, watching me in amazement. He didn't move.

I put my hand over the mouthpiece. 'See you later then,' I hissed, shooing him away with my other hand.

Nick shook his head incredulously, turned, and walked out of the front door into the garden.

'Pippa!' I hissed, turning away and cupping my hand round the mouthpiece to muffle my voice. 'What's the news?'

'Well, it's all set. They liked the photos and they're planning to start shooting on the fifth.'

'Really? Seriously? You mean it's on? YIPPEE!' I leaped up and punched the air. Through the open front door Nick's head rotated in surprise, but he strode on.

'God, that's fantastic, Pippa, absolutely brilliant! The fifth of what?'

'May, of course.'

'May? But that's – that's only a couple of weeks away, isn't it?'

'About ten days. I know it's quite soon but we're so behind schedule we've just got to get a move on. That will be all right, won't it?' Pippa sounded anxious. 'I've more or less said it's definite because you were so keen.'

'Oh yes, yes, fine.' Ten days. Christ!

'And Nick's OK about the whole thing?'

'Oh yes, delighted. Um, how much will we get for it, Pippa?'

'About seven hundred pounds, I should think, but I'll check with Bruce. D'you want to talk to him now?'

'Er, no, no, that's all right.'

Seven hundred pounds. I'd expected slightly more than that somehow. Still, it was better than nothing and it would certainly help our ailing finances.

'Oh, and Polly, could you possibly send me a list of local hotels? I'll have to arrange for the crew to stay somewhere. Any ideas?'

'Sure, there are a few places in Helston, I'll give it some thought.'

'Great. Oh, and also a local kennel for the dogs.'

'Dogs?'

'Yes, they'll have to stay somewhere too.'

'What dogs?'

'The dogs in the commercial, you moron. I told you it was for Doggy Chocs Deluxe, didn't I?'

I sat down hard on the hall chair.

'Um, yes, at least . . . well, I probably forgot. Er, how many dogs?'

'Oh, not more than twenty, I shouldn't think.'

'*Twenty!*' I gripped the banisters.

'Well, I don't think it'll be more than that, but it all depends on how many Sam wants in the charging scene.'

The charging scene! I covered my eyes with my hand and groaned. Jesus Christ – the sheep! The cows! Twenty charging dogs! Nick!

'Polly? Polly, is this OK? I really hope so because it's all arranged now and I shall be in the deepest shit imaginable if it isn't.'

I gulped. 'Um, no, no, it's fine, Pippa, leave it to me,' I croaked, 'I'll – I'll get back to you about hotels and, um,' I gasped, 'kennels.'

'Great. Speak to you soon. Sorry I haven't got time to gas

but we'll have a long gossip when I come down – I've loads to tell you, see you in ten days!'

'Look forward to it,' I said weakly.

I replaced the receiver and walked, rather shakily, upstairs. I gazed out of my bedroom window at the pastoral scene below. All was quiet, all was tranquil. In the distance I could see Nick, leaning against the tractor, talking to Larry, who was fixing a wheel. The field beyond them was dotted with sheep and young lambs, and the one beyond that with cows and their calves. In ten days' time they'd be dotted with lights, cameras, vans, trucks, a film crew, actors and twenty mad, rampaging dogs. My mouth felt inexplicably dry, my hands clammy. Blimey. What the hell had I done?

Chapter Five

Three days passed, four, five – still I hadn't told him. On the sixth day I took my courage into my trembling hands and decided tonight was the night.

I stole into Helston and bought the best fillet steak money could buy, a packet of the ubiquitous jam-tart pastry, and a tin of pâté. Originally, I'd imagined myself lovingly creating the last two components, but fear had got the better of my culinary skills and it was all I could do to slap the pâté on the fillet, cover it with frozen pastry and shove the whole lot in the oven before staggering to the wheel-back chair by the Aga and collapsing in a petrified heap.

Mrs Bradshaw, who was pretending to clean out a cupboard, was eyeing my preparations with amusement.

'Got a dinner party then, 'ave you?'

'Er, yes, something like that, Mrs Bradshaw,' I muttered, biting my nails.

'Pulling out all the stops for this one, ain't you?' she smirked. 'Made a pudding, 'ave you? Or is that frozen too?'

'What?' I was miles away – in the far field actually, wrestling with a rabid dog who'd got his jaws clasped tightly round a lamb's neck. 'A pudding? No, no that's . . . that's me!'

I leaped up. God, forget the dinner, there were some serious preparations to do – I had to go and make myself alluring, we were talking a couple of hours here.

I fled upstairs and ran a hot bath, pouring as many smellies into it as I could lay my hands on. I wallowed for a long while, letting the extract of horse chestnut do its steamy business and eyeing my tummy and thighs nervously.

Luckily, the diet I'd chosen to follow over the last six days had been amazingly successful. It was called the too-bloody-terrified-to-eat diet. Every time I'd got a morsel of food near my mouth, I'd felt as sick as a dog, which had reminded me of the twenty or so soon to be marauding through our fields, which had reminded me in turn of Nick's unamused face, which had instantly made me drop whatever it was I'd been contemplating sending down the red lane.

Consequently, I'd lost about half a stone already, a hell of a lot, but was it enough, I wondered nervously, eying the basque hanging on the back of the bathroom door. I hadn't had the nerve to try it on yet, but time would tell. I stepped out of the bath, dried myself and stepped gingerly into the garment.

Time did tell. Half an hour later I was still wriggling around on my bedroom floor, squeezing bits of recalcitrant flesh into position as I tugged on the coat hanger that I'd slotted into the zip for extra leverage.

'Breathe in and – pull!' I muttered for the umpteenth time. 'Breathe in and – pull!' Jesus, the zip must be stuck or something, or the basque must have shrunk in the wash, because this was just ridiculous! There was no way I was this fat, no way!

I was working up a sensational sweat now, my hands were dripping wet and slipping off the coat hanger every time I tugged at it, my fringe was plastered nicely to my forehead and the rest of my hair was frizzing attractively in the heat. But I wasn't giving up, no way. I gritted my teeth and tried again, wrestling with the zip. No way, José, I was *not* giving up! I breathed in so hard my chest hit my chin, gave the zip one last superhuman wrench and – yes! It rocketed up to the top. I'd done it! It was up!

I lay there beaming with relief, albeit somewhat numbly. You see, I couldn't move, I was paralysed from chest to hips. I could move my neck, my shoulders and anything bottomwards, but anything pertaining to the torso was locked into the vicelike grip of this deceptively flimsy, lacy undergarment. My waist for instance. Impossible. I simply didn't have one any more, didn't bend in the middle, I had a poker for a backbone.

There was precious little scope for breathing either, one had to sort of – well, hyperventilate really. I gave it a go. Yes – short, chuggy breaths, that was the answer, going no further than the throat, and certainly not down to the lungs or tummy, a short circuit of nose, mouth and not much else. I practised for a bit and when I'd mastered it, decided it was time to try standing up.

I wriggled over to my bed and, with a little help from my bedside table, levered myself slowly upright. I swayed slightly as everything sorted itself out – blood, heart, lungs, kidneys, liver – they were all having to relinquish their old slots and jostle for new positions and the jostling was having an unfortunate effect on my equilibrium. I steadied myself on the wall and when I was sure at least a smidgen of oxygen had got to my brain, blinked hard and prepared for the acid test.

With my shoulders necessarily pushed up somewhere near my ears and my arms swinging around like an ape, I turned and addressed the mirror. I blinked. Gosh. Well, the top half didn't look too bad, I spilled riotously over in what could almost be called a voluptuous, alluring manner. Unfortunately I spilled out at the bottom too, just as voluptuously, but not quite so alluringly. I frowned at the rolling flesh which galloped so wantonly around my thighs. Where on earth had it all come from? Some of it was stuff I'd never even seen before.

I deliberately went a bit cross-eyed, thus blurring my vision as I went for The Whole Effect. Hmmm ... The Whole Effect was rather like a particularly porky sausage in the grip of a very determined bandage, but still, I consoled myself, it was really only the top half that mattered. By the time he'd got down to this stage the basque would be coming off anyway, wouldn't it?

Suddenly I froze. Heavy footsteps were coming down the corridor towards me. Christ, Nick! I just had time to throw on a dressing gown as he poked his head around the door.

'Everything all right?' he enquired.

'Yes, fine,' I twittered nervously. 'Why?'

'No reason, just haven't seen you for a while.' He stared. 'You look awfully pink, Polly, and what's happened to your hair?'

'Oh, er, it's just gone a bit frizzy, that's all – hot bath.'

'Just what I'm going to have, see you later.' He almost went, then popped his head back. 'Incidentally, something in the oven smelled a bit suspect. I turned it off but you might take a look.' He disappeared in the direction of the bathroom.

Christ, the beef! I quickly toned down my florid face with some talc, threw on jeans and a T-shirt, and with a little help from the banisters, lowered myself painfully downstairs to see what was cooking.

Burning was more like it. I pulled it from the oven and saw at a glance that the black pastry would have to go. I picked it off with a knife and was relieved to see that it had at least protected the fillet which, though cooked to distraction, still vaguely resembled a piece of meat. I threw some broccoli into one pan, some new potatoes into another and then, all cooked out, hobbled into the drawing room in search of something horizontal on which to prostrate myself.

Breathing in an upright position was becoming a real problem now; my insides were being crushed to smithereens and only a prone position seemed to give any sort of relief. I lowered myself painfully on to the sofa, thinking that what I really wanted to do was take this bloody thing off and have a telly supper and an early night. Never mind, it would all be over soon, and no pleasure without pain, et cetera, et cetera. I lay still, trying to sneak some air into my lungs. Damn, I'd forgotten to light the candles in the dining room. I struggled to get up. Sod the candles. I collapsed on my back and shut my eyes, experiencing a bit of head rush. Five minutes later, Nick strode into the room.

'Hello, darling, feeling tired?' He bent over and dropped

a kiss on my recumbent form. 'Gosh, you're still pretty hot, are you sure you're OK?'

'Fine, fine!' I bleated.

'The kitchen smells a bit more appetising now. What are we having?'

'Oh, just a little *boeuf en cr ... boeuf en* its own, and some seasonal vegetables straight from the garden, lovingly garnished with melted butter and freshly ground black pepper. Nothing very exciting.' I smiled weakly.

'Sounds great, I could just do with a bloody great steak. Shall I lay the table?'

'It's OK, I've done it.'

'Really? Not when I last looked.'

'Oh, not in the kitchen, I thought we'd eat in the dining room.'

'Oh? Who's coming?'

'No one, I just thought it would be nice for a change.'

Nick looked surprised. 'Oh! Oh, right, fine.' He rubbed his hands together and grinned. 'Well, let's go then, shall we? I'm starving.'

'Absolutely! Let's eat!' I grinned maniacally back. I simply couldn't move.

Nick started towards the door, then turned back. 'What's wrong?'

'Nothing, nothing really, it's just I twisted my ankle today and I can't seem to put much weight on it. You couldn't sort of help me, could you?'

'Sure.' Nick hauled me up, much the same way as one would haul up a drawbridge. Plank-like. He frowned. 'Does it hurt much?'

'Good Lord, no.' I shook my head vigorously. 'No, not

much at all. You go on and I'll just go and put the finishing touches to supper.'

Walking like Arnie Schwarzenegger, all chest and pectorals, and breathing like an underwater diver, I disappeared off to the kitchen, where I immediately sensed that supper was not going to be the gastronomic delight I'd hoped for. The vegetables were not so much boiled as puréed, and the beef had a barbecued look about it. Still, there was plenty of it and Nick never really minded what he ate as long as it was abundant. I piled the plates high, tottered back into the dining room and, bending at the knees rather than the waist, lowered his plate in front of him.

'This looks great,' said Nick dubiously.

'Good.'

I tottered round and stood by my chair, eyeing it nervously. Would I be able to sit down? Let alone eat? Nick looked up at me.

'Well, come on, let's eat while it's still hot.'

'Sure.'

'Come on then, sit!' he said impatiently, grasping his knife and fork.

'I thought I might stand, actually.'

'Stand? What, to eat supper?'

'Well, it's just that my ankle—'

'Polly, your ankle will feel a damn sight better if you sit down and take your weight off it. Now come on, you're being really peculiar. What the hell's the matter?'

'Nothing, nothing.' I pulled out my chair, bent my knees, and keeping my torso ramrod straight, limbo-danced into it. Somehow I managed to slide into a semi-upright position with my buttocks perched right at the very front of the chair and my head resting on the back.

Nick regarded me over the table. He could just about see my face over the mahogany. I smiled winningly. He sighed, shook his head wearily and began his meal.

'So, um, what sort of a day have you had, darling?' I began brightly, toying with a piece of broccoli that was just about level with my nose.

'Pretty good, actually, the lambs are all doing really well now. I'll probably wean them soon, put the ewes in the meadow by the wood and move the lambs into the back field. It'll give the grass a bit of a rest too.'

'Great, great,' I croaked.

I was beginning to feel most unpleasant. My circulation had clearly been completely cut off at the tummy and I was having violent rushes of blood facewards. It was on fire, absolutely flaming, and I could hardly feel my legs.

'It's good for the grass to have a rest, is it?' I gasped.

Christ, this was hopeless, I'd never get to the pudding stage, I was in too much pain. As soon as he'd finished what he was saying about the sheep I'd whip my T-shirt off and get it over with. OK, so the seduction scene would come a little earlier than anticipated and he might not have finished his carrots, but what the hell, anything would be better than this agony.

'Oh, without a doubt, you can't keep sheep grazing a field indefinitely. It strips the goodness out and...' And so he went on. And on and on.

More and more blood was rushing round my head now. I didn't know I had so much. Feeling sick and woozy, I concentrated like mad on Nick's face, on his voice, waiting for a gap in the dialogue, willing him to pause. Of course, it wouldn't do to undress when he was in the middle of explaining the grazing rotation, but the moment there was the briefest lull, I'd be in there. I clutched the bottom of my T-shirt, ready at a moment's notice to whip it over my head, but all of a sudden I had to transfer my hands to the table to steady myself. Nick's face was getting fuzzier and fuzzier, his voice fainter and fainter.

From my perspective everything went white, my head felt as if it was going to explode and in one spectacular close-up, the carpet zoomed up to meet me. From Nick's perspective I probably went an attractive shade of purple, foamed at the mouth, and collapsed in a heap on the floor.

When I came to, I was lying on a sofa in the drawing room. I had a blanket over me and Nick was kneeling beside me, looking anxious.

'Polly? Polly, can you hear me, are you all right?' His sweet, much-loved voice was full of concern.

'Fine, fine,' I croaked. 'Much better, actually. Did I faint?'

'I'll say, you put the fear of God into me. One minute you were sitting opposite me and the next thing I knew you were flat on your back on the carpet!'

'Well, you know me,' I grinned weakly, 'any time, any place. The slightest opportunity, the least provocation.'

'Well, quite, and that's another thing, what's with the kinky underwear?'

I clutched my torso, I was naked under the blanket.

'My basque! Where is it?'

Nick held it up. 'I took it off, it was crushing the air out of you. No wonder you fainted, it left great weals on your body where those sticks had dug into you. I had no idea you were into bondage and all that sort of thing, Polly, why didn't you say?' He looked keen, if a little nervous.

I groaned. 'It's boned, that's all, to keep it up. It's not supposed to be masochistic, just sexy.'

'Really? It looks like an instrument of torture to me.'

'Well, I was a bit thinner when I last wore it, perhaps it was a bit ambitious.'

'A bit!' Nick guffawed loudly. 'I'll say! You must have used a shoe horn to get into it. I should try losing a couple of stone before you try this little number on again, Polly!'

A couple? I ground my teeth. That hurt. I sat up, clutching my blanket around me.

'Well, I'm sorry it looked so hideous,' I snapped. 'I only put it on for your benefit, you know, I don't enjoy having my insides crushed to a pulp.'

Nick looked puzzled. 'My benefit? Why?'

I bit my lip. 'Oh, it's a long story,' I muttered. Not now, Polly, this was definitely not the right time.

'Come on, darling, please tell me or I'll worry.'

Or was it? I looked at his face: anxious, concerned, loving. Yes, why not? When better, in fact? Here I was, stark naked under a blanket, having recently fainted. I was in an extremely delicate, vulnerable condition, wasn't I? He was hardly likely to ball me out, now was he?

I let the blanket fall down a bit to reveal some cleavage, gazed up at him through my eyelashes, and let my bottom lip wobble a bit.

'OK, but don't be cross, promise?' I whispered.

Big mistake. Nick regarded me grimly. 'Cut the crap, Polly, what's going on?'

Damn. I sighed. 'Well, you see, I wanted to get round you, to ask you something.'

'I gathered that, but is it so awful that you had to get dressed up like Miss Whiplash?'

'Well . . . the thing is,' I lied, 'Pippa asked me to do her an enormous favour, and in a very weak moment, I agreed.'

'What?'

'Well,' I struggled on, feeling a bit sick, 'I promised her she could sort of use the house. Just for a bit.'

He frowned. 'The house? What for?'

I squirmed, curling my toes up tight. 'Well, for a shoot, actually, a commercial. As a kind of . . . location.'

His face turned to stone. 'You what?'

'Well, yes, I know I shouldn't have done, stupid of me really, but she was desperate, you see, Nick, she'd been to see all these different houses and none of them were any good and she said this would be ideal. She was looking so down about it all and not looking forward to telling her boss she'd had a wasted journey and' – I swallowed hard – 'well, I just sort of found myself saying yes.'

Nick stared at me. 'Well, you can just sort of find yourself saying no,' he said quietly, his eyes narrowing to two little pieces of flint.

I gasped, and clutched his arm. 'What! Oh no! No, Nick, I can't, you see, I promised.'

'Don't be silly,' he snapped, shaking my hand off. 'There is absolutely no way I'm having a commercial shot here, I'm amazed you even considered it. Did you really think I'd welcome a film crew traipsing all over my house, tramping through the garden, not to mention wrecking the crops and frightening the animals? No, I'm sorry, Polly, it's out of the question and if you don't telephone Pippa right now and tell her so, I will.'

'Oh, but Nick, I can't!' I wailed, wringing my hands. 'She'll have arranged everything by now, she'll kill me! Please think it over, we'd get paid really well, you know, you could put a new roof on the barn, maybe even buy some more livestock, it would be a new lease of life for the farm!'

'Rubbish, I didn't work in advertising all those years without knowing we'd get a few hundred quid and a great deal of damage. Now pick up that phone.'

'But Nick, just think! It could be a going concern, this could be just the beginning, we could let big film companies use it, we'd get thousands, we'd – no! No, don't – all right, I'll do it!'

Nick had reached up to the shelf where the portable phone was, found Pippa's number in the address book, and was even now punching it out. I grabbed the receiver from him.

'Do it then, Polly,' he ordered.

'But—'

'*Now!*'

I gulped and slowly punched out the rest of the number. I bit the inside of my cheek, feeling truly sick. Pippa would never speak to me again, never, but it was either that or divorce. She answered.

'Hello, Pippa?' I quaked. 'It's me, Polly.'

'Hi! How's it going? Looking forward to the big day? I can't believe it's come round so soon! It's all going really smoothly this end, I got your list of hotels and kennels so I've booked all that, oh, and we've got a brilliant crew together, I can't wait to get going now! How are things with you?'

My mouth felt sticky, as if I'd been eating neat peanut butter for days. I dredged up some saliva from somewhere.

'W-e-ll, not so good, actually,' I quavered.

'Oh? Why's that?'

I snuck a look at my grim-faced husband. 'Er, well, you see, it's Nick.'

'Nick? What's wrong with him?'

For one crazy moment I nearly threw myself through this window of opportunity – yes, of course, Nick was ill, terminally ill, we couldn't possibly have a film crew traipsing round the house, he needed peace, quiet. I glanced up at the grim but healthy face beside me. The window slammed shut.

'Er, nothing,' I gulped, tightening my grip on the phone. 'He's not ill or anything but – well, the thing is, Pippa, he won't do it.'

'Do what?'

'The shoot. He won't hear of it.' I clenched my buttocks hard and shut my eyes. 'He won't even consider it. He says no, Pippa.'

There was a terrible silence.

'Pippa? Pippa?' I quavered eventually.

'I don't believe you,' she whispered. 'I thought you asked him ages ago, you said it was all agreed. You can't do this to me, Polly.'

'I know, I know,' I wailed. 'It's all my fault, but you see I kept putting it off and putting it off and actually – I've only just asked him. I'm so sorry, Pippa, really I am, but I'll make it up to you, I promise!'

'I'll lose my job,' she whispered.

'No, no, I'm sure you won't, say something awful's happened, say the cows have got foot-and-mouth, say we're riddled with ringworm, rampant with myxomatosis, say no one's allowed down here, say you'll have to go somewhere else, say—'

'Polly, you don't understand!' she shrieked. 'The crew is booked, the actors are booked, the client's coming down from Manchester and now you're telling me we don't have a location? We're talking about next week, Polly, *next week*! I won't be *able* to find a location, it's impossible!'

'But surely one of the other places you looked at would—'

'Not at a few days' notice – no, no way! And what's Josh going to say, have you thought of that?' Her voice cracked slightly. 'Have you thought about what sort of a position this puts me in? He's not just my boss, you know, he's my boyfriend and things are shaky enough as it is at the moment without me springing this on him – YOU JUST CAN'T DO THIS TO ME, POLLY!' she screamed.

I turned to Nick with eyes like saucers. I put my hand over the mouthpiece. 'I think she's going to cry,' I whispered.

I felt about two inches tall, smaller even. I felt slug-like, worm-like, I wanted to crawl away and die.

'Let me talk to her.' He took the phone, looking grim. 'Pippa, I realise this puts you in a tight spot, but this is quite literally the first I've heard of this little scheme. Polly sprung it on me a moment ago and I'm afraid there's just no way, not with spring lambs around and—' He listened. I watched his jaw drop, his eyes glaze over. 'Next week?' he said incredulously. 'Next week!' He turned to me furiously. 'Did you know it was scheduled for next week?' he hissed.

I nodded shamefacedly, unable to meet his eye. He licked his lips and addressed the receiver.

'Pippa, I had no idea ... Yes, I can see that ... Yes, terribly difficult ... Oh God, yes, the client ... No, of course not, but I still don't think ... Oh Pippa, look, please don't cry ... No, don't cry, look, I'll – I'll see what I can do ... Yes, yes, I will ... all right, yes, I promise ... It's all right, it's not your fault ... Yes ... Yes, yes all right, we'll work something out ... Yes, I'll move the animals and ... Dogs? What dogs?'

I stuffed my fist in my mouth, ducked quickly under the blanket and moaned softly.

'I see.' Even the muffling effect of the blanket couldn't disguise the steel in his voice. 'Yes, I see ... Well, what can I say? I've given you my word now, but I'm not happy. I'm not happy about this at all. How many?'

I moaned again.

'Really.' His voice was dangerously quiet. 'Well, I'll ring you at work tomorrow and find out exactly what the arrangements are ... Don't apologise, Pippa, it's not your fault ... Goodbye.'

I stayed exactly where I was, staring into the darkness, biting hard on my knuckles, not daring to move. Two seconds later the protective blanket was whipped abruptly from my face.

'Did you know there were dogs involved?' he hissed into my nose.

'Yes,' I whispered.

'And you still said yes? When we have a farm full of

87

sheep and lambs? Cows due to calf at any minute? You still said yes?' He stared at me incredulously. I couldn't look at him.

'Christ!' he muttered eventually, shaking his head. 'It simply defies belief! What were you thinking of, Polly?'

'I don't know,' I whispered.

'You don't know. I see.'

There was a terrible silence.

'Sorry,' I whispered.

This was awful, I'd never seen him so furious, so white, so quietly livid.

'You put me in an invidious position, Polly,' he said between clenched teeth. 'They're due to start shooting next week. Pippa was distraught, she'd never have found another location. I had to say yes.'

I grabbed his hand. 'Oh thank you, oh thank you so much! You didn't have to, but you did, thank you!' I kissed his hand madly but he pulled sharply away.

'Don't, Polly.'

'I promise you everything will be all right,' I whispered miserably. 'It'll be really well organised and if a dog so much as sniffs a sheep's backside I'll kill it, I swear, I'll kill it with my own bare hands, but it won't, it won't happen, it'll all go like clockwork, you'll see!'

'It had better,' he said grimly, getting to his feet, 'because I'm warning you, Polly, if any of the animals are worried in any way, or if any of the crops are trampled, I swear to God I'll have them off my land before you can say Doggy Bloody Chocs Deluxe, do I make myself clear?'

'Absolutely,' I gulped.

'I hope so. And one more thing, Polly.' His eyes bored

into me. 'Don't ever try to manipulate me like that again. I'm doing this for Pippa's sake, not yours, please remember that.'

He turned on his heel, marched out of the room and thumped up the stairs.

I sat there quaking, listening to him stomping around upstairs. My God, he was mad. Truly mad. To the uninitiated he might seem tight-lipped, even a little cross, but to the cognoscenti like me he was hopping, steaming, irrevocably mad and I knew from experience that I had to keep right out of his way. Let him blow his top in private then wait for the dust to settle. Any sort of interference at an early stage could be fatal, my head could so easily roll.

I gulped and clutched my knees. Well, that had backfired a bit, hadn't it? And it had all seemed so harmless, just a bit of fun. I bit my lip miserably. I'd put Nick in an impossible position, I could see that now, and it was only his intrinsically kind heart and concern for Pippa that had stopped him from calling the whole thing off – God, I could have cost Pippa her job, how awful of me! Suddenly I flushed with shame. How dare I push people around like that? How dare I manipulate them? What on earth was the matter with me? Why did I get these little ideas into my head and let them snowball away out of control until they were great big scheming boulders? Did other people behave like this, I wondered, or was it just me? For once I felt truly ashamed.

I lay down and tucked myself into a foetal position, shivering miserably, hating myself. It was damned chilly without any clothes on, but there was no way I was going upstairs to get any, no way I was facing Nick. I made a little nest out of the blanket and hugged Badger, who'd quivered nervously up to me, sensing the wrath of Nick that was so often vented on him for chewing the furniture, and offering a wet nose, halitosis and moral support.

I suppose I must have drifted off to sleep because when I opened my eyes the fire had completely gone out and I was absolutely frozen. I wrapped the blanket around me and stole quietly upstairs. The curtains were drawn and the great hump in the duvet indicated that Nick was sound asleep. I slipped in beside him and hugged my knees, trying to get warm. A second later an arm wound round my waist.

'You're freezing,' he murmured.

'I thought you were asleep,' I whispered back, surprised he was even talking to me, let alone touching me.

'Too busy totting up the damage a pack of marauding dogs will cause.'

'I'm really sorry, Nick, I can't tell you how awful I feel.'

'You're a total dickhead, Polly,' he muttered, but not too unkindly.

'I know, but I've got great plans to remove the dick from my head,' I whispered, vastly encouraged.

'See that you do.' He leaned over and kissed me. 'Just see that you do.'

He leaned back on his pillow as if to go to sleep, but I wound my arms round his neck, full of relief and gratitude. I began to kiss him very thoroughly. 'Thank you, thank you...' I murmured, working hard on the stony facial muscles, 'thank you so much.' I kissed away.

'Polly, if you think you can get round me like this...' he muttered into my hair.

I worked harder.

'It takes more than a kiss and a cuddle, you know...'

he grunted, 'more than that ... yes, even more than that ... that's a bit better ... better still ... keep going ... you're getting there, Poll...'

Chapter Six

During the course of the next few days Nick and I made our respective preparations for the shoot. His took the form of moving his sheep out of harm's way and squeezing as much money as possible out of the production company, eventually bumping our fee up another five hundred pounds.

'Might as well take them for all we can get,' he said grimly, having clinched the deal on the phone with Bruce. 'It's not as if they won't leave us unscathed.'

He'd just about come down from boiling point but was still at a slow, rolling simmer and only managed to keep the lid on it if he wasn't provoked. I have a habit of being unwittingly provocative so I kept well out of his way as he and Larry moved hordes of sheep and cows into distant meadows, muttering dire curses under their breath.

My own preparations were of a slightly different nature. Having felt genuinely guilty and ashamed of myself I bounced back surprisingly quickly, and on the day before the film crew were due to arrive, I bustled excitedly off to Truro where I availed myself of every conceivable beauty treatment the town had to offer.

I was plucked, waxed, pummelled, manicured, pedicured,

massaged, reflexologied and aromatherapied to within an inch of my life, before finally coming to rest at the most important venue of all, the cut, bleach and blow-dry establishment. As I settled back into my chair I bravely uttered the words every hairdresser longs to hear.

'I'd like to try something different, please,' I quavered.

On hearing these magic words my 'hair sculptor', as he was pleased to call himself, spat out his gum and flexed his wrists, his scissors flashed and he whirred into action. The result was a chunky shoulder-length bob, a wispy fringe, a head full of highlights, and not much change from £80, but it was worth it.

In fact, when I saw Nick's face as I sailed in through the back door of Trewarren armed with carrier bags, I decided it would have been cheap at twice the price. His jaw fell open and he almost dropped the current copy of *The Field* in the sink.

'Blimey,' he said slowly. 'What have you done?'

I grinned and dumped the bags on the kitchen table.

'I've done what I should have done months ago, I've taken myself in hand. D'you like it?'

Nick walked around me. 'It's great. You look like you did when I first met you.'

'Really?' I wasn't quite sure how to take this. 'But that was only three years ago, I haven't changed that much, surely?'

'Well, you were letting yourself go a bit, you know, Polly.'

'Was I?' I gasped. 'Why didn't you say so, for God's sake?'

'Oh, I don't mind, not much call for glamour-girl looks on a farm. What's in the bags?'

'Oh, just a few odds and ends.'

He grinned. 'Spent a fortune, have you? Well, it's about time you bought some new clothes, and I must say, the hair's a distinct improvement.' He grabbed an apple from the fruit bowl, took a bite out of it and made for the back door. 'See you at lunch time.' He strode out.

I beamed with delight. Talk about the right result! No more jeans and sweatshirts for me, from now on I'd swan around the farm like something out of *Vogue* – and I'd smell good too, I thought, reaching into a bag for my new Obsession spray. I squirted some on my neck. No more borrowing Nick's Right Guard deodorant and thinking that would do in the pong department – no, I'd absolutely reek of Ralph Lauren. I squirted some more on my neck, on my wrists, on the backs of my knees and up my skirt.

'Obsession,' I muttered, striking a dramatic pose, 'for the girl who's mysterious yet sexy, elusive yet sensual—'

'What's that terrible smell?'

I swung around. Sarah, my sister-in-law, had walked into my advert. She was wrinkling up her nose in disgust in the doorway.

'Oh, hi, Sarah, it's called perfume, not much call for it round here, I agree, but it's something women in civilised societies use to make themselves smell sexy and alluring. It's instead of the usual cow dung.'

'Oh, right, yes, rings a bell actually, I seem to remember in my far-off distant past squirting something like that behind my ears, when I lived in a town, of course, and wore shoes instead of clogs – gosh, I like the hair!' She circled me approvingly. 'Ooh, and what's in the bags, can I see?'

She delved in and pulled out a fuchsia pink skirt about eight inches long.

'Hey, look at this! God, how divine, but where are you going to go in it, the Young Farmers' bring-and-buy? The WI car-boot sale?' She giggled.

'Why not?' I said, grabbing it from her. 'Might shake them up a bit. From now on, Sarah, I'm changing my image. Just because I live on a farm, I don't have to look like one or smell like one – you won't recognise me, I'll be a new woman!'

Sarah sat down with a sigh. 'God, I wish I was a new woman, a completely different woman, in fact, not me at all.'

She ran her hands through her curly brown hair, her sweet, freckled face decidedly gloomy. I dumped the bags on the floor, hoping she hadn't seen the price tag on the skirt, put the kettle on for coffee and sat down opposite her.

Sarah was married to Nick's brother Tim and I was extremely fond of her. As far as female company went she'd saved my life when I'd moved down here, and not many days passed when we didn't partake of a tea bag or two in one or other kitchen. She worked her butt off in a riding stables for very little money whilst Tim tried to scrape a living from his terribly correct organic farm. They were very, very Green (in more ways than one, I thought privately) and full of high ideals and marvellous morals, but at the end of the day they were still exhausted and penniless, and as I kept telling her, what was the good of having high ideals and marvellous morals if you didn't have any fun or any dosh?

'Trooble oop stables?' I said sympathetically, passing her

a mug of coffee. 'Still shovelling shit out of some ungrateful stallion's stall? Tell them to get off their lazy hocks and do it themselves.'

She sighed. 'You know I wouldn't mind the hard work, Polly, if we just had a bit of fun now and again, but we don't. Nothing ever seems to happen around here, does it? It's just work, eat, sleep, day after day, that's all I seem to do. For God's sake, I'm only twenty-three, and Tim and I never do anything any more, we don't go out to dinner, we don't even go to the cinema. I tell you, I'm fed up.'

'Sarah! I'm shocked. You know very well there's a Friends of the Earth rally in Truro next month!'

She ground her teeth. 'Terrific. Talk about life in the fast lane.'

I grinned. 'OK, I will.'

I leaned forward conspiratorially and told her about the shoot. She listened agog, suitably impressed by the fiendish way I'd arranged it all.

'Heavens, Polly, you're unreal. Isn't Nick furious?'

'Oh no,' I said airily, 'he's very relaxed. In fact, he's rather pleased now, quite proud of me, in fact. You see, we're getting a hell of a lot of money for the location fee and we'll be able to make all sorts of improvements to the farm. Who knows, we might even plant a few trees, do our bit for the rain forests, that kind of thing.'

Sarah looked incredulous. 'Rain forests are tropical, Polly!'

'Well, we could throw in a few cheeseplants, or yukkas perhaps – but the point I'm trying to make, Sarah, is that it's all very well having wonderful plans to save the world, and I'm the first one to say that ecology and all that environmental junk is terribly important, but if you don't have the money to implement those plans—'

'I THOUGHT YOU SAID THEY WERE COMING TOMORROW!' boomed an outraged voice in my left ear.

My coffee mug nearly leaped out of my fingers as I swung round in alarm.

'Wh-what?' I faltered.

'Tomorrow, you said, well they're bloody well here today!' Nick ground his teeth. 'And d'you know where they are? Eh? Go on, have a guess.'

'Er . . . where?'

'In my bloody barley field! Apparently they thought it was a marvellous place to park, terrifically handy, thought it was grass, you see, didn't have the nous to realise that some crops do vaguely resemble grass but aren't actually quite so robust and don't take kindly to having two-ton trucks parked on top of them! Of course, they didn't even stop to consider that it might be somebody's livelihood, oh no!'

'Oh my God,' I mumbled.

'Yes, oh my God,' he seethed, 'the nightmare's begun. I've got Larry re-directing them to the top field but if you could tear yourself away from your coffee morning for two minutes you might slip down and give him a hand. I've got work to do and I haven't got time to be a bloody traffic warden! Morning, Sarah.' He slammed out again.

Sarah raised her eyebrows. 'Doesn't seem too proud at the moment,' she murmured.

'Er, no, you may be right there,' I said, getting hurriedly to my feet. 'In fact I'd better get down there before the shit hits the fan.'

'You mean that wasn't it? Blimey, I'm getting out of here.'

She quickly drained her coffee and we went our separate ways.

I ran speedily to the barley field. God! A day early! Why hadn't Pippa let me know? I couldn't help feel inordinately excited, though, as I sped down the garden, across the first field and into the meadow beyond. They were here! They'd arrived! In fact I couldn't resist a couple of gazelle-like leaps as I bounded through the long grass. As I executed the second leap I caught sight of Nick wrestling with a ewe in the adjacent field. I instantly dropped the aerobics and adopted a slow, sober walk, head hung low, face suffused with guilt.

'Get a move on, Polly,' yelled Nick over the fence. 'Instead of prancing around you could get down there and help Larry!'

'Yes, sir,' I muttered meekly, doffing an imaginary cap.

Gosh, he was a bore. So they were a day early? So what? His unwavering misanthropy about the whole thing was beginning to annoy me.

In the distance I spotted a convoy of trucks and vans trundling out of the barley field, along the dirt track, and into the field immediately below me. Larry was waving his arms around, directing them in. I ran to join him at the gate and swung on it as the first of the lorries made its way towards us. I smiled cheerily as it trundled through and two young guys in the front smiled back, giving me a wave. As the six or seven vehicles rolled through I kept the smile glued to my face, despite the dust, whilst silently appraising the occupants. He's attractive . . . she's pretty . . . so is she . . . she's not – oh look, there's Pippa—

'Pippa!'

Pippa's Alfa Romeo bounced through the gate and stopped in the middle of the field. As she got out I felt slightly nervous. We hadn't spoken since that dreadful phone call.

'Hi!' I yelled.

She ran over and hugged me warmly.

'So glad it's worked out,' she muttered in my ear, 'it would have been awful to fall out over this.'

'We wouldn't have,' I promised, 'but I'm so thrilled you're here, albeit a day early. I thought you were coming tomorrow?'

'Didn't you get my message? I left a message with some yokel woman I couldn't understand, so perhaps she didn't understand me either.'

'Mrs Bradshaw? No, she didn't mention it.'

'Probably forgot.'

Or else, I thought, had deliberately kept quiet. It hadn't escaped my notice that Mrs Bradshaw was getting a vicarious thrill out of all the friction the shoot was causing between me and Nick.

I jumped suddenly as the passenger door of the Alfa Romeo slammed shut with an almighty bang.

'Josh! Come and meet Polly!' shouted Pippa. 'That's him,' she whispered in my ear.

A grim-faced middle-aged man strode towards us. He was wearing white jeans, a denim shirt and a black leather jacket, all of which were slightly too tight and looked faintly ridiculous on his rather portly body. He had a closely cropped black beard tinged with grey and jet-black hair which was very thick at the front and sides but nonexistent in the middle – a bit of a slap-head actually. His eyes were fierce and dark.

'Where the hell did you put my Filofax, Pippa?' he stormed as he approached.

'It's in your case,' replied Pippa soothingly. 'I didn't want you to forget it so I popped it in there first thing this morning.'

'In the office, you mean,' he said quickly, eyes like daggers.

'Y-yes, in the office, of course,' faltered Pippa, flushing. 'Where else?'

'Quite,' he seethed, shortly. 'Well, for future reference, don't touch my things without telling me. I nearly had a heart attack just then, I thought I'd forgotten it.'

'Right. Sorry.'

I looked down and kicked at a tuft of grass, feeling uncomfortable.

'Um, Polly, this is Josh,' said Pippa quickly, 'Josh Drysdale, Polly Penhalligan, my best friend and chatelaine of this vast estate!'

I held out my hand. So this was Josh. This was the married man who was causing Pippa so much pain and heartache. I couldn't see it myself, he looked at least forty and would have been no great shakes at thirty. What was someone as beautiful as Pippa doing with someone as ordinary – and bad-tempered – as this?

'Hi, Pippa's told me all about you,' I said with a smile.

Pippa looked horrified.

'I – mean, what you do, you know, at work, as a producer,' I gabbled quickly.

Josh gave a tight little smile. 'She's told me about you too,' he said grudgingly.

'Well, I hope she didn't tell you how I nearly cocked up the whole bloody thing by not telling my husband you were com—'

'Um, Polly, can I show Josh around?' cut in Pippa with wide eyes and gritted teeth.

'Sure, come up to the house if you like, have a cup of—'

'Wait!' interrupted Josh, holding up his hand for quiet and cocking his ear to the car. We waited. 'Yes, I thought so,' he affirmed with a curt little nod, 'that's my phone.' He turned and ran back to the car.

Pippa rounded on me. 'Polly, *don't* tell him we nearly had a cock-up,' she hissed. 'I want him to think it's all going swimmingly!'

'Well, it is now, isn't it?'

'And *don't* act as if you know about us either!'

'Doesn't he know I know?'

'No! No one's supposed to know, it's all supposed to be incredibly secret!'

'But he's still leaving her for you, isn't he? I mean, he's not stringing you along or anything?'

'Of course not. I told you, he's mad about me, but just don't mention it, that's all!'

'OK, OK, calm down.'

'Right. So what d'you think?' she asked eagerly.

'Er ... well. He looks very nice. I mean, it's so hard to tell when I've only just met him. How old is he?'

'Forty-three. Heavenly, isn't he? D'you know, I had no idea I was into older men until I met Josh, but I tell you, Polly, I'd never go out with anyone under forty again. There are so many advantages of being with an older man, it's incredible!'

'Really?' I said doubtfully. I could only think of the

disadvantages, like the baldness, the saggy tummy, the grey hair, the pathetic attempts at trendy clothes, but I wisely held my tongue. I turned to look at him as he leaned into Pippa's car, talking on the car phone. His jacket had ridden up at the back and through his tight white jeans I could see his Father Christmas boxer shorts. I shuddered. Heavens. Rather her than me.

A moment later he rejoined us, clutching his Filofax and accompanied by someone who provoked a knee-jerk reaction in me that I haven't experienced for some time. I gasped. Jesus. Now we really were talking heavenly.

This individual was about six inches taller than Josh, about eight years younger and about a hundred times more attractive. His nut-brown hair was streaked with gold and swept back off his face, curling slightly as it came to rest on the back of his collar. His face was tanned and his hazel eyes twinkled with gold flecks, rather like his hair. He had that enviable, expensive outdoor look you only get from swimming in hot seas, taking regular skiing trips and playing a spot of polo. We were talking fit and ready for action here. He held out a suntanned hand, flashed an immaculate set of pearly whites and dazzled me with his golden eyes. I nearly fell over.

'Hi, you must be Polly. I'm Sam Weston, the director of this motley crew. I'm so sorry, we obviously parked in completely the wrong field. Is your husband going to be livid?'

I went for his extended hand enthusiastically – so enthusiastically that I nearly missed and shot up his armpit – and flashed my very best smile in return.

'Oh no, not in the least, it really couldn't matter less!' I gushed.

'Well, that's a relief, I thought perhaps he was planning to sue us before we'd even started!'

'Ha ha! Good lord no, don't be silly, he's delighted you're here, can't wait to meet you, in fact!'

'Really?'

'Yes, he used to be in the ad business himself, you see, so he's terrifically interested, can't wait to get – you know – involved again!'

'Great! Well, I'll tell you what, we need a few long shots of the house, so we'll probably stay down here for a bit, but once that's done I'll pop up and say hello, shall I? Explain what we're going to be doing?'

'Oh do, do – although, er, actually,' I said hastily, 'he's pretty busy with the sheep at the moment, but do pop up anyway, I'd love to hear your plans and, um, familiarise myself with your shooting schedule.'

I was rather pleased with this last little throwaway remark, remembered from my own days in the business.

I thought Sam looked suitably impressed, if a little surprised. 'Er, yes, of course, I'd be happy to run through the schedule with you if that's what you'd like.'

'Great! Two o'clock suit you?'

Sam looked a little taken aback. Steady, Polly, steady.

'Well, actually, we'll probably be right in the middle of shooting then, but when I get a moment I promise I'll come up.'

'Oh, yes, well, whenever,' I said quickly. 'I'm pretty busy myself, of course, got loads to do.' Stop it, Polly, you're behaving like some sort of frustrated housewife from the sticks, get a grip. I gave him an earnest, businesslike look. 'Now, is there anything I can get you? Tea? Coffee? Cold drinks for the crew?'

'Good lord no, that's kind, but we bring our own catering service.'

'Oh really? Where?'

He turned and pointed. 'Big Winnibago in the far corner there, see?'

I turned and looked in the direction he was indicating but couldn't see anyone of that description, only a large sort of caravan affair.

'I see, well if Big Winnie wants any help you be sure to let me know, OK?' I smiled winningly.

Sam looked a bit confused 'Er . . . right, thanks.'

Josh tapped him on the arm 'Sam, a word . . .'

'The big Winnibago's a catering truck, you moron,' muttered Pippa in my ear, 'not a fat tea lady.'

'Oh!' I blushed.

Sam and Josh were deep in discussion now and looked as if they were about to wander off, when suddenly Sam turned back. He smiled.

'Oh, and listen, Polly, please don't worry. I promise everything will be left just exactly as we found it, no broken fences or open gates or anything like that. We're quite capable of keeping the country code. You won't even know we've been here, we'll be no trouble at all.'

He flashed his dazzling smile straight into my eyes and I felt a certain amount of knee tremble coming on. Gosh, he was attractive, and what easy self-assurance.

'Oh, I'm quite sure you won't be,' I said breathlessly, 'and don't worry, we're delighted to have you, really!'

'Thanks, and now if you'll excuse me I must get on. See you a bit later, I hope?'

By now I was absolutely charmed to the marrow. I opened my mouth to be equally charming back but was heavily out of practice and nothing came out, at least nothing coherent, just a sort of imbecilic squawk of pleasure. Luckily he'd already turned to Josh.

'Josh, a word about the light. I'm not convinced it's quite right yet so what I propose to do is this . . .' They wandered off deep in discussion.

'Wow,' I muttered when my voice had resurfaced.

'What?' said Pippa.

'Well, he's all right, isn't he?'

'Who, Sam?'

'Yes, Sam, I think he's divine. I'm surprised you're not after him, Pippa.'

'Oh no, he's married.'

'Well, so's Josh.'

'I know, but Sam's happily married, adores his wife. Anyway, what d'you mean? What's wrong with Josh?'

'Oh, nothing, nothing,' I said hastily. 'He's lovely, I just thought Sam was more sort of your type, that's all.'

'Why, because he's tall, darkish and handsome? I'm not that obvious, Polly. Josh may not be an oil painting but he's a jolly nice guy, and looks aren't everything, you know.'

'No, no, of course not,' I said hastily. I'd obviously offended her in a big way. 'Tell you what, Pippa, I know you're supposed to eat with the crew and everything, but why don't you and Josh have supper with us tonight?'

Pippa looked pleased. 'Oh, that would be brilliant! D'you know, in all the time we've been together I've never once been able to have supper with friends or do anything normal, it's so frustrating, but – oh God, wouldn't it look a bit obvious? A bit of a foursome? I'm sure Josh would think so.'

'Well, I'll ask Sam too if you like, that way he could fill Nick in on his plans.'

'Oh, OK, good idea.' She brightened considerably and took my arm as we wandered off. 'I know you're going to love Josh when you get to know him – Nick will too, he's just his type.'

'Er, yes, I'm sure.'

Actually I couldn't think of anyone less Nick's type, he was more the type he'd run a mile from, but I'd brief him to be tolerant for Pippa's sake.

'Got to go.' Pippa squeezed my arm. 'I'm supposed to be working, remember?'

She ran off to join the others.

I sat on the fence for a while and watched. Huge lights were being lifted out of vans and erected, people were moving props about and shouting to one other, make-up was being applied, hair was being coiffed, the whole place was buzzing with glamorous, frenetic activity. After a while my bottom began to feel numb, so I took one last lingering look, jumped off the fence and hurried back to the house, fizzing inwardly. As I galloped through the long grass I noticed how green and spring-like everything was and surprised myself by leaping the fence into the garden with uncharacteristic energy. I wondered, slightly nervously, if perhaps my sap was rising too, and if so why. Well, why not, I retorted, it wasn't often a dashing film director graced my dinner table, was it? This called for some serious glamour. I'd think big. So big that eight inches of extremely small pink skirt would undoubtedly make an appearance. I hurried excitedly into the house.

Chapter Seven

'You did what!' thundered Nick over the tomato salad half an hour later.

'I asked them to supper, that's all.'

'That's all! Christ, Polly, isn't it enough that I have these people making free with my property during the day? Do you really think I want to entertain them in the evening as well?'

'Oh, for goodness' sake, Nick,' I snapped, 'stop being so bloody pompous, you're behaving like an anally retentive Guards officer! OK, so you didn't want them here in the first place, but—'

'Too right!'

'—but now that they're here, why can't you just loosen up a bit and enjoy it? It makes a change to have something going on around here, to have some fun, for God's sake!'

'Polly, you may think it's fun to be mingling with these precious arty types – and my God, are they precious, I came into my own kitchen half an hour ago to find some middle-aged trendy called Josh maniacally sponging his white jeans and wailing about a little bit of mud – but excuse me if I don't share your enthusiasm! You haven't got to trail around behind them shutting gates, mending fences—'

'They promised they wouldn't do that. Sam – he's the director – he gave me his word there'd be no damage.'

'Well, bully for Sam, a media man's word is his bond, I'm sure. Tell him to take a look at the barley field before he makes any more rash promises.'

'Nick, what exactly is wrong with being a media man?' I snarled. 'We can't all make wholesome livings in the fresh air on our inherited farms, you know. Some people have to work in offices, and correct me if I'm wrong but I believe you were once a media man yourself, or have you forgotten?'

'No, I haven't forgotten, and I absolutely hated it, as you well know, which is precisely why I find it inconceivable that you actually *invited* these detestable people down here in the first place!'

I ground my teeth and leaned over the salad, slopping vinaigrette on my T-shirt. 'Nick,' I spat, 'these "detestable people", as you so charmingly put it, include, number one, my very best friend in the world, and number two, the man she intends to spend the rest of her life with. She's *extremely* keen to introduce us to Josh and I for one am keen to get to know him!'

Nick looked aghast. 'Josh? Pippa's going out with that creep in the white jeans?'

'Er – well, yes, but actually, Nick, you're not supposed to know, so forget I said that,' I said hastily.

'Why?'

'Well, because, because—'

'Because he's married, is that it?'

'Well, yes, I suppose he is a bit,' I said, falling into Pippa's trap.

'A bit? He's either married or he's not – Christ, what is Pippa up to?'

'Oh, for heaven's sake, Nick, don't be so high and mighty!' I stormed. 'You're so unbelievably smug, aren't you? You've no idea how difficult some people's lives are. Just because everything fell neatly into place for you, it doesn't mean—'

'Coo-ee!' A little blond head popped around the door. Bruce looked from me to Nick, registering our flushed, embattled faces.

'Oh dear, having a bit of a domestic, are we? Pardon *moi*, I'll come back a bit later,' he murmured, withdrawing.

'No, no, it's all right, Bruce, come in,' I said quickly. He might at least defuse the situation. 'Did you want me?'

The head popped back. 'Well, actually, no.'

The rest of Bruce sidled in and he perched his pert little bum on the edge of the table. He pursed his lips, clasped his hands together and gazed adoringly at Nick.

'I was after the man of the house,' he purred.

Nick pushed his chair back nervously. 'Er, yes, Bruce, what can I do for you?' he said as assertively as possible.

'A *petite* favour.' Bruce cocked his head prettily on one side. '*S'il vous plaît?*'

'Er, y-yes, fire away,' said Nick, much less assertively.

Bruce produced a book from behind his back with a dramatic flourish. It was *Miller's Antiques Price Guide*.

'Well, Sam doesn't need me for the moment,' he pouted, 'more's the pity, and since I brought dear old Mr Midler down, he and I were wondering if we might just take a wee peek-a-boo at your porcelain again. Would you mind?'

'Not at all, not at all, be my guest!' Nick looked relieved. 'I'm delighted you're so keen, help yourself. You know

111

where the cabinet is, I'll just get you the key.' He stood up, took a jar down from the top of the dresser and fished it out. 'Here.'

Bruce clasped the key to his bosom. 'Too kind, too kind,' he murmured, 'and if I may be so bold, I'd like to take this opportunity to say how absolutely thrilled to bits we all are to be here and to be on the receiving end of your generous hospitality, which, I gather, knows no bounds. For, correct me if I'm wrong, but Brucey Boy heard on the grapevine that you're planning a little din-dins party for this evening! *Quel* fun!'

'Oh, well, yes, but—' I began.

'Oh yes, do come, Bruce,' cut in Nick wearily, sitting down again.

Bruce held up his hands in mock horror. 'Oh no, no, I couldn't possibly, I didn't mean—'

'No, do, you're absolutely right, our hospitality knows no bounds. In fact, it hasn't the faintest idea when to stop, it's like a bloody runaway train, and of course the more the merrier, eh, Polly? And the merrier we get the more fun we have, isn't that right?' He raised his eyebrows quizzically at me. I glared back, fuming silently.

'Well, if you're sure . . .' murmured Bruce, slipping down off the table. 'Meanwhile, I'll just pop upstairs to check out the collectables – see you anon!' He gave a dinky little wave and wiggled out, key in hand.

'You didn't have to invite him,' I snapped when he was out of earshot. 'You're just desperate for the martyr's crown now, aren't you?'

Nick sighed wearily. 'Oh, what's one more fun guy at my dinner table, Polly, and actually, contrary to what you might think, I rather like Bruce, at least he's genuine. He's a genuine poof and a genuine antiques enthusiast – fine, you know where you are. It's all these bloody phoneys swanning around pretending to be something they're not that irritates me.' He pushed his chair back and got to his feet. 'Anyway, I trust you'll be rustling up something predictably delicious for tonight's little gathering?' He grabbed his flat cap from the dresser. 'Can't wait,' he muttered grimly, before striding out of the back door, slamming it behind him.

I stared after him for a second, then, in a moment of blind fury, leaped to my feet, ran to the saucepan cupboard, pulled out the biggest one I could find and hurled it after him with a vengeance.

'AAAAARRRRGH!'

It went straight through the window next to the back door, smashing it to smithereens. My hand flew to my mouth. Oh God. I stared at the hole, aghast.

Nick was back in a moment, his face white with anger. 'Clear up this mess, Polly, and get someone in to fix the window,' he said quietly, 'and in future, if you've got something to say try to express it with words rather than resorting to primeval urges and hurling things through windows. It's rather an expensive way of communicating.'

'I – I didn't mean it to go through the—'

'JUST FIX IT!' he thundered, and slammed out again, making the door frame shudder.

I shut my eyes tight, clenched everything in my entire body – teeth, fists, toes, buttocks – and when I was sure he was out of earshot, let rip.

'SHIT SHIT BUGGER SHIT!' I shrieked, expressing myself – I thought – extremely clearly.

Then, all sworn out, I slumped in a heap at the kitchen

table, snarling into the stripped pine and thinking murderous thoughts. After a while I roused myself, poured a glass of wine and slammed around the kitchen, sweeping up the glass and muttering darkly. Why did he always have to be so *right*, I seethed, banging the dustpan on the floor. Why? Why couldn't he be wrong, just for a change, and let *me* be right? And what the hell was I going to cook tonight, eh? Eh, Delia? I pulled her roughly from the shelf and blew the dust off her spine. I flipped miserably through the pages, staring vacantly at photographs of beef stroganoff and chicken à la King, all of which were apparently foolproof, but not, of course, Polly-proof.

I looked up and stared miserably at the broken window. He'd spoiled everything, the bastard. How was I supposed to enjoy myself tonight with this little débâcle hanging over my head? How dare he speak to me like that, how *dare* he, and, more to the point, what the hell was I going to *cook*? I hurled Delia on to the floor, again expressing myself, I thought, very succinctly. She struck me as being just a bit too bleeding perfect, actually, hard to hack at the best of times but insupportable when I was feeling so incredibly imperfect myself.

I slumped down at the kitchen table again and bit the skin around my nails, hoping for a brainwave. Surprisingly, one crashed over my head remarkably quickly. Yes, of course! I ran to the phone and punched out a number.

'Sarah? Hi, it's me. Listen, are you and Tim doing anything tonight...? You're not? Well, why don't you come for supper? Nick and I are having some of the film people over, should be quite a laugh... Great! Listen, the only thing is, I was just wondering if you could sort of give me a hand, only... Oh, no, no, not the whole thing, I wouldn't hear of it, but . . . Really? You don't mind? Well, that would be terrific! Yes, if you could do the main course I'll do a pudding and a starter . . . Brilliant! Thanks so much, you've saved my life as usual, we'll be eight, by the way . . . See you then! Bye!'

I grinned and replaced the receiver. My star of a sister-in-law. She knew my limitations, and after all, she had to eat the food, so she might as well make sure it was edible. All I had to do now was nip into Helston for some smoked salmon, some wildly extravagant out-of-season straw-berries, a few tubs of Häagen Dazs ice cream, and Bob was undoubtedly my uncle.

With a skip of pleasure and forgetting entirely about the little business of getting the window fixed, I pranced out of the back door, car keys in hand, feeling positively buoyant again.

Bugger Nick, I decided as I leaped a flowerbed, I was damned if he was going to spoil my few days of fun – oh Christ, there he was, coming out of the potting shed. I immediately dropped the skippy routine and adopted the obligatory sober walk – head hung low, face contrite, et cetera, et cetera. I could feel his eyes boring into my back, radiating disapproval. What the hell was he doing sneaking up on me all the time, he was like something out of the Gestapo.

I trudged meekly round the car, shoulders hunched, and slumped disconsolately into the driving seat. I had a quick peek, caught his eye and looked forlornly away. I drove sedately past him down the drive, but as I turned into the lane and was sure he couldn't see me I snapped U2 into the cassette player, gave a whoop of pleasure, and shot off to Helston, singing at the top of my voice.

Chapter Eight

The next time I saw Nick I was charging downstairs at seven-thirty to organise supper. He grabbed my arm as I sped past.

'What the hell's that?'

'What?' I followed his incredulous gaze downwards.

'That pink thing round your bottom.'

'It's a skirt, of course.'

'But Polly, I can see your knickers!'

'No you can't, only if I bend over, I've practised in the mirror.'

'Oh well, that's a relief, let's just hope you don't drop your napkin. Are you seriously wearing it tonight?'

'Yes, of course, why not?'

Nick raised his eyebrows. 'Oh, no reason, don't mind me, I'm obviously way out of touch. I had no idea the jail-bait look was in this season.' He shook his head in disbelief and carried on upstairs.

I treated this remark with the contempt it deserved and ran on down to the kitchen. Sarah was just staggering through the back door with an enormous pheasant casserole which she dumped gratefully on the kitchen table. She was followed by a startlingly attractive girl bearing a large vegetable dish, which she too deposited.

'Oh, Polly,' gasped Sarah, collapsing in a chair, 'you'll never guess what, I walked past your film crew in the bottom field and ran into Amanda here. She's the art director and she was at school with me! We were in the same dorm! I've asked her for supper, hope you don't mind.'

'Not at all, not at all!' After all, I could hardly object when she'd cooked the thing, could I? 'Where's Tim?'

'Oh, he'll be a bit late, I'm afraid, digging potatoes.'

I smiled at Amanda, who was blinking shyly. 'Typical farmer, always late. Here, grab a chair, I'll get you a drink.'

'Thanks.' She smiled and sat down, flicking back her dark silky hair which was swept off her face in a velvet hairband. She had small, perfect features, a pink and white complexion and pale-blue eyes. She was wearing a navy-blue skirt, a sleeveless puffa jacket and pearl earrings. Very pretty, and very Sloaney, I decided.

'So you were at Benenden with Sarah?'

'Yeah, for me sins,' she said in an exaggerated Cockney accent. I'm a sucker for a silly voice myself.

'Bi' of a dump then, was it?' I bandied back.

'Yeah, couldn't wait to get out of there.' She nodded round the kitchen. 'Nice place you got 'ere, Polly.'

'Oh, ta ever so, we like it.'

'Wodja call this then – a manor?'

'Well, it's a bloody great mansion really, innit?'

'Bet it cost a bob or two. Me dad's got a place a bit like this down Purley way.'

'Purley, eh? Nice part of the world that, me nan came from Purley – 'ere,' I said, passing her a glass of wine, 'get that down yer Gregory Peck.'

I poured one for Sarah too, but when I passed it to her I noticed she'd gone very pale behind her freckles. She shook her head at me slowly. Suddenly I had a most unpleasant feeling in my tubes. Oh God.

Amanda got up and clutched her bag. 'Can I use yer lav, Polly?'

'Um, yes – yeah,' I mumbled, 'first on the left.'

'Ta.' She withdrew.

Sarah rounded on me. 'You burk!' she hissed. 'That's how she speaks!'

'Well, I realise that now,' I hissed back, 'but how was I to know? You said she was at Benenden with you, for God's sake!'

'Only for the last year. Her father made a fortune in wet fish and sent her there to iron out her vowels!'

'Didn't work, did it?' I groaned. 'Oh no, I'll have to talk like that all night now.'

Sarah was appalled. 'Polly, you can't!'

'I'll have to, otherwise she'll think I'm taking the piss – oh, er, 'ello again, found the karsy orright, did yer?'

'Yeah, thanks.'

She slipped her bag off her shoulder and started helping me arrange the smoked salmon on to plates. I noticed she'd applied some more lipstick to her rosebud mouth. She certainly was very beautiful.

'Sam coming, is 'e?' she asked nonchalantly.

'Yeah, he should be 'ere soon. Know him well, do yer?'

Sarah moaned softly and tiptoed from the room.

'Yeah, I've worked wiv him a bit over the years.'

'Nice bloke, is 'e?'

She blushed and looked a bit uncomfortable. 'He's all right,' she said shortly.

She avoided my eyes and busied herself arranging slices of lemon on the plates. I wondered if she fancied him. We worked in silence for a minute and I tried desperately to think if I knew anything about Purley or wet fish that I could use as an opening gambit, but luckily I was saved from making a complete idiot of myself by a sharp rap on the back door. We both swung around and in strode Sam, his face almost completely obscured by an enormous bunch of flowers, closely followed by Pippa, Josh and Bruce. Sam popped his head over the top of the flowers and grinned.

'And I didn't nick them from your garden either, although I must say I was sorely tempted when I saw the display out there. Touch of coals to Newcastle, I'm afraid!' He thrust them into my hands.

I laughed, feeling unaccountably flustered. 'Thanks! They're beautiful, it's a long time since anyone brought me flowers.' I hurried to a cupboard and busied myself finding a vase.

'Oh, come now,' he said, leaning lazily against the dresser and watching me closely as I arranged them too hurriedly, 'I don't believe that for one moment. Surely the farmer sits down to breakfast with a rose between his teeth every morning?' His hazel eyes twinkled.

'Hardly!' I laughed. Suddenly I remembered Amanda. 'Not on your bleedin' nellie, actually – hah hah!' I cackled like a fishwife.

My guests eyed me curiously. There was a slight pause.

'Where d'you want us then?' asked Pippa eventually. 'Shall we get out of your way?'

I nodded furiously, grinning inanely. Surely if I stuck to nodding and grinning Sam wouldn't think I was unspeakably 'cor blimey', and Amanda wouldn't think I was taking the mickey? I wasn't really enjoying this, I felt a bit clammy under the arms.

'Yes?' Pippa raised her eyebrows enquiringly, head on one side. 'Shall we get out of your way? Go-in-the-drawing-room?' She enunciated it slowly as if I was brain dead.

I nodded enthusiastically and ran to the door, gesturing like a demented traffic policeman for them to pass through. They trooped past me, looking slightly mystified, and Pippa paused to hiss in my ear, 'We're going to have to get you up to London pretty damn quickly, Polly, you've obviously been stuck in the country far too long, you're behaving like the village idiot!'

'I'll explain later,' I muttered out of the corner of my mouth, 'there's method in my madness.'

Whilst everyone else was drinking in the drawing room I slipped away and hurriedly wrote out some place cards, putting Amanda as far away from me as possible next to Nick at the far end, and Sam as close as possible, on my right. By the time I'd slipped back into the drawing room the noise level had reached a pitch that suggested that thus far, at least, the party could be deemed to be a success. Nick was leaning up against the fireplace laughing and joking with Sarah and Amanda; Josh and Pippa were screaming with laughter at something outrageous Bruce had said, and Sam was beside him, egging him on. Suddenly I felt unaccountably happy. I stood in the doorway watching for a moment. This was more like it. This was what you might call a social life. After a moment I clapped my hands and yelled at everyone to come and sit down.

We all trooped through and as everyone jostled into their places I noticed Amanda glance over and catch Sam's eye.

He smiled but she looked away quickly. She's definitely got the hots for him, I thought as I shook out my napkin, either that or they've had a ding-dong in the past.

'So, Polly,' said Sam as he settled down next to me with a grin, 'tell me, what does a married lady get up to on a vast estate like this? A tinkle on the pianoforte, perhaps? A visit to the neighbours with your calling card? A slow amble round the gardens with your parasol before collapsing on the *chaise-longue* with the vapours? Am I close?'

I laughed, but was aware he was mocking me slightly. 'Heavens, no, I wish you were! No, I'd love to play at lady of the manor but unfortunately I'm much too busy.'

'Oh really?'

'Oh yes, this place keeps me—' I broke off, suddenly recalling Pippa grilling me in a similar vein a couple of weeks ago. I wasn't going to get caught out twice. I licked my lips. 'This place keeps me pretty occupied, but I also have a – a hobby, which is terrifically time-consuming.'

'Oh? What's that?'

'Oh, it's terribly boring.' I gulped and gripped my wine glass.

'Try me.'

I caught my breath and looked wildly round the room for inspiration. Wallpaper-hanging? Carpet-laying? Table-laying? Luckily my eye caught the serried ranks of silver photograph frames arranged on the cabinet in the corner.

'Well, it's photography, actually,' I blurted. 'I'm absolutely mad about it. Snap, snap, snap, I'm at it all day!' After all, anyone can take a picture, can't they?

'No, really? How extraordinary, it's one of my passions too. What camera do you have?'

'Oh, er, well, I use all sorts really, a Canon, an Olympus, a Brownie—'

'A Brownie?' He looked astonished.

'Yes, you see, I'm a great believer in not getting too attached to one particular camera, I like to think I can get equally good results whichever one I use. It's much more of a challenge if the art is down to the photographer rather than his tools, don't you agree?' Gosh, was that *my* mouth talking? I quickly popped some smoked salmon into it before it said anything else. Its capacity to perform in public without consulting me first was getting seriously out of hand. I chewed hard.

Sam looked puzzled. 'Well, it's an interesting thought, but I must say I've always tended to use the camera that gives me the best results.' He sipped his wine thoughtfully. 'You have a dark room here, I suppose?'

'Sorry?'

'You develop them yourself?'

'Oh, good lord no, this may be deepest Cornwall but we're not that backward, no, I take them into Helston, Boots does a very good twenty-four-hour service.'

'Oh!'

'More wine?'

'Er, yes, thanks very much.' Sam looked amused, obviously enjoying my company.

'And are these your pictures?' he asked, indicating the extremely average happy holiday snaps arranged on the cabinet.

'Oh no, Nick took most of those.' An awful lot of them featured Nick, but I didn't let that bother me. 'No, mine are all upstairs. I'm rather shy about displaying them, actually.'

'Oh, come now, you mustn't be shy!' Sam scraped his

chair back a bit and rested his arm on the back of my chair. 'I'd love to see them.' He held my gaze for just a little longer than was strictly necessary.

Christ! I took a great gulp of wine and quite a lot went down my chin. Gosh, this was so exciting, he was flirting *outrageously* with me, wasn't he? He obviously fancied me something rotten.

'Oh, they're frightfully ordinary,' I warbled, desperate to get off the subject of my fascinating camera technique. 'You wouldn't be very interested – but tell me,' I cupped my chin in my hands and gave him what I hoped was a ravishing smile, 'what I really want to know is how did you get into directing?'

He smiled. 'Oh, that's a long and boring story.'

'Rubbish, I'm interested, go on.'

Sam sighed. 'Well, I suppose I worked my way up from the bottom really. It's the only way in the film world; nobody's terribly impressed by degrees or exam results. I started off as a runner when I left school – ran my little legs off, in fact – then I got a job as a second assistant, which led to first assistant, then finally someone gave me a chance to direct my first commercial. That led fairly naturally to films, of course, but I tell you, it was a hard slog getting there, you have to be prepared to work very long hours. Sally was marvellous about it but it can't have been much fun for her.'

'Sally?'

'My wife. We'd only just got married and the last thing we wanted to do was spend our evenings apart. I missed her like mad, so in the end she used to come and watch me work, sit there reading or sewing or something while I fiddled around with a camera. Then we'd go out and have a late supper. It was the only way to get on in those days, you had to put in the hours and learn how to do things practically, learn how to focus properly, how to get the lighting right, that sort of thing. Of course, being a photographer in my spare time helped enormously. It's very much a natural progression, as I'm sure you're aware, Polly.' He smiled.

I stared at him blankly. I'd been thinking about Sally. What was a natural progression?

'Oh! Oh yes, of course, it is, isn't it? Yes, I'm terribly interested in filming myself, always catch the latest directors – Visconti, Coppola, Capoletti – I've seen them all, never miss a chance to see something avant-garde.'

'Capoletti? I'm not sure I know him.'

Heavens, did I mean Capoletti, or was that a kind of pasta? Luckily, there was a slight pause as Mrs Bradshaw, whom I'd enlisted to help for the evening, replaced our empty salmon plates with pheasant. 'Oh, er, well, he's a bit of an acquired taste really, does, um, spaghetti westerns, that kind of thing.'

'Really? Well, you certainly have eclectic tastes. Do they cater for that sort of thing down here?'

'Oh yes, we have a marvellous cinema in Helston' – the fact that it showed *The Jungle Book* pretty much continuously was neither here nor there – 'marvellous, but you know what really interests me, Sam, is the actual technique of film-making. That's why I was so keen for you all to come down here, I want to immerse myself in the finer nuances, get the smell of greasepaint up my nose.'

Sam smiled ruefully. 'I'm afraid it's only a commercial, Polly.'

'Oh, I know, but I've got to start somewhere, haven't I?

And it's such a shame you're shooting the final day in London! I only found that out from Pippa earlier on today. I would have loved to have seen it through to the end, appreciated it as a whole entity and—'

I jumped as an arm went round my shoulders and a head came between me and Sam.

'I don't know what she's telling you but I wouldn't believe it if I were you. It's bound to be lies, every word of it!'

'Tim! You made it at last!' I blushed, wishing he hadn't hit the nail quite so firmly on the head. 'Sam, this is my brother-in-law Tim Penhalligan, this is Sam Weston, the director.'

Tim smiled and held out his hand. He was a smaller, softer version of Nick, nice-looking but with none of Nick's stature and presence.

'I can't believe you got my brother to agree to this commercial,' he said to Sam incredulously. 'You must have asked him at a very weak moment.'

'Well, you'll have to ask Polly about that, she engineered the whole thing.'

'I bet she did!' Tim grinned widely. 'Exactly how devious and Machiavellian did you have to be, Polly?'

'Now, Tim, don't be like that, go and sit down next to Pippa, there's a good boy. Your wife's made the most delicious pheasanty thing and it's getting cold.' I shooed him away before he had a chance to elaborate on my engineering skills.

I turned back to Sam and smiled winningly, wondering what we could talk about next. Would he be interested in the organisation of the village fête, I wondered?

'So, why don't you then?' he asked with a smile.

I jumped. 'Sorry? What?'

'The commercial, you said you'd like to see it through to the end. Why don't you come up to London for the studio shoot? Frankly, there's a lot of waiting around and not much action, but if you're interested, by all means come and watch, you'd be more than welcome.'

'Oh! Oh, well, I don't know, I mean it's quite a long way to go just to watch a commercial being shot, isn't it?'

'Sure, absolutely.' He nodded. 'I just thought I'd offer, but you're right, it's a hell of a drive just to stand around in a draughty studio.' He smiled and cupped his ear at Bruce, who was shouting something at him across the table. 'What? Missed that, Bruce.'

I stared at his profile, then down at my pheasant. Well done, Polly, you handled that beautifully, you moron. I watched him chatting and laughing with Bruce, so easy, so self-assured, so urbane, so . . . London. Suddenly I wanted to stand around in a draughty studio more than anything else in the world. I tried to catch his eye but he was deep in discussion. Bruce was waxing lyrical about the porcelain.

'You really should see it, Sam, it's out of this world!'

'So you said earlier, Brucey, but to be honest it's not really my scene.'

'Don't you like antiques?' I asked, trying to crowbar my way back into the conversation.

He turned and looked at me for a moment. 'In the right setting, yes, I do, and they look perfect here, but personally I'm more at home with the minimalist look. I'm not very keen on clutter, I like very clean lines.' He laughed. 'I'm probably a bit of a philistine but if truth be told I like everything to be bang up to date. I'm not a great one for living in the past and being surrounded by relics.'

'Oh, but these Meissen figurines are different,' gushed Bruce. 'They're mind-blowing, they belong in a museum. They must be worth a fortune, Polly!'

'Probably,' I said ruefully, 'and don't get me wrong, I love them too, but sometimes I think I'd love the money more. We need it so badly at the moment but Nick won't hear of selling anything, they've been in the family for generations, you see.'

'Oh, you couldn't sell them!' said Bruce, shocked.

Mrs Bradshaw momentarily obscured Bruce from view as she leaned in to serve some vegetables. I seized my chance.

'Sam, actually,' I murmured, leaning towards him and blushing slightly, 'I'd love to come. You're right, it would be a tremendous opportunity.'

'Really?' He grinned. 'What made you change your mind?'

'Oh, I don't know . . .' I faltered, wishing he wouldn't look at me like that. 'I – I would have said yes in the first place but I suppose I'm not used to having things sprung on me like that.'

'It's always as well to say yes to things, rather than no,' he said softly. 'It's a bit of a philosophy with me.'

'Oh, I couldn't agree more,' I said quickly, thinking I'd say yes to absolutely everything from now on.

'Good, well, I'm delighted you're coming. The last day's really quite fun, we usually go out for a few drinks after the shoot, have something to eat.'

'Oh!' I exclaimed. 'A wrap party! I've heard about those!'

'Well, not quite, we're making a Doggy Chocs commercial, not *Ben Hur*, but budget permitting we should have a

128

few laughs.' He took a sip of wine, smiled at me over his glass, then turned to talk to Sarah, who was momentarily on her own.

I drank my wine thoughtfully and wondered what his wife was like. Stunningly beautiful, I suspected, but perhaps in a rather hard way. Sharp little power suits, a dark geometric bob and bright-red Paloma Picasso lips, no doubt. Really high-powered and successful, another media whiz kid or something big in PR. I wondered what she did while her man was away shooting? Did she pine, or was she even now twinkling away in a similar vein at an elegant dinner party in London, besotting a barrister or mesmerising a management consultant – it certainly seemed to be the way the chattering classes behaved these days, and why not? It was obviously totally harmless, and great fun. Gosh, I was so out of touch. But I wondered if I'd mind if Nick chatted up the birds quite so vociferously. I watched him at the other end of the table laughing and joking with Pippa. Now, that really was harmless. He caught my eye and smiled. I smiled back, relieved that we were at least on smiling terms again.

'Nick can spare you for a couple of days, can he?' asked Sam with a grin, clearly witnessing this touching exchange of teeth.

'A – couple of days?'

He saw my face. 'Well, it's not really worth driving there and back in one day, you'll be whacked, but of course if you'd rather just come up for the morning or—'

'No, no! No, I wouldn't! I mean, you're absolutely right, I'll stay with Pippa. Yes, of course he can spare me, I don't have to ask permission, you know!'

He laughed. 'I'm sure you don't.'

'And, um, where shall I meet you?' I asked, leaning back and rummaging in the sideboard drawer behind me for a paper and pencil. 'Where do I have to go? What time?' I flipped open a pad.

Sam laughed. 'You're so efficient, Polly, I could do with a secretary like you! To be honest, I'm not absolutely sure. I haven't actually used the studio before, but I think it's somewhere in Chalk Farm. I'm sure Pippa will fill you in on the details.'

'Oh sure, I'll ask her later,' I said, nonchalantly flinging the pad and paper over my shoulder on to the floor, as if I couldn't be more relaxed about where and when I was next going to see him. I tucked into my supper and turned to chat to Bruce for a while.

After a bit, Mrs Bradshaw appeared to take more plates away. It was too much for her to carry in one go so I got to my feet and held out my hands. 'Here, let me help you.'

She stared incredulously at me and stalked past, holding on firmly to the dirty dishes. I flushed unattractively and sat down in confusion. Sam gave her a winning smile as she collected his and, to my surprise, she smiled back.

'God, that was blood out of a stone,' he muttered. 'Where did you find her, Central Casting?'

I sighed ruefully. 'Unfortunately I inherited her with the house.'

'Well, I should disinherit her if I were you. Life's too short to be bossed around in your own home.'

I stared at him. He didn't care what he said, did he? For all he knew she might be a faithful and valued old retainer. But he was right, and it was about time I said what I thought for a change too, instead of pussyfooting around people's feelings and getting my own crushed in the process. It was about time I stood up for myself. I watched as he chatted to Sarah, not quite as flirtatiously as he had with me, I was pleased to see, but still charm itself, asking questions and listening attentively to the answers as if she was the only person in the room with anything worthwhile to say.

Sarah caught my eye when he'd turned back to Bruce and did a mock swoon. 'Divine,' she mouthed, rolling her eyes.

I grinned, but felt ridiculously proprietorial. He was *my* film director, making a commercial in *my* house, so I got to be chatted up, OK? My turn came again soon enough and I made the most of it, laughing uproariously at all his jokes, twinkling merrily into his eyes and doing a great deal of crossing and uncrossing of legs, even once – in a very daring moment and hoping to God Nick hadn't seen – retrieving a deliberately dropped napkin from the floor. It was the best fun I'd had in ages.

Later that evening when everyone had gone, I took the coffee cups through to the kitchen where Mrs Bradshaw was washing up. I closed the door behind me.

'That's OK, Mrs Bradshaw, I'll do the rest, you get off home.'

She didn't budge from her position at the sink, neither did she acknowledge my remark. She simply took the cups from my hands without even looking at me and carried on washing up. I bit my lip and moved to the side of the sink where she could see me.

'I said leave it, really, I'll finish up here.'

'I'm here now, aren't I?' she growled.

'Look, I don't think you understand. I don't want you to do any more. In fact I don't want you to do anything for me ever again.'

She looked up sharply. 'What d'you mean?'

'I mean I'm letting you go, Mrs Bradshaw.'

'You can't do that!'

'Of course I can. I'll give you a month's wages, of course, but I honestly think it's best for all concerned if you leave now. You obviously don't enjoy working here, and to be perfectly honest, I don't enjoy having you. Good night, Mrs Bradshaw.' I turned and left her staring open-mouthed into the soap suds.

I closed the kitchen door softly behind me and went upstairs to the bedroom. I smiled. Yes, I was sorting my life out. It was really beginning to take shape. Nick was already in bed. I climbed in beside him.

'I've fired Mrs Bradshaw,' I whispered.

''Bout time too,' he murmured back.

'You don't mind?'

'Course not. I said you should do it, what made you suddenly decide?'

'Oh, just something Sam said. It's such a relief, I must say.'

There was a pause. 'Good,' he said gruffly. 'Anything else? Or can I go to sleep now, I've got to be up in a few hours.'

'Well . . . there is, actually. D'you mind if I go to London for a couple of days?'

'Of course not, why?'

'Well, I thought it would be fun to see the rest of the commercial being made. Sam suggested it and I'd really quite like to.' This last bit came out in a bit of a rush. There was another pause.

'Fine,' said Nick slowly, 'although I'm surprised, Polly, I thought you would have had enough of commercials from your advertising days.'

'Oh, well, yes, I certainly typed a few, but I never actually made it to a shoot, did I?'

'My fault, I'm sure,' he said drily. 'When are you off?'

'On Thursday.'

'Right. Anything else?'

'No, I don't think so.'

'Good.'

'Oh, yes,' I said a few moments later, 'I thought I might buy a camera.'

Nick made no response.

Chapter Nine

I was awoken the following morning by a scrunch of wheels on the gravel, followed by a terrific barking. I sat up in bed with a jolt. For some extraordinary reason I'd been having an erotic dream about Val Doonican, and we'd ended up in a precarious position in his rocking chair with one of his woolly cardies thrown over us, rocking for England, as it were. Understandably, I was in something of a fluster when I flew out of bed and ran to the window, not least because it had been strangely pleasurable . . . Perhaps Pippa was right about older men?

I peered out, loins still twanging perceptibly, to see a large green van parked outside on the drive. The deafening barking was coming from within and the van itself looked possessed, jumping up and down of its own accord as its canine occupants hurled themselves against the sides, howling their heads off, desperate for their liberty. I shivered and grabbed Val's cardie – I mean my dressing gown – and watched as a little pixie of a man with a green cap on jumped down from the cab and ran around to open the door at the back.

The moment he'd turned the handle the door flew open and out leaped ten or twelve dogs of various shapes and sizes, all thoroughly over-excited and barking their heads off furiously. I was relieved to see that they were all on leads and attached to two or three formidable Barbara Woodhouse-type minders who were fairly dragged out of the van after them, yelling at them in foghorn, county voices.

'Quiet, Bracken!'

'Pipe down, Sasha! PIPE DOWN, I SAY!'

'Steady, Victor! Steady!'

There were labradors, retrievers, an Alsatian, a couple of Dalmatians and God knows what else, but all of them seemed to me to be on the huge and enormous side. What was wrong with a couple of Yorkshire terriers? I gulped in alarm, threw some clothes on and ran down to the kitchen.

Nick was at the kitchen window, taking in the canine scene in a somewhat tight-lipped fashion. The noise was unreal.

'It's the doggy bit today,' I said nervously as I put the kettle on.

'Really, Polly? I'd never have guessed.'

He grabbed hold of Badger who was leaping up at the back door, barking his head off in an ecstatic, demented fashion, totally over the moon that well over a dozen dogs had suddenly got it into their heads to come and play at *his* house today.

'I'm putting Badger in his kennel,' he said grimly, dragging a wildly protesting Badger in the opposite direction to that of his playmates. 'Don't want him joining in.'

I breathed deeply as he went, exhaling slowly. Oh lord. I did hope everything was going to go smoothly. Perhaps I should go back to bed until it was all over? I made myself a piece of toast and Marmite and stood munching it at the window, watching as the dogs charged off towards the bottom field, dragging their minders behind them, still hysterical with excitement. A moment later there was a tap at the kitchen door. Sam stuck his head round.

'I know they sound outrageous, but I promise you, when it comes to the crunch they're incredibly well behaved. They've been specially trained for this sort of thing.'

'I'm glad to hear it,' I said nervously. 'They certainly make enough noise.'

'They're just a little over-excited, but don't you worry, I'm well aware that you've got livestock here and we're going to keep a really close eye on these hounds. All they've got to do is run across a field, leap a little stone wall and run towards some dog bowls. It's a cinch. We might even get it in one take, then they'll be back in the van and off home. You won't even know they've been here.' He grinned. 'Smile, Polly.'

I grinned back. 'OK, if you say so.'

'I do. Coming down to watch? I can get you a VIP seat?'

'Sure, why not?'

'See you later then, don't be too long.' He winked, then disappeared round the door.

Suddenly any misgivings I might previously have had about this morning's activity were totally forgotten. I shoved the toast in my mouth and ran upstairs in a flurry of excitement. A frantic dressing and undressing saga then took place until the bed was piled high with clothes and I was dressed in the very first outfit I'd originally thought of. I stared at my reflection. Right, make-up. I drew a line under my eyes – quite carefully for me – then added lipstick, blusher and – hang on. I eyed my reflection guiltily as the blusher brush skimmed over my cheekbones. What are you doing, Polly? I tried to meet my eyes.

Nothing, I retorted sharply, snapping the compact shut, I'm simply making the best of myself, anything wrong with that? And yes, OK, I'm enjoying myself too, anything wrong with that either? I raised my eyebrows quizzically at my reflection. God, they could do with a pluck. I hurriedly pulled some tweezers from a drawer and launched a frenzied attack, taking too much from one and having to even up the other, then taking too much from that one – and so it went on until my eyebrows had all but disappeared. It was an absorbing, painful and time-consuming exercise and by the time I'd finished and looked out of the window again, I was surprised to see that the dogs were already lined up in the bottom field, ready for the off.

There they sat, all in a row with their minders standing behind them, looking, I had to admit, remarkably quiet and well behaved. Even so, I'd be glad when it was all over.

I grabbed a jacket, ran downstairs and was about to go out when I decided I couldn't possibly take another step until I'd had a cup of coffee and a cigarette. I gulped down a scalding mug of Nescafé and was just taking the last drag of nicotine down to my Docksiders when the most terrific howling made me dash to the window.

The scene that greeted my eyes is one I hope never to see again as long as I live. First I dropped my cigarette then my jaw. I gaped incredulously. A dozen or so supposedly impeccably behaved dogs were indeed charging. But they were charging the wrong way. They were charging this way, my way, my house way. A sea of rolling eyes, open mouths, flapping ears and lolling tongues was galloping towards me, a howling mass of totally out-of-control and extremely mad dogs, and behind them, furiously giving chase, were the minders, pounding along, waving their arms, shaking their fists and making almost as much noise, but all to no avail.

Because there was no stopping these dogs. They moved as one, as a back-to-the-wilds pack, pounding along hell-for-leather and destroying everything that got in their way; hedges, fences, gates – you name it, they crashed through it, scattering chickens, geese and ducks, and leaving a cloud of feathers in their wake. I couldn't move. I was literally rooted to the spot, paralysed with fear and disbelief.

They'd almost made it to the garden, just one more fence and – sorry, one more *broken* fence – and they were in, it was the work of a moment. Through they crashed, and behind them crashed the minders, still waving their arms about and screaming futilely into the wind at the tops of their voices. In the midst of this second, human pack, I spotted a familiar figure. Nick was running like the blazes, fists clenched, face purple with fury. It was a terrifying sight. My hand flew to my mouth. 'Shit!' My intestines very nearly obeyed, they certainly curdled nastily. I clenched my buttocks guardedly.

My first, and on reflection probably best inclination was to hide. I looked around wildly – what about the cupboard under the sink? Or maybe I had time to make it down to the cellar? I could stay there for days, weeks even, sneaking up at night for food and water, Nick would never find me. I dithered, but stupidly resisted the temptation, and instead – mad impulsive fool that I am – darted to the back door.

As I opened it I screamed and leaped about a foot in the air as a small, bedraggled creature raced in, swept over my feet and fled through the kitchen. Christ, a rat! I scuttled quickly outside and ran down the path to the vegetable garden.

The marauding dogs had reached the front lawn now, or, rather, the rose garden. I could see the whites of their eyes as they galloped recklessly through it, scattering roses and trampling carefully tended lavender bushes, madness in their eyes, rose petals and saliva dripping copiously from their mouths. I waved my arms around timidly, surely they'd stop when they saw me?

'Steady, boys, steady now!' I quavered nervously.

They didn't seem to be steadying at all, if anything they seemed to be gaining momentum. Any minute now I'd be mown down, flattened by a pack of marauding dogs, but I had to stand my ground. Better to die with paw prints on my face than to face the wrath of Nick, whose livid purple features were even now bearing down on me. If anything it was a more terrifying sight than the dogs. As he crashed through the rose garden he yelled something about a door, but I couldn't quite hear.

'WHAT?' I yelled back.

The dogs shot past me, missing me by inches, and in their midst I spotted a familiar black figure, pink tongue hanging out, galloping joyously – Badger. For a moment he gave a naughty glance in my direction, then, with mad rolling eyes, thundered on by with the others.

'I SAID SHUT THE BACK DOOR!' screamed Nick, as he raced up the lawn.

I swung around but – too late. The last of the bunch, a panting golden retriever, flashed inside and out of sight. I moaned low. Ooohhhh ... divorce. Nick shot past me.

'WHY DIDN'T YOU SHUT THE BLOODY DOOR?'

'I – I didn't hear you, didn't think . . .' I stammered, but he'd gone.

He tore into the kitchen followed by the minders. One of them grabbed my arm as he went past.

'Polly!'

'Bruce!' He was as white as a sheet, his eyes wide with fear.

'Have you seen Munchkin?' he shrieked.

'Munchkin? No, not unless she was amongst that lot – Bruce, what the hell's going on, they've all gone absolutely crazy! Nick's going to kill me, it's going to be all my fault, I just know it is!'

'It's Munchkin,' wailed Bruce, wringing his hands, 'she's on heat and I completely forgot! I took her down to watch the big doggy-boys doing their stuff, thought she'd really enjoy it, you see, and – and they just went berserk! One whiff and they completely forgot what they were supposed to be doing, they just wanted to get at her! She jumped out of my arms, poor mite, and fled – she even swam through a stream – and now I don't know where she is, probably being raped and pillaged by one of those brutish hounds at this very moment! Oh God, I can't bear it!' He wrung his hands in despair.

'Oh! Oh wait, hang on a minute! I thought it was a rat but it must have been Munchkin, yes it was, soaked through – she's in the house! Quick!'

We ran inside where a trail of destruction greeted us. Chairs and tables had been tipped over, vases were smashed, pictures were askew, plants were spewing out of their pots and carpets were covered in mud. I felt physically sick and very nearly made for the cellar right there and then, but somehow I managed to get a grip and follow

Bruce and the paw marks as he raced upstairs towards the frantic howling and baying that was coming from the spare bedroom.

'Oh Munchkin! Oh my poor baby, Daddy's coming!' he gasped as we tore down the corridor and flew into the room at the end of the passage.

In this very small spare bedroom, about fourteen large dogs were going completely demented. They'd got a wardrobe surrounded and were barking and howling like crazy, scratching frantically at the carpet, climbing on top of each other, desperately trying to shove their noses underneath. Nick and one or two burly women had most of them by their collars and were doing their best to haul them off.

'I think there's a rat or something under the wardrobe,' yelled Nick above the noise, dragging a couple of dogs away. 'I had a look and I can see a couple of eyes. I'll get my gun.'

'NO!' shrieked Bruce, as he fell on Nick's arm, 'No, no! Don't! It's Munchkin!'

Nick frowned. 'Munchkin?'

'My little dog!' Bruce looked around quickly to see who was listening before confiding quietly, 'It's – it's her special time of the month, you see.'

'Her what?'

'Her delicate, ladies' time. You know,' he whispered, 'her cursey-wursey.'

Nick stared at him. 'Are you trying to tell me she's on heat?'

'Exactly.'

Nick groaned. 'Oh, Bruce, it's a wonder she hasn't been raped, she's sending these boys absolutely crazy!'

Bruce tightened his grip on Nick's arm. 'You don't think she has been raped, do you? You don't think one of these brutes has had his evil, wicked way with her?' he whimpered, his voice cracking.

Nick regarded the sex-crazed hounds surrounding us, still baying their heads off.

'Well, it would be an interesting combination, wouldn't it? What d'you fancy, Bruce, Chihuahua-Dalmatian or Chihuahua-Great Dane?'

'Oh God!' gasped Bruce, clutching his mouth. 'My poor darling!'

'Relax,' went on Nick darkly, 'unless one of these boys had the nous to hoist her up on to a chair and slip it in before she shot under the wardrobe I think it's highly unlikely.' He turned to the minders. 'Come on, let's get them out of here. Polly, you could lend a hand too if you can tear yourself away from the curtains.'

Oh God, he'd spotted me. I crept meekly out from my hiding place and grabbed a couple of labradors. Nick found a piece of rope and we managed to make some leads so the minders could drag them, protesting wildly, downstairs and back to the fields.

Bruce then spent half an hour lying on the floor trying to coax a terrified Munchkin out from under the wardrobe.

'Come on, Munchy, come on, Boofles, come to Daddy! The nasty rough boys have all gone home now, come to Daddy-kins!'

I would have liked to have stayed safely up in the bedroom with Bruce and Munchkin but Nick jerked his head curtly in the direction of the door and I meekly fell in behind him. We walked downstairs in silence and surveyed the mayhem around us. My spouse's lips were tightening by the moment and a look of furious horror and outrage was passing over his face. I had a feeling he wasn't going to be able to quell it. I was right.

'This is intolerable, Polly,' he seethed, 'absolutely intolerable!'

'But Nick, it wasn't my fault,' I quavered pathetically. 'I mean, Munchkin is Bruce's dog, she's nothing to do with me, all I did was—'

'All you did was leave the bloody door open, which I think you'll agree was really quite a contributing factor to the destruction of our house,' he seethed. 'If I were you, Polly, I wouldn't say another word on the subject, because I have a feeling I may not be able to control my temper, and I don't want to have to kill you.'

Grateful for the warning, I confined myself to surveying the debris. I dreaded to think how much it might cost to repair, but in the light of Nick's last remark thought it best not to broach the subject. Josh did it for me. He came racing through the front hall and skidded to a halt at the foot of the stairs.

'I've just heard,' he gasped. 'I'm terribly sorry, this is appalling!'

'Isn't it just,' muttered Nick darkly.

'Now look, don't worry about a thing, it'll all be put straight in a twinkling. I'll get on to our insurance company straight away, they'll be round here just as soon as I've briefed them.'

'They'd better be,' said Nick curtly. 'That vase down there in a million pieces was a very old Royal Doulton.'

'Everything will be replaced, I give you my word.'

'Something like that is irreplaceable.'

'Oh dear.' Josh scratched his head. 'I am extremely

sorry, but it really wasn't our fault. Apparently Bruce's little bitch got them all sexed up and—'

'So I gather,' snapped Nick, picking up a small tripod table and setting it straight. 'Well, please see what can be done about the superficial mess and get the house tidied up. I'll look into the more serious damage outside. Excuse me while I go and round up any animals that might have escaped to the next village and mend a few miles of fencing.' He stalked off, leaving Josh and me to cringe deeply at each other.

In the event, it was only the Royal Doulton vase that had actually been irrevocably smashed. Thankfully, everything else could be picked up, put back together, sponged down, or washed. I dragged a much-scolded and sheepish Badger back to his kennel, tying him up firmly this time. He gave me a pathetic, pleading look but I didn't melt. If I was in the dog house so was he. Various crew members arrived to clean the stair carpet, wash down the walls and generally pick up the pieces. Pippa and I rolled up our sleeves and set to work in the kitchen. We'd just finished washing the kitchen floor when Sam stuck his head round the door. His eyes were shining and a mischievous grin lit up his face.

'Where's the irate husband?' he whispered.

'He's gone to cool down.'

'Is he absolutely livid?'

'Steaming.'

'Out for blood?'

I giggled. 'Mine in particular, but probably yours too.'

'Oh hell.' He crept in, unable to keep the radiance from his smile. 'I'm terribly sorry, dreadful thing to happen, but the thing is, you see, we got the most incredible shot of the dogs! Tony managed to swing the camera round and we got them charging hell-for-leather. It looked absolutely amazing on the monitor, you should have seen it.'

'I did,' I said grimly, 'together with the whites of their eyes. I was on the receiving end of the magic.'

'Gosh, how awful, poor you. I am sorry.' Actually, he did look genuinely sorry. 'And I gather they made a bit of a mess in here – anything I can do to help? Sponge a few walls? Wash the floor, perhaps?' He looked innocently at the now gleaming, damp flagstones. 'Oh dear, I see I'm too late.'

I grinned. 'Just a touch. Don't worry, everything's under control now. To be honest, it looked worse than it was.'

'Oh, what a relief. Well, I just came to tell you that since we got the charging scene in the can so quickly we'll be off pretty soon. We're leaving Bruce behind for a couple of days to tie up a few loose ends – he wants to see his mother anyway – and he'll liaise with the insurance company for you. He'll be staying in Helston if you need him, but the rest of us will be getting out of your hair and shooting back to London in' – he looked at his watch – 'oh, about an hour's time, I suppose.'

'Oh!' My spirits sank into my boots. 'So soon?'

He smiled ruefully. I could feel Pippa's eyes on me. ''Fraid so, but we'll see you again in London, won't we? You're still on for that?'

'Oh yes, of course! Yes, I'll see you then.' My spirits made a miraculous recovery, rocketing from my ankles to my armpits in seconds. I was all smiles again, transparent or what?

He grinned. 'Good, look forward to it. See you then, Polly, and thanks again for the hospitality.'

'My pleasure,' I whispered as he pecked me on the cheek.

I watched as he disappeared round the back door and down through the garden.

Pippa stood up, put her bucket and mop in the broom cupboard, pulled her sleeves down and folded her arms in a businesslike manner. She turned to face me.

'He's married, Polly,' she said grimly.

I stared at her. 'Don't be ridiculous!' I gasped. 'So am I, happily, thanks very much!' I could feel myself blushing.

'I know, and that's why I don't want you to spoil things. I know you're a bit bored, but don't – you know – dabble, will you, Poll? It's simply not worth it.'

I gaped. 'Bloody hell!' I spluttered eventually. 'That's rich coming from you!'

'But that's precisely why I'm telling you this, don't you see?' she said earnestly. 'My situation is not a happy one, I'd give anything not to have fallen for a married man, and apart from anything else Sam's not a patch on Nick.'

'Pippa!' I exploded. 'You're way off beam here, I have *not* fallen for a married man! Just because I'm enjoying myself for a change – God, you were the one who told me to have a bit of fun, get my act together, lose weight, go blonde, shorten my skirts, get up to London – and now that I'm doing all that you go off the deep end!'

Pippa shook her head sagely. 'Polly, I know when you've got the hots for someone, you get that look in your eye.'

'What look?'

'That sort of glazed goldfish look. Also your boobs heave around like nobody's business and you hold your tummy in – come on, you definitely fancy him, any fool can see that.'

'Well, OK, maybe I do, so what? Doesn't mean I'm going to do anything about it, does it? I mean, I fancy Jeremy Paxman but I don't sniff around the *Newsnight* studio waiting for him to emerge, do I? I quite fancy the sheep-shearer in the next village in a bit-of-rough sort of way, but I don't make myself available to him every time he gets to grips with our sheep. So what if I fancy Sam? So what if I indulge in a little harmless banter, flirt with him even, where's the harm in that? Married people are allowed to talk to each other, you know, it doesn't mean we're about to embark on a full-blooded sex romp.'

'No, but—'

'Pippa, you see adultery at every corner. You live with it so you automatically assume everyone's up to it.'

Pippa opened her mouth to argue – then hesitated. She sat down at the kitchen table and sighed. Her lips compressed and she gazed past me.

'Maybe you're right,' she said softly, 'perhaps it's me. I'm so obsessed with a married man I think everyone else must be too. I'm sorry, Polly.' She looked down and abruptly covered her face with her hands. 'Oh God, what am I going to do?' she whispered.

I sat down next to her and put my arm round her. Even though it was upsetting for her I was relieved we'd got off the subject of me and were talking about her suddenly. I sighed.

'I don't know, I don't know what you're going to do. I just know it must be awful for you.'

'It's not awful, it's hell!' she snapped, looking up for a second. 'It's an absolute living hell!' She sighed and looked down again. 'Oh Polly, I don't even like myself any more. I don't like what I'm doing but I just can't help it. It's so

destructive – for Josh, for his wife, not to mention me –
God, it's tearing me apart!' She gulped. 'Look at me, I'm
falling to pieces here, and for what? He's never going to
leave her, is he?' She looked at me pleadingly, willing me to
say he might.

I hesitated. 'Well . . . put it this way, Pipps, I wouldn't set
your heart on it.' Her face crumpled. 'Isn't there anyone
else?' I said quickly. 'Anyone – you know – single? Charles
was lovely, what happened to him?'

'Charles?' She looked wistful for a moment, then shook
her head. 'Oh, I don't know, I suppose I bished it up as
usual. You just don't know how lucky you are, Polly, you
don't know what it's like to be still out there, still on the
market, still sitting on the shelf and getting staler by the
minute.'

'Pippa! You don't think like that, do you?'

'Not usually, no, but in my darker moments I do. I see
myself as a stale old bun with a few mouldy currants on top.
Only for a second, of course, then I pick myself up, brush
myself off, read a few "think positive about being single"
articles in women's magazines, remember my great job, my
friends, my sort-of relationship with my sort-of boyfriend,
and I'm all right for a bit. But it's still there, you know,
however much I disguise it, that nagging feeling that I
haven't quite got life in the bag.'

'You mean a man in the bag.'

'I suppose so,' she mumbled. 'Christ, not very feminist,
is it? What would the editor of *Cosmo* say?'

'I won't tell on you.'

'Thanks. But you see, that's why I find it so hard to see
how two married people like you and Sam can be just good
mates. I think all married people are secretly looking for a

bit on the side. But I suppose that's just me being jaundiced – sorry.'

'Forget it.' I squeezed her hand. 'I have.'

I poured her a glass of wine and she downed it practically in one. Then she looked at her watch. 'God, is that the time? I must go, Josh will kill me if I'm late.'

She quickly put on some lipstick and dragged a brush through her hair, then we hugged each other and she went on her way, off to join the crew and then back to London.

When she'd gone I got up and moved slowly round the kitchen, thinking about what she'd said. I put a few things away and wiped the last traces of dirty dog tails from the walls. I poured myself a drink. Nick came in from the farm.

'Everything all right?' His lips were still quite tight.

'Well, they've gone, thank God, and everything's shipshape and tidy again – very little damage, actually, just the vase,' I breezed as brightly as I could.

'Good,' he said shortly. 'Well done for clearing up.'

'Oh, it didn't take long.'

We smiled politely at each other, then Nick went upstairs for a bath, taking the newspaper with him. I felt guiltily glad to be on my own. I sat at the table, smoking one cigarette after another, trying hard not to think too much.

Chapter Ten

Two days later I set off for London. Nick heaved my heavy case downstairs and round to the car in the drive.

'God, how long are you going for, Polly, a fortnight?'

'Don't be silly, just a couple of days, but I couldn't decide what clothes to take so I ended up packing half my wardrobe.'

'So I see.' He slammed the boot shut. 'I hadn't realised it was a fashion parade. You'll be back by Saturday morning, won't you?'

'I'm not sure, why?'

He sighed. 'Don't you remember? I asked you to make sure you were. Foxtons are delivering a whole load of corn and feed at nine o'clock and Larry and I won't be here to check it. You know what Foxtons are like, they're bound to short-change us if no one's around, and it takes months to get them to deliver again.'

'But where will you be?'

'I told you, Polly,' he said patiently. 'Larry and I are going to Yorkshire to look at some stock. We'll have to stay over on Friday night. I told you all this yesterday while we were having supper, don't you remember?'

'Er ... well it sort of rings a bell now you mention it.'

Nick shook his head. 'Sometimes I really wonder about you. You're in another world half the time, aren't you?'

He had a point there, though it was actually more like three-quarters of the time. And funnily enough, the other world I'd been inhabiting lately was the glamorous world of stage and screen.

You see, in the space of just two short days I'd graduated from being spotted by Sam to star in his dog-food commercial to taking the leading role in his latest block-busting feature film. Of course, he'd taken a major gamble casting an unknown newcomer in the starring role, but my goodness it had paid off. The film – a sort of arty-farty English thing with lots of twirling parasols and bags of good taste, the sort of thing Helena Bonham-Whatsername does – had been a phenomenal success, so I now lived a glamorous peripatetic life flitting back and forth between Hollywood, London and Cornwall, still madly in love with my divine husband, of course, but now the darling of the film world too.

Sam, naturally, had fallen headlong at my feet, but I made sure I kept him at arm's length. Obviously we still had to go to expensive restaurants and I had to lean over tiny little tables looking beautiful and sexy to discuss scripts and things, but whilst he tried desperately to look down my top – no, too tacky – to gaze into my eyes, I remained friendly but aloof, maintaining a purely professional relationship with him at all times.

Eventually he poured out his heart to the tabloids – 'The love I can't have' by Sam Webster, 'The Forbidden Fruit I crave for' by Sam Webster – but I kept a dignified silence. I tried gently to discourage him and was only ever seen on the arm of my incredibly good-looking husband – attending first nights, accepting awards, holidaying in Antigua – the sort of thing one sees in *Hello!*, though of course we'd never stoop to that. Well, I suppose we *might* just consider one photograph in the drawing room at Trewarren with me reclining gracefully on the sofa in a gorgeous white silk affair, Nick standing proprietorially behind me, his hands resting protectively on my shoulders and two or three enchanting children playing at our feet … Ah yes, the children. I sighed. Even in my fantasies that was quite a stumbling block. Nick seemed to be saying something.

'Polly? Are you with me?' He knocked on my head. 'Is anyone at home?'

'Sorry, what?'

'I said, what's this?' He picked up a black leather box from the front seat of the car.

'Oh, that's my new camera, I bought it in Truro yesterday.'

'Really? I didn't know, you should have said, I'd have come with you to choose it.' He took it out of its case and turned it around. 'Is it a good one?'

'Oh yes, it's brilliant, the man in the shop said so, and I know Sam's got one exactly the same.'

'Ah.' Nick put it back and snapped the case shut. 'I see.' He put it down on the front seat again. He seemed strangely silent.

'See you on Saturday then?' I ventured cheerily, and went to peck him on the cheek.

'Sure.' He kissed me back, but as I turned to get in the car he suddenly grabbed hold of me and held me tight. I looked up in surprise. His face seemed troubled.

'What's wrong?'

'Nothing.' He shook his head.

I gave him a hug. 'Have a good time in Yorkshire, give my love to the cows!'

'Will do. Listen, Polly, I'm sorry if I've been rather – well, bad-tempered lately. I've blamed you for everything that's gone wrong around here and it hasn't all been entirely your fault. Sorry. You know me and my short fuse.'

I looked at him incredulously. Good grief, whatever had come over him? 'That's all right, don't be silly. Most of it was most definitely my fault, and anyway, as you well know, it's water off a duck's back with me. Most of the time I don't even listen to you.'

'I know, but . . .' He bit his lip and frowned. 'Look, Poll, are you bored down here?' He looked searchingly at me. 'Because if you are, there's nothing to stop you from doing something. I'd go along with it wholeheartedly, you know I would. I remember when you first came down you said the shops round here were lousy and talked about opening a boutique or something – you could still do that, you know. I could raise a bit of money if I had to, it wouldn't be that much of a problem, we could always sell something.'

I was amazed, and very touched. Sell something? Nick?

'That's sweet, Nick, but honestly, I went off that idea ages ago. I think I'd be even more bored sitting in a shop waiting for customers. But thanks anyway.'

His brow puckered. 'So you are bored?'

'No! No, of course not, I didn't mean it like that. It's just – well, I don't want to start another career really – not that I had much of a one in the first place. I suppose somehow I thought . . . well, I think I thought I'd be doing something else by now.'

I paused and looked at the ground, kicking a bit of gravel

around with my foot. I didn't want to bang on about it. Nick nodded and looked at the ground too.

'I know. Babies.' He put his arms around me again. 'It'll happen, Polly, really it will, there's nothing wrong with either of us and there's no reason why we shouldn't have a whole brood one day. We just have to be patient, that's all.'

'I know.'

We held each other silently. I felt rather choked up. Eventually we disentangled ourselves, Nick kissed me hard on the mouth and deposited me in the front seat. I buzzed down the window.

'See you then.'

He smiled. 'Will do. Drive carefully.'

'I will.'

I let the clutch in and moved off slowly, looking in my rear-view mirror at him standing there. He watched until I was out of sight. I waved as I rounded the corner into the lane, still feeling rather choked. Gosh, he could be sweet, couldn't he? I flicked a cassette on. Simply Red blared into action. I flicked it off. I didn't feel like that quite yet. I lit a cigarette. Odd, Nick had seemed strange, emotional ... troubled, even, so unlike him. Usually he was so – well, pragmatic. I shook my head, perhaps I was imagining it. I gave Simply Red a second chance, put my foot down and headed for the London road.

When I eventually arrived in London I made straight for the centre of the universe, Harrods car park. I had absolutely no idea where Chalk Farm was but it was bound to be somewhere central, there was no way a man like Sam would shoot a commercial in the back of beyond, was there? I dumped the car at vast expense and whizzed into Rymans for an A to Z. Blimey, Chalk Farm *was* in the back of beyond. I suddenly remembered Pippa saying something about it being a bugger to get to and it was best to drive, but I couldn't possibly get the car out now, having invested a fortune in its installation, so I dived down the Underground steps and headed north.

An hour and a half later, I emerged from beneath the ground, panting, swearing and hoping to God I was somewhere in the region of Camden Town. It had indeed been a bugger of a journey. First a suicidal commuter had to be prised from the rails three stops down before we could even begin our journey, and then our driver had taken it into his head to do a funereal crawl, perhaps as some sort of misguided mark of respect. If anything was designed to make people speak ill of the dead it was this, and the mutterings around me ranged from 'Odd how they always choose the rush hour to top themselves,' to 'selfish, inconsiderate bastard'. I must say, by the end of the journey I was very much lining up with the sentiments of the latter.

I trudged the last half a mile on foot and eventually arrived at the impossibly difficult-to-find location, which, far from the glamorous studio I'd imagined, seemed to be more of an enormous converted garage next to a fish and chip shop. Frankly, by this stage I couldn't have cared if they were shooting the commercial in a human abattoir I was so exhausted, and I crashed through the double doors like a thing possessed, crazy for a seat and even crazier for a cup of tea.

'Hi!' I gasped, stumbling into a gloomy cavernous room with one very bright spotlight shining at the other end. 'Ooof!' I collapsed gratefully on to the nearest chair, brushing off a few tapes and things so I could sit down.

'Phew! Bloody hell, Pippa, you weren't joking, were you, that was a hell of a trip!' I cried, peering around in the darkness for her.

'Ssshhhhhh!' hissed someone furiously.

'Christ, who the hell's that?'

'CUT! Damn it!'

I gulped and slid down in my chair. Oh no, they hadn't been shooting, had they? At the far end of the room the very bright light snapped off.

'Shit,' said somebody.

I gulped again. They had. An overhead light flicked on and about twenty people turned to look at me. I felt a boiling blush unfolding from my feet.

'Oh it's *you*,' Polly!' cried Pippa, appearing from the back of the room. 'Didn't you see the red light?'

'Er, sorry, what red light?'

'The one we put outside to let people know if we're shooting! Oh well, never mind, you weren't to know, you're not used to this sort of thing, but next time – oh my goodness, you look dreadful!' She peered at me. 'Look at you, you're all hot and sweaty, and look at your hair! You didn't walk here, did you? I *told* you not to walk. Honestly, you're such a moron, you never listen, do you?'

By now the entire crew, actors, technicians, Josh, and of course Sam, had turned to look at this hot, sweaty moron who never listened and had terrible hair. Vowing to disembowel Pippa later, I blustered, 'Of course I *drove*, Pippa, I'm not that stupid. I've been here *millions* of times!'

'Have you? When?'

'When I worked for Nick, of course.'

'But I thought he never took you to a—'

'Sam! Gosh, sorry I'm late, and sorry for barging in like

that.' I jumped up, brushing brusquely past Pippa with a mighty glare, and gave Sam my very best smile as he came over to greet me.

He gave me a resounding kiss on the cheek, ruffled my already extremely ruffled hair and grinned.

'Not to worry, although I must say I was beginning to get worried. This is a hellish place to find, but somehow I thought you might know it from your advertising days.'

'Of course, of course! I was just saying to Pippa, I've driven here millions of times. No, the reason I'm a bit late is I stopped off on the way to shoot a couple of rolls of film!'

I indicated the camera swinging jauntily from my neck.

'Oh, excellent,' beamed Sam, 'got to seize the moment, a good shot doesn't wait for anyone.'

'Absolutely, and you see there was this marvellously surly London Transport guard who I just couldn't resist, bags of character, so I just – well, as you said, seized the moment!'

'But I thought you drove here?'

'Oh! Oh yes, I did, but luckily he just happened to be standing *outside* the station, probably getting some fresh air, after all, it's awfully muggy on the Underground, so when I drove past and spotted him, I leaped out, and snapped away – like this—'

I stepped back and took a quick shot of Sam at an artistic angle, then flexed my fingers in a professional manner.

'Thanks, Sam, I think that was a good one.' I patted my camera knowingly and pursed my lips. 'Yep, bags of depth.'

'Er, yes, that's the idea, although you'll probably get more depth if you take the lens cap off.'

Sam reached over and pulled it off for me, but before I

had time to take this crushing blow on board he was steering me in the direction of a group of people standing by a camera.

'Now,' he went on, 'who d'you know out of this little lot? Josh and Tony, of course, and Tim who was our lighting cameraman in Cornwall, but I don't think you've met the actresses we're using in the kitchen scene – the non-canine variety, of course! This is Susan Tyler...'

I smiled and shook hands with a wholesome, motherly type holding a can of dog food.

'Hi.' She returned my smile.

'And this,' Sam went on, 'is our glamorous leading lady, in as much as you can have a leading lady in a dog-food commercial!'

Out of the shadows emerged an undoubtedly glamorous but also extremely familiar figure. I stepped back and gasped.

'Well, well,' she drawled. 'Hello, Polly, fancy seeing you here.'

'Serena!'

Sam raised his eyebrows and looked from me to Serena. 'You two know each other?'

'Oh sure,' purred Serena, 'we're old buddies. In fact Polly married one of my cast-offs, didn't you, Polly?'

There was an embarrassed silence. Serena stood watching me, looking as devastating as ever. Her slanty green eyes shot off at angles over her high cheekbones and her short blonde hair gleamed almost white. She swept it back in a practised manner, a mocking smile playing about her perfect mouth. She fair took your breath away in more ways than one. Eventually I stopped gasping at her audacity and found some wind.

'If I remember rightly,' I snapped, 'he cast *you* off, not vice versa!'

Serena's irritating girly laugh tinkled around the studio 'Gol-ly, calm down!' she tittered. 'I'm only winding you up, I see you're still as hot-headed as ever. Anyway, I seem to recall there was very little love lost between either party at the end of our relationship. But tell me, how is Nick? Still playing at being a farmer?'

I clenched my fists. 'There's no playing about it, it's a serious business, as you well know, and he's extremely well, thank you!'

'Phew!' Serena fanned her perfectly made-up face and backed away. 'You don't half heat up quickly, Polly. Try exercising a little self-control now and again.'

'I'm perfectly in control, thank you very much,' I snarled between gritted teeth, 'and I must say, I'm a little surprised to see you here, Serena – a dog-food commercial? Slumming it a bit, aren't you? Hardly Oscar-winning stuff, is it, or has your career been put on the back burner for a while?'

Serena threw back her pretty blonde head and tinkled merrily into the rafters. 'You're showing your ignorance, darling, I should keep quiet if I were you. When one has a chance to work with a director like Sam, one would do anything, simply anything – a video, a commercial, a feature film – just for the experience. It's all in the direction, you see, but I don't expect you to understand that.' She lit a cigarette, narrowed her eyes and blew the smoke into my face. 'But tell me, what about you? What brings you all the way from the sticks on your little own-some? Don't tell me you're bored with rural life already? Got a bit of time on your hands? Planted all your cabbages?

Or is Nick neglecting you, perhaps – no trouble at home, I hope?'

I was just about to biff her smartly on the nose when Sam cut in hastily. 'Er, Polly's come up to watch the commercial being made. We filmed the first day on her farm and she's very interested in camera technique, so she's here to see the conclusion.' He looked totally baffled by the shrapnel that was flying around.

Serena raised her eyebrows. 'So you filmed the first day at Trewarren? How amusing!' She turned to Sam. 'Nick and I were briefly engaged, you see, but thank God I saw the light and got out, otherwise it might have been me living in that run-down old farmhouse, can you imagine!'

I was speechless with rage and shock now. She took advantage of this and steamrollered on as I gasped for breath.

'So you're a film groupie now, are you, Polly? How extraordinary, you really must be bored. Got a bit of a taste for the high life when they were shooting down on the farm, did you? What was it that caught your eye, I wonder, or should I say,' she winked at Sam, '*who* was it? Camera technique indeed!' She threw back her head and tinkled again, before leaning forward and confiding, in an incredibly loud whisper, 'He's married, you know – happily – and she's absolutely *sweet*. I do hope you're not making a fool of yourself again?'

'Bl— Je— Wha—!' I spluttered incredulously and incoherently, before eventually managing, 'Don't be so bloody ridiculous!' What I really wanted to do was spit in her eye and kick her shins very hard. 'God, Serena, you're unreal! You're absolutely unreal! If you think for one moment I'm—'

'Er, Serena, I think you're wanted in make-up.' Sam slid between us, arms outstretched. 'And Polly, if you come this way I'll show you the monitor, I think you'll find it interesting.'

He took me firmly by the arm while the make-up girl quickly appeared to lead Serena in the other direction. I was spitting with fury.

'Bloody hell! She's a bitch! She's an absolute bitch!'

'I know, I know,' soothed Sam, 'she loves to bait, I'm afraid.'

'Don't I know it,' I seethed. 'We're old sparring partners. She used to go out with Nick but he turned her down in favour of me.' I knew it sounded childish but I wanted to set the record straight.

'Ah, I see. Yes, I got the impression you'd come to blows in the past.'

'She's utterly poisonous. She tried to pretend she was getting married to Nick in order to get rid of me, and she even got an old boyfriend of mine to try to lure me away from him. She'd stop at nothing to get her own way, she's the sort of person who should have a government health warning stamped on her forehead!'

Sam scratched his head. 'Well, I must say, from the little I know of her I'm inclined to agree with you. I thought it was rather a coup to get her for this commercial, because, as you know, she's done some pretty classy films—'

'Mostly naked,' I spat venomously.

'Well, yes, I suppose some of them required her to take her clothes off – but she's very difficult to direct. I wanted to try her out in this with a view to having her in my next film, but to tell you the truth I'm having second thoughts.

She's only got one line but you'd think she was playing Lady Macbeth the way she argues with me about it.'

'I should fire her now,' I said decisively. 'Tell her to pack her bags and get out – go on.'

I'm not normally remotely bitchy but I can really pull the stops out when it comes to Serena. Sam looked taken aback.

'Well, I can't exactly do that now. She's signed a contract and it is after all only a commercial.' He smiled. 'Anyway, let's forget about her, shall we? She's not worth it.'

The smile was desperately winning. I smiled back in what I hoped was an equally winning fashion.

'No, you're absolutely right, she's not worth it.' I put my head to one side, rested my chin on one finger and tried to look intelligent and creative.

'Sam, I was wondering if I might pick your brains on filters, only I do feel they're an integral part of photography, don't you?'

He threw his head back and laughed. 'Oh, Polly, I think you're absolutely right, filters are an integral part and I'd love to stand here all day and gas about them, but unfortunately I've got to get on. But listen, do wander around and don't be afraid to ask the crew questions, they love an enthusiastic amateur. Tony's particularly patient and amenable.' He nodded over to Tony, who I recognised from Cornwall. 'Oh, incidentally, you're still on for the party at Quaglino's tomorrow, aren't you?'

My heart sank. 'Tomorrow? I thought it was tonight.'

'No, we couldn't get a table for tonight so we booked it for tomorrow. Is that a problem?'

'No, it's just ... well, I promised Nick I'd be back by

Saturday morning, he's away and I've got to check a delivery for him. I can't drive back after dinner, it'll take forever and I'm bound to be pissed – damn.' I bit my lip miserably.

'Oh dear, what a shame.' Sam frowned. 'Well, hang on, why don't you leave the car in London and get the sleeper at about midnight? You could come up by train another day and pick the car up then, couldn't you?'

I stared at him, joy and incredulity surging within me. My goodness, he really wanted me to come, didn't he?

I gulped. 'Well – well, yes, I suppose I could – yes, why not? I'll come! And I'll pop back next week and pick up the car!' I breezed, as if popping back took a matter of minutes.

'Excellent!' He beamed. 'That's the spirit. And now if you'll excuse me' – he looked at his watch – 'I must get on, I've got loads to do and I'll have to go and placate the sulky star first – see you later, Polly!'

He whizzed off. I watched him go in a trance. He was obviously absolutely mad about me. Totally infatuated. Out of his mind with desire for my body. I gulped. I'd have to be very careful, have to play it cool, mustn't lead him on, mustn't, under any circumstances, encourage him. I was, after all, a married woman. He suddenly turned, saw me watching him and smiled. I gave him an enormous wink back, quite forgetting how cool I was going to be.

Pippa dashed by, clutching a clipboard and looking important. I seized her arm.

'Pippa, I'm coming with you!' I gabbled.

'Where?'

'To Quaglino's tomorrow! I'll leave the car in London and get the sleeper.'

'Really? Well, great, that's great.' She looked around

distractedly. 'Have you seen Serena? She needs this.' She held up a dog-food can and peered around.

'Yes, she's in make-up – oh, and that's another thing, Pippa, you didn't tell me *she* was in this. Why didn't you warn me?'

Pippa stared at me for a moment, then it dawned. 'Oh God, I'm so sorry, Polly, I completely forgot about all that business with her and Nick. I've worked with her quite a lot, you see, and all that seems so long ago now.'

'Not to me it doesn't,' I said grimly. 'I can remember her throwing her weight around at Trewarren only too well. Honestly, you might have said something.'

'Well, you'd still have come, wouldn't you?'

'Well, yes, but – well, I might have been a bit more prepared, made more of an effort clothes-wise so she didn't think I'd become a country bumpkin.'

'Oh, right.' Pippa gazed doubtfully at my suit. 'Yes, I see what you mean, sorry.'

I gasped. She was supposed to say I looked great. 'What d'you mean? What's wrong with this?' I smoothed down the skirt of my sharp little black suit.

'Oh, nothing, it's lovely, but it's a bit sort of eighties really, isn't it? A bit nipped in and shoulder pads. Anyway, I must get on, I've got heaps of things to do – see you later.'

She wafted off in her long flowing skirt, muslin blouse and bovver boots, leaving me with my mouth open. I shut it thoughtfully. I'd thought she'd looked extraordinary when I'd arrived, but I had to admit the fab look was growing on me, she had a certain groovy charm. I obviously needed a sartorial refresher course and I resolved to buy *Vogue* on the way home.

I wandered around happily, looking at the set, chatting

to Tony, marvelling at the realistic rustic kitchen made entirely from cardboard, and pausing to pat the little cocker spaniel in his basket, the only dog in this scene. I couldn't quite believe it was going to take a whole day to shoot ten seconds of commercial. Heaven knows how long it must have taken to shoot *Gone with the Wind* or something epic. It seemed to me there was an awful lot of standing around and very little action, and when there was any action Serena certainly seemed to do her damnedest to make things as difficult as possible for everybody.

In the middle of the final take she put her hands on her hips and resolutely refused to do what Sam asked her.

'I'm not kissing that bloody spaniel,' she stormed, 'it'll ruin my credibility!'

'Whatever that means,' muttered Tony, who was standing beside me.

'Serena, please,' said Sam, quickly leading her off the set and taking her over to the side, 'it's only a very short take and it would look marvellous. Apart from anything else the advertising agency have specifically asked us to do it. Couldn't you just—'

'No!' She glared at him. 'It's too much of a risk to my career. I didn't get where I am today by kissing spaniels, you know – why can't Susan do it?'

'Serena, please be reasonable,' said Sam quietly. 'I'm sure Susan would be very happy to do it, but to have a middle-aged woman kissing a dog as the end frame isn't really sexy advertising, is it? Whereas if *you* did it we could get a nice close-up on those beautiful lips all puckered and pursed and then freeze-frame on your lovely face for – oooh . . . a good three seconds while we slip the pack shot in.' He shrugged and made as if to walk away. 'But of course if you insist on Susan having the final frame, I'll just go and ask her if she'll—'

'Oh, all right, I'll do it!' snapped Serena quickly. 'Although why I have to kiss a bloody dog I don't know. I usually kiss leading men, handsome ones too – although,' she sniggered in my direction, 'I suppose I have kissed a dog or two in my time.' She sneered and flounced past us, leaving me with my mouth gaping yet again.

'Was that a reference to my husband perchance?' I gasped. 'She's got a sodding—'

'Let her go.' Sam held me back as I went to go after her. 'She's not worth bothering about, she's just a spoilt child.'

'You're telling me!' I fumed.

But he was right, she wasn't worth the effort. She didn't strike me as being particularly good at her job either. I watched as she fluffed her only line time after time. She sulked and flounced around, saying the words were stupid, and had to be constantly cajoled by Sam, who eventually got the result he wanted on about take fifteen. Finally she kissed the dog and there were sighs of relief all round as Sam declared a wrap. Serena grabbed her bag and stormed out immediately without saying goodbye to anyone.

'Stuck-up bitch,' muttered Tony.

The crew began to pack up and I followed Sam, Josh and Pippa out from the gloom of the studio into even more gloom outside. It was pouring with rain. Sam had an umbrella and we huddled underneath it, looking at the sheets of water which hit the ground and bounced back over our feet.

'We'd better make a run for the car,' said Pippa, turning up her collar. 'I'm going back to the office first, so I'll see you at home, Polly.'

'Oh, OK.' I was going to get soaked. I was just about to make a dash for the Tube when Sam caught my arm.

'Where are you parked?'

I gasped. Oh Christ. I had a car, didn't I? I'd clean forgotten.

'Oh, er . . . not far away, just down the road a bit.'

'Down which road?' We seemed to be at something of a crossroads. I looked around wildly and picked one.

'That one.'

'That's where we are, come on, let's go.'

'But—'

'Come on!'

Pippa and I huddled under the brolly and the two men ran on ahead. Two seconds later we were all gathered at Sam's Range Rover.

'Bye then!' I warbled, giving a cheery wave and making to trot on. Sam seized my arm.

'Don't be silly, it's pissing down. I'll just let these two in, then I'll walk you with the umbrella.'

'There's really no need. It's not very far, I can easily—'

'I insist, hang on.' He opened the door for the others, still holding on to my arm.

'Where is your car anyway, Polly?' asked Pippa, climbing in and looking around.

'Oh, a bit further on.'

'I can't see it.' She screwed up her eyes and peered down the road.

'Well, to tell you the truth, it's quite a *bit* further on. I couldn't park any closer so it's a few minutes' walk, but I feel like a walk so I'll see you later, bye.'

I wriggled free and made another spirited attempt to

escape but was once again intercepted by Sam, who grabbed my other arm.

'For goodness' sake, it's bucketing down. Hop in, we'll drive you to it.'

'No – no, really—'

'Don't be silly, Polly, you'll get soaked,' snapped Pippa. 'Just get in.'

My mouth felt dry and my toes began to curl. 'But I like the rain . . .' I bleated in a small voice as the authoritative film director and my best friend – who was rapidly being demoted – bundled me forcibly into the front seat. Sam ran round and jumped up the other side. He snapped his seat belt on, indicated, and pulled out.

'Now, where to?'

I gulped. He might well ask.

'Um . . . just a bit further down here . . . sort of.'

We went quite a bit further, so far in fact that we came to a junction.

He looked at me. 'Which way?'

'Er, it's . . . right here.' My tongue seemed to be stuck to the roof of my mouth. My hands felt clammy. I gazed stupefied at the cars lining the residential street as we purred along at about five miles an hour. Sam looked at me again and raised his eyebrows.

'Further?'

'Um, yes, a bit further,' I croaked.

'Blimey, you did have a walk.'

'Mmmm . . .'

We drove on in agonising silence.

'And we're looking for a red BMW, right?' he asked, peering from side to side.

I had in fact been looking for that very thing, not mine of

course, somebody else's, to borrow, as it were, but red BMWs seemed to be an endangered species in North London and I had a feeling we'd never find a spare one.

'Er, no, we're not actually.'

'We're not?'

'No, you see, it broke down so I borrowed Larry's.'

'Oh! Oh, OK, so what's that?'

'Well, I'm not too sure, to tell you the truth, but I'll recognise it when I see it.'

'You're not too sure?' Sam's mouth twitched. 'Any clues? A colour, perhaps?'

'Oh, yes, well it's sort of . . . white. Whitish-cream. Or grey.' Like my face probably, I thought, feeling rather sick and wondering if we might just pull over so I could puke out of the window. Why had I started this?

He grinned. 'Whitish-creamish-grey. Right.'

We drove on. The silence was excruciating. Sam looked at me enquiringly from time to time. I bit my lip and frowned at the mass of parked cars, concentrating like mad and willing myself to pick one.

'Oh, for heaven's sake, Polly,' snapped Pippa, exasperated, 'you haven't a clue where we are, have you? You've gone and lost the bloody car. This is just typical of Polly, Sam, absolutely typical!'

'It is not!' I stormed. How dare she? I'd have a few words with her about loyalty later. 'I know exactly where we are and I know precisely where the car is, it's – it's that one!' I cried, pointing to an innocent little whitish, creamish-grey car sitting at the side of the road minding its own business.

Sam pulled up. I jumped out thankfully.

'Bye then!' I cried, with what I hoped was a degree of finality. I slammed the door firmly.

Sam buzzed down the window. He made no move to drive on and they all watched as, despite the torrential rain, I walked very slowly to the car. Go away, I muttered to myself, as I walked around it, just damn well go *away*. But they didn't.

I pulled my keys out of my bag and waved them in the air triumphantly. 'It's all right, I've got them!' I yelled. 'Bye now!' Still they watched.

I dumped my handbag proprietorially on the roof and made a great show of finding the right key and pretending to put it in the lock. A good thirty seconds later I looked up, aware that I was sweating. Three pairs of eyes met mine.

'Always sticks a bit, nothing to worry about though! See you tomorrow!' I waved again.

Still they sat on the tarmac, staring, mesmerised, it seemed. I began to panic. Didn't they have anything better to do? Surely this was about as exciting as watching paint dry, and far nosier. Go away. Just sod off, why don't you, can't a girl even get into her car on her own?

'Everything all right?' called Sam, in a I-could-be-over-to-help-you-in-a-jiffy sort of voice. Christ, was that his door opening even now?

'Fine! Fine!' I cried.

In desperation, I straightened up and caught Pippa's eye. I looked straight at her, tilted my head to one side, opened my eyes wide until they were enormous with meaning, pursed my lips, raised my eyebrows to heaven and shook my head very slowly. It was a momentous look. She stared at me for a moment in amazement, then the penny dropped. She blanched perceptively, quickly leaned forward, and whispered something in Sam's ear. He raised his

171

eyebrows in surprise, shunted into first gear, and they moved off.

I keeled over and slumped on to the little car, joy and relief flooding within me. 'Oh, thank you, God, thank you, thank you!' I whispered to the car roof, shutting my eyes and kissing the dirty paintwork. 'Thank you a million times!'

Suddenly I jumped about a foot in the air as a large hand seized my shoulder from behind. I swung around. A huge, burly great thug of a man was towering over me. He was totally bald, with bulging pale-blue eyes and bulging forearms.

'Just what the hell d'you think you're doing!' he thundered. 'That's my car you're breaking into!'

'Oh no, is it? I mean, I – I'm terribly sorry, I thought it was mine!'

'Oh you did, did you?' He lowered his moon-like face and positioned it inches from mine. The bulging eyes nearly popped out on to the pavement. 'So where's your car then, eh? Tell me that, darlin', where's yours?'

'Well, it's, it must be—' I gesticulated wildly down the road. 'It must be a bit further down! I obviously haven't walked far enough – so silly of me, I do apologise, but it's incredibly similar to this one, almost identical in fact! I've even got those lovely fluffy things hanging from the mirror and – and that adorable froggy air freshener on the dashboard! Extraordinary, isn't it?'

'Oh yeah? And I suppose you've got "Toot if you think I'm sexy" on the back window too, have you?' He jerked his head towards the witty little sticker. I groaned inwardly. I did hope Sam hadn't seen that.

'No, no, I haven't actually.' I shook my head regretfully.

'But it's awfully good, very amusing. I must look out for one of those, I like a jokey little remark on the back of—'

'Oh, just bugger off, you silly tart – go on, bugger off!' he bellowed, giving me what for him was probably a little shove but which jolly nearly propelled me under the wheels of a passing taxi. What I wouldn't have done to be propelled into it. He advanced as I groped for my footing.

'If it wasn't pissing with rain I'd drag you down to the police station right now, and if I catch you anywhere near my car again I'll set the dog on you – Sergeant!'

On command, Sergeant, the biggest Dobermann I'd ever seen, came bounding out of the adjacent house, knocked a couple of gnomes over and threw himself against what was, happily for me, a very high wrought-iron fence. He barked furiously, baring razor-sharp teeth.

'And he doesn't take prisoners either!' bellowed my new friend as I backed away hastily. 'Just you remember that!'

'Oh I will, I will! So sorry, just a silly misunderstanding!' I turned, put my head down and galloped off down the road. I pounded along the pavements in the torrential rain and didn't stop running until I reached the Tube station.

An hour or so later I squelched miserably through Pippa's hall, soaked to the skin, my suit clinging to me, shivering like a wet puppy. Despite popping into the office, Pippa had beaten me back. She was lying with her feet up on the sofa, reading *Tatler* and watching *LA Law*. She gazed in astonishment as I dripped slowly by.

'Blimey! What happened to you?'

'Don't ask,' I said wearily, kicking my shoes off and squelching on upstairs. 'Be an angel and fetch me a large gin, would you?'

I fell into the bathroom, peeled off my sodden clothes

and turned on the taps. A few minutes later she appeared, a gin in each hand. She handed me one, and put the top of the loo seat down and sat on it.

'That wasn't your car, was it?'

I sighed. 'No, but I'm too tired and pissed off to explain. All I can say was it seemed like a good idea at the time.'

I sank back into the warm, Radoxy waters with a sigh of relief. I looked up at her.

'What did you say to Sam?'

'I said you were an extremely nervous driver and you'd be scared shitless at the prospect of us all watching you emerge from a tight parking space. I said most of the surrounding cars, including his, were in imminent danger and would probably be written off. He moved off pretty sharpish, I can tell you.'

I brought the gin to my grateful lips, took a slug and groaned. 'Oh God, now he must think I'm completely mad.'

'Probably,' said Pippa, regarding me coolly, 'but what does it matter?'

I avoided her eye and buried my face in my gin.

Chapter Eleven

I spent about two hours getting ready for the party at Quaglino's. Luckily I'd brought plenty of clothes, but for some reason nothing seemed quite right. Every so often I'd fling something on and run into Pippa's bedroom, where she was lying on her bed reading and eating an apple.

'What about this?'

Pippa looked up laconically and appraised me in my neat little black skirt with red linen jacket. She bit into her apple and shook her head.

'No. You look like a secretary.'

'Really? It's Joseph, you know, and the skirt's quite short.'

'You still look like a secretary.'

She went back to her book and I ran out, wondering if Pippa recalled that not so long ago we'd both actually been gainfully employed as secretaries. A few minutes later I was back.

'What about this then?'

She raised her eyes from her book, stuck her finger in her place and looked me up and down in my very best navy-blue suit complete with vivid red silk scarf tied jauntily at the neck.

She shook her head. 'Uh, uh.'

'Why?'

'Come fly with me.'

'Really?'

'Definitely.'

'Oh Christ!'

I ran out again and ripped it off. When I returned I had on the shocking pink micro mini and a nipped-in black velvet jacket with nothing on underneath. I was grinning confidently, I looked terrific. Pippa took one look, sighed, and got off the bed.

'Polly, where have you been?'

'Sorry? What d'you mean?'

'That sort of look went out with the ark, no one's wearing that sort of tarty power thing any more.'

'Aren't they? Oh! Well it hasn't got any shoulder pads – look.' I squished the shoulders down to prove it.

'Doesn't matter, it still looks naff – here, try these on.'

She delved in her wardrobe and threw me a bundle of clothes. I shook them out.

'What's this – a swimming costume? And . . . flares!'

'It's a body, you goon, and flares are back. I'll lend you some platforms to go with them.'

I collapsed on her bed in a heap. 'Platforms? You must be joking!'

'No, I'm not, now get it all on quickly then we can share a bottle of wine before we go.'

I ran into my bedroom, giggling, and dutifully obeyed, wriggling into the clinging Lycra.

'D'you wear pants with this body thing?' I yelled as I shimmied into it.

'Oh, Polly, for goodness' sake!'

I stared down doubtfully at the garment as it hung, unclasped, between my legs. For goodness' sake yes, or for goodness' sake no? I didn't like to ask her to be more specific for fear of incurring more incredulity about my spell in a sartorial time warp, so in the end I left the pants off, feeling more than a little outré.

Twenty minutes later, with a bottle of hastily guzzled Sancerre inside us, we piled into a taxi, looking, I thought, like a couple of born-again hippies. Pippa even had a long sleeveless cardigan on – I drew the line at that, but had added a string of beads just to show willing.

Quaglino's was already throbbing mightily when we arrived and I felt a surge of excitement as we clumped precariously down the steps in our platforms and then waded through the packed tables, turning heads as we went. Sam stood up as soon as he saw us and kissed us both roundly on the cheeks.

'Wow! You both look terrific! I like the kit, although it makes me feel incredibly old, I was wearing all that the first time around. Take a pew. You know everyone here, don't you, Polly?'

I had a quick glance around the table. I certainly knew most, Josh, Tony, Tim, Amanda – oh God, don't let me be next to her, I couldn't take the strain of dropping my aitches and crucifying my vowels all evening – Amanda's copywriter Chris, a few other crew members, Susan, but thank goodness, no Serena.

'Here, sit next to me.' Sam had obviously got one or two warmers into the bank already, he was looking decidedly pink about the cheeks and his eyes were shining. He pulled out a chair and patted it. 'I've been saving it for you,' he murmured with a wicked wink.

'Thanks.' I sat down, delighted. Pippa slipped in next to Josh.

'No Serena?' I asked as I shook out my napkin.

'No, isn't it a blessed relief? She had a more important party to go to, more star-studded, no doubt, but she's no loss.'

I grinned. 'I couldn't agree more.'

'Now – a drink? I ordered you a gin and tonic because I seemed to recall it was your tipple, but I can change it if you like.'

'No, that's fine!' He remembered my drink? I smiled up at him. He smiled back and held my eyes for an inordinately long time. Suddenly I looked away. Steady, Polly, have a good time but take it easy, you're a married woman, remember? And for goodness' sake don't get drunk. My gin and tonic arrived, I took a huge gulp out of nerves and excitement and nearly collapsed on the floor. It was practically neat gin.

'Christ!' I spluttered.

Sam patted my back as I coughed and snorted attractively into the *crudités*. 'All right?' he enquired.

'Yes thanks,' I croaked, 'bit strong, that's all.'

'They do make a rather mean cocktail here. D'you want some more tonic?'

'No! No, it's fine.' I took another hefty gulp just to prove it. I smiled nonchalantly. 'I've been drinking mean cocktails since I was a babe in arms.'

He grinned back. 'I rather imagined you had ... your health, Polly.'

Our glasses gently collided, and so again did our eyes, and this time I had the nerve to return his gaze. I mean, what the hell, we were only looking, weren't we? Just window-shopping, and in a crowded restaurant what's more, with me to be deposited on a train at midnight like Cinderella – what could be safer? I looked a bit more. God, he was attractive, in a kind of Mel Gibson playing an Argentinian polo player sort of way. I licked my lips wantonly.

'I'm so glad you decided to come this evening,' he murmured into my ear, 'it really wouldn't have been the same without you.' His lips brushed briefly against my hair.

I felt a frisson of excitement and leaned forward to come back with something equally suave yet titillating, but for some reason my tongue seemed to be well and truly tied. I wrestled with it, but we were talking bondage here.

'Th-thanks, it was nice of you to ask me,' I squeaked at last, a deep blush accompanying this incredibly sexy riposte.

Sam smiled, but politely rather than lecherously, and turned to his other side to talk to Susan, who'd plucked at his sleeve and asked him something urgently. He replied at length, giving her the benefit of his hazel eyes, and me his back.

I was furious with myself. For heaven's sake, Polly, buck up! What's happened to your sexy banter, your winning smile, your flirty little ways? Nice of you to ask me? Hell's teeth, you'll be saying thank you for having me next!

Truth was, of course, I was chronically out of practice. Not much call for sexy banter in Helston, but all I needed was a little refresher course, and speaking of refreshment – I picked up my gin and hoovered it back in one. I put the glass down and shuddered. Wow, that was strong, but it should do the trick. I had a quick look around and, managing to avoid Pippa's rather censorial eye, surreptitiously popped open a couple of buttons on my top, took a huge gulp of wine and – *voilà*! I grinned. Tongue and buttons well loosened, I was raring to go.

I practised a smoulder and murmured 'Well, hello' to myself once or twice, just to make sure my voice was deep and sexy, then turned to muscle in on the conversation Sam was having with Susan. It was quite hard because Sam had his back to me now, so I had to sort of peer round and try to catch Susan's eye. She wouldn't look at me, so I listened closely, watched her teeth and laughed when they laughed.

'Ah ha ha! Very good!' I roared.

No response. I leaned round again and smiled sweetly at Susan, who saw but didn't smile back. Cow, I thought, a huge frozen smile on my face, how could I ever have thought she was wholesome? She was about as wholesome as a packet of pork scratchings.

Determined not to be beaten I tried again and this time leaned forward until my head was practically resting on the table. *Chariots of Fire* cropped up.

'Oh, that's *such* a good film, isn't it?' I enthused loudly. 'Oh, Nigel Havers, yes, he's *fabulous*, isn't he . . . ? Oh, you know him, do you, Susan? . . . Yes, yes, *marvellous* soundtrack, simply *marvellous*, by that Greek guy – whatsisname, well anyway, *very* memorable . . .'

I roared on thus but they chatted on regardless. I flushed, hot with embarrassment now. Damn it. Quite apart from anything else I was the only person at the table not talking to anyone. How incredibly galling, had anyone noticed? I had a quick look around. Everyone but me was engrossed. Something had to be done. Quick as a flash and thinking on my feet as usual, I pulled off an earring, dropped it on the floor, then slid off my chair and disappeared under the table on a spurious errand to retrieve it. I salivated slightly at the sight of Sam's glorious long Armani-clad legs, then emerged, smiling and waving the earring triumphantly.

'Got it!' I announced to anyone who was interested. I awaited attention. Nothing. Help.

I blushed some more and nervously quaffed my wine. My spaghetti with some kind of clam and lobster sauce arrived. I frowned with intense concentration and made a great show of expertly winding it on to my fork as if I really couldn't possibly have coped with talking to anyone anyway, seeing as how I had such a delicate operation to attend to. But there's only so much attention one can give to a plateful of spaghetti and when I'd masticated every tiny morsel I put my fork down and turned to Tony next to me, eyes wide and desperate now. Not a chance, he was deep in conference with Josh. I tried to catch Pippa's eye across the table, but she was too far away. Hell. There was nothing else for it, I'd have to turn to drink.

I summoned a passing waiter, commandeered a bottle of red and treated it as my own private supply, steadily emptying and refilling my glass, as if finishing the bottle were some sort of gargantuan task I'd set myself. By the time Sam eventually turned back to me a good fifteen minutes later I was so plastered I was practically nose-diving into my *crème brûlée*.

'Sorry,' he muttered in my ear, 'I didn't mean to abandon you but Susan's having a bit of a confidence crisis at the moment. I had to reassure her, you know what actresses are like.'

'S'quite all right, don't mind me,' I slurred, with more than a hint of pissed petulance in my voice.

She was having a confidence crisis, what did he think I was having, sitting here like a lemon? But at least I had his attention, and just enough sobriety to realise that now was not the time to sulk, but rather to put my skills into action.

I pulled my hair free from behind my ears and let it fall sexily into my eyes, then I nuzzled towards him, lowering my lashes and speaking softly so he had to lean in close to hear.

'Sorry? What was that?'

'I said I really admired the way you handled Serena at the shoot,' I murmured. 'It can't be easy having temperamental actresses flouncing around on the set.'

He laughed. 'That's nothing, you should see them on a feature film. Sometimes they lock themselves in their caravans and refuse to come out for days, and not just the women. The men are just as bad, if not worse. You need to be a nanny, psychiatrist and film director all rolled into one sometimes.'

'Well, you do it awfully well,' I husked admiringly, swaying slightly in my seat as I gazed up at him. I steadied myself on the table and ran my tongue over my teeth as they stuck to my lips. Sam rested his arm around the back of my chair and regarded me thoughtfully.

'Tell me, Polly, have you ever thought about taking filming seriously? I think you have all the right instincts for it and I think you'd probably take a very fresh approach.'

I clenched my toes. This was it, this was *it*! He was going to ask me to audition for his next film – I was about to be discovered! I smiled coyly and played with some breadcrumbs on the table.

'Well, I must admit I did a fair amount of acting at

school, in fact I was a bit of a star, in a very small way, of course.' I smiled modestly.

He nodded. 'Good, so you know the basics. That's terribly important, so many young directors these days don't know a thing about acting and it helps enormously. There's a marvellous film-making course at one of the polys in London, why don't you sign up for it?'

'Er, yes, bit of a hike from Cornwall, isn't it?' I said weakly, neglecting to add that somehow I'd imagined myself on the other side of the camera.

'Well, what's to stop you being a weekly commuter? You could always stay with Pippa during the week and go home at weekends.' He raised his eyebrows enquiringly.

I gasped and took a slug of wine. Wow! He obviously wanted me all to himself during the week! Was he hot for me or what? And was it my imagination or weren't those hazel eyes just sparkling with depravity? Play it cool, Polly, I thought, blushing into my *brûlée*, he's mad about you all right, but for God's sake play it cool.

'What d'you think?' he asked.

'Well, Sam, I'm flattered, really I am, but to stay all week in London, I'm not sure how Nick would—'

'Look, Polly,' he put his hand on my arm, 'I hope you don't think I'm coming on strong or anything, it's just that – well, I find you so refreshing, so gloriously unspoilt. And I'm not bullshitting you about the directing either, I do think you'd bring a fresh approach, but I must admit I have a selfish motive too. I'd really like to see more of you, in – well, in a purely platonic way of course.' He shook his head and looked slightly bewildered. 'I don't know, I just find you so—' he paused and struggled for the right word.

Golly, what? What was I? I was absolutely agog now and

leaned forward, eager not to miss a syllable of this tantalising observation, but unfortunately he never got to the end of it because I inadvertently put my elbow on the edge of his plate and catapulted a great dollop of gooseberry fool up on to my chest.

'Damn!' I squeaked. 'Oh God, what a mess!'

'Here – let me.'

Sam reached quickly for a napkin, dipped it in some Perrier and began mopping my top, perilously close to a couple of my larger erogenous zones. I clutched the table for support and moaned softly, trying desperately to imagine he was Roy Hattersley or someone.

'Thanks!' I gasped at last. 'Silly of me!'

'Easily done,' he said, still mopping away in the lower armpit region. He grinned. 'Not making you nervous, am I?'

'God, no!' I trilled, feeling decidedly light-headed with drink and excitement. 'Me? Nervous? Not at all, don't be ridiculous.'

'Good,' he said quietly. He stopped mopping and his hand came to rest next to mine on the table. Our fingers touched and I could almost feel mine vibrate with excitement. I swallowed hard and stared at him. He held my gaze.

'Um ... look, Sam ...' I began, but quite forgot what I was going to say as his hand covered mine and held it. I felt powerless to take it away. My head said no, but my body was all for it, no self-control as Nick would say – Nick! I gulped. Would he sense that I'd indulged in guilty gazing? That I'd been mopped to within an inch of my erogenous zones? That I'd done a bit of extra-curricular hand-holding? Drunk or not, alarm bells rang loud in my head and with a staggering flash of sobriety I realised I had to act fast. Perhaps Sam had forgotten he too had a spouse? Certainly it had temporarily escaped me. His hand held mine and his eyes were getting more dangerous by the second. I had to remind him.

'And how – how is your wife?' I enquired desperately.

Sam looked surprised.

'My wife?'

'Yes, your, um, wife. Sally, isn't it?'

Sam's mouth began to twitch at the corners. He took his hand away, threw back his head and laughed out loud. He roared away for quite some time before eventually slumping back in his seat. He wiped his eyes and groaned, shaking his head.

'Oh God, Polly, you do make me laugh. That's what I like about you, you have absolutely no guile at all, do you? You just say exactly what comes into your head. My wife is fine and you're absolutely right, I'm getting way out of line here. Sorry, I've probably had one too many of these,' he indicated his gin, 'and I have to admit, I do find you incredibly attractive.' He shrugged and gave me a lopsided smile. 'Sorry, but there it is, can't help myself. If it's not too corny, you're a real breath of fresh air in this fuggy, pseudo-sophisticated London atmosphere. I can't tell you what a glorious change it is to talk to someone like you after the luvvie people I spend my time with, but believe me, that's as far as it goes. I've never cheated on my wife in my life and I don't intend to start now, even,' he grinned and winked, 'with someone as delectable and enticing as yourself.' He raised his glass enquiringly at me. 'OK? Friends?'

I grinned back and raised my glass. I wasn't sure about the lack of guile, I'd always thought I'd had buckets of it, but this was much better, this I could cope with. 'Friends,' I agreed, 'and I'm sorry I brought your wife up in such a cack-handed manner, but I did just think it might be as well to – you know – keep our matrimonial obligations to the forefront of our minds and not to forget that we do owe it to our partners to—'

'Hey, hey, enough!' Sam was grinning and backing away in mock terror now. He held up his hands. 'I promise I'll never so much as smile at you again, I'll never even glance in your general direction! Dib dib dib, dob dob dob, scout's honour, you've made your point, Polly!' He wiped his mouth on his napkin and got to his feet. 'In fact I'm backing off right now.'

'Oh!' I felt suddenly disappointed. 'Wh-where are you going?'

He grinned. 'To the loo. I'll be right back.'

'Ah.' I smiled. 'Right, good.'

He went. I leaned back in my seat and sighed. Shame. Pity I'd had to nip him in the bud like that, but it had to be done. I frowned as I cradled my wine glass, taking the occasional sip. Odd that there really didn't seem to be any middle ground with this flirting lark. As far as men were concerned it was very definitely a means to an end and not an art to be savoured and perfected. Such a waste, and so unlike France, where it's practically a national pastime. I mean look at that Cointreau ad. That smoothie Frenchman's been at it for years – stroking crystal glasses suggestively, giving his bird smouldering, sexy looks over the dinner table, banging on about an inimitable blend of 'erbs and spices – it's never got him anywhere but he still seems to be enjoying himself. What a pity the English are so – I jumped as someone tapped my shoulder.

'Eh? What?' I swung around.

'Wake up, Polly, there's a plan afoot to move on.'

Sam was smiling down at me from behind my chair. I looked around dreamily. Everyone else appeared to be standing up too but they weren't smiling. Coats were on, bags were on shoulders, hands were in pockets, in fact the entire table were standing behind their chairs looking at me in a rather disapproving manner.

'Wh-what? What's going on?' I enquired from my slumped position. It occurred to me that I couldn't even begin to move without some help, I was positively welded to my chair. I spotted someone familiar.

'Where are we going, Pippa?' Her face swam in and out of focus.

'Well, one or two people are going on to Annabel's, but personally I'm going home to bed, and I think perhaps you should come too, Polly, and get the train in the morning.' She looked at me meaningfully.

I giggled. 'What, with you and Josh? Three in a bed, you mean?'

I sniggered. Gosh, I was on form tonight. Then I saw her face. It was white, ashen even. Oh Christ. I stumbled to my feet and crashed towards her, knocking over a couple of chairs on the way.

'Pippa! Oh Pippa, I'm so sorry, I didn't mean to say that, it just slipped out!'

'I've no idea what you're talking about,' hissed Pippa, 'but I'm going home – on my own – right now. Are you coming?'

'Oh, Pippa, I'm so sorry, I completely forgot no one was supposed to know!' I wailed, making it much worse, but Pippa was already halfway out of the restaurant with Josh stalking out behind her. I went to go after her but Sam put a restraining hand on my arm.

'Leave her, wait till she's calmed down a bit.'

'She hates me!' I wailed.

'Course she doesn't. Besides, it's no big deal, we all knew anyway.'

'Really?'

'Sure, it's been going on for months, and it's probably a good thing it's out in the open now, certainly from Pippa's point of view.'

I considered this. He was right. I cheered up immeasurably.

'Yes, of course, you're right. Gosh, she'll probably even thank me tomorrow!'

'Exactly. Now come on, forget about Pippa and Josh, let's go dancing.'

'Really? Now?' I peered at my watch. 'I've got to get a train at some point.'

The point was, when? I couldn't actually see what the devil the big and little hands were up to, they seemed to be rotating at an alarming rate. I knew I should have gone for digital. I turned to Sam for assistance.

'Er, any idea what the time is?'

'Oh, it's quite early, you'll make it easily, don't worry.'

'Will I?' I lurched and clung to his arm to steady myself. 'Will I really?'

'I'll personally put you on the train myself. Now come on, let's go and get a taxi.'

'What a dominant man you are,' I murmured, knocking back the remains of my wine and clinging to his arm like a limpet as we ascended the perilous staircase to the front door.

'I like my men like that, dominant and forceful, mmmmm . . . lovely, only – shhhh,' I held a wobbly finger to my lips and it slipped attractively up my nose as I stumbled on the steps, 'keep it shtum. We girls aren't supposed to like that cave-man-hunter-gatherer bit any more, we're supposed to go weak at the knees for the caring-sharing lark. Well, stuff that for a game of soldiers, give me a great big dominant man any time, only' – I looked around for fear of being overheard – 'for God's sake keep it quiet,' I hissed. 'If any of those open-toed feminists found out there'd be hell to pay, know what I mean?'

Sam grinned and guided me through the door. 'Your secret is safe with me, Polly, I won't breathe a word.'

He bundled me into a purring taxi and I fell into a bucket seat. Amanda, Chris and Sam made up the party. I looked around.

'What – just us? Isn't anyone else coming?'

'They've all dun a bunk,' grinned Amanda. 'Couldn't 'ack the pace, most likely.'

I groaned inwardly. Oh no, Amanda again. 'Yeah, well blimey, wot a load of par'y poopers, eh? Gorblimey, the night's still bleedin' well young, innit? Wot the 'ell are they playin' at, eh? I mean, lawks a mercy, apples an' pears, whistle an' flute—' Suddenly I felt weak, I couldn't keep it up.

'Um, listen, Amanda.' I leaned forward – a huge mistake in the bucket seat of a taxi – and nose-dived into her lap. She helped me up and deftly swapped places with me.

''Ere, you sit 'ere, you need it more than I do.'

'Thanks – I mean, ta – I mean, listen, Amanda, I've got a terrible confession to make.'

'Oh yeah?'

'Yeah – yes. You see, the thing is I'm not really like you at all.'

'Come again?'

'I mean, I don't – you know – speak like you do, actually. I'm sorry, but the thing is I'm really quite posh, well, a little bit posh, and I'm certainly not a Cockney – not that you are either, of course.'

Even in my highly intoxicated state I was dimly aware that making fun of someone's regional accent was neither politically nor socially correct, but it was a very dim awareness, and anyway, it was out now.

There was a terrible silence. Chris and Sam stared at their feet, Amanda stared at me. I gulped. Oh hell, what was she going to do, punch me on the nose? Or perhaps something altogether more sinister? I clutched my kneecaps possessively. After all, she could well be related to the Kray twins.

Suddenly she let out a bellow of laughter. She threw her head back and roared into the roof of the taxi.

'It's all right, I sussed you! You were so bad at it. I mean, blimey, I might be an East London girl but I'm not the blinkin' Pearly Queen, you know!'

More raucous laughter followed this declaration and I joined in, nervously at first, but then wholeheartedly, and then of course I couldn't stop. In fact the pair of us didn't stop roaring and gasping until we fell out of the taxi at Berkeley Square, helpless with hysteria.

Sam gripped my arm and steadied me as I lurched around on the pavement, holding my stomach.

'Here we are, girls,' he said, ushering us down the steps. 'Steady now, Polly, you'll rupture something if you're not careful.'

'Oh God, that was so funny,' I gasped weakly as Sam held the door open for me. 'It's made me positively thirsty!'

'Er, d'you think perhaps you should have something soft, Polly, maybe a Perrier?' said Sam, following me rather anxiously as I headed in a determined, if not entirely straight line for the bar.

'Water? Don't be ridiculous. I want to drink it, not swim in it – waiter! Oi, waiter, one large gin and tonic please!' I yelled, totally out of control now. I banged the bar and tried to climb on to a stool but it was awfully high and I fell off.

'Waiter!' I shouted, trying to scramble up the stool again.

'Er, it's OK, Polly, I'll get the drinks,' said Sam, prising me off the stool as I clambered up the side and steering me towards a little table. 'You sit down here.'

'So dominant, so charming,' I muttered, giving him a winning smile as I lowered myself rather precariously into a chair.

He turned to Amanda. 'Amanda, what would you like?'

'No thanks, Sam, actually I've just spotted some really old mates of mine over there, d'you mind if I go and join them for a sec?'

'No, no, fine, we'll see you later.'

She disappeared with Chris in tow.

Sam returned from the bar with our drinks and sat down opposite me. 'So ... just the two of us.' He smiled. 'Perfect. Cheers.'

I smiled back, but had the feeling it was more of a drunken leer, so I buried my face in my gin. This one hadn't even been near a tonic bottle but luckily my taste buds were totally anaesthetised so I knocked it back without a problem. The only problem seemed to be coming from my loins. I staggered to my feet.

'Got to go to the loo,' I mumbled, and off I stumbled, knocking over a couple of chairs on the way and cannoning into quite a few people who didn't seem to be able to walk in straight lines.

It took me ages to find the ladies' and when I did I was a little taken aback to see a couple of men already *in situ*. They looked equally surprised to see me, so I gave them an icy glare and made a mental note to inform the management that whilst mixed loos might be a liberated concept I didn't think it would work until men could be trained not to pee in the basins like that. Disgusting. Not being such an exhibitionist myself I crashed into a cubicle to relieve myself, but once relieved, I encountered a problem. Getting the Lycra body unpopped at the crutch had been simple enough, but getting it done up again was a different matter. I had to half crouch down and sort of lean forward and peer, and then for some reason my fingers wouldn't work the poppers.

'Oh come on, come on,' I whispered urgently, but it was no good. All manual dexterity had deserted me. Not only that, but every time I adopted the obligatory skiing position needed to get to grips with the thing, the blood would rush to my head and I'd cannon forward, hitting my head violently on the loo door. When this had happened more than twice a plummy male voice enquired from without – rather impertinently I thought – 'Are you all right in there?'

'Fine, thank you,' I informed him icily. Christ, can't a girl even snap her knickers together in peace?

Eventually I gave up and just tucked the tails hastily inside my trousers, thinking that whoever had invented this extraordinary bit of kit had a lot to answer for. I lurched out of the door to a wash basin and steadied myself on the porcelain. More men were wandering around now, giving me the oddest looks, but I expect they just fancied me. I ignored them all disdainfully and studied my reflection. Heavens, I looked terrible. My hair was all over the place and the bloods of my eyes were only slightly whiteshot. I dragged a comb through my hair, added some lipstick which conveniently matched my eyes, then stumbled out again, bursting back into the nightclub like an unguided missile and cannoning straight into warm human flesh.

'Look out!'

'Ooops, sorry!' I steadied myself against the female I'd embraced. She had a beautiful face with large brown eyes and long dark silky hair, and by golly she looked familiar.

'Polly!'

I tried desperately to focus. 'Good grief.' I squinted. 'Lottie!'

'What on earth are you doing here, and why were you in the men's? Heavens, you look terrible!'

'Do I? Oh well, never mind.' I grinned up at my erstwhile flatmate and hugged her warmly, grateful for something friendly to hang on to. 'I'm having a terrific time!'

We wobbled precariously. 'Hey, steady – gosh, you look completely plastered. Are you all right? Is Nick with you?' She looked around for my husband.

'No, no, I'm with Sham, he's a film director,' I confided happily.

Lottie frowned. 'Sham? But where's Nick?'

'Oh, he's busy farming. Now, don't you worry, it's not

like that, Lottie, it's all strictly above board. It's just that he thinks I've got hidden talents, you see, thinks I've got the makings of a marvellous director, so he's giving me the benefit of his vast expertise.'

'I bet he is,' she said drily.

'Oh Lottie, don't be like that, come and meet him!' I dragged her bodily over to our table. 'Sam,' I called loudly, perhaps too loudly, because quite a few people turned round. 'Hey, Sam, stand up please, I want you to meet one of my very best friends in the whole world, Lottie – shit, I've forgotten your name.'

'Parker,' she put in helpfully, 'and don't shout, Polly.'

'Parker, that's it, she got married, you see, lost her real name which was why I couldn't remember it, oh, and Lottie, this is Sam Weston, an *extremely* famous film director, you've heard of him, of course, haven't you?'

'Well—'

'Oh God, Lottie, you're *hopeless*, he's done *loads* of things, haven't you, Sam? Come on, what have you done?' I bellowed. 'Tell her what you've done! Come on!'

Suddenly I had to grip hold of the back of a chair as I swayed violently and experienced a rush of blood to the head. Too much shouting, probably. I wondered if I could possibly walk around the front of the chair and get my bottom on to its seat.

Sam was on his feet now, shaking Lottie by the hand. 'I assure you I haven't done anything remotely memorable, there's no reason why you should have heard of me.'

Lottie smiled. 'I'm afraid I don't get to the cinema much these days.'

'I don't blame you, most of it's rubbish.'

'Hey, Lottie, sit down!' I'd finally managed to park my

own bottom and was keen for others to join me. It was making me dizzy looking up at them. 'Sam, oi, Sam, how about getting a drink for Lottie, where are your manners, eh?' I yelled. The people at the next table turned to stare at me.

'Er, sure – what can I get you, Lottie?'

'Oh no, not for me,' said Lottie, waving her hand. 'I've got one over there, I'm with a party from the office – oh, here's one of them. Polly, you remember Peggy, don't you?'

An extremely large American colleague of Lottie's came bounding up, fairly shaking the floorboards as she bounced to a halt. Remember her? I'd nearly fallen asleep on her. Nick and I had once spent a mind-numbing evening in her company at a party of Lottie's where she'd singlehandedly bored for America. All night long we'd been treated to her views on Ikea furniture, Marks and Spencer pre-cooked meals, Benetton jumpers, Sainsbury's *crème fraiche* and the joys of Mars Bar ice creams. Now I can shop till I'm sick, but this girl had me beaten into a paper bag. Nick and I had finally escaped, reeling and gasping into the night, vowing never again to accept an invitation without having a full dossier on the other guests first. She grinned toothily at me.

'Polly, hi! How y'doing? Hey, I love your beads. You must tell me where you got them, I'd love to take some back to the States. You wouldn't believe it but it's just impossible to get hold of that kind of thing out there, weird, isn't it? What d'you think of this dress, by the way?' She glanced down at the snot-green tent affair she was wearing. 'Bet you can't guess where I got it?' she asked gleefully.

'Harvey Nicks?' I hazarded meekly, knowing full well

that that was what she wanted to hear but that Oxfam was nearer the mark.

'Wrong! Marks and Spencer, fourteen ninety-nine, don't you think that's just incredible value?'

'Incredible,' I agreed weakly.

Peggy smiled with satisfaction and looked around ominously, as if searching for somewhere to park her heavily upholstered derrière and continue this fascinating retail discussion. Sam looked alarmed, as well he might. Luckily I was alive to the situation.

'Oh, er, Lottie, is that the rest of your crowd from the office over there?' I asked, peering into the middle distance. 'I think they're waving to us,' I lied.

'Where?' Lottie strained to see.

'There, behind that pillar, they're beckoning to you, I think.'

'Really? I can't see, but perhaps we'd better go, they'll be wondering where we are. Come on, Peggy.' She seized Peggy's huge arm and bent down to peck me on the cheek.

'Listen, are you really all right, Polly?' she hissed in my ear.

'Yes, of course, why?'

'Because you look absolutely out of your head, that's why. D'you want me to get you a taxi or anything?' She looked worried.

'Don't be ridiculous, I'm having a whale of a time!'

'Really?'

'Bloody hell, Lottie, I haven't had so much fun in ages!'

'Well, if you're sure . . .' She looked doubtful. 'Only I know you . . .'

'Course I'm sure, now get back to the rest of your crowd – go on!'

She laughed. 'Bugger off, you mean. All right, but take it easy, OK?'

I grinned and waved her on her way, winking conspiratorially at Sam as she went. We settled down into another cosy gaze. This time I tried out a sort of come-hither one, complete with languid licking of lips. It was a huge success, I think, judging by the way he guffawed with pleasure. I wriggled happily in my seat. This was bliss. It was weeks, months – no, years even – since I'd felt this way. Silly, light-headed, frivolous, irresponsible – drunk, even – but why not? I was still young, wasn't I?

Sam leaned forward, looking a bit concerned. 'Polly, would you rather make a move now? Your train's not for a while yet, but I'll wait with you at the station if you like. We could get a cup of coffee?'

'But we've only just got here. There's still bags of time, isn't there?'

'Sure, but you look a bit tired.'

'Me? Tired? Rubbish, I'm having a brilliant time!'

He smiled and looked at his watch. 'OK, if you're sure, but you'd better not have any more to drink. I just hope yours is the last stop on the line because I can't see you waking up for it. I'll have to hang a notice round your neck – "Wake me up at Truro".'

'Like Paddington Bear.'

He smiled and took my hand. 'Just like a little bear.'

I let him take my hand. That was OK, I decided. After all, we'd held hands before, so we weren't breaking new ground. I sighed blissfully as he stroked my fingers. God, he was attractive. If I wasn't married and in love with Nick . . . He smiled and I smiled back. I couldn't think why I hadn't thought of this before, I mean, the world must be full of gorgeous married men, why stop at this one? Why not find some more? There must be loads of them with time on their hands, ready and willing for a bit of innocuous eye contact and platonic hand-holding, why not make it a pastime? A sort of hobby? I wondered if Nick would be prepared to put some money into a little scheme if I went into business. Set myself up as an expert, give lessons, that sort of thing – after all, he'd offered to set me up in a shop, hadn't he? I was just idly wondering if a council grant would be possible when I found myself being dragged to my feet. Neither my feet nor the rest of my body wanted to move an inch.

'Come on,' said a voice in my ear, 'just one dance then I'll put you on that train. I just want to hold you once in my arms before you go.'

I couldn't even speak now, let alone put up any resistance, so I let myself be half dragged, half carried to the dance floor. Once there, I fell into his arms. I didn't like to tell him it was a mistake but I knew it was, I'd felt much better sitting down. People seemed to be cannoning into us from all over the place, so I hung on tight and buried my face in his shoulder.

I felt awfully sick but didn't like to open my mouth to tell him so in case I gave a practical demonstration. Coloured lights were swirling horribly above me and the music was unbearably loud. I shut my eyes tight. I was dimly aware that the tails of my body had crept out and were hanging down on the wrong side of my trousers, but there was absolutely nothing I could do about it. Sartorial elegance be damned, I had more important things to contend with, like how to stay upright.

Whitney Houston pounded urgently into my ears. My

head was throbbing. Sam held me close and stroked my hair. If only I was sober enough to enjoy it, but I really did feel terribly ill.

'Sam, I . . .' I whispered into the pounding music, looking up into his face.

He smiled down at me and I realised that he must have thought I was lifting my face to be kissed. He bent his head and his lips brushed mine, warm and soft, but definitely unwelcome in the light of my condition. I gritted my teeth. Please don't let me be sick now, oh please God, not now! It was important that he didn't kiss me again so I kept my head buried in his shoulder, praying that the dance would end soon and we could get far enough away from the pounding music for me to tell him how ill I felt. All of a sudden I knew I couldn't wait till the end of the record. I had to act fast or I was going to disgrace myself in a very big way and make a terrible mess all over the dance floor.

'Sam, I feel awful,' I muttered, 'I must—' I made an almighty effort to wrench myself free of his arms but, sadly, simultaneously lost the fight. The one I'd been waging to stay upright. The flashing lights fell from the ceiling in a dazzling display of colour and the dance floor came up to meet them. Ceiling and floor collided with an almighty flash of white. After that, there was nothing. Just blackness.

Chapter Twelve

When I came to, I was lying in a bed that wasn't mine, in a room I didn't recognise. My head was throbbing like a waiting taxi and my eyes ached in their sockets. I opened them slowly. Where the hell was I? Battling through a wave of pain and nausea I tried to work it out. The curtains were drawn, but it was light. I narrowed my eyes. Too light. I peered around nervously. The room was smart, a tasteful grey and white colour scheme prevailed, but it was tomb-like, impersonal, and it smacked of efficiency – a hospital perhaps? Private, of course, I thought, glancing down at the inch-thick carpet. I hoped to God Nick had kept up the BUPA payments. Two seconds later I realised that glancing at the carpet had been a huge mistake, as my tummy rose to my throat like a high-speed lift and I clutched my mouth.

'Nurse, nurse!' I yelled, looking around wildly. I was about to be very ill and I needed a bowl, or preferably a bucket, right now.

'NURSE!' I shrieked in panic.

No nurse, and no handy red button with which to summon one. Damn. Still clutching my mouth, I sat up and swung my legs over the side of the bed. There was a door, slightly ajar, to my left. A bathroom? I bolted towards it, hoping it wasn't a wardrobe as it had been on one disastrous occasion at a house party in Scotland, but happily, instead of encountering a row of shining Churchill brogues, I encountered a shining marble bathroom instead. I made it to the loo with seconds to spare and was violently, and repeatedly, sick.

I clutched the porcelain to steady myself and sank down gingerly on to the cold tiled floor. I shivered. It occurred to me that I hadn't a stitch on. I grabbed a towel from a rail and pulled it around me, shaking now and feeling extremely ill. This was extraordinary. Where on earth was I, and why was I naked? It was a pretty rum sort of hospital that liked their patients starkers, wasn't it? I looked around, desperate for clues.

The bathroom was a riot of marble and chrome, with so many gleaming surfaces and sparkling taps it made your eyes ache to look at it. Perhaps this doubled as an operating theatre? The lights were certainly bright enough and there were plenty of marble slabs for surgery, handy really, because I was going to need some in my brain quite soon. 'Oooooh . . . Christ!' I moaned and clutched my head.

Holding it carefully, as if bits might spill out, I hobbled gingerly back to bed. I lay down and turned on my side. Surely a nurse would come soon, to check I was OK. I hoped so, I certainly couldn't go looking for one in my condition. I stared at the hygienic-looking bedside table beside me. Nine o'clock, said my watch.

Through the table's glass top I spotted a little black Bible. I blinked. Heavens, that was a bit pessimistic, wasn't it? Was it handily placed there for the last rites, perhaps? Didn't give one much faith in the medical team, did it? I stared at the spine of the book underneath it. *A Guide To*

London's Night Spots. I blinked again. Wow. One minute the inmates were on their deathbeds and the next they were dancing round their handbags. Talk about kill or cure.

Suddenly I had a nasty thought. I sat bolt upright and stared at the dressing table. There was a tray with a tea pot on it, and some cups, two cups, and round the rim of the cups something was written in green – The Royal ... something ... Hotel. Oh! I gulped. A hotel! Not a hospital at all, but – what was I doing in a hotel? How had I got here? I racked my addled brain and tried desperately to piece together the happenings of the previous night.

Well, first we'd all gone out to dinner, that much was clear, then a few of us had gone on to Annabel's, and then ... what next? I frowned. Somewhere along the line I remembered getting stupendously drunk and dancing with Sam, but then what? Well, then I woke up in a hotel bedroom with no clothes on, that's what. I froze. Oh my God! I clapped my hand over my mouth. Had I slept with him? Had I? My eyes grew huge with fear. No! No, I couldn't have, because if I had – well, where was he now?

I sprang from the bed with hitherto unimaginable alacrity, rushed to the wardrobe and flung it open. Empty. I ran to the curtains and swept them aside, hastily shutting them again as a startled passer-by got a full-frontal. No, he definitely wasn't here, which was a rattling good sign, because if, *if* by any catastrophic chance anything untoward *had* occurred – God forbid – well, then he'd certainly be here now, wouldn't he? Being even more untoward? I mean, who forks out for a hotel room for only one bunk-up, for heaven's sake? Hardly worth the effort, is it? No, he'd definitely still be here, demanding his early-morning rights.

I paced nervously round the room, looking for clues. I

sorted out my clothes which were scattered about. No boxer shorts amongst them – good. I peeked cautiously in the waste-paper basket – nothing rubber and unspeakable in there. Excellent, things were looking up. I sat down on the bed, relief flooding over me. Yes, of course, I'd obviously missed the last train and had been parked here by some good samaritan to sleep off my alcoholic stupor – what a relief!

I flopped back thankfully on the bed, and as I did so a piece of paper flew off the bedside table. It fluttered about in the breeze my flop had created and then spiralled slowly down to the floor like a sycamore seed. I watched as it landed. My heart just about stopped beating. I jumped off the bed and fell on it. My hand shook as I spread it out.

Saturday, 7.00 a.m.

Darling Polly,

Thank you for a wonderful evening. Sorry you missed your train, but it was worth it, wasn't it? Had to dash off early this morning but I'll ring you soon.

Love always, Sam.

I stared at the paper in disbelief. I read it again. Seven a.m., it said, so he'd been here . . . all night. My hand flew to my mouth and something cold gripped my heart. I'd slept with him. I must have done. My stomach curdled with revulsion. I dropped the piece of paper and it fluttered down to the carpet again. I stared at it, stunned.

Then I picked it up again. 'It was worth it, wasn't it?' The words swam in and out of focus. I tried to think what that meant. Did it necessarily mean that . . . yes, of *course* it did, Polly, what else *could* it mean? Oh God! I sank to my knees on the carpet, hid my face in my hands and doubled up in agony like a footballer who's been kneed in the groin. How could I? How *could* I have gone to bed with him? Had I really been that drunk, was it possible?

I lay down on my side, holding myself, shivering with cold and self-pity. I pulled my towel around me and stared at the grey carpet, which was getting less tasteful by the minute. I felt numb. I simply couldn't believe I'd done it. As I lay there, something green and shiny caught my eye. It was sticking out from under the bed, right by my shoes. I pulled it out. It was an empty champagne bottle. I sat up and looked around. Sure enough, sitting on the dressing table was a champagne glass. I glanced wildly around the room and there, on the windowsill, just behind the curtain, was another. Only this one had lipstick on the rim. I got shakily to my feet, walked over and picked it up. Pink lipstick. My lipstick. Clearly these had been our pre-, and possibly post-, coital drinks.

I sat down on the little stool by the dressing table, put my head in my hands and wept. I hated myself. I just wanted to die. Tears streamed down my face and I let them fall unchecked. I'd broken my marriage vows, I'd been unfaithful to Nick, I'd – Nick! Suddenly I froze. I sat bolt upright like a pin in a bowling alley and my tears stopped in mid-stream. Hell! No! It was Saturday! Saturday morning, and I should be in Cornwall, not dying gracefully in a London hotel room! I should be checking the Foxtons delivery, Nick would kill me – Jesus!

I scrambled to my feet and raced to my bundle of clothes, grabbing bra, body, trousers, shirt and – oh God, plat-forms. I scrambled into them. Infidelity might find me doubled up on the floor in agony but the impending wrath of my husband had me throwing my clothes on, grabbing my handbag, dragging a comb through my hair and bolting out of that room in three minutes flat.

I tore along the corridor and down the stairs, nearly breaking my ankle in my ridiculous shoes. Should I go by train or collect the car? But the car was – heavens, where was the car? I racked my brain as I hobbled down the stairs. Oh Lord, the car was still in Harrods car park, wasn't it? I couldn't possibly go and get it now, I probably owed them about a million pounds! No, I'd just have to ring later and explain I'd had a terrible accident, been hit by a truck in Knightsbridge or – no, a Bentley – and hadn't been able to pick it up. It would take much too long to go along and lie my way out of it now, though. I'd get the train.

I ran through the lobby, looking straight ahead and hoping to God I'd be spared the indignity of being stopped to pay the bill. No one batted an eyelid so I pushed through the revolving doors and ran out into the sunlit street. Cars screeched around me, honking their horns madly.

'Taxi!' I yelled, as a proximate one nearly bowled me over.

'Jesus Christ!' bellowed the driver. 'You want to die?'

'Wouldn't mind,' I muttered, climbing in. 'Paddington, please, I'm in a tearing hurry.'

'So I see.'

I sank back in the black leather and caught my breath. I looked around. Mayfair. Definitely Mayfair. A discreet yet expensive little hotel just off Dover Street, a stone's throw from Annabel's – he probably used it all the time, the bastard. I ground my teeth miserably. It was all becoming horribly plain. He'd deliberately got me plastered – hadn't he been tipping gin down my throat all evening? Then he'd got rid of everyone else, and just when I was more or less unconscious he'd taken me back to a hotel and violated me – raped me even!

'Rape!' I yelped, clutching my mouth. The taxi driver looked at me in horror in his rear-view mirror.

'I never bleedin' touched you!'

'Oh, no, no, it's all right, not you, um, someone else.'

'Blimey,' he said shortly. A second later he looked in the mirror again. 'What, you mean you've been . . . ?' he asked nervously.

'No, no, forget it,' I said quickly. 'I'm rehearsing for a play, learning my lines, forget I said anything.'

'Ah.' He looked faintly reassured.

I stared out of the window, wishing it were true, but this was no rehearsal, this was real life. Perhaps I should go to the police? Get him arrested, bound over, imprisoned – anything to keep him off the streets, to keep him from doing it again. I frowned. From doing what again? What exactly had happened?

I rummaged around in my bag and pulled the note out. 'It was worth it, wasn't it?' Crikey. That sounded very much as if I'd been a willing participant, as if I'd enjoyed it. Would that stand up in court? I mean, I couldn't remember a damn thing, so perhaps I had enjoyed it? And had he really been tipping gin down my throat? I had one or two hazy recollections of him actually trying to restrain my alcohol intake. I hastily stuffed the note back in my bag. Perhaps I wouldn't go to the police after all. And perhaps I'd burn that note, or eat it even, before it was used in evidence against me.

At Paddington I bought a ticket, raced over to a kiosk for some cigarettes, and belted over to platform six. By some lucky chance a train had just pulled in and was throbbing away impatiently, waiting to set off again. I climbed aboard. It was relatively empty so I found a window seat and sank down into a corner. The train chugged slowly out of the station.

With shaking hands I took a cigarette from my pack, lit it, and managed to spill the rest of the packet on the floor. As I scrambled around under seats picking them up, someone tapped me on the shoulder.

'No smoking in here, young lady!'

I looked up from beneath a seat. A bumptious little man in half-moon glasses was glaring over his pinstriped stomach at me, thumbs lodged in waistcoat pockets. He was a dead ringer for Captain Mainwaring. I stared at him. This was no ordinary cigarette, this was keeping me from throwing myself off a moving train, didn't he know that?

'I'm an addict,' I informed him. 'Have to have one every ten minutes or I pass out, I've got a doctor's certificate to prove it.'

He looked a little taken aback, but soon recovered. 'Well, you shouldn't be travelling by train then, should you? Go on,' he waved his hand imperiously, 'put it out.'

'I also get very sick, it's the withdrawal symptoms, you see.'

He went purple. 'Just put the blasted thing out or I'll have you thrown off the train!'

He probably would, too. 'Well, don't blame me if I throw up on your shoes,' I warned icily.

He flinched but sat down opposite to spy on me, tucking his highly polished shoes well under the seat. I took one last, lingering, defiant drag, then threw it out of the window. I glared at him. Yet another member of the smoking police with nothing better to do than persecute people who just wanted a quiet fag in peace. Unbelievable. He shook his *Telegraph* out noisily and peered over it every now and then just to make sure I hadn't lit another.

I ignored him and stared out of the window. My mind boomeranged back to Sam. What the devil was his game? Wasn't he supposed to be a happily married man? What about his sacred marriage vows? I mean, for goodness' sake, it had just been a harmless little flirtation, not a full-blown adulterous wham-bam-thank-you-mam, hadn't he realised that? Hadn't he? I squirmed in my seat. I had a nasty feeling in my waters. Had it, I wondered, been in any way my fault? Had I, perhaps . . . led him on? I'd certainly been aware that he fancied me and – well, yes, OK, I probably *had* led him on, but had I led him on so far that it was inconceivable we wouldn't go all the way? Was I in fact . . . to blame?

'Oh God . . .' I groaned, and hid my face in my hands.

Tears began to trickle down my nose. I let them fall unchecked. I peered through my fingers. Captain Mainwaring was spying on me, looking rather alarmed. Yes, I thought savagely, this is what you've done to me, this is what an addict looks like deprived of her fix. I'll be having a cold chicken next, or a turkey, or whatever it's called. I hope you're thoroughly ashamed of yourself.

I stared out of the window, my cheeks sopping wet. Would Nick guess? Would he find out? And if he did, would he ever feel the same way about me again? And even if he didn't find out, it would still be hanging over us, wouldn't it, because I'd know. I gazed out at the tower blocks, the graffiti, the inner-city decay. It all swept by in the drizzling rain.

Odd, I reflected, resting my forehead on the window, how one night can change your entire life, especially one you can't even remember. Yesterday I hadn't a care in the world, now I had a truckload. I felt numb with shock, with shame, and with the pain that was still rattling around in my head. I also felt desperately tired, which was odd, considering I'd just woken up. Clearly, it had been an eventful night. I shut my eyes and listened to the wheels rattling beneath me. Faster than fairies, faster than witches . . . I let my mind go blank and let sleep wash over me, a defence mechanism I've always been able to employ, no matter how dire the circumstances.

I think I must have slept for a long time because when I woke up there had been quite a dramatic scene change. Inside the carriage Captain Mainwaring had disappeared, and outside the rain had stopped and the sky was clear and blue, with only the odd wispy little cloud racing through it. Green hills swept up from the track, horses nodded and flicked flies with their tails, cows tugged at the wet grass. It looked a lot more like home. Suddenly London and all its horrors seemed a long way away. I sat up. My head had stopped throbbing and I didn't feel sick any more. In actual fact I felt a lot better. I got the note out of my handbag again and spread it on my knee. I dissected it word by word.

'7.00 a.m.,' it read. Yes, well, OK, there was no escaping the fact that he'd spent the night with me, but *how* exactly? Shouldn't we be careful not to jump to conclusions here? Shouldn't we, in fact, read between the lines just a smidgen more? For example, thus:

'Darling Polly' – well he would call me darling, wouldn't he? I mean, all those luvvie types do, look at Richard

Attenborough, he probably calls the milkman darling, so nothing odd about that. 'Thank you for a wonderful evening' – evening, mind, not night – why hadn't I noticed that before? My heart lifted a millimetre. 'Sorry you missed your train, but it was worth it, wasn't it?' – i.e., the fun we'd had that *evening*, the party at Quaglino's, the dancing at Annabel's, the laughs, the jokes. 'Had to dash off early this morning' – no inclination to stay, note – 'but I'll ring you soon. Love always' – luvvie language again – 'Sam.'

I stared at the paper as if I'd never seen it before. No mention of a night of debauchery, no mention of sex, no mention of anything other than the fact that we'd had a good evening. I'd missed the train and he'd kindly deposited me in a hotel room and stayed with me. Why had I automatically assumed the worst? I mean, after all, if I couldn't remember doing anything, it was pretty unlikely, wasn't it?

Well! I sank back in my seat, quite weak with relief. What on earth had I been worrying about? Nothing had happened and Sam – bless him – had been an absolute saint! What else could he have done? He could hardly have taken me home, could he, burst in at midnight and called up the stairs to the wife – 'Sorry darling, this is Polly, we've been in Annabel's having a mild flirtation, she's a bit plastered and she's missed her train, all right if she kips on the sofa?'

No, no, that wouldn't have gone down at all well, so naturally he'd booked me into a hotel and then stayed with me, just in case – well, just in case I swallowed my tongue, or some puke, or anything else that comatose drunks are wont to swallow.

I smiled, I beamed, I almost laughed! Oh joy! It was all

so simple! Sam had been a white knight! Why, if it hadn't been for him I might have woken up on a bench at Paddington station with all the other inebriates. I had a great deal to thank him for, a great deal. I'd write, yes, I'd write him a little note when I got home, just to say thanks. I'd send it to his office, though, I thought hastily, didn't want his wife to get the wrong end of the stick.

At long last the train chugged into Truro station. With a n.uch lighter heart I jumped off and dashed across to another platform, where I caught a slow, chugging, comforting train to Helston and then, eventually, a taxi home.

As the taxi rounded the stone gates to Trewarren and swept up the gravel drive, I peered nervously over the driver's shoulder from the back seat. Was Nick's Range Rover in the drive? I hoped not. He wasn't due back until this evening, but it was already four o'clock and you never quite knew with Nick. He was so bloody efficient, he could have gone to Yorkshire, bought the cattle and been back by yesterday lunch time. I breathed a huge sigh of relief as I saw the empty drive. Thank goodness.

I leaped out of the taxi and ran up the stone steps two at a time. The front door was still double locked so he definitely wasn't back, good. Feeling decidedly carefree for a girl who not so long ago had been perilously close to suicide, I raced around the house, turning lights on, drawing curtains and rolling around on beds. Then I threw bits of food on the kitchen floor, pulled all the loo paper off the rolls, flushed it down the loos, left the empty rolls hanging and generally made it look as if I'd been back for hours.

When the house looked suitably chaotic I grabbed a Barbour from the back hall and scampered down to the farm to check the delivery. I swung back the huge Dutch barn door and flicked on the light. The whole place was piled high with sacks of grain, corn and maize and great black bags full of silage. I found the list that Nick had left me, pulled it off the nail in the wall and began the long, tedious task of counting the sacks and checking everything off.

Half an hour later I emerged beaming and confident into the early-evening sunshine. All present and correct for once, definitely a first for Foxtons and a hell of a relief for me. I slammed the barn door behind me and skipped back to the house.

In a fit of enthusiasm I got a couple of chicken breasts out of the freezer, defrosted them in the microwave, then poured a tin of tomatoes, a few mushrooms and a slug of wine over the top of them and shoved them back in the microwave. Could be interesting. Then I mashed up some bananas, poured cream on top, gave it a layer of sugar and browned it under the grill. Terrific! Gosh, cooking was tiring, though. I was just sitting down at the kitchen table and helping myself to a glass of wine, when the back door gave a familiar rattle. It stuck, as usual, then flew open and in walked Nick.

'Darling!' I sprang up much too guiltily and knocked over my glass of wine.

'Careful!' Nick grabbed it before it rolled off and smashed on the floor.

'Sorry,' I said breathlessly, mopping it up with newspaper. 'I'm just so pleased to see you!'

I threw my arms round his neck and hugged him hard, burying my face in his jacket and breathing in its gorgeous tweedy, Nick-like smell. I reached up and kissed his mouth.

'Well, what a welcome!' laughed Nick, giving me a hug. 'I shall have to go away more often if it provokes such a homecoming. What's the matter, didn't you enjoy your little jaunt to London?'

'Oh, it was OK,' I said, turning away and busying myself peeling some potatoes, 'but I really think I've had it with London, you know. I mean, restaurants and nightclubs are all very fine now and again, but I don't think it's really me. I'm much happier in the country, couldn't wait to get home, actually.'

'Well, you know my feelings on that score,' said Nick, sitting down and helping himself to a glass of wine. 'I wouldn't care if I never saw the inside of a nightclub again as long as I lived. Which one did you go to?'

I felt my colour rising. 'Which what?' I peeled potatoes furiously.

'Which nightclub?'

'Oh . . . er, Annabel's.'

'What, on Thursday?'

'Y-yes, Thursday – ouch!' I'd cut myself with the knife. Blood spurted out. I sucked my finger. Nick reached up and pulled the first-aid box off the top of the dresser. He took out a plaster.

'Come here, idiot.'

I held out my hand.

'So who's a member then, not Pippa, surely?'

I met his eyes briefly as he bandaged my finger, then looked down. 'Um, no, not Pippa. Sam, I suppose.'

'Ah. Sam.'

I looked at him quickly. 'What does that mean? Ah, Sam?'

He grinned and put the box away. 'Nothing really, it's

just his name crops up quite a lot these days, doesn't it? God, what's this?' He was peering into the microwave now.

'Oh, it's just a chicken casserole thing I made.' What did he mean about Sam? Did he suspect anything?

'*Just* a chicken casserole thing? Blimey. Chicken on its own is a major breakthrough in this kitchen and a casserole thing is positively a gastronomic delight. What's happened to the fish fingers? Did they finally get up and walk away? And what's this?' He stuck his finger in the bowl of bananas and looked amazed. 'Pudding? Good heavens, Polly, what have you been up to? Haven't got a guilty conscience by any chance, have you? Any minute now the doorbell's going to ring and a man from Interflora will thrust some roses into my hands!'

'Don't be silly!' I blustered, pink with indignation and horror. 'I just felt a bit peckish, that's all. Aren't you hungry?' I put the casserole on the table.

'Starving,' he said, sitting down and helping himself to a chicken breast. He grinned. 'Just winding you up, Poll, can't you take it any more?'

'Course I can!' I declared, slipping in opposite him and helping myself with a cheery grin. I chewed grimly. Bit close to the bone, that's all, I thought.

After supper I collapsed on the sofa in the sitting room and flicked on the TV. I put my feet up and let the cathode rays wash over me. It had been a busy old day one way and another. Nick lit a fire. It was early May, but it cheered the room. A film had just started about a blind woman left alone in an enormous house, fumbling from room to room whilst unbeknown to her a serial killer with a penchant for the partially sighted crept around after her, moving things so she tripped up and making creepy noises. It was right up my street, although I watched most of it from behind a cushion. I found half a bar of stale Fruit and Nut tucked down the side of the sofa and nibbled away at it, waiting nervously for the murderer to pounce. Nick watched for five minutes, pronounced it utter drivel, and went upstairs to have a bath.

A few minutes later he was down again. The murderer had just cornered the blind woman in the airing cupboard, so I was well and truly glued to my cushion. I turned round and saw Nick's face. It was as white as a sheet.

'It's all right,' I whispered, 'her brother's just arrived in his car, he's got a gun.'

Nick didn't seem to register this. He looked most peculiar. I put my cushion down and sat up.

'What's wrong?'

He stared at me, his face ghostly. 'We've been burgled,' he said.

Chapter Thirteen

I dropped the cushion. 'What!'

'We've been burgled. I walked past the blue room upstairs and the door was wide open. When I went in I noticed the cabinet was open too. It's completely empty, cleared out, every single piece of porcelain has gone.' His voice was odd, strained.

'No! I don't believe it!'

'Go and see for yourself.' He sat down rather abruptly on the sofa opposite. He looked shattered.

I stared at him. 'Nick, how appalling! Has anything else gone?'

'I don't know. I daren't look.'

He put his head in his hands. I jumped up and sat beside him, putting my hand on his knee. I'd never seen him like this.

'You must phone the police,' I urged.

He raised his head and stared at me, looking a bit dazed. He didn't seem to hear.

'Nick—'

'Yes, yes, of course, you're right, I'll do it now.'

He jumped up, suddenly back to his normal, assertive self, and disappeared into the hall. I followed him, feeling suddenly cold. I pulled my jumper down over my hands and folded my arms tightly across my chest as I listened to him briefing the local police station. Fat lot of good they'd be, I thought bitterly. Directing the traffic in Helston was pretty much beyond them. Nick put the receiver down.

'Right, well they're on their way. We'd better go and see what else is missing. Come on.'

He turned and led the way upstairs, still white as a sheet. I scurried after him. Gosh, how awful. Quite apart from being extremely valuable, the porcelain had been in the Penhalligan family for generations. Nick's great-grandfather had started the collection by giving a figurine to his wife as a wedding present, and every year after that he'd presented her with a different piece. Each one had a provenance and usually a fascinating story about how and where he'd managed to acquire it. In terms of sentimental value they were priceless. I felt sick to my stomach, so heaven knows how Nick must be feeling. What on earth would his mother say?

'What will Hetty say?' I whispered as we went into the blue room together.

'God only knows,' he said grimly. 'Bastards, look at this.' He pointed to the empty cabinet. The door was wide open.

'My God, there must have been about thirty pieces in there!'

'Thirty-two.'

'But how did they get the door open? Was the lock smashed?' I went up to look.

'Don't touch it!' Nick grabbed my arm. 'Just in case there are fingerprints on it. No, look, the key's still in the lock.'

'What! They had the key? But – there are only two keys, aren't there?'

'Exactly. Mum's, and this one which is ours, it's got the blue ribbon on it.'

'So they took it from the jug?'

He shrugged. 'Must have done.'

'So it's someone we know, someone who knows where we keep it. Nick, how awful, how creepy!'

'Or someone who's heard about where we keep it – let's face it, the blue jug on the dresser isn't exactly the safest place in the world.' He shook his head. 'God, I could kick myself, I kept meaning to put it back in the safe but I just never got round to it.'

He started prowling around the room, pulling open cupboards and searching through drawers. This was the room where anything remotely valuable was kept. I followed tentatively.

'Anything else missing?' I asked, anxiously peering over his shoulder as he rifled through a drawer.

'Nope, not as far as I can tell. The watches are still here and they haven't touched the stamp collection – go and check your jewellery, Polly, oh, and the silver downstairs.' He had a clenched calmness now, he was back in control.

I ran down the corridor and into our bedroom with a hammering heart. How beastly, and how horrid to think someone had been rooting around in our house, our home, going through our things. It made me feel sick just thinking about it. I pulled my jewellery box out of a drawer and opened it. I don't really have much, but I'm desperately attached to the few pieces Nick has given me and one or two brooches of Granny's. Thank goodness, it was all there. I put it back in the drawer and ran down to the dining room.

The silver candlesticks were still in the middle of the table and the usual array of odds and ends was all present and correct on the sideboard. I was just looking through the cutlery when the doorbell rang. I dropped the knives and forks and ran to the front door. Two rather bored-looking policemen stood on the doorstep, one of them was leaning against a pillar.

'Mrs Penhalligan? enquired the elder of the two.

'Yes, thank goodness you're here,' I gasped. 'Quick, come in, we've been burgled, isn't it awful!'

The pair moved slowly through the hall, gazing around and taking in all the portraits and the huge chandelier.

'There's a lot of it about, madam,' observed the elder one lugubriously. 'In here?' He indicated the drawing room.

'Yes, yes, go in, my husband's just checking to see if anything else has been taken, he'll be down in a minute.' I followed hard on their heels. 'What d'you mean, there's a lot of it about? Has there been a spate of burglaries in the area or something? Have you any idea who it is? Is it a gang? D'you think we'll ever get our stuff back?'

They made straight for the fire, toasting their bottoms and looking around the room with interest.

'It's a little early to answer all those questions, madam, certainly without more detailed information,' said the elder man pompously. 'We'll start when your husband gets down, shall we?' He picked up a little silver snuff box from a table, looked at it with interest, turned it around and put it down again.

'You've got some nice stuff here, Mrs Penhalligan,' he observed.

'Yes, yes, we have, um, you said there's a lot of it about – round here, d'you mean?' I persisted.

'All I meant, madam,' he said with weary indifference, 'is that burglary is a very common occurrence these days.' He pursed his lips, clasped his hands behind his back, rocked back on his heels and resumed his appraisal of the room.

'Not for us it isn't,' I retorted darkly, 'and not when it's thirty-odd pieces of priceless porcelain either. I do hope you're not going to write that off as a common occurrence. This collection has been in the family for centuries, we must get it back, it's absolutely imperative!' My voice rose rather hysterically.

I felt a hand on my shoulder. 'Take it easy, Polly, come and sit down.' Nick led me over to a sofa.

The policemen sat opposite us. I glared at them.

'My wife and I are in need of a drink, but I don't suppose you'll join us?'

'No thank you, sir,' declined the elder one, taking off his cap, 'not whilst we're on duty, got to keep our wits about us, you see!' He grinned moronically.

Yes, that must be a full-time job, I thought sardonically as Nick handed me a large gin. What hope did we have of getting our loot back with this pair of country bobbies? God, the younger one was even stifling a yawn now, not too keen on night duty, perhaps? Missing the football on the telly, maybe? Well, bad luck, Ploddie, I thought, eyeing him grimly, you've got work to do now.

Plod the elder wearily took a notebook from his top pocket, then he patted a few more pockets and eventually extracted a pencil. He licked the end and slowly flicked through his little black book.

'Now. Suppose you tell me exactly when you discovered that the collection was missing, sir?'

'Just now,' said Nick patiently, 'just before I telephoned you.'

'What, just before? Or about five minutes before?'

'Er, well, yes, about then.'

'Shall I write ten o'clock then, sir?' he asked, pencil poised, eyebrows raised.

'No, it was about three weeks ago actually,' I burst in angrily, 'but we've only just got around to telephoning you, been too busy, you see. For goodness' sake, what difference does it make?'

'OK, Polly,' Nick said gently, 'I'll deal with this.' He took my hand. I was trembling.

The Plods stared at me open-mouthed. Eventually Plod the elder cleared his throat. 'We have to go through the formalities, madam,' he said stiffly, 'for our notes, you see.' He indicated his little book.

'Well, be a bit quicker about it, can't you?' I muttered.

He turned his watery gaze on Nick. 'What exactly did you discover was missing, sir?'

'Thirty-two pieces of antique Meissen, mostly figurines. I can give you a more detailed description later.'

'Valuable?'

'Very,' said Nick through clenched teeth.

'And, er, was this said collection in a safe?'

'Well, no, it was in a glass cabinet, actually.'

'A glass cabinet?' He raised his eyebrows.

'Yes, I know that probably sounds a bit crazy to you but they've always been kept there, so that we can see them.

Not much point in having beautiful objects if you can't look at them, is there?'

'That's a matter of opinion really, sir,' murmured Plod the elder, exchanging a knowing look with his gormless companion. 'And, er, was this said cabinet, by any happy coincidence, locked?'

Nick flushed. 'Of course it was.'

'And the lock had been smashed?'

'No, the key was in the lock. Whoever it was had found our key and used it.'

At this, Plod the younger raised his head. He awoke from his dream and turned his sleepy eyes on his partner. One of them flickered ever so slightly as if he were alive.

'Ah ha!' he murmured knowingly. Heavens, he could speak.

His partner nodded sagely and, leaning in, confided to Nick in a conspiratorial whisper, 'It's too early to say for certain, sir, but what you've told us so far gives us reason to believe that this was an inside job, someone who knew the house, who knew where the key was kept.'

'Oh, brilliant!' I snapped scathingly. 'Truly amazing deduction. Funnily enough we'd come to the same staggering conclusion ourselves in about two seconds flat!' God, these people were morons, where were MI5, CID – where was Morse when we needed him most? The policeman looked at me in amazement.

'OK, Poll,' soothed Nick, 'calm down, they're just doing their job.'

I ground my teeth but managed to hold my tongue. The Plods turned away, pointedly excluding me, and addressed themselves exclusively to the man of the house.

'Anything else missing, sir?' purred Plod the elder.

'Not as far as I can tell, but I'll have to have a thorough look later.'

'And as far as you've been able to check – no broken windows? Signs of forced entry?'

'No, nothing, although the downstairs loo window was slightly ajar, but that's not unusual and it's too small for anyone to get through anyway.'

Plod the elder pursed his lips. 'Hrmmm...' He jotted something down, murmuring 'Open...win...dow' as he wrote. He looked up sharply. 'Now. Burglar alarm?'

'Er, no.'

'Locks on the windows?'

Nick shifted awkwardly. 'Well, most of them don't shut properly anyway, they're so old, so it would be a waste of time locking them.'

The policeman stared. 'Don't shut properly? Really?' He gave a sardonic little smile. 'I wonder, sir, you didn't actually leave the front door open for them, did you?'

I was on my feet in an instant. 'Oh, so it's our fault, is it?' I stormed. 'Because we don't live in a house with bars on the windows and Rottweilers circling the grounds, it's our fault if our property is violated, is that it? Well, funnily enough, we choose to live like this, in a home, not a prison, and why shouldn't we, it's a free country, isn't it!'

'Polly—' Nick put his hand on my arm.

'Well, honestly, it's ridiculous! They've been here about twenty minutes now and all they've done is yawn, state the bleeding obvious and blame us!' I rounded on them. 'You should be after them! Giving chase, radioing for help, pursuing them across country, climbing over walls, jumping ditches, instead of sitting here on your bums scratching your heads and taking notes!' I couldn't help it, I couldn't bear to see them make Nick feel so guilty, knowing how desperately upset he was.

The Plods declined even to acknowledge this outburst. They politely examined their notebooks as if the mad wife had unfortunately, and embarrassingly, escaped from the West Wing. They focused their attention even more pointedly on Nick, shifting their bottoms as they turned towards him. I fumed silently.

'Now, sir,' went on Plod the elder, 'you've been here all day, I take it?'

'No, I've been away for a couple of days on a business trip, I got back at about six o'clock tonight. My wife has also been away, but she got back last night.'

Suddenly my fumes evaporated. I sat very still. Plod the elder turned to me.

'Is that right, Mrs Penhalligan? You got back last night?'

My tongue seemed to be welded to the roof of my mouth. I unstuck it, it tasted rather as I imagined dog poo would. 'Er . . . yes,' I whispered, 'last night.'

'I'm sorry? I didn't quite catch that.'

I cleared my throat. 'Sorry. Yes, I got back last night.'

'And you'd been away for . . .?'

'J-just one night. Thursday.'

'And were you also away Thursday night, sir?'

'No, I was here, I left on Friday at about lunch time. You see, that's what I don't understand, the house was only empty on Friday afternoon and I can't believe anyone would have had the nerve to break in in broad daylight, especially with our various farm hands wandering around, but I suppose they must have done, unless it happened last night while Polly was asleep. What an awful thought, darling.' He took my hand.

'Awful,' I murmured. The whole thing was awful, appalling, actually. I felt hot all over, I seemed to have been ambushed by pints of red-hot blood and every part of my anatomy was either burning like fire or wet and clammy, except my mouth, of course, which was extremely dry. Plod the elder turned to me.

'At about what time did you go to bed on Friday night, madam?'

'I – I'm not sure.'

'Approximately, darling,' coaxed Nick gently. 'I know it's horrible to imagine someone prowling around while you slept, but do try and remember. Was it about ten? Or eleven?'

'Er, yes. About ten. Or eleven. About ten-thirty,' I whispered, pulling a cushion on to my lap and using it to wipe the perspiration from my hands.

'And nothing disturbed you all night?' Plod the elder's eyes bored into mine. How could I ever have found them watery and insipid? They seemed to burn like laser beams, and his questions, which had previously seemed so banal and inconsequential, now seemed terrifyingly probing and inquisitorial.

'You didn't get up to go to the bathroom? Or go downstairs for a glass of water? Nothing like that?'

'No, nothing like that,' I whispered. Was he trying to trap me?

'You stayed in bed all night?'

I licked my lips. 'Yes, all night.'

Well, that was true enough, wasn't it? I thought desperately. I had been in bed all night. All right, it hadn't been *my* bed, but it had been a bed. Another man's bed. I felt sick for the umpteenth time that day. Nick's precious porcelain collection had been stolen whilst I lay next to another man in a hotel bedroom, and now I was lying like a dog to save my own miserable skin. Even by my extremely low standards this was unspeakably shameful. I stared at my shoes. Guilt seemed to be leaking out of them, all over the polished floorboards and the Persian carpet. I daren't look up. My toes were sliding around in my docksiders now, slippy with perspiration. Was this what was known as perjury? I wondered. Lying to the law like this? Was it a treasonable offence? Could I be arrested?

The navy-blue legs opposite me were straightening. The Plods were getting to their feet, notebooks were snapping shut and, thank God, they appeared to be talking to Nick rather than me. I took advantage of this brief respite and wiped a few beads of sweat from my forehead. My hair was frizzing dramatically.

'Now, sir,' Plod the elder was saying, 'we'd like to have a look around in a minute if we may – check the windows, look at the cabinet, that sort of thing – but first of all, could you tell me who exactly has a key to this house?'

'Well, aside from ourselves there's my mother, Hetty Penhalligan, she lives in Gweek, and my brother Tim, whose farm is next door to ours. I think that's it.'

'No, Mrs Bradshaw has one,' I muttered.

'Oh yes, our daily.'

'Ex-daily,' I reminded him.

Plod the elder raised his eyebrows. 'Ex?'

'Yes, I fired her last week.'

'Did you now? And she still has a key?'

'I suppose she has, I certainly don't remember asking for it back.'

'Ah ha!' He pursed his lips and nodded importantly. Revenge Motive flashed like a neon sign on his forehead.

'I really can't see Mrs Bradshaw taking a cabinetful of antique china,' said Nick wearily. 'If she felt like taking something out of spite – and I'm quite sure she wouldn't – she'd be far more likely to nick the video, something she could sell.'

'Well, we have to explore every possibility, sir, follow every lead. In our line of work, no stone can be left unrolled or it won't gather moss. If you want to see the trees in the woods, you've got to be alive to every possibility,' he said pompously, comprehensively mixing every single metaphor he could think of.

He pocketed his notebook. 'And now if you'd be so kind as to furnish me with Mrs Bradshaw's address, I'll have one of my men interview her just as soon as possible.'

He made it sound as if he had a force of thousands at his disposal, whereas in actual fact one or other of these two goons would be round at her house dunking a digestive in a cup of tea and discussing The Mad Woman of Trewarren just as soon as they'd finished here.

Nick showed them round the rest of the house, then saw them to the front door. I was very relieved to see them go. He came back from the hall looking pale and drawn. He stood with his back to the fire, massaged his eyes with the heels of his hands, yawned widely and shoved his fists despondently in his pockets.

'I'm knackered.'

I reached out and touched his arm. 'Me too. Let's go to bed.'

'Good idea. We'll sleep on it.'

We turned out the lights and went slowly upstairs. Nick shut the blue-room door as we passed. We undressed in silence, got into bed and lay still, our minds whirring. I stared into the darkness.

'Odd, isn't it, that nothing else is missing,' mused Nick eventually.

'Mmmm ... I mean, it's not as if the silver isn't valuable, or the stamps. You'd think if someone was going to go to the trouble of breaking in they'd snap up as many goodies as possible.'

'Unless they were particularly interested in the porcelain and knew where they could sell it on. It's incredibly difficult to get rid of a collection like that unless you have contacts and you know the antique world. You can't just leak thirty-odd pieces of Meissen on to the market, people in the know would immediately smell a rat.'

'So ...' I said, thinking aloud, 'it's got to be someone who knows the antique world ... who knew where the key was kept ... and who also knew that we were away!' I raised myself up on to my elbows, feeling quite excited.

'Who knew *I* was away,' corrected Nick.

'I – I mean, who knew you were away,' I stammered, flushing in the darkness and lowering myself hastily back on to my pillow. That'll teach you to be a smart arse, Polly.

'But you must admit,' I went on a moment or two later, 'it sounds very much like someone who knows us.'

Nick sighed wearily. 'Not necessarily. Word spreads very quickly in the country, especially in a small village. Mrs Bradshaw might inadvertently have let it slip that the key was kept in the jug and then somebody could easily have overheard in the pub that Larry and I were going to look at cattle for a couple of days. They've only got to put two and two together, and bingo.'

'I bet Mrs Bradshaw's thrilled to bits,' I said bitterly. 'Word will have reached the village by now and she'll be rubbing her hands with glee, revelling in our misfortune.'

'Don't be silly,' said Nick, turning over to go to sleep. 'Mrs Bradshaw might be a sour old bag but she's always been tremendously loyal. I'm sure she'll be horrified when she hears.'

'Don't you believe it,' I said grimly.

'We'll see. G'night.'

'Night.'

I turned over and shut my eyes, but for once my defence mechanism failed me. Sleep evaded me, and I tossed and turned fitfully, eventually resorting to my secret supply of Curly Wurlys under the bed. I sucked one after another, shut my eyes tight and eventually, in the early hours, drifted off to sleep. Despite my fitful sleep I managed to have quite a good dream which involved me rescuing Prince Harry from under the wheels of a speeding taxi in Pall Mall. As a result I became Princess Diana's new b.f. and had loads of chummy lunches with her in San Lorenzo's. Prince Charles was also incredibly grateful and I became his new confidante too – apparently he found me a refreshing change from Laurens Van der Post. I was just trying to patch things between him and Diana, when the doorbell rang.

'Oh Lord,' I murmured sleepily, raising my eyebrows at Charles, 'I do hope it's not that blasted Camilla again.'

'There's someone at the door,' said an equally sleepy voice in my ear.

'What? Charles? Nick? Oh God, what time is it?' I rolled over and peered at the clock.

'Seven o'clock. I'll go,' groaned Nick. He sat up, yawned, scratched his head vigorously, then threw on some clothes and went downstairs.

I lay very still, straining to hear and hoping to God it wasn't the police again, wanting to know if I'd kindly accompany them to the station. A few minutes later I heard my mother-in-law's unmistakably deep baritone voice resounding confidently and emphatically up from the kitchen. Hetty! I felt quite weak with relief.

I gave Nick a few minutes to break the news then put on my dressing gown and went downstairs to greet her. I hoped she wasn't going to be too upset, I was extremely fond of her. I needn't have worried, Hetty was as unpredictable as ever.

'Polly, darling!' she boomed as I shuffled sleepily into the kitchen. 'Wonderful news! I heard at six-thirty this morning, it's absolutely the talk of the village. Isn't it simply marvellous!'

I blinked. Hetty was perched on our kitchen table, swinging her legs excitedly, her dark eyes and dark bobbed hair shining brightly. She was dressed, as usual, in her own alternative, inimitable style. Today she'd chosen a pair of corduroy knickerbockers, an England rugby shirt, a red silk scarf for her neck and a tweed Baker Boys cap for her head. A cigarette was poised in her bejewelled fingers and she carried the whole arresting ensemble off with effortless style and panache. I groped around in the larder, searching for a new box of tea bags.

'Er, marvellous, Hetty? Are you sure?'

'Of course, it's fabulous news!'

'Don't be ridiculous, Mum,' snapped Nick, banging the kettle on the Aga. 'How can it be?'

'Well, think about it, darling,' she boomed, flicking ash nonchalantly into a saucer. 'There's no way you'd ever have sold all that ghastly old china, and quite right, you can't sell off the family silver, I wouldn't have done either, although your father and I were sorely tempted at times – but, well! Now that it's been *stolen*, that's *quite* a different matter, isn't it?'

'Is it?' I poured boiling water into the teapot with a rather unsteady hand.

'Well, of *course* it is,' insisted Hetty, 'don't you see? It must be insured for *thousands*, so this way you get all the loot, with none of the guilt – terrific!' She kicked her heels up gleefully and beamed triumphantly.

I grinned. I had to admit she had a point. We'd never have sold the porcelain, but now that it had gone walkabout – well! How much was it insured for? I wondered. I raised my eyebrows enquiringly at Nick.

'Don't be absurd, Mum,' he snapped. 'I'd much rather have the porcelain, and I'm going to make every effort to get it back!'

'Oh well, suit yourself,' sighed Hetty with a shrug. 'I personally think it's a blessing in disguise, couldn't bear the stuff, actually, it took so bloody long to dust, and just when you'd finished you had to start all over again. I'd much rather have had the money, would have used it for something fun – a gazebo perhaps, or an amusing statue in the garden.' She took a sip of tea. 'Yuck!' She made a face. 'Revolting – any coffee going, Polly? I need something strong and dark in the mornings, can't be doing with this Earl Grey chappie, he wouldn't have been my type at all, insipid and chinless, I bet.'

'Oh, sorry, Hetty, here—' I threw some Nescafé into a mug, poured boiling water on and handed it to her.

'Marvellous, darling – spot of brandy, perhaps? Awfully chill for May, isn't it?'

I giggled and added a splash of cooking brandy.

Nick raised his eyebrows. 'It's only seven o'clock, Mum.'

'Don't be a boring old fart, darling, the French would have knocked back a couple of cognacs by now – cheers! Here's to the insurance money!' She winked and I stifled a giggle.

'Now' – she lit another cigarette while the previous one was still smoking in the saucer and leaned forward conspiratorially – 'any ideas? Any inkling as to who it might be? I gather the key was used so it must be someone from around here, don't you think? Someone local who knew the house? Shall we make a list? Isn't it thrilling!'

'Hardly,' said Nick grimly. 'It's bloody irritating and pretty unpleasant too. D'you realise Polly could have been badly hurt? As far as we can tell it happened on Friday night while Polly was alone here. I hate to think what might have happened if she'd disturbed them.'

'My dear!' Hetty turned to me in surprise. 'You were here? I had no idea! I thought you were in London!'

'Er, no, I got back on Friday evening,' I mumbled into my tea.

'Really?' Hetty looked puzzled. 'That's odd. I rang on

Friday night, but there was no answer. What time did you get back?'

'Oh, er, about nine,' I muttered, pitching it fairly late.

'But I rang at about quarter to ten! There was this marvellous programme on the television, I wanted you to watch it so I—'

'Oh, I was – having a bath. I heard the telephone but couldn't be bothered to get out to answer it.' I buried my flushing face in my mug. This was horrible, just horrible.

'Oh, what a shame, you'd have loved this, it was a David Attenborough thing all about the praying mantis – fascinating. Did you know, for example, that after they've had nooky, the female *eats* the male? Just pops him in her mouth and swallows him whole – isn't that terrific! You see, once he's done the business he's totally redundant as far as she's concerned, so she just has him for her supper, a little post-coital snackette, as it were – isn't it killing! I think I shall have to ring Harrods pet department and order a couple!'

I tried to grin, but my mouth twitched with terror. This was awful. These were really dirty lies now, not just the harmless little whitish-grey ones I'm wont to pepper my life with – no, these were thumping great black ones. I busied myself slicing some bread, my hand shaking. Luckily Hetty started prattling away again. I turned to get some bacon out of the fridge, keeping my eyes down, and, when I deemed it safe, turned to Nick and said as normally as possible, 'Bacon sandwich, darling?'

'Please.'

Was it my imagination or did he give me the strangest look? No, I was getting paranoid. The telephone rang and Nick went to the hall to answer it. Good. Phew, this was getting much too hairy for my liking. I fried the bacon and listened whilst Hetty outlined her list of prime suspects.

'Well, for a start there's Tom Rawlings at the butcher's, I wouldn't put it past him at all. He knows the house and he's delivered here loads of times so he could *easily* have seen the key in the jug, *and* he absolutely loathes us because I caught him fiddling the bill once and switched the account to the butcher's in Helston, *and* his silly fool of a wife likes to think she dabbles in antiques although in actual fact she wouldn't know a Queen Anne cachepot from a Victorian piss-pot – oh yes, the pair of them are high on my list of possibilities.' She nodded sagely, narrowed her eyes and took a long drag from her cigarette.

'*Then* of course' – she looked for the saucer, couldn't find it so leaned back and flicked her ash in the sink – 'there's Mrs Bradshaw, who I was *delighted* to hear you'd fired! Should have done it myself long ago – sour old bag – it was only loyalty to her poor old henpecked husband who worked on the farm that made me keep her on. Mind you, she drove him to an early grave, he probably would have thanked me if I'd given her the boot. Yes,' she mused, taking another long, thoughtful drag, 'Mrs Bradshaw, a little too obvious at first glance, perhaps, but...' She sat up straight suddenly. 'How about this – suppose she put someone up to it? Eh, Polly? What d'you think?'

'Er, sorry? What did you say?' I gave her an ashtray. I was finding it hard to concentrate.

'Mrs Bradshaw, suppose she put someone up to it?'

'Well, yes, I suppose it's a possibility.'

'Of course it is! A very distinct one at that, and shall I tell you who that someone might be?'

'Do, Hetty,' I said, sitting down wearily and putting three bacon sandwiches on the table.

She leaned forward eagerly. 'Ted Simpson,' she whispered.

'What, that enormous great chap from the hardware shop?'

'Exactly. And d'you know why?' I shook my head and bit into my sandwich. 'Well, I'll tell you. Not only is he practically bankrupt, but *apparently* he used to work for a house-clearance company in London so he's got plenty of contacts in the antiques world, but even more pertinent – and get this – word in the village is that Simpson and Mrs Bradshaw are having a ding-dong!'

'No!' I abandoned my sandwich, agog now. 'But he's enormous, and she's so tiny!'

'Precisely! Isn't it disgusting? That hideous great whale of a man with that shrivelled little prune of a woman – imagine! How d'you think they do it – with her perched on top like a little gnat, or with him on top squashing the life out of her? Or do you suppose he suspends himself from some sort of trapeze from the ceiling so as not to crush her, or even – goodness, what's the matter, darling?'

She broke off as Nick came back into the kitchen. His face looked strange, twisted almost.

'Nick, what is it?' I quickly got up and went to him but he seemed almost to back away. He thrust his hands in his pockets, he wouldn't look at me.

'That was Tim. He'd heard, of course, from one of his farm hands, he was ringing to commiserate. But he said he was here on Saturday morning, Polly, he brought us some vegetables, early, at about seven-thirty. He rang the doorbell but no one answered. Then he came back about an hour later, just in case you'd been asleep, there was still no answer. Eventually he used his key to get in and left the vegetables in the pantry. He said the house was deserted.' At last he turned to look at me, his eyes full of pain. 'Where were you, Poll?'

Chapter Fourteen

I was a rat and his eyes were the trap. He pinned me with them. I looked at the floor, and then rather desperately at the skirting boards, hoping perhaps for a handy little rat hole through which to slip, but there was no escape. The eyes had me.

'Well, Polly?'

I licked my lips. 'It's a long story,' I whispered.

There was a terrible silence.

'Oooohhh!' breathed someone excitedly to my left. 'You naughty girl, Polly, what *have* you been up to?'

Hetty had blown her cover. For a moment there I think both Nick and I had actually forgotten about her. Her eyes were wide with wonder, her face agog.

'Come on, Mum, we'll see you later,' said Nick, thrusting her latest handbag, a tartan rucksack affair, into her arms and hustling her towards the door.

Hetty pouted and dug her heels in. 'But darling, I want to hear where Polly was, oh come on, don't be a spoilsport,' she wailed as she was dragged across the floor, physically outmanoeuvred.

'Polly, do tell, where were you?' she asked breathlessly, swivelling her head round a hundred and eighty degrees as she was bundled past me.

'Come on,' said Nick, holding her in a vicelike grip with one hand and reaching for the door handle with the other. But just as he was about to grab it, the door flew open of its own accord. Sarah stuck her head round.

'Hello there, thought I'd pop in for coffee. I say, terrible news about the burglary, who d'you think it was? Any theories?' She raised her eyebrows and looked from one face to another – one guilty, one grim, one bursting with excitement – then she took in the half-nelson grip Nick had on his mother.

'Bad moment?' she ventured.

'Not great,' agreed Nick. 'Mum was just leaving, actually, and Polly and I have something we want to discuss. Could you come back later, Sarah?'

'Sure, no problem,' she said, not moving an inch. 'What d'you need to discuss? Is it the burglary?'

'No, they're having a domestic!' hissed Hetty loudly. 'Nick's just found out that Polly stayed out all Friday night, imagine!'

'Really?' Sarah's eyes grew round. 'Goodness, Polly, where were you?'

'Out, please!' said Nick, depositing Hetty on the doorstep and bundling Sarah off with her. 'Out, out, OUT!'

'Pop round later, Polly!' yelled Hetty as the door shut on the pair of them – slammed, actually.

Through the glass I saw them give one last lingering look in our direction before turning away, heads bent together, whispering furiously as they went down the path. What I wouldn't have given to have been on the other side of that door, whispering with them. I began to clear the table, frantically burying my head in the dishes.

'Now,' said Nick calmly, turning to face me, 'if it's not too much to ask, perhaps you'd be good enough to let me be the first to know what the hell's going on here, before Mum and Sarah spread tidings of our impending divorce throughout the county!'

'Oh, don't be silly, they wouldn't do that!' I said, desperately trying to change the subject. 'They're very well meaning really, and if their tongues do tend to wag a bit it's only because they're taking an interest and—'

'Terrific, so am I,' interrupted Nick, grabbing my arm and turning me around to face him. 'Come on,' he said grimly, 'spill the beans.'

I started to tremble. I was holding a pile of dirty plates which began to clatter uncontrollably.

'Just let me get rid of these,' I muttered, 'before I spill them instead.'

I bent down to load the dishwasher, hiding my flushing face in its stainless-steel depths and desperately playing for time. When I stood up I had a feeling my time had run out, but I had one last shot.

'Look, Nick, it's an awfully long story and I'm feeling so hot and bothered, would you mind terribly if I just had a quick bath first and then I could—'

'Get your story straight? Think of a few lies with which to embellish it? No, Polly, you couldn't, I want it NOW!' He banged the table with his fist, his face livid. 'Where were you?' he asked in a dangerously quiet way.

I sat down, it was a must, my legs just wouldn't do their supporting act any longer.

'Sit down,' I mumbled. I couldn't possibly look up at that man-mountain towering above me. He sat. I licked my lips, they were like sandpaper.

'I was . . . still in London.'

'At Pippa's?' he asked, somewhat hopefully.

I hesitated, sensing an escape route here. It would be the work of a moment to ring Pippa and make her corroborate, but something stopped me – Nick's face. It was deadly, but at the same time vulnerable, frightened even. I couldn't lie to him any more. After all, as far as I knew I hadn't done anything wrong. In fact, I was convinced I was totally in the clear, nothing had happened at all. I'd tell him everything, he'd just have to understand, of course he would. He loved me, didn't he, and didn't he always say honesty was the best policy?

'No, not at Pippa's – look, Nick, I'm going to tell you exactly what happened and I swear to God this is the truth, OK?'

'Fire away,' he said, tight-lipped.

'But it's most important you believe me,' I urged. 'Promise me you will, because – well, what I'm going to say may not exactly *sound* like the truth.'

He looked at me squarely. I tried to look back equally squarely but ended up looking all sort of sideways.

'Get on with it, Polly.'

'And if I look shifty now it's only because you make me very nerv—'

'Just get on with it, will you!'

'OK, OK.' I gulped and pulled my dressing gown around me. 'Right.' I licked my hellishly dehydrated lips. 'Well, there was this party in a restaurant, you see, on the Friday night, after the shoot.'

Nick looked puzzled. 'Which you went to?'

'Well, yes I did, actually, but only because everyone kept asking me to go. I was sort of – persuaded into it.'

'But you were supposed to be back here on Friday night, you knew that.'

I nodded. 'To check the delivery on Saturday morning, I know, I know, but – well, I had this brainwave, you see!' I looked at him eagerly, hoping he'd share my enthusiasm. 'I thought – why not leave the car in London, get the sleeper after the party and still be back in time to check the stock on Saturday! Brilliant, eh?'

Nick looked more incredulous than enthusiastic. 'You left the car in London? I thought you'd just put it away in the garage or something – Christ, Polly, you must have wanted to go to this party very badly.'

'Well, yes,' I shifted uncomfortably. 'I suppose I did, but – only because it was going to be such *fun*.' I grabbed his hand, desperate for him to understand. 'And it was so long since I'd been to anything remotely like that, and I've missed that part of my life a bit – not much, of course, not much at all, in fact, but just a bit – and I thought, well, just for once – damn it, why not?'

Nick pulled his hand away. 'Why not indeed,' he said drily. 'I had no idea you were suffering such with-drawal symptoms for your good-time-girl days.' He looked pained.

'Oh no, I'm not! No, not at all really, it's just that now and again – well, obviously I can see how superficial it all is but sometimes I miss that buzz, that little thrill of excitement, that feeling you get when you're out with loads of people having a good time, there's something so—'

'Polly, could we debate the pros and cons of London's social scene some other time? Just get to the point. You went to the party, and . . . ?'

I sighed and lit my third cigarette of the morning. 'Well, after that, a few of us went on to Annabel's.'

'I thought you said that was Thursday night?'

I dredged up yet more saliva.

'I lied,' I said in a small voice.

'I see,' he said in an icy one.

I swallowed hard. This was going very badly, very badly indeed, and I hadn't even got to the horrendous bit. I desperately wanted to get it over and done with so I speeded up.

'So as I said, we went on to Annabel's – me, Amanda, Chris and S-Sam.' There, I'd said it. I hurried on. 'And of course there was lots of dancing and drinking and that sort of thing and – oh yes, *lots* of drinking, actually, I got incredibly drunk, Nick, absolutely steaming, in fact I was—'

'How unusual,' he cut in sarcastically.

'No, but I was really *spectacularly* drunk.' It was imperative he understood I was in no way responsible for my actions. 'To the point where I was' – I looked down at my hands – 'practically unconscious.'

'Really.' I felt his eyes burn into me. 'And then?'

I twisted my hands together miserably. 'Well, that's just it, I don't know, I've got absolutely no idea how what happened next actually . . . happened.'

'How d'you mean? What did happen next?'

'I don't know!' I gazed at him desperately, willing him to understand. 'Because the next thing I knew, I was waking up in bed the next morning.'

'Where?'

'In a . . . hotel bedroom,' I whispered.

There was a horrible silence.

'With Sam?' His voice was weird, strangled.

I dared not look at him. I pulled at a thread in my towelling dressing gown.

'No, not with Sam, but – well, he'd obviously been there. At some point. There was a note, you see . . .' I trailed off miserably.

'Give it to me.'

With a hand like blancmange I reached behind me to the dresser, pulled my handbag down, rummaged around for the crumpled note and handed it to him. He spread it out on the table. I watched his face as he read it. It went white. He handed it back to me.

'I see.' He got up and went towards the door.

'Wh-where are you going?' I stammered.

'Out.'

'But I haven't finished! I have to tell you why I—'

'You mean there's more!' Nick swung around. His face was like a mask, like someone else's face, not my husband's.

'Still more?' he whispered. 'Jesus, Polly, you really know how to kick a man when he's down, don't you? I don't believe this, I just don't believe it!'

'But you don't understand!' I wailed. 'I didn't do it!'

He just stared at me.

'Don't you see?' I pleaded. 'I don't *remember* anything, nothing at all! I just woke up and found this on the bedside table, so – so if I don't remember, well, I can't have done anything wrong, can I?'

'So – what, you expect me to believe he raped you while you lay there unconscious? D'you want me to phone the police, Polly?'

'No, but—'

'Or – or perhaps nothing happened at all? Maybe he tucked you up in bed, read you a bedtime story, made you some cocoa and then curled up quietly on the floor. Is that more to your liking?'

'Well, perhaps not on the floor, but—'

'Oh, on the bed? But no funny business? Ah, I see, there's a sporting chance he just lay down beside you, is there? Oh yes, of course, it's all becoming crystal clear now, a platonic little sleep-in, babes in the wood, a kind of mixed dorm, is that it?'

I felt his tone lacked a certain conviction. I shifted uncomfortably.

'Well, it's possible, isn't it?'

'Oh, quite possible, quite possible, and tell me, Polly, the "wonderful evening" he refers to – what are your theories on that? Was he perhaps referring to your sparkling conversation? Your witty line in repartee? Or do you have any other ideas?'

'Well,' I whispered, 'I wondered perhaps if it was . . .'

'Yes? Go on, I'm keen to learn?'

'Well, a combination really, you know – chatting, laughing, joking, dancing—'

'Dancing! Yes, of course, why not? You've always created quite a stir on the dance floor, haven't you? Your dancing! Why not indeed?'

'Oh Nick,' I said desperately, 'I know it all sounds a bit odd, but—'

'A bit odd? A BIT ODD!' he bellowed.

He leaned his hands on the table and stuck his face close to mine. I shrank down in my seat.

'Polly, I just don't believe this. You sit down at the breakfast table one Sunday morning and cool as a cucumber tell me a story about how you spent the night in a hotel room with a man I very much suspected you had the hots for anyway—'

'Now that's not—'

'Let me finish!' he yelled. I gulped. 'You tell me you woke up the next morning and found this note' – he flicked it across the table as if it were a piece of dog shit – 'saying what a wonderful lover you were and what a marvellous time you'd given him—'

'But it doesn't—'

'Yes it *does*, Polly, clear as daylight I'm afraid, and then you expect me to believe you had convenient amnesia between the hours of midnight and seven a.m. and that because you don't *remember* anything, nothing actually happened? D'you honestly expect me to swallow that?'

His incredulous face was inches from mine now. I'd never seen him so angry, not even back in the bad old days of Penhalligan and Waters when he was my exacting boss and I was his useless secretary and he balled me out on a regular basis. Nothing had ever remotely prepared me for this. I quaked in my slippers and tried desperately to defend myself.

'Well, I know it *sounds* a little far-fetched, a little unbelievable even—'

'A little far-fetched? Polly, it's downright lies and you know it!'

His eyes had me pinned again. I shrank, I slithered, I ducked and weaved, but there was no getting out of the line of fire.

'Don't forget, Polly, I know you,' he hissed. 'I know you inside out, and God knows you've told some whoppers in your time, but this really is the biggest, isn't it? This really takes the biscuit. Tell me, I'm genuinely intrigued, what exactly were you wearing when you woke up?'

'Wh-what was I wearing?'

'Yes, do tell.'

'Well . . . I was . . .'

'Naked?'

I hung my head, shame overwhelming me now, filling every crevice, every nook, every toenail.

'I see. And you still don't know what happened?'

I shook my head miserably.

'Well, let me enlighten you, Polly, let me fill you in. It's like this. You went to bed with him. You went to bed with Sam. You took advantage of the fact that your husband was away on a business trip and you bonked another man whom you'd fancied for some time. Not a very original scenario, I grant you, and a pretty cheap and nasty one at that, but one that you obviously had no qualms about participating in. In fact I'd go so far as to say you almost planned the whole thing.'

I couldn't look at him, this seemed so unfair, and yet, what could I say? Had I? Had I done it? I stared at the floor, my eyes filling with hot tears. Nick saw my shamed face and took it as an admission of guilt. He straightened up and shook his head slowly.

'Jesus,' he whispered. His face, which had been firm and furious up to now, suddenly wobbled precariously. His mouth trembled, his eyes watered.

'This time, you've just gone too far,' he said in a shaky voice.

He got up and walked out of the kitchen, banging the back door behind him. I stared at the door for a second, then my head dropped on to the table and I burst into tears.

My heart broke into the stripped pine. After the few first terrible convulsions, I dragged myself up and ran after him. Sobbing and heaving, I flung open the back door and raced down the garden path, dressing gown flying, but he was striding fast. I ran through the vegetable patch in my bare feet and eventually caught up with him in the lettuces. I grabbed his sleeve.

'No! No!' I sobbed, clinging to his arm. 'It wasn't like that, really it wasn't, you don't understand, you must let me explain! I don't *know* what happened, but it wasn't that! I know I'm a terrible liar, but Nick, I promise I'm not lying this time, I'm not, you *must* believe me, I'm telling the truth, I'm telling the truth!'

He tried to shake me off but I clung to his arm like a puppy with a rubber toy, tenacious, desperate, sobbing. Eventually he prised my fingers off one by one and pushed me away. Not hard, but definitely away. We stood facing each other a few feet apart. The tears were streaming down my face now, my shoulders were shaking and my breath was coming in gasps. I'm not sure, but I think he was crying too.

'Nick, please . . .' I sobbed, holding out my hand.

'I'll be staying at Tim's tonight. We'll make other arrangements later,' he whispered.

With that he turned on his heel and left me standing there. I watched him go, then covered my face with my hands and sank to my knees in the lettuces.

Chapter Fifteen

I must have sat there for some time, because when I tried to get up my legs were stiff and numb from being doubled up beneath me and my dressing gown was sopping wet and covered in mud. I pulled it around me, shaking with cold and misery. As I knotted the cord, I noticed a tiny black spider scrambling furiously along it, frantic and lost amongst a mass of blue towelling. I flicked him on to the mud and he sped away on more familiar terrain, just a wrong turning in an otherwise ordinary day. As I turned and stumbled back to the house I saw Larry mending a fence in the far field. He looked up, waved and smiled, just an ordinary day for him too. Life, for the rest of the planet, seemed to be going on as normal, why was mine falling apart?

I went into the kitchen and sat down carefully, holding myself tightly. I rested my head on the table. I couldn't even cry now. I stared at the remains of the breakfast things in front of me. The blue tea pot was inches from my nose. Was it only this morning I'd been pouring tea from it? Funny, it seemed like days ago. It had a crack, I saw, just at the top, by the handle. Odd, I'd never noticed that before. I shut my eyes and heard Nick's voice in my head. 'I'll be staying at Tim's tonight. We'll make other arrangements later.' What other arrangements? What did that mean? Separate rooms? Separate houses? Separate lives?

I turned my head, leaned my other cheek on the table and stared at the fridge minus its magnets. Minus its finger paintings. I felt my guts knot themselves into a tight little ball and my face buckled. Did I say I was all cried out? The tears flowed silently down my cheeks. This was so unreal, I just couldn't believe it was happening. Nick . . . my Nick, was I losing him? Had I lost him already? It was something I'd never, ever envisaged. I'd assumed we'd be together forever, have children together, grow old together, and now, in the space of just a few days, it was all over. What had happened?

I buried my head in my arms and groaned. I'd cocked it up, that's what. A loving husband, a beautiful house, security, love, happiness – it hadn't been enough for me, had it? No, I'd wanted more. Not much more, of course, just a little bit, nothing big enough to trouble the happy home, but enough to bring a small frisson of excitement now and then. A secret, something to think about in quiet, private moments – when I was drying my hair, or driving to the shops, or listening to a slushy record, or before I went to sleep at night – something to hug to myself, or more precisely, someone. And someone to be thinking about me, too.

And of course, if that someone had ever got out of hand, if Sam had come on a bit strong, for instance, why, then I'd have been wide-eyed with innocent amazement.

'Heavens, Sam, you mean you thought that you and I might one day . . . oh! Golly, so sorry to have misled you, to have wasted your time, but you see I've got this husband

. . . Love him? I adore him! Worship the ploughed fields he tramples on – didn't I mention it?'

I probably would have shot him one last hot look full of the promise of what might have been, given a tantalising flick of the long blonde hair that never lay on his pillow and then left him to stew in his own frustrated juices, longing for me, lusting after me. Yes, that had been about the size of it, hadn't it, Polly? Hadn't that been the big idea? Well, blow me if it hadn't backfired in one hell of a big way.

I dragged myself up from the table and moved slowly through the kitchen to the hall. I went to go upstairs but the mirror at the foot of the banisters stopped me. I stared. God, I looked like I'd been beaten up. My jaw wobbled and another tear made its way rather self-consciously down my cheek. I brushed it away roughly and scowled fiercely at my reflection.

'Oh, for heaven's sake, get a grip,' I hissed. 'Who are you to feel sorry for yourself, you've brought it all on yourself, haven't you? Shut *up*, you silly fool, stop blubbing and bloody well *do* something about it, all right?'

But what? I rested my burning face against the mirror. My head felt so thick, so gummed up, I couldn't even begin to think. I had to make Nick believe me, that much was clear – he'd never forgive me, not in a million years, so I had to make him believe me. I turned my forehead against the cool glass. If only I could remember what had actually happened, if only I hadn't been so out of it, so drunk. I mean, if I didn't know, how on earth could Nick be expected to?

Suddenly I froze and eyeballed myself in the mirror. A gem of an idea was scuttling across my retina. Blimey. Of course! Yes, of course, you idiot, ask Sam, just jolly well *ask* him! And if it transpires that you did indulge in any naughtiness – as I was rapidly coming to suspect I had – well then, just get him to lie! Get him to ring Nick and say it hadn't happened at all, that I'd fallen asleep and he hadn't laid a finger on me!

I frowned and bit the skin around my thumbnail. But why should he do that, why should he lie? I thought hard. Because – because if he didn't, I'd – I'd tell his wife! I gasped and clapped my hand over my mouth, my eyes huge with horror, stunned by my own treachery. Goodness, Polly, what an awful person you've become! I gazed in wonder at my reflection, wondering if it showed. I hesitated, but only for a moment. No, damn it, this was no time to be moral and whimsical, my marriage was at stake. It was a brilliant idea, absolutely brilliant.

Today was Sunday and I couldn't possibly ring Sam at home, but I'd do it tomorrow morning. Yes, absolutely first thing, just as soon as he got into his office. I set my mouth in a determined line and regarded my reflection. Things were looking distinctly upward. Well all right, not distinctly, but marginally, because you see I had a plan, and there's nothing I like more in a crisis than a plan.

The following morning I woke up alone. I had a brief sob into the pillow about this sorry state of affairs, then I remembered my plan. I sat up straight and forced myself to think positive. I looked at the clock. Eight-thirty. At nine o'clock I'd phone. I grabbed my muddy dressing gown from the floor, pulled it around my shoulders and sat watching the minutes tick by. I lit a cigarette – couldn't find an ashtray so commandeered the top of a deodorant spray and wedged it precariously in the bedding. I took one deep, thoughtful drag and murmured a brief rehearsal of what I might say to Sam on the phone.

'Er, hello there, Sam, it's Polly . . . Fine thanks, and you? . . . Good. Sorry to bother you but there's something I'd like to clear up. Did we do it last Friday night? . . . Ah, we did, I rather suspected as much. Listen, old boy, sorry to be a nuisance, but get on the blower and lie through your teeth to my husband, would you, or before you can say alimony I'll be round at your place spilling the beans to her indoors, all right?'

I gulped and took another deep drag of nicotine. Well, something like that anyway. My cigarette-holding fingers were shaking violently, bad sign. I suspected this was going to be rather an awkward phone call, but on the other hand it had to be done. At nine o'clock on the dot I bit my lip and punched out Sam's work number. A rather plummy receptionist answered.

'Eu, helleu, Rocket Productions?'

'Yes, could I speak to Sam Weston, please?'

'Aim afraid he's not in the office today, he's aight shooting.'

'Oh! Where's he shooting? Can you give me the number?'

'Aim afraid Mr Weston doesn't like to be disturbed on a shoot.'

'I'm sure he won't mind under the circumstances,' I purred sweetly. 'We're making a film together. Could you put me through to his office please, I'll speak to his assistant.'

'Jarst one moment,' she said icily.

There were a few clicks and gurgles, then another girl answered.

'Production?'

'Hello,' I said briskly, 'look, sorry to bother you, but it's imperative I get hold of Sam Weston right away, I'm making a war-torn documentary about the Bosnian Kurds and I need to discuss the rushes with him immediately. Could you get his telephone number for me, please, it's rather urgent. My name's Kate Adie, by the way.'

There was a pause. 'Polly?'

'Pippa! Oh, Pippa, it's you, I didn't recognise you, oh, thank goodness. Listen, I must speak to Sam, where is he?'

'Sam's on location at the moment.' She sounded hostile, even more hostile than the receptionist, in fact. Crikey. I frowned, then suddenly remembered.

'Oh gosh, Pippa, I'm so sorry!' I gasped. 'I'm so sorry about what I said in the restaurant about you and Josh, but you see I was incredibly drunk! It was stupid and – and horrid, I know that, but Pippa, I was out of my tree, and so many awful things have happened to me since then that I just completely forgot to ring and apologise, please forgive me, please!'

'It was totally out of order, I've never been so embarrassed in all my life.' Her voice was icy.

'Oh I know, I know,' I wailed, 'but it'll never happen again, honestly, please forgive me, Pipps, please?'

There was a pause, and then a sigh. 'You really are a dickhead, aren't you, Polly?'

She forgave me. 'Oh thank you, thank you! And you're right, I am a dickhead, I really am, and you're so sweet, so—'

'Oh, all right. Spare me the effusive gushing, just *think* next time, OK?'

'OK, OK!' I agreed wholeheartedly. 'And thank you so—'

'Shut *up*, Polly.'

'Right, right.' I cowered. 'Was Josh, um, furious?'

'Livid. He got in his car and raced off without me. I tried to follow in a taxi but I lost him. I don't know where he went but it wasn't home. I sat outside his house for ages waiting for his car to draw up, but he never appeared.'

'Oh Pipps, I'm so sorry,' I said in a small voice.

She sighed. 'Well, actually, as it turned out it wasn't so terrible. When I got into work everyone said they couldn't understand what the fuss was all about because they all knew anyway. It doesn't make things any easier but I suppose at least we can be a bit more open about things here, I don't have to skulk around quite so much.'

'You see! Oh good, I'm so glad! So it's all turned out rather well, then?'

'I wouldn't go as far as that,' snapped Pippa tersely. 'I'm certainly not about to thank you, if that's what you mean!'

'No, no, of course not,' I muttered meekly.

'But what happened to you? Did you get your train?'

I groaned. 'Oh Pippa, it's awful, simply awful, so much has happened I just can't tell you. Nick hates me, I think he's leaving me, in fact, and he's right, I'm a ghastly person, rotten through and through, a liar, a cheat, a—'

'*What!* He's leaving you? But he knew all that stuff when he married you, didn't he? The cheating and the lying and—'

'Oh yes, of course, but he didn't know I was an adulteress, did he? He didn't know I'd go to bed with Sam, he didn't know about my nasty, rotten, conniving—'

'YOU WHAT! You went to bed with Sam? Polly, what the hell's going on?'

Out tumbled the whole sordid story, punctuated by much sniffing, sobbing, nose-blowing and pauses to light more cigarettes. When I'd finished there was a silence at the other end.

'Pippa? Are you still there?'

'Yes, I'm still here, but I'm practically on the floor. God, you've really gone and done it this time, haven't you?'

'I know, I know!' I wailed.

'What on earth are you going to do?'

'Well, first of all I've got to speak to Sam and find out exactly what happened.'

'I should have thought that was fairly obvious.'

'Well, yes, OK, but – I wondered if he could be persuaded to pretend otherwise.'

'What, to lie?'

'Er, sort of, yes.'

'To Nick? Heavens, Polly, talk about a tangled web and all that. Why don't you just come clean for once?'

'Oh yes, brilliant,' I snapped. 'I came clean yesterday and look where it got me, practically in the divorce courts. No, I've got to speak to him, it's the only way.'

'Well, you've got a slight problem, he's somewhere on the Nile.'

'The Nile! What the hell's he doing there?'

'Shooting a commercial for Turkish delight, he'll be back in about two weeks.'

'I can't wait that long, I could be divorced by then!'

'Well, I've got a few telephone numbers, but they're moving around a lot and it might be quite difficult to trace him.'

'Give them to me,' I said desperately. 'I'll try them all.'

'Cost you a fortune, Polly,' said Pippa dubiously.

'Oh, what does money matter when my marriage is at stake!' I cried dramatically.

I wrote down all the numbers and promised to report back if I had any news. A couple of hours later, when my index finger was numb from punching out twenty-digit numbers and my voice hoarse from shouting at ignorant Egyptian hotel receptionists who couldn't even speak the Queen's English for heaven's sake, I finally put the phone down in despair. I traipsed miserably downstairs, poured myself a large gin and tonic, cut some cucumber slices for my puffy little eyes and trailed back to bed again. It was quite clear that getting hold of Sam was going to be very tricky. I'd tried every hotel between Aswan and Cairo and the answer was always the same. 'He not due here till next week,' or, 'He been, he gone now, he go yesterday.' Eventually, knocked out by the mother's ruin and soothed by the cucumber eye patches, I went back to sleep, resolving that in the afternoon, with a rested brain and finger, I'd track him down if it was the last thing I did.

Unfortunately, as I discovered later, this was not to be. After shrieking at a whole new batch of receptionists and then reporting back to Pippa, it transpired that there'd been a complete change of plan and the entire film crew were now actually *on* the Nile, on a boat which stopped whenever and wherever the director felt like filming, but with no firm schedule.

'How can he do this to me?' I screeched to Pippa. 'I need to speak to him right now!'

'Well, he'll definitely be in Cairo in a couple of weeks,' soothed Pippa, 'no question about it. They're shooting the pack shot there and that's where the client's waiting, complete with pristine box of Turkish delight in his hot little hand. So don't worry, you'll get hold of him then. Just for once in your life be patient, Polly, OK?'

Easy for her to say, I thought gloomily, putting the phone down. It wasn't her life that was in the balance here, was it?

The next two weeks were purgatory. Nick worked on the farm but slept and ate at Tim and Sarah's. I never saw him. I stayed inside and basically took to my bed, just popping down to the kitchen now and then for supplies, which I then squirrelled away in a little store under my bed. I curled up miserably under the duvet, mentally ticked the days off as they went by, and generally felt that there was nothing much to live for, let alone get up for. I tried to diet but seemed to put on more weight than ever, which might have had something to do with the fact that the only exercise I got was reaching for my cigarettes.

Apart from smoking a lot, I cried a lot and talked tearfully on the phone to Pippa, who did her best to console me, but who, I could tell, felt that the dice were not exactly loaded in my favour. Sarah, I knew, felt much the same. She crept over to see me every day, feeling horribly divided between Nick and me.

She'd assured me on her first visit that the whole village knew of the marital tiff and were on tenterhooks, dying to know the outcome – would he come back? Paul, the newsagent, had even opened a book on it. Apparently the odds were against me, but that could have had something to do with the fact that the current story sweeping the village was that I'd got out of my head on Ecstasy at an acid house party and then bonked an entire rugger team.

As Sarah was one of the few people privy to a conversation with Nick these days, I awaited her daily visits with bated breath. One day, at the beginning of the third week, she crept in as usual at around eleven o'clock. I sat up eagerly, wrapped my distinctly grubby dressing gown around me and peered through the dark glasses which hid my puffy eyes.

'How is he?' I whispered, before she'd even got a foot through the door. 'Pining for me yet, d'you think?'

''Fraid not, Polly,' she said, a mite too cheerfully for my liking, brushing some ash off the bed cover before she sat down. 'He was up with the lark this morning and ate a hearty breakfast. Actually he was on quite good form for a change. Of course,' she added quickly, seeing my face fall, 'he's probably faking it, he's probably eating his heart out, but you know Nick, he'd never show it.'

I nodded dumbly. 'Sure.' I slumped back down on the pillows and stared out of the window.

Sarah got up and swept some crumbs on to the floor. 'God, this bed's disgusting, crumbs and ash and – oh yuck, toenails too! You are a slob, Polly, when did you last change the duvet cover?'

'Oh, I don't know,' I muttered miserably, reaching down beside my bed for the Coco Pops packet and pulling out a handful of cereal. I crunched away gloomily. 'Last month, I think. Does he mention me, Sarah?'

'Christ,' she muttered, moving hastily on to a chair. 'Er, well, not exactly, but then I think that's pretty significant, don't you? It's as if he can't bear to mention your name in case – well, in case it hurts too much.'

'Or in case he pukes,' I muttered. 'What's in the Le Creuset thing?' I'd spotted a casserole dish by her feet.

'Oh, I thought you probably weren't eating properly so I brought you a stew, we had some last night.'

'Stew? On a weekday? Gosh, he'll never come back if he gets used to your cooking. Give him beans on toast every night like I do. You're an angel for bringing it, Sarah, but honestly, I'm trying to diet, I'm getting so fat.'

'Well, it's hardly surprising since you live on Coco Pops – and what's that aerosol thing you keep squirting in your mouth?'

'Whipped cream,' I said, giving my tonsils a quick squirt. 'Easier than going downstairs to get the milk. These are my staples, Sarah, just a little cereal and cream every day. I'm cutting out all the frivolous luxuries like bread and—'

'Fruit and vegetables, yes, I know. It's no wonder you're putting on weight – and look at all these empty chocolate boxes!' She cruelly swept the duvet aside to reveal my secret store.

'They're not all empty,' I protested sulkily. 'Here, have one.' I pushed a box in her direction.

'No thanks, I know you, if it's still sitting there it'll be because it's marzipan or something disgusting and it'll have a chunk out of it where you've tried it and put it back. Anyway, I thought you hadn't got out of bed for ages. Where did you get them from?' She giggled. 'Secret admirer? Someone who goes in for the distressed-bag-lady look, eh?'

'Very funny, and for your information I did actually get out of bed one day last week. I went into Helston to get my split ends cut.' I sniffed. 'I felt so lonely and miserable I just had to have some sort of physical contact, even if it was only with a complete stranger who stroked my hair and snipped the ends off.' I turned to face the wall. 'And guess who I ran into as I was coming out of the salon?'

'Who?'

'Nick,' I whispered. 'We practically bumped into each other. He didn't say a word. I opened my mouth to say hello but I shut it when I saw his eyes. Cold and hard. He just looked straight through me and walked on by without saying anything.' I pulled my hanky out from under my pillow and snuffled into it. 'What have I got to live for, Sarah? Just tell me that, eh?'

Sarah sighed. 'Look, Polly, he's bound to be feeling like that at the moment, just give him some time, OK? And you know something?'

'What?'

'You'd feel much better if you got up and got your act together. You could clear up this pigsty of a room for a start. I mean, look at it!' She swept her hand around in disgust. 'You can hardly move for dirty washing and overflowing ashtrays. I've never seen so many cigarette butts in one room – and look at all these empty Mr Kipling boxes! I don't know how you can bear to live like this! And look at that dressing gown you're still wearing, it's filthy, why don't you wash it?'

'Washing machine's broken,' I said gloomily.

'Well, get a plumber!'

I bit my nail. 'Don't scold me, Sarah, I'm just not up to it.'

'Take it off and give it to me,' she sighed. 'I'll wash it and give it back to you tomorrow.'

I dutifully slipped out of it and handed it to her. She took it gingerly and bundled it up by the door ready to take. I huddled under the duvet with nothing on and watched as she began sweeping all the debris into the waste-paper basket, emptying ashtrays and picking up clothes. She stubbed out a couple of cigarette ends smouldering peacefully away in the top of the deodorant spray.

'Apart from anything else you'll go up in flames if you're not careful!' she scolded.

'And who would care?' I retorted. 'Who would care if I died right now, certainly not Nick, he hasn't even bothered to enquire how I am, I could be dead already and he wouldn't even know about it!'

Sarah stooped to pick up a mouldy banana skin that was nestling in one of my suede shoes. She straightened up and looked at me rather impatiently.

'If you don't mind me saying so, Polly, I think you're taking this self-indulgent bit a mite too far. I mean, no one can actually blame Nick for avoiding you, seeing as you were the one who opted for the extra-marital sex in the first place.'

'Whose side are you on, Sarah?'

'No one's, but you must admit he's got a point, and anyway, you wouldn't want him to come and see you now, would you? Imagine if he walked in and found you in this revolting state.'

'Well, he's not going to, is he? I mean, let's face it, Sarah, he's never going to come back, is he?' My voice cracked.

Sarah busied herself grinding out more cigarettes. She didn't look at me.

'Well, is he?' I pleaded.

She sighed. 'I don't know. I really don't, Poll. I think he's talked to Tim but Tim won't tell me anything because he thinks it'll go straight back to you, which it probably would.'

I was shocked. 'There's no probably about it, Sarah, of course it would!'

'All right, all right, of course it would. But you're right, he's not going to walk back in just like that. Nick's got some pretty uncompromising views about the sanctity of marriage.' She picked up a mug with two inches of solid blue mould at the bottom. 'Shall I soak this for you?'

'Oh, throw it away,' I said miserably, 'it'll never come off.'

Sarah ignored this directive and put it in my washbasin, running the hot tap over it. I groaned and bashed my head on the pillow.

'You know, Sarah, everything would be all right if I could just talk to Sam and find out what happened! I've got to speak to him in Cairo, I've just got to!'

'And if he says you did sleep together you're still going to ask him to lie through his teeth?'

'You bet,' I said grimly, 'it's the only way.'

Sarah sighed and folded her arms. 'Well, you know my views on that topic. I mean, wouldn't it be easier to just – well, to just sort of – stick to the truth?' She had the grace to ask this somewhat hesitantly, knowing how diametrically it went against the grain.

'Oh sure, *easier*,' I scoffed, 'but hopelessly ineffectual, and anyway, sometimes,' I went on piously, 'one has to take the hard route in life, however unpleasant it might be. One can't always take the easy way out, you'll learn that one day. No, no, this calls for some carefully thought-out subterfuge.'

She shrugged and threw open a window. 'Oh well, you know best. Phew, that's better. God, you can hardly see for smoke in here!'

'Atmosphere,' I mumbled.

'And what are you doing with these binoculars?' She picked them up off the windowsill.

'Oh, that's so I can see Nick when he's working in the fields. It's the only time I get to catch a glimpse of him now, and to think, I used to be able to see him every minute of the day!' My voice rose dramatically and I sniffed into my hanky, poking it up under my dark glasses to dab my eyes.

Sarah sighed and sat down patiently on the bed beside me. 'Oh dear, you are in a bad way, aren't you?'

I nodded miserably, sniffing wildly. She patted my hand, then looked at her watch. She shook her head.

'Listen, I'm really sorry, Poll, but I must go in a sec, I've got a new showjumping pupil arriving at the stables soon. Will you be all right?'

'Yes, I'll be fine,' I whispered, smiling bravely. 'Oh, and er – leave the stew if you like, Sarah,' I added quickly, seeing her tuck it under her arm. 'You never know, I might feel up to it a bit later on.'

'That's the spirit,' she said, putting it on a chest of drawers. 'It'll do you good. And just think, Polly, tomorrow you'll be able to speak to Sam and sort out exactly what happened. Odd the way these film people change their schedules all the time. I thought he was supposed to be in Cairo today?'

'No, it was always tomorrow. He arrives at the hotel on Tuesday.'

'But it's Tuesday today, Polly.'

I went pale. 'Don't be silly, it's Monday.'

'No.' Sarah shook her head emphatically. She pulled a diary out of her handbag, flipped through, then brandished it in my face. 'Look, definitely Tuesday.' I nearly fainted with shock.

'My God! It can't be true! You mean I'm sitting here wasting precious hours gabbling to you when I could be talking to him?'

'You've been in bed too long, Poll, lost a day along the way somewhere.'

'Out! Out!' I screamed, shooing her away. 'I've got to ring him right now, quick, Sarah, go away!'

'All right, I'm going, I'm going,' she said, making hastily for the door. One hand was already on the phone, the other scrabbling around on my bedside table for the important piece of paper I'd scribbled the number on.

Sarah picked up the dirty dressing gown and scuttled out, but a second later her head popped back around the door. 'Oh, and you will let me know how it goes, won't you?' she said eagerly.

'Yes!' I screeched. 'Just go!'

She went.

With a very shaky hand I punched out the number. I listened nervously as it rang and rang. Eventually someone answered.

''Allo?'

'Yes, I'd like to speak to Mr Sam Weston, please,' I said breathlessly. 'I believe he's staying with you.'

'Heh? Speak up?' It was a terrible line.

'MR SAM WESTON!' I shouted.

'Ah yes, he in his room.'

I sat bolt upright. 'He is? Terrific! Put me through, please!'

'Ah no, he resting, he say he no want to be disturbed.'

'Do you know who I am?' I screeched.

'Heh?' The line was getting worse.

'DO YOU KNOW WHO I AM?'

'No, but Meester Weston, he say—'

'I don't give a damn what he say! I'm Helena Bleeding-Bonham-Carter, that's who, Mr Weston's leading lady no less, and if you don't put me through right now I shall abandon Mr Weston's picture and go to Hollywood and make one with Harrison Ford and Great Britain will hold you personally responsible for the collapse of its film industry! You'll find yourself impaled on top of one of your precious pyramids if you're not careful. Now put me through!'

I thought I might have gone slightly over the top as far as the old prima donna bit was concerned, but it certainly did the trick. It scared the living daylights out of Abdul and two seconds later Sam answered his phone.

'Sam Weston?' The line was even worse. 'Hello, Sam? It's me, Polly, can you hear me?'

'Hello? Who's that?'

'It's me! POLLY!' I yelled, almost eating the mouthpiece.

'Polly! Darling, listen, I'm so sorry I had to dash off like that the other morning, do forgive me, I'd much rather have woken up beside you but I had to go to the office to organise this blasted shoot!'

'Doesn't matter, doesn't matter at all – listen, Sam, are you on your own? Can you talk?'

'What? Speak up, Polly, this line is appalling, you want to what?'

'TALK! It's about that night at the hotel. It's very

important, Sam. I need to know what happened, because you see I can't remember!'

'Become a member? Darling, it's a hotel, not a club. Very smart, I agree, but—'

'NO!' I screeched, feeling rather faint from shouting. 'I said I can't remember! Did we do it, Sam?'

'What?'

'DID WE DO IT?'

'Darling, I want to do it too, I'm aching for you right now, absolutely aching! And Polly, let's see each other the moment I'm back, we've been apart too long already. I can't wait to take you in my arms and—'

'NO!' I screeched, feeling sick with both fear and a strained larynx. 'I don't want to do it again, I want to know if we did it at all! If we made LOVE!'

'Ah, love.' He sighed. 'D'you know it felt very much like that for me too, isn't it extraordinary? I've never in my life strayed out of my marriage, Polly, and to be honest I expected to wake up the next morning with terrible feelings of guilt and awful misgivings, but I didn't. I can't help it, I just didn't, and now I can't stop thinking about you. When am I likely to see you again – can I phone? I haven't liked to in case Nick answered but—'

I groaned and bashed my head against the headboard a few times. The way this convoluted conversation was going there seemed little doubt that I should essentially fear the worst and slit my wrists right now, but, call me old-fashioned, I still wanted confirmation that the evening had indeed been consummated. I got the mouthpiece so close it was practically nudging my tonsils and yelled, 'DID WE HAVE SEX?'

'Sorry?'

'SEX, damn you, SEX SEX SEX!'

As I screeched these last few words I heard a faint click behind me. I turned around to see Nick standing in the doorway. I stared at him aghast, and simultaneously heard a voice in my right ear saying, 'Oh, sex! Yes, of course we did, darling, you were tremendous! It was absolutely wonderful, I've never felt so close to someone in my entire life, I just wish I wasn't a million miles away and could—'

I gasped and slammed down the phone. Nick was staring at me, ashen-faced, a muscle twitching away in his left cheek. It seemed to me that my last, highly compromising words were still echoing round the room. I jumped up and ran to him.

'Oh no, Nick, it's not what you think!'

He shook me off and pulled a case down from the top of the wardrobe. He began to fill it with clothes.

'No? I take it that was Sam?'

'Y-yes, it was, but—'

'But what, Polly?' he said, throwing things in the case. 'God, I had no idea you were so frustrated, you've obviously got a problem.'

'But you don't understand, I—'

'Oh really?' He turned to face me, his face white and deadly. 'I walk into my bedroom to get some more clothes and find you sitting up in bed, stark naked, screaming, "Sex! Sex! Sex!" down the phone to some guy you bedded a couple of weeks ago. What do you expect me to think?' He shook his head grimly. 'I obviously haven't been able to satisfy you, Polly, I had no idea you were so highly sexed.'

I groaned and fell to my knees on the floor, clutching my head and bashing it on the carpet.

'No!' I groaned. 'No, it's not like that, really it isn't! For a start, the only reason I've got nothing on is because my dressing gown is filthy and Sarah's taken it away to – WHAT ARE YOU DOING!'

I screamed as he reached into the back of the wardrobe and pulled out a gun. I ducked, covering my head with my hands.

'Don't be bloody silly, Polly, it's for the rats in the barn, not the rat in the house.'

I gulped, peering through my fingers. He rested it against the wall while he snapped his case shut. Heavens, for a moment there I thought I was going to be on the receiving end of a *crime passionnel*. Then he picked up the case in one hand and the gun in the other and marched to the door.

'Oh Nick, please . . .' I whispered, as he walked away.

'Oh Nick, please what?' he hissed, suddenly turning on his heel.

I tried to meet his eyes but couldn't. I stared down at my bare knees, lost for words. There was a silence.

'Nothing to say?' he asked softly. He walked back. 'Well, perhaps while I'm here you could explain our phone bill which I picked up from the hall table not a few moments ago.' He took it out of his pocket and threw it on the floor beside me. 'No less than fourteen itemised phone calls and all of them to Egypt. Is that where your boyfriend is at the moment?'

'Nick, he's not my—'

'IS THAT WHERE HE IS?'

'Yes, but you don't understand,' I wailed. 'I was just trying to get hold of him, to ask him something, I wasn't trying to—'

'I understand perfectly, Polly,' he interrupted icily. 'I understand that this was anything but a one-night stand and that you're speaking to him constantly and probably thinking about him every minute. You're infatuated with him, aren't you? God, you're nothing but a nasty, cheap little cheat.'

'Nick, I—'

'Yes you are, Polly, and you know it.' He sat down slowly on the arm of a chair and shook his head. 'You know,' he said softly, looking past me, 'when I married you, I have to admit I found your cock-eyed view of life rather endearing. Call me foolish, but I always thought your propensity to be so economical with the truth was just a harmless, quirky trait in your character.' He shrugged. 'If anything, I found it rather charming and lovable, I certainly didn't see it as anything sinister. But this isn't charming and lovable, Polly, this is just downright devious.' He narrowed his eyes at me. I tried to meet them but had to look away. 'You're corrupt, Polly, you know that? You slip from one lie to the next without even knowing what the truth is half the time. You go through life in a haze of half-truths, white lies, and now downright deception. Well, I've had enough. I'm getting out. I've had it with your nasty, cruel little games, go and inflict them on someone else. I'm sure Sam would be a willing partner, he's obviously cheating on his wife too.'

'You're wrong, Nick, you're so wrong,' I whispered. 'If you could just let me explain for one moment I could—'

'Polly, no!' he snapped fiercely. 'Enough! I've told you, I just don't want to *hear* any more! I'm quite sure you could fabricate your way out of this one like you've fabricated your way out of everything else, but to be honest, just hearing your voice, just hearing you *attempt* it makes me feel sick now!'

His face screwed up in disgust and I gazed at him in

horror. I could feel the tears rushing to my eyes. I made him feel sick. I actually made him feel physically sick.

'Now what I propose,' said Nick, rearranging his features with difficulty and speaking calmly, 'is that you should find yourself somewhere else to live. There's no rush, and you don't have to start looking immediately, but start thinking about it, please. I'm quite happy to stay with Tim and Sarah for as long as it takes, but you must see that we can't live together any more. You're entitled to a decent-sized place, so don't go looking at hovels. Somehow, I'll find the money to run two houses.' He paused. 'If it means I have to sell this place,' he went on, slightly shakily, 'then so be it.'

I gasped. My God. He hated me so much that he was prepared to sell his beloved house just to get rid of me. There was no holding the tears now, they streamed down my cheeks, and splashed on to my bare knees.

'No histrionics please, Polly,' said Nick quietly, getting to his feet. 'I dare say you won't be short of places to stay. I'm quite sure your boyfriend will look after you.' He walked to the door and made as if to go out, but before he did he turned. Our eyes met. His hard, but nonetheless hurt and haunted, mine streaming with tears.

'Shame on you, Polly,' he whispered, 'shame on you.' And with that, he walked out.

Chapter Sixteen

I don't remember much about the next couple of days. I lay in bed and lurched from one bout of crying to the next, feeling shocked and dazed. I couldn't actually believe this was happening to me. I stayed in my room and drew the curtains, staring into space, sleeping a bit, but eating nothing. I didn't answer the telephone and I didn't answer the doorbell, I just lay there, hugging my pillow, my face turned to the wall.

Sarah had a key so she still came to see me, but she didn't say much on these visits. There wasn't an awful lot to say. She just sat by the bed and patted my hand. Now and again she tried to get me to eat, but they were half-hearted attempts because even she knew it was useless. My marriage was over and I just wasn't up to eating. She'd heard the news from Tim and she knew it was final. Nick wasn't a man to make idle threats so there was no point in trying to make me think positive and I didn't ask her to.

We sat in silence most of the time, except when I cried, but after a while she began to make tentative suggestions about places I might go and look at with a view to living in. She'd seen a nice cottage for sale in Polzeath, apparently, but just mentioning moving out only provoked a fresh bout of tears, so eventually she gave up on that too. She simply arrived, made sympathetic noises, cleared up my room and left food parcels by the bed as if I were a little old lady and she were Meals on Wheels.

On one such day, about a week after Nick's dreadful pronouncement, she was creeping round the room, stooping to pick up tear-sodden tissues and cigarette ends, when she suddenly straightened.

'Oh, I almost forgot why I came today, I mean apart from trying to tidy up and get you to eat a bit. I've got some news!'

I turned my head away from the wall and looked at her with blank eyes. 'Is it Nick?' I whispered. 'Has he said something?'

'Oh, er, no, 'fraid not, Polly, it's not Nick. No, it's about the burglary.'

'Oh, that.' I turned away again. Gosh, all that seemed so long ago now, and so unimportant.

'Don't you want to know?'

'Go on then,' I sighed, 'tell me.'

'Well, apparently they've arrested someone!'

I turned back and raised myself up very slightly on my pillows. 'Really? Who?'

'Ah, you see!' said Sarah gleefully. 'You *are* interested.'

'Only because it took place in my – my husband's house,' I said shakily. 'Go on, Sarah, spill the beans, who is it?'

'Well, it's one of those film-crew people, you know, who came here. I think he actually came to supper that time, I'm just trying to think of his name.' She frowned.

I sat up a bit more. 'Really? God, who is it?'

Her face cleared. She snapped her fingers. 'I remember now! It's that poofy guy, Australian name . . .'

I sat bolt upright. 'Not Bruce!'

'That's it, Bruce!'

'Oh no.' I shook my head. 'No, you must have got it wrong, Sarah.'

'No, it's definitely Bruce the police have got, I heard Nick talking to the police last night and he was amazed too, he kept saying – Bruce? Surely not! So there you go, quite a piece of news, eh?' She grinned, clearly delighted she'd managed to get some sort of reaction from the corpse in the bed aside from more tears or a noncommittal whisper. 'They arrested him a couple of days ago apparently, I think they're holding him in London, but – oh, I know, Polly, why don't you ring Hetty? She knows all about it and I know she's dying to speak to you.'

'No, I couldn't,' I said, shaking my head and sinking back into my pillows again. 'Not Hetty.'

'Look,' said Sarah gently, sitting down beside me, 'please speak to her. You and I both know that Hetty is the last person to take sides. She loves you, Polly, she really does, and not just because you married her son, and she's desperate to talk to you, to comfort you. Please give her a ring, she's too afraid to ring here.'

I sighed. 'I'd like to speak to her too,' I said softly, 'but not about me and Nick, I can't discuss that.'

'Well, say that, then, say you just want to talk about the burglary. Honestly, Polly, you've got to get out of bed at some point, you can't stay here forever.'

'I'm not staying in bed forever, I'm getting up the day after tomorrow. I'm going to London.'

'Oh?' She looked amazed. 'Why?'

'Sam's back, that's why. I'm going to give it one last shot.'

'What – get him to lie about that night? Polly, I honestly think that even if you *can* get him to talk to Nick, Nick's gone beyond the point of listening to anything. He's going to guess it's all a huge invention dreamed up between the two of you and—'

'But it's worth a try, isn't it?' I cut in desperately. 'I mean, anything's worth a try. I know it's hopeless but I've got to have one last attempt to save my marriage.'

'OK, OK,' she said hastily, seeing my eyes water. 'Have a go, see what he says, at least it will get you out of bed. But please, Polly, do talk to Hetty, you've got no quarrel with her, have you? And she's so worried about you.' She gazed at me beseechingly.

I sighed. 'OK,' I muttered, 'I'll ring her when you've gone.'

'Brilliant,' beamed Sarah, hastily making for the door before I could change my mind. 'Now don't forget, will you, do it now.'

The door shut behind her and I heard her running downstairs. Bruce. Blimey, who would have thought? And why? I wondered. I bit the skin round my thumbnail, then reached for the phone. I hesitated. Hetty was the kindest, wackiest and most sublime of mother-in-laws, but she was nonetheless my mother-in-law. How was I supposed to explain that the reason her son had walked out on me was that I'd been up to no good with another man?

Suddenly I grabbed the receiver decisively. No, I had to do it, I couldn't lie in bed and hide from people forever. I punched out her number. She answered straight away in her dark-brown throaty voice.

'Hello?'

'Hetty, it's me, Polly,' I said somewhat shakily.

'Polly! Darling, how lovely, I've been dying to ring but – well, you know, haven't liked to, what with one thing and another.'

'I know, and it's my fault, I should have rung you sooner, but I felt awkward. Listen, I'd love to come and see you, but would you mind awfully if we didn't talk about me and Nick?'

'Of course! I couldn't agree more, too boring for words, and anyway I think he's behaved abysmally. Fancy moving out lock, stock and barrel after only one tiny little indiscretion on your part, I mean, really! Incidentally, hate to be nosy, but this indiscretion, it wasn't really a whole rugby team, was it? Only Mrs Parker at the dairy swears it was but I told her it was far more likely to be one of those glamorous film people. I can't really see you as the rugger-bugger type and I don't honestly think you've got the stamina for a whole team of virile young—'

'Hetty,' I interrupted sternly.

'What? Ah, yes, right. Sorry, darling, I'll try to mind my own business, shall I?' She sighed wistfully. 'Awfully hard though.'

'I can imagine,' I sympathised. 'I'd be the same, and just for the record, no it was *not* a rugger team. But look – what I do want to talk to you about is the burglary.'

'My dear! Isn't it too exciting? Come over at once and I'll tell all.'

Half an hour later, having washed my hair and put on make-up for the first time in weeks, I borrowed Larry's car and drove over to Hetty's cottage.

Hetty had moved out of Trewarren just after Nick's father had died. The house had been left to Nick on her death, but she'd asked him to take over immediately, saying it was much too big for her and that she found it too sad and empty now that her husband had gone. Much to Nick and Tim's horror she'd found herself a tumbledown cottage just outside Gweek and insisted on buying it. No surveyor in Cornwall would swing a plumb line at it, it was so rotten and derelict, but Hetty had been adamant and within a twinkling had bought it. In fact, it was a sensible decision. She'd needed to do something with her grief and had poured all her energy into lovingly restoring it until she'd transformed it into the house it was today – the showpiece of the village.

There it stood at the bottom of the hill, a welcoming sight as one approached the village. The new wing that she'd so cleverly added looked as if it had been there for ever, the brand-new thatched roof was weathering nicely, sparkling leaded windows poked out from under the eaves and the whole thing was painted the palest shade of putty. It was surrounded by a beautiful cottage garden full of lupins, delphiniums, honeysuckle and climbing roses.

Inside, the original warren of tiny dark rooms had become one enormous, bright, airy ground floor, and upstairs had likewise said goodbye to its dividing walls to become a huge circular gallery with all the bedrooms and bathrooms running into each other. There were no doors to speak of and any staying guests had to leave their inhibitions firmly at home, but as Hetty said – who needs doors?

I peered through the bay window and rapped on the stable door – no bell, of course.

'Hetty, coo-ee!'

'Come in!' she yelled from within.

I stepped in and was simultaneously taken aback. All the

rugs on the floor had gone and in their place were green floorboards. Actually they were clearly in the throes of being painted green, because in the far corner of the room I spotted Hetty, crouching low and eagerly covering what remained of the wood with copious amounts of emerald paint. She was dressed in a rather elegant Noël Coward silk paisley dressing gown, a pair of trainers and a New York Yankees baseball cap. I don't think I've ever seen Hetty without a hat, she probably wears one to bed. As usual, most of the ensemble was spattered with paint.

'Darling!' She turned around, beamed and waved her paintbrush in the air. 'Be with you in a minute, but I must just finish this bit of grass.'

She bent down again and carefully added what was obviously a crucial finishing touch.

'There!' She straightened up. 'Like it?' she asked proudly, cocking her head to one side and eyeing her handiwork.

'Er ... well, it's certainly unusual, Hetty. All right to step on it or is it still wet?' I gingerly tiptoed in.

'Oh no, that bit's dry, I did it yesterday. Isn't it divine? I'm going to add some daisies later, and a few poppies, just scatter them liberally around. It'll be just like strolling though a summer meadow,' she said dreamily.

I looked down doubtfully. 'I suppose it will, but won't it get a bit chipped? With people walking on it?'

'Oh yes, possibly,' she said airily, wiping her hands on her dressing gown, 'but I'll probably be bored with it by then so I'll change it to something else – a beach, maybe, with shells and a spot of seaweed. Anyway, sit down, darling, and I'll get us both a large drinky – God, I could use it, I'm exhausted!'

She strode off to what passed as the kitchen but was actually a stove, a sink and a few cupboards in the far corner. A woman after my own heart, Hetty thought cooking was wildly overrated and didn't believe in setting aside a whole room for it. I meanwhile installed myself in a large, squashy blue sofa, by the fire which Hetty lit – for colour, darling – even in August. I glanced around and couldn't help noticing that the grass seemed to be growing up the side of most of the furniture too.

'So what's he like, this Bruce chap?' foghorned Hetty from what was effectively the other side of the house, but then she'd never been one to let a little thing like distance come between her and conversation.

'Terribly nice,' I yelled back, but my voice doesn't have quite the same resonance, as her answer confirmed.

'What? A complete bastard? I bet he is. I'm so disappointed I didn't meet him, everyone in the village is asking me about him and I'm having to make it up, rather like you do, Polly.' She marched back armed with two hefty gins and handed one to me.

'Oh, thanks very much!' I said indignantly.

She flopped down at the other end of the sofa and opened her eyes wide.

'Oh, but I'm right behind you, darling, I mean, why tell the boring truth when you can get away with a good lie? But do tell, is he mean and conniving? Has he got a pinched, sly little face and slitty, piggy eyes like this' – she twisted her features accordingly – 'only that's how I'm pitching it to everyone at the moment.'

'Well don't,' I said, sipping my gin, 'because he's not like that at all. He's got a lovely face – angelic even, with big blue eyes. He's such a waste. When I first saw him I couldn't stop hitching my skirt up and sucking my cheeks in until I realised the only cheeks he was interested in were the ones in Nick's jeans.'

'Ah yes, I gathered he was a poof. Awfully amusing company on the whole, but they can be a bit sly, you know,' observed Hetty sagely, as if she were describing a completely different species.

'No, but he's not, that's just it. When you elbow your way through his rather whimsical ways you realise he's an absolute darling underneath, very kind and sincere, and actually if anything rather insecure. Nick and I both really liked him and Nick spent quite a bit of time with him.' I shook my head. 'I really can't believe he's done this. The police down here must have got it wrong, you know their alarming propensity to get everything wrapped round their necks.'

'Not this time.' Hetty pursed her lips. 'No, for once they've done their homework. They've got conclusive proof. You see, apparently he was stupid enough to give a piece of the porcelain to his mother for a birthday present – I mean, for heaven's sake!'

'What!'

'I promise you it's true, his mother's in a hospice somewhere near here—'

'In Truro, she used to live in Penrith.'

'Precisely, well it turns out she was rather grand at one time and had an amazing porcelain collection – not as amazing as ours, of course, but still, quite good stuff – but when Bruce's father died she was clobbered by death duties and had to sell it all.'

'D'you know, I think Bruce mentioned that,' I said slowly, suddenly remembering.

'Exactly, which is why it all makes sense. You see, according to Mrs Parker—'

'The fount of all knowledge and inventor of rugby anecdotes,' I put in sourly.

'Well, quite, but no, this time it's gospel. According to her the poor old dear is absolutely riddled with cancer and your chap Bruce is beside himself with grief. She's clearly dying, so Bruce thinks – wouldn't it be wonderful to give her something really special on what will obviously be her last birthday, something beautiful that she can hold in her hands and get some sort of final pleasure from? So what does the poor silly boy go and do? He visits her in hospital and gives her a piece of the porcelain he's nicked from us – sorry, darling, from you – the week before.'

'Good grief, he must be mad!'

'Totally, but wait, there's more.' Hetty leaned in eagerly and took an enthusiastic drag from her cigarette, thrilled to have such a captive audience.

'Presumably he told her to keep very quiet about it, to hide it and keep it a secret, but of course, as soon as he'd gone she couldn't resist showing it off around the ward. Well, eventually one of the nurses saw it and suspected it might be worth a bit, she'd also read about the burglary at our place in the local paper, so she put two and two together and tipped off the police. They arrived hotfoot, checked it out, and Bruce was arrested that afternoon at his flat in London.' Hetty sat back looking frightfully smug. 'You see? Caught red-handed, *in flagrante*, fingers in the till and absolutely with his trousers down – what further proof do you need?' She raised her eyebrows and stubbed her cigarette out triumphantly in the geranium pot behind her.

I shook my head incredulously. 'God, I just can't believe it, it's ludicrous, how could he have been so stupid? And what on earth made him take the whole lot, Hetty? Surely if all he wanted was one piece to give to his mother before she died he could have slipped that away easily, we probably wouldn't have noticed for ages.'

'Ah, but you see it *wasn't* enough, he needed the rest of it too.'

'Why?'

'Because' – Hetty leaned forward eagerly to deliver her *pièce de résistance* – 'he was being blackmailed!' she hissed.

'What!'

'I promise you it's true. The police searched his flat and found all these blackmail notes – you know, letters cut out of newspapers and stuck on to Basildon Bond paper, that sort of unspeakable stuff.'

'God, how horrid! What did they say?'

'Oh, ghastly things about how perverted his sexual preferences were and how disgusting it was that he was gay, but the main thrust of it was – if you'll excuse the expression – that if he didn't cough up with some money soon, his mother would be told.'

'What, that he was gay? Surely she knew that?'

'Apparently not. According to Mrs Parker's niece who lives in Penrith' – I rolled my eyes to heaven but she swept on – 'Bruce is an only child, and was a very late arrival. So just imagine, right? He's got elderly parents who absolutely dote on him – the child they thought they'd never have and all that – and then, *quelle horreur!* He discovers he's gay! Now how d'you think a sweet old couple living in the depths of conservative Cornwall are going to take that piece of news? Not quite on the chin, I can assure you. So, naturally, Bruce keeps quiet. His gay world is up in London so there's no reason why they should ever find out, and when he comes to visit them at weekends he plays the dutiful bachelor son, presumably dropping all his camp ways, and they're none the wiser.' Hetty took a quick swig of gin and licked her lips. 'Of course, the father's dead now so there's only the mother, and now *she's* dying too, so why shatter her illusions when she's only got weeks to live?'

I nodded. 'I couldn't agree more, but – God, how ghastly, you mean some vile bastard is threatening to spill the beans while she's on her deathbed?'

'Precisely. Isn't it unspeakable?'

'It's horrendous.'

We both sank into our gins. I stared at the fire. Poor Bruce, sitting in a prison cell somewhere with all this hanging over his head. Somehow it seemed to eclipse even my own monumental problems.

'But you see, what I want to know,' said Hetty, cradling her gin thoughtfully, 'is how he got into the cabinet in the first place without breaking the lock? How on earth did he know where the key was kept?'

'Oh, that's easy,' I said miserably. 'Nick and I practically showed him where it was. He was very interested in the porcelain so Nick let him go up and look at it on his own. In fact, if I remember rightly, Nick even took the key down from the dresser in front of him.' I shook my head. 'Gosh, we practically talked him into it, I'm surprised we didn't help him pack his swag bag.'

'Nonsense,' said Hetty briskly, 'you just trusted him, that's all. How were you to know he was up there pricing it all with his Miller's guide with a view to selling it on?'

'He did have a Miller's guide too,' I remembered gloomily. I took another gulp of gin. 'Poor Bruce. I almost wish he'd got away with it.'

'Polly!'

'Well, he obviously needed that china more than we did.'

She sighed. 'That's true, I suppose.'

We were silent for a while, staring at the fire as it crackled away in the grate. I shifted position, tucking my feet up under me.

'But how do the police think he got into the house? Have they worked that one out? There was no sign of what they so pompously call "a forced entry", was there?'

Hetty stubbed her cigarette out. 'Well, I think they're still working on that one but apparently they've got enough conclusive proof without it to lock him up for quite some time.'

'Where have they got him at the moment?'

'Oh, he's not behind bars yet, he's out on bail. He's got to wait for his court case to come up first.'

'Oh! So he's not in a cell or anything?'

'Oh no, I imagine he's at home, sweating it out. I think he's free to come and go as he pleases as long as he doesn't leave the country or anything.'

I stared at her and put my gin down slowly on the table. 'I'll go and see him then,' I said suddenly.

'Polly!' Hetty looked alarmed. 'You can't do that, he's – well, he's a hardened criminal. I mean, he stole from you, after all.'

'Yes, but it's totally understandable, isn't it, Hetty? I mean, think about it, if you had some awful secret which you knew would break your mother's heart and some bastard was threatening to break it to her on her deathbed, you'd move heaven and earth to do something about it, wouldn't you? You might even steal, I know I would. God, I think it's outrageous!'

I quickly collected my cigarettes and lighter from the table and popped them in the pocket of my denim shirt.

'No, I must go and see him, tell him I understand – especially since it was me he stole from. At least if he knows I'm on his side and I forgive him it might make him feel a little bit better.' I got up to go.

Hetty looked up at me anxiously. 'Polly, I'm really not sure you should. I'm sure burglar and burgled don't usually fraternise before the court case.'

'Maybe not usually, but this is an unusual case. In fact – I think I'll go up today. I was going to go the day after tomorrow anyway to see Sa—' Hetty's eyes glinted with excitement, she held her breath. 'Er – well, to see someone else,' I finished.

Hetty looked disappointed. She stood up and pulled her dressing gown around her. 'Ah. Oh well, if you were going anyway – but do be careful, my dear, he might be feeling awfully bitter and resentful, you don't want him to take it out on you.'

'Don't worry, I can take care of myself. I'll ring him up first and if he sounds murderously inclined I won't go.'

We walked to the door. Hetty took my arm.

'D'you know, Hetty,' I said with a smile, 'I feel a bit better now. It's probably an awful thing to say but other people's problems can sort of put yours into perspective, can't they? For the first time in over two weeks I've got something positive to do.' I pecked her on the cheek. 'Thanks for the drink, I'm glad I came.'

'You'll let me know what happens, won't you?' she said

anxiously, opening the stable door for me. 'And don't go to his flat or anything, meet him in a bar, or a restaurant – somewhere public.'

'Don't worry, I'll be fine.' I smiled and shut the bottom half of the stable door after me. Hetty leaned over it.

'Oh, and good luck with your other little assignation too,' she said slyly. 'Who did you say you were meeting in London?'

I grinned. 'I didn't. Bye, Hetty.' I waved cheerily and ran off down the garden path.

Hetty stood and watched as I got into the car. I drove off and she waved till I was out of sight. As I roared back to Trewarren I delved around in the glove compartment and found an ancient bag of Opal Fruits. I sucked one thoughtfully. It was true. Strangely enough, I did feel a bit better now that I had something other than myself to focus on, and anyway, I shifted uncomfortably in my seat, being in bed for so long had practically given me bed sores.

When I got home I ran upstairs to the bedroom to pack a bag, but as I pulled a case off the top of the wardrobe, for some reason I suddenly had to drop it and sit down very quickly on the floor. God. Yuck. I put my head between my knees. I felt most peculiar, rather woozy and sort of – sick. I sat there for a minute or two, then, when I deemed it safe, got up and had a glass of water. I steadied myself on the basin. Clearly my body wasn't used to all this frenzied activity, having spent such a long time horizontal on a mattress.

After a moment I felt better so I flung open the case and ran around the room, throwing things in – as usual I packed for about a month, much preferring to travel heavy in case of a sartorial emergency. Then I sat on it, snapped it shut and ran downstairs to ring Pippa. She wasn't at her desk – out at a meeting or something important – so I left a message to say I was coming to stay. Then I rang Sarah and told her I was going away for a few days.

'What shall I tell Nick?' she asked doubtfully.

'What's it got to do with him?' I snapped. 'I mean, he's left me, hasn't he? I can come and go as I please now, can't I?' As I said it I remembered Hetty had said exactly the same about Bruce. So I was out on bail too, was I? Conditional discharge pending the court case. The divorce court case. I saw red.

'Tell him to go to hell!' I stormed.

Sarah gasped. 'Oh Polly, you don't mean that!'

I sat down on the hall chair and bit my lip miserably. 'No, you're right. I don't.' My eyes filled with tears and I fiddled with my wedding ring. I sighed. 'OK,' I said after a while, 'tell him I've gone to see Bruce, that I've taken the old Renault, and tell him . . . tell him I love him very much.'

There was a pause. 'He's just come in actually, Polly, you could tell him yourself if you like,' she said quietly.

I hesitated. 'No. No, he won't want to speak to me. You do it for me, Sarah. Bye.'

I put the receiver down, brushed away a rogue tear that had somehow escaped down my cheek and pulled myself together. Right. No time for that sort of nonsense now, I had things to do, places to go, people to – oh, shut up, Polly, just get a move on. I grabbed my car keys from the hall table, picked up my case and ran down to the farm to get the car.

As I beetled down the muddy track to the yard I smiled fondly. For there, mouldering away quietly under a tree, was Rusty, my dear old green Renault. He heralded from my single, girl-about-town days and we'd had some good times together. He was retired now, of course, and his principal role in life these days was to transport chickens and ducks to market. I patted his old bonnet and jumped in. I instantly jumped out again. The nauseating pong of chicken shit was enough to make anyone gag, but with the BMW in London, needs must. I brushed half a ton of straw and muck off the driver's seat, then I held my breath, got in, turned the poor old engine over and rattled off to London.

Even in his heyday Rusty had never been much of a speed merchant, but sitting in a wet field with only the occasional trip to market had really taken the edge off him. We vibrated our way precariously up the M4 with me urging him on, cajoling just a few more miles an hour out of him whilst he complained noisily.

When I eventually arrived at Pippa's house it was way after midnight and I was exhausted. I parked the car without bothering to lock it, tottered gratefully up the path, delighted I'd made it in one piece, and rang the bell.

Pippa was yawning away in her dressing gown when she opened the door. She looked very bleary-eyed.

'I thought you were never coming,' she said. 'I was just about to leave a note on the door saying "The key's under the flowerpot" but then I thought that was probably a bit silly.'

'Just a bit, unless you want the whole of Kensington hopping into bed with you.'

'I wouldn't mind,' she said gloomily as I followed her into the sitting room. 'It would certainly make a change. No one's hopped into my bed for about two weeks now.' She flopped down dejectedly on a sofa.

'What, no Josh?' I threw off my jacket and curled up next to her.

'No, he's making himself very scarce these days – family problems, so he says.'

She grimaced and poured out a couple of glasses of wine from a half-empty bottle. I noticed there was already an empty Frascati bottle nestling on the sofa beside her, which would explain the bloodshot eyes. She handed me a glass.

'Here, help me finish this. Actually, I think his wife suspects and now he's showing his true colours and running home with his tail between his legs every night. Bastard.' She knocked back her drink in a couple of gulps and poured herself another one.

I looked at her admiringly. 'Atta-girl, Pippa, looks like you've finally seen the light.'

She sighed. 'Not really, I know he's a pig all right but I'm still in love with him, so it doesn't really help much, does it?' She gave me a sad little smile. 'And anyway,' she went on defensively, 'he does actually have some family problems, it's not a complete lie, his sister isn't well at all.'

I pulled a long face. 'Bit weak, isn't it?'

'Well, no, she's really ill actually, and they're twins so he's very close to her. In fact,' she looked around furtively as if someone might be listening, 'it's a deadly secret, but apparently she might have AIDS.'

'AIDS! Blimey, do be careful, Pippa!'

'What?' She looked blank for a second then rolled her eyes to heaven. 'Oh, for goodness' sake, you're not one of those people who still thinks you can get it from loo seats, are you?'

'Er, no, don't be silly, of course not, but – well, all the same.' I hastily took a slug of wine. 'How did she get it?'

Pippa shrugged. 'Who knows? Someone at work said it was a blood transfusion – it's not the sort of thing you ask, is it, especially since I'm not really supposed to know. Anyway, enough about me, what about poor old Bruce? Have you heard?'

'Yes, Hetty told me, that's why I've come up. Isn't it awful?'

Pippa shook her head. 'Dreadful.'

'How is he?'

'Well, when I spoke to him yesterday he sounded practically hysterical. I could hardly make out what he was saying he was crying so much.'

'Crying?'

She nodded. 'I hate it when men cry, don't you?'

I thought of Nick with tears in his eyes and gulped. 'Yes, but then Bruce isn't really – you know, macho, is he?'

'No, but he's still a man.' She sighed. 'Anyway, at least he's not in a ghastly cell or anything. Sam and Josh put up the bail for him, ten grand they had to find.'

'Really? That much? Gosh, that was nice of them.'

'Well, everyone's terribly fond of Bruce, you know. We rang Sam in Egypt and he's coming back a day early to see him. He instructed the bank to make the money available and apparently he knows a brilliant barrister who's going to act for him.'

'Oh well, that's something. Bruce is going to need all the help he can get.' I sipped my wine thoughtfully. 'So Sam's coming back tomorrow, is he?' I sat up straight and compressed my lips. 'Right. I'll go and see him.'

Pippa gave me a strange look. 'Polly, you're not still . . .'

'What?'

'Well, you're not still keen on him or anything, are you?'

'Aarrrhh!' I shrieked and nearly hurled my wine glass across the room. Instead I threw a cushion. 'No, I'm not bloody keen on him! I'm keen on my husband and I'm keen on saving my marriage, actually! I told you, I've got to go and see him to get him to talk to Nick and – oooohh!' Suddenly I doubled up and clutched my tummy.

Pippa jumped up in alarm. 'God, I'm sorry, I didn't mean to upset you, honestly – heavens, Polly, what's wrong?'

I stuck my head between my knees. 'I don't know,' I mumbled from somewhere near my ankles. 'I just feel a bit odd. It's been happening quite a bit lately.'

'What sort of odd?' Pippa knelt down beside me.

'Sort of ... faint. And sick. Very sick, actually – ooohh . . .' I moaned again and swooned sideways.

Pippa straightened up beside me and pulled her dressing gown around her. She narrowed her eyes. 'Faint and sick, eh? Really. And how long have you been feeling like this?'

'Oh, I don't know, just a couple of days really. In the mornings mostly, when I get up.'

There was a silence. I eyeballed the carpet for a moment, then slowly brought my head up from between my knees. I looked at her.

'Oh Pippa, you don't think . . .'

'When's your period due, are you late?'

'Oh God, I don't know!'

'Well think, should it be about now?'

'Well, I'm not sure, I'd have to check – oh God, I feel really sick now – quick, get me a calendar!' I clutched my mouth.

Pippa looked doubtful. 'Polly, if you're going to be sick I

really don't think a colander's quite the thing to catch the—'

'No, not a colander, you berk, a calendar – get me a calendar so I can check my dates!'

Pippa got up hastily and ran to the kitchen. A second later she was back with a diary. She rammed it under my nose – 'Here.'

I flicked frantically through the pages, counting back and then counting forward again. I threw it on the floor and groaned.

'Oh my God!' I held my head.

'What?'

'I'm ten days late!'

'Ten days! Really? But that's brilliant, Polly! You must be pregnant!' She bent down and hugged me enthusiastically. 'Gosh, how fantastic, oh I'm so pleased! Imagine, you're going to have a baby!'

I hid my face in my hands and groaned again.

She frowned. 'What's the matter? Aren't you pleased? I thought it's what you wanted, you've been banging on about it for ages.'

'Yes, I do, I *do* want it, I'd love to have a baby.' I looked up at her desperately. 'But Pippa, don't you see? If I'm pregnant, well then – whose is it?'

She stared at me for a moment, aghast. 'Oh God . . . you mean it could be . . .'

'Exactly!'

'Oh!'

Chapter Seventeen

Pippa looked aghast. 'You mean . . .'

'It might not be Nick's,' I whispered, 'it might be Sam's.'

'Oh!'

She stared at me for a moment, then grabbed my hand urgently. 'Think back, Polly, think back about four weeks ago, could it be Nick's? Did you two see any action around that time?'

I frowned, desperately trying to remember. It would have been just before I came up to London. We weren't getting on desperately well, but even so . . . I shrugged.

'I'm not sure, yes, quite possibly, but I can't really remember – oh, please let it be his!' I wailed, wringing my hands.

'And when did you go to bed with Sam?' urged Pippa. 'Think, Polly, that would have been about . . . ?'

I gulped and nodded. 'Just over three weeks ago.' I put my head in my hands.

Pippa put her arms around me and gave me a squeeze. 'Now don't you worry, that doesn't necessarily mean it's his, it could easily be Nick's. We'll sort this out, you'll see. Everything will be fine.' She was doing her best to sound convincing but failing miserably.

I stared at the carpet in a daze. Suddenly I looked up at her. 'I don't want to get rid of it,' I said quickly. 'I've wanted this baby for too long. I'm not having an abortion!'

'Of course you won't have to get rid of it,' she said staunchly. Then she hesitated. 'But suppose – I mean, what if you knew for sure that it was Sam's, would you then?'

'Oh God, I don't know, I just don't know! I mean, what if it grew up to look just like Sam? Totally different from Nick or me – with hazel eyes and brown hair, wouldn't that be awful? Nick would be sure to guess and he'd hate the child and hate me, although of course he hates me anyway and it's not as if he's coming back, but if he did – oh Christ, what a mess!' I burst into noisy tears at the thought of this ghastly scenario.

'Well, that's why I was wondering if it wouldn't be better to—'

'No! No, I can't get rid of it!' I wailed. 'I can't possibly – what if it is Nick's after all? What if I'm carrying his baby and I pull the plug on it, that would be totally horrendous too!' I sniffed hard and wiped my nose on my sleeve. 'Oh God, I need a hanky,' I muttered.

Pippa jumped up and came back a second later brandishing a loo roll. I pulled off about nine sheets, wrapped them round my hand and blew my nose noisily.

'You know, Pippa,' I muttered, stuffing the paper up my sleeve, 'this has got to be about the worst thing that's ever happened to me, and let's face it, some pretty dire things have happened over the years.' I rummaged in my bag for a cigarette and fumbled with the packet but my fingers were shaking too much for me to get one out.

'Light one for me would you, Pipps, and pour me another drink while you're at it.'

Pippa looked doubtful. 'Er . . . well, you shouldn't really, you know.'

'Shouldn't what?'

'Do either. Drink or smoke. I mean, in your condition.'

I looked at her, appalled. 'Really? Oh no, no of course not, you're right, how frightful!' This really was a shaker, almost as bad as being pregnant. I struggled to come to terms with it. 'How will I ever survive? They're my only pleasures in life at the moment.'

'Well, have one quick fag to steady your nerves, but make that the last one you have.'

'Right.'

She lit one for me but I only took a couple of drags before I was overcome with guilt.

'Poor little thing,' I muttered, stubbing it out, 'it's going to have enough problems without me adding to them before it's even born.'

I sighed gloomily as Pippa poured the last of the Frascati into her glass.

'Of course,' she said, sipping it thoughtfully, 'you are only ten days late, maybe you're not pregnant at all.'

'No such luck,' I said darkly. 'I'm always bang on time, I'm like bloody Big Ben, never a second late.'

'Even so, just in case – hang on a minute.' Pippa stubbed her cigarette out, jumped up and ran out of the room. I heard her thumping away up the stairs and running along the corridor to her room. I sank back in the sofa and rested my throbbing head, which felt as if it was going to explode. I closed my eyes. What a nightmare . . . what a complete and utter nightmare. Perhaps if I shut my eyes for long enough I'd fall asleep and the whole ghastly problem would go away . . .

A second later I heard her thumping downstairs again. I opened my eyes to see her standing over me waving a magic wand, a huge grin on her face.

'Look what I've found!'

'Don't tell me,' I said bitterly, 'you've joined the Magic Circle and now you're going to cast a few spells and make a baby disappear.'

'Don't be silly. It's a pregnancy test, you just pee on it and if you're pregnant it goes bright blue in about a nanosecond.'

'So what are you doing with it?'

'Oh, I had a scare a few weeks ago. It was negative, thank God. I'm telling you, Polly, it would be my worst nightmare, a baby – imagine!' She rolled her eyes in horror then saw my face darken. 'Oh! Oh, sorry, I didn't mean it like that, of course a baby would be lovely at, um, at the right time, it's just that – well, you know, Josh being married and everything . . .' She trailed off.

'So is Sam,' I said grimly, grabbing the wand from her and stalking down the passage to the loo, 'and so am I, and so is Nick and – oh God, this is awful!'

I slammed the door and looked doubtfully at the stick in my hand. I opened the door again.

'Pippa?'

'What?'

'Is this the same stick you used?'

'Oh, don't be an idiot, you get two sticks in the box. I haven't given you a part-worn pregnancy test!'

'Oh. Right.'

I shut the door and got on with it. Sure enough it went bright blue before I'd even had a chance to pull my knickers up. I dragged my feet back to the sitting room.

'They don't give you much time to get used to the idea, do they?' I said gloomily. 'I thought I'd at least have time to plan the nursery, think of a colour scheme, decide on a theme for the borders – you know, ducks or teddies, pink or blue, that kind of thing.' I stuck the wand under her nose. 'Positive?'

'Positive, couldn't be bluer. You're up the duff, Polly, no doubt about that!' she confirmed cheerfully.

I sank into a chair and groaned. 'No wonder I feel so lousy. Honestly, this pregnancy lark isn't all it's cracked up to be at all, talk about propaganda. I'm supposed to be blooming, aren't I? Well, all I feel is blooming sick and blooming tired. Unbelievably tired actually, lie-down-on-the-pavement tired – and just look at my boobs! I wondered why I'd turned into Samantha Fox overnight. I tell you my heart goes out to her now, lugging these pendulous melons around is no joke.'

Pippa peered at me. 'You don't look any bigger than normal.'

'Oh Pippa, I'm huge! Absolutely huge! I'm practically busting my bra here, can't you see? I'll have to go to Peter Jones tomorrow and get a new one.'

'I should wait a bit,' said Pippa knowingly. 'They're going to get an awful lot bigger than that, you know.'

'Are they?' I asked, glancing down in horror.

'Oh yes.' She nodded sagely. 'It's one of the occupational hazards. By the time you're about nine months you'll be carting them around in a hammock, you won't be able to see your feet for bosoms.'

'Oh, thanks very much,' I snapped. 'Since when did you become such an authority? And incidentally, d'you think you could put your cigarette out? It's making me feel a bit queasy.' It wasn't, but it was making me feel awfully envious.

'Gosh, sorry,' she said, quickly stubbing it out. She looked at me in concern. 'Hey, are you sure you're all right? Not going to be sick, are you? D'you want to put your feet up or anything?'

'Oh don't be so rid—' I stopped abruptly. 'Well ... yes actually, now you come to mention it, perhaps I am feeling a little delicate – yes, if you could just pull that stool up for my feet ... thanks – oh, and that cushion, for behind my head ... bit to the left ... down a bit ... perfect, thanks.' I leaned back in the chair, hands resting delicately on my tummy, looking pained and wan.

Pippa hovered over me anxiously. 'Cup of tea? I think I've got rosehip somewhere, isn't that what pregnant women drink? I'd have to hunt around a bit but I don't mind.'

'Would you? You are an angel, Pippa, thanks so much ...' I muttered weakly. Pippa trotted off dutifully.

'Oh – and a piece of toast and honey would be lovely if you could manage it,' I called feebly after her, 'and three sugars in my tea, please, got to keep my strength up.'

I settled back into my cushions. This at least was some compensation for my ghastly predicament. I'd no idea pregnant women got such perks. I wondered if I could get a tea-and-toast-bearing punka wallah on the National Health. I shut my eyes and tried to think. What on earth was I going to do about all this? I simply had to have a plan. By the time Pippa came back laden with tea and toast a few minutes later, I had at least formed what you might call a quarter-baked one. I sat up.

'I'm going to go and see Sam tomorrow,' I said decisively. 'First thing.'

Pippa put down the tray and sighed. 'Is there really any point? I mean, I know you've set your heart on him phoning Nick and telling him nothing happened that night, but d'you really think he's going to want to get involved?'

'Well sure, he may not *want* to get involved, but...' I hesitated.

Pippa stiffened. 'Polly! You're not going to tell him you're pregnant, are you?'

I shifted uncomfortably. 'Er, it had occurred to me. Don't you think I should?' I hazarded guiltily.

'No. I don't,' she said firmly. 'It would certainly get him on the phone double-quick denying all responsibility, but—'

'Exactly!' I interrupted, eyes shining. 'My thoughts exactly!'

'*But*,' she carried on sternly, 'what if it *is* his? What if it's his baby after all?' She shook her head firmly. 'No, Polly, you can't do that, you'd just be fooling yourself, fooling him, fooling everybody, in fact. No, you've got to wait until you know for sure who the father of this child is. Don't breathe a word of this to Sam *or* Nick, until you know.' She leaned forward and took a bite out of my toast.

'But how am I ever going to find out?' I wailed, dropping my toast and feeling sick with fear now. 'It's all very well for you to say that, but how am I ever going to know?'

She helped herself to my abandoned toast and chewed away, looking rather blank for once. We gazed at each other. We were a bit out of our depth here. None of our friends were even remotely pregnant yet, I was very much a trailblazer.

'Can they tell before it's born, d'you think?' I said hopefully. 'Do blood tests or something? Or what about this new DNA thing, isn't that supposed to sort out who you are?'

'I think that's more to do with fingerprints,' said Pippa doubtfully, 'and I'm not sure a three-week-old foetus even has fingers, let alone prints, and anyway, how would you get to them?'

'Well, all right,' I conceded, 'perhaps not DNA, but blood tests then, or urine samples or – yes I know – one of those scan things.'

Pippa looked at me incredulously. 'Those "scan things" just show you an ultrasound picture of the baby. You don't think you're going to spot a family resemblance, do you?'

'Well, Nick's got an awfully big nose, that's bound to show up.'

'Oh, don't be ridiculous, he grew that much later! He probably didn't have it as a baby, let alone as a foetus.'

'Well, you think of something then!' I cried desperately, on the verge of hysteria now.

Pippa licked some honey off her fingers thoughtfully. 'Trouble is . . .' she said slowly, 'I may be way off beam here, but I have an awful feeling they can't really tell until it's actually born.'

'No! Don't say that, that can't be true! Think of all the things they can do with unborn babies these days – heart surgery in the womb with laser beams, kidney transplants – all that kind of thing, there was a programme about it the other night. I mean, if they can do that then surely they can discover a tiny little thing like who the father is, surely that's not too much to—'

'Oh!' Pippa suddenly grabbed my hand. She went a bit bug-eyed and trance-like. 'Hang on!'

''What? What is it?' I pounced eagerly.

'I've got a brilliant idea! Of course, I don't know why I didn't think of it before.'

'What?'

'Go and see Mr Taylor!'

'Who's Mr Taylor?'

'He's the most divine gynie in the whole world. I went to see him ages ago when I had a dodgy smear test – he's fabulous, Polly, you'll adore him, he looks just like Peter Bowles!' Her eyes glazed over with lust.

I groaned. 'Pippa, I'm not really in the market for falling for Peter Bowles look-alikes, I just want to know who the father of my unborn child is.'

'Well, if anyone can tell you, he can. He's written loads of books about infertility and that sort of thing, he's a real authority—'

'Pippa, I'm not infertile, I'm sodding pregnant!'

'I know, but same field, honestly, Poll. I promise you he's brilliant, he'll probably be able to tell just by glancing at you. I'm sure if you can work out the exact dates you had sex with both Nick and Sam he'll be able to tell whose it is just from the size of the foetus.'

I went cold. 'You mean . . . I'll have to tell him? About – you know – there being two men and everything?'

'Well, how else are you going to find out?'

I cringed. 'He'll think I'm a dreadful tart.'

'Probably, but you'll never see him again so what does it

matter?' She lit a cigarette and blew the smoke out airily. God, it was all right for her.

'Where is he then?' I asked suspiciously. 'Croydon or somewhere?'

I had visions of a ghastly back-street abortionist, right at the top of some dirty lino-covered stairs, probably with one of those beaded curtains for a door. Inside a grotty little room with peeling wallpaper would be a low rickety bed covered in a blood-red blanket, and all around the room, hanging from the walls, would be a glistening array of lethal-looking tools of the trade. I shuddered.

'Don't be silly. He's in Harley Street, he's absolutely kosher. I'll make an appointment for you tomorrow.'

I sighed. 'OK. I suppose I ought to go anyway to find out when it's due and what I ought to be doing. I expect he'll say I have to stay in bed and eat most of the time, won't he? I probably should be eating now – you know, for two and all that. Got any biscuits, Pippa?'

'I haven't actually, and anyway,' she said doubtfully, 'I'm not sure that's right. I have a feeling they like you to exercise these days rather than lie around. My cousin went up Scafell Pike when she was six months pregnant.'

'Really?' I sat up in alarm. 'Christ, I'm not doing that!'

'You don't *have* to, you idiot, it's not compulsory, she just wanted to.'

'Oh, right.'

'Anyway,' she said briskly, getting to her feet and pulling her dressing gown around her, 'go along and see Taylor, he'll tell you all you need to know. Meanwhile, I'm going to bed, and so should you, it's nearly two o'clock you know.'

'Is it? Gosh.' I looked at my watch. 'So it is.' I got up wearily. 'Thanks, Pippa, I don't know what I'd do without you.'

She grinned and put her arm around my shoulders. 'Don't mention it, all part of the service at this exclusive little hotel.'

We went slowly upstairs.

'You know, Pippa, this should have been one of the happiest days of my life. Of our lives,' I added quietly. 'Nick and I have been waiting for this for so long, imagine how thrilled he'd have been if – well, if everything had been different.'

She gave me a hug at the top of the stairs as we got to the spare room. 'I know, but try not to think about that, just get some sleep. Everything's going to be fine, really it is.'

I nodded gloomily, wishing I could share her optimism. I crawled under the duvet and shut my eyes, and as usual drifted off to sleep almost immediately, but unfortunately it wasn't the deep, peaceful, dreamless sleep I'd hoped for. In fact it was a complete nightmare.

I dreamed I was in the kitchen at Trewarren – at least, I think it was me, I was so huge with pregnancy I hardly recognised myself – but yes, there I was, an immense, bloated monster of a woman, staggering and reeling around the kitchen, one hand lodged in the small of my back, the other clutching on to the furniture. We were talking *big* with child. As I manoeuvred my enormous bulk around I suddenly stopped short, gasped, clutched my huge stomach and sank with a piercing shriek into a ginormous heap of blubber on the kitchen floor.

'Help!' I bleated. 'Somebody help! I'm having contractions!'

Sure enough a ghastly rumbling sound like Mount Vesuvius about to erupt heralded a shuddering and shaking from my enormously swollen belly. It began to vibrate violently like a washing machine on final spin.

'H-e-l-p!' I shrieked feebly, holding on to the table leg as I vibrated around the kitchen floor. 'Help me, I'm having a baby! Somebody *help*!'

Just then I heard the back door fly open behind me – thank God! Someone was here! I peered over my shoulder, but – oh no, it was Mrs Bradshaw! She stood over me, arms folded, eyes glinting dangerously, as I bounced around painfully on the quarry-tiled floor.

'What seems to be the trouble, Mrs Penhalligan? Tummy ache? Something you've eaten, perhaps?'

'N-no!' I gasped, throbbing away like a pneumatic drill now and hanging on to both table legs for fear of shuddering right out of the back door. 'I'm h-having a b-baby!'

'Oh, is that all?' she said with a sardonic little smile. 'Let's have a look then.'

She knelt down and rolled up her sleeves in a business-like manner. A horrifically loud rumble greeted her as the tummy mountain went into vibration overdrive. It looked like a huge possessed blancmange which any minute now would explode and decorate the walls in a riot of glorious technicolour.

'Help! Get it out!' I shrieked.

'Now hold still, Mrs Penhalligan,' she said, hoicking up the marquee that passed as my skirt. 'Let's see what we've got in here.'

I shut my eyes tight.

'Brace yourself!' she cried cheerfully as, like a magician

producing a rabbit from a hat, she reached up and pulled something out.

'Aaargh!' I shrieked.

'Oh look,' she observed, dangling it under my nose by its feet, 'it's a little boy!'

I stared. It was indeed a little boy, but little only as compared to a grown man. This boy was about six years old, dressed from head to toe in prep school uniform complete with cap and satchel, and the living image of Sam Weston.

'Aaagh!'

'Now now,' admonished Mrs Bradshaw, 'he's just a mite overdue, that's all, let's have a bit of stiff upper lip, shall we. You're not the first woman in the world to have a baby, you know – oops, hold still, I think there's another one in here!'

Sure enough, within a twinkling, she'd produced another identical six-year-old.

'Twins!' she announced joyfully, before thrusting her hand up again. 'Triplets!' She pulled out another. 'Quads!' And then another, and another, until eventually the whole kitchen was knee deep in grinning mini Sam Weston look-alikes.

'No!' I screamed. 'No more! No more!'

'Oh yes,' Mrs Bradshaw assured me, eyes gleaming sadistically, 'plenty more where they came from.'

'No! Please, no more!' I shouted as my shoulders began to vibrate too. I felt as if my head was going to pop off. I opened my eyes and found myself staring at Pippa who had me by the shoulders and was shaking me awake.

'Polly! Polly, wake up!'

I was sitting up in bed, screaming like a banshee.

'What's wrong, what is it?' she cried.

'Oh God,' I groaned, flopping down on to my pillows, 'what a nightmare! I've just given birth to twenty-four Sam Westons!'

'Good Lord, you never do things by halves, do you, Polly? Never mind, you just lie down and take it easy, I'll go and get you a cup of tea.'

She disappeared and I pushed the covers off. I was boiling hot but sopping wet. A few minutes later she returned with the tea.

'Bad dream then?' she said cheerfully.

'You could say that,' I muttered, hoovering up the tea gratefully. My mouth was totally devoid of saliva and I felt as if someone had squirted my eyeballs with vinegar.

'You're dressed,' I observed, eyeing her smart suit and make-up incredulously.

'Well, it is nine o'clock,' she said, looking at her watch, 'and actually, I really must go, I've got a meeting this morning and I'm going to be late. How d'you feel?'

'Oh, awful,' I groaned, 'absolutely awful. Wrung out, knackered, exhausted.'

Pippa looked puzzled. 'But you've only just woken up, how can you be tired?'

'Pippa, you'd be tired if you'd just given birth twenty-four times, and of course I am pregnant, remember, so naturally I feel sick too.' I lay back on the pillow looking weak and delicate.

She frowned. 'Polly, you don't think you're getting this pregnancy lark a bit out of proportion, do you? I mean, you're effectively only a few weeks pregnant, you don't think your symptoms might be, well – psychosomatic? I seem to remember my cousin didn't feel sick until she was at least—'

'Oh, your bloody cousin!' I stormed, sitting up abruptly. 'I expect she was scampering up Everest, baking flapjacks and running a multi-million-pound conglomerate at the same time as giving birth, well, bully for her, but we're not all superwomen, you know – in fact, if you don't mind I'd rather not hear any more about your sodding cousin, she's making me feel worse by the minute.' I flopped back down on the bed, feeling extremely sorry for myself.

Pippa didn't even bother to answer. She smoothed her skirt down, then adjusted her hair in the mirror. 'Right, well I've got to go to work now, but I'll ring you from the office and arrange for you to see Taylor, OK?'

'And Sam,' I whispered, gazing up at her beseechingly, 'I've got to see Sam.'

'OK, and Sam. I'll try to put lunch with you in his diary. Oh, and don't forget why you came up in the first place, will you?'

'Why?'

'To see Bruce, of course.'

'Oh help,' I groaned, 'I'd forgotten about him.'

'Well, do try to see him, it would really help him a lot.'

I raised my eyebrows at her. 'Oh it would, would it?' I dragged myself wearily out of my pit. 'Oh well, I'm glad about that, I'm glad I've got time in my fun-packed life to lend a helping hand where it's needed. It's really not important that my own little world is falling to pieces around me, no no, there are plenty of other people with far more screwed-up lives – poor deserving souls – and help them I must. Dib dib dib, dob dob dob, lend a hand, Mother bleeding Teresa, that's me.'

I staggered to the bathroom and brushed my teeth with a vengeance, spitting the toothpaste out viciously. Pippa was already thumping away downstairs, sensibly ignoring my tirade.

'Have fun!' she yelled cheerfully, slamming the door behind her. I scowled into the mirror.

An hour or so later the telephone rang. I dragged myself out of a hot bath, grabbed a towel and ran dripping down the stairs to answer it. It was Pippa with my itinerary for the day.

'Right, got a pen?' she barked. God, she was efficient.

'Er, yes.' I scrabbled around in my bag on the hall chair and found my eyeliner.

'Good, now listen. Mr Taylor will see you at three o'clock, seventy-two Harley Street, got that?'

'Today? Already?' I scribbled away in black kohl. 'Not exactly in demand then, is he? Hasn't exactly got all the pregnant women in London beating a path to his door.'

'He had a cancellation,' said Pippa patiently. 'It's either today or in three weeks' time, take it or leave it.'

'OK, OK,' I mumbled. I was dimly aware I was behaving badly. 'Thanks, Pipps.'

'And Sam's in a meeting at the moment, but he says he'll meet you for lunch. One o'clock, Daphne's, Draycott Avenue, OK?'

'Really? He agreed? Did you tell him why?'

'Oh yes, I said you were carrying his unborn child and you had some paternity papers you'd like him to sign – of course I bloody didn't, what do you take me for?'

'All right, all right – and Bruce?'

'Forty-two Sugden Street, W6.' She reeled off a telephone number. 'Got that?'

'Yep.'

'Got to fly now, see you tonight. Busy day, eh?'

'Just a bit,' I said grimly. 'Thanks, though.'

I put the receiver down. Right. I looked at the names and places on the piece of paper in front of me and sighed. I really didn't feel like coping with any of it this morning. I made a cup of coffee, then threw it down the sink in case caffeine was bad for the bump, and made some disgusting rosehip tea instead. I took a sip, gagged, threw that down the sink too, then looked at the piece of paper again. Bruce had to be dealt with first. I picked up the phone and dialled his number.

It rang for ages and ages and I began to feel heady with relief. He wasn't in, he wasn't there, but at least I'd tried. I was just about to put it down when he answered. Damn.

'Yes? Who is it?' he bleated in a tearful whisper. I softened immediately. He was in a bad way.

'Bruce? It's Polly, Polly Penhalligan.'

'Polly!' He gave a strangled sob and then burst into tears. 'Oh Polly, please don't hate me, it's all a terrible mistake, please don't hate me!'

'I don't hate you, Bruce,' I said gently. 'Calm down. I just wondered if I could come and see you, to see how you are. Would that be all right? Would you like that?'

There was a pause. 'Really? You want to see me? Yes, I'd like that, I would.'

'D'you want to meet me somewhere? For a coffee or something?'

'Um, I'd rather not, Polly, only I don't like to go out much at the moment, I feel safer here, you see. Could you possibly come to the flat?'

'Sure, no problem,' I said, forgetting what I'd promised Hetty. 'I'll be over in about an hour then, shall I?'

'OK. Oh – but Polly, n-no bully boys or anything like that? Just you?' He was frightened, really frightened. I remembered the ghastly threatening letters.

'Of course not, Bruce, just me. Get the coffee on, or even something stronger. I have a feeling we're both going to need it.'

Chapter Eighteen

It took me ages to find Bruce's flat. There was a tennis tournament at Queen's Club and West Kensington was choked with traffic, so I had to leave the car miles away and perform – even by my standards – some pretty creative parking. The space I eventually found would have been more suitable for a three-year-old's tricycle, and I got very wet under the armpits as I pulled and pushed at the wheel, desperately trying to squeeze Rusty in. Eventually I succeeded – albeit with two wheels on the pavement – got out, slammed the door and legged it, keen to distance myself as quickly as possible from the improbably parked heap of rust.

With an A to Z under my nose I then map-read my way round a labyrinth of roads; through a mews, down an alley, under an arch, round a corner and, finally, up what looked like some fire-escape steps to the third floor of a dismal-looking block of flats. Taking the lift had been an option, but when the doors had slid back to reveal a menacing-looking steel box of alarmingly beaten up and graffitied proportions and stinking thoroughly of urine, I'd instantly opted for the climb.

I then made my way cautiously along the outside concrete walkway, keeping an eye out for pit bulls and

Alsatians. I wasn't too keen to meet one but I was keen to give the tenants the benefit of the doubt apropos the pong in the lift. This was definitely not the most salubrious of establishments. Was it council, I wondered? Every flat had the same blue door with a small pane of reinforced glass and at each window a net curtain seemed to twitch as I passed. Eventually I came to Bruce's door, number 42. I pressed the bell. His curtain twitched briefly too and I caught a quick glimpse of his face. A second later he opened the door.

He looked awful. His eyes were huge and sunken, with enormous dark circles underneath, and his normally golden face was ashen and unshaven. He clutched at the lapels of his blue silk dressing gown, which aside from some rather dirty pink mules was all he appeared to be wearing. He blinked nervously.

'Come in,' he whispered, glancing furtively over my shoulder as if to check no one else was with me. He quickly ushered me in.

'I won't kiss you,' he said, shutting the door behind me. 'I'm a bit of a mess this morning.'

I smiled and kissed him warmly on the cheek anyway. 'You look fine, Bruce, if a little tired.'

'Here, let me take your jacket.'

'Thanks.'

I let him take it off my shoulders while I looked around. The front door led directly into the sitting room, which also seemed to be the dining room, and judging by the large silk screen emblazoned with peacocks sectioning off the far end of the room, possibly the bedroom too.

I stared. It was an extraordinary place. The whole room was literally full of childhood memorabilia. There were teddy bears everywhere; sitting on chairs, perched on shelves and all over the wallpaper and curtains. Hanging from the picture rails were rows of string puppets – clowns, Pinocchios, harlequins – all with their limbs dangling and their heads lolling as if their necks were broken. There was also a staggering display of china animals – again, mostly teddies, but with a fair sprinkling of dogs, cats and rabbits thrown in for good measure. These were displayed on what I believe are known as 'occasional tables', except that in this instance there was nothing occasional about them, in fact at a conservative estimate I'd say there were no fewer than fifteen dotted about the room.

I blinked in astonishment. My limited experience of gays, gained chiefly from my advertising days, had led me to believe they were a predominantly tasteful lot, given rather to the minimalist and the trendy, but this place couldn't have been more kitsch if it tried. It was also, somehow, terribly sad, as if a little boy had never grown up. Bruce was hovering next to me. I had the feeling some sort of reaction was called for.

'What a . . . lovely room!' I gasped eventually, totally at a loss.

'Thank you,' he whispered. 'Come and sit down.'

He weaved expertly through a sea of clutter and scooped Munchkin up from the only comfortable-looking chair, by the gas fire. He patted the seat.

'Sit here. I'll go and get some coffee.'

'Thanks.'

I clutched my handbag nervously to my chest, tucked my bottom in – I'm nowhere near as sylph-like as Bruce – and weaved precariously around the obstacle course of tiny, ornament-laden tables, hoping my broad beam wasn't going to send something flying. Bruce watched my progress with an expert's eye and then padded out in his slippers to what was obviously a galley kitchen.

I sat down and watched him go. How odd. He'd seemed so flamboyant, so glamorous, so – well, gay – in Cornwall, yet here in this melancholy little flat he just seemed rather small and forlorn.

I looked around. Fighting for space amongst the china animals on the table beside me were a few photographs. They were all of a sweet-looking elderly couple, sometimes with Bruce smiling beside them, sometimes without. I picked one up and looked at it. Bruce came back with the coffee.

'Mummy and Daddy,' he said, handing me a mug. His hand was shaking.

'I thought so.' I smiled and put the photo down. 'You're very like your mother. How is she?' I asked gently.

He shuffled into a seat opposite and tugged his dressing gown down over his bony knees.

'Not good,' he said with a sigh, 'not good at all. Of course, all this business has made her much worse.'

'She knows?'

'Some of it. Not all of it, she doesn't know for instance that I might go to prison.' His eyes filled with tears and he stared into his coffee.

I looked away, giving him a second to wrestle with his lower lip. Something else was different about him too, but I couldn't quite put my finger on it. Then I realised – of course, his voice! All the campness had gone and there were no effete little mannerisms either. He was a different person – more like half a person, in fact, and now I understood why his parents had never known. I reached across and touched his arm gently.

'It may not come to that, Bruce. I mean, there were some incredibly – whassicalled – mitigating circumstances, weren't there? After all, you were being blackmailed, the court's bound to take that into consideration, you might just get a fine or be let off with a caution, and of course it was only your first offence, wasn't it?'

Bruce raised his eyes from his coffee and stared at me. 'No, Polly, it wasn't my first offence, because I didn't do it. Why doesn't anyone believe me!' His voice rose hysterically.

I shifted uncomfortably in my seat. 'Well, it's not that we don't believe you, it's just that – well, the thing is, Bruce, your fingerprints were all over the cabinet, the police said so, and—'

'Of course they were!' he broke in angrily. 'I was probably the last person to look at the stuff, before the burglary, I mean. Don't you remember? Nick gave me the key and said I could help myself—' He blushed at his unfortunate phrase. 'I mean, have a look.'

'Yes, I know, but' – I hesitated – 'that also means that you were one of the few people who knew where the key was kept, and the key was definitely used, so, um . . .' I trailed off nervously.

'Oh come on, anyone with half a brain could have found it in that jug, and besides, there must have been other people who knew where it was kept.'

'Well, yes, Nick and me, of course, and Hetty and Tim – oh, and Sarah.'

'No one else? Please think, Polly,' he urged. 'It might just help me.'

'Well, Mrs Bradshaw knew.'

'Who's she?'

'My old daily.'

'Well then? Why does everyone automatically assume it has to be me?'

'Well' – I licked my lips nervously – 'perhaps it's got something to do with the piece of porcelain you gave to your mother? I mean, you must admit, that's pretty incriminating, isn't it?' I asked hesitantly.

'But I didn't give it to her! Honestly, Polly, you've got to believe me!'

'You didn't? Oh, so um ... how did it get there, d'you think?' I asked, trying hard not to sound interrogative.

'I don't know!' he wailed, frantically twisting his fingers together. 'I just don't know! The first I heard of it – before I even knew about the burglary and before the police had arrested me – was when Mummy rang to thank me for some piece of china she'd found. She kept rabbiting on about how she'd woken up about an hour after I'd left her and there it was, sitting on her bedside table, all wrapped up with "Love from Bruce" written on a tag in my handwriting. She kept thanking me over and over again, one minute saying it was too much and the next saying how beautiful it was – she was nearly crying, she was so pleased.

'I didn't have a clue what she was talking about, I didn't even know it was a piece of your porcelain. To be honest I thought she'd gone completely doolally – she is getting rather senile these days – and in the end, just to calm her down – because she was getting so agitated and confused when I denied it – I said yes, OK, I had given it to her after all. She was delighted, of course, and I thought no more about it – thought I'd just ring back later and have a quiet word with one of the nurses and sort it out. I even wondered if one of them had bought it, wrapped it up and sent it from me, because I'd only given her some chocolates for her birthday – well, there's not a great deal she needs in there, you see.' He paused for breath and took a gulp of his coffee.

'Well, of course I completely forgot about it, and the next thing I knew the police were banging on my door, telling me I had the right to remain silent but anything I did say would be taken down and used in evidence against me!' His voice rose to a hysterical sob. 'I simply couldn't believe it! They wouldn't even let me speak to her – still won't, even now, it's one of the conditions of my bail. They say I'll try to persuade her to lie, to say it wasn't me, but all I want to do is to find out the truth.' He gazed at me, his pained, hollow eyes wide with anguish. Then, abruptly, he hung his head and looked down at his pink slippers.

'But none of this really matters you know, Polly,' he whispered sadly. 'I could handle all of it, the whole ghastly mess, if it weren't for the fact that she's dying and they won't let me see her. Suppose she asks for me and they won't let me go and I'm not there when she – oh God, it's just too awful to contemplate!' He gave a strangled sob and broke down completely, clutching Munchkin to his chest and sobbing into her fur.

I dashed over and knelt beside him, putting my arm around him. I could feel his bony shoulders shaking and heaving under his dressing gown. Munchkin whimpered as he held her too tightly but made no effort to escape. Eventually Bruce shuddered to a halt and started to sniff.

He released his grip on Munchkin, who frantically licked his hand, and I sat back as he rummaged for a hanky down the side of his chair. He pulled one out and blew his nose noisily.

'Someone hates me very much, don't they, Polly?' he muttered, staring at me with red-rimmed eyes. 'Someone's really got it in for me, first the letters and now this.'

'Well yes.' I licked my lips, I had to tread carefully here. 'The letters are awful, simply horrid, but you see, Bruce, that's one of the reasons the police think you did it, because you were being blackmailed. They think you needed the money.'

'Well, I did need money, yes of course I did, but I'd never *steal* for it.' He looked at me in amazement. 'Never! And certainly not from people like you and Nick whom I like and respect – what do you take me for?'

I gulped and sat on my hands, feeling ashamed. 'I'm sorry, Bruce, it's just ... well it's so terribly difficult wh-when all the evidence sort of points to you.'

Bruce compressed his lips and sniffed huffily. 'Maybe so, but it would be nice to think people would have a little more faith in one, regardless of the evidence.'

He wiped his nose with his hanky, regarding me reproachfully over the top of it. I looked away guiltily. We were both silent for a moment. I gazed down at the carpet, a ghastly, patterned nylon affair. I looked up quickly, hating myself for noticing it. I racked my weary brains, trying desperately to think of a way out for him.

'I suppose the nurses didn't see anyone else lurking round her bed that day, did they?' I asked tentatively. 'Anyone suspicious?'

He shook his head. 'No one. The only people who visit

are me and a few old ladies from her village, neighbours, that sort of thing. Anyone else would stand out like a sore thumb and they say there was no one unusual that day.'

He gave a deep sigh and sank back in his chair, picking abstractedly at some stuffing that was coming out of the upholstered arm. Then he looked up and gave me a wry little smile.

'It's very simple, Polly. I've been framed. Quite comprehensively and cleverly framed, and there's not a damn thing I can do about it.'

I frowned. 'Oh Bruce, surely not, there's no one who hates you that much, is there? Enough to let you take the rap for this?'

He shrugged and looked down at Munchkin's head as he stroked it with his finger.

'Hard to say really. No one exactly springs to mind but you'd be surprised at the number of people who hate people like me.' He found my eyes. 'Queers, I mean. Shit-shovellers, uphill gardeners, whatever you want to call us.'

I winced and looked away, embarrassed by his blatancy. He sat up straight and rearranged his dressing gown, suddenly composed.

'Oh yes, we know what people think of us. A lot of people still think Hitler had the right idea, they'd like to see us herded into gas chambers and incinerators. And I don't necessarily mean loony extremists, I mean normal, every-day, common or garden people who pretend to be terribly liberated and free-thinking but who would secretly like to see all of us dirty, AIDS-ridden buggers exterminated once and for all. Wiped out.'

'Oh come on, Bruce,' I muttered uncomfortably, 'not in this day and age.'

'You'd be surprised. Decent people like you will find it hard to believe but I can assure you it's true.' He smiled sadly. 'That's why, when you ask me if I can think of anyone in particular, it's rather hard to be specific.'

I gazed up at him from the floor where I was kneeling. All of a sudden he'd acquired a certain dignity, dressed even as he was in his dressing gown and slippers. I looked down abruptly, feeling momentarily ashamed of the arrogance of my own heterosexual community. There must have been times when I'd giggled at Bruce, ridiculed him even, because – well, he set himself *up* to be ridiculed. But seeing him now, in this heart-rendingly childish flat, sensing the chaos and turbulence that must have been within him from an early age as he struggled to come to terms with his sexuality and, when he finally did, his bravery in sparing his elderly parents that particular confession, I felt rather small. And his outrageously camp behaviour which he could evidently turn on and off – it was almost as if he put that on to give other people an excuse to laugh at him, to make *them* feel better, not him. It was a defence mechanism all right, but in defence of whom? I looked at his feet in their pink mules, so white and cold-looking, so vulnerable.

A silence fell. I tried to think of something that might help him. Anything.

I cleared my throat. 'I don't suppose you've got an alibi for that Friday night, have you?' I ventured hopefully.

He smiled ruefully. 'No such luck. I was fast asleep in bed at the boarding house where I was staying, but the police say I could easily have slipped out and got back in again because the landlady had given me a key.' He grinned suddenly. 'It's a great shame you're such a sound sleeper,

Polly. If only you'd woken up you might have seen it wasn't me!'

'Er, yes, quite,' I said nervously and quickly rummaged around for a change of subject. I didn't particularly want to get embroiled in my whereabouts on that Friday night.

'Um, is there anything I can get you, Bruce? Anything I can do, some shopping perhaps?'

He leaned forward. 'There is something, actually.'

Oh Lord, I'd rather imagined I was enquiring rhetoric-ally. I hoped it wasn't going to be anything too demanding, I had rather a lot on my plate at the moment. 'Er, yes, of course, what is it?'

'Well, if I do – you know – go away, would you look after Munchkin for me? Only, if she can't be with me I'd like her to be in the country where she's got lots of space to run around, with people who like animals. Would you mind, Polly?'

I gulped. 'No, of course not, Bruce, I'd be glad to have her.'

I wasn't too sure what a dog of Munchkin's size was going to do with a thousand acres of Cornish countryside, but since Nick would undoubtedly have kicked me out by then anyway, it was purely academic.

'Good, I know you'll look after her properly, but do remember she's got an awfully delicate tummy. She's allergic to eggs – they make her frightfully sick – but she's rather partial to a little poached chicken – oh, and lightly grilled fish. I'll give you her diet sheet, of course.'

'Super,' I said weakly.

Oh, this was terrific. Absolutely marvellous. Not only would I be a homeless, single parent with a baby to look after but I'd also have a dog with a delicate tummy and a propensity to puke, so not only would I be covered in baby sick but chihuahua icky-poo too. I'd obviously just have to wear a plastic mac all day and sponge myself down at regular intervals, when I wasn't poaching chicken for one or breastfeeding the other, of course. I simply couldn't wait.

And where were we all supposed to live? Eh? Would somebody like to answer me that one, please? It was all very well Nick saying I should go and look at houses, but there was no way I was going to live in Cornwall if I couldn't live with Nick at Trewarren, no way! And since there was also no way he could possibly afford to buy me anything in London without selling Trewarren – which I would never in a million years allow him to do – that left me up the creek without a home really, didn't it? Perhaps I should just get a Sainsbury's trolley to put baby, dog and belongings in, then I could drift around London in my puke-covered mac looking for suitable bus shelters. I sighed and leaned back on the heels of my hands, staring miserably at the teddies on the shelf above me.

Then I had an idea. Oh! I sat up abruptly. Hang on a minute – I had a quick look around – on second thoughts, perhaps we could live here. I wouldn't have to decorate because it already looked exactly like a nursery, so Junior would get the right vibes, Munchkin wouldn't have to be uprooted – an experience which would no doubt play havoc with her delicate digestive system – and Nick could perhaps pay Bruce a small amount of rent which would come in jolly handy when he came out of the clink! Yes, all in all it would suit us very well! A perfect little *pied-à-terre* for three homeless waifs and strays. I sat up eagerly.

'Bruce?'

'Hmmm?' He turned to me with sorrow-laden eyes.

I sat back again. 'Er . . . nothing.'

One peek at those eyes made me hold my tongue. Some other time perhaps. It might, after all, look a trifle callous to ask for the keys to his flat before he was even banged up.

Once more we lapsed into gloomy silence, both pre-occupied with our respective shattered lives. Eventually I looked at my watch and sighed.

'I must go, Bruce, I'm meeting Sam in half an hour.'

He nodded and got to his feet, retying his dressing-gown cord with something that smacked vaguely of determination.

'And I must get dressed,' he said decisively. 'For the first time in three days actually, awful I know, but up to now I haven't really felt there was much to get dressed for. Talking to you has made me feel a lot better, Polly, you're a real tonic.'

'Oh good,' I said, dragging myself up from the floor. 'I'm glad about that.'

The mere fact that it had depressed the hell out of me was neither here nor there, of course. What did it matter that I felt even more like sticking my head in an oven if one poor soul felt like removing his?

'Actually I know the feeling,' I said, suddenly wanting to out-gloom him. 'I didn't get dressed for about two weeks recently, didn't even get out of bed,' I bragged, as I weaved my way back through the tables.

'Really? Why?' He opened the door for me.

'Oh, er, it's a long story,' I muttered, back-pedalling like mad. 'I won't bore you with the details, I think you've got enough to contend with at the moment.' I smiled. 'Chin up, Bruce, I'll give you a ring in a couple of days, OK?'

He nodded. 'Thanks, Polly. Oh, and give my love to Sam, won't you? He guaranteed my bail, you know. Tell him I'm seeing his barrister tomorrow.'

I pecked his unshaven cheek. 'I will. Now you take care, and ring me if you need anything, I'm staying with Pippa.'

'Will do. Thanks for bothering to come and see me.' His voice cracked slightly at this and tears, I noticed with alarm, were surfacing again.

I hurriedly gave him a hug and then without looking back moved smartly down the walkway to the stairs, giving a cheery little backwards wave as I went. I simply couldn't cope with any more waterworks today, his, mine, or anybody else's. I clattered quickly down the fire-escape steps, feeling horribly guilty but desperate to get as far away as possible from that sad little flat. God, poor Bruce, talk about a shedful of problems, and far from lightening my own load it seemed to have added a couple of tons to it. In fact it made me want to hire an articulated lorry to cart it around in.

I jumped the last few steps and ran to the end of the street, grateful to be out in the sunshine again. As I ran along I groped in my bag for my A to Z and peered at the grid reference for my next little rendezvous, my tête-à-tête with Sam. Draycott Avenue, off Walton Street, Brompton Cross end. It wasn't too far from Pippa's, so I'd dump the car at her house and get the tube. There was no way I'd be able to park in Draycott Avenue. Right. I snapped the A to Z shut and sighed grimly. Oh yes, I was under no illusions about this little débâcle. If I'd thought the encounter with Bruce had been a headache I was well aware that it was nothing to the severe migraine this one was going to induce.

Nevertheless, I trotted dutifully off to my car, shooting only the occasional reproachful glance at the open blue skies above me as I went. Why me, God, why me?

Chapter Nineteen

Sam was already sitting at a corner table when I walked into the restaurant twenty minutes late. He didn't see me come in and I caught him glancing at his watch as I made my way towards him. He looked up, saw me, and got eagerly to his feet, knocking his chair over backwards as he did so. He looked a bit embarrassed at his lack of cool and laughed as he picked it up and kissed me roundly on the cheek.

'Just wrecking the joint. It's great to see you!'

His face was tanned from his Egypt trip, his eyes with their amber flecks sparkled brilliantly and his hair was streaked with gold. He certainly looked devilishly handsome and terribly boyish, but I was pleased to note that my heart didn't even miss a semiquaver.

I smiled. 'Good to see you too, Sam.'

'Here, let me.' He rushed around to pull my chair out and took my jacket as I wriggled out of it. He hung it on the back of my chair.

'Thanks.' I sat down.

'Drink?' he asked eagerly, sitting down opposite me again and indicating the carafe of red on the table.

'Please.'

The burgundy liquid glugged delightfully into my glass.

It was very definitely just what I needed right now, but as I raised it greedily to my lips I realised it was also very definitely just what I shouldn't be having. I took a miserable little sip then put it down. Christ. How on earth was I supposed to get through a lunch of such awesomely tricky proportions without a cigarette *or* a drink? It occurred to me that Sam was looking more than a little keen and that I might have to give him the heave-ho, something I hadn't really contemplated. Not only that, but I was also going to have to ask him to do some pretty outrageous lying. I seized my paper napkin and began shredding it maniacally.

'So!' began Sam joyfully, folding his arms on the table and leaning across. 'How've you been? How's tricks, as they say?' He beamed. 'You look terrific, incidentally!'

'God, I look a mess,' I ran my hands through my hair, 'but I'm fine, fine,' I nodded, cranking up a nervous smile.

'Good.' Sam leaned over the table and grabbed my hand enthusiastically, nearly knocking a vase of flowers over. 'It's wonderful to see you again, Polly, it's been so long!'

'I – I know, Sam, it's been ages. Um, how – how was Egypt?' I asked, desperately wanting to get off the subject of our long separation.

He sat back and sighed. 'Oh, so-so. Hard work and incredibly hot.' He shook his head. 'Too hot, in fact, and I'm not sure I got the result I was after. It's impossible to work in those sort of conditions.'

'I can imagine. Still, you look well,' I observed, 'got a good tan.'

He grinned. 'Well, it's pretty hard to keep out of the sun, you get a tan whether you want one or not.'

'Yes, um . . . I suppose you do.'

I followed up this sparkling piece of repartee with a festive smile and then buried my head in the menu. When I looked up Sam was watching me carefully. I had the impression he knew all was not well. I scrunched the remains of my napkin into a tight ball and wished to God I'd rehearsed just one tiny sentence of what I was going to say before I'd got here. How idiotic of me not to have thought this through. I desperately rooted around for another inconsequential gambit, just one more, then I'd come to the point, really I would. Our voices clashed.

'Sorry I was a bit—' I began.

'Look, Polly—' he started.

We laughed.

'Go on, what were you . . . ?'

'No, no, you first,' he insisted.

'Well, I was just going to say sorry if I was a bit late. I went to see Bruce and I got rather held up, stayed longer than I meant to but it was jolly difficult to get away.'

'God, I can imagine. Good for you for going, though, I'm not sure I could have faced it. Poor Bruce, how is he?'

'Desperate. Frightened out of his mind, and I don't blame him either.'

'No, absolutely, I'd be terrified.' Sam shook his head in horror. 'Awful business, simply ghastly. Apart from anything else, I can't think what possessed him to *do* it. I mean, it's just so unlike old Bruce, he's the last person in the world one would imagine doing something dodgy, and if he was so short of money he could have come to me, I'm sure we could have sorted something out, an advance on his salary or something. I had no idea he had money problems.'

'Oh, I don't think he did, and I don't think he did it either.'

'What?'

'I don't think he stole the porcelain.'

'Really? But I thought the police were more or less convinced – didn't he leave fingerprints all over the place, and Pippa said something about giving a piece to his mother?'

'Oh that,' I said dismissively, 'no no, that's nonsense. He doesn't know anything about it, it was obviously planted there by someone else to get him into trouble.'

Sam looked surprised. 'Really? Is that what the police think?'

'No, but it's what I think.'

'Gosh, well I just hope you're right, for Bruce's sake. I must say, I had my doubts about the whole thing all along, couldn't *believe* it when I heard. Old Bruce just hasn't got the nerve, he'd run a mile from anything that smacked of trouble.'

'Exactly, and I'm sure it'll all come out in court and he'll be completely vindicated. I gather you've got him a brilliant barrister, is that right?'

'Peter Summers, yes, he's a friend of mine and by all accounts he's shit hot. Bruce wanted some idiot of a hack lawyer to take the case, someone his father had known who's about ninety years old now and hasn't practised for years, but I wouldn't hear of it.'

'Quite right, he needs the best defence he can get, and you've put up the bail too?'

'Well, the company's guaranteed it but at the end of the day it's my dosh, I suppose – well, mine and Josh's since he's the other shareholder.' He frowned. 'Had a bit of a job persuading old Josh, actually.'

'Really? Why?'

'Oh, I don't know. I suppose he thought ten grand was a bit steep, and it's not as if he and Bruce are bosom pals either.'

'Oh? I didn't know.'

'Oh, it's nothing drastic, just a bit of a personality clash, that's all. Josh thinks Bruce is a bit of a pain in the arse – in more ways than one, if you know what I mean!' He grinned. 'But anyway, we're not really here to talk about Bruce, are we? Don't we have more personal matters to discuss?' His smile was warm. He leaned across the table and took my hand. 'Polly, I—'

'Look, Sam,' I said, interrupting him abruptly, 'd'you mind if I go first? Only – well I've got a few things I need to say, to – you know, get off my chest.'

'Sure, sure! Go ahead.' He sat back in surprise.

I took a deep breath and leaned forward. 'Well, the thing is . . . the thing is, I – I think you're a terrific guy. Really I do.' I nodded emphatically. 'But I'm afraid I'm just not on for any of this.'

'Any of what?'

'Any of this – well, any of this adultery lark. You see, in the first place I never actually intended to do it, can't think what possessed me, as a matter of fact, and in the second place – well, I just love my husband too much, it's as simple as that. Oh God, I'm awfully sorry, Sam, this is all coming out wrong, but the bottom line is I'm afraid it just can't go on.'

There was a silence. Beautifully put, Polly, beautifully put.

Sam licked his lips. 'I see,' he said quietly, playing with the stem of his wine glass. 'A one-night stand, is that it?'

'Sam, I'm sorry but you must see that it's just not right! You're married, and I'm married – although I'm not so sure about that any more, but that's another story – but the point is, well, the point is it was just a moment of madness really, wasn't it?' I pleaded.

He looked slightly pained. 'What a lovely turn of phrase you have, Polly,' he muttered.

'Oh Lord, I'm sorry, I'm not doing this very well, I don't mean to sound so heartless.' I took a deep breath and started again. 'What I mean is that it's got nothing whatsoever to do with you. If you were the sexiest, handsomest, most divine man in the world – which of course you are,' I added hastily, 'but even if you were Mel Gibson or – or that divine English actor with the floppy hair, Hugh someone, for example, I'd *still* have to turn you down because I'm just too in love with Nick. I'm just not on for any of this extra-marital stuff.' I shook my head. 'I'm sorry if I'm not being very tactful here, but I don't know how else to say it.'

Sam pursed his lips and stared at the tablecloth. He gave a wry little smile. 'I had a feeling you were going to say something like this, actually,' he said quietly. 'Half expected it in a way, that's why I was nervous about seeing you. And you're right, Polly, you're absolutely right. This *is* madness, but it's a madness I would have continued with, I'm afraid.' He looked up quickly. 'I'm obviously a much weaker character than you are.' He shrugged. 'I'm sorry, I just can't help it, I'm crazy about you.'

He ran his fingers through his hair and continued staring bleakly at the tablecloth.

I gulped. Oh hell. This was much worse than I'd ever envisaged. I clenched my toes. Why the bloody hell had he fallen for me like this?

'Sam, I'm so sorry,' I said softly. 'I had no idea you felt so strongly. I'd never have come barging in and trampled all over your feelings in such a heartless way, but I somehow imagined you'd feel the same. I mean, after all you and Sally—'

'I know,' he interrupted, looking up sharply, 'I know. Sally and I have a terrific marriage and I'm still very much in love with her. I've never done this before, never ever.' He shook his head vigorously. 'This is the first time in our entire marriage I've ever – well, I've ever cheated, that's the only word for it, isn't it? And I know I'm being weak and foolish but – God,' he ran his hands through his hair, 'it's been such a long time since I've had this feeling, this incredible buzz of happiness and excitement! And of course it's frightfully addictive. I think I knew it was crazy but I just wanted it to continue for a bit longer.' He took a gulp of wine and gazed at me intently. Suddenly he grinned. 'But you're right, Polly, it can't go on, and sooner or later I would have realised that. I just wanted to prolong my fool's paradise for a while.'

I sighed. 'Oh, Sam—'

He took my hand and shook his head, smiling. 'Don't feel bad, you're right, you're doing the sensible thing. It's much better that we finish it now when it's not too painful, rather than in a year or so's time when it might have been so much harder.'

'Absolutely,' I muttered, nodding hard. I took a huge gulp of wine. A year or so's time! Blimey, he'd had some pretty permanent ideas about the two of us, hadn't he?

He smiled. 'You're a lovely girl, Polly, you know that? You're fresh, beautiful and sometimes just downright hilarious. You made me feel about ten years younger that night, I'll never forget it.'

'Ah yes, well, Sam, that's one of the things I want to talk to you about actually, if you don't mind.'

'What d'you mean?'

'Well, I wondered if you could perhaps shed some light on one or two rather grey areas I have concerning our – um, our encounter. In the hotel.'

'Sure, fire away.' He looked puzzled.

'What happened?'

He frowned. 'Sorry?'

'What happened that night?'

He stared at me. 'What d'you mean?'

'I mean, I can't remember.'

'What . . . not at all? Nothing?' He looked shocked.

'Not a sausage, if you'll excuse the allusion.'

He looked at me in alarm. 'Good grief, Polly, you mean—'

'I mean I have absolutely no recollection of our night of passion, none whatsoever.' I gave this a moment to permeate his boggling brain cells, then leaned in urgently.

'Listen, Sam, the last thing I remember about that night is dancing a clinchy number with you in Annabel's. I remember feeling exceedingly drunk and I remember thinking I wanted to sit down, or go to the loo, or pass out, or *something*, but then all I've got is a complete blank. As far as I'm concerned we then fast forward to the following morning where I wake up alone in a hotel bedroom, the only clue to my recent behaviour being a coded message by my bed.'

He stared at me, aghast. 'That's it?'

'That's it.'

'Heavens,' he muttered, 'good grief, Polly, that's appalling. I feel awful. I mean, I knew you were drunk, plastered even – and so was I – but I had no idea you weren't even remotely *compos mentis*, I promise you, I'd *never* have taken advantage of—'

'Ah!' I pounced hopefully. 'So you took advantage?'

'Absolutely not!' He looked offended. 'I was going to say I wouldn't have taken advantage of the situation had I known the extent of your inebriation, but I had no idea. Hell, Polly, you were all for it. I mean, you were the one who instigated it, for God's sake!'

My jaw dropped. 'I was?'

'Certainly you were.'

'But I thought – hang on, didn't I faint or something? I could have sworn I went a bit woozy on the dance floor.'

'Oh sure, you did, and I sat you down and got you a glass of water, but you recovered in seconds and that's when you dragged me outside. You hailed a taxi and insisted it took us to a hotel.'

'No!'

'Yes, and you were the one who went for my flies in the back of the cab, you tried to take my trousers off, you even tried to take your own trousers off until I stopped you. The taxi driver nearly threw us out, it was hysterical!'

'I don't believe it.'

'I promise you it's true, but – God, does this all come as a complete surprise? What about in the lift at the hotel? Don't you remember trying to re-create that scene in *Fatal Attraction*? You sort of jumped into my arms yelling "Take me, take me!" but I was laughing so much I dropped you – remember? And then in the bedroom – gosh, you made so much *noise*! All that shouting and whooping and waving your bra around your head like a football rattle, shouting "Here we go, here we go!" – Polly, you *must* remember!'

I made a strange retching sound and bit my knuckles. 'No!' I gasped. 'No, I don't. Did I? Gosh, how *awful*! I'm so *sorry*, Sam, how *embarrassing*.'

'Don't be ridiculous, I loved it. I haven't had a night like that for ages. I mean, phew, hot stuff or what, I didn't know if I was coming or going. I was like a boy of eighteen that night, I even impressed myself!' His eyes were shining now. 'It puts my batting average up beyond belief, talk about a personal best, I must have—'

'Yes, thank you, Sam,' I groaned, hiding my burning face in my hands. 'Spare me the score card, would you? I get the idea, you surpassed yourself.'

'Oh Lord, I'm sorry, Polly,' he said quickly, 'I didn't mean to get – you know – crude, but you did ask and it really was the most terrific night. But what a shame you don't remember. What a waste.' He looked slightly hurt, then suddenly his brow puckered as if he were recalling something. 'I suppose,' he said, nodding slowly, 'yes, I suppose if I'm absolutely honest with myself I'd have to admit I was a little surprised when you fell asleep on top of me like that, right in the middle of that last frenzied bout of lovemaking. All of a sudden you just went limp and heavy and started snoring in my ear. I had to prise you off, which was quite difficult under the circumstances, seeing as how we were still very much connected – attached, if you like – and, well, I'm not saying you're a heavy girl, Polly, but I was a bit worried I wouldn't be able to shift you, actually. Thought I'd have to call a porter.'

I gave a faint but audible whimper at this point, seized my wine glass and threw its contents down my throat. It was no good, if I didn't get some alcohol into my bloodstream pretty damn fast I was going to die of shame right here on the spot, and if I went the baby went with me so it might just as well have a drink with me instead. God, how awful! I'd collapsed like a beached whale on *top* of him! Yuck, how repulsive! Sam's mouth was still moving, he was obviously still shedding light. I listened in a daze.

'. . . but up until then you were game for anything. At one point you asked me to get on all fours and make a noise like Thomas the Tank Engine.'

'No!'

'Oh yes,' Sam nodded emphatically, 'definitely Thomas the Tank Engine, you were quite specific.'

'God! And did you?'

'Well, I had a go, I gave a sort of feeble *peep-peep*, which seemed to go down rather well actually. You did quite a bit of toot-tooting back and kind of chugged round the bed a bit. Said you were Gordon.'

'Jesus!'

'Then you wanted to ring room service and send down for some sex food.'

'What the hell's that?'

'You may well ask.' He frowned and scratched his head sheepishly. 'It came as a bit of a surprise to me too. You were babbling a bit by this stage but I seem to recall you thought an assorted fruit bowl might do the trick.'

'No!' I gasped in horror. 'What on earth was I *thinking* of?'

'Lord knows,' he said wistfully, 'but I wish we had, the very idea got me pretty feverish, I can tell you.'

'Oh God,' I groaned. 'Oh Sam, how awful, what must you think of me?'

He grinned. 'I think you're a pretty game girl actually, it made me realise I'd been leading a frightfully tame love life. Couldn't stop thinking about it the whole time I was in Egypt, but – don't you remember *any* of this?' he asked incredulously.

'No,' I muttered, staring down at my hands, shame filling every part of me.

'And can't you even *imagine* doing all that?'

'Oh yes,' I whispered miserably, 'that's no problem, that's the awful thing. Given the right amount of alcohol and a little encouragement it's all entirely possible, I'm afraid. I'm only surprised I didn't treat you to some naked abseiling or a flying trapeze act.'

He looked at me wistfully. 'Really? I'd have loved that. Still, I think you made up for it. I love that thing you do with your toes, by the way.'

I froze, my eyes huge with terror. 'What thing?' I breathed, paralysed with dread.

'You know,' he winked conspiratorially, 'that . . . thing. Come on, Polly, you must have done it before, it's absolute dynamite.' He grinned salaciously and wiggled his fingers on the tablecloth. 'This little piggy went to—'

'Stop, *stop*!' I shrieked. I shut my eyes tight and stuffed my fingers in my ears. 'No more!'

After a moment I opened my eyes cautiously. His mouth, thank goodness, was firmly shut in a rather hurt little line. I slowly removed my fingers from my ears.

'No more, really, Sam,' I said in a shaky whisper. 'I – I don't want to know.'

'Well, I'm sorry, but you did ask, I was only trying to enlighten you,' he said in a wounded tone.

'And I'm most grateful, really I am, but if it's all right with you I think I'd rather be left in the dark as far as the rest of the evening's concerned. I'm quite sure my imagination can fill in the blanks, it's already boggling out of my earholes as it is.' I drained my wine glass, feeling rather faint. 'Oh Sam,' I whispered, 'you've no idea how awful this is.'

'Don't be ridiculous, Polly, it was wonderful!'

'No, but – you don't understand. I have to think of Nick.'

'Well of course, and I have to think of Sally, but what's done is done, it's no good wishing it had never happened. And look at it this way,' he went on brightly, 'if you can't remember a thing about it then you almost have a clear conscience, don't you? It's almost as if it never happened, practically puts you in the clear, doesn't it?'

'Practically,' I whispered, 'apart from one tiny detail.'

'What's that?'

I gulped. 'Nick knows.'

'What!'

I nodded dumbly. 'He knows.'

Sam's jaw dropped, his eyes grew wide with alarm. 'But – but how on earth did he find out?'

'I . . . told him.'

'You *told* him? Polly! What on earth were you thinking of?'

'Well,' I muttered, avoiding Sam's gaze, which was one of undiluted horror, 'he found out I wasn't at home that night. It was the night of the burglary, you see, and the police were round questioning us, and when they'd gone – well, it just all came out, I *had* to tell him. I suppose I thought he'd understand,' I said miserably. 'I thought he'd believe me when I said I couldn't remember what had happened but – he didn't. He was furious. He's left me actually,' I whispered, 'moved out. I'm on my own.'

Sam could hardly speak 'You told him?' he blustered eventually. 'You actually told him you spent the night with me? Did you say it was me?' he added quickly.

I nodded without looking up.

He shook his head in despair. 'Oh Polly, *Polly*, what were you *thinking* of?'

'I don't know!' I wailed. 'I know it sounds ridiculous, and obviously in retrospect – well *certainly* in retrospect, particularly now I've found out what happened – I wish I hadn't, but at the time I didn't even know I'd snogged you, for God's sake! Let alone wrestled you to the ground in a lift, got you chuffing round the bed like a steam engine and performed some sort of gruesome Fergie-meets-David-Mellor toe-job on you. I didn't have a clue! And I suppose I thought he'd think the best of me. But he didn't,' I went on in a small voice, 'he thought the worst, and obviously he was right.'

'Jesus,' muttered Sam.

I looked up earnestly. 'So the thing is, Sam, I want you to talk to him. Please, you've got to, it's the only thing that's going to get me out of this mess. You've got to swear nothing frisky happened, say I passed out or something and – and you just spent the night beside me making sure I was OK. You must,' I pleaded, 'don't you see? He's never going to forgive me and it's the only thing that'll save my marriage now. You're my last hope!'

Tears were springing into my eyes. I could feel them, hot and salty and swimming around at the bottom ready to fall. 'Please!' I begged. 'Please say you'll do it!'

Sam lit a cigarette. He shook his head slowly. 'Polly, you're asking the impossible, you really are. How can I possibly get involved? This is between you and Nick now. You've told him you spent the night with me, I can't just turn around and lie to him, pretend nothing happened. He'd never believe me, I'd feel a complete tosser. Anyway, you wouldn't lie to Sally if I asked you to, would you?'

'Oh yes!' I said eagerly. 'If you wanted me to I could do it easily, no problem at all, honestly, pop round if you like!'

Sam raised his eyebrows. 'Well, I'm sorry,' he said flatly, 'but it's just not my style. I can't tell a bare-faced lie just like that, I really can't.'

'But it's only a tiny little one,' I pleaded, 'a sort of off-white one, and anyway,' I went on angrily, 'this is no time to be moral, Sam, this is my sodding marriage we're talking about, damn you!'

He began to look huffy. 'There's no need to be like that, Polly.'

'Sorry, sorry,' I said quickly, realising this was no way to cajole him into anything. 'I'm just a bit desperate, that's all.'

'But – what on earth made you tell him in the first

place?' he said, looking mystified. 'I mean, what did you think he'd say, for heaven's sake? Oh never mind, Polly, don't let it happen again? Or – good for you, have one on me?'

'No,' I groaned, 'no, of course not.'

'Or perhaps you thought he'd imagine we just did a bit of innocent hand-holding? Read each other poetry in bed? Played a bit of Scrabble, perhaps? Hell's teeth, he's a *man*, Polly, he knows what goes on. Did you really think he'd give you the benefit of the doubt when you said you were pissed out of your mind and ended up in a hotel bedroom with another man? God, I'm surprised he's not coming after me.' He took a rather feverish drag on his cigarette.

'Well, I—'

'And as for roping me in on this . . .' He shook his head vigorously. 'He's a big chap, your Nick, he'll – he'll knock my teeth into my head, it'll be pistols at dawn, he'll—'

'Oh no, you don't have to see him,' I said quickly, 'just ring him up and explain nicely over the phone. You don't have to come within a hair's breadth of him, but you must understand, my life dep—'

'No, Polly,' he said firmly, cutting me short. 'I'm afraid I'm just not for it. I'm not getting involved and that's that.'

He helped himself to another glass of wine and downed it decisively. He looked rather cross and petulant now.

I stared at him, the tears ready to brim over. 'You mean . . . you won't do it?'

He sighed. 'Oh Polly, please' – he took my hand – 'don't do that, don't give me the emotional blackmail bit. I'm so fond of you, you know that, but I just can't do it.

As far as I'm concerned it happened, it was wonderful – beautiful even – and I'd dearly love for it to happen again. I'm not going to deny it, it makes it so – well, cheap.'

'It was,' I muttered softly.

'Sorry?'

'Nothing. Forget it, I'm sorry, we're obviously both coming at this from completely different angles. You see it as a night to remember and I see it as a night to – well . . . Never mind.'

A silence engulfed us. I stared at the tablecloth in a daze. A few minutes later a waiter materialised beside us.

'So sorry to have kept you waiting, there's been a slight delay in the kitchen,' he purred. 'Can I take your order?'

I don't think it had occurred to either of us that we'd sat there for about half an hour with diddly-squat to eat. Suddenly I didn't feel in the slightest bit hungry, in fact I felt positively sick at the thought, for emotional and biological reasons.

I shook my head. 'I've lost my appetite,' I muttered.

The waiter looked concerned. 'Is madam all right? Can I get you some water, perhaps?'

I looked up. He was a young chap, with a nice open face. He was worried, how sweet.

'No, I – I'm fine,' I faltered, trying to smile.

'Could you give us a moment?' asked Sam. 'You see, I'm not sure we're going to—'

'No, we're not,' I put in decisively, 'at least I'm not.'

'What, nothing at all?' asked Sam, in concern. 'Not even a quick spaghetti?' he suggested.

'Not even a quick anything,' I muttered between

347

clenched teeth. Then I remembered my manners. 'No thanks, Sam, I'm not really very hungry.'

'I'm sorry,' said Sam to the waiter, 'could I just pay for the wine?'

'Of course, I'll get the bill, sir.'

He took one last look at my pale face, then disappeared. I stared at the tablecloth. Sam shifted around uncomfortably. He cleared his throat and gave a nervous laugh.

'That suits me, actually, I've got so much to do at the office. You know what it's like when you've been away. My desk looks like bloody Snowdonia!'

I nodded dumbly. I couldn't speak.

He leaned over. 'Polly, don't hate me,' he mumbled. 'I'm sorry, but what more can I say? I simply don't want to get involved, you can't blame me for that, surely?'

I didn't look up. I shook my head. 'No . . .' I said slowly, 'I suppose not, but I just sort of thought . . . hoped really . . .'

The waiter came back with the bill. Sam quickly paid in cash and stood up. He helped me on with my jacket and we walked outside.

When we got on to the pavement, the light hit me. It was a beautiful day. I blinked hard against the sun and bit my lip, tears were imminent. Sam saw and took me in his arms. He hugged me close.

'I'm sorry I've caused you so much pain,' he muttered, 'it's the last thing in the world I wanted to do.'

A cab cruised past with its light on. I broke away from Sam's embrace and stuck my hand out to stop it. Suddenly I just wanted to get away. It screeched to a halt in front of us and I went to open the door and scramble in. I turned back as I was halfway inside. Sam was standing with his hands thrust in the pockets of his overcoat. He looked hurt, miserable.

'Sorry to rush off, Sam, but there's nothing more to say really, is there?'

He gave a rather bleak smile. 'It would appear not.'

'Um, can I give you a lift? I'm going to Harley – Oxford Street to do some shopping.'

'Well, you could drop me at Knightsbridge Tube if you could bear to sit next to me for another five minutes.' He grinned.

I managed to smile back. 'Don't be ridiculous, of course I could, get in.'

Must we prolong the agony? I thought miserably as he sat down next to me. I felt dumb with despair and I wanted to be alone. The cab pulled away. I was dimly aware that Sam was making a stab at polite conversation but I was unable to concentrate on a word. I stared out of the window as the shops flashed by in all their Knightsbridge glory. I'd lost Nick. Lost him. And it was all my fault. And much as I hated Sam for refusing to comply, it was crazy of me to blame him, I could see that. I looked up. His face was pale with tension, he was looking at me anxiously.

'Are you all right, Polly? I feel absolutely dreadful, really I do, but—'

'It's OK, Sam,' I said wearily, 'it's not your fault. Don't lose any sleep over it.'

We drove the rest of the way in silence. As we drew up at the Tube station he leaned across to kiss me. I think it would have landed on my lips but the cab lurched to a halt and he missed. We laughed nervously as he ended up somewhere round my ear. He smiled ruefully as he got out of the cab. I pulled down the window.

'Bye then, Polly,' he said. 'Don't think badly of me, I'll certainly always have wonderful memories of you.'

I cranked up a tepid smile. 'Bye, Sam.'

The cab pulled away. If only he knew, I thought bitterly, sinking back into the black leather upholstery, if only he knew I might be carrying his child, he wouldn't be so keen not to get involved then, would he? Oh no, he'd be on the blower to Nick before you could blink, denying all knowledge of our night of passion, disclaiming any sort of responsibility. Or would he? I gazed out of the window. Perhaps I was being too hard on him. After all, he'd wanted to carry on the relationship, perhaps he'd have wanted me big with child too? Who knows. But I wasn't about to find out.

The taxi lurched up to some lights, taking my delicate tummy with it. I breathed in hard through my nose and gulped back the bile. Thankfully, the moment passed and I sighed the sigh of the fated as we trundled north towards my next assignation, the third appointment on my fun-packed agenda. Oh yes, I was in for even more thrills and spills now, because what was my next blind date? A trip to the gynaecologist. As Cilla would say, what a lorra fun that was going to be. I groaned.

'Whereabouts in Oxford Street, love?' yelled the driver, cocking his ear at the glass partition.

'Actually I want Harley Street – hang on, I'll give you the number.'

I reached down to the floor for my bag and it was then that I saw the case. A silver, typically posey, film director's attaché. Oh no, he'd left his case behind! I looked around wildly, almost as if to catch him and fling it out of the window, but of course he was long gone. I leaned back in despair. Christ, now I'd have to *get* it to him somehow, have to bloody *see* him again. I bashed my head hard against the headrest.

'Aaaaargh!'

'Sorry, love? What number was that?'

'Oh, hang on.' I rummaged around for the bit of paper. 'Seventy-two,' I yelled.

I gazed out of the window and it was with a profound sense of relief that it dawned on me. No, I didn't have to see him at all, all I had to do was give the blasted thing to Pippa, who could take it with her to the office in the morning. Phew. Well, thank heaven for small – and we're talking minuscule here – mercies. I sighed as the taxi headed north.

Chapter Twenty

Having skipped lunch I was of course far too early for my appointment with Mr Taylor. I walked aimlessly up and down Harley Street, sat waifishly on doorsteps and eventually trudged dejectedly into number 72 with still about half an hour to spare.

To my surprise the receptionist informed me with a bright, white smile that it was in fact my lucky day. And I'd had no idea! There was I thinking that this was the day to contemplate suicide in more than just a half-hearted fashion, when all the time my luck was in. I questioned her further and it transpired that Mr Taylor was running at least twenty minutes early so I only had about five minutes to kill. Ah. I went gloomily into the oak-panelled waiting room and, as it turned out, killed time quite fittingly by sticking imaginary pins into the only other patient in the room.

The girl in question was about my age and luminous with pregnancy. She had pretty blonde curls, a contented, Madonna-like smile on her rosy-cheeked face and was wearing a terribly twee maternity smock, strewn with daisy chains. Every so often she'd stroke her swollen tummy protectively, giving me the benefit of not just a wedding ring and an engagement ring but a serious whopper of an eternity ring too.

I stared at her, sick with jealousy. That should have been *me* over there, happily pregnant with a loving husband to go home to, hand heavy with rocks. She looked across and smiled. A nice, comradely, we're-both-in-this-together smile. Now, under normal circumstances I'd have been over there like a shot – comparing morning-sickness bouts, asking her the best place to buy outsized bras, enquiring about the likelihood of piles – but as it was I could only twist my face into what I hoped was a smile but was probably more of a homicidal grimace, make sure my own rings – albeit smaller and fewer – were well on display too and bury my head firmly in *Country Life*. I caught her look of disappointment as the chance of a cosy mother-to-be chat proved not-to-be. God. When did I get to be so mean and twisted?

I flicked miserably through the vast houses for sale at the front of the magazine, remembering how I used to pore over them, salivating with longing, dreaming of living in just such a pile. Of course, now I did, but for how much longer? How much longer would it be before Nick decided he could quite easily live without a cheating, scheming, conniving little hussy and sue for divorce on the grounds of adultery?

Once he discovered I was pregnant of course, that's how long. Nick was no fool, he'd know the baby was Sam's. I mean, let's face it, two years of bonking for Britain with my husband had resulted in absolutely zilch in the way of a bun in the Aga, but one night of steaming sex with a fabulously fertile film director and *wham*! Here I was, up the duff without a paddle and down at the gynie clinic before you could say knife. Knife! I jumped. No. No way. No way was I losing this baby, not while there was still a chance, however remote, that it might be Nick's.

Out of the corner of my eye I spotted a white coat gliding silently towards me. It stopped beside me.

'Mr Taylor will see you now,' murmured a discreet female voice in my ear.

'Thank you,' I muttered nervously.

I got up too quickly and sent at least three magazines flying. As I bent down to pick them up, my bag slipped off my shoulder on to the floor. It flew open and various odds and ends spilled out, including a witty paperback Pippa had lent me to cheer me up, entitled *101 Ways To Have an Orgasm*. I flushed, hurriedly shoved everything back in, straightened up, and as I swung the bag back on to my shoulder again, caught White Coat full in the stomach with it.

'Oof,' she groaned, but faintly and decorously.

'Sorry,' I muttered, puce now.

'Take your time,' she murmured, with enviable composure.

I hid my flushing face and scampered after her as she silently glided away again. As I hurried up the stairs behind her I noticed a ladies' loo on the landing.

'Just popping in here for a moment,' I mumbled.

She nodded politely and I scurried in, principally because it had suddenly occurred to me that I might reek of booze. I'd only had a couple of glasses but judging by the innocent demeanour of Daisy Chain downstairs that was a couple more than the mighty Mr Taylor was used to smelling on his patients' breath, and I did, after all, want to create a good impression.

I rummaged around in my bag, found my Gold Spot and

had a good squirt, tugged down my rather too short skirt – what on earth had possessed me to wear it? – and was about to leave when I realised I was so nervous I had to have a quick pee. I rushed into a cubicle, sat down, but – oh hell, there was no loo paper. I rummaged around furiously at the bottom of my bag, aware that white coat was tapping her foot impatiently outside, but also aware that I *had* to have some loo paper, I was having an examination for God's sake. Fortunately, right at the bottom of my bag I found a grotty rolled-up ball of tissue with bits of fluff and gunge stuck to it. It looked as if it had been there for a hundred years. I hurriedly used it and scurried out again.

White Coat was well on her way up to the next landing. 'Mrs Penhalligan to see you, Mr Taylor,' she announced, opening a door.

Blimey, hang on, I thought, bounding after her two at a time. I quickly scuttled past her into the room. She shut the door behind me and I stood there, panting and flustered, not quite making the entrance I'd envisaged.

The room was large and light with a high, heavily corniced ceiling and gracious french windows leading on to a balcony which overlooked the street. Mr Taylor was sitting with his back to the windows behind an enormous leather-topped desk. He stood up and stuck out his hand and I was almost blinded by the simultaneous flash of teeth, cuff links, gold watch, tie pin and silk accessories.

He was indeed a dead ringer for Peter Bowles, and my God was he dapper. His black, military-style moustache gleamed with good health – even Brylcreem perhaps – his immaculate, but slightly too loud pinstriped suit looked fresh from Savile Row, and his yellow silk tie matched his yellow silk handkerchief which I had no doubt matched his yellow silk underpants.

'Mrs Penhalligan,' he beamed, 'delighted . . . do, please,' he purred, indicating for me to sit opposite him.

I sat down nervously, still puffing and blowing a bit, and watched as he rearranged himself in his chair, pulling up his trouser legs before he lowered his bottom, flicking his arms out to push up his sleeves and then adjusting his cuffs so that j-u-s-t the right amount of shirt protruded. Thus arranged, he folded his arms neatly on his desk and leaned forward, brown eyes twinkling.

'So,' he purred smoothly, 'what can I do for you this sunny afternoon?'

I gulped. Bugger. Bugger, bugger, bugger. This was a big mistake, why had I let Pippa talk me into this? Why hadn't I gone to some tweedy old professor who would have listened sympathetically to my tale of woe, patted my hand reassuringly and assured me all would be well, instead of this obvious ladykiller in the flashy suit? How was I supposed to unburden myself to *him*, for heaven's sake? I mean, it shouldn't be allowed, he was a *gynaecologist*, for crying out loud, he was going to – well, you know. And look at those eyes. Twinkling away all come-hitherishly – it was obscene. Not that he was my type, of course, not at all, but still, he had a certain raffish charm and one simply didn't *want* to be charmed, however raffishly, when one's legs were sticking out at undignified angles. One wanted to be as detached as possible from the whole ghastly business – plan one's dinner party, rearrange the furniture, contemplate one's summer wardrobe – that kind of thing.

'Er . . . Mrs Penhalligan?' His expensively coiffured head was cocked enquiringly to one side. 'Are you with me?'

Shit. I crossed my legs in what I hoped was a rather businesslike manner and cleared my throat.

'Yes. Well, the thing is, Mr Taylor, I appear to be pregnant.' Good start, Polly, tell it like it is.

He beamed across at me. 'Excellent, excellent, that's the sort of thing we like to hear in this surgery. That's what we're here for!'

We? I looked around nervously, wondering if more Peter Bowles look-alikes were suddenly going to spring out from behind the furniture.

'Pleased, are you?' he enquired, still beaming. 'Feeling pretty chuffed? Rightly so, rightly so!'

God, he was jolly.

'Er, yes, sort of, but—'

'Jolly good, jolly good! Takes a bit of getting used to, of course, but it's a big event in anyone's life. Husband pleased?'

'Well—'

'Excellent, excellent.' He nodded, and started scribbling away on a pad. He paused, and looked up, pen and eyebrows raised. 'Done a test?'

'Sorry?'

'Pregnancy test, done one yet?'

'Oh, yes – yes I have, actually.'

'Good, when was that?'

'Um, yesterday.'

'Remember which one?'

We were well into clipped, ex-army, staccato speak now, and by God it was catching.

'Don't actually, went blue, though, 'bout thirty seconds.'

'Splendid, splendid.' He scribbled furiously then beamed up again.

'Now. Last period, Mrs Penhalligan. Any idea? Got a date? Got a clue?'

'Have actually, wrote it in my diary, April the twenty-sixth.'

'April twenty-sixth!' he exclaimed as if it was some kind of magical date. 'Marvellous! Now, if you'll just bear with me while I have a little ... look ...' He picked up a chart and ran a finger down a line of dates. 'That'll be ... yes! Baby due February third, tremendous!' he declared joyfully. God, anyone would think it was his.

'Third all right?' he enquired.

'Er, yes, fine.' What did he expect me to say? No, actually, I'm having my roots done?

'Good.' He threw the chart in a drawer and shut it with a flourish. 'Now.' He folded his arms and leaned across the desk with a smile. 'How's Mum? Feel OK? No sickness? No gippy tummy?'

'Um, a bit, in the mornings – oh, and evenings sometimes.'

He compressed his lips and nodded, scribbling furiously. 'Only to be expected, dry biscuits, sips of water, don't get up too quickly, soon pass. Four months max. Anything else? Aches and pains?'

'N-no, but—'

'Good, excellent, Charlotte's all right?'

I looked at him in bewilderment. Who the devil was Charlotte and how the hell was I supposed to know how she was?

'Sorry?'

'Queen Charlotte's all right? Got to have it somewhere!'

'Oh! Y-yes, fine.'

'Good, good, book you in then. Now.' He held up his

359

hand and proceeded to tick off on his fingers what were clearly key points. 'No smoking, no drinking – within reason, of course.' He winked. 'Couple of glasses of wine now and then won't hurt you – but no illegal substances, eh? Ha ha! Lots of fresh fruit and veg but go easy on the soft cheese, other than that, life goes on as normal, OK? So! There we are. All seems to be present and correct, Mrs Penhalligan, see you again in six weeks' time!' He beamed, stood up and stuck out his hand. Jesus.

'Th-that's it?' I asked incredulously.

He looked puzzled. 'Sorry?'

'That's it? You're not going to examine me or anything?'

He shuffled his papers busily, shaking his head. 'No, no real need, if your period's late and you've had a positive result from a test, well, Bob's your uncle generally.' He looked up abruptly. 'Unless of course you'd like me to examine you? Feel more reassured, perhaps? Some women do?'

'Well, I—'

'Fine! Fine! No problem, hop up over there in that case.' He indicated a bed with a curtain half drawn around it in the corner. 'No problem at all, let's have a quick look at you.'

Hop up? A quick look? God, this chap was like greased lightning, no wonder he was running early, he only allotted twenty seconds to each patient and then no doubt charged like a wounded rhino. This little interview had probably cost me well over a hundred pounds already, just for telling me what I already knew.

Nevertheless, his alacrity was infectious. He'd really got me going now. I flew behind the curtain, ripped my skirt, tights and pants off in one untidy bundle, threw them on the floor and in double-quick time jumped up and hit the deck, ready for action, so to speak. The curtain swept aside.

'Now...' he murmured, and went to a little table to peruse his instruments.

I gulped and shut my eyes, preparing to think of England and hoping to God I wouldn't fart at a crucial moment. I went into my usual gynie-visit deep-breathing exercises and was well on the way to feeling reasonably relaxed, when all of a sudden I had a thought. I opened my eyes. Hang on a minute – this was absurd, I had to tell him why I was here! There were specific things I needed to know, this was no routine check-up and I had to tell him so before he was telling me to hop back down again and it was too late!

'Wait!' I sat bolt upright.

He was poised for action beside me, jacket off, Marigolds on, an instrument of torture poised in his rubber-gloved hand. His eyebrows shot into his hairline. This man was a consummate eyebrow-raiser.

'Sorry?'

I swung my legs over the side of the bed.

'Just wait a minute, please, you're going so fast I can hardly think. You see, there was a specific reason why I came to see you today, not just to confirm my pregnancy but to ask you a very important question.'

'Oh?'

'Yes, only you haven't let me get a word in edgeways!'

He looked abashed and lowered his tool. 'Gosh. So sorry, Mrs Penhalligan, so used to this first visit being purely routine – do go on, I do apologise.'

'Yes, well, thank you,' I said in a peeved tone, rather milking this moment of moral superiority. It was, after all, the only one I was going to get. I cleared my throat.

'The thing is, I need to know something about the baby.'

'Y-e-s,' he folded his arms and nodded slowly and carefully, 'and what is it exactly you need to know? I'm sure it's absolutely fine, by the way, nothing to worry about at all.'

'No, it's not that, it's – well . . .' I bit my lip and shifted around from one cold buttock to the other on the hard bed, staring down at my toes. I looked up. 'It's about the father.'

'The father? Oh! Oh goodness me, yes, father's are always welcome. Consultations, examinations, scans – oh yes, no problem there, do bring the father.' He beamed and picked up his instrument again. 'Shall we go on?'

'Er, no, no, it's not about bringing the father, it's about . . . knowing who the father is.'

He frowned. 'Rather lost me there, Mrs Penhalligan – I know the father, do I? Is that it? Penhalligan, Penhalligan – army chap, was he? Blues and Royals?'

'N-no, you don't know him,' I licked my incredibly dry lips, 'it's more to do with the fact that – I don't know him.'

He shook his head, bewildered. 'Really losing me completely now, I'm afraid, Mrs P' – heavens, he was even abbreviating my name now – 'you're surely not telling me – no. No, of course not, do excuse me.'

'What? What were you going to say?' I pounced eagerly. Please God let him be the one to say it rather than me.

He nervously smoothed down his moustache and looked embarrassed.

'I – I was going to say . . . surely you're not saying you don't know who the father is?'

'That's it! That's it exactly!'

He stared at me incredulously. 'What . . . not at all?'

I met his eyes and felt myself flushing scarlet with shame. I quickly looked down. My toenails, appropriately enough, were crimson too.

'Well, I've narrowed it down to two,' I whispered.

'Good lord.' He whistled. 'Yes, I see. Yes, quite a predicament. Quite, um, distressing.' He pursed his lips and frowned, looking hugely embarrassed. 'Dear me, yes, and – well, extraordinary,' he murmured, 'you don't seem . . . anyway.'

I looked up quickly. He was fiddling with his cuff links.

'Don't seem what?' I demanded. 'Don't seem the type? Don't seem like the sort of girl who sleeps around and doesn't know who the father of her child is?' My voice rose hysterically. 'Well, I'm not, Mr Taylor, I'm not! I'll have you know this was a totally uncharacteristic and unprecedented departure from the straight and narrow path I usually stick to, a one-in-a-million drunken encounter with a good-for-nothing bastard who I'm quite convinced took complete advantage of me. I don't love him and he doesn't love me and I hope to goodness this is my husband's child and not his and – oh God, this is all so awful!' I covered my face with my hands and burst into tears.

Within a twinkling a blue and white striped Gieves and Hawkes arm had whizzed around my shoulders and a yellow silk hanky was thrust into my hands.

'There, there, it's all going to be fine,' he murmured, 'you'll see, these things always sort themselves out, it'll be fine.'

Ah, there they were at last, the magic, comforting words they obviously all learn at medical school but are so bloody economical with. What had taken him so long? So soothing, yet so tear-provoking too.

'Oooh, no it *won't*!' I blubbed into the glorious silk hanky which I felt sure had never in its life been used for practical purposes. 'It's such a mess! What on earth am I going to *do*?'

A fresh flood followed this outburst, plus more reassuring shoulder-hugging from Peter Bowles. I sobbed and sniffled into his hanky and all the time I was breaking down part of me couldn't quite believe I was doing it. Heavens, Polly, in front of a suave Harley Street consultant? All over his immaculate pinstripe? Naked from the waist down? – me, not him, of course. But it was no good. The floodgates had never officially been opened on this subject, but now that they were it was damned hard to shut them again.

Eventually, though, the tears subsided enough for me to at least be able to see and the sobs became mere gasps and hiccups. Peter Bowles patted my hand.

'Now you just sit there quietly for a second and I'll be back in just a mo with a nice cuppa tea.'

He disappeared and I tried desperately to get a grip on myself. I blew my nose, wiped my eyes and shoved my hair behind my ears, attempting at least to look a little more presentable, but it was jolly difficult to look even remotely dignified sitting there as I was without my skirt on and with just my T-shirt protecting my vitals. I pulled it down, frantically trying to cover my thighs which are only fit to be seen in the dark and then only fleetingly. I spotted a handy blanket at the end of the bed and hurriedly pulled it across them. By the time Peter Bowles returned bearing hot, sweet tea, I had at least gained some sort of control and composure.

'Thank you,' I whispered, taking the cup and saucer from him and sipping thirstily.

'Now then,' he said kindly, perching beside me on the bed, 'what are we going to do about all this, eh?'

I shook my head. 'I don't know,' I whispered, 'I really don't.'

'Do you want to keep the baby?'

'Oh yes, yes I want to keep it – at least, I'm pretty sure I do. When you've told me who it belongs to I'll know for sure, of course.'

He frowned. 'Sorry?'

'Well, you can do that, can't you? Take a blood test or something? My husband's AB negative which is pretty rare, so if we took some blood from the baby and it turned out to be the same, well, that would be terrific, wouldn't it? Then we'd be almost sure it was his.'

Peter Bowles pursed his lips and looked at the floor. Then he folded his arms and turned to look at me.

'Mrs Penhalligan,' he said gently, 'there is absolutely no way of knowing who the father of your child is before it's born.'

I stared at him, aghast.

'What?' I whispered. 'No way of knowing? But there must be!'

He shook his head. ''Fraid not.'

'But – but what about all those tests you do – amniocen-whatsit and – and all those blood tests and things?'

'Amniocentesis is about extracting fluid, not blood. It tells us if the baby has Down's syndrome and it can also tell us the sex of the child. The blood tests we do are samples of *your* blood, not the baby's, to check for other abnor-malities. There isn't one test that is actually done on the baby itself, it would be too dangerous, you see, and we certainly wouldn't attempt anything simply to find out who the father is.'

'So ... what you're telling me is ... there's no way of knowing?' I stared at him in horror.

'No way at all, I'm afraid. The only thing we can do is try to work out the date of conception. Did you sleep with both men in the middle of your cycle?'

I cringed deeply. Must he be so basic? I supposed he must. 'Yes,' I whispered.

'Within weeks or days of each other?'

I clenched my toes and squirmed. 'Days,' I breathed, 'possibly two days, I think.' Oh God, please let me die now. I dared not look but I knew the eyebrows were well raised.

'Hmmmmm...' he murmured, 'in that case I'm afraid there really is no way of knowing.'

I think I must have looked awfully shaken, because he squeezed my hand.

'Sorry,' he said gently. 'What I suggest you do is make a decision as soon as possible as to whether or not you want to keep the baby. The sooner you make that decision the better it is all round, for you and the foetus. You do see that, don't you?'

I nodded, not trusting myself to speak. Suddenly the baby had become a foetus.

'And if it's all right with you,' he went on, standing up, 'I think I'd still like to make that examination, just to make absolutely sure. Is that OK?' he asked gently, his brisk army manner totally evaporated now.

'Yes, of course, Mr Bowles,' I whispered.

He frowned. 'Taylor, actually.'

'I – I mean Taylor.'

I took the blanket off my thighs, swung my legs back on to the bed again and lay down, dumb with disbelief. No way of knowing? No way at all? What on earth was I going to do?

Peter Bowles put his Marigolds on again and I lay there, staring blankly at the elaborate plaster cornicing on the ceiling. God, what a mess. I sighed. Well, at least I had plenty to think about as he went about his business, I had enough problems to fill an entire woman's magazine. What must he think of me?

I swivelled my head slightly to the left and took a sneaky look at his face. Inscrutable, of course. Another thing they all learn at medical school. How to make a gynaecological examination without betraying the slightest trace of emotion. But, suddenly, he frowned. He seemed to take a closer look, then he reached behind him to a little table and picked up what looked like ... a pair of tweezers. Tweezers! What the hell were they for? I raised my head slightly from the bed and watched, fascinated, as he used them to remove something ... from within my person. Heavens! From inside? Surely not. What the hell was it? Had something fallen out? Had the *baby* fallen out? He turned away, tweezers in hand, and, still frowning, gingerly dropped whatever it was ... in the waste-paper bin. Bloody hell, in the *bin*? What *was* it?

'Um, wh-what was that?' I ventured querulously.

He shook his head, lips pursed. 'Noo ... nothing, nothing at all.'

'No, really, I'd like to know, what was it?'

'Nothing of any consequence, nothing to worry about.' He resumed his examination.

I stared at him, incredulous. Nothing of any conse-quence? He removes something from *inside* me, chucks it in the bin and says it's nothing of any consequence? Jesus!

He straightened up and slipped his gloves off in a businesslike manner.

'All finished, Mrs Penhalligan, and yes, you are most definitely pregnant, cervix very swollen. If you'd like to pop your clothes back on I'll just go and write a few notes. Take your time.'

He slipped around the curtain, drew it back again for me, and disappeared to his desk.

I sat up, slipped off the bed and grabbed my clothes, hurriedly tugging them back on. Then I cocked an ear to the curtain to make sure he wasn't coming back, and tiptoed over to the bin in the corner.

I peered in. It was empty. How extraordinary, empty, except for – wait a minute, a small piece of paper at the bottom. I reached in and picked it out. I turned it over in my hand and stared at it. It was a Green Shield stamp. I frowned, completely foxed. A Green Shield stamp? Up my whatsit? Surely not. Suddenly I went cold. My jaw dropped. I clapped my hand to my mouth. Oh good grief! It must have been stuck to the tissue! The grotty one I'd found at the bottom of my handbag, it must have been stuck to it along with all the other bits of fluff and gunge, probably been there for centuries! Oh God, fancy having a Green Shield stamp up my – what must he think?

I swept the curtain aside and hurried to his desk.

'Mr Taylor, I—'

'Won't keep you a moment...' he purred, cutting me short. His dark head was bent low, he was writing studiously. I bit my lip. What did it say? What was he writing? I craned my neck but I couldn't see. I could imagine, though. 'Doesn't ... know ... who ... the ... father ... of the ... child ... is ... and keeps Green ... Shield ... stamps—' I couldn't bear it.

'L-look, Mr Taylor, about the stamp, you see the thing is, there wasn't any loo paper downstairs so I used an old tissue at the bottom of my handbag and – and I think it must have—'

'No need, Mrs Penhalligan,' he said, shaking his head vehemently, still writing away, 'no need at all, really.'

'No, but—'

'Now then.' He looked up abruptly and gave me a bright smile. 'I'd like to see you again in about another six weeks just to make sure everything's going smoothly, so let's see now, that would be . . .' He consulted his diary.

'But I really would like to explain about the—'

'July the sixteenth. That suit?'

He didn't want to know. He simply didn't want to know, did he? And who could blame him? Wasn't it enough of a shock to an eminent gynaecologist to have a patient who didn't know who the father of her child was without wishing to know why she should feel the need to secrete ancient voucher stamps so snugly about her person? And why did it have to be Green Shield? So naff, so common, so very un-Harley Street?

I bit my lip and stared at my shoes, suffused with shame. Peter Bowles neatly recapped his pen and arranged it, just so, above his papers. He flicked out his arms, realigned his cuffs, folded his arms and smiled in a most professional way.

'Y-e-s, well, that seems to be all for the moment, Mrs Penhalligan. I'll see you again on the sixteenth and, if I don't hear anything to the contrary, I'll book you into Queen Charlotte's, OK? I do hope everything sorts itself out. I'm quite sure – well, I'm quite sure you'll soon come to terms with your rather, ahem, unusual situation.' He coughed nervously. 'Now, any questions? Good, good,' he said, getting smartly to his feet and thus forestalling any other horrendous enquiries I might have. He stuck his hand out. 'Look forward to seeing you on the sixteenth then. Goodbye!'

His smile was kind, but I couldn't meet it. I stared red-faced at his leather-topped desk, like an errant child in a headmaster's study. I nodded and extended my hand, hoping he'd make contact with it without me having to look up. He did.

'Thank you so much,' I whispered when he'd released it, 'see you on the sixteenth.'

I picked up my bag and Sam's case, turned around, and shuffled miserably from the room.

Chapter Twenty-one

That evening I was ambushed by a premature attack of morning sickness. I lay on Pippa's sofa with a bucket poised on the carpet beneath me, feeling incredibly sorry for myself. Pippa was on the floor beside me in her dressing gown, painting her toenails with meticulous attention. I watched as her brushstrokes swept slowly up and down.

'Remind me never to take medical advice from you again, Pippa,' I muttered bitterly, 'not even if I'm dying. I'll arrange my own doctors from now on, thanks very much. Incidentally, could you give that a rest for a sec? The fumes are going right up my nose.'

'Nearly finished,' said Pippa, hastily applying a few final strokes. She screwed the top on the varnish and sat up. 'Well, I'm sorry, I was only trying to help, and so what if he is charming? It's better than having some repulsive old toad examine you, isn't it?'

'No, it isn't, give me a repulsive old toad any day, at least it doesn't matter if you make a complete fool of yourself.'

I tried not to gag as she waved her feet in the air to dry them and I got another noxious whiff.

'And if you must do that I'd move away from the bucket if I were you,' I whispered. 'I'm not sure how good my aim is.'

Pippa got up hurriedly and plumped down in an armchair opposite. She stretched her legs out and surveyed her sparkling red toes.

'I must admit old Taylor is rather yummy, just my type now that I'm into older men. Did he mention me at all? Ask how my blood pressure was or anything? It always seems to rocket when I visit him.'

'No, he didn't,' I snapped, 'we had enough to talk about without getting on to your very minor problems, it wasn't even as if he could solve mine!'

Pippa frowned. 'Yes, I must say that does seem a bit rum. I mean, if they can do all that amazing *in vitro* stuff you'd think they could sort out a tiny technicality like who the father of your child is, wouldn't you?'

'I have an idea one is supposed to have an inkling oneself, at least that's the impression he gave me,' I said grimly. 'God, what's that revolting smell?'

'It's a packet of crisps, Polly,' she said patiently. 'Can't I even eat a packet of crisps in my own home?'

'Not when they smell like rotting armpits you can't, please put them away, Pippa, unless you want a technicolour carpet.' I clutched my mouth dramatically and rolled my eyes.

She sighed and screwed the top of the bag shut. 'It's all very well but I'm really hungry, you know. I haven't had supper yet because you can't stand the smell of baked beans, I can't paint my nails, I can't fry sausages—'

'Don't even mention sausages,' I whispered, gulping back the bile.

'But I thought this sickness lark was supposed to be restricted to mornings. How come you get it in the evenings too?'

'I don't know, Pippa,' I groaned, resting my head on the arm of the sofa, 'and I'm sorry, really I am. I know it's frightfully inconvenient of me and I apologise for feeling so lousy, so sick, so tired, so permanently nauseous, so tummy-churningly wretched. It must be awful for you.'

'Oh, it's OK,' said Pippa cheerily, lighting a cigarette and somehow missing my shovel-load of sarcasm, 'I don't really mind. It might be nice to open the fridge door now and then without you collapsing in a heap and shrieking for the smelling salts though. D'you think it would be all right if I did it now? You're not going to smell the salami long-distance, are you, only if I don't make myself a sandwich soon I'll expire.'

'No, no,' I muttered, 'you go and stuff your face, see if I care.'

'D'you want anything?'

'You could bring me a dry biscuit to nibble on, I might just be able to manage that. If it's not too much trouble, of course.'

'No trouble at all!'

She got up with an alacrity that made me wince and bounded off to the kitchen. I groaned and shut my eyes. A few minutes later she was back with a plate piled high with dead meat. She sidled guiltily past, tossing me a biscuit as she went.

'All right if I eat in here?' she asked, ostentatiously scraping her chair right back. 'I mean, right in the corner, practically in the garden?'

'Sure, sure, just don't be surprised if I honk, that's all.'

I moaned low and half closed my eyes. Pippa regarded me thoughtfully as she munched her salami sandwich. Suddenly she put her plate down.

'Can I have a feel?'

'What?'

'Your tummy, can I feel it?' She jumped up and knelt down beside me, pulling up my jumper.

'Pippa, for goodness sake, I'm only a few weeks pregnant, you're not going to feel anything!'

'Even so . . .' She put her hand on my tummy. 'Weird, isn't it,' she said after a moment, 'to think there's something in there. How does it feel? D'you feel different? I mean, apart from sick, d'you feel like you're carrying a baby?'

Suddenly I felt rather important. I sat up and adopted a slightly superior tone. 'Well, yes, I suppose one does feel a bit special, rather – you know, chosen.'

'Chosen? God, anyone would think you were the Virgin Mary!'

'Hardly,' I said grimly, 'but all the same, yes, I do feel incredibly blessed.' I smiled serenely and stroked my tummy like the girl in the waiting room had, trying hard to re-create the Madonna look.

'Is that why you're looking so gormless?' Pippa kneaded around with her hand looking for action. 'Is it kicking yet? Can you feel it?'

'No, of course not,' I snapped, dispensing with the blessed look, 'it's only about the size of a pea, for goodness sake – ouch, geddoff, that hurt! In fact,' I reflected, 'that's how I like to think of it at the moment.'

'What, as a pea?'

'Well, some sort of vegetable, not a baby at any rate, not until I know more about it. A little potato perhaps, or a carrot.'

'Gosh, it would be a bit disappointing to give birth to an

eight-pound carrot, wouldn't it? Imagine lugging it around for nine months thinking it was a baby then out pops a carrot.'

'It would come out pretty easily though, wouldn't it? Just the right shape!' We giggled.

Suddenly I frowned and pulled my jumper down. 'And that's another thing, Pippa, this giving birth lark. I'm not at all sure about it.'

She sat back on her heels. 'What d'you mean?'

'Well, I'm not very good at pain, as a matter of fact I've got an extremely low threshold, some people have, you know.'

'Oh, it'll be a breeze, don't worry about it. All you need is the right birthing partner to spur you on, keep your pecker up.'

'What the hell's a birthing partner?'

'Oh, it's someone who sprays you with water and warms your feet up and brings along sandwiches – oh, and plays soothing music, that kind of thing.'

I frowned. 'Music? What, on a guitar or something?'

'No, idiot, on a tape recorder, unless you particularly want a live guitarist. I'm sure it can be arranged.'

'So who is this person?' I felt none the wiser and had visions of a Cat Stephens look-alike droning away on a guitar in the corner of my delivery room, occasionally pausing to eat a sandwich, fiddle with my feet or spray me with water.

Pippa looked a bit uncomfortable. 'Er, well, actually it's your husband, but of course in your rather unusual situation . . .'

I sat bolt upright. 'Oh help! You mean I haven't got a birthing partner? You're right! I can't have Nick and I certainly don't want Sam – oh Pippa, what am I going to do, I can't possibly have this baby on my own!'

'Well, don't panic, I'm pretty sure it doesn't necessarily have to be your husband, I'm sure it could be – I know!' Suddenly her eyes shone dangerously. 'It could be me!'

'Er, well, Pippa, I'm not sure if—'

'Yes! Of course, I'd be brilliant...' She was gazing rapturously into space now and I could tell she'd already got herself kitted out in the Florence Nightingale garb and was mopping my fevered brow yelling 'PUSH! PUSH!' at the same time as maintaining feverish eye contact with the dreamy white-coated doctor in charge.

'Yes, well, we'll see shall we, Pippa?' I said a trifle nervously. 'Actually I wondered if I might try the whole thing unconscious, some people do do that, don't they?'

Pippa frowned. 'I think if you have a Caesarean it's possible, but I'm pretty sure you're only allowed one of those if your pelvis is too small to squeeze the baby out, and I hardly think, Polly,' she looked doubtfully at my distinctly child-bearing hips, 'you'd qualify on that score.'

I sighed. 'Oh well, that's out then, I'll just have to rely on pain relief. They have all sorts of knock-out drops these days, don't they?'

'Oh yes, they'll toss you the occasional aspirin as you writhe around in agony.'

'Aspirin!' I gasped.

'No, idiot, you can have an epidural, it paralyses you from the neck down.'

My eyes grew wide with fear.

'Oh, not permanently, at least not in most cases, although my sister knew someone who—'

'Thank you, Pippa,' I said quickly, 'I'd rather not know.'

'Oh, it's perfectly safe as long as it's put in by a competent anaesthetist, and as long as they can get it *in* in time, of course.'

'What d'you mean?'

'Well, you might not make it to the hospital, you might drop the baby in the back of the car, or on the bus or—'

'Oh thanks, really dignified.'

'Well, don't you remember Jane Hutchinson's sister? Hers popped out in Sainsbury's car park! Luckily the car-park attendant had done a St John's Ambulance course so he had a vague idea and managed to sort of pull it out, but God,' she rolled her eyes dramatically, 'she'd have been snookered if it hadn't been for him.'

'Oh terrific, so if I get some oily car-park attendant officiating at what should be the most poignant and moving moment in my life I should count my blessings, is that it?'

'Well, you have to be prepared for all eventualities,' said Pippa sagely. 'I mean, what about Kate Rawlinson?'

'What about Kate Rawlinson?' I said warily. I had the impression Pippa was getting a vicarious kick out of dredging up these horror stories. 'Had hers in a public loo, did she? With the lavatory attendant as her birth partner?'

'Oh no, she was in hospital, but she wasn't on the labour ward because they thought she wasn't going to have it for ages and it was only when a passing doctor stuck his hand up to check everything was OK that he discovered the baby was on its way and the cord was wrapped around its neck!'

'Is that good?'

'Of course not, you idiot, it could strangle itself! No, it was awful, but luckily the doctor managed to slip his fingers under the cord to stop it getting any tighter, but then they had to somehow get her to the labour room which was two floors down!' Pippa's eyes were shining now as she relived the horror. She leaned forward. 'So guess what?'

'What?' I muttered nervously.

'Well, the doctor had to keep his hand right up – literally elbow deep – and they pushed her into the lift with him still attached and then when they got out they had to run really fast down loads of corridors, and she was bouncing around all over the place and this doctor *still* had his hand right—'

'Thank you, Pippa, that will DO!' I screeched with my hands over my ears. 'I simply don't want to *know* about any more nightmare deliveries if it's all right with you, I mean *we're* here for God's sake, our mothers must have done it, there must be some women who have these things without a hitch, mustn't there?'

Pippa pursed her lips and gave this some thought. Eventually she shook her head. 'Not to my knowledge, Polly.'

I sighed. 'Oh well, I'll manage somehow I suppose.'

I sank back on the sofa and had just about rested my head when the phone rang, making me jump. It was right by my ear but I simply didn't have the energy to swing around and get it. Pippa reached over and picked it up.

'Hello? . . . Oh hi! . . . Yes, she is, hang on a minute.' She clamped her hand over the mouthpiece and grinned. 'It's the father of your unborn child!'

I ground my teeth together. 'Which one?' I hissed.

'The married one!' Her grin was getting bigger.

'Pippa . . .' I eyed her dangerously.

'OK, sorry, it's Sam.'

I glared at her as I took the receiver, hauling myself over

on to my tummy and up on to my elbows. I felt like I had a sack of potatoes on my head.

'Hello?' I said weakly. Surely we'd said all we had to say?

'Hello, Polly?' He sounded anxious. 'Listen, you haven't by any chance got my case, have you, only I think I left it in the taxi.'

'You did, and I have. It's right here actually.' I eyed the fiercely trendy silver case sitting under the table next to my legs and aimed a vicious little kick at it.

'Oh, thank goodness for that, what a relief, I thought I'd lost it! Thanks for picking it up, could you possibly ask Pippa to bring it in with her tomorrow?'

'Sure, I was going to do that anyway.'

'Great, thanks so much. Oh, and Polly,' he lowered his voice slightly, 'listen, there's some pretty confidential stuff in there regarding the company, so if you could give it to Pippa in the morning when she leaves, rather than now, I'd be grateful, only I don't really want her to, well—'

'To look? Sam, as if she would!'

'No, no, of course not, silly of me even to mention it, but you know what it's like, some people like to snoop a bit, not Pippa, of course, but – well, you know!' He laughed nervously. 'Thanks, Polly . . .'

'Not at all, goodbye, Sam,' I said, with what I hoped was grim finality.

I put the receiver down, leaned across and picked up the case. I swung it round by its handle. Big mistake, Sam, big mistake.

I grinned across at Pippa. 'Guess what?'

'What?'

'This here case contains some awfully crucial information pertaining to your company, Pipps.'

'Oooh, really? Is that what he said? Hang on, I'll just go and get a yoghurt and then we'll open it, shall we?'

'Thought you might say that.'

She crammed the last of the evil-smelling salami into her mouth and dashed out to the kitchen for some nice sour milk to taunt me with. The moment she'd gone the phone rang again.

'Pippa!' I yelled.

'Can't you get it?' she bellowed from the kitchen, but dashed back, grumbling, to pick it up.

'Hello? . . . Oh hi!' She clamped her hand over the mouthpiece. 'It's the father again.'

'Sam?'

'No! Guess again!' She giggled. I could see she was finding this hard to resist.

'I'm going to kill you later!' I hissed.

She composed herself with difficulty. 'Sorry, it's Nick.'

'Nick!' I felt the blood drain from my face. 'What does he want?'

'Well, I don't know, talk to him, for God's sake, he's not going to eat you!' She rammed the receiver into my trembling hands.

'H-hello?' I whispered.

'Polly? It's me.' He sounded fierce. 'Look, I got some convoluted message from Mum saying you'd gone off to London to investigate the burglary, is that right?'

'Well, I just thought I'd—'

'Well *don't*. For God's sake, it's not for you to poke your nose into this, it's the police's job and apart from anything else it could be bloody dangerous. She said you had some hairbrained idea about going to see Bruce, I couldn't believe it! You haven't seen him yet, have you?'

'Oh, er, no, no, of course not.'

'Good, I absolutely forbid it. Who knows what state of mind he might be in? If he's guilty he'll be furious at being caught and if he's not guilty he'll be bitter as hell at being arrested. If you go skipping round there offering tea and sympathy, he might just go ballistic, so don't go, OK?'

A tiny glimmer of hope shone out of a very dark sky. 'No, darling, I won't, and sweet of you to worry.'

'Don't push your luck, Polly, I just don't want to have to pick up the pieces, that's all.'

I gulped. 'Oh. Right.'

There was a pause.

'Um, how are you, Nick?'

'I'm fine,' he said shortly. 'Except that a fox got into the chicken run last night and killed most of the laying stock, that didn't improve my temper, I can tell you.'

'Oh dear,' I said lamely.

'Yes, eleven dead and feathers everywhere. Doesn't exactly add to the gaiety of nations, does it? Incidentally, have you found anywhere to live yet? Sarah said there was quite a nice house over at Polzeath.'

I couldn't speak for a moment.

'Polly?'

'Y-yes, that's right, I'll go and look at it when I get back.'

'Good. No rush, but decent houses don't hang around for long, you know, it'll get snapped up. Anyway, remember what I said about Bruce. Goodbye.'

He put the phone down.

I lowered the receiver back into its slot, feeling awfully sick. Tears welled in my eyes.

'What happened, what did he say?'

'He – he asked me if I'd found anywhere to live,' I whispered. The tears began to topple over the brink.

'Oh! Oh dear. Is that why he rang?'

'No, he rang to tell me not to go and see Bruce.'

'Bit late for that.'

'Exactly, but don't tell him. He thought it might be dangerous.'

'Well, that's good news,' Pippa said brightly. 'He obviously cares, don't you think?'

'He might care enough not to want to see me decapitated but he doesn't care enough to want me back, that's for sure,' I whispered. I wiped my wet face with the back of my hand and sighed. 'Said he didn't want to have to pick up the pieces.' I slumped back on the sofa. 'He was awfully terse.'

'Oh well, you know Nick, he's not exactly the gushing type, is he? At least he rang. Now come on, buck up,' said Pippa hastily, trying to ward off a fresh flow of tears, 'let's have a look at this.'

She picked Sam's case up from under where I'd dropped it, pulled it up on to her lap and flipped the lid open. I watched gloomily as she riffled through the papers. I'd completely lost interest now, and anyway, it all looked deadly dull to me. Nick, my Nick . . . he'd sounded so cold, like a stranger. And he wanted me out of the way as soon as possible. I stared into space trying to gulp back tears as Pippa flipped through the papers. Every so often she'd exclaim as she came across a new snippet of gossip.

'Oh really? Gosh, that's interesting – a merger's possible apparently . . . oh, with Bazooka Films . . . Hey it looks like Marion's finally going to be fired, 'bout time too, she's lazy and good-for-nothing, all she does is paint her nails – ooh look, his Filofax, I bet he's lost without this.'

She went to put it back but I grabbed it from her.

'Polly!' She looked shocked.

'What?'

'You're not going to look at it, are you?'

'Well, you're going through his case.'

'That's different, a Filofax is – well, it's like a diary.'

'Oh don't be silly, it's just a notebook really – ooh look, photos.'

'That's Sally,' said Pippa, instantly abandoning her principles and peering round over my shoulder. 'Pretty, don't you think?'

'Very,' I said, staring at the rather shy-looking girl with long blonde hair and freckles who smiled back at me from a deckchair in her garden.

'And that's not actually awfully good of her,' said Pippa, 'she's a stunner in the flesh, oh look, there's one tucked in behind it, maybe that's better.'

She pulled out a tiny snapshot. 'Oh!'

'What?' I peered over. 'Oh! Golly.'

It was a photo of Serena Montgomery. We stared at the picture, then at each other.

'How very odd...' said Pippa slowly. 'What on earth d'you think he's doing with a picture of her in his wallet?'

'Could it be for casting purposes, or something? I mean he does use her quite a lot in his films, perhaps it's to remind him what she looks like?'

'In his Filofax though? Behind a picture of his wife?'

We gazed at each other.

'Pippa, you don't think...'

'Oh no. Surely not. He doesn't even know her that well, at least that's what he says.'

'Makes quite a point of saying it too, doesn't he?' I said

slowly. 'Always telling someone how he doesn't know her very well and doesn't like her much either. Odd how she crops up in all his films and commercials though, isn't it? Methinks he doth protest too much.'

Pippa looked shocked. 'But Polly, he's a happily married man!'

'But is he, Pippa? I mean, the more I think about it the more I wonder. I saw him at lunchtime today and to be honest he was desperate to have an affair with me, and if he'd have one with me, well, why not other girls as well?'

'But I thought he said it had never happened before, that you were the first?'

'He did, but then if you think about it, he would, wouldn't he? He's not going to admit he's always played around with other women, is he?'

'I suppose not . . . golly, I always thought he was happily married.'

'I'm beginning to think he's about as happily married as Prince Charles.'

'So you reckon he's cheating on Sally?'

'Well, of course he's cheating on her, we know that much from the high jinks he got up to with me, so why not with Serena too?'

'Crikey. Serena.'

We stared at the photo. Pippa shook her head. 'I don't know, they just seem so unlikely . . .'

'Only because he pretends to bitch about her so much, but when you think about it – glamorous film director, beautiful actress, what could be more obvious?'

Pippa raised her eyebrows. 'What indeed?'

We peered at the photo again. It was a tiny black-and-white shot of Serena sitting by a pool, no doubt in some exotic location, throwing back her beautiful blonde hair and laughing into the camera, displaying perfect white teeth.

'You've got to admit, she is pretty gorgeous,' said Pippa. 'I suppose he just couldn't resist her. I expect he was bowled over by her when they were away shooting somewhere, just couldn't help himself.'

'Mmm, she's certainly got the capacity to twist men round her little finger. Look what happened to Nick, he went out with her for ages before he saw the light. Still, Serena and Sam. That's quite a turn-up for the books, isn't it? I wonder if his wife knows?'

'Doubt it,' said Pippa. 'I'm sure she thinks he's totally faithful – oh God, there's the phone again, it's like the blasted BT exchange tonight and I bet it's not for me either.' She reached across. 'Hello?'

I tensed up, wondering which of my possible impregnators it might be this time.

'Oh hi, Amanda, how are you?'

I relaxed. Thank goodness. I stared down at the photo again. Sam and Serena. Who would have thought? I had a quick flick through the diary section of the Filofax and, sure enough, now and again I spotted a discreet little 'S' in the lunch and evening sections. And to think, he'd been hoping to pop a little 'P' in as well. He really was a bit of a lad, wasn't he?

'Polly? Yes, she's right here, hang on.'

I looked up. 'For me?' I mouthed. She nodded. I frowned and took the phone.

'Hello?'

'Polly, it's me, Amanda, how you doin'?'

'Er, fine, fine thank you.'

'Good. Listen, I wondered if you'd got time to meet me for a quick drink, only I need to have a little chat with you about this an' that.'

'With me?'

'Yeah, if you don't mind.'

'Er, sure. When did you have in mind?'

'Well, I'm still at work but I'll be driving past Pippa's place at about nine o'clock, so why don't I meet you down the Scarsdale?'

'Tonight? Why not tomorrow or—'

'Can't wait, I'm afraid, for one thing I'm off on location tomorrow, but apart from anything else I've gotta get something off me chest.'

I froze. Jesus! I swallowed hard. 'Er, righto then, I'll meet you there at nine. Um, what's it about, Amanda?'

'It's about Sam. See you later, Polly.' She rang off.

I replaced the receiver slowly and stared at Pippa.

'What?' she asked.

I licked my rather dry lips. 'She wants to meet me,' I whispered, 'to talk about Sam.'

'What about Sam?'

'Well, I don't know, do I? But – oh God, Pippa, she sounded really odd, really – well, cross actually.'

'But why doesn't she just come here for a drink?'

'I think she wants to see me alone,' I whispered. 'Oh Pippa, I think I know what this is all about – she's going to kill me, I know she is!'

'Don't be silly, why on earth should she do that?'

'Because I've seen the way she looks at him.'

'At who?'

'At Sam! She's having an affair with him, I'm convinced. Or she's *had* an affair with him and he's spurned her, or she *wants* to have an affair with him or – or something, anyway, I'm absolutely sure of it. She's found out about our night of passion and she's coming to get me!' I went cold. 'Of course! She saw me dancing with him in Annabel's and she probably saw us leave together – oh Pippa, what am I going to do?'

Pippa looked very confused. 'But ... I thought we'd decided he was having an affair with Serena?'

'Well, why not Amanda too? I mean, he slotted me in, so why not her as well?'

'But—'

'And don't tell me he's happily married!' I shrieked. 'The man's clearly a sex maniac. He should be in that clinic in Hollywood, the one Michael Douglas went into for sex addiction, he's quite obviously a nymphomaniac!'

Pippa frowned. 'I think only women can be nymphomaniacs.'

'Typical, if it's a woman she's a maniac, if it's a man it's something medical, an addiction – but, oh God, Pippa this is awful, she's coming to sort me out!' I wrung my hands in terror.

'Don't be silly, Amanda's not violent.'

'How d'you know? She's from the East End, isn't she? I mean, that's where her roots are and that's where the underworld is. She's coming to warn me off, fill me in – d'you know what she said? She said she wanted to get something off her chest, that's probably rhyming slang for dead meat or something.'

Pippa frowned. 'Doesn't even rhyme...'

'It probably doesn't have to!' I shrieked. I was getting a bit hysterical now. 'The really nasty ones probably don't, to make them more sinister.'

'Now, Polly, you really are overreacting, I'm sure there's some perfectly simple explanation. Just relax, will you?'

'Easy for you to say,' I muttered grimly, 'you're not the one she wants to kneecap.'

Suddenly I had an idea. I curled up defiantly on the sofa and buried my head under a cushion.

'I feel sick.'

Pippa regarded me severely. 'Polly, Amanda is a friend of mine, you can't stand her up. You're meeting her in a crowded pub, for heaven's sake, there's absolutely no way you can come to any harm. You're going, OK?'

I stayed rooted to my cushion for a moment, then stupidly looked up and caught her eye. It was enough. I banged my head on the arm of the sofa and groaned.

'OK,' I muttered, 'I'm going.'

Chapter Twenty-two

Half an hour later, feeling like death in a sweatshirt and clutching a warm tonic water to my chest, I perched nervously in a corner of the crowded pub. I watched the door, wide-eyed with apprehension, and every time it opened I jumped off my chair. After ten minutes of this rather tiring, bottom-numbing gymnastics, I decided I'd had enough. I drained my tonic and looked at my watch. Ten past nine. Surely I'd done my bit? I'd waited a while and she hadn't shown, couldn't I creep off home to bed with impunity now? Two more minutes, my conscience told me, then I'd be away.

I sat back and a couple of likely lads propping up the bar leered over in my general direction. They had to be very desperate or very drunk, I looked like something out of *EastEnders*. I glared back and scratched my chin with my wedding-ring finger, wishing I had a T-shirt with 'Bog off I'm pregnant' written on it. They leered again, had a quick confab and looked perilously close to swaggering over, which frankly was all I needed right now. I glared as icily as I could and was just about to pick my nose to really put them off when the door opened and Amanda walked in. I was almost pleased to see her.

'Sorry I'm late,' she breezed, with not too much of a

murderous smile, 'got a bit held up.' She eyed my empty
glass. 'Blimey, you've obviously been 'ere ages, sorry 'bout
that. Another gin?'

'Er, just a tonic, please.'

She raised her eyebrows. 'Not like you, is it?'

I smiled weakly. 'No, I suppose not.'

She shrugged. 'OK, back in a mo.'

She put her case down, flung her jacket over the back of a
chair and elbowed her way determinedly to the bar, taking
no nonsense at all from the two grinning idiots supporting it
and looking like a woman who was used to pushing people
out of the way. I couldn't help noticing that her arms
looked awfully strong in her skimpy black T-shirt, in fact
she looked worryingly fit all over. I wondered if she worked
out? Pumped iron or something?

I reached nervously for a cigarette, not to smoke, you
understand, just to fondle. Recently I'd found that it
helped just to be in contact with one, to hold it, gaze at it
and basically reassure myself that this was just a temporary
lull in my smoking career, that they hadn't disappeared
from my life forever. I was nervously smelling one and
rolling it around in my hands when Amanda came back.
She put the drinks down and pulled a lighter out of her
pocket.

'Here.' The flame flickered in my face.

'Er, no, it's OK,' I said, putting the ciggie back in my
bag, 'I'll smoke it later.'

She sat down next to me. 'I've got masses if yer short.'

'No, no, I've got loads, it's just that I'm – trying to give
up.'

'What's this, Polly, no gin, no fags, not pregnant or
anything, are you?'

'No!' I gasped. 'No, good lord no, of *course* not! No, I'm just on a bit of a health kick at the moment. Pregnant! Ha! What a joke!'

I lifted my tonic water to my nervous lips and realised my hand was shaking perceptibly. You idiot, Polly, for goodness sake be careful, if she finds out you're carrying Sam's baby she'll probably finish you off right here and now. I surreptitiously sidled round the table a bit, wondering which way I should duck if she took a swing at me.

'So how've you bin?' she asked, convivially enough.

'Fine, fine,' I croaked, cranking up a smile.

She lit a cigarette and I watched enviously as the smoke flew in a perfect straight line over my head. I craned my nostrils skywards and inhaled deeply, hoping to catch a gratuitous whiff.

'A-and you?' I faltered, remembering my manners.

'Oh, not so bad, up to me eyeballs in work, but there you go, better than being bored out of yer skull, innit?'

'Yeah, yeah, I s'pose it is.' Oh no, Polly, don't slip into that again. 'Yah, right,' I brayed hastily, 'absolutely nothing worse than being bored is there? Simply gha-a-stly.'

She looked at me carefully. I gulped. Now she probably thought I was taking the mickey. I flushed and threw back my tonic water, chucking most of it down my sweatshirt. She handed me a hanky.

'Listen, Polly,' she said as I mopped away, 'I wanna ask you something.'

'Oh yes?' I croaked casually, studiously avoiding her eye.

'You might think this is none of my business, but are you havin' an affair wiv Sam?'

I gasped and looked up, eyes – hopefully – full of shock and horror.

'Good lord, no! Gosh, what a question – with Sam? Good gracious me, no, perish the thought, of course not!'

She eyed me speculatively. 'What about that night in Annabel's then? Or just after, to be more specific?'

'Wh-what about it?'

'Come on, I saw the way you were lookin' at him, I saw you dancing wiv him too, you'd even started to take yer kit off, yer underwear was hangin' out all over the place.'

'It was a body,' I muttered.

'Well, whatever it was it was all over the shop, and you were definitely overexcited, practically had yer tongue round his tonsils. I couldn't bear to watch so I went to the lav and when I came back you'd both dun a bunk. What did you do, slip off to a hotel or something?'

'Oh God, Amanda . . .'

'Well did you? Come on, I'm not gonna spit in your eye or anything, I just need to know, did you go off wiv him or what?'

I sighed. I couldn't look at her. I was also beginning to suffer from the rather debilitating effects of sobriety. It had been a good eight hours since I'd had a drink. I picked up a beer mat and twisted it nervously in my hands.

'Look,' I muttered, 'it was a big mistake, all right? I was incredibly drunk, we both were. These things happen.' I licked my lips.

'What things?'

I shrugged miserably. 'You know . . .' I sighed. 'Yes, all right, we did go to a hotel. For the night.' I looked up, her eyes were pinning me to the wall. 'But honestly, I didn't have a clue what was going on, I was completely out of it. I mean, you were there, you must have seen how drunk I was. I promise you, Amanda, it wasn't my fault!'

My voice sounded shrill, guilty. I avoided her eyes. I knew it, I *knew* it. She was in love with him, she was having an affair with him. She was the other woman, and as far as she was concerned I was the other, *other* woman. Well, the other, other, *other* woman, actually, counting Serena. There seemed to be rather a lot of us about.

She ground her cigarette out in what I considered to be an incredibly threatening manner, leaving both hands free for nail-flexing. I couldn't help noticing that they were long, red and very sharp and I therefore took the precaution of cunningly placing both my feet to one side of my chair, thus poised for a quick getaway.

Amanda narrowed her eyes and nodded thoughtfully. 'We thought it was you.'

I jumped. We? Hang on a minute, just how many other women were there? Did he have a harem or something? How many concubines had I upset here, a dozen or so?

'Drive up from Cornwall a lot, do you?' she asked casually. ''Bout twice a week? Tuesdays and Fridays usually, innit?' She gave a twisted little smile. 'I'll say this for you, Polly, you've certainly got stamina, hell of a long way for a quick bonk.'

She lit a fresh cigarette and blew the smoke over my head, but only just.

'Don't be ridiculous,' I spluttered, coughing a bit under the smoke. 'I don't come up to bonk Sam, I don't usually come up at all actually, and anyway – what's it got to do with you?'

That was brave, Polly, foolhardy more like. I clenched my buttocks and prepared to duck the left hook.

She smiled sardonically. 'Fair enough, but just remember, we've got your number. We know what you're up to.'

It was this *we* business that was so damned intimidating. Any minute now I expected a whole posse of women to appear at the table, fold their arms and glare threateningly at me.

Amanda frowned and shook her head. 'We were really surprised when we found out it was you. I mean, there you are with that lovely bloke of yours and that bloody great house, and you go riskin' it all for some two-bit affair. Whadja wanna do that for? You must be out of your head.'

'I'm not! I don't! For goodness sake, you've got it all wrong. I'm *not* having an affair with him, and anyway, what's all this *we* lark, who else knows about this?'

'Oh, just me and Sally,' said Amanda calmly.

I gasped. 'Sally? You've told Sally?'

'She guessed.'

'What – about you, too?'

She frowned. 'Whadja mean, about me, too?'

'Well, you're having an affair with him, aren't you?'

She stared at me. 'What?'

'You and Sam, you're having a ding-dong, aren't you?'

She looked at me in amazement, then abruptly threw back her head and hooted with laughter.

'You must be joking! Me and Sam? Do me a favour, he's my idea of a complete tosser!' She hooted some more, then wiped her eyes. 'No, I wouldn't touch him with a bargepole, but Sally's me best mate, you see.'

'Your what?'

'Yeah, we were at college together, shared a flat too.'

I stared at her. 'So that's why you kept giving him funny looks, I thought you were after him.'

'After him? God, I'd run a mile in the other direction! No, I can't stand the bloke and 'e knows it, which is why 'e goes all shifty when I'm around. He's sussed out I'm on to him, you see, knows 'e has to be really careful when I'm around. Sally's suspected for ages but 'e's always denied it and she's never been able to catch him out. He's a clever little bastard, really covers his tracks.' She grimaced at me. 'Oh, you're not the first, not by a long shot. Sally reckons he's been at it for years but she's never been able to prove it. 'E's never slipped up before, you see, not once. Until now of course, until you.' She blew another line of smoke centimetres above my head. ''E went a bit too far in public this time, didn't he? Got a bit overconfident, like. So now we know.'

'Oh no you don't,' I retorted, 'you don't know the half of it! I might have had a ghastly one-night stand with him but that was it! I am not, repeat *not* having an affair with him, you can believe what you damn well like but it's the truth!'

She sighed. 'Look, Polly, I like you, really I do, and I don't wanna interrogate you, but Sally's me mate, right? And she's desperate for some information. You'd do the same in my position, wouldn't you?'

'Well, if it was absolutely necessary, but I'm telling you, Amanda, you're way off the mark here, you've totally lost the plot. *I'm* not having an affair with him, but if you like,' I paused slightly here for dramatic effect, 'I can tell you who is.'

She frowned. 'But I thought you just said you *did* go to a hotel and bonk the living day—'

'Yes, all right, all right – I did, but it was just one night, that's all. If you want to know who's rocking his socks off on a permanent basis I'll tell you, it's Serena Montgomery.'

'Serena Montgomery? Don't be soft,' she scoffed.

'It's true, I promise you, at least we're pretty sure it is.' I rather enjoyed my own little 'we' there.

'We?'

'Yes, me and Pippa. He was careless enough to leave his Filofax lying around and we found a cute little picture of her in the back, together with a fair smattering of S's in the lunch and dinner sections of his diary. She's definitely your girl, Amanda.'

'But he doesn't even like her – at least . . .'

'Exactly. As you said, clever little bastard, isn't he? Even goes so far as to pretend he hates her.'

She frowned. 'Now I come to think of it, out in Aswan . . .'

'Come again?'

'At the shoot on the Nile, he was always mouthing off at her for not knowing her lines and then draggin' her off for private little rehearsals an' that, raising his eyes to heaven as he went. But they didn't appear again for hours on end . . .' She stared into her drink. 'And they were always goin' off to check out locations together and – oh yeah, hang on, they both liked early nights, didn't they! Did a lot of ostentatious yawning and then disappeared while the rest of us were still partying – damn, why didn't I think of it before?'

'Because you were too busy thinking it was me, I suppose.'

She looked surprised. 'Yeah, I suppose I was.' She had

the grace to look abashed. 'Sorry, Polly, been a bit hasty I suppose, but Sally's in such a state, you see, always crying an' that, and I really wanted to help her nail him this time. She's had it up to here with his lies, she really has.'

'Would she divorce him then?'

'If she found out the truth I reckon she might. Sally's big problem has always been that she loves him too much, that's why she's never been able to leave him. She hides from the truth, see, kids herself he's working late when he doesn't pitch up till midnight, but just recently she's been toughening up a bit, says she wants to know what he's up to. I reckon if she actually had some cast-iron proof she'd do something about it, kick him out once and for all.'

'And Sam wouldn't want that? I mean, if he leads this extraordinary double life why doesn't he just leave anyway? What's the point of staying with Sally?'

'Because Sally's got all the dosh, he'd be penniless.'

'What?'

'Yeah, Sam owes so much money it's untrue. Sally's his second wife, you see, 'e's still paying maintenance to number one and putting his two kids from that marriage through public school.'

'God, I had no idea, he keeps that very quiet.'

'Well he would, wouldn't he? Sally owns the house, the car, probably even the company. Her old man set Sam up when they got married, so there's no way he'd be able to get his hands on that money. He'd probably have to pay maintenance too, 'cos Sally's never really worked, and considering 'e's completely stony broke, he'd be in a bit of a pickle really, wouldn't he?'

'But surely his films, his career—'

Amanda scoffed. 'Listen, Sam's career is only going one

way at the moment, down the bleedin' plughole. He's a nobody in the film world, a washout, a has-been.'

'But I thought – God, I thought he was famous. I mean, he made that film – what was it called?'

'Yeah, *Marengo*, a low-budget, culty little film that was a surprise hit about seven years ago, but he's done bugger all since then apart from a series of major flops. Why d'you think he makes all these terrible commercials? Not exactly high art, are they? No, he's desperate to claw some cash together.'

'Gosh, I had no idea, he comes across as such a groovy film director.'

'Well, that's his image, innit? He's got to keep up the front, got to keep the girls in the dark, can't have them knowing he's just a sad old has-been, can he? I mean, let's face it, that's what you fell for, wasn't it, the famous film director bit?'

I looked sheepish. 'I suppose so.'

She shrugged. 'Well, there you go.' She stubbed out her cigarette. 'But it's a long way from the truth. My guess is he's up to his eyeballs in debt and he's absolutely terrified Sally's gonna find out about all his indiscretions and haul him off to the divorce courts. Then he'd really be up the creek.'

'Serve him right,' I muttered. I remembered how I'd sat opposite him at lunch and listened to him telling me how crazy he was about me, how miserable he'd be without me. What a load of crap, he couldn't care less about me, he'd just wanted a repeat performance of our sex-crazed night together. I shuddered.

'Exactly,' Amanda leaned forward eagerly, 'serve him right. Listen, Polly, would you do something for me?'

I eyed her nervously. 'What?'

'Would you go and see Sally? Tell 'er about what happened to you?'

I nearly fell off my chair. 'What! Go and see Sally? Amanda, you must be mad!'

'Look, she's not out for blood or anything, but she's doin' her nut trying to find out the truth and you've got – well, you've got first-hand experience, like, haven't you?'

'Yes, but I don't particularly want to share it with his—'

'And you could spill the beans about Serena too. I mean, let's face it, at the moment she thinks you're the one having the ding-dong with him so you could at least let yourself off *that* hook, put her straight on that score, as it were.' She eyed me carefully. 'I sort of think you owe it to her.'

I gasped. 'I do?'

'Well, you wouldn't like it if someone bonked your old man, would you?'

'Well no, but—'

'Well then. Go on, Polly, you can do it.'

'But – why can't you? I mean, couldn't you just report back, say you've seen me and—'

'I'm off to the States tomorrow,' she said briskly, stubbing her cigarette out, 'an' I hardly think she's gonna want to hear all this over the telephone, do you? But I'll tell you what, I'll ring 'er up and let 'er know you're coming to see 'er, how 'bout that?'

'But—'

'Come on, Polly, it's the least you can do.'

I had a nasty feeling this girl was used to getting her own way. Talk about persistent. She fixed my eyes with hers like a couple of drawing pins, nailing them to the wall while the rest of me squirmed around in my seat. Was there no way out of this? Suddenly I spotted one, a tiny little exit sign. I lunged for it.

'OK,' I said, nodding and smiling warmly, 'I'll go and see her.'

'Good on yer, girl!' she said heartily and went to slap me on the back, but I instinctively ducked when I saw her hand coming and she cuffed me round the head instead.

'Blimey, sorry, you moved!'

'It's OK,' I mumbled, straightening my hair.

'Here's the address,' she said, busily scribbling the name of a smart Chelsea street down on the back of an envelope, '. . . and her phone number.'

'Great, great,' I said, picking it up and grinning broadly, still clinging like billyo to my big idea. It was quite a good one as it happened, very simple. You see, I wouldn't go. I just wouldn't go. I'd pretend I would, but I wouldn't. Amanda would be out of the country tomorrow and hopefully, by the time she got back, so would I. Somewhere far-flung, somewhere remote, somewhere incredibly inaccessible, maybe even somewhere hot. I'd like to get something out of this ghastly fiasco, even if it was only a suntan. I pocketed the address, a plastic smile still spread broadly across my face.

'Super, well I'll go and see her tomorrow then, shall I?' I said brightly, getting to my feet.

She eyed me cautiously. 'You will go, won't you, Polly?'

'Yes, of course I will,' I assured her, 'first thing probably, straight after breakfast, pop round for coffee, get it over and done with. And now,' I looked at my watch and sighed regretfully, 'I'm afraid I really must go because I haven't got a key and I don't want to keep Pippa up too late.'

'Oh right.' She drained her drink. 'Well, I've got to go to the lav, so you go on, don't wait for me.'

'Righto!' I chortled merrily, grabbing my bag and scuttling for the door. I turned and gave her a cheery wave. 'Have a good time in the States then, bye!'

I was out, out and running. I scurried up the dark street, clutching my handbag to my chest, my heart thumping away high up in my ribcage. Heavens, what a nightmare, what a complete and utter nightmare! And what a narrow escape! Lucky I was such a quick thinker. How many other people could have extricated themselves from such a tight spot quite so brilliantly?

I rounded the corner at a canter and set off down the home straight, panting heavily now. I mean, did she think I was mad? Totally stark staring mad? What – go and confess to the wronged wife? Have a quiet word with her indoors? Pop round for coffee and say, 'Oh, by the way, I appear to have rogered your husband, only once, mind, and I can't remember a thing about it, but if you're interested I can give you the name and address of someone who's been *much* naughtier than me, rogered him on a *much* more regular basis – mmm, lovely coffee, is it filter?' Oh no, no thanks, not likely.

I dashed up the path to Pippa's front door, found the spare key under the geranium pot and bounded up the stairs two at a time, quite forgetting my delicate condition. I threw my clothes on the floor, dived under the duvet and pulled it up high over my head. Oh no, I had quite enough on my plate without tipping that particular can of worms on to it as well, thank you very much. I shut my eyes tight. Sorry, Amanda, nice try an' all that, but sorry, no.

Chapter Twenty-three

I hadn't really been serious about fleeing the country, but the more I thought about it as I lay in bed the next morning, the more I decided it wasn't such a bad idea. What was the point of going home right now? What did I have to look forward to apart from a big empty house and the odd telephone call from Nick enquiring as to whether I'd found a house to live in and how soon could I get out of his? I felt my eyes fill up at this but gulped down the tears determinedly. No, Polly. No more falling apart at the seams. Instead I was going to get away from all this aggro, even if it was only for a week or two. Yes, I'd take a little break, a little holiday. When had I ever needed one more? I asked myself. I couldn't be more tired and run down if I tried. I huddled under the duvet, staring at the cracks in the attic ceiling, warming nicely to my plan.

I'd go somewhere hot, of course, no point whatsoever in going away if I didn't come back with a suntan, but it didn't have to be too remote, just Spain, or maybe Greece, or – hang on, were they hot enough at this time of year? In May? There was no doubt about it, it had to be absolutely sizzling.

I jumped out of bed and ran downstairs in my dressing gown to quiz Pippa on southern European meteorology.

Big mistake. As I bustled into the kitchen, full of my newest plan, I caught her red-handed. She was standing with her back to me by the stove and as she heard my footsteps she turned quickly. I saw her eyes. Huge with guilt. She was clutching the evidence in her hands and damn nearly dropped it right there on the floor, but instead she panicked, and quickly rammed the whole thing into her mouth. The biggest, greasiest, doorstep of a bacon sandwich you've ever seen in your life. Her eyes were still wide with fear as she chomped away frantically, butter oozing down her chin.

'Sorry,' she mumbled through half a pig, spraying me copiously with crumbs, 'thought you were still in bed!'

She grabbed an air freshener from the windowsill and began spraying furiously.

'No, don't!' I yelped, heaving on lavender and bacon grease. 'Just open the back door!'

She ran to push it open but it was too late. I was already running fast in the other direction, arriving just too late to deposit last night's dry biscuit and tonic water in the downstairs loo. I mopped up the floor and emerged a few minutes later looking very green around the gills.

'Thanks a bunch, Pippa,' I whispered.

'Sorry,' she muttered guiltily, taking my arm as I tottered back into the kitchen, clutching the furniture, 'thought I'd be able to get rid of the evidence before you came down.'

With a little help from my friend I gingerly lowered myself into a chair and rested my cheek on the kitchen table.

'Sorry about the pong in the loo,' I muttered.

'Couldn't matter less,' she assured me, ever the hostess.

She sat down opposite me and regarded my slumped form anxiously.

'You know, it's going to be bloody difficult to keep this pregnancy thing from everyone when you get back to Trewarren. You've got morning sickness written all over you. You'll be heaving in the post office and fainting in the dairy and it'll be round the village in no time, Nick's sure to hear.'

'I know,' I said, raising my head a couple of inches, 'which is precisely why I'm not going back yet.'

'Oh?' Pippa looked alarmed, perhaps not relishing the prospect of an enforced starvation diet continuing in her own home.

'Oh no, it's OK, I'm not staying here,' I assured her, 'I've got a cunning plan.'

'Oh really? What's that then?' Pippa looked even more nervous. She knew my plans of old.

I sat up and wrapped my dressing gown around me decisively.

'It's simple, I'm going to skip the country for a couple of weeks and go somewhere hot. I'll lie on a beach with a pile of books and come back refreshed, rejuvenated and with an incredible suntan. Then I'll go home and flaunt my suntanned body around the village and everyone will tell Nick how amazing I'm looking. I'll make sure all the eligible men in the village chase after me – I'll resist their advances, of course – but Nick will get wind of it and he'll be wild with jealousy. He'll come storming round to demand to know what's going on, see how gorgeously brown I am and how wonderfully blonde and sunstreaked my hair is, be absolutely mesmerised and forgive me unreservedly for having had a fling with Sam.'

'He will?' Pippa looked incredulous.

'Well.' I hesitated. 'OK, perhaps not, but it's worth a try, isn't it?' I pleaded desperately.

'Well, I'm not sure. I can't help thinking there are some socking great holes in your logic. For a start there are precisely no eligible men in your village, and secondly the chances of Nick being mesmerised by a mere suntan are pretty remote, aren't they?'

'Well, all right, you come up with something then!' I snapped. 'I'm trying to be positive here. Sure, we both know that the reality of the situation is I'll be holed up in a council flat as a single parent with a baby to look after, but for God's sake, give me some positive vibes! I'm trying to look on the bright side.'

'Well, I'm all for looking on the bright side, Polly, but—'

'But in this case there isn't a bright side because I'm married to a highly principled, uncompromising man who is never in a million years going to overlook the fact that his wife committed adultery with another man. Is that it?' I demanded savagely, my jaw wobbling.

'Er, well—'

'Yes, Pippa, I know that, but if I kept that thought in my mind every waking moment, first of all I'd go barking mad and then I'd slit my wrists, wouldn't I?'

'Well, crikey, don't do that,' she muttered hastily. 'Heavens, Polly, I didn't mean to upset you, I mean – yes, yes have a holiday! I think it's a great idea, marvellous! Wish I'd thought of it myself.'

'Good,' I said shakily, gaining control of my jaw, and blinking back the tears. 'Right. That's settled then. Hand me the phone, would you? I'm going to ring the estate agents right now and ask them to book me a flight tomorrow. I want to go somewhere hot, cheap and absolutely sizzling with harmful ultraviolet rays.'

'Travel agents,' corrected Pippa, handing me the phone, 'and here, before you land me with a bill for directory inquiries, I've got Thomas Cook in my address book.'

I punched out the number she dictated and waited impatiently as it rang in my ear. Pippa frowned.

'Polly, I don't want to be a killjoy, but wouldn't it be better to get the baby business sorted out *before* you go away? Only I can't help thinking that when you come back you'll be really quite pregnant, and if you decide you don't want to go ahead with it it'll be a darned sight more difficult to do anything about—'

'Hello, Thomas Cook?' I shut my eyes and held up my hand to silence my critic on the opposite side of the table.

'Yes, I'd like a flight and a hotel please, preferably tomorrow and most certainly to somewhere radiating temperatures in excess of thirty degrees. D'you think Greece would fit the bill? . . . Twenty-five degrees? No, not hot enough, I'm afraid, I won't get third-degree burns in that. Where else have you got? . . . Where? Lanzarote?' I looked at Pippa. 'We've been there, haven't we?' I hissed, my hand over the mouthpiece.

She nodded and shoved two fingers in her mouth in a puke-making gesture.

I turned back to the girl. 'Bit grotty, isn't it? I seem to recall discos throbbing to "The Birdy Song" and heaving with bimbos in white high heels and ankle chains who thought a banana daiquiri was the ultimate in sophistic . . . Thirty-two degrees, eh?' I raised my eyebrows at Pippa.

'Well, that certainly meets the requirements in the burning-flesh department, bugger the banana daiquiris, d'you have any vacancies? . . . Would you? Terrific, thanks so much, as soon as possible? . . . Brilliant, it's Polly Penhalligan and I'm on eight, seven, two, five, nine, six, one. Speak to you in a mo then, bye.'

I put the receiver down and grinned.

'Lanzarote, she's ringing me back in a sec to confirm the booking, then I'll just pop round and sign the cheque. I'm off! I'm off tomorrow, Pippa! Sun, sea, sand and – well, no, none of that, of course, had quite enough of that recently, but God, I'm so excited! Something's actually going right for a change!' I clapped my hands together gleefully.

Pippa screwed up her face in disgust.

'Hate to put you off but it's the pits, Polly, don't you remember? It's not just the Sharons, it's the beaches. Black volcanic sand that sticks to your suntan lotion whenever a force eight gale blows, which I seem to remember is most of the time – we couldn't work out why we were the only idiots on the beach until we stood up and realised we'd gone a shade darker than we intended. The only other lunatic lying there was that drunk who was unconscious most of the day until he lurched past us, pausing only to throw up in my sunhat.'

'I know, I know, but all I need is the sun and hopefully one of those comfortable lounger things by a hotel pool. I won't even see the beach if I'm lucky, and I can wear dark glasses to blot out the rest of the punters, and who am I to complain about puke? I'll be puking with the best of them – oh no, nothing can stop me now. I'm really excited, it'll be brilliant, I'll relax, read some books – oh Pippa, why don't you come? Take some time off and get away from work and Josh for a bit, surely you could—'

The phone rang.

'That'll be for me!' I squeaked, grabbing it.

'Hello, is that Polly Penhalligan?' said a girl's voice.

'Yes, that's right, is it OK, is it booked?'

'Um, my name's Sally.'

'Oh, right, right, fine, Sally, you're my tour operator or something, are you? Sweet of you to introduce yourself but to be honest I'm not sure I want the whole package-deal bit – you know, camp fires on the beach and ging-gang-goolie, I'm just after a quiet—'

'My name's Sally Weston.'

'Marvellous, terrific, Sally but – oh! Sally Weston?'

I gazed at Pippa in terror. She clapped her hand dramatically over her mouth, eyes huge with horror, and backed away in the direction of the fridge. It occurred to me to simply drop the receiver and do likewise, perhaps climbing into it and shutting the door behind me, but by the time I'd got any sort of muscle co-ordination together Mrs Weston was already addressing my right ear.

'I hope it's not a bad time, not too early or anything?' she was saying hesitantly.

'Er, no, no, it's fine,' I gasped, 'fine!'

'I can quite understand that you don't want to get involved in all this, but I'd be so grateful ... you see, Amanda told me she'd spoken to you but she wasn't sure if you'd really come and see me and – well, you're my only hope of finding out something concrete about m-my husband.'

She sounded shaky, uncertain. This wasn't the voice of a bitter, vengeful wife, but all the same ...

'Look, I'm sorry,' I muttered, 'but I really don't think it's any of my—'

'Oh please don't say no, please, this is so important. I must talk to you! I know what happened between you and Sam, and I swear I don't hold it against you. I know – well, I know how persuasive he can be. Please, Polly, please just pop round for a moment, or maybe I could come to you?'

By now the palm of my hand was sweating up a treat and I had to hold the receiver in a vicelike grip to stop it slipping from my grasp. I rolled mad, expressive eyes at Pippa, who rolled mad, sympathetic ones back.

'Look, um, the thing is, Mrs Weston, if Amanda's told you about m-me and your husband, well, I'm not sure that there's an awful lot more I can add.'

'But I must talk to you about Serena. Amanda said you were convinced that she's the real – you know – protagonist in all this.'

'But it's all very much conjecture, nothing definite, and—'

'But you found a picture? In his Filofax, is that right?' she persisted.

'Well yes, but—'

'Please, I – I must have it, I must have some sort of proof to dangle in front of him, could I possibly have it? Could I? Could you bring it round? In the Filofax?'

She sounded really desperate, but blimey – not deliver the Filofax back to Sam? Take it round to the wife complete with photo of bird? Did I have that much of a death wish?

'I – I really don't think I'm in any position to—'

'Look, what d'you owe him?' Suddenly she was more

assertive. 'If what Amanda told me is true he took advantage of you when you were completely and utterly plastered, as I'm sure he's taken advantage of many other girls. Let's face it, he's taken advantage of me all our married life,' she said sadly.

I didn't say anything for a moment, but I could feel myself weakening. Perhaps she felt it too.

'OK,' she urged, 'don't bring the Filofax, I can see that puts you in a difficult position, just bring the photo. It doesn't have to be anything to do with you then, I'll just say I found it and took it out a few days ago, that way you can return the Filofax and you're in the clear, what d'you say?'

I bit my lip. She was right, what did I owe him? Thanks to him, my life was now one huge, comprehensive mess.

'OK . . .' I said slowly, 'I'll just bring the photo.'

'Oh, thank you so much!' she breathed quickly, before I had a chance to reconsider. 'I'm so grateful, really I am, and I know it's a dreadful thing to ask but I'm desperate, you see, really desperate!'

Yeah, so am I, I thought as I put the phone down having promised to be there in about an hour, really desperate. I'm an abandoned wife too, you know, and I'm big with child, but no one rushes round to my house to offer to sort out my life for me, do they?

Nevertheless, half an hour later, Pippa duly trotted off to work, case in hand, complete with Filofax but minus the photograph.

'What if he notices?' she hissed in terror as I handed it to her at the front door. 'What if it's the first thing he checks for?'

'Well, he can hardly ask you, can he? He can hardly say "What's happened to that photo of my bird, the one I keep tucked behind the picture of my wife?"'

'I suppose not, but even so—'

'Bluff it out,' I said airily. 'Just say you haven't the faintest idea what he's talking about. Bye, Pipps, have a nice day.'

She still looked unconvinced so I gave her a little push and she set off hesitantly down the path, case in hand. Halfway down she turned back and walked towards me.

'What now?' I said, exasperated.

'I was just going to tell you that Lottie phoned last night,' she said huffily, 'when you were out. She was worried about you.'

'Oh, sorry, thanks, Pippa. I'll ring her later. Sorry.'

I shut the door and bit my lip. I hadn't spoken to Lottie since that night at Annabel's and I felt guilty about it, but I knew how deeply disappointed she'd be in me. Lottie was one of my dearest friends but she was incurably sensible and ran her life in a very orderly fashion. If she knew how comprehensively I was lousing mine up she'd be horrified. I'd ring her when I got back from my holiday, when hopefully things had settled down a little bit. I'd ring my parents then too, I decided. I hadn't liked to worry them by telling them about Nick and me, and whenever I spoke to Mummy on the phone I just pretended everything was fine, but I'd come clean as soon as I got back from Lanzarote.

I sighed and picked up the photograph of Serena from the hall table. I stared at it for a moment. She really was jolly pretty. I popped it quickly in my bag, grabbed my car keys and slammed out of the house. Then I ran down the path, jumped into Rusty and set off for Chelsea.

Chapter Twenty-four

Oh, very nice, Sam, very nice indeed. I sat in the car, gazing up at the elegant white façade of a magnificent Chelsea town house. Five or six storeys of sartorial splendour in a quiet garden square just a stone's throw from the bustling King's Road, an estate agent would no doubt eulogise. Quite a lot to give up, one way and another, no wonder our Sam was clinging on by his fingernails. I sat there for a moment, biting my own and collecting my few remaining wits. I had a feeling I was going to need them. Except that the longer I sat there the more witless I felt, so in the end I told myself that if I stayed there for precisely one minute longer something unspecified but totally horrendous would happen to Nick or my parents. It always did the trick. I gazed at the second hand on my watch and, with ten seconds to spare, jumped out of the car, ran up the six or seven marble steps which led to the black front door and fell on the brass bell. It was shrill and feverish, which suited my mood.

Sally had clearly been sitting on the doormat waiting for me, because the door swung back before I could take my finger off the brass. She stood there, framed in the doorway, and I instinctively took a step backwards. Pippa had been right. The picture didn't do her justice at all, she really was extraordinarily pretty in a slightly sixties flower-child kind of way.

She was tiny, with bottom-length blonde hair which was rather tangled and a too-long fringe which fell into her eyes. She had a small, heart-shaped face and enormous slate-grey eyes which blinked nervously at me. Her pencil-slim figure was poured into a tight black Lycra dress which clung everywhere, emphasising the fact that her hips and tummy were nonexistent. Her legs were long and brown and her feet were bare. I gulped. She looked rather like I look in my most outrageous fantasies. What the devil was Sam up to? Didn't he know that girls like this with rich daddies to match don't grow on trees?

She gave a hesitant smile. 'You must be Polly, come in.'

'Yes, that's right, thanks,' I muttered.

She wafted gracefully off down a bright-yellow hall smothered in prints and watercolours, a tiny black figure with a sheet of blonde hair shimmying in her wake, her bare feet padding silently in the deep blue carpet. Effortlessly elegant. I lumbered clumsily after her in my clogs and the extraordinary attire of smocked blouse and long peasant skirt which for some reason I'd deemed fit for the occasion. I felt like The Thing from the Swamp. I must have been about six inches taller than her and twice as wide. I tried to sag at the knees and lower my bottom a bit to decrease my height but there was damn all I could do about my width.

At the end of the hall she turned a corner and led me into a large, white, predominantly marble kitchen. At the far end were two enormous french windows which were flung wide on to a walled garden absolutely bursting with white roses.

'Oh! What a beautiful garden!' I exclaimed, in spite of my nerves.

She smiled shyly. 'Roses are my passion. I spend most of the day out there, pruning them, feeding them and generally fussing over them. I practically go to bed with them!' She laughed and then gasped, pulling herself up short. It wasn't perhaps the most innocuous of opening gambits, bearing in mind the nature of my visit.

I flushed and she turned away, also blushing hotly, but somehow prettily pink as opposed to my own retired-general purple. She grabbed the kettle and hid her face in the sink as she filled it.

'Coffee?'

'Please, if you're having one.'

Damn. Why had I said that? Why hadn't I just slammed the photo down on the breakfast bar and taken to my heels? It would take a good three minutes for the kettle to boil, another five for the coffee to cool down and a good seven or so to drink it without scalding the roof of my mouth. Why couldn't I ever think before I spoke?

'We'll, um, sit down and chat when I've made the coffee, shall we?' she said nervously.

'Fine, fine!'

And thus she unwittingly condemned us to an embarrassing silence. We'd made a pact, you see, no talking till coffee time, and boy had she filled the kettle full. She twiddled her hair and gazed fixedly at it, willing it to boil. I cast around for an equally fascinating diversion, eventually plumping in desperation for the spice rack on the wall. I stared at it as if I'd never seen one before, gazing with rapt absorption at the rows of little labelled bottles. If roses were her passion, spices were clearly mine. Rosemary, sage, oregano – gosh, how I marvelled.

At last the bloody thing boiled and she shakily poured out two mugs of coffee and splashed some milk in. We sat down on either side of the breakfast bar and, out of relief, both spoke at once.

'You're not quite—'

'How long have you—'

We laughed. It broke the tension.

'Go on,' I said, 'what were you . . . ?'

'No, you first.'

'Oh, I was just going to ask you how long you'd lived here, it's such a beautiful house.'

'Three years. Since we got married.' She blushed again, perhaps thinking this wasn't quite the moment to shove her marriage down my throat. 'And – and I was just going to say,' she hurried on, 'that you weren't quite what I'd expected.'

'Oh! Really?' What on earth *had* she expected, I wondered? I abruptly brought the boiling coffee nervously to my mouth, predictably scalding myself.

'Um, what did you expect?' I asked, licking my sore lips.

'Oh, I don't know, someone . . . more obvious, I suppose, you know, short skirt, loads of make-up, that kind of thing.' She eyed me nervously.

I grinned. 'Tarty, you mean?'

She giggled. 'I suppose so.' Suddenly she looked anxious. 'Not that I thought you'd be a tart, of course, just the clothes, I – oh, I don't know . . .' She trailed off miserably.

'I put this lot on on purpose, actually,' I said, gazing

down at the strange ethnic gear I'd raided from Pippa's wardrobe. 'I wanted to look – well, homely, I suppose, a bread-baker. Didn't want to seem like a threat. I think I was trying to say – don't worry, I've got a husband of my own at home, I don't want yours.' I grinned.

Her eyes widened. 'No! D'you know, before you came round I was wearing almost exactly what you've got on now, but I changed into this spray-on number so you wouldn't think I was the down-trodden wife who couldn't keep a husband!'

'You're not serious! What, you like this kind of hippy gear?'

She nodded. 'I love it.'

'It's yours, pending my flatmate's permission of course. I can't wait to get out of it, but I'd die for your little black dress – not that I'd have a hope of getting into it!'

We giggled, laughed really, and it was such a release. All at once a cosier, more comradely atmosphere prevailed. We sipped our coffee and grinned across at each other. I'd been waiting for her to ask for the photograph but suddenly I reached into my bag and slipped it over the counter to her.

'Here. It's a very good photo, she's not that pretty,' I lied.

She smiled. 'Course she is, I've seen her in films, but thanks anyway.'

She picked it up and stared at it for a moment. 'This is good . . .' she said slowly, 'this is . . . sort of working.'

'What d'you mean?'

She looked up. 'I had a feeling if I saw some hard proof, some tangible evidence of his infidelity, I might be able to love him less, and d'you know, I was right. I can almost feel the last cloying traces of my love slipping away.' She gulped. 'I can almost begin to realise what a complete bastard he is.'

'Well, that's a start,' I mumbled uncertainly. I wasn't quite sure what sort of a line I should take on this, he was after all her husband and I wasn't convinced I should be too swift to denounce him as an out-and-out villain. 'I mean,' I stumbled on, 'he has – well, misbehaved rather, hasn't he?'

She reached up and shoved the photo between the pages of a cookery book on the shelf above her. She grinned.

'Just a bit. D'you know, I've fallen for his lies for two whole years now? That's how long I've known about his affairs. And for all I know he might well have started dabbling the moment he took his marriage vows.'

'Blimey.' I was silenced for a moment. 'So, there've been, um, quite a lot then, have there?' I asked tentatively. I wasn't exactly sure how deeply I should delve, but she had, after all, brought it up. 'I mean, not just one or two?'

She smiled ruefully. 'Hardly. There've been loads, hundreds probably. Let's put it this way, it hasn't just been you and Serena by a long shot.'

I rather balked at being put in the same category as Serena, but I let it pass.

'Let me see.' She held up her elegant fingers and ticked them off one by one. 'First there was Samantha in accounts, a tacky little office affair, under the desk and behind the photocopier probably; then there was Rosy who lives around the corner, lots of frantic coupling in Battersea Park, according to one of my neighbours; then there was Charlotte, the wife of one of his best friends – I think they mostly got it together in the afternoons in a hotel in Westbourne Grove; oh, and let's not forget Trisha who works in the pub down the road, God knows where they did it, in the cellar with the beer barrels probably.' She shrugged. 'There've been plenty more, I've lost count actually, but those are the ones I've known about for certain.'

'Crikey, he must have been rushed off his feet!'

She gave a bitter little smile. 'Oh, our Sam likes a hectic social life.'

'But haven't you ever confronted him?' I was stunned. How could anyone live like this?

'Loads of times, but up until now I've never had any proof, and whenever I've accused him he's just categorically denied it. He's very careful, you see, never slips up. Oh, I've had lots of weird telephone calls late at night where the person at the other end just slams the phone down when they get me answering instead of him, but I've never actually seen him with anyone, never found any letters, any photos – until now, of course.'

She took the cookery book down from the shelf and studied the photo again.

'And he's always maintained that I'm just a bored, paranoid housewife, with nothing better to do than imagine him in a compromising clinch with a floozy.' I blanched again at this indirect allusion but obviously imperceptibly because she carried on. 'But it's funny,' she mused, 'I went on loving him all the same.'

She stared beyond my head out into the garden for a second, then turned back to me.

'Can you believe that? Throughout all the lies, the deceit, I loved him and pretended to myself that it wasn't happening, forced it out of my mind.'

'And now?' I asked. I could tell she wanted to talk, get it all out of her system. 'D'you still love him now?'

She sighed and looked down at the photograph again. Her eyes narrowed thoughtfully and her lips compressed. She shrugged.

'I'm not sure,' she said softly. 'No ... yes ... a bit ... nothing like as much as I did. I'm getting better anyway, I'm definitely on the mend. This helps.'

She took one last look, then tossed the photo defiantly into the book and slammed it shut.

'Thanks for bringing it, I know you didn't want to, but it might just give me the impetus I need to kick him out this time.'

'Well, in that case I'm glad I did.'

We smiled at each other. I drained my coffee and suddenly there didn't seem to be a lot more to say. I started to slip off my stool and reach for my bag on the floor.

'Well, I'll—'

'More coffee?' she asked abruptly, picking up both our mugs and raising her eyebrows, rather hopefully I thought. I hesitated. She wanted me to stay, wanted to talk. I put my bag down.

'Please,' I nodded, 'that would be nice.'

Why not? The worst was over and it was actually rather pleasant sitting here in her sunny kitchen bitching about her errant husband. She looked pleased and began spooning out the Nescafé with alacrity.

'So what about you?' she asked, pouring in the hot water. 'Have you ever been in love with a bastard? What about your husband, is he the reason you looked further afield? Were you getting your own back or something?'

'Oh no,' I said quickly, 'quite the opposite. He hates that sort of thing – you know, philandering, playing around.'

'Oh.'

Her face fell. I could tell she felt alone. The only betrayed wife in the world. I quickly rallied.

'But – but I've been involved with loads of other bastards in my time, oh gosh yes, plenty, men who'd make Sam look like an absolute beginner, in fact.'

I wasn't lying either, I thought, shuddering as I recalled Harry Lloyd-Roberts, my boyfriend before Nick. He fitted the bill perfectly, and how.

'Oh yes!' I nodded vigorously, warming to my theme. 'I've been betrayed quite comprehensively in my time, *and* I refused to believe it was happening. My friends had to literally rub my nose in it to make me face facts. I only knew about one of his flings but he probably had countless others behind my back. God, I was such a fool.' I stared into space, remembering the bad old days.

'Not half as much of a fool as I've been, I bet,' she whispered.

I looked back at her quickly and was aghast to see a tear trickling down her face.

'Oh God, I'm so sorry,' I gasped, 'that was so tactless, thoughtless. I didn't mean you were a fool, I just meant—'

'It's OK.' She gave a watery smile and wiped away the tear. 'I know what you meant. But I am a fool, there's no two ways about it.'

'Oh, now come on, where's that fighting spirit of just a second ago? That's all in the past! Like you said, you've got hard proof now, you can shove the photo under his nose, kick him where it hurts and then kick him out of the house. Tell him to bugger off and to conduct his sordid little affairs under someone else's roof!'

'Oh yes, I fully intend to do that, but that's not what I

meant about being a fool. You see, I haven't just let him walk all over me, I've let him trample me. Body and soul.' She looked up, her eyes full of tears. 'I'm not actually sure I'll ever recover.' Her chin wobbled dangerously.

'Course you will!' I said staunchly. 'It's just a matter of time. You're bound to feel hurt and vulnerable at the moment, that's only natural, but you'll see, before long some gorgeous hunk will come along and sweep you off your—'

'No, Polly.' She frowned and shook her head. 'I'm not just talking about Sam being unfaithful, it's more than that. It's—' She gulped and bit her lip. Then she brushed another tear roughly off her cheek and looked at me defiantly.

'You see, I wanted children,' she said in a rather demanding tone.

I jumped. 'Well, yes, of course, who doesn't, me too, although funnily enough now that I am pre—' I nearly gagged on my tongue, 'preparing to ride at Badminton, I've rather gone off the idea!' I gabbled, my heart thumping madly.

I flushed. Christ, you idiot, Polly, what the hell d'you think you're doing? Luckily she didn't seem to have registered that I was either big with her husband's child or the next Lucinda Prior-Palmer. She was miles away with her own problems.

'As soon as we got married I wanted them. Thought I'd get pregnant straight away, and when nothing happened after a year or so I began to panic.'

'I know the feeling,' I muttered, 'been there, done that.'

'Sam said I was being ridiculous, said I was too impatient and it was bound to happen sooner or later if I just stopped worrying about it.'

'So did Nick,' I said quickly, pleased I could join her on at least one agony trip, 'that's exactly what he said.'

'Of course, Sam had two children from his first marriage, so he wasn't nearly as fussed as I was. I think he only said he wanted more because I did. And I really did. I got quite hysterical about it, in fact. I think I secretly knew that our marriage was a sham and I thought a baby would help, bring us closer together, or perhaps give me a focus for my love.' She shook her head. 'Crazy.'

'But understandable,' I ventured.

She shrugged. 'Maybe. Anyway, after a while I started to go for tests. Minor ones at first, blood tests, that kind of thing, then I started to take my temperature every morning to see if I was ovulating, it's supposed to rise, you know—'

I nodded. 'Only too well.'

She sighed. 'Well, then we got on to more serious things. I had an operation in hospital to check my tubes were open – they were. Then I had a scan to look at my womb – that was fine. Then the doctors started talking about IVF and I had to have all sorts of other tests and examinations to see if it would be possible, if I was suitable – and so it went on. There seemed to be no end to the different ways they could poke, prod and peer at my reproductive organs. I can't tell you how traumatic it was, Polly, physically and emotionally. I was a complete wreck.'

'God, I can imagine, and I only got to the thermometer stage.'

'And the worst of it was that every time they did a test they'd come back with the same reply – as far as we can tell there's absolutely nothing wrong with you, Mrs Weston, just keep trying.'

'But that's good, surely?'

'No, you see I *wanted* there to be something wrong. I wanted there to be a reason, I felt the doctors could do something about it then, put it right, make whatever it was that wasn't working *work*!' She slammed the palm of her hand down hard on the counter. 'You see, I just felt so bloody helpless. I was dying inside, there was this ghastly void, and there was nothing I could *do* about it, nothing I could do to *help* myself.'

'And Sam? Wasn't he supportive or anything?'

'Oh, Sam was wonderful. We talked endlessly, he reassured me, calmed me down – gave me hope, actually, because he was so thoroughly convinced everything would be fine. But you see, he wasn't the one going through the humiliating rigmarole and he'd already fathered two children, so he was completely in the clear.'

She paused and pulled a lock of hair out from behind her ear. She began twiddling it furiously around her finger.

'Then one day,' she said softly, 'I went to one of those Christmas charity fairs – you know the kind of thing, lots of worthy Sloanes selling you totally pointless but frightfully tasteful things like tartan bottle warmers and inedible game pies.'

I grinned. 'I know the ones.'

'Anyway, there I was, on the point of being talked into parting with the best part of fifty quid for a wooden box with a chicken on it to stash my loo rolls in, when suddenly I turned and bumped into someone I hadn't seen for years. She used to be quite a mate, actually, but she was also a great friend of Sam's first wife so we'd rather diplomatically lost touch.' She paused and sucked the end of her hair into a point, gazing avidly at the marble breakfast bar as she remembered. 'She had her baby with her, on her hip, a little girl with red tights and blonde curly hair. Divine. I was playing with her, cuddling her, totally enchanted. I must have murmured something about wishing I had one of my own, because I can see this girl's face now, full of pity, concern. Poor you, she said, isn't there anything they can do? I remember being surprised, because I'd kept my tests deadly secret, but I assumed she'd just guessed. "No," I said, "we've tried everything, but nothing seems to work." She stared at me. "But can't they just reverse it?" she asked. I stared back at her. "Reverse what?" I said. She looked away, embarrassed. I remember feeling the blood literally drain from my face, down my neck, through my body. I grabbed her arm. "Reverse what?" I said, "reverse *what*?" She licked her lips, trapped. "The – the snip," she said nervously, "I – I thought Sam had had a vasectomy, after his children with Veronica, but I must have got it wrong..."' Sally gulped, her eyes wide, staring past me now, her face ashen. 'I remember gazing at her with my mouth open. She was pink, flustered. Then she quickly leaned over and kissed me goodbye, saying she had to dash. She bustled away with her baby, covered in confusion.'

She bit her lip and looked down at her lap. 'I don't remember leaving that fair,' she whispered, 'don't know how I got home. All I remember is sitting here, on this stool, in this kitchen, waiting for him to come home. It was early afternoon and he wasn't due back till about six, but I sat here all that time, hour after hour as it got darker and darker, not putting any lights on, just waiting, waiting. When he finally opened the front door I flew at him. I ran down the hall and almost took off, landing on top of him, ranting, raving, pulling at his clothes, his hair, anything I could get at, screaming like a mad thing. Two years of agony and torment came out in a matter of seconds. I remember his face, white, trapped. He sank down on his knees right there on the doormat and covered his face so I couldn't see his shame. But I didn't have to, I could smell it, it was all over him. Then he cried. Hot tears, flowing down his cheeks, he broke down completely, told me everything.

'He said he'd wanted to marry me so much but thought I wouldn't have him if I'd known he couldn't give me children. Said he'd tried to have the vasectomy reversed and it had failed. That he hadn't been able to tell me, that it had killed him. Not as much as it had killed *me*, I remember shrieking, still pummelling him with my fists. He said he'd never imagined I'd want children so badly, that I'd go to the lengths I had. He said it had been horrific to watch me go through it all, to pick me up from the hospital each time I had an operation, knowing I was on a hiding to nothing. Said it had been a nightmare for him.'

She gave a twisted little smile. 'He clung on to me like a baby, and after a while I just let him. I gave up, effectively. One minute I was punching him, kicking him, screaming at him, and the next I threw in the towel. I just sort of went limp and let him cling to me. He sobbed into my hair and kissed my face, desperate, tortured kisses. We held on to each other, crying. He said he'd done it because he loved me so much, couldn't bear to lose me. Then finally he asked me to forgive him. He was on his knees, right there on the doormat.' Sally looked past me, her eyes full of pain. 'And I forgave him,' she whispered, 'because – because I still loved him, you see, and I wasn't strong enough not to. I'd forgiven him his infidelity by turning a blind eye and finally I forgave him his cowardice and his cruelty. Just like that.'

Her face was blank, a mask. At last she found my eyes. 'So you see,' she whispered, 'that's how much of a bastard he is, and that's how much of a fool I am.'

There was a silence. I stared at her, wide-eyed, all sorts of conflicting emotions battling for supremacy within me. Pain at her pain – I couldn't remember when I'd been so moved by someone's anguish, but neither could I remember feeling quite so hysterically, madly, unbearably, deliriously happy. I breathed deeply, trying desperately to quell it, to keep it down, to control my overwhelming desire to shriek with joy. Sam had had the snip. Sam was incapable. Sam was firing blanks. Sam was not by any stretch of the imagination the father of my child, which by a deft process of elimination meant that Nick most definitely was. I clenched everything I possessed very hard – buttocks, teeth, knees – and shut my mouth very tightly, but it was no good. A strangled, joyous, whinny-like noise still escaped my lips.

'Hrmmmm!' I squealed, and then again, 'Hraaa! Hrmmmm!'

Sally looked at me in horror.

'Sorry!' I gasped, but the moment I spoke I lost control of my mouth and it split my face into a mad, helpless grin.

'So sorry!' I yelped again, desperately wrestling with my facial muscles and trying hard to think about starving children in Ethiopia, multiple pile-ups on the motorway, anything horrendous. Didn't work.

'Can't help it!' I gasped, shaking my head helplessly, my face writhing with joy. 'Hrmmmm! Ye! Ha!' A succession of weird strangled yelps continued to escape me.

Sally looked first astonished, then desperately hurt. 'Wh-what's so—' she began in confusion.

I quickly reached over and seized her hand. 'Oh, I'm so sorry!' I gasped. 'I'm so sorry, what must you think of me? But please believe me, it's got nothing whatsoever to do with what you've just told me, I think that's the most horrific story I've ever heard, ghastly, barbaric, awful – but, oh God, I can't tell you what good news it is for me!'

She looked at me aghast. 'G-good news? But how can it – what on earth d'you mean?'

I had to tell her. There was no other way. I gripped her hand tight, eyes shining.

'I'm pregnant,' I breathed.

Her face twisted momentarily in envy and I winced at the pain I was giving her. Then she shrugged and looked confused. 'S-so . . . ?'

'So I slept with Sam.'

Suddenly her face cleared. 'Oh! So you mean you thought – oh!'

'Exactly!'

'You thought—'

'Thought! I was sodding convinced!' I yelped. I was desperate to do some full-blooded yelping now.

'Oh no, no way. No chance of that at all.'

'Because he's impotent!' I screeched. 'He's flaming well impotent, isn't he?'

She gave a wry smile. 'No chance of that either, unfortunately, but he's certainly infertile, if that's what you mean.'

'YE-HAA!' I screeched, loud and clear, punching the air with my fist. 'YE-HA, YE-HA, YE-HA! HE'S INFERTILE! YE-HA! AR-R-RIBA!'

It was no good, I couldn't help it, I simply couldn't keep it in any more.

'Oh, I'm so sorry,' I gasped when I'd finished, clapping my hand over my mouth, 'but I just can't help it. I'm afraid. I've been worried for so long, desperately worried. Nick and I have been trying for ages, I was convinced it couldn't be his, that it had to be Sam's, and now it's not! It's not, is it?'

She grinned. 'Most definitely not. Go on, go ahead, do a war dance or something.'

I breathed deeply, in and out, in and out, and shook my head furiously, gaining control. 'No, no, I'm fine now, honestly.'

My face, I knew, was wreathed in smiles, my eyes were shining uncontrollably, that was enough for her to cope with at the moment. I'd do my war dance later, out in the street perhaps, or if I didn't make it that far, on the marble steps just outside the front door.

Suddenly she leaned across and patted my hand. She smiled. 'I'm pleased for you, really I am.' She looked surprised. 'Actually, I meant that too, I wasn't just saying it.'

'Course you weren't, you're far too nice.'

'Not that nice, I'm afraid. I'd still rather it was me. I still want what you've got, and I can't have.'

'But you can!' I said eagerly. 'You *can* have babies, you know you can, there's absolutely nothing wrong with you. Gosh, you've had a complete bloody overhaul! Everything's been flushed out and polished up till it's absolutely gleaming, you're probably as fertile as a gerbil now. And I just know that once you're shot of Sam you'll meet someone, someone totally divine, who's going to want to marry you and look after you and have babies with you and you'll only have to *look* at him and you'll be pregnant,

431

you'll end up with loads! Hundreds! Too many! They'll all be running around this kitchen drawing on the immaculate walls before you can say bugger off up to your rooms!'

She laughed. 'We'll see,' she said.

Her laugh died away quickly, though, and her smile faded. She looked down at her wedding ring and twisted it. Suddenly I went cold. I knew she wasn't completely over him, wasn't completely cured. I wondered then if she'd ever really leave him.

A silence fell. We sat there, opposite each other, gripping our mugs of cold coffee, both preoccupied with our own thoughts. Me with my intoxicating joy – a baby, *our* baby, our first of *many* babies, he'd have to forgive me now, he'd just *have* to – and her with her pain. Suddenly it came billowing over the counter towards me like a thick, enveloping fog and I realised my own vibes must be doing the same. There didn't seem to be much point in sticking around rubbing in my happiness. I drained my freezing coffee in a quick gulp and slipped quietly off my stool.

'I'd better go.'

She looked up, and came back from a long way away. She nodded and gave a faint smile. 'Sure.'

I gathered my things together, still tingling with excitement, and followed her back down the yellow hall, trying hard not to skip, not to jig, not to leap in the air and punch it mightily.

As we went, we passed the open door to the drawing room and I caught a quick glimpse of a beautiful, high-ceilinged, pale-yellow room. The lemon walls were crowded with pictures, oil paintings mostly, all originals, and at ground level there were gorgeous, covetable, faded antiques scattered around on the Persian rugs. It was elegant yet comfortable and not too imposing. However hard I tried my house would never have that effortless grace.

'How beautifully you've done it,' I breathed. 'You really have got quite an eye.'

She looked surprised and followed my gaze. 'The drawing room? Oh, that's not me at all, I'm much more interested in the garden. No, this is all Sam's idea.'

I frowned, and stepped forward to take a closer look. 'Really? But this is all old stuff, isn't it? Antiques? I thought he wasn't interested in that sort of thing, he told me he was only into the really modern look, state-of-the-art and all that.'

Sally threw back her head and hooted. 'Sam? He told you that? God, you must be joking, he lives for all this antiquated rubbish, can't get enough of it. He's always off at some auction house or another buying more junk to clutter up the place with. He's obsessed by it, if he was here now he'd tell you precisely where each piece came from, when it was made and whether it's true to its period or not. That's his pride and joy over there, he spends hours with his head in that,' she said, pointing to an elegant Queen Anne corner cupboard.

'What – that cupboard?'

'Oh no, not the cupboard, what's inside it. I'll show you.' She walked over and took a key from a china box on the shelf above it. Then she bent down and fitted it into the lock. I followed her, my heart pounding. The door swung back.

'There,' she said with a slight sneer, 'his precious collection. Sometimes I think I'm only here to finance his obsession.'

I gazed inside. All four shelves were crammed fit to

bursting with the most exquisite collection of porcelain figurines I'd ever seen outside of Trewarren.

'Meissen!' I breathed.

Chapter Twenty-five

'That's right, how did you know?' asked Sally in surprise.

'Oh, um, Nick likes it,' I muttered, my mind racing. 'We used to have one or two pieces.'

'Oh really? Oh well, Sam's a complete fanatic, you should see him sitting here on the floor every Saturday morning with all these figures spread out around him, polishing every piece lovingly with his little yellow duster.'

'But . . . is it all his?' I asked, picking up an artisan figure and turning it around in my hand. 'Did he collect all this?'

'Oh no, I only call it his collection because he's the one who takes an interest, but in actual fact it's all mine, my grandfather left it to me, he was mad about porcelain. All this furniture was his too, in fact,' she said, looking around. 'We've added very little. Just a couple of chairs over there, oh – and that mirror. You see, it sounds ridiculous but we've never really had much money, we were given the house but it's so expensive to run and Sam doesn't make very much. I suppose we look as if we're loaded because of all these antiques and things, but it all belongs to my family.'

'I see . . .' I said slowly, as she locked the cupboard. My heart was still pounding. 'But, Sam knows a lot about antiques, does he? I mean, porcelain in particular?'

'Oh yes, he's a bit of an expert in his own quiet way. He's always up at the V and A, nosing around, and whenever we go abroad we always have to trudge around a few dreary museums and peer at their bits and pieces. It's more than a hobby really, it's an all-consuming passion. His *other* all-consuming passion,' she added caustically, popping the key back in the china box.

'Gosh,' I said, following her out to the hall again and trying hard not to sound too interested. 'I had no idea he was such a – a whassicalled, aficionado.'

'Well, why should you? He keeps it very much to himself, doesn't really talk about it, can't think why.'

I can! I thought tremulously.

'Perhaps he thinks nosing round stuffy old museums doesn't quite go with the trendy-film-director image,' she went on, opening the front door for me.

Perhaps, I thought, but perhaps not.

Sally smiled shyly as we stood on the step together, blinking in the sunlight.

'Thanks for coming round, Polly, it can't have been easy, but I really appreciate it, and honestly, I'm really happy about your news.'

I smiled back. 'I'm glad I came.' *So* glad, I thought privately.

We kissed each other on the cheek and I ran across the road. I waved as I got into my car. She stood on the steps, a tiny blonde figure in her little black dress, watching as I pulled off.

I drove sedately down the road, keeping an eye on her in my rear-view mirror, but as soon as I knew I was out of sight I gave a great whoop of delight. I hit the gas, and shot off down the road. Bloody hell! What a morning! What an unbelievably riveting morning! I took my hands off the steering wheel for a second and gazed at them in wonder. They were trembling! They were actually trembling with excitement, and why not? I mean, God, first of all – and here I threw back my head and gave another great shout of joy into the roof of the car – Sam was not the father of my child, that much was wonderfully, beautifully, blissfully clear! He might strut around like a highly sexed tom cat, like a walking, talking sperm bank, but his missiles were all doing U-turns the moment they'd been fired. Hoo-bleeding-ray!

I looked down at my tummy and took a hand off the steering wheel for a second, stroking it gently, gazing with wonder, with awe almost. I was pregnant. By my husband. No one else. A radiant smile spread dreamily across my face. What a wonderfully warm feel— Oh Christ! I hastily dropped the radiant smile and put my hand back on the wheel as I narrowly missed colliding with a double-decker bus. Horns blared and obscenities were mouthed but I was much too excited to care.

Because what about that other revelation? What about that, eh? So much for Sam the modernist man. What an equally intriguing discovery that had been. Our Sam was no more a trendy minimalist than the entire *Antiques Roadshow* team put together, he was a history man, a heavily-into-antiques-and-porcelain man, a *Meissen* man no less!

I turned for Pippa's house, feverish with excitement now, all thoughts of rushing off to Thomas Cook to book my holiday in Lanzagrotty totally forgotten. Oh no, I couldn't lie on a beach getting sand in my eyes, I had to lie quietly in a darkened room and think, think, think!

But what did it all mean, though? So what if Sam was a

Meissen expert, could it just be one huge coincidence? I shook my head. No, it was much too huge for my liking, much too staggeringly colossal. I set my mouth in a grim line as I drove fast and furiously through the back streets of Chelsea, my mind whirring. Oh yes, make no mistake about it, Sam was up to his neck in the nicking of our precious porcelain, and I was the super sleuth who was going to nail him!

I careered up to some red lights, just managing to stop in time, and gripped the steering wheel hard as I tried desperately to think of some more incriminating evidence. I was pretty sure I had to have a bit more than just the fact that he was a Meissen enthusiast to go to the police. I mentally ticked off a few starters in my head.

Right, first of all, Sam had no money. He was stony broke, that much was clear, so he needed the loot. Secondly, he'd know how to get rid of the stuff. He obviously had his finger on the pulse of the porcelain market so he'd know when and where to pass it on without arousing suspicion – probably knew every collector in the country. Thirdly . . . I bit my lip and frowned. Thirdly, on the night of the burglary he'd been two hundred miles away, holed up in a hotel room with yours truly, much too drunk to drive and much too late to catch the last train to Cornwall, which would have gone hours ago. Damn! I punched the steering wheel hard. How the hell had he done it then?

I stared out of the window at the row of shops I'd pulled up in front of. Unless . . . unless he hadn't actually done it himself. The lights went green, I shunted into first gear and shot off. Yes, of course, brilliant! Sam wouldn't actually want to get his own hands dirty, would he? No, he'd have an accomplice, a lackey, someone who'd do the job for him. But who could that be? Did Sam know someone in Cornwall, perhaps? Someone who'd run the risk? I sighed. The list could be endless, he might know every light-fingered crook in the West Country for all I knew. He probably knew a hell of a lot of antique dealers, and if Lovejoy was anything to go by they were all a pretty dodgy lot.

I roared up the road to Pippa's house in a state of high excitement, parked – well, screeched to a halt – and ran up the garden path. I found the spare key under the pot, bustled importantly into the sitting room and grabbed a piece of paper and a pencil to take notes. I sat down purposefully on the sofa, all ready to think.

I chewed the end of my pencil. Now think, Polly, think. I gazed into space. Nothing much seemed to be happening. I pursed my lips. What would be the most thought-provoking position? I wondered. I swung my legs up and lay down with my head on the arm of the sofa. Then I shut my eyes. Huge mistake, I began to feel a bit sleepy. I quickly got up and sat with my head between my knees so that lots of blood could flow into my brain and help things along. I frowned at the carpet. Now come on, Polly, think. *Think*!

I bashed my head with my fist. Why was I so slow? Where the hell had I been when God had been handing out the little grey cells? Round the back of the bike sheds, probably, having a quick fag and touching up my lipstick. I groaned in frustration. Why couldn't I be one of those people who only had to look at a puzzle and it snapped into place? Like those eggheads on *Countdown* who did conundrums in under twenty seconds, or people who did

The Times crossword while they were waiting for the toast
to pop up. Why couldn't I be more like . . . Nick! Yes, of
course, Nick! He'd know. I'd ring him. He'd know *exactly*
what to do.

I leaped up with a little squeak of joy and ran to the
phone, delighted to have such a good excuse to speak to
him. I was halfway through punching out Tim and Sarah's
number, however, when I hesitated and lowered the
receiver. Should I be doing this? How would he react to
hearing from me? As far as I was concerned he was my
darling husband, father of my unborn child, no less, but as
far as he was concerned I was still public enemy number
one, the unfaithful hussy of a wife.

All the same, I thought, slowly bringing the receiver
back up to my ear, this was surely something Nick should
know about, wasn't it? We were talking about his precious
porcelain collection here, it might even lead to him getting
it back, he'd thank me for that, wouldn't he? It would help
to – you know, ingratiate me, wouldn't it?

I finished dialling and listened with some trepidation as it
rang at the other end. I cleared my throat nervously, but
after a while trepidation turned to frustration as no one
answered. I tried Trewarren but it just rang and rang there
too. Oh, come on, Nick, where are you, how come you're
never *there*? Finally the answering machine clicked into
action.

'Hello, this is Nicholas Penhalligan, I'm sorry we're
not . . .' and so on. I listened dreamily. It was a pleasure to
hear his voice. Suddenly I realised I was beyond the beep.

'Oh, er, Nick?' I began clumsily. Oh help, why hadn't I
thought out what I was going to say? 'Um, it's Polly here,
your wife – obviously enough!' I giggled nervously, then

cleared my throat and struggled to sound sensible. 'Um, look, the thing is I've got this idea, well, more of a suspicion really. I think it's possible – well, I'm almost certain actually – that Sam's somehow connected with our burglary, because I've found out that he's got loads of Meissen in his house – don't you think that's weird? And he obviously really knows his stuff – his porcelain stuff, I mean,' I added quickly. 'Er, so that's it really. I'm going to do some more investigating but I really need to speak to you, for – well, for advice really. Um, bye then.'

I put the receiver down. Terrible, Polly, really terrible. Totally convoluted and inarticulate. I sighed. Oh well, what did he expect from a pregnant woman? I looked at my watch. Ten past one. He'd surely come back for some lunch soon, I'd just nip to the shops and get some food, then I'd sit by the phone for the rest of the day and wait for him to ring.

I raced up to the High Street, bought some provisions, then ran back to the house. I set up camp by the phone in the hall and nibbled a piece of raw broccoli, quite disgusting, but full of folic acid, apparently, good for a baby's brain, or back, or something. Now that I knew about this baby's illustrious parentage I'd decided it had to be on the receiving end of something slightly more nutritious than dry biscuits.

I nibbled away and stared at the phone. Eventually my bottom got sore from sitting on the hard chair so I commandeered the portable phone and lay down on the sofa with it by my nose. I watched it closely. I rang the operator once or twice just to check it was still working. I carried it around with me. It had lunch with me. It watched a lot of television with me. It even had a bath with me.

By the time Pippa's key turned in the door at six-thirty I'd clocked up almost five hours of solid telephone watching without so much as a tinkle from Nick, and I was almost going berserk. I fell on her as she came through the front door, relieved that at last *somebody* in the world would be forced to listen to my story.

'Oh Pippa, thank goodness you're back, I've got so much to tell you – you won't believe what sort of a day I've had, you just won't believe what's happened!'

Pippa dumped her bag and jacket on the hall chair and gazed at me rather dreamily. Her cheeks were pink and her eyes were shining.

'Really?' she said in a distracted manner. 'I've got some news too . . .'

She smoothed her hair in the hall mirror, gazing abstractedly at her reflection. She looked radiant. Suddenly she turned and grabbed my hand. She beamed.

'Oh Polly, something most extraordinary has happened, something so unbelievably wonderful I still can't really believe it's true! Come on, let's go and get a glass of wine and you can tell me your news, then I'll tell you mine!'

She dragged me into the kitchen, fairly skipping with excitement, and reached for a bottle of wine in the fridge.

'You first!' she trilled. 'I want to save mine till last!' She shoved the corkscrew in and screwed furiously.

'Well, first of all,' I said, perching on the edge of the table, 'Sam's not the father of this baby, Nick is.' I grinned. 'Sam's had a vasectomy.'

'What!' She popped the cork out and almost dropped the bottle. 'Are you sure? Did Sally say so? Oh Polly, that's terrific!' She put the bottle down and hugged me. 'I'm so pleased! You must be delighted.'

'I am, ecstatic, and I can't wait to tell Nick about the baby. I think he might see things differently now, don't you?' I asked anxiously.

'Of course he will!' she said staunchly. 'Once he knows he's going to be a father he'll forgive you anything.'

'Well, hopefully,' I said nervously, twiddling my hair round my finger. 'But listen, Pippa' – I slipped off the table and sat down in a chair – 'there's something else, something really quite serious.'

'What?' She poured out a couple of glasses and sat down opposite me. 'You look all sort of strict and headmistressy, what is it?'

'Sam collects Meissen china, I saw his collection at his house.'

Pippa frowned. 'So?'

'Meissen, Pippa, the same porcelain that was stolen from Trewarren, don't you see?'

'See what?'

'Well, he has to be involved somehow, doesn't he? I mean, it's much too much of a coincidence. D'you think I should ring the police or something?'

She stared at me. 'And say what? That Sam collects the same china as you, so therefore he nicked yours? Don't be ridiculous, Polly, Sam's not a thief, and anyway he was with you on the night of the burglary, wasn't he?'

'Well yes, but that doesn't stop him from being involved, does it? He probably got someone else to do it.'

'What, you think he masterminded the whole operation from the dance floor of Annabel's while some Cornish tea leaf was doing his dirty work? Don't be absurd, it's just a coincidence, and anyway what about Bruce, what about the bit he gave to his mother? Or d'you think that was really

Sam in disguise? Mincing around the hospital in a pair of tight jeans and a blond wig, hoping Bruce's mum wouldn't suss him?'

'Now don't be flippant, Pippa, this is serious—'

'Well tell me then, tell me how you think he did it.'

'Well . . .' I scratched my head. I'd been so sure, so convinced. I struggled to get back to my train of thought.

'Yes?' she demanded.

'Now hang on a minute, Pippa, you're confusing me. I had some good ideas earlier, just let me think a minute—'

'Oh, for goodness sake, Polly, forget it, will you? It's absurd. Totally crazy. And anyway,' she seized my hand across the table, 'what about my news – just listen to this! Guess what?'

'What?'

'Josh is leaving his wife!'

'Oh! Oh, that's . . . wonderful, Pippa.'

'Isn't it fantastic? When he got home last night she confessed that she'd been unhappy for ages and was having an affair with some guy at work – Josh had no idea! She wants her man to move in with her, so Josh is going to come and live here.'

'Really? What, here with you?'

'Yes, of course, why not? And guess what, Polly, he hinted – only hinted, mind – that when the divorce comes through, we might even get married. Married!' She leaped up and danced around the kitchen, clutching the bottle of wine to her chest. 'Aren't I just the luckiest girl in the world? Aren't I? God, I can't believe it! There's only one thing, though.' She sat down again and looked anxious. 'D'you think we can still get married in a church? Because Josh has been married before? D'you think I can still have the whole ivory silk and orange blossom bit? Do you? Only I really want all that.'

'Well, I—'

'Actually I have a feeling it's OK so long as the vicar jumbles the vows up a bit. My cousin married a divorcee and she had the works, but I seem to remember the words were a bit different, which is fine by me, I don't mind what Josh says so long as "I do" is tucked in somewhere – oh, and all his worldly goods, of course!' She giggled. 'Oh, and Polly, you can be my bridesmaid, or – no, you're married – my matron of honour! My *pregnant* matron of honour. Gosh, you'll probably be about nine months by then, you can waddle up the aisle after me, what a scream! Oh, isn't it brilliant, isn't it just fantastic?' She leaped up and did a few pirouettes round the kitchen.

'It's great news, Pippa, really it is.' I forced a smile. I couldn't help thinking that Josh wasn't exactly leaving his wife, she was kicking him out. But it wasn't just that, there was something else, something about Josh, something nagging . . .

'Listen,' I said, 'sorry to harp on, but about Sam, d'you really think I shouldn't just mention it to the police? I mean, that he's a collector?'

Pippa stopped in mid-twirl. 'No, I don't think you should.' She stared at me. 'You know what you're doing, Polly? You're trying to get back at him. You're trying to pin something on him because he got you drunk and then went to bed with you. You're just pissed off with him, aren't you? You haven't got the slightest bit of proof, for heaven's sake, you just know he collects the same china as you! And anyway, what about my news? What about my life, for a change, did you hear what I said? Josh and I might be getting married. Isn't that marvellous, or doesn't my life matter?'

'Of course it does and I'm thrilled for you if . . . well, if that's what you want.'

She stared at me. 'Of course it's what I want, it's what I've always wanted, you know that. What's the matter, don't you like him or something?'

'Of course I do, it's just – oh, I don't know, forget it.'

'What? It's just what?'

'Well . . . it's nothing really, it's just – well, you know how he doesn't get on with Bruce?'

'Yes, so what?'

'Well, I just thought—' I licked my lips, I was getting into really deep water here. 'Forget it, Pippa, it's nothing.'

Pippa sat down and narrowed her eyes. 'No, come on, Polly, what? I'd really like to know. So what if he doesn't get on with Bruce?'

I squirmed around on my chair. 'Well, I just wondered . . . whether he had anything to do with it – but forget it, Pippa, I'm way out of line here, I—'

'No, no, I will *not* forget it! Hang on a minute now, you think Josh had something to do with the burglary? You think he framed Bruce, is that it?'

'Well, I—'

'Because his sister got Aids from a blood transfusion and as a result he can't bear homosexuals? You think that because of that he and Sam framed Bruce and nicked your china, is that it?' She gazed at me for a moment, then sat back in her chair, her eyes widening with comprehension. She nodded slowly.

'Ah yes, of course, I've got it now! You think that when he stormed out of the restaurant that night he went down to

Cornwall to steal your porcelain. Then he passed it on to Sam and together they framed Bruce, that's it, isn't it?'

'Look, I know it sounds far-fetched, but—'

'Far-fetched? Polly, it's obscene! For your information Josh was very upset that night because his sister had taken a turn for the worse. When he left the restaurant he went straight to the hospital. He spent the whole night sitting by her bed, holding her hand, comforting her and mopping her up as she threw up all night. If you need an alibi,' she said, looking cold and furious now, 'I'm quite sure the nurses at the hospital will verify his story. Why don't you go and ask them? St Stephen's, Fulham Road, go on, ask them!' She was white now and her lips had all but disappeared.

I put my head in my hands and groaned. 'Oh God, Pippa, I'm sorry, I'm so sorry!' I wailed. 'I had no idea. What must you think of me? I just – oh, I don't know, I've obviously got this whole thing completely wrapped round my neck.'

'You certainly have,' said Pippa, her voice trembling a bit. 'I can't think what's got into you. These are my *friends* you're talking about. Josh is my *boy*friend, for God's sake, and Sam is an extremely good mate, added to which they've both got responsible jobs in the film industry – they're not petty thieves! Christ, you'll be accusing me next. Perhaps you think Josh popped into the hospital for ten minutes then he and I *both* charged down to Cornwall and robbed you blind, is that it?'

'No, of *course* not, Pippa, of course not, and I'm so sorry, really I am—'

'And what about Bruce? I mean, I know you like him, but take it from me, he is one hell of a mixed-up kid, and if you want my *very* candid opinion – which up until now I wouldn't have voiced, but seeing as how you've forced me into it – I wouldn't put it past him at all. Not at all!'

She lit a cigarette, puffing the smoke out fast and furiously and shaking the match out vigorously. She was clearly upset. She waggled her finger at me.

'You know what you're doing here, Polly? You're trying to clear the people you *do* like and pin it on the people you *don't* like, don't you realise that? It's crazy!'

I stared at her. She was right, of course. I was behaving like a loony, like some sort of amateur Sherlock Holmes. Whatever was I thinking of? I shook my head.

'Oh God, I'm sorry,' I said miserably. 'I don't know what's the matter with me, I seem to be seeing the worst in everyone at the moment. It must be this pregnancy lark. I think Josh is great, really I do, and I'm desperately sorry about his sister. Pippa, I'm so sorry, just call me hormonal, OK?' I gazed at her beseechingly.

She glared at me fiercely, then looked away. After a minute she looked back. She grinned abruptly. 'OK, forget it.' She pushed the wine bottle over the table. 'Life's too short. Here, have another glass of wine, it might relax those hormones.'

'I think I'd better,' I muttered, sloshing some into my glass. 'I certainly need something.' I shook my head. 'I just can't think what got into me.'

'Forget it, I said. Oh, and listen – Josh is taking me out to dinner tonight, can I borrow your pink skirt?'

'My short one? I thought you said it was *passé*. What happened to all your flowing robes?'

She went pink. 'Oh yes, well actually Josh says he likes me best in minis.' She grinned ruefully. 'And let's face it, who am I really trying to please here?'

448

I grinned back. 'Who indeed?'

She looked at her watch and jumped up. 'Must go and have a bath, he'll be here in a minute, will you dig it out for me then?'

'Sure.'

She disappeared upstairs.

I sighed heavily and traced my finger around a knot of wood in the pine table. What did I want to get involved in all this detective malarkey for anyway? What business was it of mine who stole the china, it was for the police to sort out, wasn't it? I had my baby to think of now, our baby. I couldn't rush around the country exposing villains. I sipped my wine thoughtfully. I'd go home tomorrow, go and face Nick. Tell him about the baby. Ask him to forgive me. Sort my life out. Go to antenatal classes, decorate the nursery, be normal for a change. I began to feel excited. The little yellow room next to ours would make a great nursery, lots of light. I'd make it beautiful, have a border, ducks and rabbits – no, teddies, pink and blue, just to hedge my bets. Oh, and a mobile, lots of mobiles, and Winnie the Pooh pictures all over the walls.

Just then the phone rang.

'I'll get it!' I screeched upstairs to Pippa, who was running her bath. Nick, it had to be Nick. I'd tell him I was coming home. No, *ask* him if I could come home. I ran to the hall.

'Hello?' I said breathlessly.

'Hello, Polly? It's Lottie.'

'Oh! Hi, Lottie.' I tried to keep the severe disappointment from my voice.

'Where the hell have you been? I've been trying to track you down for ages. Nick was most elusive when I spoke to him last night, said he hadn't a clue what you were up to. What's going on, have you had a row or something?'

'Er, well, yes, a bit. Something like that – sorry, Lotts, I've been meaning to ring you but—'

'And how are you feeling? Gosh, I've only just heard, you don't still feel ghastly, do you?'

I frowned. How the devil did she know?

'Er, not too bad, still feel pretty sick in the mornings actually, but how did you know?'

'In the mornings? What, every morning? How *awful*! Polly, you must see a doctor, I told Nick and he agreed.'

'Nick?' I breathed. 'You told Nick?'

'Well, of course, I thought you would have told him already actually, but he had no idea. Polly, you *must* go and see someone, it's not right to feel sick every morning.'

'Isn't it? I thought it was fairly normal, but – but hang on a minute, Lottie, who told you?' I stammered.

'Peggy, I ran into her in the street the other day.'

'PEGGY!' I screeched. 'How the hell does *she* know?'

'Well, she saw you leave, she asked me how you were, said she'd never seen anyone in such a terrible state.'

'L-leave where?' I babbled helplessly, totally at a loss.

'The club, of course, Annabel's – remember? Tom and I left before you but Peggy said she saw you go.'

'Ah yes.' I was beginning – slowly – to see the light. 'Yes, I was pretty drunk that night.'

'Pretty drunk? Peggy said you were unconscious!'

Well, she would, wouldn't she, I thought savagely, she probably only drank orange juice, and now she was running around telling tales out of school about me, filtering them back to Nick, no less.

'Well, all right,' I conceded, 'paralytic actually.'

'No, Polly, she said you were actually unconscious.'

I frowned. 'What?'

'Yes, she said you had to be carried out, literally lifted out of the club, by that guy you were with, that film director chappie. Peggy went over to ask if she could help and he said something about you being prone to fainting from tiredness and that you had jet lag or something. She didn't think anything of it because she doesn't know you very well, but when she told me I couldn't believe it! I've never known you faint and as for jet lag – where the hell had you been to get that?'

I sat down heavily on the chair in the hall, trying hard to accommodate all this.

'Are you sure, Lottie?' I whispered.

'Positive! Peggy said the doorman at Annabel's helped carry you to a taxi, said he'd seen some pretty plastered people in his time but you really took the biscuit.'

Christ! I made a mental note not to frequent that particular joint for a while.

'And you're still feeling sick? Every morning? That's terrible! You must go for a check-up, really.'

'Oh! Oh er, no – no, that's something else.'

'What?'

'Oh, um, nothing really, nothing at all. It's almost gone now anyway, a bug sort of thing. Tummy bug. Listen, Lottie, I've really got to dash now, thanks so much for ringing.'

'Why have you got to dash?'

'Well, I've got this – this person coming round, odd-job man – ooops – there's the doorbell now, must be him. Thanks for ringing, Lottie, bye.'

'But—'

'Bye!'

I put the phone down. I stared at the floor. Unconscious. Jesus! Not just a little the worse for wear, a bit tiddly-tight, a trifle woozy, but out for the count. The bastard. The complete and utter bastard. Sally had been right, he was totally unscrupulous, unspeakably vile. What sort of a man would get a girl so disastrously drunk that she couldn't even speak, let alone stand, then carry her to the nearest hotel and proceed to have his wicked way? I felt physically sick, and this time it was nothing to do with the hormones. This was rape then, wasn't it? This wasn't just a drunken one-night stand, this was a ghastly – I sat up straight, my eyes bulged – yes, it was a date-rape! God, I'd been date-raped!

I gasped. I clutched my mouth, horror and revulsion rising within me. I managed to stagger to my feet but my legs were like jelly.

'Rape!' I whispered, gasping for breath and clutching the banisters. All at once I found some air.

'RAPE! R-A-P-E!' I screeched at the top of my voice.

There was a great sploosh of water from the landing above me. The bathroom door flew open, hit the wall with a resounding crash, and Pippa came hurtling down the stairs, stark naked and streaming with water.

'Where? Where is he? What happened?' she shrieked, grabbing an umbrella from the stand in the hall and brandishing it wildly.

'Rape!' I squeaked again, collapsing into the chair and clutching my head. 'Ooh, Pippa, I've been raped!'

She seized my shoulders. 'Oh Polly! Oh my poor darling! Where is he, has he gone?' She looked around wild-eyed. 'Which way did he go?' She flung open the front door and brandished the brolly, clearly ready to pursue him down the street stark naked.

'Oh – no,' I gasped, 'not just now, ages ago. It was Sam, but I've only just found out!'

Pippa stared at me. She slowly lowered the umbrella. Then she shut the front door. Her jaw slackened.

'Sam?

'Yes, I've only just found out, that night in the hotel, he raped me!'

Pippa put the umbrella back in the stand. She sighed heavily and folded her bare arms against her bare chest. 'Oh God, Polly, not that again. Is that what you got me out of the bath for? You think Sam raped you now, do you?'

'Yes, yes! Because listen, Pippa,' I babbled, 'Lottie's friend Peggy was in Annabel's that night, she saw me leave with him, she said I was unconscious!'

'Really?' Pippa looked grim. 'Well you probably were, does that really come as a complete surprise? I mean, let's face it, you do tend to shift the liquor and it's not unheard of for you to lose it in the leg department as a result. For God's sake, Polly, that Peggy girl's as straight as they come, she probably saw you reeling around a bit and couldn't believe her puritanical eyes.' She raised her eyebrows. 'All right if I go back to my bath now? I mean, there's no one you actually want me to clobber over the head, is there? No one's brains you want me to beat to a pulp? Only I'm freezing to death here. As you might have noticed, I've got nothing on.' She shivered violently.

'But Pippa—'

'Listen.' She looked at me sternly. 'Sam is undoubtedly a bit of a lad and I'm quite sure he got you plastered and then coerced you into bed, but that's not quite the same thing as rape, is it?'

'But it explains why I don't remember anything,' I wailed, wringing my hands hysterically. 'It explains everything!'

Pippa grabbed a coat from the coat stand and wrapped it around herself. Her teeth were chattering now. She knelt down beside me.

'It explains nothing,' she said gently. 'OK, maybe you did pass out momentarily and then perhaps you came round in the taxi or something, who knows? But honestly, Polly, I wouldn't make a big thing of it, because believe me, it won't sound good. I mean, think about it, it's a classic, isn't it? A girl feels guilty about an extramarital bunk-up, she broods on it for a while, feels bitter and resentful and then eventually, ages after the event, accuses the guy of raping her.'

I stared at her.

'Well, that's about the size of it, isn't it? And believe me, that's certainly how it's going to look. And anyway,' she said with a quizzical smile, 'I thought he was a thief? Two minutes ago you were convinced he was a burglar, now he's a rapist.' She cocked her head to one side. 'I mean, which is it, Polly? Know what I mean?'

I gulped and stared at the floor.

She grinned, gave my hand a quick squeeze and then with chattering teeth turned and leaped back up the stairs two at a time to the bathroom.

'Look, I'll talk to you about it in a minute when I'm out of my bath, OK?' she yelled. 'But I'm freezing to *death* here!'

I watched her go. The bathroom door slammed. I heard the radio go on. I sat dumbly, staring at my reflection in the hall mirror opposite. A rapist or a thief. A thief or a rapist. My eyes stared back at me. Yes, I wondered, which indeed? I set my mouth in a grim line. And why not both? Far-fetched? We'll soon see about that. Forget about it? No way. I'd had a feeling all along there'd been something very fishy about that night, and now I was going to prove it.

I waited until I heard Pippa splashing away happily in the bath again, then I stood up and quietly plucked my car keys from the hall table. I silently opened the front door, tiptoed around it and shut it softly behind me. Then, with my heart thumping wildly, I ran down the garden path to my car.

Chapter Twenty-six

I closed the car door softly behind me and glanced anxiously up at the house to see if Pippa was looking out of the window. I didn't want to have to explain myself, she thought I was mad enough as it was and she'd think I'd gone completely doolally if I told her where I was going, but I'd had an idea. I was going to go to the hotel. I was going to go and find out if anyone remembered me from that Friday night, find out what sort of condition I'd been in. The only trouble was, apart from the fact that it was a reasonably classy joint in Mayfair, I was a little vague as to its exact location. There was going to be a certain amount of trial and error involved here. Duke Street? I wondered. Stratton Street, perhaps? I started the car. Somewhere like that anyway. Maybe if I meandered around the vicinity it would all come flooding back.

I roared off to Mayfair, trying hard not to think about Sam in case I was sick all over the steering wheel, and instead concentrated like mad on trying to remember which particular road the taxi had picked me up from on that fateful morning-after-the-night-before. I drove slowly round and round Berkeley Square, peering anxiously down side streets and feeling more and more unsure and confused. Suddenly, on a gut impulse, I hung a left. I parked the car on a yellow line and dashed up Mount Street.

I ran towards Grosvenor Square, glancing up at the tall, elegant buildings which towered on either side of me. It hadn't been a large hotel, that much I remembered, and it was just a hunch, but I had a feeling it was somewhere around . . . here! I skidded to a halt and gazed up at the ancient red-brick building I'd stopped in front of. It was definitely a hotel – albeit a discreet one, just a tiny gold plaque on the outside to let its punters in on the secret – but was it the right one?

I pushed through the smoked-glass doors and peered dubiously around the reception area. It didn't actually look terribly familiar and I was just about to go when – oh yes! Hang on a minute. I stared down at the carpet. It was royal blue with a tiny gold fleur-de-lis pattern on it. That pattern, surely I remembered it from the towels in the bathroom? I crouched down and took a closer look, peering at it.

'Yes, brilliant, Polly, right first time, this is it!' I exclaimed, much to the astonishment of a group of jabbering Japanese tourists who were clustered at the reception desk.

They instantly broke off from their animated discussion and bustled over to have a look. Had they overlooked some fascinating ancient carpet? A first-class tourist attraction in front of their very noses, right here in the hotel? I smiled and nodded.

'Seventeenth century,' I whispered, 'genuine Aubusson.'

They instantly erupted into an excited babble and thousands of yen's worth of camera equipment whirred into action. I left them to snap and flash furiously as I hurried over to the now empty reception desk.

There didn't appear to be anyone about so I banged the little gold bell and shouted 'Hello! Hello!' once or twice.

After a minute a pale, rather bored-looking young man appeared from a back office. I had the feeling he hadn't liked the urgent way I'd rung his bell because he took his time to arrive at the desk and peered down his nose superciliously at me.

'Hello,' I said rather breathlessly, 'um, d'you remember me?'

He raised a laconic eyebrow. 'Should I, modom?' he enquired in an unnaturally plummy voice.

'Well, hopefully, yes, you see I was in here – well, I think I was in here – about four weeks ago with – with a friend of mine. It was a Friday night and I believe I was rather, you know, out of it. Ring any bells?'

He regarded me coolly. 'I'm afraid not. An awful lot of people stay in this 'otel, modom, as I'm sure you'll appreciate. Just the one night was it? You and your, er, friend?' he said with a sneer.

One of these days, I decided, I'd tell one of these snotty-nosed receptionists or shop assistants who worked in smart London joints and looked at you as if you were a pile of poo when you walked in that they weren't fooling anyone, because that's exactly what they were, *receptionists*, for God's sake, *shop* assistants. They could be as superior as they damn well liked while they were in Mayfair but I was pretty sure at the end of the day they went home to their bedsits in Kilburn, dropped their h's, crucified their vowels and ate Vesta curries on their laps in front of *Brookside*.

However, I pretended I hadn't understood the implication and smiled sweetly. 'That's it, just the one night.'

'Name of?' he said wearily, flicking through a large diary on the counter.

'Penhalligan and, er, Weston. Or possibly just Weston – yes, Mr and Mrs Weston.'

He pursed his lips to hide another sneer.

'Yes...' He ran a finger down the entry for Friday 8th. 'Here it is, Mr Weston and Mrs Penhalligan.' He snapped the book shut.

'Oh! Really? Did I sign it then?'

He sighed and opened the book again. 'You tell me, modom,' he muttered, swivelling the book around for me to see.

I shook my head. 'No, that's not my writing.'

'Must be your friend's then,' he purred.

'Yes, must be. Good, so we were definitely here, that's a start. Were you on the desk that night, by any chance?'

'I was, as it happens.'

'But you don't remember me?'

'As I said, modom, an awful lot of people pass through these—'

'Here, what about this then?'

I ruffled up my hair, smudged my lipstick across my face and pulled my T-shirt off one shoulder. He looked alarmed. I slumped forward on his desk, rolled my eyes and stuck my tongue out of the corner of my mouth, frothing a bit. He started to back away in horror, but then abruptly stopped. He peered, stepped forward, and took a closer look. His face cleared.

'Oh blimey! Yeah, yeah, hang on a minute, it's all coming back!' Suddenly we were in Kilburn. 'Yeah, I've got it!' he said cheerfully, waggling his finger at me. 'I didn't recognise you at first wiv your clothes on an' that, but you were the bird wot was carried in wiv her undies hanging out!'

'Er, yes, yes, quite possibly, was I actually carried in?'

'More or less, yeah. I mean 'e had 'is arm around you and was sort of draggin' you along, but you couldn't stand up. An' then while 'e signed the register 'e propped you up on that sofa over there but you kept toppling over, like. You was in a terrible state, terrible!'

'Really,' I breathed, 'go on.'

'Well, I asked your bloke wevver I should call a doctor, like, but he said no, you often got like that an' you just needed a good night's sleep. Said it was a mixture of jet lag and booze, but I tell you, I've seen some pretty godawful drunks in my time and you looked more than half cut to me, your eyes were rollin' round your 'ead somefing terrible. It was 'orrible! Maria said we shouldn't 'ave let you in in that state, but he'd paid the bill and was up them stairs before we could say 'ang on a minute, mate!'

'I knew it!' I cried, slapping the counter with my hand. 'I knew I had to be a hospital case to let him bring me here, the bastard – and did you see him leave too? In the morning?'

'Nah, my shift finished about ten minutes after you arrived. Maria took over. She shut the place up for the night then manned the desk till I came back on at about nine the next morning. You can ask her if you like.'

'Is she around?'

''Ang on.' He poked his nose into the back office. 'Maria!'

461

A moment later a Spanish girl popped her head round. '*Si?*'

'You know that flash git wot carried that bird in 'ere a few Fridays ago, the one that was right out of 'er tree, well this is 'er. She wants to know if you saw the bloke leave the next morning.'

She sidled up to the desk and nodded nervously. '*Si*, I see heem go.'

'At about seven, was it?' I asked.

'Ah, no no, the same night, at about half the twelve.'

I frowned. 'That night? Are you sure?'

'*Si, si*, I was just locking up all ze windows and he come queekly down the back stairs. I don't zink he was even seeing me, it was very dark because all the lights were off then. He didn't leave by the front door though, he went out of ze back, through ze fire escape. I started to go after heem, to tell heem he no get back in again, all locky up, but he ran off to a car.'

'Yes?' I breathed.

'Well, he get in. He get into ze car and they drive off really fast, all screechy tyres, so I no get a chance to tell him he no get back in the hotel again.'

'They? There was someone else?'

'*Si, si*, driving the car.'

'What did he look like, did you see? Blond, dark, a beard, anything?'

'Ah, no no, not a man, a girl, I recognise her!'

'You did!'

'*Si!* I see her in feelms of course, the feelm star lady!'

'Serena Montgomery?' I breathed.

'*Si*, that's it!' Maria nodded and grinned. 'Beeg surprise for me, I can tell you!'

I leaned heavily on the desk, suddenly needing some support. Serena. I gazed at the mahogany. Serena, blimey.

'Big surprise for me too, Maria,' I muttered.

Mr Kilburn peered at me nervously. ''Ere, you all right, luv? D'you wanna glass of water or somefing, not gonna collapse on us again or anyfing, are you?'

I slowly raised myself up from his desk. 'What? Oh, no. No, I'm fine ... fine ...'

Suddenly I swung around to Maria and grabbed her arm. 'Listen,' I said urgently, 'would you swear to that in court? You know, what you've just told me, would you swear to it?'

Maria backed away, her eyes huge with fear.

Mr Kilburn stepped in protectively. ''Ere, don't you freaten her, she ain't done nuffing wrong.'

'No, no, of course she hasn't, it's just – oh, never mind, it probably won't be necessary. Thank you, though, thank you so much!' I seized Maria's hand and shook it warmly. 'You've been a great help!'

On a sudden impulse I grabbed Mr Kilburn's hand too and pumped that up and down, beaming widely. 'Thank you, thank you very much!'

They both looked at me in astonishment and retreated back towards their office, their eyes wide with wonder. I turned on my heel and, skirting round the group of fascinated Japanese tourists, who were still on their hands and knees peering at the carpet, legged it out of the hotel.

I leaped the front steps in one, fell over, picked myself up and raced down Mount Street back to my car. I could hardly do my seat belt up my hands were shaking so much, and it took quite a few stabs to get the key in the ignition, but once in, I crashed the gears with a vengeance and roared off in a state of high excitement. My mind was absolutely fizzing.

Of course! It all made perfect sense. Sam had obviously slipped me something totally lethal in Annabel's, something quite a lot stronger than a double gin and tonic, thank you very much. Oh yes, we were talking drugs here, heavy duty ones too, because whatever it was had clearly knocked me senseless. Then he'd carted my limp body off to the hotel and booked us both in, making damn sure I was registered under Penhalligan and also making absolutely sure that we were well and truly noticed.

Oh, I could see it all now, the amorous drunken couple returning from the nightclub, out of their minds with booze, hanging on to each other, reeling around the reception area making a hell of a racket. Me, already half undressed and practically comatose on the sofa, and Sam, ringing the bell, roaring his head off and acting the drunken lothario whose sole intention appeared to be to get his plastered bird up those stairs as quickly as possible and bonk the living daylights out of her.

Once upstairs he'd obviously taken my clothes off – I gripped the steering wheel hard and bit back the bile: please God that had been the extent of his lechery, please God he hadn't raped me just for the hell of it – and scribbled the note which purported to have been written at seven the next morning.

Then, when he thought the coast was clear, he'd slipped down the back stairs to Serena, who was revving up the car at the back of the hotel. Together they'd whizzed off down to Cornwall – which at that time of night in a fast car would only have taken about four hours – arriving at Trewarren in plenty of time to relieve us of our precious porcelain.

And of course, I thought bitterly, cutting straight across the traffic into Piccadilly and leaving a blare of angry horns in my wake, Serena was the perfect accomplice, wasn't she? Oh yes, she knew the house inside out, she knew every inch of it from her days with Nick and was bound to know where the key to the porcelain cupboard was kept. All she had to do was reach up to the top of the dresser, slip her long, elegant fingers into the jug, produce the key with a triumphant little smirk and swing it in Sam's admiring face on one of her sharp red nails. I ground my teeth.

Badger, of course, would have been an absolute push-over, not that he was much of a guard dog anyway, but he probably gave her a rapturous welcome. So how had they got into the house? I wondered. I shook my head. No matter, that was a minor detail, I had most of the jigsaw in place and it all fitted perfectly. I thumped my forehead with the palm of my hand and groaned. Oh, you moron, Polly, why didn't you think of all this before?

I swung right at Scotch Corner, frantically imagining the scenario. I saw them running down Trewarren's staircase together, swag bag in hand. I saw them darting quickly across the drive to their car, stashing the bag safely in the boot and jumping into the front seat. Then I saw them roaring back to London amidst gales of triumphant laughter, stealing the occasional kiss on the motorway, stroking each other's thighs perhaps, ruffling each other's hair, oh so incredibly pleased with themselves. Finally I saw Sam arriving back home that morning at about ten o'clock, looking suitably shamefaced and sheepish, leading poor Sally to imagine he'd had another of his frequent nights out on the tiles.

And of course, if the shit did happen to hit the fan, if

someone did bother to ask Sam where the devil he'd been that Friday night, he had the perfect alibi. How could he possibly have had anything to do with the burglary at Trewarren when he'd been holed up with the lady of the very same house in a smart hotel in Mayfair? Oh yes, if Serena had been the perfect accomplice then I'd been the perfect alibi. God, how they must have laughed. I clenched my teeth and shook my head. Very clever, my little love birds, very clever indeed!

I roared up to Pippa's house and due to lack of space parked at a ludicrous angle with the front wheels practically in her garden. Yep, there was no doubt about it, I thought, slamming the car door behind me, it had been an absolutely brilliant plan. Fiendish even, and if it hadn't been for Maria – and me, of course – they might just have got away with it. Thank goodness for Maria! Thank goodness for me! I hurried up the garden path.

So what were they planning to do now? I wondered. Lie low for a bit and then sneak the stuff on to the market gradually? Go abroad, perhaps, and live off their ill-gotten gains? Not so fast, my little darlings, I thought grimly as I rooted around under the flowerpot for the key, not so blinking fast!

The first thing I'd do, I decided, as I let myself in, was ring the police. Not the crappy old Cornish police but Scotland Yard or MI5 or something. I mean heavens, we were in London now, there was nothing parochial about this enquiry any more. This was of national importance, the press would be on to it in a moment. I could see the headlines now – 'Missing Meissen Mystery – Film Star and Director Charged'. Oh yes, the tabloids would have a field day, and of course they'd want to speak to me, interview me, take a few pictures, that kind of thing. Naturally I'd be frightfully modest, pepper my story with lots of 'Oh, it was nothing's, and – oh gosh, wouldn't Nick be proud? He'd be beside himself!

I shut the door behind me. The house was in darkness. It was well past ten o'clock now and Pippa had obviously gone out for dinner with Josh and forgotten to leave any lights on. Poor Pippa, how awful of me to accuse Josh like that, especially just as she'd got the happy ending she'd dreamed of. I was so pleased it wasn't him, I could get excited with her now, work out possible wedding plans, go shopping for a dress, perhaps, choose her flowers, organise the brides-maids, that kind of thing. I felt along the wall for the light switch but when I flicked it down, nothing happened. The bulb had obviously blown.

Muttering darkly, I felt my way round to the sitting room and bent down to turn on the little lamp on the table just inside the door. As I fumbled for the switch halfway down the flex, my hand brushed against something warm, something – moving. I pulled back sharply – God, a hand! I clutched my throat with a scream. In an instant the lamp came on by itself. I screamed again, louder this time, and my hands flew up to my mouth. I stared in horror. Because there, sitting in the armchair with his hand on the light switch, was Sam.

Chapter Twenty-seven

His amber eyes looked almost yellow in the sudden bright light, his face pale and twisted with loathing. I backed away.

'Sam!' I gasped.

'Hello, Polly,' he said softly, 'how nice to see you.'

The words were slightly slurred and his mouth only just managed to articulate them. I saw at a glance that he was extremely drunk.

'H-how did you get in?' I stammered.

'Same way as you, I expect, first geranium pot on the left. Very careless of Pippa, especially in these dangerous times. Anyone could get in. Anyone.'

There was something deeply menacing about this statement. He licked his front teeth, unsticking them from his bloated, dehydrated lips, then he swayed a bit to one side and steadied himself with his hand on the arm of the chair. God, he was out of his head.

I gulped and scuttled to the far end of the room where I perched on the arm of the sofa. I didn't want to sink too deeply into a chair in case I needed to get up and do some fast running. I quickly leaned across and flicked on another table lamp, noticing as I did so that all the curtains were drawn. Pippa never bothered.

'Oh yes, the spare key,' I twittered nervously, 'yes of course, very silly, I – I must tell her about it, you're right. Um – did you want to see her? Only I think she's gone out with Josh.'

'She has. Won't be back till late. No, it's you I want to see, Polly.' He was breathing heavily now and sweating profusely, his skin looked damp and waxy. 'Just you. You little bitch.'

The venom in these few short words made me flinch. A cold hand gripped my heart. He'd come to get me, to silence me. He'd found out that I'd been nosing around and he'd come to rip out my tongue.

'Now, now, Sam,' I said nervously, 'there's no need to be like that, let's try and discuss this in a civilised fashion, shall we?'

'Civilised!' he spat. 'Don't talk to me about civilised, you with your dirty, scummy little tricks. You went to see my wife this morning, didn't you?'

Oh that! Gosh, I almost breathed a sigh of relief. I'd forgotten about that, he surely wasn't going to kill me because I'd been to see Sally, was he?

'Showed her a photograph, didn't you? Stolen, incidentally, from my private diary. That was pretty bloody civilised of you, wasn't it?'

On second thoughts, perhaps he was going to kill me, his eyes were twitching maniacally and he was grinding his teeth in an alarming manner. Thanks, Sally, I thought, inching back up the arm of the sofa, thanks a bunch, really terrific of you to drop me in it. I tried a lie.

'Well actually, Sam, that's not quite the way it was, you see—'

'Oh, don't give me that cock-and-bull story she tried

about finding it weeks ago!' he hissed. 'I know damn well it was in my Filofax when I left my case in that taxi, you just rifled through it and thought – Gosh, a photo, I wonder if Sam's wife has seen this – and then you clasped it in your hot little hand and toddled off to show it to her, didn't you? You conniving little bitch, you just couldn't wait to get even. Just because your marriage was shot to bits you thought you'd pop round and blast a few holes in mine!'

'Sam, it wasn't like that, really it wasn't. She asked me to take it round, rang me up and begged me to, and I didn't tell her anything she didn't already know. I promise I—'

'You're a fucking LIAR!' he bellowed, and thumped the wall with his fist.

There was a terrifying silence. I watched as a tiny hairline crack appeared in the paintwork. How long would it be before one of those appeared in my head? He started to lever himself out of his chair. Quite soon, obviously, I thought with a gulp, really quite soon. I felt cold with fear.

'Now look, Sam,' I whispered, 'let's not get this thing out of proportion, shall we? I mean, it would be silly to fall out over—'

'You're just an interfering little busybody,' he hissed, struggling to his feet, 'with nothing better to do than—' Suddenly he stopped. He sank back into his chair again. His shoulders sagged and his head dropped like a stone into his hands. He tugged savagely at his hair, pulling at the roots.

'She's leaving me, you know,' he muttered, 'or should I say,' he gave a hollow laugh, 'she's throwing me out. Not that it matters,' he went on almost to himself, 'I was going anyway, little cow. But not yet ... not quite yet ... fouls things up a bit, you see ... all a bit ... sudden.'

There was a silence, he seemed scarcely aware of my presence. I gazed at him in wonder. Was this really the same Sam? The glamorous, fun-loving guy I'd met in Cornwall, oozing charm and bonhomie? The mighty film director? My, how he'd fallen. He looked up abruptly. I could see the veins pumping away in his forehead. He stared at me.

'You see, I like to be in control, Polly,' he said quietly. 'I don't like other people taking the initiative, it upsets me, d'you know what I mean? It's for me to decide when I want to go, when I want to leave my own house. I don't like it when little bitches like you take it upon themselves to decide for me, I take it very personally, d'you understand?'

'Yes, but—'

'DO YOU UNDERSTAND?'

'Yes, yes!' I yelped. 'I understand!'

Christ, he wasn't just drunk, he was stark staring mad. I gripped my knees to stop them from shaking, my heart was pounding furiously.

His head dropped back into his hands and he began massaging his temples. He started mumbling to himself, it was as if he'd forgotten about me again. I breathed deeply and licked my lips, plucking up the courage to speak steadily, to calm him down. I was pretty sure that was the received wisdom with maniacs.

'I do see, Sam, really I do,' I began tremulously, 'but honestly, Sally wasn't even particularly upset. She knew about Serena, she knew about all the others – God, she'd even heard about you and me, can you believe it?' I laughed nervously. 'So soon!'

He looked up abruptly. His top lip curled. 'About you?

472

Don't make me laugh. Don't flatter yourself, Polly, I wouldn't touch you if you were the last woman on earth.'

A great tidal wave of relief washed through me but I tried my best to be outraged.

'How dare you!'

'Oh, it's quite true,' he sneered. 'If you must know, you make me want to vomit, have done since I met you. I knew what you were the moment I saw you, a bored, frustrated little housewife, spoilt rotten by your husband and bored to tears with your big house in the country and all your money. You just loved playing lady bountiful with the film crew, didn't you? Got such a cheap little thrill out of it all, being so gracious and magnanimous, having us all up to dinner at the big house, wearing a skirt that didn't even cover your pants and then flirting outrageously with me in front of your husband – you got yourself worked up into a right little lather, didn't you? Trying to prove you still had some go in you, trying your damnedest to get me into bed – you were desperate to commit adultery with the first attractive man who came your way. It was pathetic, you made me feel quite ill, if you must know.'

'How dare you!' I stormed. I glared at him. 'Christ, you've got a nerve to talk about adultery, you with your string of women, your sordid little flings – if anyone's pathetic around here it's you! Oh yes, I admit I flirted with you, and maybe I was a bit bored, but it was all totally harmless, there was no way I was contemplating an affair, no way! And as for blasting holes in your perfect marriage, you did that yourself the moment you left the altar! You've been seeing other women since you put a ring on Sally's finger and now you're knocking off that jumped-up two-bit floozy who couldn't act her way out of a paper bag! And I make you quite ill now, do I? Not exactly what you said in Daphne's, if you remember you said you were crazy about me.'

'Oh, that was so perfect,' he sneered. 'There I was thinking I was going to have to get rid of you subtly, and before I could get a word in edgeways you handed it to me on a plate! "Oh Sam,"' he mimicked, '"I'm so sorry but this simply can't go on!" All I had to do was pretend to be heartbroken and off you trotted. Serena and I had quite a chuckle about it that night, I can tell you.'

'I bet you did, but don't be too sure she isn't laughing at you too, Sam.'

'What d'you mean?' he said quickly.

'Oh come on, d'you really think she's in love with you? She's an opportunist, you must know that by now, she's out for what she can get, true love doesn't come into it.'

He stared at me for a second, then looked away.

'You don't know what you're talking about,' he muttered.

I was startled. Had I hit a nerve? Had things started to go wrong between the little love birds already? I pounced.

'Oh, don't I? I know her extremely well actually, in fact I could write a book about her nasty, conniving, calculating little ways. She's totally manipulative, Sam, she uses people – men especially – and when she's finished with them she just flushes them straight down the loo without a second thought. I bet she's done that to you, hasn't she? I bet you're somewhere in the S-bend even now and you haven't the faintest idea how you got there, am I right?'

I cocked my head sideways to see his face. It crumpled briefly, then he resumed his grim contemplation of the carpet. I straightened up.

'Well, I wouldn't be too hard on yourself if I were you,' I said softly. 'That's always the way it is with Serena, most people don't find out they've been shafted until it's too late. Bad luck, Sam.'

Call me foolhardy but suddenly he didn't frighten me any more. I saw him for what he really was. A coward. A weak, pathetic man who didn't have the guts to say no, who let the tide wash him this way and that as he floated aimlessly through life. Only this time, the tide hadn't just washed him round the corner to Rosy, or through the next office to Samantha in accounts, it had taken him to Serena. Serena, the wrecker, who with her lantern of bright blonde hair had beckoned him on, luring him towards her, tempting him with her beauty and her fame, but who was ultimately poised to dash him on the rocks and smash him to smithereens when she'd finished with him. I looked at him now, savagely massaging his brow, sweat gushing from every pore. God, he was a wreck already.

Had he really meant to lose Sally, I wondered, or had he just let his affair with Serena get out of hand? Had he really meant to jettison his film career and become a petty thief, or had he just been too weak and too greedy to say no when Serena had shown him a way to pay off his crippling debts at the same time as relieving the only man who'd ever dumped her of his family heirlooms? Oh yes, I detected Serena's hand at the back of all this, no doubt about it. And for how long would she be sticking around with the failed film director? Just long enough for him to serve his purpose and leak the porcelain on to the market, I suspected. And looking at him now, I knew he suspected it too.

'You're talking crap, Polly,' he muttered eventually.

'Am I?' I folded my arms. 'Oh, well in that case I hope you'll be very happy together. You and Miss Montgomery.'

He didn't answer me.

'I suppose you'll get married then, will you? I mean as soon as Sally gives you a divorce?' He didn't look up, but the circles he was rubbing on his forehead were becoming frenetic. 'I don't suppose Sally will want to hang around, will she?' I went on. 'I dare say she'll want to get everything sorted out as quickly as possible, get her life back together again, sell the house perhaps, make a new start, that kind of—'

'Shut up!' he hissed suddenly, shooting me a glare. 'Just shut up, will you!' He looked down again but not before I'd seen the despair in his eyes. He shook his head.

'Such a mess...' he whispered, 'such a godawful ... terrible ... mess ... got to think...'

I sat quietly and let him think, let him stew in his rancid juices. After a while he muttered something inaudible. I leaned forward.

'What?'

'I said I need a cigarette.'

'Actually I don't smoke any more,' I said nonchalantly, crossing my legs and rearranging my skirt. Gosh, I felt almost in control here, soon it would be time to ask him to leave.

'GET ME A FUCKING CIGARETTE!' he bellowed.

Did I mention control? I leaped up like a cat who's been sat on and scampered out to the hall. I looked around wildly. Pippa's briefcase was still sitting on the chair where she'd left it. I ran to it, snapped it open, rummaged around furiously and found a half-empty packet of Silk Cut at the bottom. As I took them out, I noticed her Dictaphone. I stared at it for a moment. Suddenly the house seemed awfully quiet and still, just the hall clock ticking away behind me. I felt ridiculously brave. I took the Dictaphone out and with a trembling hand pressed the record button, then I carefully lodged it behind the case, out of sight.

I went back into the sitting room, handed Sam the cigarettes and a lighter and walked, rather shakily, back to the far end of the room, where I perched on the arm of the sofa again. Sam lit a cigarette and pocketed the rest. I cleared my throat.

'So you didn't sleep with me after all that night at the hotel?' I said clearly.

'No I bloody—' Suddenly he halted. He narrowed his eyes and blew the smoke out thoughtfully in a thin stream. The full implications of admitting to how revolting he found me gathered in his eyes.

'No I didn't,' he said shortly. 'You were far too drunk. I put you to bed and, er, tried to sort of get you interested, but you were totally out of it. I just went to sleep next to you in the end.' He took another deep drag on his cigarette and exhaled through his nostrils, watching me carefully.

'Not what you said in the restaurant the other day.'

'No.' He licked his lips. 'No, I – well, I suppose I wanted to shake you up a bit, give you something to think about.'

'And you stayed with me all night? Left early the next morning?'

'That's right,' he said slowly, 'at about seven. You got the note, didn't you?'

'Yes, I got the note.'

There was a tense silence. The room felt oddly still. He watched me warily, the veins throbbing away in his wet forehead. I summoned up what little courage I possessed.

'You were seen, Sam,' I said hoarsely.

'What?'

'You were seen leaving the hotel at about twelve-thirty that night. You ran down the back stairs and went out of the fire exit at the back. Maria, one of the maids at the hotel, saw you go.'

The few remaining traces of colour in his face drained clear away. He stared at me. I'd got him. The satisfaction was immense but short-lived, like me probably. What did I have, a death wish or something?

He got unsteadily to his feet and advanced towards me. I quickly got up and backed away towards the french windows.

'Her word against mine,' he breathed, advancing slowly. 'Who d'you think cuts the most ice, a maid who can hardly speak the lingo, or an eminent film director, who, it transpires, was simply nipping into the garden for a quick cigarette before going back to his room five minutes later? The mere fact that she didn't see me return is neither here nor there, is it?'

'No, no, you're right,' I said quickly, slipping round the side of the sofa, 'neither here nor there. Absolutely right, couldn't agree with you more.'

The fact that she saw him get into a car and drive off at top speed with Serena was not to be mentioned under any circumstances, not unless I wanted to be bludgeoned to death on the carpet with one of Pippa's Conran candlesticks.

I crept round the sofa as he stalked me, our eyes locked in combat. I felt my way around with my hands, not daring to lose his gaze for an instant.

'Y-you know you're absolutely right, Sam,' I whispered.

'The maid was probably very tired and she obviously got it all wrong. After all, it was very late, she was probably daydreaming or – or hallucinating or something. I'm sure there's a perfectly rational explanation, nothing to worry about at all. I mean, as you say, she's just a maid who can't even speak English, there's no way they're going to get you just on her say-so, is there?'

He stopped and stared at me from the other end of the sofa, his yellow eyes burning into mine.

'Get me for what?'

I swallowed hard. Christ! Why couldn't I just keep my mouth shut?

'Get me for what?' he repeated evenly.

'F-for . . . for nothing really, Sam, nothing. I meant, um, for not paying your bill, perhaps, or – or—'

'I paid my bill,' he hissed, circling the sofa. 'What are you blabbing about, Polly, what do you know?' He was gaining on me now. 'You interfering little cow, what the hell d'you think you're—'

Suddenly the doorbell rang, interrupting his stream of abuse. We both froze in mid-creep and stared at one another. Sam looked alarmed.

'I – I must get that,' I whispered, taking one very brave but futile step towards the door.

'Don't even think about it,' he breathed, instantly welding me to the spot.

'B-but I must, it might be Pippa, she might have forgotten her key or something, or it might be—'

It rang again, long, loud and shrill, cutting short my nervous babble. We gazed at one another, transfixed, like a couple of statues. Then there was silence. Oh God, please don't go away, I thought desperately, digging my nails into the palm of my clammy hand. Whoever you are, please don't go away!

We listened. The silence continued. Sam's mouth began to twitch triumphantly. He took a step towards me, when abruptly – the bell rang again. This time a series of short, sharp, urgent blasts.

We both stared at the door. The whole house seemed to reverberate to the shrill, persistent summons. Then silence again. I bit my lip. Please don't go, please don't *go*. There was a rustle, then – footsteps. Retreating footsteps, going back up the garden path. I felt my heart sink through the floor. Sam's face lifted with relief.

'Oh what a shame,' he said, smiling nastily. 'They've gone. Bad luck, Polly, looks like you're on your own.'

He swayed slightly and grabbed the back of the sofa to steady himself. 'Now,' he said quietly, 'you were saying?'

'W-was I?'

'Yes.' He moved towards me. 'Oh yes, you were, about how "they" were going to get me, remember? Get me for what?'

He was close now and I could see hundreds of tiny beads of sweat glistening on his forehead and upper lip. His tawny hair was streaked with dark and stuck to his temples.

'Oh, er, nothing,' I gasped. 'Nothing at all, it was just a – a figure of speech, really, an expression, can't think what I meant at all!'

He gazed at me intently. 'You know something, don't you?'

He was almost upon me now. I kept going back, but ultimately I was going to hit the wall. Like now. I flattened my hands against it and slid sideways towards the front door.

'What the hell do you know?' he breathed into my face.

'Nothing!' I yelped. 'Don't know anything!'

'You think I stole your precious porcelain, don't you?' he hissed.

'No, no, of course not,' I whimpered.

He stared at me for a moment, then his top lip curled.

'Oh, what does it matter?' he spat scornfully. 'Say what you like, no one will ever believe you. We were too clever, and you were too stupid and drugged up to the eyeballs with the little beverage I slipped you to know what the hell was going on. Do your worst, Polly, it won't get you anywhere, we outsmarted the lot of you.'

I slid slowly along the wall towards the door again, feeling my way with my hands. He crept after me, shadowing me all the time, sneering contemptuously into my face.

'You and your stupid, trusting husband who leaves his keys lying around where anyone can find them, the dopey police in that backward village of yours, Brucey the Botty with his convenient passion for porcelain and his big homosexual secret that he wanted kept from Mummy at all costs, making him ripe for a spot of blackmailing. Oh yes, it all dovetailed together very nicely indeed, thank you very much, and there's not a damn thing you can do about it now.'

He rested his hands on the wall on either side of my head, stopping me in my slide towards the door and, ultimately, the free world. Then he brought his head down level with mine. Our noses were practically touching. His was wet with sweat and his eyes had a touch of madness in them. I felt sick with fear.

'And don't think it bothers me one iota if Serena sticks

around or not,' he hissed into my face. 'Silly bitch – I've got no illusions about her, never have had. I used her as much as she used me. She got the Meissen out but at the end of the day I'll be the one selling it on, and when I do, *I'll* be the one holding the purse strings and she can come crawling to *me* for a change.'

He thumped his chest for emphasis, swayed and gripped my shoulders to steady himself. I cringed at his touch and felt myself begin to shake under his hands. He tightened his grip and leaned forward. His yellow eyes were huge and staring, his teeth bared like a dog's. I retched as a mixture of sweat and gin-soaked breath shot up my nose.

'And don't think anyone's going to believe your little fairy story either, Polly,' he breathed. 'You squeak about being drugged and they'll think you're just an adulteress who's trying to save her marriage. Too many people saw you with your undies hanging out that night, too many people saw you being carried upstairs, they all knew what a rollicking good time I was going to give you. You mention drugs and the police will smell a guilty conscience a mile off.' He shook my shoulders. 'But then you won't be mentioning anything to the police, will you, Polly?'

I stared at him, I couldn't speak.

'Will you?' he repeated, shaking me a bit harder. 'Come on, Polly, speak up, I can't hear you.' He inclined his ear to my lips.

I shut my eyes and let out a strangled sob, but still I couldn't utter. My voice seemed to be wedged in my throat somewhere, along with my heart. I was dumb with fear.

'I said, won't they, Polly?' He shook me roughly this time, and my head bashed against the wall.

I covered my face with my hands, whimpering. I was

shaking violently now. He grabbed my hands and yanked them away from my face.

'You won't be mentioning anything, WILL YOU, POLLY!' he bellowed into my face, shoving me backwards.

I gasped with pain as my head struck the wall again. I stared up into his bulging yellow eyes, his gritted teeth and his white face, dripping with sweat. He was terrifying, but he was desperate too. Suddenly I knew I had one chance and one chance only. I dug deep for courage, opened my mouth and summoned up all the breath in my body.

'H-E-E-L-P!' I shrieked at the top of my voice.

Sam stared at me in fury. He raised his hand, I ducked, and suddenly there was a resounding smash. A brick came hurtling through the front window, sending glass flying everywhere.

'Christ al—' I ducked as pieces of glass sprayed around the room and the brick landed with a crash in the fireplace.

'What the—' Sam stepped back in alarm.

I gazed in astonishment as the yellow chintz curtain at the front window was ripped roughly from its brass rail. There was a jagged hole where the glass had been smashed. Through the hole, from the dark night beyond, a hand appeared. A man's hand. It swiftly unfastened the broken window and flung it open. Two hands then gripped the top of the frame, and a pair of very familiar blue-jeaned legs dropped deftly into the room, crunching glass underfoot. They were followed by an even more familiar torso and head. I gave a strangled sob, wrenched myself free from Sam's grasp and flew across the room.

'Nick!' I shrieked, as I ran into his arms.

Chapter Twenty-eight

I buried my face in his shoulder and sobbed into his jumper. He held me close for a moment then pulled away and lunged towards Sam, who was making a desperate dash for the door. He fell on his legs and rugby-tackled him to the ground. They wrestled for a moment, but it wasn't much of a contest. Nick was stronger and fitter and Sam was too drunk to put up much of a fight. Before he knew what had hit him, Sam was flat on his face on the floor, his nose pressed hard into the Axminster, his arms pinned behind him full-nelson style with Nick sitting firmly astride his back.

'Get out of that, you bastard!' gasped Nick, wrenching one of Sam's arms a bit further towards his head.

'Aarh! You're breaking my arm!' screeched Sam.

'I'd like to break your bloody neck!' Nick gave the arm another jerk. 'You creep!'

Just then a little blond head popped through the window. 'Safe to come in yet?' said a nervous voice.

'Get in here, Bruce,' yelled Nick, 'you could give me a hand!'

Bruce climbed tentatively through the broken window. 'I'm not too sure I'd be much help, actually. I do hope you've got him firmly, I was never much of a one for wrestling.'

'Just be ready to help if I shout, OK?'

I, meanwhile, had rushed to the dresser and picked up a large Chinese vase which I held high, poised over Sam's head.

'Shall I? Shall I?' I shrieked excitedly.

'Don't be silly, Polly,' panted Nick, 'we don't want to kill him, just immobilise him. Go and phone the police, for God's sake.'

'Oh! Right.' I put the vase down with a twinge of disappointment, but at the mention of the police Sam gave one last desperate heave. Nick struggled to keep him down.

'Quick, sit on his legs, both of you!' he ordered.

Bruce and I scampered round and sat, with great pleasure, and as hard as we possibly could, on the backs of his shins. Sam struggled, but I for one was no lightweight. We'd got him.

'You bastards!' he screamed. 'You've got nothing on me, you've no right to do this!'

'Oh, haven't we?' I retorted. 'He stole our porcelain, Nick, he just admitted the whole thing. He wasn't with me at all on that Friday night, it was him and Serena, they did it together!'

'I suspected as much,' said Nick through gritted teeth. 'The police in Helston were beginning to put two and two together, said it was just a matter of time before they had enough evidence to pull him in.'

'You mean,' spluttered Bruce incredulously, 'he – he tried to frame me?'

'That's about the size of it, Bruce,' agreed Nick.

'You bastard!' screeched Bruce, bouncing up and down

hard on Sam's shins. 'You pretended you were so concerned and all the time you were trying to get me put away. How dare you!'

'Crap,' spluttered Sam into the carpet, 'it's all hearsay, won't stand up in court. You've got nothing on me, nothing!'

'Tell that to the police when they get here,' said Nick grimly. 'OK, Polly, I've got him now, run and phone.'

I leaped up and ran to the hall, but as I picked up the receiver a police siren came wailing round the corner and up the road. Through the stained-glass window in the front door I could see a blue flashing light. It stopped right outside the house. A car door slammed and then another – heavens, were they here already? I flung open the front door to see two burly policemen legging it up the path towards me.

'You all right, luv?' one of them panted. 'Your neighbour rang to say she'd heard smashing glass, thought it might be an intruder, a burglar.'

'Yes! Yes, you're right, in there, quick!' I squeaked.

They pushed past me into the sitting room. I scurried after them.

'All right, sir,' said the larger policeman to Nick, kneeling down and grabbing Sam's hands, 'you can let go now, I've got him.'

Nick got up and Bruce leaped off Sam's legs, scurrying quickly back behind Nick, out of harm's way. The two policemen heaved Sam to his feet. They clamped his hands behind his back and snapped a pair of handcuffs on him.

'Right, mate, I'm arresting you on suspicion of burglary at Fifty-two Stanbridge Villas, Kensington—'

'Don't be bloody ridiculous!' screeched Sam.

'—You are not obliged to say anything, but anything you do say will be taken down and used in—'

'Er, excuse me,' cut in Nick, 'you're absolutely right, he is a burglar, but he hasn't actually burgled this house.'

'Course I bloody haven't!' exploded Sam. 'Haven't burgled any bloody house! I'll have you for false arrest! I'll sue you, I'll sue the lot of you!'

The policeman frowned. 'But . . . he came through the window?'

'Well, no, actually I did,' said Nick. 'You see—'

'You see, it's a set-up!' screeched Sam. 'I was simply sitting here minding my own business, talking to Polly, when these two idiots came crashing through the window like the bloody SAS! Talk to them about breaking and entering, not me! I want my solicitor here right now, I'm not saying another word until he gets here! Treating me like some sort of petty thief, it's outrageous, get these handcuffs off me right now!'

The policeman looked bewildered. 'So this bloke isn't a burglar?'

'Oh yes,' I assured them, 'he's a burglar all right, but not a petty thief. He didn't break in here to steal the video or anything, he's wanted in connection with a haul of Meissen porcelain that went missing from our house in Cornwall recently, about two hundred thousand pounds worth, in fact. If you check with the police in Helston they'll fill you in on all the details. This is most definitely your man, Sergeant, he's just admitted to it, his accomplice, by the way, is a Miss Serena Montgomery. Shall I write that down for you?'

The policeman looked dumbfounded. 'The actress?' He took off his cap and scratched his head. 'With all due respect, madam, I'm not sure we can arrest this man just on your say-so, let alone a famous actress, especially on suspicion of a crime committed all the way down in Cornwall. We're going to need a bit more evidence, a bit more proof, like.'

'Hang on a minute, you've got it!' I squealed, suddenly running to the hall. I grabbed the Dictaphone and dashed back.

'Here,' I cried breathlessly, 'it's all here! I got every word of it! At least I hope I did.'

I pressed the rewind button. Five men stared at me open-mouthed; the police in astonishment, Nick in wonder, Bruce in joy and Sam in absolute horror. I snapped the play button at random. Please God, let it work.

'. . . Say what you like, no one will ever believe you,' sang Sam's dulcet tones. 'We were too clever, and you were too stupid and drugged up to the eyeballs with—'

'Yes! Yes!' yelped Bruce, jumping up and down and clapping his hands with glee. 'Got him!'

'Give me that!' screeched Sam, making a lunge for the tape recorder.

'Oh no you don't, mate,' said the policeman, roughly yanking him back. He took the Dictaphone from me. 'Thanks, luv, I'll take this for the time being.'

'I think you'll find there's everything you need there, Officer,' I beamed, bouncing around a bit. 'Let me know if you need any more information, won't you, if the recording gets a bit faint I'm sure I can fill in the gaps. Oh, and incidentally, he used quite a lot of threatening behaviour, violence even, that might not come over too clearly on the tape, but I can certainly tell you all about it. I might even have some bruises to show you.' I pulled my T-shirt off my shoulder to have a look where Sam had shaken me, but rather disappointingly there didn't seem to be much of a mark.

'You bitch,' breathed Sam between clenched teeth, 'I'll get you for this. I'll, I'll—'

'Yeah, yeah, all right, all right, save it for your court appearance, mate,' said the policeman. 'Come on, you're nicked.' He shoved Sam over to his younger colleague. 'Take him to the car, Bob, and wait for me there. I just want to listen to the rest of this tape in case this lady needs to explain any of it.'

'Right you are, sir.'

The other policeman gave Sam a gratuitous shove in the back and pushed him towards the door. Sam turned and gave me one last contemptuous glare before he was propelled through the front door and led away into the night. Bruce and I watched through the broken window.

'Good riddance to you, you bastard!' yelled Bruce as Sam was hustled up the garden path.

'Right then, let's see what we've got here, shall we?' The policeman sat down on the sofa and wound back the tape. I came away from the window and waited anxiously. Nick stood behind me and put his hand on my shoulder as the recording began. I needn't have worried, it was all there. From Sam bragging about blackmailing Bruce, to drugging me in the nightclub, stealing the porcelain with Serena, and finally my piercing scream as he threatened me. When the tape finished there was a silence. Nick squeezed my shoulder hard. Suddenly I realised I was shivering. The policeman opened the recorder and took out the cassette.

'Thank you, madam, I think that's all pretty self-explanatory. I'll look after this, if you don't mind.' He pocketed the cassette and stood up. He grinned. 'How very neat, a taped confession, I wish all our arrests were as easy as this.' He patted his breast pocket with satisfaction. 'Helston, you say?' he asked Nick as he made for the door.

'That's right, speak to an Inspector Carter at the station there, he'll fill you in on all the details.'

'Right you are, sir, will do. Goodnight to you all.' He touched his cap briefly and made for the door.

When he'd gone Bruce turned to me, his eyes shining with tears. He grabbed my hand. 'Polly, I – I don't know how to thank you, if it hadn't been for you I don't know what would have happened, I might have gone to jail!'

I patted his hand. 'Think nothing of it, Bruce,' I gave a wry smile, 'all part of the Polly Penhalligan super-sleuth service. But I must say, I can't quite believe I did that, I mean, I can't quite believe I had the nerve to tape him.'

'Neither can I,' admitted Nick admiringly. 'You took a hell of a risk. What if he'd popped into the hall and seen that thing recording? I hate to think what he'd have done to you.'

'So do I. Thank God you arrived when you did. But how come you were both out there anyway?'

'Well, I came up from Cornwall to find out what the hell was going on here – I'd had an extraordinary conversation with Lottie and a weird message from you on the answering machine – and when I arrived I found Bruce sitting outside in his car.'

'I'd just come round to talk to you, Polly,' said Bruce. 'I'd had a really bad day and I needed a shoulder to cry on, and you were the only person I could think of who wouldn't mind the fact that it was so late. I rang the bell loads of times but nobody answered.'

'Oh, so that was you ringing the bell?'

'Yes, and when I got no reply I thought I'd just sit in the car and wait for you to come back from wherever you were, then Nick showed up.'

'Bruce was just telling me there was no one in when we heard the most almighty scream. That's when we came crashing through.'

'Well,' grinned Bruce, 'Nick came crashing through, I was what you might call the rear party.'

'Crucial,' smiled Nick, 'couldn't have done it without you, Bruce.'

'Well, thank heavens you did come in then, I think I was about to have my brains bashed in.'

'Don't.' Nick grabbed me and held me close. I buried my face in his neck. He smelt of fresh air and hay lofts. We stayed like that for a minute, clutching each other, holding on. Then we remembered Bruce. We pulled apart sheepishly.

'Oh, don't mind me,' said Bruce with a grin, 'go for the full-blooded reunion, I was just off anyway.'

'Just off? Where?' I asked.

'To see my mother. I'm going to drive down there now.'

'Now? In the middle of the night?'

'Why not?' he said defiantly. 'She hasn't got much longer to – well. Let's just say I want to make sure I make it in time. If I leave it till tomorrow morning it might be too late.'

'But – what about your bail?' asked Nick. 'Are you allowed to do that?'

'Probably not, but since it was so obviously Sam who stole the porcelain, and not me, what does it matter? The whole story will be out by tomorrow and presumably the police will drop the charges so there won't be any bail, will there? They can hardly accuse me of concocting false evidence with my mother if there's nothing to concoct, can they?'

Nick grinned. 'No, I suppose not. But – will you get into the nursing home at this time of night?'

'Well, it'll be about five or six in the morning by the time I get there, and I guess it'll all be locked up, but the windows are usually open. I'll climb in and sit by her bed. I want to be there when she wakes up.' He looked calm and determined.

Nick smiled. 'Good for you, Bruce. I'm so glad it's turned out like this.'

'So am I,' said Bruce with a heartfelt smile. 'Never been so relieved in my life!' He held out his hand rather shyly to Nick. 'Well, goodbye then, and thanks for everything.'

Nick shook it heartily. 'Goodbye, and good luck.'

He turned to me and gave me a great big hug. 'Thanks again, Polly,' he whispered.

'Bye, Bruce.' I squeezed him hard. 'Give my love to your mother, won't you?'

'Will do.'

He gave us one last triumphant wave and then turned and left. We heard him run, or maybe even skip down the path to his car. The engine turned over and he roared off.

When he'd gone the room seemed strangely silent. Nick took my hand.

'Polly, I'm so sorry,' he whispered.

I turned in surprise. 'But why should you be—'

'Shh . . .' He lifted my chin gently and his lips found mine. We kissed. A long, tremulous kiss, full of the sense of being apart for too long, of nearly losing each other. The great boulder of distrust and unhappiness that had kept us apart had finally been rolled away, but not before we'd both caught a glimpse of what life would have been like without each other. We'd had a near miss. Tears of joy and relief sprang to my eyes as we drew apart. They flowed down my face.

'Sorry,' I sniffed, wiping them away. 'I'm just crying because I'm so pleased to see you, ridiculous, I know.'

Nick hugged me back to him again. 'I know,' he muttered into my ear, 'and so much of this has been my fault. Can you ever forgive me?'

I pulled away in surprise and wiped my eyes. 'What for?' I sniffed.

'For not believing you. When I heard on that tape how that creep had drugged you and dumped you in that hotel room – Christ, you could have gone into a coma or something, you could have died!'

'Could I?' I gasped in alarm, my eyes wide with horror. 'Could I really? What – swallowed my tongue, gagged on my vomit or something?'

'Well, it's possible, but let's not dwell on it, it didn't happen, thank God.'

'No. Thank God,' I muttered, feeling a bit shaky. It hadn't occurred to me that I might have had a bit of a close shave. I shuddered. 'But – what I still don't really understand is why you came up here in the first place. Why didn't you ring?'

He sat down on the sofa and dragged me down next to him. 'I was worried, Poll, I came up to see what on earth was going on. First of all I had this weird telephone call from Lottie, last night, in fact. She kept asking me if you were all right because a friend of hers had seen you being carried out of Annabel's by some film director, said you were actually unconscious. Well, that really made me think, I can tell you. Then I got your garbled message on the answering machine about how you were beetling off to investigate Sam, and that worried the hell out of me. The Helston police had already said they thought he and Serena might be involved in some way and I had visions of you waltzing round to his house and confronting him, only to be boffed on the head and dumped in the Thames in a black bin liner. I wasn't far wrong as it happened, was I? I hate to think what he might have done if I hadn't been outside, you don't half jump in feet first, Polly. I rang at lunch time to tell you to back off and stay away from him, but there was no answer.'

I groaned. 'Oh God, I popped to the shops for literally two minutes.'

'Well anyway, by that stage I was so hyped up and worried I couldn't just sit around in Cornwall waiting for you to get to the phone, so I jumped in the car and drove up here. Bruce was sitting outside when I arrived. We were just saying we thought we recognised Sam's Range Rover in the road and how odd it was that your car was here too – parked, incidentally at a most artistic angle in the front garden – when we heard a scream. That's when I came through the window.'

'Thank God you did, he was about to rearrange my face.'

'Was he?' Nick sat up and looked alarmed. 'He didn't really hurt you, did he?' he asked anxiously.

I grinned. 'Nah, you know me, tough as old boots. He just shoved me around a bit and scared me half to death, that's all, nothing serious. I was jolly glad to see you when I did, though, things were certainly getting a bit hectic. He's an absolute nutter, you know, Nick, I really thought he was going to kill me.'

'Don't.' Nick held me close. 'I wish I'd punched his lights out instead of just twisting his arm.'

'Should have let me brain him with that vase.'

'Couldn't be sure you wouldn't miss and get me instead. You never could aim, Polly.'

I grinned and snuggled up to him. Suddenly I pulled back and frowned.

'What did you mean about the police in Helston getting on to him? How did they know?'

'Oh, old Mrs Bradshaw started to cough.'

'Mrs Bradshaw!' I sat up. 'What did she have to do with it?'

'Quite a lot, actually. Serena and Sam popped round to her house that Saturday night and collected the keys from her prior to lifting the Meissen.'

'What! She gave them the keys? To our house? But why?'

Nick grinned. 'Because she hates your guts, darling, or so I was reliably and eagerly informed by the entire village. Furious with you for firing her, apparently. It also turns out that she stayed pretty thick with Serena, two of a kind I suppose, and of course she'd never really forgiven me for marrying you instead of her.'

'Don't I know it?' I said grimly. 'She never could get used to charring for an erstwhile secretary instead of a Hollywood movie star.'

'More Pinewood than Hollywood, but I know what you mean. So anyway, when Serena asked her for the key she was pleased and flattered to be asked to do a favour, I imagine.'

'But did she know they were going to rob us blind?'

'Apparently not. Serena just told her she needed to collect a few things from the house, stuff that belonged to her that I'd been too mean to give back – or some such spurious excuse. Anyway, she handed the key over without a murmur, and then, rather cleverly, Serena got her involved even deeper, making it hard for her to extricate herself and say she knew nothing about the burglary.'

'Why, what did Serena do?'

'She asked her to go to the nursing home where Bruce's mother was and put a package on her bedside table. Old Ma Bradshaw didn't know what it was all about or what was in the package, but again I reckon she was flattered to be asked and much too much in awe of Serena to say no. Anyway, off she toddled with this piece of porcelain in her bag, and of course no one turned a hair when she wandered into the hospice. There are so many old dears wandering around visiting each other she just blended into the scenery. Just another geriatric in a plastic mac clutching a Co-op bag. All she had to do was pass by Bruce's mother's bed when she was asleep, slip it on the bedside table, and waddle away again.'

'So that's how they did it,' I breathed. 'The sneaky bastards, and they blackmailed Bruce to make it look as if he was really desperate for money.'

'Exactly. But when Bruce was arrested, old Mrs B began to put two and two together. She realised what she'd done and began to wobble a bit. Apparently she got hold of Serena, who put the fear of God into her by saying she was in much too deep to get out and would definitely go to prison for her part in it if she so much as breathed a word.'

'God, poor old Mrs B, I almost feel sorry for her.'

'Well, quite, it was a pretty dirty trick, and of course Mrs Bradshaw was so terrified she kept quiet. Then the other day old Ted Simpson popped over to her place with a bottle of cherry brandy which the two of them sank together, and that's when she started to blab. She burst into tears and told Ted all about it. Of course, Ted promptly told Mrs Stanley at the post office, Mrs Stanley told her daughter, her daughter told her husband and her husband went to the police.'

'My God! The Helford mafia!'

'Quite, never underestimate the power of the village gossips. Anyway, the police went round and questioned her and she got herself into a complete paddy, cried like a baby but resolutely refused to say a word. But she didn't have to really, it was pretty obvious there was something going on. Even so, the police still didn't have enough evidence to arrest Sam and Serena, so they were just biding their time and waiting for the pair of them to slip up, to start shifting the gear on to the market.'

'Typical,' I said bitterly. 'All those boneheads in Helston ever do is bide their time. No killer instinct.'

'Well anyway, that's why I shot up here so quickly. Last night Inspector Carter tipped me off that Sam might be involved and I had ghastly visions of him getting completely desperate and finishing you off. Black bin liners, as I said.'

'You're not kidding, he's an absolute maniac, and completely unscrupulous too. My God, when I think of how he nearly ruined Bruce. He pretended to be so sympathetic – paying his bail, getting him a barrister—'

'Who, incidentally, turns out to be Sam's best man, so he's hardly likely to shaft his best mate, is he?'

'Really? Gosh, and I bet Bruce had a perfectly decent

barrister all along.' I shook my head. 'God, I d̲
what I ever—' I broke off abruptly.

Nick grinned. 'Saw in him?'

'No, no, of course not, I wasn't going to say that,' I sai̲
quickly, desperately trying to fight the raging blush which
was doing its best to liven up my features. I bit my lip.
'Well, all right, perhaps I was, but the only reason I liked
him was – well, I respected him, for his work, his films. Yes,
I must admit I admired him and I—'

'Fantasised about him?' Nick was still grinning.

'No! No, of *course* not!' I was purple now.

Nick laughed. 'It's OK, Polly, it's not a crime. It would
be a pretty stoic husband or wife who never thought about
anyone of the opposite sex apart from their spouse.'

I gasped. 'Nick!'

He roared with laughter. 'I said think, not do! Thinking
doesn't constitute adultery, does it? Which is why ostens-
ibly there was nothing wrong with you wearing that
obscene pink skirt, dousing yourself in Chanel, lounging
provocatively all over the dining table and generally flirting
outrageously with that creep, because of course you never
intended the flirting to go any further, did you?' He raised
his eyebrows quizzically at me.

'No!' I gasped. 'No, of course not, not in a million years!'

'Good. Just checking.' His mouth twitched.

I flushed to my toes and stared at the carpet. 'Sorry,' I
mumbled. 'Gosh, was I that obvious? I'm really sorry,
Nick.'

'Don't be. It's over now and I'm just winding you up.
Anyway, I'm the one who should be apologising.'

'Why?'

'For not believing you when you said you couldn't

remember what had happened that night in London. Trouble was, Poll,' he frowned and scratched his head, 'it sounded like such an incredibly lame excuse. Like one of your typically terrible, extraordinarily bad lies.'

I grinned. 'Brilliant. The one and only time I tell the truth, it sounds like a lie. Terrific, isn't it? I might just as well stick to lying, I'm obviously better at it.'

'Speaking of which,' he said, reaching into his pocket, 'perhaps you could do some fast talking about this one?' He handed me a piece of paper.

'What is it?' I asked, unfolding it.

'It's a bill from Harrods car park, where your BMW has apparently been residing in splendour for over three weeks now. What d'you suggest, Polly, a remortgage on the house, perhaps? Sell all the Meissen that we're hopefully about to recover?'

'Oh my God!' My hand flew to my mouth. 'Nick, I can explain, I just completely forgot – well, no not forgot exactly, I knew it was there but – yes, I know! I thought – I thought Pippa was going to pick it up! Yes, that's it, I seem to remember asking Pippa to get it out for me while I was away, she must have—'

'Polly, don't even *think* about wheedling your way out of this one!' laughed Nick, squeezing me hard.

'Ouch!' I gasped. 'Careful!' I pulled his arm away.

He sat back in surprise. 'What? Did I hurt you?'

'Oh no, it's just that—' I stared at him. Was this a good time? I'd been so terrified about breaking the news in case he thought the baby was Sam's, but now that Sam was well out of the frame, now that Nick knew that nothing could possibly have happened...

I smiled. 'I'm pregnant.'

He stared at me. 'You're what?'

'I'm pregnant,' I repeated, somewhat shyly. God, I was starting to blush again. 'You know, having a baby.'

He dropped his hands from my waist and his jaw dropped too.

'You are?' His eyes were wide with wonder. 'Really?'

'Yes, really!' I laughed. 'Don't look so astonished, Nick, it was bound to happen one day, you kept telling me so, remember?'

He smiled, slowly and broadly. The smile became a beam, stretching right across his face. 'You're pregnant!' he breathed. He kissed me hard on the mouth but the beam didn't waver for a moment. I grinned back. We held hands, gazing at each other like a couple of teenagers. Suddenly his eyes narrowed. He looked at me carefully.

'You're sure about this, are you, Polly? I mean, you've been to see the doctor? Only I can just see you with some makeshift chemistry set, sending litmus paper blue and test tubes pink and getting thoroughly convinced you're up the duff when in actual fact you're just a bit late or—'

'Of course I'm sure, and the word is gynaecologist, actually. I saw him a couple of days ago, I'm four or five weeks pregnant now,' I said proudly.

Nick peered at my tummy in wonder. 'Wow. A month old. Hello, little chap.'

'Or chap-ess,' I corrected him.

'Oh absolutely, or chap-ess. So – what's that then, a February baby?'

'Something like that.' I grinned.

'Try to get it all over with before I start lambing, would you?'

'Nick!' I bashed him with a cushion.

He laughed and held me close. 'Oh, Poll, I'm so pleased!' Suddenly he drew back. 'And you feel all right?' he asked, looking concerned. 'Not sick or anything?'

'Oh no, that's more or less passed now. I was as sick as a dog for a while, though, but – oooh, d'you know, now you come to mention it' – I put my hand to my throat and looked a bit pained – 'it seems to have come back. I do feel a bit queasy.'

'Really? Glass of water?' he asked, getting up anxiously.

'Mmmm, please, might help – oh, and while you're there, maybe a small piece of toast, with a smidgen of honey. Oh, and a chocolate biscuit if it's not too much trouble.'

Nick hastened to the kitchen.

'Oh, and Nick?'

He hurried back, a glass of water in his hand.

'Before you make the toast, d'you think you could just move that stool so I can put my feet up on it? Perfect – oh, and that cushion for my head . . . right a bit, down a bit . . . lovely . . . and perhaps you could find a rug or something for my knees? Super. Oh, is that my water? Thanks very – hey, what are you – hey, not on my face! Oh God, Nick, not down my – aaarh! All down my neck! Ugh, you bastard, I'll get you for that, I'll get you!'

A Married Man

Catherine Alliott

When Lucy Fellowes is offered a dream house in the country she leaps at the chance. It's hard enough living in London on an uncertain income, but when you're widowed with two small boys it's even harder. And anyway, a rural retreat will bring her closer to Charlie. Charlie? The only man in four years to make her heart beat faster. Perfect. Or it would be. If only he didn't belong to someone else . . .

A wickedly witty new novel about how complicated relationships get when you grow up, from the best-selling author of *Rosie Meadows regrets* . . . and *Olivia's Luck*.

'Alliott's skilled handling of such delicate, difficult and deep material marvellously counterpoints the Cotswolds comic archetypes and provides psychological depth and shadow to the sparky surface action. Sensitive, funny and wonderfully well-written.' Wendy Holden, *Daily Express*

0 7472 6722 7

headline

Rosie Meadows regrets . . .

Catherine Alliott

Well, what could I say? If he was smitten then I could be too, and I sank back into the whole cosy relationship with a monumental sigh of relief. I didn't have to try too hard, didn't have to be too witty, too amusing, too beautiful . . . It was like landing on a feather mattress after all those years of being Out There.

Three years down the line, however, Rosie's beginning to think that 'cosy' isn't all it's cracked up to be. Bridge parties have never really been her thing, and it would be nice to feel beautiful just once in a while. Enough is enough. It's time to get her life back.

'Alliott's *joie de vivre* is irresistible' *Daily Mail*

'Hilarious and full of surprises' *Daily Telegraph*

'A joy . . . you're in for a treat' *Express*

0 7472 5786 8

headline

Olivia's Luck

Catherine Alliott

When Olivia's husband Johnny announces, 'I don't care what colour you paint the hall, I'm leaving,' Olivia is understandably devastated. Left with an eccentric troop of builders camping in her back garden, a ten-year-old daughter with 'attitude' and a neurotic neighbour intent on foisting cast-off men in her direction, Olivia's dream home is suddenly less than dreamy.

Will Johnny ever come back, and if he doesn't, will her luck ever change?

Olivia's Luck is the brilliant new novel from the bestselling author of *The Old-Girl Network*, *Going Too Far*, *The Real Thing* and *Rosie Meadows regrets* . . .

'I literally couldn't put this down. An addictive cocktail of wit, frivolity and madcap romance' *Time Out*

'Alliott's joie de vivre is irresistible' *Daily Mail*

'Hilarious and full of surprises' *Daily Telegraph*

'Great fluff' *Company*

'Compulsive and wildly romantic' *Bookseller*

0 7472 5787 6

headline

Now you can buy any of these other bestselling books by **Catherine Alliott** from your bookshop or *direct from her publisher*.

FREE P&P AND UK DELIVERY
(Overseas and Ireland £3.50 per book)

A Married Man	£6.99
Olivia's Luck	£6.99
Rosie Meadows regrets . . .	£6.99
The Real Thing	£6.99
Going Too Far	£6.99
The Old-Girl Network	£6.99

TO ORDER SIMPLY CALL THIS NUMBER

01235 400 414

or visit our website: <u>www.madaboutbooks.com</u>

Prices and availability subject to change without notice.